GEORGE
MACDONALD

The
Fantastic
Imagination
of

GEORGE
MacDONALD

Volume I

Essays
The Portent
At the Back of the North Wind
The Flight of the Shadow

COACHWHIP PUBLICATIONS
Landisville, Pennsylvania

The Fantastic Imagination of George MacDonald, Vol. I
Copyright © 2008 Coachwhip Publications

ISBN 1-930585-61-6
ISBN-13 978-1-930585-61-4

Cover Image: Forest near Kilchurn Castle, Scotland (CC: Gustavo Naharro)
Title Page Accent: © Dzmitry Stankevich

Coachwhipbooks.com

Contents

The Imagination

(1867)

The Imagination: Its Functions and Its Culture

There are [those] in whose notion education would seem to consist in the production of a certain repose through the development of this and that faculty, and the depression, if not eradication, of this and that other faculty. But if mere repose were the end in view, an unsparing depression of all the faculties would be the surest means of approaching it, provided always the animal instincts could be depressed likewise, or, better still, kept in a state of constant repletion. Happily, however, for the human race, it possesses in the passion of hunger even, a more immediate saviour than in the wisest selection and treatment of its faculties. For repose is not the end of education; its end is a noble unrest, an ever renewed awaking from the dead, a ceaseless questioning of the past for the interpretation of the future, an urging on of the motions of life, which had better far be accelerated into fever, than retarded into lethargy.

By those who consider a balanced repose the end of culture, the imagination must necessarily be regarded as the one faculty before all others to be suppressed. "Are there not facts?" say they. "Why forsake them for fancies? Is there not that which may be *known?* Why forsake it for inventions? What God hath made, into that let man inquire."

We answer: To inquire into what God has made is the main function of the imagination. It is aroused by facts, is nourished by facts, seeks for higher and yet higher laws in those facts; but refuses to regard science as the sole interpreter of nature, or the laws of science as the only region of discovery.

We must begin with a definition of the word *imagination,* or rather some description of the faculty to which we give the name.

The word itself means an *imaging* or a making of likenesses. The imagination is that faculty which gives form to thought—not necessarily uttered form, but form capable of being uttered in shape or in sound, or in any mode upon which the senses can lay hold. It is, therefore, that faculty in man which is likest to the prime operation of the

9

power of God, and has, therefore, been called the *creative* faculty, and its exercise *creation*. *Poet* means *maker*. We must not forget, however, that between creator and poet lies the one unpassable gulf which distinguishes—far be it from us to say *divides*—all that is God's from all that is man's; a gulf teeming with infinite revelations, but a gulf over which no man can pass to find out God, although God needs not to pass over it to find man; the gulf between that which calls, and that which is thus called into being; between that which makes in its own image and that which is made in that image. It is better to keep the word *creation* for that calling out of nothing which is the imagination of God; except it be as an occasional symbolic expression, whose daring is fully recognized, of the likeness of man's work to the work of his maker. The necessary unlikeness between the creator and the created holds within it the equally necessary likeness of the thing made to him who makes it, and so of the work of the made to the work of the maker. When therefore, refusing to employ the word *creation* of the work of man, we yet use the word *imagination* of the work of God, we cannot be said to dare at all. It is only to give the name of man's faculty to that power after which and by which it was fashioned. The imagination of man is made in the image of the imagination of God. Everything of man must have been of God first; and it will help much towards our understanding of the imagination and its functions in man if we first succeed in regarding aright the imagination of God, in which the imagination of man lives and moves and has its being.

As to *what* thought is in the mind of God ere it takes form, or what the form is to him ere he utters it; in a word, what the consciousness of God is in either case, all we can say is, that our consciousness in the resembling conditions must, afar off, resemble his. But when we come to consider the acts embodying the Divine thought (if indeed thought and act be not with him one and the same), then we enter a region of large difference. We discover at once, for instance, that where a man would make a machine, or a picture, or a book, God makes the man that makes the book, or the picture, or the machine. Would God give us a drama? He makes a Shakespeare. Or would he construct a drama more immediately his own? He begins with the building of the stage itself, and that stage is a world—a universe of worlds. He makes the actors, and they do not act,—they *are* their part. He utters them into the visible to work out their life—his drama. When he would have an epic, he sends a thinking hero into his drama, and the epic is the soliloquy of his Hamlet. Instead of writing his lyrics, he sets his birds and his maidens a-singing. All the processes of the ages are God's science; all the flow of history is his poetry. His sculpture is not in marble, but in living and speech-giving forms, which pass away, not to yield place to those that come after, but to be perfected in a nobler studio. What he has done remains, although it vanishes; and he never either forgets what he has once done, or does it even once again. As the thoughts move in the mind of a man, so move the worlds of men and women in the mind of God, and make no confusion there, for there they had their birth, the offspring of his imagination. Man is but a thought of God.

If we now consider the so-called creative faculty in man, we shall find that in no *primary* sense is this faculty creative. Indeed, a man is rather *being thought* than *thinking,* when a new thought arises in his mind. He knew it not till he found it there, therefore he could not even have sent for it. He did not create it, else how could it be the surprise that it was when it arose? He may, indeed, in rare instances foresee that something is coming, and make ready the place for its birth; but that is the utmost relation of consciousness and will he can bear to the dawning idea. Leaving this aside, however, and turning to the *embodiment* or revelation of thought, we shall find that a man no more *creates* the forms by which he would reveal his thoughts, than he creates those thoughts themselves.

For what are the forms by means of which a man may reveal his thoughts? Are they not those of nature? But although he is created in the closest sympathy with these forms, yet even these forms are not born in his mind. What springs there is the perception that this or that form is already an expression of this or that phase of thought or of feeling. For the world around him is an outward figuration of the condition of his mind; an inexhaustible storehouse of forms whence he may choose exponents—the crystal pitchers that shall protect his thought and not need to be broken that the light may break forth. The meanings are in those forms already, else they could be no garment of unveiling. God has made the world that it should thus serve his creature, developing in the service that imagination whose necessity it meets. The man has but to light the lamp within the form: his imagination is the light, it is not the form. Straightway the shining thought makes the form visible, and becomes itself visible through the form.[1]

In illustration of what we mean, take a passage from the poet Shelley.

[1] "We would not be understood to say that the man works consciously even in this. Oftentimes, if not always, the vision arises in the mind, thought and form together."

In his poem *Adonais,* written upon the death of Keats, representing death as the revealer of secrets, he says:—

"The one remains; the many change and pass;
  Heaven's light for ever shines; earth's shadows fly;
  Life, like a dome of many coloured glass,
  Stains the white radiance of eternity,
  Until death tramples it to fragments."

This is a new embodiment, certainly, whence he who gains not,
for the moment at least, a loftier feeling of death, must be dull either
of heart or of understanding. But has Shelley created this figure, or
only put together its parts according to the harmony of truths already
embodied in each of the parts? For first he takes the inventions of his
fellow-men, in glass, in colour, in dome: with these he represents life
as finite though elevated, and as an analysis although a lovely one.
Next he presents eternity as the dome of the sky above this dome of
coloured glass—the sky having ever been regarded as the true symbol
of eternity. This portion of the figure he enriches by the attribution
of whiteness, or unity and radiance. And last, he shows us Death as
the destroying revealer, walking aloft through the upper region, tread-
ing out this life-bubble of colours, that the man may look beyond it
and behold the true, the uncoloured, the all-coloured.

But although the human imagination has no choice but to make
use of the forms already prepared for it, its operation is the same as
that of the divine inasmuch as it does put thought into form. And if it
be to man what creation is to God, we must expect to find it operative
in every sphere of human activity. Such is, indeed, the fact, and that
to a far greater extent than is commonly supposed.

The sovereignty of the imagination, for instance, over the region
of poetry will hardly, in the present day at least, be questioned; but
not every one is prepared to be told that the imagination has had
nearly as much to do with the making of our language as with
"Macbeth" or the "Paradise Lost." The half of our language is the work
of the imagination.

For how shall two agree together what name they shall give to a
thought or a feeling? How shall the one show the other that which is
invisible? True, he can unveil the mind's construction in the face—that
living eternally changeful symbol which God has hung in front of the
unseen spirit—but that without words reaches only to the expression
of present feeling. To attempt to employ it alone for the conveyance
of the intellectual or the historical would constantly mislead; while
the expression of feeling itself would be misinterpreted, especially

with regard to cause and object: the dumb show would be worse than
dumb.

But let a man become aware of some new movement within him.
Loneliness comes with it, for he would share his mind with his friend,
and he cannot; he is shut up in speechlessness. Thus

> He *may* live a man forbid
> Weary sevennights nine times nine,

or the first moment of his perplexity may be that of his release.
Gazing about him in pain, he suddenly beholds the material form of
his immaterial condition. There stands his thought! God thought it
before him, and put its picture there ready for him when he wanted
it. Or, to express the thing more prosaically, the man cannot look
around him long without perceiving some form, aspect, or movement
of nature, some relation between its forms, or between such and himself which resembles the state or motion within him. This he seizes
as the symbol, as the garment or body of his invisible thought, presents it to his friend, and his friend understands him. Every word so
employed with a new meaning is henceforth, in its new character, born
of the spirit and not of the flesh, born of the imagination and not of
the understanding, and is henceforth submitted to new laws of growth
and modification.

"Thinkest thou," says Carlyle in "Past and Present," "there were
no poets till Dan Chaucer? No heart burning with a thought which it
could not hold, and had no word for; and needed to shape and coin a
word for—what thou callest a metaphor, trope, or the like? For every
word we have there was such a man and poet. The coldest word was
once a glowing new metaphor and bold questionable originality. Thy
very ATTENTION, does it not mean an *attentio,* a STRETCHING-TO? Fancy
that act of the mind, which all were conscious of, which none had yet
named,—when this new poet first felt bound and driven to name it.
His questionable originality and new glowing metaphor was found
adoptable, intelligible, and remains our name for it to this day."

All words, then, belonging to the inner world of the mind, are of
the imagination, are originally poetic words. The better, however, any
such word is fitted for the needs of humanity, the sooner it loses its
poetic aspect by commonness of use. It ceases to be heard as a symbol, and appears only as a sign. Thus thousands of words which were
originally poetic words owing their existence to the imagination, lose
their vitality, and harden into mummies of prose. Not merely in literature does poetry come first, and prose afterwards, but poetry is the
source of all the language that belongs to the inner world, whether it

be of passion or of metaphysics, of psychology or of aspiration. No poetry comes by the elevation of prose; but the half of prose comes by the "massing into the common clay" of thousands of winged words, whence, like the lovely shells of by-gone ages, one is occasionally disinterred by some lover of speech, and held up to the light to show the play of colour in its manifold laminations.

For the world is—allow us the homely figure—the human being turned inside out. All that moves in the mind is symbolized in Nature. Or, to use another more philosophical, and certainly not less poetic figure, the world is a sensuous analysis of humanity, and hence an inexhaustible wardrobe for the clothing of human thought. Take any word expressive of emotion—take the word *emotion* itself—and you will find that its primary meaning is of the outer world. In the swaying of the woods, in the unrest of the "wavy plain," the imagination saw the picture of a well-known condition of the human mind; and hence the word *emotion*.[2]

But while the imagination of man has thus the divine function of putting thought into form, it has a duty altogether human, which is paramount to that function—the duty, namely, which springs from his immediate relation to the Father, that of following and finding out the divine imagination in whose image it was made. To do this, the man must watch its signs, its manifestations. He must contemplate what the Hebrew poets call the works of His hands.

"But to follow those is the province of the intellect, not of the imagination." —We will leave out of the question at present that poetic interpretation of the works of Nature with which the intellect has almost nothing, and the imagination almost everything, to do. It is unnecessary to insist that the higher being of a flower even is dependent for its reception upon the human imagination; that science may pull the snowdrop to shreds, but cannot find out the idea of suffering hope and pale confident submission, for the sake of which that darling of the spring looks out of heaven, namely, God's heart, upon us his wiser and more sinful children; for if there be any truth in this region of things acknowledged at all, it will be at the same time acknowledged that that region belongs to the imagination. We confine ourselves to that questioning of the works of God which is called the province of science.

---

[2] This passage contains only a repetition of what is far better said in the preceding extract from Carlyle, but it was written before we had read (if reviewers may be allowed to confess such ignorance) the book from which that extract is taken.

"Shall, then, the human intellect," we ask, "come into readier contact with the divine imagination than that human imagination?" The work of the Higher must be discovered by the search of the Lower in degree which is yet similar in kind. Let us not be supposed to exclude the intellect from a share in every highest office. Man is not divided when the manifestations of his life are distinguished. The intellect "is all in every part." There were no imagination without intellect, however much it may appear that intellect can exist without imagination. What we mean to insist upon is, that in finding out the works of God, the Intellect must labour, workman-like, under the direction of the architect, Imagination. Herein, too, we proceed in the hope to show how much more than is commonly supposed the imagination has to do with human endeavour; how large a share it has in the work that is done under the sun.

"But how can the imagination have anything to do with science? That region, at least, is governed by fixed laws."

"True," we answer. "But how much do we know of these laws? How much of science already belongs to the region of the ascertained—in other words, has been conquered by the intellect? We will not now dispute your vindication of the *ascertained* from the intrusion of the imagination; but we do claim for it all the undiscovered, all the unexplored." "Ah, well! There it can do little harm. There let it run riot if you will." "No," we reply. "Licence is not what we claim when we assert the duty of the imagination to be that of following and finding out the work that God maketh. Her part is to understand God ere she attempts to utter man. Where is the room for being fanciful or riotous here? It is only the ill-bred, that is, the uncultivated imagination that will amuse itself where it ought to worship and work."

"But the facts of Nature are to be discovered only by observation and experiment." True. But how does the man of science come to think of his experiments? Does observation reach to the non-present, the possible, the yet unconceived? Even if it showed you the experiments which *ought* to be made, will observation reveal to you the experiments which *might* be made? And who can tell of which kind is the one that carries in its bosom the secret of the law you seek? We yield you your facts. The laws we claim for the prophetic imagination. "He hath set the world *in* man's heart," not in his understanding. And the heart must open the door to the understanding. It is the far-seeing imagination which beholds what might be a form of things, and says to the intellect: "Try whether that may not be the form of these things;" which beholds or invents *a* harmonious relation of parts and operations, and sends the intellect to find out whether that be not *the* harmonious relation of them—that is, the law of the phenomenon it contemplates. Nay, the poetic relations themselves in the phenomenon may suggest to the imagination the law that rules its scientific life. Yea, more than this: we dare to claim for the true, childlike, humble imagination, such an inward oneness with the laws of the universe that it possesses in itself an insight into the very nature of things.

Lord Bacon tells us that a prudent question is the half of knowledge. Whence comes this prudent question? we repeat. And we answer, From the imagination. It is the imagination that suggests in what direction to make the new inquiry—which, should it cast no immediate light on the answer sought, can yet hardly fail to be a step towards final discovery. Every experiment has its origin in hypothesis; without the scaffolding of hypothesis, the house of science could never arise. And the construction of any hypothesis whatever is the work of the imagination. The man who cannot invent will never discover. The imagination often gets a glimpse of the law itself long before it is or can be *ascertained* to be a law.[3]

[3] This paper was already written when, happening to mention the present subject to a mathematical friend, a lecturer at one of the universities, he gave us a corroborative instance. He had lately guessed that a certain algebraic process could be shortened exceedingly if the method which his imagination suggested should prove to be a true one—that is, an algebraic law. He put it to the test of experiment—committed the verification, that is, into the hands of his intellect—and found the method true. It has since been accepted by the Royal Society.

Noteworthy illustration we have lately found in the record of the experiences of an Edinburgh detective, an Irishman of the name of McLevy. That the service of the imagination in the solution of the problems peculiar to his calling is well known to him, we could adduce many proofs. He recognizes its function in the construction of the theory which shall unite this and that hint into an organic whole, and he expressly sets forth the need of a theory before facts can be serviceable:—

"I would wait for my 'idea.' ... I never did any good without mine. ... Chance never smiled on me unless I poked her some way; so that my 'notion,' after all, has been in the getting of it my own work only perfected by a higher hand."

"On leaving the shop I went direct to Prince's Street,-of course with an idea in my mind, and somehow I have always been contented with one idea when I could not get another; and the advantage of sticking by one is, that the other don't jostle it and turn you about in a circle when you should go in a straight line." [Since quoting the above I have learned that the book referred to is unworthy of confidence. But let it stand as illustration where it cannot be proof.]

The region belonging to the pure intellect is straitened: the imagination labours to extend its territories, to give it room. She sweeps
across the borders, searching out new lands into which she may guide
her plodding brother. The imagination is the light which redeems from
the darkness for the eyes of the understanding. Novalis says, "The
imagination is the stuff of the intellect"—affords, that is, the material upon which the intellect works. And Bacon, in his "Advancement
of Learning," fully recognizes this its office, corresponding to the foresight of God in this, that it beholds afar off. And he says: "Imagination is much akin to miracle-working faith."[4]

In the scientific region of her duty of which we speak, the Imagination cannot have her perfect work; this belongs to another and
higher sphere than that of intellectual truth—that, namely, of full-
globed humanity, operating in which she gives birth to poetry—truth
in beauty. But her function in the complete sphere of our nature, will,
at the same time, influence her more limited operation in the sec-
tions that belong to science. Coleridge says that no one but a poet
will make any further *great* discoveries in mathematics; and Bacon
says that "wonder," that faculty of the mind especially attendant on
the child-like imagination, "is the seed of knowledge." The influence
of the poetic upon the scientific imagination is, for instance, especially present in the construction of an invisible whole from the hints
afforded by a visible part; where the needs of the part, its uselessness, its broken relations, are the only guides to a multiplex harmony,
completeness, and end, which is the whole. From a little bone, worn
with ages of death, older than the man can think, his scientific imagination dashed with the poetic, calls up the form, size, habits, peri-
ods, belonging to an animal never beheld by human eyes, even to the
mingling contrasts of scales and wings, of feathers and hair. Through
the combined lenses of science and imagination, we look back into
ancient times, so dreadful in their incompleteness, that it may well
have been the task of seraphic faith, as well as of cherubic imagination, to behold in the wallowing monstrosities of the terror-teeming
earth, the prospective, quiet, age-long labour of God preparing the
world with all its humble, graceful service for his unborn Man. The
imagination of the poet, on the other hand, dashed with the imagination of the man of science, revealed to Goethe the prophecy of the
flower in the leaf. No other than an artistic imagination, however,

---

[4] We are sorry we cannot verify this quotation, for which we are indebted to Mr. Oldbuck the Antiquary, in the novel of that ilk. There
is, however, little room for doubt that it is sufficiently correct.

fulfilled of science, could have attained to the discovery of the fact that the leaf is the imperfect flower.

When we turn to history, however, we find probably the greatest operative sphere of the intellectuo-constructive imagination. To discover its laws; the cycles in which events return, with the reasons of their return, recognizing them notwithstanding metamorphosis; to perceive the vital motions of this spiritual body of mankind; to learn from its facts the rule of God; to construct from a succession of broken indications a whole accordant with human nature; to approach a scheme of the forces at work, the passions overwhelming or upheaving, the aspirations securely upraising, the selfishnesses debasing and crumbling, with the vital interworking of the whole; to illuminate all from the analogy with individual life, and from the predominant phases of individual character which are taken as the mind of the people—this is the province of the imagination. Without her influence no process of recording events can develop into a history. As truly might that be called the description of a volcano which occupied itself with a delineation of the shapes assumed by the smoke expelled from the mountain's burning bosom. What history becomes under the full sway of the imagination may be seen in the "History of the French Revolution," by Thomas Carlyle, at once a true picture, a philosophical revelation, a noble poem.

There is a wonderful passage about *Time* in Shakespeare's "Rape of Lucrece," which shows how he understood history. The passage is really about history, and not about time; for time itself does nothing—not even "blot old books and alter their contents." It is the forces at work in time that produce all the changes; and they are history. We quote for the sake of one line chiefly but the whole stanza is pertinent.

> "Time's glory is to calm contending kings,
>   To unmask falsehood, and bring truth to light,
>   To stamp the seal of time in aged things,
>   To wake the morn and sentinel the night,
>   To wrong the wronger till he render right;
>   To ruinate proud buildings with thy hours,
>   And smear with dust their glittering golden towers."

To wrong the wronger till he render right. Here is a historical cycle worthy of the imagination of Shakespeare, yea, worthy of the creative imagination of our God—the God who made the Shakespeare with the imagination, as well as evolved the history from the laws which that imagination followed and found out.

In full instance we would refer our readers to Shakespeare's historical plays; and, as a side-illustration, to the fact that he repeatedly represents his greatest characters, when at the point of death, as relieving their overcharged minds by prophecy. Such prophecy is the result of the light of imagination, cleared of all distorting dimness by the vanishing of earthly hopes and desires, cast upon the facts of experience. Such prophecy is the perfect working of the historical imagination.

In the interpretation of individual life, the same principles hold; and nowhere can the imagination be more healthily and rewardingly occupied than in endeavouring to construct the life of an individual out of the fragments which are all that can reach us of the history of even the noblest of our race. How this will apply to the reading of the gospel story we leave to the earnest thought of our readers.

We now pass to one more sphere in which the student imagination works in glad freedom—the sphere which is understood to belong more immediately to the poet.

We have already said that the forms of Nature (by which word *forms* we mean any of those conditions of Nature which affect the senses of man) are so many approximate representations of the mental conditions of humanity. The outward, commonly called the material, is *informed* by, or has form in virtue of, the inward or immaterial—in a word, the thought. The forms of Nature are the representations of human thought in virtue of their being the embodiment of God's thought. As such, therefore, they can be read and used to any depth, shallow or profound. Men of all ages and all developments have discovered in them the means of expression; and the men of ages to come, before us in every path along which we are now striving, must likewise find such means in those forms, unfolding with their unfolding necessities. The man, then, who, in harmony with nature, attempts the discovery of more of her meanings, is just searching out the things of God. The deepest of these are far too simple for us to understand as yet. But let our imagination interpretive reveal to us one severed significance of one of her parts, and such is the harmony of the whole, that all the realm of Nature is open to us henceforth—not without labour—and in time. Upon the man who can understand the human meaning of the snowdrop, of the primrose, or of the daisy, the life of the earth blossoming into the cosmical flower of a perfect moment will one day seize, possessing him with its prophetic hope, arousing his conscience with the vision of the "rest that remaineth," and stirring up the aspiration to enter into that rest:

"Thine is the tranquil hour, purpureal Eve!
But long as godlike wish, or hope divine,

Informs my spirit, ne'er can I believe
That this magnificence is wholly thine!
—From worlds not quickened by the sun
A portion of the gift is won;
An intermingling of Heaven's pomp is spread
On ground which British shepherds tread!"

Even the careless curve of a frozen cloud across the blue will calm some troubled thoughts, may slay some selfish thoughts. And what shall be said of such gorgeous shows as the scarlet poppies in the green corn, the likest we have to those lilies of the field which spoke to the Saviour himself of the care of God, and rejoiced His eyes with the glory of their God-devised array? From such visions as these the imagination reaps the best fruits of the earth, for the sake of which all the science involved in its construction, is the inferior, yet willing and beautiful support.

From what we have now advanced, will it not then appear that, on the whole, the name given by our Norman ancestors is more fitting for the man who moves in these regions than the name given by the Greeks? Is not the *Poet*, the *Maker*, a less suitable name for him than the *Trouvère*, the *Finder?* At least, must not the faculty that finds precede the faculty that utters?

But is there nothing to be said of the function of the imagination from the Greek side of the question? Does it possess no creative faculty? Has it no originating power?

Certainly it would be a poor description of the Imagination which omitted the one element especially present to the mind that invented the word *Poet.*—It can present us with new thought-forms—new, that is, as revelations of thought. It has created none of the material that goes to make these forms. Nor does it work upon raw material. But it takes forms already existing, and gathers them about a thought so much higher than they, that it can group and subordinate and harmonize them into a whole which shall represent, unveil that thought.[5]

---

[5] Just so Spenser describes the process of the embodiment of a human soul in his Platonic "Hymn in Honour of Beauty."

"She frames her house in which she will be placed
Fit for herself . . .
And the gross matter by a sovereign might
Tempers so trim . . .
For of the soul the body form doth take;
For soul is form, and doth the body make."

The nature of this process we will illustrate by an examination of the well-known *Bugle Song* in Tennyson's "Princess."

First of all, there is the new music of the song, which does not even remind one of the music of any other. The rhythm, rhyme, melody, harmony are all an embodiment in sound, as distinguished from word, of what can be so embodied—the *feeling* of the poem, which goes before, and prepares the way for the following thought— tunes the heart into a receptive harmony. Then comes the new arrangement of thought and figure whereby the meaning contained is presented as it never was before. We give a sort of paraphrastical synopsis of the poem, which, partly in virtue of its disagreeableness, will enable the lovers of the song to return to it with an increase of pleasure.

The glory of midsummer mid-day upon mountain, lake, and ruin. Give nature a voice for her gladness. Blow, bugle.

Nature answers with dying echoes, sinking in the midst of her splendour into a sad silence.

Not so with human nature. The echoes of the word of truth gather volume and richness from every soul that re-echoes it to brother and sister souls.

With poets the *fashion* has been to contrast the stability and rejuvenescence of nature with the evanescence and unreturning decay of humanity:—

> "Yet soon reviving plants and flowers, anew shall deck the plain;
> The woods shall hear the voice of Spring, and flourish green again.
> But man forsakes this earthly scene, ah! never to return:
> Shall any following Spring revive the ashes of the urn?"

But our poet vindicates the eternal in humanity:—

> "O Love, they die in yon rich sky,
> They faint on hill or field or river:
> Our echoes roll from soul to soul,
> And grow for ever and for ever.
> Blow, bugle, blow, set the wild echoes flying;
> And answer echoes, answer, Dying, dying, dying."

Is not this a new form to the thought—a form which makes us feel the truth of it afresh? And every new embodiment of a known truth must be a new and wider revelation. No man is capable of seeing for himself the whole of any truth: he needs it echoed back to him from every soul in the universe; and still its centre is hid in the Father of Lights. In so far, then, as either form or thought is new, we may grant

the use of the word Creation, modified according to our previous defi-
nitions.

This operation of the imagination in choosing, gathering, and vitally
combining the material of a new revelation, may be well illustrated
from a certain employment of the poetic faculty in which our greatest
poets have delighted. Perceiving truth half hidden and half revealed
in the slow speech and stammering tongue of men who have gone
before them, they have taken up the unfinished form and completed
it; they have, as it were, rescued the soul of meaning from its prison
of uninformed crudity, where it sat like the Prince in the "Arabian
Nights," half man, half marble; they have set it free in its own form,
in a shape, namely, which it could "through every part impress."
Shakespeare's keen eye suggested many such a rescue from the tomb—
of a tale drearily told—a tale which no one now would read save for
the glorified form in which he has re-embodied its true contents. And
from Tennyson we can produce one specimen small enough for our
use, which, a mere chip from the great marble re-embodying the old
legend of Arthur's death, may, like the hand of Achilles holding his
spear in the crowded picture,

"Stand for the whole to be imagined."

In the "History of Prince Arthur," when Sir Bedivere returns after
hiding Excalibur the first time, the king asks him what he has seen,
and he answers—

"Sir, I saw nothing but waves and wind."

The second time, to the same question, he answers—

"Sir, I saw nothing but the water wap, and the waves wan."[6]

---

[6] The word *wap* is plain enough; the word *wan* we cannot satisfy
ourselves about. Had it been used with regard to the water, it might
have been worth remarking that wan, meaning dark, gloomy, turbid,
is a common adjective to a river in the old Scotch ballad. And it might
be an adjective here; but that is not likely, seeing it is conjoined with
the verb *wap*. The Anglo-Saxon *wanian,* to decrease, might be the
root-word, perhaps, (in the sense of *to ebb,*) if this water had been
the sea and not a lake. But possibly the meaning is, "I heard the water whoop or wail aloud" (from *Wópan*); and "the waves whine or
bewail" (from *Wánian* to lament). But even then the two verbs would
seem to predicate of transposed subjects.

This answer Tennyson has expanded into the well-known lines—

"I heard the ripple washing in the reeds,
 And the wild water lapping on the crag;"

slightly varied, for the other occasion, into—

"I heard the water lapping on the crag,
 And the long ripple washing in the reeds."

But, as to this matter of *creation,* is there, after all, I ask yet, any genuine sense in which a man may be said to create his own thought-forms? Allowing that a new combination of forms already existing might be called creation, is the man, after all, the author of this new combination? Did he, with his will and his knowledge, proceed wittingly, consciously, to construct a form which should embody his thought? Or did this form arise within him without will or effort of his—vivid if not clear—certain if not outlined? Ruskin (and better authority we do not know) will assert the latter, and we think he is right: though perhaps he would insist more upon the absolute perfection of the vision than we are quite prepared to do. Such embodiments are not the result of the man's intention, or of the operation of his conscious nature. His feeling is that they are given to him; that from the vast unknown, where time and space are not, they suddenly appear in luminous writing upon the wall of his consciousness. Can it be correct, then, to say that he created them? Nothing less so, as it seems to us. But can we not say that they are the creation of the unconscious portion of his nature? Yes, provided we can understand that that which is the individual, the man, can know, and not know that it knows, can create and yet be ignorant that virtue has gone out of it. From that unknown region we grant they come, but not by its own blind working. Nor, even were it so, could any amount of such production, where no will was concerned, be dignified with the name of creation. But God sits in that chamber of our being in which the candle of our consciousness goes out in darkness, and sends forth from thence wonderful gifts into the light of that understanding which is His candle. Our hope lies in no most perfect mechanism even of the spirit, but in the wisdom wherein we live and move and have our being. Thence we hope for endless forms of beauty informed of truth. If the dark portion of our own being were the origin of our imaginations, we might well fear the apparition of such monsters as would be generated in the sickness of a decay which could never feel—only declare— a slow return towards primeval chaos. But the Maker is our Light.

One word more, ere we turn to consider the culture of this noblest faculty, which we might well call the creative, did we not see a something in God for which we would humbly keep our mighty word:—the fact that there is always more in a work of art—which is the highest human result of the embodying imagination—than the producer himself perceived while he produced it, seems to us a strong reason for attributing to it a larger origin than the man alone—for saying at the last, that the inspiration of the Almighty shaped its ends.

We return now to the class which, from the first, we supposed hostile to the imagination and its functions generally. Those belonging to it will now say: "It was to no imagination such as you have been setting forth that we were opposed, but to those wild fancies and vague reveries in which young people indulge, to the damage and loss of the real in the world around them."

"And," we insist, "you would rectify the matter by smothering the young monster at once—because he has wings, and, young to their use, flutters them about in a way discomposing to your nerves, and destructive to those notions of propriety of which this creature—you stop not to inquire whether angel or pterodactyle—has not yet learned even the existence. Or, if it is only the creature's vagaries of which you disapprove, why speak of them as *the* exercise of the imagination? As well speak of religion as the mother of cruelty because religion has given more occasion of cruelty, as of all dishonesty and devilry, than any other object of human interest. Are we not to worship, because our forefathers burned and stabbed for religion? It is more religion we want. It is more imagination we need. Be assured that these are but the first vital motions of that whose results, at least in the region of science, you are more than willing to accept." That evil may spring from the imagination, as from everything except the perfect love of God, cannot be denied. But infinitely worse evils would be the result of its absence. Selfishness, avarice, sensuality, cruelty, would flourish tenfold; and the power of Satan would be well established ere some children had begun to choose. Those who would quell the apparently lawless tossing of the spirit, called the youthful imagination, would suppress all that is to grow out of it. They fear the enthusiasm they never felt; and instead of cherishing this divine thing, instead of giving it room and air for healthful growth, they would crush and confine it—with but one result of their victorious endeavours— imposthume, fever, and corruption. And the disastrous consequences would soon appear in the intellect likewise which they worship. Kill that whence spring the crude fancies and wild day-dreams of the young, and you will never lead them beyond dull facts—dull because their relations to each other, and the one life that works in them all, must remain undiscovered. Whoever would have his children avoid this arid region will do well to allow no teacher to approach them—not even of mathematics—who has no imagination.

"But although good results may appear in a few from the indulgence of the imagination, how will it be with the many?"

We answer that the antidote to indulgence is development, not restraint, and that such is the duty of the wise servant of Him who made the imagination.

"But will most girls, for instance, rise to those useful uses of the imagination? Are they not more likely to exercise it in building castles in the air to the neglect of houses on the earth? And as the world affords such poor scope for the ideal, will not this habit breed vain desires and vain regrets? Is it not better, therefore, to keep to that which is known, and leave the rest?"

"Is the world so poor?" we ask in return. The less reason, then, to be satisfied with it; the more reason to rise above it, into the region of the true, of the eternal, of things as God thinks them. This outward world is but a passing vision of the persistent true. We shall not live in it always. We are dwellers in a divine universe where no desires are in vain, if only they be large enough. Not even in this world do all disappointments breed only vain regrets.[7] And as to keeping to that which is known and leaving the rest—how many affairs of this world are so well-defined, so capable of being clearly understood, as not to leave large spaces of uncertainty, whose very correlate faculty is the imagination? Indeed it must, in most things, work after some fashion, filling the gaps after some possible plan, before action can even begin. In very truth, a wise imagination, which is the presence of the spirit of God, is the best guide that man or woman can have; for it is not the things we see the most clearly that influence us the most powerfully; undefined, yet vivid visions of something beyond, something which eye has not seen nor ear heard, have far more influence than any logical sequences whereby the same things may be demonstrated to the intellect. It is the nature of the thing, not the clearness of its

---

7   "We will grieve not, rather find
        Strength in what remains behind;
        In the primal sympathy
        Which, having been, must ever be;
        In the soothing thoughts that spring
        Out of human suffering;
        In the faith that looks through death,
        In years that bring the philosophic mind."

outline, that determines its operation. We live by faith, and not by sight. Put the question to our mathematicians—only be sure the question reaches them—whether they would part with the well-defined perfection of their diagrams, or the dim, strange, possibly half-obliterated characters woven in the web of their being; their science, in short, or their poetry; their certainties, or their hopes; their consciousness of knowledge, or their vague sense of that which cannot be known absolutely: will they hold by their craft or by their inspirations, by their intellects or their imaginations? If they say the former in each alternative, I shall yet doubt whether the objects of the choice are actually before them, and with equal presentation.

What can be known must be known severely; but is there, therefore, no faculty for those infinite lands of uncertainty lying all about the sphere hollowed out of the dark by the glimmering lamp of our knowledge? Are they not the natural property of the imagination? there, *for* it, that it may have room to grow? there, that the man may learn to imagine greatly like God who made him, himself discovering their mysteries, in virtue of his following and worshipping imagination?

All that has been said, then, tends to enforce the culture of the imagination. But the strongest argument of all remains behind. For, if the whole power of pedantry should rise against her, the imagination will yet work; and if not for good, then for evil; if not for truth, then for falsehood; if not for life, then for death; the evil alternative becoming the more likely from the unnatural treatment she has experienced from those who ought to have fostered her. The power that might have gone forth in conceiving the noblest forms of action, in realizing the lives of the true-hearted, the self-forgetting, will go forth in building airy castles of vain ambition, of boundless riches, of unearned admiration. The imagination that might be devising how to make home blessed or to help the poor neighbour, will be absorbed in the invention of the new dress, or worse, in devising the means of procuring it. For, if she be not occupied with the beautiful, she will be occupied by the pleasant; that which goes not out to worship, will remain at home to be sensual. Cultivate the mere intellect as you may, it will never reduce the passions: the imagination, seeking the ideal in everything, will elevate them to their true and noble service. Seek not that your sons and your daughters should not see visions, should not dream dreams; seek that they should see true visions, that they should dream noble dreams. Such out-going of the imagination is one with aspiration, and will do more to elevate above what is low and vile than all possible inculcations of morality. Nor can religion herself ever rise up into her own calm home, her crystal shrine, when

one of her wings, one of the twain with which she flies, is thus broken
or paralyzed.

> "The universe is infinitely wide,
>   And conquering Reason, if self-glorified,
>   Can nowhere move uncrossed by some new wall
>   Or gulf of mystery, which thou alone,
>   Imaginative Faith! canst overleap,
>   In progress towards the fount of love."

The danger that lies in the repression of the imagination may be
well illustrated from the play of "Macbeth." The imagination of the
hero (in him a powerful faculty), representing how the deed would
appear to others, and so representing its true nature to himself, was
his great impediment on the path to crime. Nor would he have succeeded in reaching it, had he not gone to his wife for help—sought
refuge from his troublesome imagination with her. She, possessing
far less of the faculty, and having dealt more destructively with what
she had, took his hand, and led him to the deed. From her imagination, again, she for her part takes refuge in unbelief and denial, declar-
ing to herself and her husband that there is no reality in its representations; that there is no reality in anything beyond the present effect
it produces on the mind upon which it operates; that intellect and
courage are equal to any, even an evil emergency; and that no harm
will come to those who can rule themselves according to their own
will. Still, however, finding her imagination, and yet more that of her
husband, troublesome, she effects a marvellous combination of ma-
terialism and idealism, and asserts that things are not, cannot be,
and shall not be more or other than people choose to think them. She
says,—

> "These deeds must not be thought
>   After these ways; so, it will make us mad."

> "The sleeping and the dead
>   Are but as pictures."

But she had over-estimated the power of her will, and under-esti-
mated that of her imagination. Her will was the one thing in her that
was bad, without root or support in the universe, while her imagination was the voice of God himself out of her own unknown being. The
choice of no man or woman can long determine how or what he or
she shall think of things. Lady Macbeth's imagination would not be

repressed beyond its appointed period—a time determined by laws of her being over which she had no control. It arose, at length, as from the dead, overshadowing her with all the blackness of her crime. The woman who drank strong drink that she might murder, dared not sleep without a light by her bed; rose and walked in the night, a sleepless spirit in a sleeping body, rubbing the spotted hand of her dreams, which, often as water had cleared it of the deed, yet smelt so in her sleeping nostrils, that all the perfumes of Arabia would not sweeten it. Thus her long down-trodden imagination rose and took vengeance, even through those senses which she had thought to subordinate to her wicked will.

But all this is of the imagination itself, and fitter, therefore, for illustration than for argument. Let us come to facts.—Dr. Pritchard, lately executed for murder, had no lack of that invention, which is, as it were, the intellect of the imagination—its lowest form. One of the clergymen who, at his own request, attended the prisoner, went through indescribable horrors in the vain endeavour to induce the man simply to cease from lying: one invention after another followed the most earnest asseverations of truth. The effect produced upon us by this clergyman's report of his experience was a moral dismay, such as we had never felt with regard to human being, and drew from us the exclamation, "The man could have had no imagination." The reply was, "None whatever." Never seeking true or high things, caring only for appearances, and, therefore, for inventions, he had left his imagination all undeveloped, and when it represented his own inner condition to him, had repressed it until it was nearly destroyed, and what remained of it was set on fire of hell.[8]

Man is "the roof and crown of things." He is the world, and more. Therefore the chief scope of his imagination, next to God who made him, will be the world in relation to his own life therein. Will he do better or worse in it if this imagination, touched to fine issues and having free scope, present him with noble pictures of relationship and duty, of possible elevation of character and attainable justice of behaviour, of friendship and of love; and, above all, of all these in that life to understand which as a whole, must ever be the loftiest

[8] One of the best weekly papers in London, evidently as much in ignorance of the man as of the facts of the case, spoke of Dr. MacLeod as having been engaged in "whitewashing the murderer for heaven." So far is this from a true representation, that Dr. MacLeod actually refused to pray with him, telling him that if there was a hell to go to, he must go to it.

aspiration of this noblest power of humanity? Will a woman lead a
more or a less troubled life that the sights and sounds of nature break
through the crust of gathering anxiety, and remind her of the peace
of the lilies and the well-being of the birds of the air? Or will life be
less interesting to her, that the lives of her neighbours, instead of
passing like shadows upon a wall, assume a consistent wholeness,
forming themselves into stories and phases of life? Will she not hereby
love more and talk less? Or will she be more unlikely to make a good
match—? But here we arrest ourselves in bewilderment over the word
good, and seek to re-arrange our thoughts. If what mothers mean by
a *good* match, is the alliance of a man of position and means—or let
them throw intellect, manners, and personal advantages into the same
scale—if this be all, then we grant the daughter of cultivated imagination may not be manageable, will probably be obstinate. We hope
she will be obstinate enough.[9] But will the girl be less likely to marry
a *gentleman,* in the grand old meaning of the sixteenth century? when
it was no irreverence to call our Lord

"The first true gentleman that ever breathed;"

or in that of the fourteenth?—when Chaucer teaching "whom is
worthy to be called gentill," writes thus:—

"The first stocke was full of rightwisnes,
  Trewe of his worde, sober, pitous and free,
  Clene of his goste, and loved besinesse,
  Against the vice of slouth in honeste;
  And but his heire love vertue as did he,
  He is not gentill though he rich seme,
  All weare he miter, crowne, or diademe."

Will she be less likely to marry one who honours women, and for
their sakes, as well as his own, honours himself? Or to speak from

---

[9] Let women who feel the wrongs of their kind teach women to be
high-minded in their relation to men, and they will do more for the
social elevation of women, and the establishment of their rights,
whatever those rights may be, than by any amount of intellectual
development or assertion of equality. Nor, if they are other than mere
partisans, will they refuse the attempt because in its success men
will, after all, be equal, if not greater gainers, if only thereby they
should be "feelingly persuaded" what they are.

what many would regard as the mother's side of the question—will the girl be more likely, because of such a culture of her imagination, to refuse the wise, true-hearted, generous rich man, and fall in love with the talking, verse-making fool, *because* he is poor, as if that were a virtue for which he had striven? The highest imagination and the lowliest common sense are always on one side.

For the end of imagination is *harmony*. A right imagination, being the reflex of the creation, will fall in with the divine order of things as the highest form of its own operation; "will tune its instrument here at the door" to the divine harmonies within; will be content alone with growth towards the divine idea, which includes all that is beautiful in the imperfect imaginations of men; will know that every deviation from that growth is downward; and will therefore send the man forth from its loftiest representations to do the commonest duty of the most wearisome calling in a hearty and hopeful spirit. This is the work of the right imagination; and towards this work every imagination, in proportion to the rightness that is in it, will tend. The reveries even of the wise man will make him stronger for his work; his dreaming as well as his thinking will render him sorry for past failure, and hopeful of future success.

To come now to the culture of the imagination. Its development is one of the main ends of the divine education of life with all its efforts and experiences. Therefore the first and essential means for its culture must be an ordering of our life towards harmony with its ideal in the mind of God. As he that is willing to do the will of the Father, shall know of the doctrine, so, we doubt not, he that will do the will of The Poet, shall behold the Beautiful. For all is God's; and the man who is growing into harmony with His will, is growing into harmony with himself; all the hidden glories of his being are coming out into the light of humble consciousness; so that at the last he shall be a pure microcosm, faithfully reflecting, after his manner, the mighty macrocosm. We believe, therefore, that nothing will do so much for the intellect or the imagination as *being good*— we do not mean after any formula or any creed, but simply after the faith of Him who did the will of his Father in heaven.

But if we speak of direct means for the culture of the imagination, the whole is comprised in two words—food and exercise. If you want strong arms, take animal food, and row. Feed your imagination with food convenient for it, and exercise it, not in the contortions of the acrobat, but in the movements of the gymnast. And first for the food.

Goethe has told us that the way to develop the aesthetic faculty is to have constantly before our eyes, that is, in the room we most frequent, some work of the best attainable art. This will teach us to refuse

the evil and choose the good. It will plant itself in our minds and become our counsellor. Involuntarily, unconsciously, we shall compare
with its perfection everything that comes before us for judgment. Now,
although no better advice could be given, it involves one danger, that
of narrowness. And not easily, in dread of this danger, would one
change his tutor, and so procure variety of instruction. But in the
culture of the imagination, books, although not the only, are the readi-
est means of supplying the food convenient for it, and a hundred books
may be had where even one work of art of the right sort is unattainable, seeing such must be of some size as well as of thorough excellence. And in variety alone is safety from the danger of the convenient food becoming the inconvenient model.

Let us suppose, then, that one who himself justly estimates the
imagination is anxious to develop its operation in his child. No doubt
the best beginning, especially if the child be young, is an acquaintance with nature, in which let him be encouraged to observe vital
phenomena, to put things together, to speculate from what he sees to
what he does not see. But let earnest care be taken that upon no matter
shall he go on talking foolishly. Let him be as fanciful as he may, but
let him not, even in his fancy, sin against fancy's sense; for fancy has
its laws as certainly as the most ordinary business of life. When he is
silly, let him know it and be ashamed.

But where this association with nature is but occasionally possible, recourse must be had to literature. In books, we not only have
store of all results of the imagination, but in them, as in her work-
shop, we may behold her embodying before our very eyes, in music of
speech, in wonder of words, till her work, like a golden dish set with
shining jewels, and adorned by the hands of the cunning workmen,
stands finished before us. In this kind, then, the best must be set before the learner, that he may eat and not be satisfied; for the finest
products of the imagination are of the best nourishment for the begin-
nings of that imagination. And the mind of the teacher must mediate
between the work of art and the mind of the pupil, bringing them
together in the vital contact of intelligence; directing the observation
to the lines of expression, the points of force; and helping the mind
to repose upon the whole, so that no separable beauties shall lead to
a neglect of the scope—that is the shape or form complete. And ever
he must seek to *show* excellence rather than talk about it, giving the
thing itself, that it may grow into the mind, and not a eulogy of his
own upon the thing; isolating the point worthy of remark rather than
making many remarks upon the point.

Especially must he endeavour to show the spiritual scaffolding or
skeleton of any work of art; those main ideas upon which the shape is

constructed, and around which the rest group as ministering dependencies.

But he will not, therefore, pass over that intellectual structure without which the other could not be manifested. He will not forget the builder while he admires the architect. While he dwells with delight on the relation of the peculiar arch to the meaning of the whole cathedral, he will not think it needless to explain the principles on which it is constructed, or even how those principles are carried out in actual process. Neither yet will the tracery of its windows, the foliage of its crockets, or the fretting of its mouldings be forgotten. Every beauty will have its word, only all beauties will be subordinated to the final beauty—that is, the unity of the whole.

Thus doing, he shall perform the true office of friendship. He will introduce his pupil into the society which he himself prizes most, surrounding him with the genial presence of the high-minded, that this good company may work its own kind in him who frequents it.

But he will likewise seek to turn him aside from such company, whether of books or of men, as might tend to lower his reverence, his choice, or his standard. He will, therefore, discourage indiscriminate reading, and that worse than waste which consists in skimming the books of a circulating library. He knows that if a book is worth reading at all, it is worth reading well; and that, if it is not worth reading, it is only to the most accomplished reader that it *can* be worth skimming. He will seek to make him discern, not merely between the good and the evil, but between the good and the not so good. And this not for the sake of sharpening the intellect, still less of generating that self-satisfaction which is the closest attendant upon criticism, but for the sake of choosing the best path and the best companions upon it. A spirit of criticism for the sake of distinguishing only, or, far worse, for the sake of having one's opinion ready upon demand, is not merely repulsive to all true thinkers, but is, in itself, destructive of all thinking. A spirit of criticism for the sake of the truth—a spirit that does not start from its chamber at every noise, but waits till its presence is desired—cannot, indeed, garnish the house, but can sweep it clean. Were there enough of such wise criticism, there would be ten times the study of the best writers of the past, and perhaps one-tenth of the admiration for the ephemeral productions of the day. A gathered mountain of misplaced worships would be swept into the sea by the study of one good book; and while what was good in an inferior book would still be admired, the relative position of the book would be altered and its influence lessened.

Speaking of true learning, Lord Bacon says: "It taketh away vain admiration of anything, *which is the root of all weakness.*"

The right teacher would have his pupil easy to please, but ill to satisfy; ready to enjoy, unready to embrace; keen to discover beauty, slow to say, "Here I will dwell."

But he will not confine his instructions to the region of art. He will encourage him to read history with an eye eager for the dawning figure of the past. He will especially show him that a great part of the Bible is only thus to be understood; and that the constant and consistent way of God, to be discovered in it, is in fact the key to all history.

In the history of individuals, as well, he will try to show him how to put sign and token together, constructing not indeed a whole, but a probable suggestion of the whole.

And, again, while showing him the reflex of nature in the poets, he will not be satisfied without sending him to Nature herself; urging him in country rambles to keep open eyes for the sweet fashionings and blendings of her operation around him; and in city walks to watch the "human face divine."

Once more: he will point out to him the essential difference between reverie and thought; between dreaming and imagining. He will teach him not to mistake fancy, either in himself or in others, for imagination, and to beware of hunting after resemblances that carry with them no interpretation.

Such training is not solely fitted for the possible development of artistic faculty. Few, in this world, will ever be able to utter what they feel. Fewer still will be able to utter it in forms of their own. Nor is it necessary that there should be many such. But it is necessary that all should feel. It is necessary that all should understand and imagine the good; that all should begin, at least, to follow and find out God.

"The glory of God is to conceal a thing, but the glory of the king is to find it out," says Solomon. "As if," remarks Bacon on the passage, "according to the innocent play of children, the Divine Majesty took delight to hide his works, to the end to have them found out; and as if kings could not obtain a greater honour than to be God's playfellows in that game."

One more quotation from the book of Ecclesiastes, setting forth both the necessity we are under to imagine, and the comfort that our imagining cannot outstrip God's making.

"I have seen the travail which God hath given to the sons of men to be exercised in it. He hath made everything beautiful in his time; also he hath set the world in their heart, so that no man can find out the work that God maketh from the beginning to the end."

Thus to be playfellows with God in this game, the little ones may gather their daisies and follow their painted moths; the child of the kingdom may pore upon the lilies of the field, and gather faith as the

birds of the air their food from the leafless hawthorn, ruddy with the
stores God has laid up for them; and the man of science

> "May sit and rightly spell
>   Of every star that heaven doth shew,
>   And every herb that sips the dew;
>   Till old experience do attain
>   To something like prophetic strain."

The Fantastic Imagination

(1893)

The Fantastic Imagination

That we have in English no word corresponding to the German Märchen, drives us to use the word Fairytale, regardless of the fact that the tale may have nothing to do with any sort of fairy. The old use of the word Fairy, by Spenser at least, might, however, well be adduced, were justification or excuse necessary where need must.

Were I asked, what is a fairytale? I should reply, Read Undine: that is a fairytale; then read this and that as well, and you will see what is a fairytale. Were I further begged to describe the fairytale, or define what it is, I would make answer, that I should as soon think of describing the abstract human face, or stating what must go to constitute a human being. A fairytale is just a fairytale, as a face is just a face; and of all fairytales I know, I think Undine the most beautiful.

Many a man, however, who would not attempt to define a man, might venture to say something as to what a man ought to be: even so much I will not in this place venture with regard to the fairytale, for my long past work in that kind might but poorly instance or illustrate my now more matured judgment. I will but say some things helpful to the reading, in right-minded fashion, of such fairytales as I would wish to write, or care to read.

Some thinkers would feel sorely hampered if at liberty to use no forms but such as existed in nature, or to invent nothing save in accordance with the laws of the world of the senses; but it must not therefore be imagined that they desire escape from the region of law. Nothing lawless can show the least reason why it should exist, or could at best have more than an appearance of life.

The natural world has its laws, and no man must interfere with them in the way of presentment any more than in the way of use; but they themselves may suggest laws of other kinds, and man may, if he pleases, invent a little world of his own, with its own laws; for there is that in him which delights in calling up new forms—which is the nearest, perhaps, he can come to creation. When such forms are new embodiments of old truths, we call them products of the Imagination; when they are mere inventions, however lovely, I should call them the work of the Fancy: in either case, Law has been diligently at work.

His world once invented, the highest law that comes next into play is, that there shall be harmony between the laws by which the new world has begun to exist; and in the process of his creation, the inventor must hold by those laws. The moment he forgets one of them, he makes the story, by its own postulates, incredible. To be able to live a moment in an imagined world, we must see the laws of its existence obeyed. Those broken, we fall out of it. The imagination in us, whose exercise is essential to the most temporary submission to the imagination of another, immediately, with the disappearance of Law, ceases to act. Suppose the gracious creatures of some childlike region of Fairyland talking either cockney or Gascon! Would not the tale, however lovelily begun, sink once to the level of the Burlesque—of all forms of literature the least worthy? A man's inventions may be stupid or clever, but if he does not hold by the laws of them, or if he makes one law jar with another, he contradicts himself as an inventor, he is no artist. He does not rightly consort his instruments, or he tunes them in different keys. The mind of man is the product of live Law; it thinks by law, it dwells in the midst of law, it gathers from law its growth; with law, therefore, can it alone work to any result. Inharmonious, unconsorting ideas will come to a man, but if he try to use one of such, his work will grow dull, and he will drop it from mere lack of interest. Law is the soil in which alone beauty will grow; beauty is the only stuff in which Truth can be clothed; and you may, if you will, call Imagination the tailor that cuts her garments to fit her, and Fancy his journeyman that puts the pieces of them together, or perhaps at most embroiders their button-holes. Obeying law, the maker works like his creator; not obeying law, he is such a fool as heaps a pile of stones and calls it a church.

In the moral world it is different: there a man may clothe in new forms, and for this employ his imagination freely, but he must invent nothing. He may not, for any purpose, turn its laws upside down. He must not meddle with the relations of live souls. The laws of the spirit of man must hold, alike in this world and in any world he may invent. It were no offence to suppose a world in which everything repelled instead of attracted the things around it; it would be wicked to write a tale representing a man it called good as always doing bad things, or a man it called bad as always doing good things: the notion itself is absolutely lawless. In physical things a man may invent; in moral things he must obey—and take their laws with him into his invented world as well.

"You write as if a fairytale were a thing of importance: must it have meaning?"

It cannot help having some meaning; if it have proportion and harmony it has vitality, and vitality is truth. The beauty may be plainer in it than the truth, but without the truth the beauty could not be, and the fairytale would give no delight. Everyone, however, who feels the story, will read its meaning after his own nature and development: one man will read one meaning in it, another will read another.

"If so, how am I to assure myself that I am not reading my own meaning into it, but yours out of it?"

Why should you be so assured? It may be better that you should read your meaning into it. That may be a higher operation of your intellect than the mere reading of mine out of it: your meaning may be superior to mine.

"Suppose my child ask me what the fairytale means, what am I to say?"

If you do not know what it means, what is easier than to say so? If you do see a meaning in it, there it is for you to give him. A genuine work of art must mean many things; the truer its art, the more things it will mean. If my drawing, on the other hand, is so far from being a work of art that it needs THIS IS A HORSE written under it, what can it matter that neither you nor your child should know what it means? It is there not so much to convey a meaning as to wake a meaning. If it do not even wake an interest, throw it aside. A meaning may be there, but it is not for you. If, again, you do not know a horse when you see it, the name written under it will not serve you much. At all events, the business of the painter is not to teach zoology.

But indeed your children are not likely to trouble you about the meaning. They find what they are capable of finding, and more would be too much. For my part, I do not write for children, but for the child-like, whether of five, or fifty, or seventy-five.

A fairytale is not an allegory. There may be allegory in it, but it not an allegory. He must be an artist indeed who can, in any mode, produce a strict allegory that is not a weariness to the spirit. An allegory must be Mastery or Moorditch.

A fairytale, like a butterfly or a bee, helps itself on all sides, sips every wholesome flower, and spoils not one. The true fairytale is, to my mind, very like the sonata. We all know that a sonata means something; and where there is the faculty of talking with suitable vagueness, and choosing metaphor sufficiently loose, mind may approach mind, in the interpretation of a sonata, with the result of a more or less contenting consciousness of sympathy. But if two or three men sat down to write each what the sonata meant to him, what approximation

to definite idea would be the result? Little enough—and that little
more than needful. We should find it had roused related, if not identical, feelings, but probably not one common thought. Has the sonata
therefore failed? Had it undertaken to convey, or ought it to be expected to impart anything defined, anything notionally recognisable?

"But words are not music; words at least are meant and fitted to
carry a precise meaning!"

It is very seldom indeed that they carry the exact meaning of any
user of them! And if they can be so used as to convey definite meaning, it does not follow that they ought never to carry anything else.
Words are live things that may be variously employed to various ends.
They can convey a scientific fact, or throw a shadow of her child's
dream on the heart of a mother. They are things to put together like
the pieces of dissected map, or to arrange like the notes on a stave. Is
the music in them to go for nothing? It can hardly help the definiteness of a meaning: is it therefore to be disregarded? They have length,
and breadth, and outline: have they nothing to do with depth? Have
they only to describe, never to impress? Has nothing any claim to
their use but definite? The cause of a child's tears may be altogether
undefinable: has the mother therefore no antidote for his vague misery? That may be strong in colour which has no evident outline. A
fairytale, a sonata, a gathering storm, a limitless night, seizes you
and sweeps you away: do you begin at once to wrestle with it and ask
whence its power over you, whither it is carrying you? The law of each
is in the mind of its composer; that law makes one man feel this way,
another man feel that way. To one the sonata is a world of odour and
beauty, to another of soothing only and sweetness. To one, the cloudy
rendezvous is a wild dance, with a terror at its heart; to another, a
majestic march of heavenly hosts, with Truth in their centre pointing
their course, but as yet restraining her voice. The greatest forces lie
in the region of the uncomprehended.

I will go farther.—The best thing you can do for your fellow, next
to rousing his conscience, is—not to give him things to think about,
but to wake things up that are in him; or say, to make him think things
for himself. The best Nature does for us is to work in us such moods in
which thoughts of high import arise. Does any aspect of Nature wake
but one thought? Does she ever suggest only one definite thing? Does
she make any two men in the same place at the same moment think the
same thing? Is she therefore a failure, because she is not definite? Is
it nothing that she rouses the something deeper than the understanding—the power that underlies thoughts? Does she not set feeling, and
so thinking at work? Would it be better that she did this after one
fashion and not after many fashions? Nature is mood-engendering,

thought-provoking: such ought the sonata, such ought the fairytale to be.

"But a man may then imagine in your work what he pleases, what you never meant!"

Not what he pleases, but what he can. If he be not a true man, he will draw evil out of the best; we need not mind how he treats any work of art! If he be a true man, he will imagine true things; what matter whether I meant them or not? They are there none the less that I cannot claim putting them there! One difference between God's work and man's is, that, while God's work cannot mean more than he meant, man's must mean more than he meant. For in everything that God has made, there is a layer upon layer of ascending significance; also he expresses the same thought in higher and higher kinds of that thought: it is God's things, his embodied thoughts, which alone a man has to use, modified and adapted to his own purposes, for the expression of his thoughts; therefore he cannot help his words and figures falling into such combinations in the mind of another as he had himself not foreseen, so many are the thoughts allied to every other thought, so many are the relations involved in every figure, so many the facts hinted in every symbol. A man may well himself discover truth in what he wrote; for he was dealing all the time things that came from thoughts beyond his own.

"But surely you would explain your idea to one who asked you?"

I say again, if I cannot draw a horse, I will not write THIS IS A HORSE under what I foolishly meant for one. Any key to a work of imagination would be nearly, if not quite, as absurd. The tale is there not to hide, but to show: if it show nothing at your window, do not open your door to it; leave it out in the cold. To ask me to explain, is to say, "Roses! Boil them, or we won't have them!" My tales may not be roses but I will not boil them.

So long as I think my dog can bark, I will not sit up to bark for him.

If a writer's aim be logical conviction, he must spare no logical pains, not merely to be understood, but to escape being misunderstood; where his object is to move by suggestion, to cause to imagine, then let him assail the soul of his reader as the wind assails an aeolian harp. If there be music in my reader, I would gladly wake it. Let fairytale of mine go for a firefly that now flashes, now is dark, but may flash again. Caught in a hand which does not love its kind, it will turn to an insignificant ugly thing, that can neither flash nor fly.

The best way with music, I imagine, is not to bring the forces of our intellect to bear upon it, but to be still and let it work on that part of us for whose sake it exists. We spoil countless precious things by intellectual greed. He who will be a man, and will not be a child, must—he cannot help himself—become a little man, that is, a dwarf. He will, however need no consolation, for he is sure to think himself a very large creature indeed.

If any strain of my "broken music" make a child's eyes flash, or his mother's grow for a moment dim, my labour will not have been in vain.

The Portent

(1864)

1
My Boyhood

My father belonged to the widespread family of the Campbells, and possessed a small landed property in the north of Argyll. But although of long descent and high connection, he was no richer than many a farmer of a few hundred acres. For, with the exception of a narrow belt of arable land at its foot, a bare hill formed almost the whole of his possessions. The sheep ate over it, and no doubt found it good; I bounded and climbed all over it, and thought it a kingdom. From my very childhood, I had rejoiced in being alone. The sense of room about me had been one of my greatest delights. Hence, when my thoughts go back to those old years, it is not the house, nor the family room, nor that in which I slept, that first of all rises before my inward vision, but that desolate hill, the top of which was only a wide expanse of moorland, rugged with height and hollow, and dangerous with deep, dark pools, but in many portions purple with large-belled heather, and crowded with cranberry and blueberry plants. Most of all, I loved it in the still autumn morning, outstretched in stillness, high uplifted towards the heaven. On every stalk hung the dew in tiny drops, which, while the rising sun was low, sparkled and burned with the hues of all the gems. Here and there a bird gave a cry; no other sound awoke the silence. I never see the statue of the Roman youth, praying with outstretched arms, and open, empty, level palms, as waiting to receive and hold the blessing of the gods, but that outstretched barren heath rises before me, as if it meant the same thing as the statue—or were, at least, the fit room in the middle space of which to set the praying and expectant youth.

There was one spot upon the hill, half-way between the valley and the moorland, which was my favourite haunt. This part of the hill was covered with great blocks of stone, of all shapes and sizes—here crowded together, like the slain where the battle had been fiercest; there parting asunder from spaces of delicate green—of softest grass. In the centre of one of these green spots, on a steep part of the hill, were three huge rocks—two projecting out of the hill, rather than standing up from it, and one, likewise projecting from the hill, but lying across the tops of the two, so as to form a little cave, the back of which was the side of the hill. This was my refuge, my home within a home, my study—and, in the hot noons, often my sleeping chamber, and my house of dreams. If the wind blew cold on the hillside, a hollow of lulling warmth was there, scooped as it were out of the body of the blast, which, sweeping around, whistled keen and thin through the cracks and crannies of the rocky chaos that lay all about; in which confusion of rocks the wind plunged, and flowed, and eddied, and withdrew, as the sea-waves on the cliffy shores or the unknown rugged bottoms. Here I would often lie, as the sun went down, and watch the silent growth of another sea, which the stormy ocean of the wind could not disturb—the sea of the darkness. First it would begin to gather in the bottom of hollow places. Deep valleys, and all little pits on the hill-sides, were well-springs where it gathered, and whence it seemed to overflow, till it had buried the earth beneath its mass, and, rising high into the heavens, swept over the faces of the stars, washed the blinding day from them, and let them shine, down through the waters of the dark, to the eyes of men below. I would lie till nothing but the stars and the dim outlines of hills against the sky was to be seen, and then rise and go home, as sure of my path as if I had been descending a dark staircase in my father's house.

On the opposite side the valley, another hill lay parallel to mine; and behind it, at some miles' distance, a great mountain. As often as, in my hermit's cave, I lifted my eyes from the volume I was reading, I saw this mountain before me. Very different was its character from that of the hill on which I was seated. It was a mighty thing, a chieftain of the race, seamed and scarred, featured with chasms and precipices and over-leaning rocks, themselves huge as hills; here blackened with shade, there overspread with glory; interlaced with the silvery lines of falling streams, which, hurrying from heaven to earth, cared not how they went, so it were downwards. Fearful stories were told of the gulfs, sullen waters, and dizzy heights upon that terror-haunted mountain. In storms the wind roared like thunder in its caverns and along the jagged sides of its cliffs, but at other times that uplifted land—uplifted, yet secret and full of dismay—lay silent as a cloud on the horizon.

I had a certain peculiarity of constitution, which I have some reason to believe I inherit. It seems to have its root in an unusual delicacy of hearing, which often conveys to me sounds inaudible to those about me. This I have had many opportunities of proving. It has likewise, however, brought me sounds which I could never trace back to their origin; though they may have arisen from some natural operation

which I had not perseverance or mental acuteness sufficient to discover. From this, or, it may be, from some deeper cause with which
this is connected, arose a certain kind of fearfulness associated with
the sense of hearing, of which I have never heard a corresponding
instance. Full as my mind was of the wild and sometimes fearful tales
of a Highland nursery, fear never entered my mind by the eyes, nor,
when I brooded over tales of terror, and fancied new and yet more
frightful embodiments of horror, did I shudder at any imaginable
spectacle, or tremble lest the fancy should become fact, and from behind the whin-bush or the elder-hedge should glide forth the tall swaying form of the Boneless. When alone in bed, I used to lie awake, and
look out into the room, peopling it with the forms of all the persons
who had died within the scope of my memory and acquaintance. These
fancied forms were vividly present to my imagination. I pictured them
pale, with dark circles around their hollow eyes, visible by a light
which glimmered within them; not the light of life, but a pale, greenish phosphorescence, generated by the decay of the brain inside. Their
garments were white and trailing, but torn and soiled, as by trying
often in vain to get up out of the buried coffin. But so far from being
terrified by these imaginings, I used to delight in them; and in the
long winter evenings, when I did not happen to have any book that
interested me sufficiently, I used even to look forward with expectation to the hour when, laying myself straight upon my back, as if my
bed were my coffin, I could call up from underground all who had
passed away, and see how they fared, yea, what progress they had made
towards final dissolution of form—but all the time, with my fingers
pushed hard into my ears, lest the faintest sound should invade the
silent citadel of my soul. If inadvertently I removed one of my fingers,
the agony of terror I instantly experienced is indescribable. I can compare it to nothing but the rushing in upon my brain of a whole churchyard of spectres. The very possibility of hearing a sound, in such a
mood, and at such a time, was almost enough to paralyse me. So I
could scare myself in broad daylight, on the open hillside, by imagining
unintelligible sounds; and my imagination was both original and fertile
in the invention of such. But my mind was too active to be often subjected to such influences. Indeed life would have been hardly endurable
had these moods been of more than occasional occurrence. As I grew
older, I almost outgrew them. Yet sometimes one awful dread would seize
me—that, perhaps, the prophetic power manifest in the gift of second
sight, which, according to the testimony of my old nurse, had belonged
to several of my ancestors, had been in my case transformed in kind
without losing its nature, transferring its abode from the sight to the
hearing, whence resulted its keenness, and my fear and suffering.

2
The Second Hearing

One summer evening, I had lingered longer than usual in my rocky
retreat: I had lain half dreaming in the mouth of my cave, till the shadows of evening had fallen, and the gloaming had deepened half-way
towards the night. But the night had no more terrors for me than the
day. Indeed, in such regions there is a solitariness for which there
seems a peculiar sense, and upon which the shadows of night sink
with a strange relief, hiding from the eye the wide space which yet
they throw more open to the imagination. When I lifted my head, only
a star here and there caught my eye; but, looking intently into the
depths of blue-grey, I saw that they were crowded with twinkles. The
mountain rose before me, a huge mass of gloom; but its several peaks
stood out against the sky with a clear, pure, sharp outline, and looked
nearer to me than the bulk from which they rose heaven-wards. One
star trembled and throbbed upon the very tip of the loftiest, the central
peak, which seemed the spire of a mighty temple where the light was
worshipped—crowned, therefore, in the darkness, with the emblem of
the day. I was lying, as I have said, with this fancy still in my thought,
when suddenly I heard, clear, though faint and far away, the sound as
of the iron-shod hoofs of a horse, in furious gallop along an uneven
rocky surface. It was more like a distant echo than an original sound.
It seemed to come from the face of the mountain, where no horse, I
knew, could go at that speed, even if its rider courted certain destruc-
tion. There was a peculiarity, too, in the sound—a certain tinkle, or clank,
which I fancied myself able, by auricular analysis, to distinguish from
the body of the sound. Supposing the sound to be caused by the feet of a
horse, the peculiarity was just such as would result from one of the
shoes being loose. A terror—strange even to my experience—seized
me, and I hastened home. The sounds gradually died away as I descended
the hill. Could they have been an echo from some precipice of the
mountain? I knew of no road lying so that, if a horse were galloping
upon it, the sounds would be reflected from the mountain to me.

The next day, in one of my rambles, I found myself near the cottage of my old foster-mother, who was distantly related to us, and was a trusted servant in the family at the time I was born. On the death of my mother, which took place almost immediately after my birth, she had taken the entire charge of me, and had brought me up, though with difficulty; for she used to tell me, I should never be either folk or fairy. For some years she had lived alone in a cottage, at the bottom of a deep green circular hollow, upon which, in walking over a healthy table-land, one came with a sudden surprise. I was her frequent visitor. She was a tall, thin, aged woman, with eager eyes, and well-defined clear-cut features. Her voice was harsh, but with an undertone of great tenderness. She was scrupulously careful in her attire, which was rather above her station. Altogether, she had much the bearing of a gentle-woman. Her devotion to me was quite motherly. Never having had any family of her own, although she had been the wife of one of my father's shepherds, she expended the whole maternity of her nature upon me. She was always my first resource in any perplexity, for I was sure of all the help she could give me. And as she had much influence with my father, who was rather severe in his notions, I had had occasion to beg her interference. No necessity of this sort, however, had led to my visit on the present occasion.

I ran down the side of the basin, and entered the little cottage. Nurse was seated on a chair by the wall, with her usual knitting, a stocking, in one hand; but her hands were motionless, and her eyes wide open and fixed. I knew that the neighbours stood rather in awe of her, on the ground that she had the second sight; but, although she often told us frightful enough stories, she had never alluded to such a gift as being in her possession. Now I concluded at once that she was seeing. I was confirmed in this conclusion when, seeming to come to herself suddenly, she covered her head with her plaid, and sobbed audibly, in spite of her efforts to command herself. But I did not dare to ask her any questions, nor did she attempt any excuse for her behaviour. After a few moments, she unveiled herself, rose, and welcomed me with her usual kindness; then got me some refreshment, and began to question me about matters at home. After a pause, she said suddenly: "When are you going to get your commission, Duncan, do you know?" I replied that I had heard nothing of it; that I did not think my father had influence or money enough to procure me one, and that I feared I should have no such good chance of distinguishing myself. She did not answer, but nodded her head three times, slowly and with compressed lips—apparently as much as to say, "I know better."

Just as I was leaving her, it occurred to me to mention that I had heard an odd sound the night before. She turned towards me, and looked at me fixedly. "What was it like, Duncan, my dear?"

"Like a horse galloping with a loose shoe," I replied.

"Duncan, Duncan, my darling!" she said, in a low, trembling voice, but with passionate earnestness, "you did not hear it? Tell me that you did not hear it! You only want to frighten poor old nurse: some one has been telling you the story!"

It was my turn to be frightened now; for the matter became at once associated with my fears as to the possible nature of my auricular peculiarities. I assured her that nothing was farther from my intention than to frighten her; that, on the contrary, she had rather alarmed me; and I begged her to explain. But she sat down white and trembling, and did not speak. Presently, however, she rose again, and saying, "I have known it happen sometimes without anything very bad following," began to put away the basin and plate I had been using, as if she would compel herself to be calm before me. I renewed my entreaties for an explanation, but without avail. She begged me to be content for a few days, as she was quite unable to tell the story at present. She promised, however, of her own accord, that before I left home she would tell me all she knew.

The next day a letter arrived announcing the death of a distant relation, through whose influence my father had had a lingering hope of obtaining an appointment for me. There was nothing left but to look out for a situation as tutor.

3

My Old Nurse's Story

I was now almost nineteen. I had completed the usual curriculum of study at one of the Scotch universities; and, possessed of a fair knowledge of mathematics and physics, and what I considered rather more than a good foundation for classical and metaphysical acquirement, I resolved to apply for the first suitable situation that offered. But I was spared the trouble. A certain Lord Hilton, an English nobleman, residing in one of the midland counties, having heard that one of my father's sons was desirous of such a situation, wrote to him, offering me the post of tutor to his two boys, of the ages of ten and twelve. He had been partly educated at a Scotch university; and this, it may be, had prejudiced him in favour of a Scotch tutor; while an ancient alliance of the families by marriage was supposed by my nurse to be the reason of his offering me the situation. Of this connection, however, my father said nothing to me, and it went for nothing in my anticipations. I was to receive a hundred pounds a year, and to hold in the family the position of a gentleman, which might mean anything or nothing, according to the disposition of the heads of the family. Preparations for my departure were immediately commenced. I set out one evening for the cottage of my old nurse, to bid her good-bye for many months, probably years. I was to leave the next day for Edinburgh, on my way to London, whence I had to repair by coach to my new abode—almost to me like the land beyond the grave, so little did I know about it, and so wide was the separation between it and my home. The evening was sultry when I began my walk, and before I arrived at its end, the clouds rising from all quarters of the horizon, and especially gathering around the peaks of the mountain, betokened the near approach of a thunderstorm. This was a great delight to me. Gladly would I take leave of my home with the memory of a last night of tumultuous magnificence; followed, probably, by a day of weeping rain, well suited to the mood of my own heart in bidding farewell to the best of parents and the dearest of homes. Besides, in common

with most Scotchmen who are young and hardy enough to be unable
to realise the existence of coughs and rheumatic fevers, it was a positive pleasure to me to be out in rain, hail, or snow.

"I am come to bid you good-bye, Margaret; and to hear the story
which you promised to tell me before I left home: I go to-morrow."

"Do you go so soon, my darling? Well, it will be an awful night to
tell it in; but, as I promised, I suppose I must."

At the moment, two or three great drops of rain, the first of the
storm, fell down the wide chimney, exploding in the clear turf-fire.

"Yes, indeed you must," I replied.

After a short pause, she commenced. Of course she spoke in Gaelic;
and I translate from my recollection of the Gaelic; but rather from
the impression left upon my mind, than from any recollection of the
words. She drew her chair near the fire, which we had reason to fear
would soon be put out by the falling rain, and began.

"How old the story is, I do not know. It has come down through
many generations. My grandmother told it to me as I tell it to you;
and her mother and my mother sat beside, never interrupting, but
nodding their heads at every turn. Almost it ought to begin like the
fairy tales, Once upon a time,—it took place so long ago; but it is too
dreadful and too true to tell like a fairy tale.—There were two brothers,
sons of the chief of our clan, but as different in appearance and disposition as two men could be. The elder was fair-haired and strong,
much given to hunting and fishing; fighting too, upon occasion, I dare
say, when they made a foray upon the Saxon, to get back a mouthful
of their own. But he was gentleness itself to every one about him, and
the very soul of honour in all his doings. The younger was very dark
in complexion, and tall and slender compared to his brother. He was
very fond of book-learning, which, they say, was an uncommon taste
in those times. He did not care for any sports or bodily exercises but
one; and that, too, was unusual in these parts. It was horsemanship.
He was a fierce rider, and as much at home in the saddle as in his
study-chair. You may think that, so long ago, there was not much fit
room for riding hereabouts; but, fit or not fit, he rode. From his reading
and riding, the neighbours looked doubtfully upon him, and whispered
about the black art. He usually bestrode a great powerful black horse,
without a white hair on him; and people said it was either the devil
himself, or a demon-horse from the devil's own stud. What favoured
this notion was, that, in or out of the stable, the brute would let no other
than his master go near him. Indeed, no one would venture, after he had
killed two men, and grievously maimed a third, tearing him with his
teeth and hoofs like a wild beast. But to his master he was obedient
as a hound, and would even tremble in his presence sometimes.

"The youth's temper corresponded to his habits. He was both gloomy and passionate. Prone to anger, he had never been known to forgive. Debarred from anything on which he had set his heart, he would have gone mad with longing if he had not gone mad with rage. His soul was like the night around us now, dark, and sultry, and silent, but lighted up by the red levin of wrath and torn by the bellowings of thunder-passion. He must have his will: hell might have his soul. Imagine, then, the rage and malice in his heart, when he suddenly became aware that an orphan girl, distantly related to them, who had lived with them for nearly two years, and whom he had loved for almost all that period, was loved by his elder brother, and loved him in return. He flung his right hand above his head, swore a terrible oath that if he might not, his brother should not, rushed out of the house, and galloped off among the hills.

"The orphan was a beautiful girl, tall, pale, and slender, with plentiful dark hair, which, when released from the snood, rippled down below her knees. Her appearance formed a strong contrast with that of her favoured lover, while there was some resemblance between her and the younger brother. This fact seemed, to his fierce selfishness, ground for a prior claim.

"It may appear strange that a man like him should not have had instant recourse to his superior and hidden knowledge, by means of which he might have got rid of his rival with far more of certainty and less of risk; but I presume that, for the moment, his passion overwhelmed his consciousness of skill. Yet I do not suppose that he foresaw the mode in which his hatred was about to operate. At the moment when he learned their mutual attachment, probably through a domestic, the lady was on her way to meet her lover as he returned from the day's sport. The appointed place was on the edge of a deep, rocky ravine, down in whose dark bosom brawled and foamed a little mountain torrent. You know the place, Duncan, my dear, I dare say."

(Here she gave me a minute description of the spot, with directions how to find it.)

"Whether any one saw what I am about to relate, or whether it was put together afterwards, I cannot tell. The story is like an old tree—so old that it has lost the marks of its growth. But this is how my grandmother told it to me.—An evil chance led him in the right direction. The lovers, startled by the sound of the approaching horse, parted in opposite directions along a narrow mountain-path on the edge of the ravine. Into this path he struck at a point near where the lovers had met, but to opposite sides of which they had now receded; so that he was between them on the path. Turning his horse up the course of the stream, he soon came in sight of his brother on the ledge before him. With a suppressed scream of rage, he rode head-long at him, and ere he had time to make the least defence, hurled him over the precipice. The helplessness of the strong man was uttered in one single despairing cry as he shot into the abyss. Then all was still. The sound of his fall could not reach the edge of the gulf. Divining in a moment that the lady, whose name was Elsie, must have fled in the opposite direction, he reined his steed on his haunches. He could touch the precipice with his bridle-hand half outstretched; his sword-hand half outstretched would have dropped a stone to the bottom of the ravine. There was no room to wheel. One desperate practicability alone remained. Turning his horse's head towards the edge, he compelled him, by means of the powerful bit, to rear till he stood almost erect; and so, his body swaying over the gulf, with quivering and straining muscles, to turn on his hind-legs. Having completed the half-circle, he let him drop, and urged him furiously in the opposite direction. It must have been by the devil's own care that he was able to continue his gallop along that ledge of rock.

"He soon caught sight of the maiden. She was leaning, half faint-ing, against the precipice. She had heard her lover's last cry, and although it had conveyed no suggestion of his voice to her ear, she trembled from head to foot, and her limbs would bear her no farther. He checked his speed, rode gently up to her, lifted her unresisting, laid her across the shoulders of his horse, and, riding carefully till he reached a more open path, dashed again wildly along the mountain-side. The lady's long hair was shaken loose, and dropped trailing on the ground. The horse trampled upon it, and stumbled, half dragging her from the saddle-bow. He caught her, lifted her up, and looked at her face. She was dead. I suppose he went mad. He laid her again across the saddle before him, and rode on, reckless whither. Horse, and man, and maiden were found the next day, lying at the foot of a cliff, dashed to pieces. It was observed that a hind-shoe of the horse was loose and broken. Whether this had been the cause of his fall, could not be told; but ever when he races, as race he will, till the day of doom, along that mountain-side, his gallop is mingled with the clank of the loose and broken shoe. For, like the sin, the punishment is awful: he shall carry about for ages the phantom-body of the girl, knowing that her soul is away, sitting with the soul of his brother, down in the deep ravine, or scaling with him the topmost crags of the towering moun-tain-peaks. There are some who, from time to time, see the doomed man careering along the face of the mountain, with the lady hanging across the steed; and they say it always betokens a storm, such as this which is now raving around us."

I had not noticed till now, so absorbed had I been in her tale, that the storm had risen to a very ecstasy of fury.

"They say, likewise, that the lady's hair is still growing; for, every time they see her, it is longer than before; and that now such is its length and the headlong speed of the horse, that it floats and streams out behind, like one of those curved clouds, like a comet's tail, far up in the sky; only the cloud is white, and the hair dark as night. And they say it will go on growing till the Last Day, when the horse will falter and her hair will gather in; and the horse will fall, and the hair will twist, and twine, and wreathe itself like a mist of threads about him, and blind him to everything but her. Then the body will rise up within it, face to face with him, animated by a fiend, who, twining her arms around him, will drag him down to the bottomless pit."

I may mention something which now occurred, and which had a strange effect on my old nurse. It illustrates the assertion that we see around us only what is within us: marvellous things enough will show themselves to the marvellous mood.—During a short lull in the storm, just as she had finished her story, we heard the sound of iron-shod hoofs approaching the cottage. There was no bridle-way into the glen. A knock came to the door, and, on opening it, we saw an old man seated on a horse, with a long slenderly-filled sack lying across the saddle before him. He said he had lost the path in the storm, and, seeing the light, had scrambled down to inquire his way. I perceived at once, from the scared and mysterious look of the old woman's eyes, that she was persuaded that this appearance had more than a little to do with the awful rider, the terrific storm, and myself who had heard the sound of the phantom-hoofs. As he ascended the hill, she looked after him, with wide and pale but unshrinking eyes; then turning in, shut and locked the door behind her, as by a natural instinct. After two or three of her significant nods, accompanied by the compression of her lips, she said:—

"He need not think to take me in, wizard as he is, with his disguises. I can see him through them all. Duncan, my dear, when you suspect anything, do not be too incredulous. This human demon is of course a wizard still, and knows how to make himself, as well as anything he touches, take a quite different appearance from the real one; only every appearance must bear some resemblance, however distant, to the natural form. That man you saw at the door was the phantom of which I have been telling you. What he is after now, of course, I cannot tell; but you must keep a bold heart, and a firm and wary foot, as you go home to-night."

I showed some surprise, I do not doubt; and, perhaps, some fear as well; but I only said, "How do you know him, Margaret?"

"I can hardly tell you," she replied; "but I do know him. I think he hates me. Often, of a wild night, when there is moonlight enough by

fits, I see him tearing around this little valley, just on the top edge—
all round; the lady's hair and the horses mane and tail driving far
behind, and mingling, vaporous, with the stormy clouds. About he
goes, in wild careering gallop; now lost as the moon goes in, then visible far round when she looks out again—an airy, pale-grey spectre,
which few eyes but mine could see; for, as far as I am aware, no one
of the family but myself has ever possessed the double gift of seeing
and hearing both. In this case I hear no sound, except now and then a
clank from the broken shoe. But I did not mean to tell you that I had
ever seen him. I am not a bit afraid of him. He cannot do more than
he may. His power is limited; else ill enough would he work, the mis-
creant."

"But," said I, "what has all this, terrible as it is, to do with the
fright you took at my telling you that I had heard the sound of the
broken shoe? Surely you are not afraid of only a storm?"

"No, my boy; I fear no storm. But the fact is, that that sound is
seldom heard, and never, as far as I know, by any of the blood of that
wicked man, without betokening some ill to one of the family, and
most probably to the one who hears it—but I am not quite sure about
that. Only some evil it does portend, although a long time may elapse
before it shows itself; and I have a hope it may mean some one else
than you."

"Do not wish that," I replied. "I know no one better able to bear it
than I am; and I hope, whatever it may be, that I only shall have to
meet it. It must surely be something serious to be so foretold—it can
hardly be connected with my disappointment in being compelled to
be a pedagogue instead of a soldier."

"Do not trouble yourself about that, Duncan," replied she. "A soldier
you must be. The same day you told me of the clank of the broken
horseshoe, I saw you return wounded from battle, and fall fainting
from your horse in the street of a great city—only fainting, thank God.
But I have particular reasons for being uneasy at your hearing that
boding sound. Can you tell me the day and hour of your birth?"

"No," I replied. "It seems very odd when I think of it, but I really
do not know even the day."

"Nor any one else; which is stranger still," she answered.

"How does that happen, nurse?"

"We were in terrible anxiety about your mother at the time. So ill was
she, after you were just born, in a strange, unaccountable way, that you
lay almost neglected for more than an hour. In the very act of giving birth
to you, she seemed to the rest around her to be out of her mind, so wildly
did she talk; but I knew better. I knew that she was fighting some evil
power; and what power it was, I knew full well; for twice, during her pains,

I heard the click of the horseshoe. But no one could help her. After her delivery, she lay as if in a trance, neither dead, nor at rest, but as if frozen to ice, and conscious of it all the while. Once more I heard the terrible sound of iron; and, at the moment, your mother started from her trance, screaming, 'My child! my child!' We suddenly became aware that no one had attended to the child, and rushed to the place where he lay wrapped in a blanket. Uncovering him, we found him black in the face, and spotted with dark spots upon the throat. I thought he was dead; but, with great and almost hopeless pains, we succeeded in making him breathe, and he gradually recovered. But his mother continued dreadfully exhausted. It seemed as if she had spent her life for her child's defence and birth. That was you, Duncan, my dear.

"I was in constant attendance upon her. About a week after your birth, as near as I can guess, just in the gloaming, I heard yet again the awful clank—only once. Nothing followed till about midnight. Your mother slept, and you lay asleep beside her. I sat by the bedside. A horror fell upon me suddenly, though I neither saw nor heard anything. Your mother started from her sleep with a cry, which sounded as if it came from far away, out of a dream, and did not belong to this world. My blood curdled with fear. She sat up in bed, with wide staring eyes and half-open rigid lips, and, feeble as she was, thrust her arms straight out before her with great force, her hands open and lifted up, with the palms outwards. The whole action was of one violently repelling another. She began to talk wildly as she had done before you were born, but, though I seemed to hear and understand it all at the time, I could not recall a word of it afterwards. It was as if I had listened to it when half asleep. I attempted to soothe her, putting my arms round her, but she seemed quite unconscious of my presence, and my arms seemed powerless upon the fixed muscles of hers. Not that I tried to constrain her, for I knew that a battle was going on of some kind or other, and my interference might do awful mischief. I only tried to comfort and encourage her. All the time, I was in a state of indescribable cold and suffering, whether more bodily or mental I could not tell. But at length I heard yet again the clank of the shoe A sudden peace seemed to fall upon my mind—or was it a warm, odorous wind that filled the room? Your mother dropped her arms, and turned feebly towards her baby. She saw that he slept a blessed sleep. She smiled like a glorified spirit, and fell back exhausted on the pillow. I went to the other side of the room to get a cordial. When I returned to the bedside, I saw at once that she was dead. Her face smiled still, with an expression of the uttermost bliss."

Nurse ceased, trembling as overcome by the recollection; and I was too much moved and awed to speak. At length, resuming the conversation, she said: "You see it is no wonder, Duncan, my dear, if, after all this, I should find, when I wanted to fix the date of your birth, that I could not determine the day or the hour when it took place. All was confusion in my poor brain. But it was strange that no one else could, any more than I. One thing only I can tell you about it. As I carried you across the room to lay you down, for I assisted at your birth, I happened to look up to the window. Then I saw what I did not forget, although I did not think of it again till many days after,—a bright star was shining on the very tip of the thin crescent moon."

"Oh, then," said I, "it is possible to determine the day and the very hour when my birth took place."

"See the good of book-learning!" replied she. "When you work it out, just let me know, my dear, that I may remember it."

"That I will."

A silence of some moments followed. Margaret resumed:—

"I am afraid you will laugh at my foolish fancies, Duncan; but in thinking over all these things, as you may suppose I often do, lying awake in my lonely bed, the notion sometimes comes to me: What if my Duncan be the youth whom his wicked brother hurled into the ravine, come again in a new body, to live out his life on the earth, cut short by his brother's hatred? If so, his persecution of you, and of your mother for your sake, is easy to understand. And if so, you will never be able to rest till you find your fere, wherever she may have been born on the face of the earth. For born she must be, long ere now, for you to find. I misdoubt me much, however, if you will find her without great conflict and suffering between, for the Powers of Darkness will be against you; though I have good hope that you will overcome at last. You must forgive the fancies of a foolish old woman, my dear."

I will not try to describe the strange feelings, almost sensations, that arose in me while listening to these extraordinary utterances, lest it should be supposed I was ready to believe all that Margaret narrated or concluded. I could not help doubting her sanity; but no more could I help feeling very peculiarly moved by her narrative.

Few more words were spoken on either side, but after receiving renewed exhortations to carefulness on my way home, I said good-bye to dear old nurse, considerably comforted, I must confess, that I was not doomed to be a tutor all my days; for I never questioned the truth of that vision and its consequent prophecy.

I went out into the midst of the storm, into the alternating throbs of blackness and radiance; now the possessor of no more room than what my body filled, and now isolated in world-wide space. And the thunder seemed to follow me, bellowing after me as I went.

Absorbed in the story I had heard, I took my way, as I thought, homewards. The whole country was well known to me. I should have said, before that night, that I could have gone home blindfold. Whether the lightning bewildered me and made me take a false turn, I cannot tell; for the hardest thing to understand, in intellectual as well as moral mistakes, is how we came to go wrong. But after wandering for some time, plunged in meditation, and with no warning whatever of the presence of inimical powers, a brilliant lightning-flash showed me that at least I was not near home. The light was prolonged for a second or two by a slight electric pulsation; and by that I distinguished a wide space of blackness on the ground in front of me. Once more wrapped in the folds of a thick darkness, I dared not move. Suddenly it occurred to me what the blackness was, and whither I had wandered. It was a huge quarry, of great depth, long disused, and half filled with water. I knew the place perfectly. A few more steps would have carried me over the brink. I stood still, waiting for the next flash, that I might be quite sure of the way I was about to take before I ventured to move. While I stood, I fancied I heard a single hollow plunge in the black water far below. When the lightning came, I turned, and took my path in another direction.

After walking for some time across the heath, I fell. The fall became a roll, and down a steep declivity I went, over and over, arriving at the bottom uninjured.

Another flash soon showed me where I was—in the hollow valley, within a couple of hundred yards from nurse's cottage. I made my way towards it. There was no light in it, except the feeblest glow from the embers of her peat fire. "She is in bed," I said to myself, "and I will not disturb her." Yet something drew me towards the little window. I looked in. At first I could see nothing. At length, as I kept gazing, I saw something, indistinct in the darkness, like an outstretched human form.

By this time the storm had lulled. The moon had been up for some time, but had been quite concealed by tempestuous clouds. Now, however, these had begun to break up; and, while I stood looking into the cottage, they scattered away from the face of the moon, and a faint vapoury gleam of her light, entering the cottage through a window opposite that at which I stood, fell directly on the face of my old nurse, as she lay on her back, outstretched upon chairs, pale as death, and with her eyes closed. The light fell nowhere but on her face. A stranger to her habits would have thought she was dead; but she had so much of the appearance she had had on a former occasion, that I concluded at once she was in one of her trances. But having often heard that persons in such a condition ought not to be disturbed, and feeling quite sure she knew best how to manage herself, I turned, though reluctantly, and left the lone cottage behind me in the night, with the death-like woman lying motionless in the midst of it.

I found my way home without any further difficulty, and went to bed, where I soon fell asleep, thoroughly wearied, more by the mental excitement I had been experiencing than by the amount of bodily exercise I had gone through.

My sleep was tormented with awful dreams; yet, strange to say, I awoke in the morning refreshed and fearless. The sun was shining through the chinks in my shutters, which had been closed because of the storm, and was making streaks and bands of golden brilliancy upon the wall. I had dressed and completed my preparations long before I heard the steps of the servant who came to call me.

What a wonderful thing waking is! The time of the ghostly moonshine passes by, and the great positive sunlight comes. A man who dreams, and knows that he is dreaming, thinks he knows what waking is; but knows it so little, that he mistakes, one after another, many a vague and dim change in his dream for an awaking. When the true waking comes at last, he is filled and overflowed with the power of its reality. So, likewise, one who, in the darkness, lies waiting for the light about to be struck, and trying to conceive, with all the force of his imagination, what the light will be like, is yet, when the reality flames up before him, seized as by a new and unexpected thing, different from and beyond all his imagining. He feels as if the darkness were cast to an infinite distance behind him. So shall it be with us when we wake from this dream of life into the truer life beyond, and find all our present notions of being, thrown back as into a dim, vapoury region of dreamland, where yet we thought we knew, and whence we looked forward into the present. This must be what Novalis means when he says: "Our life is not a dream; but it may become a dream, and perhaps ought to become one."

And so I looked back upon the strange history of my past; sometimes asking myself,— "Can it be that all this really happened to the same me, who am now thinking about it in doubt and wonder?"

4
Hilton Hall

As my father accompanied me to the door, where the gig, which was to carry me over the first stage of my journey, was in waiting, a large target of hide, well studded with brass nails, which had hung in the hall for time unknown—to me, at least—fell on the floor with a dull bang. My father started, but said nothing; and, as it seemed to me, rather pressed my departure than otherwise. I would have re-placed the old piece of armour before I went, but he would not allow me to touch it, saying, with a grim smile,—

"Take that for an omen, my boy, that your armour must be worn over the conscience, and not over the body. Be a man, Duncan, my boy. Fear nothing, and do your duty."

A grasp of the hand was all the good-bye I could make; and I was soon rattling away to meet the coach for Edinburgh and London. Seated on the top, I was soon buried in a reverie, from which I was suddenly startled by the sound of tinkling iron. Could it be that my adversary was riding unseen alongside of the coach? Was that the clank of the ominous shoe? But I soon discovered the cause of the sound, and laughed at my own apprehensiveness. For I observed that the sound was repeated every time that we passed any trees by the wayside, and that it was the peculiar echo they gave of the loose chain and steel work about the harness. The sound was quite different from that thrown back by the houses on the road. I became perfectly famil-iar with it before the day was over.

I reached London in safety, and slept at the house of an old friend of my father, who treated me with great kindness, and seemed alto-gether to take a liking to me. Before I left he held out a hope of being able, some day or other, to procure for me what I so much desired—a commission in the army.

After spending a day or two with him, and seeing something of London, I climbed once more on the roof of a coach; and, late in the afternoon, was set down at the great gate of Hilton Hall. I walked up the broad avenue, through the final arch of which, as through a huge Gothic window, I saw the hall in the distance. Everything about me looked strange, rich, and lovely. Accustomed to the scanty flowers and diminutive wood of my own country, what I now saw gave me a feeling of majestic plenty, which I can recall at will, but which I have never experienced again. Behind the trees which formed the avenue, I saw a shrubbery, composed entirely of flowering plants, almost all unknown to me. Issuing from the avenue, I found myself amid open, wide, lawny spaces, in which the flower-beds lay like islands of colour. A statue on a pedestal, the only white thing in the surrounding green, caught my eye. I had seen scarcely any sculpture; and this, attracting my attention by a favourite contrast of colour, retained it by its own beauty. It was a Dryad, or some nymph of the woods, who had just glided from the solitude of the trees behind, and had sprung upon the pedestal to look wonderingly around her. A few large brown leaves lay at her feet, borne thither by some eddying wind from the trees behind. As I gazed, filled with a new pleasure, a drop of rain upon my face made me look up. From a grey, fleecy cloud, with sun-whitened border, a light, gracious, plentiful rain was falling. A rainbow sprang across the sky, and the statue stood within the rainbow. At the same moment, from the base of the pedestal rose a figure in white, graceful as the Dryad above, and neither running, nor appearing to walk quickly, yet fleet as a ghost, glided past me at a few paces, distance, and, keeping in a straight line for the main entrance of the hall, entered by it and vanished.

I followed in the direction of the mansion, which was large, and of several styles and ages. One wing appeared especially ancient. It was neglected and out of repair, and had in consequence a desolate, almost sepulchral look, an expression heightened by the number of large cypresses which grew along its line. I went up to the central door and knocked. It was opened by a grave, elderly butler. I passed under its flat arch, as if into the midst of the waiting events of my story. For, as I glanced around the hall, my consciousness was suddenly saturated, if I may be allowed the expression, with the strange feeling—known to every one, and yet so strange—that I had seen it before; that, in fact, I knew it perfectly. But what was yet more strange, and far more uncommon, was, that, although the feeling with regard to the hall faded and vanished instantly, and although I could not in the least surmise the appearance of any of the regions into which I was about to be ushered, I yet followed the butler with a kind of indefinable expectation of seeing something which I had seen before; and every room or passage in that mansion affected me, on entering it for the first time, with the same sensation of previous acquaintance which

I had experienced with regard to the hall. This sensation, in every case, died away at once, leaving that portion such as it might be expected to look to one who had never before entered the place.

I was received by the housekeeper, a little, prim, benevolent old lady, with colourless face and antique head-dress, who led me to the room prepared for me. To my surprise, I found a large wood-fire burning on the hearth; but the feeling of the place revealed at once the necessity for it; and I scarcely needed to be informed that the room, which was upon the ground floor, and looked out upon a little solitary grass-grown and ivy-mantled court, had not been used for years, and therefore required to be thus prepared for an inmate. My bedroom was a few paces down a passage to the right.

Left alone, I proceeded to make a more critical survey of my room. Its look of ancient mystery was to me incomparably more attractive than any show of elegance or comfort could have been. It was large and low, panelled throughout in oak, black with age, and worm-eaten in many parts—otherwise entire. Both the windows looked into the little court or yard before mentioned. All the heavier furniture of the room was likewise of black oak, but the chairs and couches were covered with faded tapestry and tarnished gilding, apparently the superannuated members of the general household of seats. I could give an individual description of each, for every atom in that room, large enough for discernable shape or colour, seems branded into my brain. If I happen to have the least feverishness on me, the moment I fall asleep, I am in that room.

5
Lady Alice

When the bell rang for dinner, I managed to find my way to the drawing-room, where were assembled Lady Hilton, her only daughter, a girl of about thirteen, and the two boys, my pupils. Lady Hilton would have been pleasant, could she have been as natural as she wished to appear. She received me with some degree of kindness; but the half-cordiality of her manner towards me was evidently founded on the impassableness of the gulf between us. I knew at once that we should never be friends; that she would never come down from the lofty table-land upon which she walked; and that if, after being years in the house, I should happen to be dying, she would send the housekeeper to me. All right, no doubt; I only say that it was so. She introduced to me my pupils; fine, open-eyed, manly English boys, with something a little overbearing in their manner, which speedily disappeared in relation to me. Lord Hilton was not at home. Lady Hilton led the way to the dining-room; the elder boy gave his arm to his sister, and I was about to follow with the younger, when from one of the deep bay windows glided out, still in white, the same figure which had passed me upon the lawn. I started, and drew back. With a slight bow, she preceded me, and followed the others down the great staircase. Seated at table, I had leisure to make my observations upon them all; but most of my glances found their way to the lady who, twice that day, had affected me like an apparition. What is time, but the airy ocean in which ghosts come and go!

She was about twenty years of age; rather above the middle height, and rather slight in form; her complexion white rather than pale, her face being only less white than the deep marbly whiteness of her arms. Her eyes were large, and full of liquid night—a night throbbing with the light of invisible stars. Her hair seemed raven-black, and in quantity profuse. The expression of her face, however, generally partook more of vagueness than any other characteristic. Lady Hilton called her Lady Alice; and she never addressed Lady Hilton but in the same ceremonious style.

I afterwards learned from the old house-keeper, that Lady Alice's position in the family was a very peculiar one. Distantly connected with Lord Hilton's family on the mother's side, she was the daughter of the late Lord Glendarroch, and step-daughter to Lady Hilton, who had become Lady Hilton within a year after Lord Glendarroch's death. Lady Alice, then quite a child, had accompanied her stepmother, to whom she was moderately attached, and who had been allowed to retain undisputed possession of her. She had no near relatives, else the fortune I afterwards found to be at her disposal would have aroused contending claims to the right of guardianship.

Although she was in many respects kindly treated by her step-mother, certain peculiarities tended to her isolation from the family pursuits and pleasures. Lady Alice had no accomplishments. She could neither spell her own language, nor even read it aloud. Yet she de-lighted in reading to herself, though, for the most part, books which Mrs. Wilson characterised as very odd. Her voice, when she spoke, had a quite indescribable music in it; yet she neither sang nor played. Her habitual motion was more like a rhythmical gliding than an ordi-nary walk, yet she could not dance. Mrs. Wilson hinted at other and more serious peculiarities, which she either could not, or would not describe; always shaking her head gravely and sadly, and becoming quite silent, when I pressed for further explanation; so that, at last, I gave up all attempts to arrive at an understanding of the mystery by her means. Not the less, however, I speculated on the subject.

One thing soon became evident to me: that she was considered not merely deficient as to the power of intellectual acquirement, but in a quite abnormal intellectual condition. Of this, however, I could myself see no sign. The peculiarity, almost oddity, of some of her re-marks, was evidently not only misunderstood, but, with relation to her mental state, misinterpreted. Such remarks Lady Hilton gener-ally answered only by an elongation of the lips intended to represent a smile. To me, they appeared to indicate a nature closely allied to genius, if not identical with it—a power of regarding things from an original point of view, which perhaps was the more unfettered in its operation from the fact that she was incapable of looking at them in the ordinary common-place way. It seemed to me, sometimes, as if her point of observation was outside of the sphere within which the thing observed took place; and as if what she said, had a relation, occasionally, to things and thoughts and mental conditions familiar to her, but at which not even a definite guess could be made by me. I am compelled to acknowledge, however, that with such utterances as these mingled now and then others, silly enough for any drawing-room young lady; which seemed again to be accepted by the family as proofs that she was not altogether out of her right mind. She was gentle and kind to the children, as they were still called; and they seemed reasonably fond of her.

There was something to me exceedingly touching in the solitariness of this girl; for no one spoke to her as if she were like other people, or as if any heartiness were possible between them. Perhaps no one could have felt quite at home with her but a mother, whose heart had been one with hers from a season long anterior to the development of any repulsive oddity. But her position was one of peculiar isolation, for no one really approached her individual being; and that she should be unaware of this loneliness, seemed to me saddest of all. I soon found, however, that the most distant attempt on my part to show her attention, was either received with absolute indifference, or coldly repelled without the slightest acknowledgment.

But I return to the first night of my sojourn at Hilton Hall.

6
My Quarters

After making arrangements for commencing work in the morning, I took my leave, and retired to my own room, intent upon carrying out with more minuteness the survey I had already commenced:
several cupboards in the wall, and one or two doors, apparently of
closets, had especially attracted my attention. Strange was its look as
I entered—as of a room hollowed out of the past, for a memorial of
dead times. The fire had sunk low, and lay smouldering beneath the
white ashes, like the life of the world beneath the snow, or the heart
of a man beneath cold and grey thoughts. I lighted the candles which
stood upon the table, but the room, instead of being brightened looked
blacker than before, for the light revealed its essential blackness.

As I cast my eyes around me, standing with my back to the hearth
(on which, for mere companionship's sake, I had just heaped fresh
wood), a thrill ran suddenly throughout my frame. I felt as if, did it
last a moment longer, I should become aware of another presence in
the room; but, happily for me, it ceased before it had reached that
point; and I, recovering my courage, remained ignorant of the cause
of my fear, if there were any, other than the nature of the room itself.
With a candle in my hand, I proceeded to open the various cupboards
and closets. At first I found nothing remarkable about any of them.
The latter were quite empty, except the last I came to, which had a
piece of very old elaborate tapestry hanging at the back of it. Lifting
this up, I saw what seemed at first to be panels, corresponding to those
which formed the room; but on looking more closely, I discovered
that this back of the closet was, or had been, a door. There was nothing unusual in this, especially in such an old house; but the discovery
roused in me a strong desire to know what lay behind the old door. I
found that it was secured only by an ordinary bolt, from which the
handle had been removed. Soothing my conscience with the reflection that I had a right to know what sort of place had communication
with my room, I succeeded, by the help of my deer-knife, in forcing

back the rusty bolt; and though, from the stiffness of the hinges, I
dreaded a crack, they yielded at last with only a creak.

The opening door revealed a large hall, empty utterly, save of dust
and cobwebs, which festooned it in all quarters, and gave it an appearance of unutterable desolation. The now familiar feeling, that I had
seen the place before, filled my mind the first moment, and passed
away the next. A broad, right-angled staircase, with massive banis-
ters, rose from the middle of the hall. This staircase could not have
originally belonged to the ancient wing which I had observed on my
first approach, being much more modern; but I was convinced, from
the observations I had made as to the situation of my room, that I
was bordering upon, if not within, the oldest portion of the pile. In
sudden horror, lest I should hear a light footfall upon the awful stair,
I withdrew hurriedly, and having secured both the doors, betook myself to my bedroom; in whose dingy four-post bed, with its carving
and plumes reminding me of a hearse, I was soon ensconced amidst
the snowiest linen, with the sweet and clean odour of lavender. In
spite of novelty, antiquity, speculation, and dread, I was soon fast
asleep; becoming thereby a fitter inhabitant of such regions, than
when I moved about with restless and disturbing curiosity, through
their ancient and death-like repose.

I made no use of my discovered door, although I always intended
doing so; especially after, in talking about the building with Lady
Hilton, I found that I was at perfect liberty to make what excursions I
pleased into the deserted portions.

My pupils turned out to be teachable, and therefore my occupation was pleasant. Their sister frequently came to me for help, as there
happened to be just then an interregnum of governesses: soon she
settled into a regular pupil.

After a few weeks Lord Hilton returned. Though my room was so
far from the great hall, I heard the clank of his spurs on its pavement.
I trembled; for it sounded like the broken shoe. But I shook off the
influence in a moment, heartily ashamed of its power over me. Soon I
became familiar enough both with the sound and its cause; for his
lordship rarely went anywhere except on horseback, and was booted
and spurred from morning till night.

He received me with some appearance of interest, which immediately stiffened and froze. Beginning to shake hands with me as if he
meant it, he instantly dropped my hand, as if it had stung him.

His nobility was of that sort which stands in constant need of repair.
Like a weakly constitution, it required keeping up, and his lordship
could not be said to neglect it; for he seemed to find his principal
employment in administering continuous doses of obsequiousness to

his own pride. His rank, like a coat made for some large ancestor, hung loose upon him: he was always trying to persuade himself that it was an excellent fit, but ever with an unacknowledged misgiving. This misgiving might have done him good, had he not met it with renewed efforts at looking that which he feared he was not. Yet this man was capable of the utmost persistency in carrying out any scheme he had once devised. Enough of him for the present: I seldom came into contact with him.

I scarcely ever saw Lady Alice, except at dinner, or by accidental meeting in the grounds and passages of the house; and then she took no notice of me whatever.

7

The Library

One day, a week after his arrival, Lord Hilton gave a dinner-party to some of his neighbours and tenants. I entered the drawing-room rather late, and saw that, though there were many guests, not one was talking to Lady Alice. She appeared, however, altogether unconscious of neglect. Presently dinner was announced, and the company marshalled themselves, and took their way to the dining-room. Lady Alice was left unattended, the guests taking their cue from the behaviour of their entertainers. I ventured to go up to her, and offer her my arm. She made me a haughty bow, and passed on before me unaccompanied. I could not help feeling hurt at this, and I think she saw it; but it made no difference to her behaviour, except that she avoided everything that might occasion me the chance of offering my services.

Nor did I get any further with Lady Hilton. Her manner and smile remained precisely the same as on our first interview. She did not even show any interest in the fact that her daughter, Lady Lucy, had joined her brothers in the schoolroom. I had an uncomfortable feeling that the latter was like her mother, and was not to be trusted. Self-love is the foulest of all foul feeders, and will defile that it may devour. But I must not anticipate.

The neglected library was open to me at all hours; and in it I often took refuge from the dreariness of unsympathetic society. I was never admitted within the magic circle of the family interests and enjoyments. If there was such a circle, Lady Alice and I certainly stood outside of it; but whether even then it had any real inside to it, I doubted much. Nevertheless, as I have said, our common exclusion had not the effect of bringing us together as sharers of the same misfortune. In the library I found companions more to my need. But, even there, they were not easy to find; for the books were in great confusion. I could discover no catalogue, nor could I hear of the existence of such a useless luxury. One morning at breakfast, therefore, I asked

Lord Hilton if I might arrange and catalogue the books during my leisure hours. He replied:—

"Do anything you like with them, Mr. Campbell, except destroy them."

Now I was in my element. I never had been by any means a book-worm; but the very outside of a book had a charm to me. It was a kind of sacrament—an outward and visible sign of an inward and spiritual grace; as, indeed, what on God's earth is not? So I set to work amongst the books, and soon became familiar with many titles at least, which had been perfectly unknown to me before. I found a perfect set of our poets—perfect according to the notion of the editor and the issue of the publisher, although it omitted both Chaucer and George Herbert. I began to nibble at that portion of the collection which belonged to the sixteenth century; but with little success. I found nothing, to my idea, but love poems without any love in them, and so I soon became weary. But I found in the library what I liked far better—many romances of a very marvellous sort, and plentiful interruption they gave to the formation of the catalogue. I likewise came upon a whole nest of the German classics which seemed to have kept their places undisturbed, in virtue of their unintelligibility. There must have been some well-read scholar in the family, and that not long before, to judge by the near approach of the line of this literature; happening to be a tolerable reader of German, I found in these volumes a mine of wealth inexhaustible. I learned from Mrs. Wilson that this scholar was a younger brother of Lord Hilton, who had died about twenty years before. He had led a retired, rather lonely life, was of a melancholy and brooding disposition, and was reported to have had an unfortunate love-story. This was one of many histories which she gave me. For the library being dusty as a catacomb, the private room of Old Time himself, I had often to betake myself to her for assistance. The good lady had far more regard than the owners of it for the library, and was delighted with the pains I was taking to re-arrange and clean it. She would allow no one to help me but herself; and to many a long-winded story, most of which I forgot as soon as I heard them, did I listen, or seem to listen, while she dusted the shelves and I the books.

One day I had sent a servant to ask Mrs. Wilson to come to me. I had taken down all the books from a hitherto undisturbed corner, and had seated myself on a heap of them, no doubt a very impersonation of the genius of the place; for while I waited for the housekeeper, I was consuming a morsel of an ancient metrical romance. After waiting for some time, I glanced towards the door, for I had begun to get impatient for the entrance of my helper. To my surprise, there stood Lady Alice, her eyes fixed upon me with an expression I could not comprehend. Her face instantly altered to its usual look of indifference, dashed with the least possible degree of scorn, as she turned and walked slowly away. I rose involuntarily. An old cavalry sword, which I had just taken down from the wall, and had placed leaning against the books from which I now rose, fell with a clash to the floor. I started; for it was a sound that always startled me; and stooping I lifted the weapon. But what was my surprise when I raised my head, to see once more the face of Lady Alice staring in at the door! yet not the same face, for it had changed in the moment that had passed. It was pale with fear—not fright; and her great black eyes were staring beyond me as if she saw something through the wall of the room. Once more her face altered to the former scornful indifference, and she vanished. Keen of hearing as I was, I had never yet heard the footstep of Lady Alice.

8
The Somnambulist

One night I was sitting in my room, devouring an old romance which I had brought from the library. It was late. The fire blazed bright; but the candles were nearly burnt out, and I grew sleepy over the volume, romance as it was.

Suddenly I found myself on my feet, listening with an agony of intention. Whether I had heard anything I could not tell; but I felt as if I had. Yes; I was sure of it. Far away, somewhere in the labyrinthine pile, I heard a faint cry. Driven by some secret impulse, I flew, without a moment's reflection, to the closet door, lifted the tapestry within, unfastened the second door, and stood in the great waste echoing hall, amid the touches, light and ghostly, of the cobwebs set afloat in the eddies occasioned by my sudden entrance.

A faded moonbeam fell on the floor, and filled the place with an ancient dream-light, which wrought strangely on my brain, and filled it, as if it, too, were but a deserted, sleepy house, haunted by old dreams and memories. Recollecting myself, I went back for a light; but the candles were both flickering in the sockets, and I was compelled to trust to the moon. I ascended the staircase. Old as it was, not a board creaked, not a banister shook—the whole felt solid as rock. Finding, at length, no more stair to ascend, I groped my way on; for here there was no direct light from the moon—only the light of the moonlit air. I was in some trepidation, I confess; for how should I find my way back? But the worst result likely to ensue was, that I should have to spend the night without knowing where; for with the first glimmer of morning, I should be able to return to my room. At length, after wandering into several rooms and out again, my hand fell on a latched door. I opened it, and entered a long corridor, with many windows on one side. Broad strips of moonlight lay slantingly across the narrow floor, divided by regular intervals of shade.

I started, and my heart swelled; for I saw a movement somewhere—I could neither tell where, nor of what: I was only aware of motion. I stood in the first shadow, and gazed, but saw nothing. I sped across the light to the next shadow, and stood again, looking with fearful fixedness of gaze towards the far end of the corridor. Suddenly a white form glimmered and vanished. I crossed to the next shadow. Again a glimmer and vanishing, but nearer. Nerving myself to the utmost, I ceased the stealthiness of my movements, and went forward, slowly and steadily. A tall form, apparently of a woman, dressed in a long white robe, appeared in one of the streams of light, threw its arms over its head, gave a wild cry—which, notwithstanding its wildness and force, had a muffled sound, as if many folds, either of matter or of space, intervened—and fell at full length along the moonlight. Amidst the thrill of agony which shook me at the cry, I rushed forward, and, kneeling beside the prostrate figure, discovered that, unearthly as was the scream which had preceded her fall, it was the Lady Alice. I saw the fact in a moment: the Lady Alice was a somnambulist. Startled by the noise of my advance, she had awaked; and the usual terror and fainting had followed. She was cold and motionless as death. What was to be done? If I called, the probability was that no one would hear me; or if any one should hear—but I need not follow the course of my thought, as I tried in vain to recover the poor girl. Suffice it to say, that both for her sake and my own, I could not face the chance of being found, in the dead of night, by common-minded domestics, in such a situation.

I was kneeling by her side, not knowing what to do, when a horror, as from the presence of death suddenly recognized, fell upon me. I thought she must be dead. But at the same moment, I hear, or seemed to hear, (how should I know which?) the rapid gallop of a horse, and the clank of a loose shoe.

In an agony of fear, I caught her up in my arms, and, carrying her on my arms, as one carries a sleeping child, hurried back through the corridor. Her hair, which was loose, trailed on the ground; and, as I fled, I trampled on it and stumbled. She moaned; and that instant the gallop ceased. I lifted her up across my shoulder, and carried her more easily. How I found my way to the stair I cannot tell: I know that I groped about for some time, like one in a dream with a ghost in his arms. At last I reached it, and descending, crossed the hall, and entered my room. There I placed Lady Alice upon an old couch, secured the doors, and began to breathe—and think. The first thing was to get her warm, for she was cold as the dead. I covered her with my plaid and my dressing-gown, pulled the couch before the fire, and considered what to do next.

9
The First Waking

While I hesitated, Nature had her own way, and, with a deep-drawn sigh, Lady Alice opened her eyes. Never shall I forget the look of mingled bewilderment, alarm, and shame, with which her great eyes met mine. But, in a moment, this expression changed to that of anger. Her dark eyes flashed with light; and a cloud of roseate wrath grew in her face, till it glowed with the opaque red of a camellia. She had almost started from the couch, when, apparently discovering the unsuitableness of her dress, she checked her impetuosity, and remained leaning on her elbow. Overcome by her anger, her beauty, and my own confusion, I knelt before her, unable to speak, or to withdraw my eyes from hers. After a moment's pause, she began to question me like a queen, and I to reply like a culprit.

"How did I come here?"

"I carried you."

"Where did you find me, pray?"

Her lip curled with ten times the usual scorn.

"In the old house, in a long corridor."

"What right had you to be there?"

"I heard a cry, and could not help going."

"Tis impossible.—I see. Some wretch told you, and you watched for me."

"I did not, Lady Alice."

She burst into tears, and fell back on the couch, with her face turned away. Then, anger reviving, she went on through her sobs:—

"Why did you not leave me where I fell? You had done enough to hurt me without bringing me here."

And again she fell a-weeping.

Now I found words.

"Lady Alice," I said, "how could I leave you lying in the moonlight? Before the sun rose, the terrible moon might have distorted your beautiful face."

"Be silent, sir. What have you to do with my face?"

"And the wind, Lady Alice, was blowing through the corridor windows, keen and cold as the moonlight. How could I leave you?"

"You could have called for help."

"Forgive me, Lady Alice, if I erred in thinking you would rather command the silence of a gentleman to whom an accident had revealed your secret, than be exposed to the domestics who would have gathered round us."

Again she half raised herself, and again her eyes flashed.

"A secret with you, sir!"

"But, besides, Lady Alice," I cried, springing to my feet, in distress at her hardness, "I heard the horse with the clanking shoe, and, in terror, I caught you up, and fled with you, almost before I knew what I did. And I hear it now—I hear it now!" I cried, as once more the ominous sound rang through my brain.

The angry glow faded from her face, and its paleness grew almost ghastly with dismay.

"Do you hear it?" she said, throwing back her covering, and rising from the couch. "I do not."

She stood listening with distended eyes, as if they were the gates by which such sounds entered.

"I do not hear it," she said again, after a pause. "It must be gone now." Then, turning to me, she laid her hand on my arm, and looked at me. Her black hair, disordered and entangled, wandered all over her white dress to her knees. Her face was paler than ever; and her eyes were so wide open that I could see the white all round the large dark iris.

"Did you hear it?" she said. "No one ever heard it before but me. I must forgive you—you could not help it. I will trust you, too. Take me to my room."

Without a word of reply, I wrapped my plaid about her. Then bethinking me of my chamber-candle, I lighted it, and opening the two doors, led her out of the room.

"How is this?" she asked. "Why do you take me this way? I do not know the place."

"This is the way I brought you in, Lady Alice," I answered. "I know no other way to the spot where I found you. And I can guide you no farther than there—hardly even so far, for I groped my way there for the first time this night or morning—whichever it may be."

"It is past midnight, but not morning yet," she replied, "I always know. But there must be another way from your room?"

"Yes, of course; but we should have to pass the housekeeper's door—she is always late."

"Are we near her room? I should know my way from there. I fear
it would not surprise any of the household to see me. They would say—
'It is only Lady Alice.' Yet I cannot tell you how I shrink from being
seen. No—I will try the way you brought me—if you do not mind going back with me."

This conversation passed in low tone and hurried words. It was
scarcely over before we found ourselves at the foot of the staircase.
Lady Alice shivered, and drew the plaid close round her.

We ascended, and soon found the corridor; but when we got
through it, she was rather bewildered. At length, after looking into
several of the rooms, empty all, except for stray articles of ancient
furniture, she exclaimed, as she entered one, and, taking the candle
from my hand, held it above her head—

"Ah, yes! I am right at last. This is the haunted room. I know my
way now."

I caught a darkling glimpse of a large room, apparently quite fur-
nished; but how, except from the general feeling of antiquity and
mustiness, I could not tell. Little did I think then what memories—
old, now, like the ghosts that with them haunt the place—would ere
long find their being and take their abode in that ancient room, to
forsake it never more. In strange, half-waking moods, I seem to see
the ghosts and the memories flitting together through the spectral
moonlight, and weaving mystic dances in and out of the storied windows and the tapestried walls.

At the door of this room she said, "I must leave you here. I will
put down the light a little further on, and you can come for it. I owe
you many thanks. You will not be afraid of being left so near the
haunted room?"

I assured her that at present I felt strong enough to meet all the
ghosts in or out of Hades. Turning, she smiled a sad, sweet smile,
then went on a few paces, and disappeared. The light, however, remained; and I found the candle, with my plaid, deposited at the foot
of a short flight of steps, at right angles to the passage she left me in.
I made my way back to my room, threw myself on the couch on which
she had so lately lain, and neither went to bed nor slept that night.
Before the morning, I had fully entered that phase of individual development commonly called love; of which the real nature is as great
a mystery to me now, as it was at any period previous to its evolution
in myself.

10
Love and Power

When the morning came, I began to doubt whether my wakeful-
ness had not been part of my dream, and I had not dreamed the whole
of my supposed adventures. There was no sign of a lady's presence
left in the room.—How could there have been?—But throwing the plaid
which covered me aside, my hand was caught by a single thread of
something so fine that I could not see it till the light grew strong. I
wound it round and round my finger, and doubted no longer.

At breakfast there was no Lady Alice—nor at dinner. I grew uneasy, but what could I do? I soon learned that she was ill; and a weary
fortnight passed before I saw her again. Mrs. Wilson told me that she
had caught cold, and was confined to her room. So I was ill at ease,
not from love alone, but from anxiety as well. Every night I crept up
through the deserted house to the stair where she had vanished, and
there sat in the darkness or groped and peered about for some sign.
But I saw no light even, and did not know where her room was. It
might be far beyond this extremity of my knowledge; for I discovered
no indication of the proximity of the inhabited portion of the house.
Mrs. Wilson said there was nothing serious the matter; but this did
not satisfy me, for I imagined something mysterious in the way in
which she spoke.

As the days went on, and she did not appear, my soul began to
droop within me; my intellect seemed about to desert me altogether.
In vain I tried to read. Nothing could fix my attention. I read and re-
read the same page; but although I understood every word as I read,
I found when I came to a pause, that there lingered in my mind no
palest notion of the idea. It was just what one experiences in attempting to read when half-asleep.

I tried Euclid, and fared a little better with that. But having now
to initiate my boys into the mysteries of equations, I soon found that
although I could manage a very simple one, yet when I attempted one
more complex—one in which something bordering upon imagination

was necessary to find out the object for which to appoint the symbol to handle it by—the necessary power of concentration was itself a missing factor.

But although my thoughts were thus beyond my control, my duties were not altogether irksome to me. I remembered that they kept me near her; and although I could not learn, I found that I could teach a little.

Perhaps it is foolish to dwell upon an individual variety of an almost universal stage in the fever of life; but one exception to these indications of mental paralysis I think worth mentioning.

I continued my work in the library, although it did not advance with the same steadiness as before. One day, in listless mood, I took up a volume, without knowing what it was, or what I sought. It opened at the Amoretti of Edmund Spenser. I was on the point of closing it again, when a line caught my eye. I read the sonnet; read another; found I could understand them perfectly; and that hour the poetry of the sixteenth century, hitherto a sealed fountain, became an open well of refreshment, and the strength that comes form sympathy. What if its second-rate writers were full of conceits and vagaries, the feelings are very indifferent to the mere intellectual forms around which the same feelings in others have gathered, if only by their means they hint at, and sometimes express themselves. Now I understood this old fantastic verse, and knew that the foam-bells on the torrent of passionate feeling are iris-hued. And what was more—it proved an intellectual nexus between my love and my studies, or at least a bridge by which I could pass from the one to the other.

That same day, I remember well, Mrs. Wilson told me that Lady Alice was much better. But as days passed, and still she did not make her appearance, my anxiety only changed its object, and I feared that it was from aversion to me that she did not join the family. But her name was never mentioned in my hearing by any of the other members of it; and her absence appeared to be to them a matter of no moment or interest.

One night, as I sat in my room, I found, as usual, that it was impossible to read; and throwing the book aside, relapsed into that sphere of thought which now filled my soul, and had for its centre the Lady Alice. I recalled her form as she lay on the couch, and brooded over the remembrance till a longing to see her, almost unbearable, arose within me.

"Would to heaven," I said to myself, "that will were power!"

In this concurrence of idleness, distraction, and vehement desire, I found all at once, without any foregone resolution, that I was concentrating and intensifying within me, until it rose almost to a command,

the operative volition that Lady Alice should come to me. In a moment
more I trembled at the sense of a new power which sprang into conscious being within me. I had had no prevision of its existence, when
I gave way to such extravagant and apparently helpless wishes. I now
actually awaited the fulfilment of my desire; but in a condition ill-
fitted to receive it, for the effort had already exhausted me to such a degree, that every nerve was in a conscious tremor. Nor had I long to wait.

I heard no sound of approach: the closet-door folded back, and in
glided, open-eyed, but sightless pale as death, and clad in white,
ghostly-pure and saint-like, the Lady Alice. I shuddered from head to
foot at what I had done. She was more terrible to me in that moment
than any pale-eyed ghost could have been. For had I not exercised a
kind of necromantic art, and roused without awaking the slumbering
dead? She passed me, walking round the table at which I was seated,
went to the couch, laid herself down with a maidenly care, turned a
little on one side, with her face towards me, and gradually closed her
eyes. In something deeper than sleep she lay, and yet not in death. I
rose, and once more knelt beside her, but dared not touch her. In
what far realms of life might the lovely soul be straying! What mysterious modes of being might now be the homely surroundings of her
second life! Thoughts unutterable rose in me, culminated, and sank,
like the stars of heaven, as I gazed on the present symbol of an absent
life—a life that I loved by means of the symbol; a symbol that I loved
because of the life. How long she lay thus, how long I gazed upon her
thus, I do not know. Gradually, but without my being able to distinguish the gradations, her countenance altered to that of one who
sleeps. But the change did not end there. A colour, faint as the blush
in the centre of a white rose, tinged her lips, and deepened; then her
cheek began to share in the hue, then her brow and her neck. The
colour was that of the cloud which, the farthest from the sunset, yet
acknowledges the rosy atmosphere. I watched, as it were, the dawn of
a soul on the horizon of the visible. The first approaches of its far-off
flight were manifest; and as I watched, I saw it come nearer and
nearer, till its great, silent, speeding pinions were folded, and it looked
forth, a calm, beautiful, infinite woman, from the face and form sleeping before me.

I knew that she was awake, some moments before she opened her
eyes. When at last those depths of darkness disclosed themselves,
slowly uplifting their white cloudy portals, the same consternation
she had formerly manifested, accompanied by yet greater anger, followed.

"Yet again! Am I your slave, because I am weak?" She rose in the
majesty of wrath, and moved towards the door.

"Lady Alice, I have not touched you. I am to blame, but not as you think. Could I help longing to see you? And if the longing passed, ere I was aware, into a will that you should come, and you obeyed it, forgive me."

I hid my face in my hands, overcome by conflicting emotions. A kind of stupor came over me. When I lifted my head, she was standing by the closet-door.

"I have waited," she said, "to make a request of you."

"Do not utter it, Lady Alice. I know what it is. I give you my word—my solemn promise, if you like—that I will never do it again." She thanked me, with a smile, and vanished.

Much to my surprise, she appeared at dinner next day. No notice was taken of her, except by the younger of my pupils, who called out,—

"Hallo, Alice! Are you down?"

She smiled and nodded, but did not speak. Everything went on as usual. There was no change in her behaviour, except in one point. I ventured the experiment of paying her some ordinary enough attention. She thanked me, without a trace of the scornful expression I all but expected to see upon her beautiful face. But when I addressed her about the weather, or something equally interesting, she made no reply; and Lady Hilton gave me a stare, as much as to say, "Don't you know it's of no use to talk to her?" Alice saw the look, and colouring to the eyes, rose, and left the room. When she had gone, Lady Hilton said to me,—

"Don't speak to her, Mr. Campbell—it distresses her. She is very peculiar, you know."

She could not hide the scorn and dislike with which she spoke; and I could not help saying to myself, "What a different thing scorn looks on your face, Lady Hilton!" for it made her positively and hatefully ugly for the moment—to my eyes, at least.

After this, Alice sat down with us at all our meals, and seemed tolerably well. But, in some indescribable way, she was quite a different person from the Lady Alice who had twice awaked in my presence. To use a phrase common in describing one of weak intellect—she never seemed to be all there. There was something automatical in her movements; and a sort of frozen indifference was the prevailing expression of her countenance. When she smiled, a sweet light shone in her eyes, and she looked for the moment like the Lady Alice of my nightly dreams. But, altogether, the Lady Alice of the night, and the Lady Alice of the day, were two distinct persons. I believed that the former was the real one.

What nights I had now, watching and striving lest unawares I should fall into the exercise of my new power! I allowed myself to

think of her as much as I pleased in the daytime, or at least as much
as I dared; for when occupied with my pupils, I dreaded lest any ab-
straction should even hint that I had a thought to conceal. I knew
that I could not hurt her then; for that only in the night did she enter
that state of existence in which my will could exercise authority over
her. But at night—at night—when I knew she lay there, and might be
lying here; when but a thought would bring her, and that thought was
fluttering its wings, ready to spring awake out of the dreams of my
heart—then the struggle was fearful. And what added force to the
temptation was, that to call her to me in the night, seemed like calling
the real immortal Alice forth from the tomb in which she wandered
about all day. It was as painful to me to see her such in the day, as it
was entrancing to remember her such as I had seen her in the night.
What matter if her true self came forth in anger against me? What
was I? It was enough for my life, I said, to look on her, such as she
really was. "Bring her yet once, and tell her all—tell her how madly,
hopelessly you love her. She will forgive you at least," said a voice
within me. But I heard it as the voice of the tempter, and kept down
the thought which might have grown to the will.

11
A New Pupil

One day, exactly three weeks after her last visit to my room, as I was sitting with my three pupils in the schoolroom, Lady Alice entered, and began to look on the bookshelves as if she wanted some volume. After a few moments, she turned, and, approaching the table, said to me, in an abrupt, yet hesitating way,

"Mr. Campbell, I cannot spell. How am I to learn?"

I thought for a moment, and replied: "Copy a passage every day, Lady Alice, from some favourite book. Then, if you allow me, I shall be most happy to point out any mistakes you may have made."

"Thank you, Mr. Campbell, I will; but I am afraid you will despise me, when you find how badly I spell."

"There is no fear of that," I rejoined. "It is a mere peculiarity. So long as one can think well, spelling is altogether secondary."

"Thank you; I will try," she said, and left the room. Next day, she brought me an old ballad, written tolerably, but in a school-girl's hand. She had copied the antique spelling, letter for letter.

"This is quite correct," I said; "but to copy such as this will not teach you properly; for it is very old, and consequently old-fashioned."

"Is it old? Don't we spell like that now? You see I do not know anything about it. You must set me a task, then."

This I undertook with more pleasure than I dared to show. Every day she brought me the appointed exercise, written with a steadily improving hand. To my surprise, I never found a single error in the spelling. Of course, when, advancing a step in the process, I made her write from my dictation, she did make blunders, but not so many as I had expected; and she seldom repeated one after correction.

This new association gave me many opportunities of doing more for her than merely teaching her to spell. We talked about what she copied; and I had to explain. I also told her about the writers. Soon she expressed a desire to know something of figures. We commenced arithmetic. I proposed geometry along with it, and found the latter especially fitted to her powers. One by one we included several other necessary branches; and ere long I had four around the schoolroom table—equally my pupils. Whether the attempts previously made to instruct her had been insufficient or misdirected, or whether her intellectual powers had commenced a fresh growth, I could not tell; but I leaned to the latter conclusion, especially after I began to observe that her peculiar remarks had become modified in form, though without losing any of their originality. The unearthliness of her beauty likewise disappeared, a slight colour displacing the almost marbly whiteness of her cheek.

Long before Lady Alice had made this progress, my nightly struggles began to diminish in violence. They had now entirely ceased. The temptation had left me. I felt certain that for weeks she had never walked in her sleep. She was beyond my power, and I was glad of it.

I was, of course, most careful of my behaviour during all this period. I strove to pay Lady Alice no more attention than I paid to the rest of my pupils; and I cannot help thinking that I succeeded. But now and then, in the midst of some instruction I was giving Lady Alice, I caught the eye of Lady Lucy, a sharp, common-minded girl, fixed upon one or the other of us, with an inquisitive vulgar expression, which I did not like. This made me more careful still. I watched my tones, to keep them even, and free from any expression of the feeling of which my heart was full. Sometimes, however, I could not help revealing the gratification I felt when she made some marvellous remark—marvellous, I mean, in relation to her other attainments; such a remark as a child will sometimes make, showing that he has already mastered, through his earnest simplicity, some question that has for ages perplexed the wise and the prudent. On one of these occasions, I found the cat eyes of Lady Lucy glittering on me. I turned away; not, I fear, without showing some displeasure.

Whether it was from Lady Lucy's evil report, or that the change in Lady Alice's habits and appearance had attracted the attention of Lady Hilton, I cannot tell; but one morning she appeared at the door of the study, and called her. Lady Alice rose and went, with a slight gesture of impatience. In a few minutes she returned, looking angry and determined, and resumed her seat. But whatever it was that had passed between them, it had destroyed that quiet flow of the feelings which was necessary to the working of her thoughts. In vain she tried: she could do nothing correctly. At last she burst into tears and left the room. I was almost beside myself with distress and apprehension. She did not return that day.

Next morning she entered at the usual hour, looking composed, but paler than of late, and showing signs of recent weeping. When we were all seated, and had just commenced our work, I happened to look up, and caught her eyes intently fixed on me. They dropped instantly, but without any appearance of confusion. She went on with her arithmetic, and succeeded tolerably. But this respite was to be of short duration. Lady Hilton again entered, and called her. She rose angrily, and my quick ear caught the half-uttered words, "That woman will make an idiot of me again!" She did not return; and never from that hour resumed her place in the schoolroom.

The time passed heavily. At dinner she looked proud and constrained; and spoke only in monosyllables.

For two days I scarcely saw her. But the third day, as I was busy in the library alone, she entered.

"Can I help you, Mr. Campbell?" she said.

I glanced involuntarily towards the door.

"Lady Hilton is not at home," she replied to my look, while a curl of indignation contended with a sweet tremor of shame for the possession of her lip.— "Let me help you."

"You will help me best if you sing that ballad I heard you singing just before you came in. I never heard you sing before."

"Didn't you? I don't think I ever did sing before."

"Sing it again, will you, please?"

"It is only two verses. My old Scotch nurse used to sing it when I was a little girl—oh, so long ago! I didn't know I could sing it."

She began without more ado, standing in the middle of the room, with her back towards the door.

> Annie was dowie, an' Willie was wae:
> What can be the matter wi' siccan a twae?
> For Annie was bonnie's the first o' the day,
> And Willie was strang an' honest an' gay.
>
> Oh! the tane had a daddy was poor an' was proud;
> An' the tither a minnie that cared for the gowd.
> They lo'ed ane anither, an' said their say—
> But the daddy an' minnie hae pairtit the twae.

Just as she finished the song, I saw the sharp eyes of Lady Lucy peeping in at the door.

"Lady Lucy is watching at the door, Lady Alice," I said.

"I don't care," she answered; but turned with a flush on her face, and stepped noiselessly to the door.

"There is no one there," she said, returning.

"There was, though," I answered.

"They want to drive me mad," she cried, and hurried from the room.

The next day but one, she came again with the same request. But she had not been a minute in the library before Lady Hilton came to the door and called her in angry tones.

"Presently," replied Alice, and remained where she was.

"Do go, Lady Alice," I said. "They will send me away if you refuse."

She blushed scarlet, and went without another word.

She came no more to the library.

12
Confession

Day followed day, the one the child of the other. Alice's old paleness and unearthly look began to reappear; and, strange to tell, my midnight temptation revived. After a time she ceased to dine with us again, and for days I never saw her. It was the old story of suffering with me, only more intense than before. The day was dreary, and the night stormy. "Call her," said my heart; but my conscience resisted.

I was lying on the floor of my room one midnight, with my face to the ground, when suddenly I heard a low, sweet, strange voice singing somewhere. The moment I became aware that I heard it I felt as if I had been listening to it unconsciously for some minutes past. I lay still, either charmed to stillness, or fearful of breaking the spell. As I lay, I was lapt in the folds of a waking dream.

I was in bed in a castle, on the seashore; the wind came from the sea in chill eerie soughs, and the waves fell with a threatful tone upon the beach, muttering many maledictions as they rushed up, and whispering cruel portents as they drew back, hissing and gurgling, through the million narrow ways of the pebbly ramparts; and I knew that a maiden in white was standing in the cold wind, by the angry sea, singing. I had a kind of dreamy belief in my dream; but, overpowered by the spell of the music, I still lay and listened. Keener and stronger, under the impulses of my will, grew the power of my hearing. At last I could distinguish the words. The ballad was Annie of Lochroyan; and Lady Alice was singing it. The words I heard were these:—

Oh, gin I had a bonnie ship,
And men to sail wi' me,
It's I wad gang to my true love,
Sin' he winna come to me.

Lang stood she at her true love's door,
And lang tirled at the pin;

At length up gat his fause mother,
Says, "Wha's that wad be in?"

* * * * * * *

Love Gregory started frae his sleep,
And to his mother did say:
"I dreamed a dream this night, mither,
That maks my heart right wae.

"I dreamed that Annie of Lochroyan,
The flower of a' her kin,
Was standing mournin' at my door,
But nane wad let her in."

I sprang to my feet, and opened the hidden door. There she stood, white, asleep, with closed eyes, singing like a bird, only with a heartful of sad meaning in every tone. I stepped aside, without speaking, and she passed me into the room. I closed the door, and followed her. She lay already upon the couch, still and restful—already covered with my plaid. I sat down beside her, waiting; and gazed upon her in wonderment. That she was possessed of very superior intellectual powers, whatever might be the cause of their having lain dormant so long, I had already fully convinced myself; but I was not prepared to find art as well as intellect. I had already heard her sing the little song of two verses, which she had learned from her nurse. But here was a song, of her own making as to the music, so true and so potent, that, before I knew anything of the words, it had surrounded me with a dream of the place in which the scene of the ballad was laid. It did not then occur to me that, perhaps, our idiosyncrasies were such as not to require even the music of the ballad for the production of rapport between our minds, the brain of the one generating in the brain of the other the vision present to itself.

I sat and thought:—Some obstruction in the gateways, outward, prevented her, in her waking hours, from uttering herself at all. This obstruction, damming back upon their sources the out-goings of life, threw her into this abnormal sleep. In it the impulse to utterance, still unsatisfied, so wrought within her unable, yet compliant form, that she could not rest, but rose and walked. And now, a fresh surge from the sea of her unknown being, unrepressed by the hitherto of the objects of sense, had burst the gates and bars, swept the obstructions from its channel, and poured from her in melodious song.

The first green lobes, at least, of these thoughts, appeared above the soil of my mind, while I sat and gazed on the sleeping girl. And now I had once more the delight of watching a spirit-dawn, a soul-rise, in that lovely form. The light flushing of its pallid sky was, as before, the first sign. I dreaded the flash of lovely flame, and the out-burst of regnant anger, ere I should have time to say that I was not to blame. But when, at length, the full dawn, the slow sunrise came, it was with all the gentleness of a cloudy summer morn. Never did a more celestial rosy red hang about the skirts of the level sun, than deepened and glowed upon her face, when, opening her eyes, she saw me beside her. She covered her face with her hands; and instead of the words of indignant reproach which I dreaded to hear, she mur-mured behind the snowy screen: "I am glad you have broken your promise."

My heart gave a bound and was still. I grew faint with delight. "No," I said; "I have not broken my promise, Lady Alice; I have struggled nearly to madness to keep it—and I have kept it."

"I have come then of myself. Worse and worse! But it is their fault."

Tears now found their way through the repressing fingers. I could not endure to see her weep. I knelt beside her, and, while she still covered her face with her hands, I said—I do not know what I said. They were wild, and, doubtless, foolish words in themselves, but they must have been wise and true in their meaning. When I ceased, I knew that I had ceased only by the great silence around me. I was still look-ing at her hands. Slowly she withdrew them. It was as when the sun breaks forth on a cloudy day. The winter was over and gone; the time of the singing of birds had come. She smiled on me through her tears, and heart met heart in the light of that smile.

She rose to go at once, and I begged for no delay. I only stood with clasped hands, gazing at her. She turned at the door, and said;

"I daresay I shall come again; I am afraid I cannot help it; only mind you do not wake me."

Before I could reply, I was alone; and I felt that I must not follow her.

13
Questioning

I laid myself on the couch she had left, but not to sleep. A new pulse of life, stronger than I could bear, was throbbing within me. I dreaded a fever, lest I should talk in it, and drop the clue to my secret treasure. But the light of the morning stilled me, and a bath in ice-cold water made me strong again. Yet I felt all that day as if I were dying a delicious death, and going to a yet more exquisite life. As far as I might, however, I repressed all indications of my delight; and endeavoured, for the sake both of duty and of prudence, to be as attentive to my pupils and their studies as it was possible for man to be. This helped to keep me in my right mind. But, more than all my efforts at composure, the pain which, as far as my experience goes, invariably accompanies, and sometimes even usurps, the place of the pleasure which gave it birth, was efficacious in keeping me sane.

Night came, but brought no Lady Alice. It was a week before I saw her again. Her heart had been stilled, and she was able to sleep aright.

But seven nights after, she did come. I waited her awaking, possessed with one painful thought, which I longed to impart to her. She awoke with a smile, covered her face for a moment, but only for a moment, and then sat up. I stood before her; and the first words I spoke were:

"Lady Alice, ought I not to go?"

"No," she replied at once. "I can claim some compensation from them for the wrong they have been doing me. Do you know in what relation I stand to Lord and Lady Hilton? They are but my stepmother and her husband."

"I know that."

"Well, I have a fortune of my own, about which I never thought or cared—till—till—within the last few weeks. Lord Hilton is my guardian. Whether they made me the stupid creature I was, I do not know; but I believe they have represented me as far worse than I was, to keep people from making my acquaintance. They prevented my going on with my lessons, because they saw I was getting to understand things, and grow like other people; and that would not suit their purposes. It would be false delicacy in you to leave me to them, when you can make up to me for their injustice. Their behaviour to me takes away any right they had over me, and frees you from any obligation, because I am yours.—Am I not?"

Once more she covered her face with her hands. I could answer only by withdrawing one of them, which I was now emboldened to keep in my own.

I was very willingly persuaded to what was so much my own desire. But whether the reasoning was quite just or not, I am not yet sure. Perhaps it might be so for her, and yet not for me: I do not know; I am a poor casuist.

She resumed, laying her other hand upon mine:—

"It would be to tell the soul which you have called forth, to go back into its dark moaning cavern, and never more come out to the light of day."

How could I resist this?

A long pause ensued.

"It is strange," she said, at length, "to feel, when I lie down at night, that I may awake in your presence, without knowing how. It is strange, too, that, although I should be utterly ashamed to come wittingly, I feel no confusion when I find myself here. When I feel myself coming awake, I lie for a little while with my eyes closed, wondering and hoping, and afraid to open them, lest I should find myself only in my own chamber; shrinking a little, too—just a little—from the first glance into your face."

"But when you awake, do you know nothing of what has taken place in your sleep?"

"Nothing whatever."

"Have you no vague sensations, no haunting shadows, no dim ghostly moods, seeming to belong to that condition, left?"

"None whatever."

She rose, said "Good-night," and left me.

14
Jealousy

Again seven days passed before she revisited me. Indeed, her visits had always an interval of seven days, or a multiple of seven, between.

Since the last, a maddening jealousy had seized me. For, returning from those unknown regions into which her soul had wandered away, and where she had stayed for hours, did she not sometimes awake with a smile? How could I be sure that she did not lead two distinct existences?—that she had not some loving spirit, or man, who, like her, had for a time left the body behind—who was all in all to her in that region, and whom she forgot when she forsook it, as she forgot me when she entered it? It was a thought I could not brook. But I put aside its persistency as well as I could, till she should come again. For this I waited. I could not now endure the thought of compelling the attendance of her unconscious form; of making her body, like a living cage, transport to my presence the unresisting soul. I shrank from it as a true man would shrink from kissing the lips of a sleeping woman whom he loved, not knowing that she loved him in return.

It may well be said that to follow such a doubt was to inquire too curiously; but once the thought had begun, and grown, and been born, how was I to slay the monster, and be free of its hated presence? Was its truth not a possibility?—Yet how could even she help me, for she knew nothing of the matter? How could she vouch for the unknown? What news can the serene face of the moon, ever the same to us, give of the hidden half of herself turned ever towards what seems to us but the blind abysmal darkness, which yet has its own light and its own life? All I could hope for was to see her, to tell her, to be comforted at least by her smile.

My saving angel glided blind into my room, lay down upon her bier, and awaited the resurrection. I sat and awaited mine, panting to untwine from my heart the cold death-worm that twisted around it, yet picturing to myself the glow of love on the averted face of the beautiful spirit—averted from me, and bending on a radiant companion all the light withdrawn from the lovely form beside me. That light began to return. "She is coming, she is coming," I said within me. "Back from its glowing south travels the sun of my spring, the glory of my summer." Floating slowly up from the infinite depths of her being, came the conscious woman; up—up from the realms of stillness lying deeper than the plummet of self-knowledge can sound; up from the formless, up into the known, up into the material, up to the windows that look forth on the embodied mysteries around. Her eyelids rose. One look of love all but slew my fear. When I told her my grief, she answered with a smile of pity, yet half of disdain at the thought,

"If ever I find it so, I will kill myself there, that I may go to my Hades with you. But if I am dreaming of another, how is it that I always rise in my vision and come to you? You will go crazy if you fancy such foolish things," she added, with a smile of reproof.

The spectral thought vanished, and I was free.

"Shall I tell you," she resumed, covering her face with her hands, "why I behaved so proudly to you, from the very first day you entered the house? It was because, when I passed you on the lawn, before ever you entered the house, I felt a strange, undefinable attraction towards you, which continued, although I could not account for it and would not yield to it. I was heartily annoyed at it. But you see it was of no use—here I am. That was what made me so fierce, too, when I first found myself in your room."

It was indeed long before she came to my room again.

15

The Chamber of Ghosts

But now she returned once more into the usual routine of the family. I fear I was unable to repress all signs of agitation when, next day, she entered the dining-room, after we were seated, and took her customary place at the table. Her behaviour was much the same as before; but her face was very different. There was light in it now, and signs of mental movement. The smooth forehead would be occasionally wrinkled, and she would fall into moods which were evidently not of inanity, but of abstracted thought. She took especial care that our eyes should not meet. If by chance they did, instead of sinking hers, she kept them steady, and opened them wider, as if she was fixing them on nothing at all, or she raised them still higher, as if she was looking at something above me, before she allowed them to fall. But the change in her altogether was such that it must have attracted the notice and roused the speculation of Lady Hilton at least. For me, so well did she act her part, that I was thrown into perplexity by it. And when day after day passed, and the longing to speak to her grew, and remained unsatisfied, new doubts arose. Perhaps she was tired of me. Perhaps her new studies filled her mind with the clear, gladsome morning light of the pure intellect, which always throws doubt and distrust and a kind of negation upon the moonlight of passion, mysterious, and mingled ever with faint shadows of pain. I walked as in an unresting sleep. Utterly as I loved her, I was yet alarmed and distressed to find how entirely my being had grown dependent upon her love; how little of individual, self-existing, self-upholding life, I seemed to have left; how little I cared for anything, save as I could associate it with her.

I was sitting late one night in my room. I had all but given up hope of her coming. I had, perhaps, deprived her of the somnambulic power. I was brooding over this possibility, when all at once I felt as if I were looking into the haunted room. It seemed to be lighted by the moon, shining through the stained windows. The feeling came and went suddenly, as such visions of places generally do; but this had an indescribable something about it more clear and real than such resurrections of the past, whether willed or unwilled, commonly possess; and a great longing seized me to look into the room once more. I rose with a sense of yielding to the irresistible, left the room, groped my way through the hall and up the oak staircase—I had never thought of taking a light with me—and entered the corridor. No sooner had I entered it, than the thought sprang up in my mind— "What if she should be there!" My heart stood still for a moment, like a wounded deer, and then bounded on, with a pang in every bound. The corridor was night itself, with a dim, bluish-grey light from the windows, sufficing to mark their own spaces. I stole through it, and, without erring once, went straight to the haunted chamber. The door stood half open. I entered, and was bewildered by the dim, mysterious, dreamy loveliness upon which I gazed. The moon shone full upon the windows, and a thousand coloured lights and shadows crossed and intertwined upon the walls and floor, all so soft, and mingling, and undefined, that the brain was filled as with a flickering dance of ghostly rainbows. But I had little time to think of these; for out of the only dark corner in the room came a white figure, flitting across the chaos of lights, bedewed, besprinkled, bespattered, as she passed, with their multitudinous colours. I was speechless, motionless, with something far beyond joy. With a low moan of delight, Lady Alice sank into my arms. Then, looking up, with a light laugh— "The scales are turned, dear," she said. "You are in my power now; I brought you here. I thought I could, and I tried, for I wanted so much to see you—and you are come." She led me across the room to the place where she had been seated, and we sat side by side.

"I thought you had forgotten me," I said, "or had grown tired of me."

"Did you? That was unkind. You have made my heart so still, that, body and soul, I sleep at night."

"Then shall I never see you more?"

"We can meet here. This is the best place. No one dares come near the haunted room at night. We might even venture in the evening. Look, now, from where we are sitting, across the air, between the windows and the shadows on the floor. Do you see nothing moving?"

I looked, but could see nothing. She resumed:—

"I almost fancy, sometimes, that what old stories say about this room may be true. I could fancy now that I see dim transparent forms in ancient armour, and in strange antique dresses, men and women, moving about, meeting, speaking, embracing, parting, coming and going. But I was never afraid of such beings. I am sure these would not, could not hurt us."

If the room was not really what it was well fitted to be—a rendez-vous for the ghosts of the past—then either my imagination, becoming more active as she spoke, began to operate upon my brain, or her fancies were mysteriously communicated to me; for I was persuaded that I saw such dim undefined forms as she described, of a substance only denser than the moonlight, flitting, and floating about, between the windows and the illuminated floor. Could they have been coloured shadows thrown from the stained glass upon the fine dust with which the slightest motion in such an old and neglected room must fill its atmosphere? I did not think of that then, however.

"I could persuade myself that I, too, see them," I replied. "I cannot say that I am afraid of such beings any more than you—if only they will not speak."

"Ah!" she replied, with a lengthened, meaning utterance, expressing sympathy with what I said; "I know what you mean. I, too, am afraid of hearing things. And that reminds me, I have never yet asked you about the galloping horse. I too hear sometimes the sound of a loose horse-shoe. It always betokens some evil to me; but I do not know what it means. Do you?"

"Do you know," I rejoined, "that there is a connection between your family and mine, somewhere far back in their histories?"

"No! Is there? How glad I am! Then perhaps you and I are related, and that is how we are so much alike, and have power over each other, and hear the same things."

"Yes. I suppose that is how."

"But can you account for that sound which we both hear?"

"I will tell you what my old foster-mother told me," I replied. And I began by narrating when and where I had first heard the sound; and then gave her, as nearly as I could, the legend which nurse had recounted to me. I did not tell her its association with the events of my birth, for I feared exciting her imagination too much. She listened to it very quietly, however, and when I came to a close, only said:

"Of course, we cannot tell how much of it is true, but there may be something in it. I have never heard anything of the sort, and I, too, have an old nurse. She is with me still. You shall see her some day."

She rose to go.

"Will you meet me here again soon?" I said.

"As soon as you wish," she answered.

"Then to-morrow, at midnight?"

"Yes."

And we parted at the door of the haunted chamber. I watched the flickering with which her whiteness just set the darkness in motion, and nothing more, seeming to see it long after I knew she must have turned aside and descended the steps leading towards her own room. Then I turned and groped my way back to mine.

We often met after this in the haunted room. Indeed my spirit haunted it all day and all night long. And when we met amid the shadows, we were wrapped in the mantle of love, and from its folds looked out fearless on the ghostly world about us. Ghosts or none, they never annoyed us. Our love was a talisman, yea, an elixir of life, which made us equal to the twice-born,—the disembodied dead. And they were as a wall of fear about us, to keep far off the unfriendly foot and the prying eye.

In the griefs that followed, I often thought with myself that I would gladly die for a thousand years, might I then awake for one night in the haunted chamber, a ghost, among the ghosts who crowded its stained moonbeams, and see my dead Alice smiling across the glimmering rays, and beckoning me to the old nook, she, too, having come awake out of the sleep of death, in the dream of the haunted chamber. "Might we but sit there," I said, "through the night, as of old, and love and comfort each other, till the moon go down, and the pale dawn, which is the night of the ghosts, begin to arise, then gladly would I go to sleep for another thousand years, in the hope that when I next became conscious of life, it might be in another such ghostly night, in the chamber of the ghosts."

16
The Clanking Shoe

Time passed. We began to feel very secure in that room, watched as it was by the sleepless sentry, Fear. One night I ventured to take a light with me.

"How nice to have a candle!" she said as I entered. "I hope they are all in bed, though. It will drive some of them into fits if they see the light."

"I wanted to show you something I found in the library to-day."

"What is it?"

I opened a book, and showed her a paper inside it, with some verses written on it.

"Whose writing is that?" I asked.

"Yours, of course. As if I did not know your writing!"

"Will you look at the date?"

"Seventeen hundred and ninety-three! You are making game of me, Duncan. But the paper does look yellow and old."

"I found it as you see it, in that book. It belonged to Lord Hilton's brother. The verses are a translation of part of the poem beside which they lie—one by Von Salis, who died shortly before that date at the bottom. I will read them to you, and then show you something else that is strange about them. The poem is called Psyche's Sorrow. Psyche means the soul, Alice."

"I remember. You told me about her before, you know."

"Psyche's sighing all her prison darkens;
  She is moaning for the far-off stars;
  Fearing, hoping, every sound she hearkens—
  Fate may now be breaking at her bars.

  Bound, fast bound, are Psyche's airy pinions:
  High her heart, her mourning soft and low—
  Knowing that in sultry pain's dominions

Grow the palms that crown the victor's brow;

That the empty hand the wreath encloses;
Earth's cold winds but make the spirit brave;
Knowing that the briars bear the roses,
Golden flowers the waste deserted grave.

In the cypress-shade her myrtle groweth;
Much she loves, because she much hath borne;
Love-led, through the darksome way she goeth—
On to meet him in the breaking morn.

She can bear—

"Here the translation ceases, you see; and then follows the date, with the words in German underneath it— 'How weary I am!' Now what is strange, Alice, is, that this date is the very month and year in which I was born."

She did not reply to this with anything beyond a mere assent. Her mind was fixed on the poem itself. She began to talk about it, and I was surprised to find how thoroughly she entered into it and understood it. She seemed to have crowded the growth of a lifetime into the last few months. At length I told her how unhappy I had felt for some time, at remaining in Lord Hilton's house, as matters now were.

"Then you must go," she said, quite quietly.

This troubled me.

"You do not mind it?"

"No. I shall be very glad."

"Will you go with me?" I asked, perplexed.

"Of course I will."

I did not know what to say to this, for I had no money, and of course I should have none of my salary. She divined at once the cause of my hesitation.

"I have a diamond bracelet in my room," she said, with a smile, "and a few guineas besides."

"How shall we get away?"

"Nothing is easier. My old nurse, whom I mentioned to you before, lives at the lodge gate."

"Oh! I know her very well," I interrupted. "But she's not Scotch?"

"Indeed she is. But she has been with our family almost all her life. I often go to see her, and sometimes stay all night with her. You can get a carriage ready in the village, and neither of us will be missed before morning."

I looked at her in renewed surprise at the decision of her invention. She covered her face, as she seldom did now, but went on:

"We can go to London, where you will easily find something to do. Men always can there. And when I come of age—"

"Alice, how old are you?," I interrupted.

"Nineteen," she answered. "By the way," she resumed, "when I think of it—how odd!—that"—pointing to the date on the paper— "is the very month in which I too was born."

I was too much surprised to interrupt her, and she continued:

"I never think of my age without recalling one thing about my birth, which nurse often refers to. She was going up the stair to my mother's room, when she happened to notice a bright star, not far from the new moon. As she crossed the room with me in her arms, just after I was born, she saw the same star almost on the tip of the opposite horn. My mother died a week after. Who knows how different I might have been if she had lived!"

It was long before I spoke. The awful and mysterious thoughts roused in my mind by the revelations of the day held me silent. At length I said, half thinking aloud:

"Then you and I, Alice, were born the same hour, and our mothers died together."

Receiving no answer, I looked at her. She was fast asleep, and breathing gentle, full breaths. She had been sitting for some time with her head lying on my shoulder and my arm around her. I could not bear to wake her.

We had been in this position perhaps for half an hour, when suddenly a cold shiver ran through me, and all at once I became aware of the far-off gallop of a horse. It drew nearer. On and on it came—nearer and nearer. Then came the clank of the broken shoe!

At the same moment, Alice started from her sleep and, springing to her feet, stood an instant listening. Then crying out, in an agonised whisper,— "The horse with the clanking shoe!" she flung her arms around me. Her face was white as the spectral moon which, the moment I put the candle out, looked in through a clear pane beside us; and she gazed fearfully, yet wildly-defiant, towards the door. We clung to each other. We heard the sound come nearer and nearer, till it thundered right up to the very door of the room, terribly loud. It ceased. But the door was flung open, and Lord Hilton entered, followed by servants with lights.

I have but a very confused remembrance of what followed. I heard a vile word from the lips of Lord Hilton; I felt my fingers on his throat; I received a blow on the head; and I seem to remember a cry of agony from Alice as I fell. What happened next I do not know.

When I came to myself, I was lying on a wide moor, with the night wind blowing about me. I presume that I had wandered thither in a state of unconsciousness, after being turned out of the Hall, and that I had at last fainted from loss of blood. I was unable to move for a long time. At length the morning broke, and I found myself not far from the Hall. I crept back, a mile or two, to the gates, and having succeeded in rousing Alice's old nurse, was taken in with many lamentations, and put to bed in the lodge. I had a violent fever; and it was all the poor woman could do to keep my presence a secret from the family at the Hall.

When I began to mend, my first question was about Alice. I learned, though with some difficulty—for my kind attendant was evidently unwilling to tell me all the truth—that Alice, too, had been very ill; and that, a week before, they had removed her. But she either would not or could not tell me where they had taken her. I believe she could not. Nor do I know for certain to this day.

Mrs. Blakesley offered me the loan of some of her savings to get me to London. I received it with gratitude, and as soon as I was fit to travel, made my way thither. Afraid for my reason, if I had no employment to keep my thoughts from brooding on my helplessness, and so increasing my despair, and determined likewise that my failure should not make me burdensome to any one else, I enlisted in the Scotch Greys, before letting any of my friends know where I was. Through the help of one already mentioned in my story, I soon obtained a commission. From the field of Waterloo, I rode into Brussels with a broken arm and a sabre-cut in the head.

As we passed along one of the streets, through all the clang of iron-shod hoofs on the stones around me, I heard the ominous clank. At the same moment, I heard a cry. It was the voice of my Alice. I looked up. At a barred window I saw her face; but it was terribly changed. I dropped from my horse. As soon as I was able to move from the hospital, I went to the place, and found it was a lunatic asylum. I was permitted to see the inmates, but discovered no one resembling her. I do not now believe that she was ever there. But I may be wrong. Nor will I trouble my reader with the theories on which I sought to account for the vision. They will occur to himself readily enough.

For years and years I know not whether she was alive or dead. I sought her far and near. I wandered over England, France, and Germany, hopelessly searching; listening at tables-d'hôte; lurking about mad-houses; haunting theatres and churches; often, in wild regions, begging my way from house to house; I did not find her.

Once I visited Hilton Hall. I found it all but deserted. I learned that Mrs. Wilson was dead, and that there were only two or three servants in the place. I managed to get into the house unseen, and made my way to the haunted chamber. My feelings were not so keen as I had antici- pated, for they had been dulled by long suffering. But again I saw the moon shine through those windows of stained glass. Again her beams were crowded with ghosts. She was not amongst them. "My lost love!" I cried; and then, rebuking myself, "No; she is not lost. They say that Time and Space exist not, save in our thoughts. If so, then that which has been, is, and the Past can never cease. She is mine, and I shall find her—what matters it where, or when, or how? Till then, my soul is but a moon-lighted chamber of ghosts; and I sit within, the dreari- est of them all. When she enters, it will be a home of love. And I wait— I wait."

I sat and brooded over the Past, till I fell asleep in the phantom- peopled night. And all the night long they were about me—the men and women of the long past. And I was one of them. I wandered in my dreams over the whole house, habited in a long old-fashioned gown, searching for one who was Alice, and yet would be some one else. From room to room I wandered till weary, and could not find her. At last, I gave up the search, and, retreating to the library, shut myself in. There, taking down from the shelf the volume of Von Salis, I tried hard to go on with the translation of Pysche's Sorrow, from the point where the student had left it, thinking it, all the time, my own unfin- ished work.

When I woke in the morning, the chamber of ghosts, in which I had fallen asleep, had vanished. The sun shone in through the win- dows of the library; and on its dusty table lay Von Salis, open at Pysche's Trauer. The sheet of paper with the translation on it, was not there. I hastened to leave the house, and effected my escape be- fore the servants were astir.

Sometimes I condensed my whole being into a single intensity of will—that she should come to me; and sustained it, until I fainted with the effort. She did not come. I desisted altogether at last, for I bethought me that, whether dead or alive, it must cause her torture not to be able to obey it.

Sometimes I questioned my own sanity. But the thought of the loss of my reason did not in itself trouble me much. What tortured me almost to the madness it supposed was the possible fact, which a return to my right mind might reveal—that there never had been a Lady Alice. What if I died, and awoke from my madness, and found a clear blue air of life, a joyous world of sunshine, a divine wealth of delight around and in me—but no Lady Alice—she having vanished with all the other phantoms of a sick brain! "Rather let me be mad still," I said, "if mad I am; and so dream on that I have been blessed.

Were I to wake to such a heaven, I would pray God to let me go and live the life I had but dreamed, with all its sorrows, and all its despair, and all its madness, that when I died again, I might know that such things had been, and could never be awaked from, and left behind with the dream." But I was not mad, any more than Hamlet; though, like him, despair sometimes led me far along the way at the end of which madness lies.

17
The Physician

I was now Captian Campbell, of the Scotch Greys, contriving to live on my half pay, and thinking far more about the past than the present or the future. My father was dead. My only brother was also gone, and the property had passed into other hands. I had no fixed place of abode, but went from one spot to another, as the whim seized me—sometimes remaining months, sometimes removing next day, but generally choosing retired villages about which I knew nothing.

I had spent a week in a small town on the borders of Wales, and intended remaining a fortnight longer, when I was suddenly seized with a violent illness, in which I lay insensible for three weeks. When I recovered consciousness, I found that my head had been shaved, and that the cicatrice of my old wound was occasionally very painful. Of late I have suspected that I had some operation performed upon my skull during my illness; but Dr. Ruthwell never dropped a hint to that effect. This was the friend whom, when first I opened my seeing eyes, I beheld sitting by my bedside, watching the effect of his last prescription. He was one of the few in the profession, whose love of science and love of their fellows combined, would be enough to chain them to the art of healing, irrespective of its emoluments. He was one of the few, also, who see the marvellous in all science, and, therefore, reject nothing merely because the marvellous may seem to predominate in it. Yet neither would he accept anything of the sort as fact, without the strictest use of every experiment within his power, even then remaining often in doubt. This man conferred honour by his friendship; and I am happy to think that before many days of recovery had passed, we were friends indeed. But I lay for months under his care before I was able to leave my bed.

He attributed my illness to the consequences of the sabre-cut, and my recovery to the potency of the drugs he had exhibited. I attributed my illness in great measure to the constant contemplation of my early history, no longer checked by any regular employment; and my recovery in equal measure to the power of his kindness and sympathy, helping from within what could never have been reached from without.

He told me that he had often been greatly perplexed with my symptoms, which would suddenly change in the most unaccountable manner, exhibiting phases which did not, as far as his knowledge went, belong to any variety of the suffering which gave the prevailing character to my ailment; and after I had so far recovered as to render it safe to turn my regard more particularly upon my own case, he said to me one day,

"You would laugh at me, Campbell, were I to confess some of the bother this illness of yours has occasioned me; enough, indeed, to overthrow any conceit I ever had in my own diagnosis."

"Go on," I answered; "I promise not to laugh."

He little knew how far I should be from laughing.

"In your case," he continued, "the pathognomonic, if you will excuse medical slang, was every now and then broken by the intrusion of altogether foreign symptoms."

I listened with breathless attention.

"Indeed, on several occasions, when, after meditating on your case till I was worn out, I had fallen half asleep by your bedside, I came to myself with the strangest conviction that I was watching by the bedside of a woman."

"Thank Heaven!" I exclaimed, starting up, "She lives still."

I need not describe the doctor's look of amazement, almost consternation; for he thought a fresh access of fever was upon me, and I had already begun to rave. For his reassurance, however, I promised to account fully for my apparently senseless excitement; and that evening I commenced the narrative which forms the preceeding part of this story. Long before I reached its close, my exultation had vanished, and, as I wrote it for him, it ended with the expressed conviction that she must be dead. Ere long, however, the hope once more revived. While, however, the narrative was in progress, I gave him a summary, which amounted to this:—

I had loved a lady—loved her still. I did not know where she was, and had reason to fear that her mind had given way under the suffering of our separation. Between us there existed, as well, the bond of a distand blood relationship; so distant, that but for its probable share in the production of another relationship of a very marvellous nature, it would scarcely have been worth alluding to. This was a kind of psychological attraction, which, when justified and strengthened by the spiritual energies of love, rendered the immediate communication of certain feelings, both mental and bodily, so rapid, that almost the consciousness of the one existed for the time in the mental circumstances of the

other. Nay, so complete at times was the communication, that I even
doubted her testimony as to some strange correspondence in our past
history on this very ground, suspecting that, my memory being open
to her retrospection, she saw my story, and took it for her own. It
was, therefore, easy for me to account for Dr. Ruthwell's scientific
bewilderment at the symptoms I manifested.

As my health revived, my hope and longing increased. But although
I loved Lady Alice with more entireness than even during the latest
period of our intercourse, a certain calm endurance had supervened,
which rendered the relief of fierce action no longer necessary to the
continuance of a sane existence. It was as if the concentrated orb of
love had diffused itself in a genial warmth through the whole orb of
life, imparting fresh vitality to many roots which had remained leafless in my being. For years the field of battle was the only field that had
borne the flower of delight; now nature began to live again for me.

One day, the first on which I ventured to walk into the fields alone, I
was delighted with the multitude of the daisies peeping from the grass
everywhere—the first attempts of the earth, become conscious of
blindness, to open eyes, and see what was about and above her. Everything is wonderful after the resurrection from illness. It is a resurrection of all nature. But somehow or other I was not satisfied with
the daisies. They did not seem to me so lovely as the daisies I used to
see when I was a child. I thought with myself, "This is the cloud that
gathers with life, the dimness that passion and suffering cast over the
eyes of the mind." That moment my gaze fell upon a single, solitary, red-
tipped daisy. My reasoning vanished, and my melancholy with it, slain
by the red tips of the lonely beauty. This was the kind of daisy I had
loved as a child; and with the sight of it, a whole field of them rushed
back into my mind; a field of my father's where, throughout the multitude, you could not have found a white one. My father was dead; the
fields had passed into other hands; but perhaps the red-tipped gowans
were left. I must go and see. At all events, the hill that overlooked the
field would still be there, and no change would have passed upon it.
It would receive me with the same familiar look as of old, still fronting
the great mountain from whose sides I had first heard the sound of that
clanking horseshoe, which, whatever might be said to account for it,
had certainly had a fearful connection with my joys and sorrows both.
Did the ghostly rider still haunt the place? or, if he did, should I hear
again that sound of coming woe? Whether or not, I defied him. I would
not be turned from my desire to see the old place by any fear of a
ghostly marauder, whom I should be only too glad to encounter, if
there were the smallest chance of coming off with the victory.

As soon as my friend would permit me, I set out for Scotland.

18
Old Friends

I made the journey by easy stages, chiefly on the back of a favourite black horse, which had carried me well in several fights, and had come out of them scarred, like his master, but sound in wind and limb. It was night when I reached the village lying nearest to my birth place.

When I woke in the morning, I found the whole region filled with a white mist, hiding the mountains around. Now and then a peak looked through, and again retired into the cloudy folds. In the wide, straggling street, below the window at which I had made them place my breakfast-table, a periodical fair was being held; and I sat looking down on the gathering crowd, trying to discover some face known to my childhood, and still to be recognized through the veil which years must have woven across the features. When I had finished my breakfast, I went down and wandered about among the people. Groups of elderly men were talking earnestly; and young men and maidens who had come to be fee'd, were joking and laughing. They stared at the Sassenach gentleman, and, little thinking that he understood every word they uttered, made their remarks upon him in no very subdued tones. I approached a stall where a brown old woman was selling gingerbread and apples. She was talking to a man with long, white locks. Near them was a group of young people. One of them must have said something about me; for the old woman, who had been taking stolen glances at me, turned rather sharply towards them, and rebuked them for rudeness.

"The gentleman is no Sassenach," she said. "He understands everything you are saying."

This was spoken in Gaelic, of course. I turned and looked at her with more observance. She made me a courtesy, and said, in the same language:

"Your honour will be a Campbell, I'm thinking."

"I am a Campbell," I answered, and waited.

"Your honour's Christian name wouldn't be Duncan, sir?"

"It is Duncan," I answered; "but there are many Duncan Campbells."

"Only one to me, your honour; and that's yourself. But you will not remember me?"

I did not remember her. Before long, however, urged by her anxiety to associate her Present with my Past, she enabled me to recall in her time-worn features those of a servant in my father's house when I was a child.

"But how could you recollect me?" I said.

"I have often seen you since I left your father's, sir. But it was really, I believe, that I hear more about you than anything else, every day of my life."

"I do not understand you."

"From old Margaret, I mean."

"Dear old Margaret! Is she alive?"

"Alive and hearty, though quite bedridden. Why, sir, she must be within near sight of a hundred."

"Where does she live?"

"In the old cottage, sir. Nothing will make her leave it. The new laird wanted to turn her out; but Margaret muttered something at which he grew as white as his shirt, and he has never ventured across her threshold again."

"How do you see so much of her, though?"

"I never leave her, sir. She can't wait on herself, poor old lady. And she's like a mother to me. Bless her! But your honour will come and see her?"

"Of course I will. Tell her so when you go home."

"Will you honour me by sleeping at my house, sir?" said the old man to whom she had been talking. "My farm is just over the brow of the hill, you know."

I had by this time recognised him, and I accepted his offer at once.

"When may we look for you, sir?" he asked.

"When shall you be home?" I rejoined.

"This afternoon, sir. I have done my business already."

"Then I shall be with you in the evening, for I have nothing to keep me here."

"Will you take a seat in my gig?"

"No, thank you. I have my own horse with me. You can take him in too, I dare say?"

"With pleasure, sir."

We parted for the meantime. I rambled about the neighbourhood till it was time for an early dinner.

19
Old Constancy

The fog cleared off; and, as the hills began to throw long, lazy shadows, their only embraces across the wide valleys, I mounted and set out on the ride of a few miles which should bring me to my old acquaintance's dwelling.

I lingered on the way. All the old places demanded my notice. They seemed to say, "Here we are—waiting for you." Many a tuft of hare-bells drew me towards the roadside, to look at them and their children, the blue butterflies, hovering over them; and I stopped to gaze at many a wild rosebush, with a sunset of its own roses. The sun had set to me, before I had completed half the distance. But there was a long twilight, and I knew the road well.

My horse was an excellent walker, and I let him walk on, with the reins on his neck; while I, lost in a dream of the past, was singing a song of my own making, with which I often comforted my longing by giving it voice.

> The autumn winds are sighing
> Over land and sea;
> The autumn woods are dying
> Over hill and lea;
> And my heart is sighing, dying,
> Maiden, for thee.
>
> The autumn clouds are flying
> Homeless over me;
> The homeless birds are crying
> In the naked tree;
> And my heart is flying, crying,
> Maiden, to thee.
>
> My cries may turn to gladness,

And my flying flee;
My sighs may lose the sadness,
Yet sigh on in me;
All my sadness, all my gladness,
Maiden, lost in thee.

I was roused by a heavy drop of rain upon my face. I looked up. A cool wave of wind flowed against me. Clouds had gathered; and over the peak of a hill to the left, the sky was very black. Old Constancy threw his head up, as if he wanted me to take the reins, and let him step out. I remembered that there used to be an awkward piece of road somewhere not far in front, where the path, with a bank on the left side, sloped to a deep descent on the right. If the road was as bad there as it used to be, it would be better to pass it before it grew quite dark. So I took the reins, and away went old Constancy. We had just reached the spot, when a keen flash of lightning broke from the cloud overhead, and my horse instantly stood stock-still, as if paralysed, with his nostrils turned up towards the peak of the mountain. I sat as still as he, to give him time to recover himself. But all at once, his whole frame was convulsed, as if by an agony of terror. He gave a great plunge, and then I felt his muscles swelling and knotting under me, as he rose on his hind legs, and went backwards, with the scaur behind him. I leaned forward on his neck to bring him down, but he reared higher and higher, till he stood bolt upright, and it was time to slip off, lest he should fall upon me. I did so; but my foot alighted upon no support. He had backed to the edge of the shelving ground, and I fell, and went to the bottom. The last thing I was aware of, was the thundering fall of my horse beside me.

When I came to myself, it was dark. I felt stupid and aching all over; but I soon satisfied myself that no bones were broken. A mass of something lay near me. It was poor Constancy. I crawled to him, laid my hand on his neck, and called him by his name. But he made no answer in that gentle, joyful speech—for it was speech in old Constancy—with which he always greeted me, if only after an hour's absence. I felt for his heart. There was just a flutter there. He tried to lift his head, and gave a little kick with one of his hind legs. In doing so, he struck a bit of rock, and the clank of the iron made my flesh creep. I got hold of his leg in the dark, and felt the shoe. It was loose. I felt his heart again. The motion had ceased. I needed all my manhood to keep from crying like a child; for my charger was my friend. How long I lay beside him, I do not know; but, at length, I heard the sound of wheels coming along the road. I tried to shout, and, in some measure, succeeded; for a voice, which I recognised as that of my farmer-friend, answered cheerily. He was shocked to discover that his expected guest was in such evil plight. It was still dark, for the rain was falling heavily; but, with his directions, I was soon able to take my seat beside him in the gig. He had been unexpectedly detained, and was now hastening home with the hope of being yet in time to welcome me.

Next morning, after the luxurious rest of a heather-bed, I found myself not much the worse for my adventure, but heart-sore for the loss of my horse.

20
Margaret

Early in the forenoon, I came in sight of the cottage of Margaret. It lay unchanged, a grey, stone-fashioned hut, in the hollow of the mountain-basin. I scrambled down the soft green brae, and soon stood within the door of the cottage. There I was met and welcomed by Margaret's attendant. She led me to the bed where my old nurse lay. Her eyes were yet undimmed by years, and little change had passed upon her countenance since I parted with her on that memorable night. The moment she saw me, she broke out into a passionate lamentation such as a mother might utter over the maimed strength and disfigured beauty of her child.

"What ill has he done—my bairn—to be all night the sport of the powers of the air and the wicked of the earth? But the day will dawn for my Duncan yet, and a lovely day it will be!"

Then looking at me anxiously, she said,

"You're not much the worse for last night, my bairn. But woe's me! His grand horse, that carried him so, that I blessed the beast in my prayers!"

I knew that no one could have yet brought her the news of my accident.

"You saw me fall, then, nurse?" I said.

"That I did," she answered. "I see you oftener than you think. But there was a time when I could hardly see you at all, and I thought you were dead, my Duncan."

I stooped to kiss her. She laid the one hand that had still the power of motion upon my head, and dividing the hair, which had begun to be mixed with grey, said: "Eh! The bonny grey hairs! My Duncan's a man in spite of them!"

She searched until she found the scar of the sabre-cut.

"Just where I thought to find it!" she said. "That was a terrible day; worse for me than for you, Duncan."

"You saw me then!" I exclaimed.

"Little do folks know," she answered, "who think I'm lying here like a live corpse in its coffin, what liberty my soul—and that's just me—enjoys. Little do they know what I see and hear. And there's no witchcraft or evil-doing in it, my boy; but just what the Almighty made me. Janet, here, declares she heard the cry that I made, when this same cut, that's no so well healed yet, broke out in your bonny head. I saw no sword, only the bursting of the blood from the wound. But sit down, my bairn, and have something to eat after your walk. We'll have time enough for speech."

Janet had laid out the table with fare of the old homely sort, and I was a boy once more as I ate the well-known food. Every now and then I glanced towards the old face. Soon I saw that she was asleep. From her lips broke murmured sounds, so partially connected that I found it impossible to remember them; but the impression they left on my mind was something like this,

"Over the water. Yes; it is a rough sea—green and white. But over the water. There is a path for the pathless. The grass on the hill is long and cool. Never horse came there. If they once sleep in that grass, no harm can hurt them more. Over the water. Up the hill." And then she murmured the words of the psalm: "He that dwelleth in the secret place."

For an hour I sat beside her. It was evidently a sweet, natural sleep, the most wonderful sleep of all, mingled with many a broken dream-rainbow. I rose at last, and, telling Janet that I would return in the evening, went back to my quarters; for my absence from the mid-day meal would have been a disappointment to the household.

When I returned to the cottage, I found Margaret only just awaked, and greatly refreshed. I sat down beside her in the twilight, and the following conversation began:

"You said, nurse, that, some time ago, you could not see me. Did you know nothing about me all that time?"

"I took it to mean that you were ill, my dear. Shortly after you left us, the same thing happened first; but I do not think you were ill then."

"I should like to tell you all my story, dear Margaret," I said, conceiving a sudden hope of assistance from one who hovered so near the unseen that she often flitted across the borders. "But would it tire you?"

"Tire me, my child!" she said, with sudden energy. "Did I not carry you in my bosom, till I loved you more than the darling I had lost? Do I not think about you and your fortunes, till, sitting there, you are no nearer to me than when a thousand miles away? You do not know my love to you, Duncan. I have lived upon it when, I daresay, you did not care whether I was alive or dead. But that was all one to my love.

When you leave me now, I shall not care much. My thoughts will only return to their old ways. I think the sight of the eyes is sometimes an intrusion between the heart and its love."

Here was philosophy, or something better, from the lips of an old Highland seeress! For me, I felt it so true, that the joy of hearing her say so turned, by a sudden metamorphosis, into freak. I pretended to rise, and said:

"Then I had better go, nurse. Good-bye."

She put out her one hand, with a smile that revealed her enjoyment of the poor humour, and said, while she held me fast:

"Nay, nay, my Duncan. A little of the scarce is sometimes dearer to us than much of the better. I shall have plenty of time to think about you when I can't see you, my boy." And her philosophy melted away into tears, that filled her two blue eyes.

"I was only joking," I said.

"Do you need to tell me that?" she rejoined, smiling. "I am not so old as to be stupid yet. But I want to hear your story. I am hungering to hear it."

"But," I whispered, "I cannot speak about it before any one else."

"I will send Janet away. Janet, I want to talk to Mr. Campbell alone."

"Very well, Margaret," answered Janet, and left the room.

"Will she listen?" I asked.

"She dares not," answered Margaret, with a smile; "she has a terrible idea of my powers."

The twilight grew deeper; the glow of the peat-fire became redder; the old woman lay still as death. And I told all the story of Lady Alice. My voice sounded to myself as I spoke, not like my own, but like its echo from the vault of some listening cave, or like the voices one hears beside as sleep is slowly creeping over the sense. Margaret did not once interrupt me. When I had finished she remained still silent, and I began to fear I had talked her asleep.

"Can you help me?" I said.

"I think I can," she answered. "Will you call Janet?"

I called her.

"Make me a cup of tea, Janet. Will you have some tea with me, Duncan?"

Janet lighted a little lamp, and the tea was soon set out, with "flour-scons" and butter. But Margaret ate nothing; she only drank her tea, lifting her cup with her one trembling hand. When the remains of our repast had been removed, she said:—

"Now, Janet, you can leave us; and on no account come into the room till Mr. Campbell calls you. Take the lamp with you."

Janet obeyed without a word of reply, and we were left once more alone, lighted only by the dull glow of the fire.

The night had gathered cloudy and dark without, reminding me of that night when she told me the story of the two brothers. But this time no storm disturbed the silence of the night. As soon as Janet was gone, Margaret said:—

"Will you take the pillow from under my head, Duncan, my dear?"

I did so, and she lay in an almost horizontal position. With the living hand she lifted the powerless arm, and drew it across her chest, outside the bed-clothes. Then she laid the other arm over it, and, looking up at me, said:—

"Kiss me, my bairn; I need strength for what I am going to do for your sake."

I kissed her.

"There now!" she said, "I am ready. Good-bye. Whatever happens, do not speak to me; and let no one come near me but yourself. It will be wearisome for you, but it is for your sake, my Duncan. And don't let the fire out. Don't leave me."

I assured her I would attend to all she said. She closed her eyes, and lay still. I went to the fire, and sat down in a high-backed armchair, to wait the event.—There was plenty of fuel in the corner. I made up the fire, and then, leaning back, with my eyes fixed on it, let my thoughts roam at will. Where was my old nurse now? What was she seeing or encountering? Would she meet our adversary? Would she be strong enough to foil him? Was she dead for the time, although some bond rendered her return from the regions of the dead inevitable?—But she might never come back, and then I should have no tidings of the kind which I knew she had gone to see, and which I longed to hear!

I sat thus for a long time. I had again replenished the fire—that is all I know about the lapse of the time—when, suddenly, a kind of physical repugnance and terror seized me, and I sat upright in my chair, with every fibre of my flesh protesting against some—shall I call it presence?—in its neighbourhood. But my real self repelled the invading cold, and took courage for any contest that might be at hand. Like Macbeth, I only inhabited trembling; I did not tremble. I had withdrawn my gaze from the fire, and fixed it upon the little window, about two feet square, at which the dark night looked in. Why or when I had done so I knew not.

What I next relate, I relate only as what seemed to happen. I do not altogether trust myself in the matter, and think I was subjected to a delusion of some sort or other. My feelings of horror grew as I looked through or rather at the window, till, notwithstanding all my resolution and the continued assurance that nothing could make me turn my back on the cause of the terror, I was yet so far possessed by a feeling I could neither account for nor control, that I felt my hair rise upon my head, as if instinct with individual fear of its own—the only instance of the sort in my experience.—In such a condition, the sensuous nerves are so easily operated upon, either from within or from without, that all certainty ceases.

I saw two fiery eyes looking in at the window, huge, and wide apart. Next, I saw the outline of a horse's head, in which the eyes were set; and behind, the dimmer outline of a man's form seated on the horse. The apparition faded and reappeared, just as if it retreated, and again rode up close to the window. Curiously enough, I did not even fancy that I heard any sound. Instinctively I felt for my sword, but there was no sword there. And what would it have availed me? Probably I was in more need of a soothing draught. But the moment I put my hand to the imagined sword-hilt, a dim figure swept between me and the horseman, on my side of the window—a tall, stately female form. She stood facing the window, in an attitude that seemed to dare the further approach of a foe. How long she remained thus, or he confronted her, I have no idea; for when self-consciousness returned, I found myself still gazing at the window from which both apparitions had vanished. Whether I had slept, or, from the relaxation of mental tension, had only forgotten, I could not tell; but all fear had vanished, and I proceeded at once to make up the sunken fire. Throughout the time I am certain I never heard the clanking shoe, for that I should have remembered.

The rest of the night passed without any disturbance; and when the first rays of the early morning came into the room, they awoke me from a comforting sleep in the arm-chair. I rose and approached the bed softly.

Margaret lay as still as death. But having been accustomed to similar conditions in my Alice, I believed I saw signs of returning animation, and withdrew to my seat. Nor was I mistaken; for, in a few minutes more, she murmured my name. I hastened to her.

"Call Janet," she said.

I opened the door, and called her. She came in a moment, looking at once frightened and relieved.

"Get me some tea," said Margaret once more.

After she had drunk the tea, she looked at me, and said,

"Go home now, Duncan, and come back about noon. Mind you go to bed."

She closed her eyes once more. I waited till I saw her fast in an altogether different sleep from the former, if sleep that could in any sense be called.

As I went, I looked back on the vision of the night as on one of those illusions to which the mind, busy with its own suggestions, is always liable. The night season, simply because it excludes the external, is prolific in such. The more of the marvellous any one may have experienced in the course of his history, the more sceptical ought he to become, for he is the more exposed to delusion. None have made more blunders in the course of their revelations than genuine seers. Was it any wonder that, as I sat at midnight beside the woman of a hundred years, who had voluntarily died for a time that she might discover what most of all things it concerned me to know, the ancient tale, on which, to her mind, my whole history turned, and which she had herself told me in this very cottage, should take visible shape to my excited brain and watching eyes?

I have one thing more to tell, which strengthens still further this view of the matter. As I walked home, before I had gone many hundred yards from the cottage, I suddenly came upon my own old Constancy. He was limping about, picking the best grass he could find from among the roots of the heather and cranberry bushes. He gave a start when I came upon him, and then a jubilant neigh.

But he could not be so glad as I was. When I had taken sufficient pains to let him know this fact, I walked on, and he followed me like a dog, with his head at my heel; but as he limped much, I turned to examine him; and found one cause of his lameness to be, that the loose shoe, which was a hind one, was broken at the toe; and that one half, held only at the toe, had turned round and was sticking right out, striking his forefoot every time he moved. I soon remedied this, and he walked much better.

But the phenomena of the night, and the share my old horse might have borne in them, were not the subjects, as may well be supposed, that occupied my mind most, on my walk to the farm. Was it possible that Margaret might have found out something about her? That was the one question.

After removing the anxiety of my hostess, and partaking of their Highland breakfast, a ceremony not to be completed without a glass of peaty whisky, I wandered to my ancient haunt on the hill. Thence I could look down on my old home, where it lay unchanged, though not one human form, which had made it home to me, moved about its precincts. I went no nearer. I no more felt that that was home, than one feels that the form in the coffin is the departed dead. I sat down in my old study-chamber among the rocks, and thought that if I could but find Alice she would be my home—of the past as well as of the future;—for in her mind my necromantic words would recall the departed, and we should love them together.

Towards noon I was again at the cottage.

Margaret was sitting up in bed, waiting for me. She looked weary, but cheerful; and a clean white mutch gave her a certain company-air. Janet left the room directly, and Margaret motioned me to a chair by her side. I sat down. She took my hand, and said,

"Duncan, my boy, I fear I can give you but little help; but I will tell you all I know. If I were to try to put into words the things I had to encounter before I could come near her, you would not understand what I meant. Nor do I understand the things myself. They seem quite plain to me at the time, but very cloudy when I come back. But I did succeed in getting one glimpse of her. She was fast asleep. She seemed to have suffered much, for her face was very thin, and as patient as it was pale."

"But where was she?"

"I must leave you to find out that, if you can, from my description. But, alas! it is only the places immediately about the persons that I can see. Where they are, or how far I have gone to get there, I cannot tell."

She then gave me a rather minute description of the chamber in which the lady was lying. Though most of the particulars were un-known to me, the conviction, or hope at least, gradually dawned upon me, that I knew the room. Once or twice I had peeped into the sanc-tuary of Lady Alice's chamber, when I knew she was not there; and some points in the description Margaret gave set my heart in a tremor with the bare suggestion that she might now be at Hilton Hall.

"Tell me, Margaret," I said, almost panting for utterance, "was there a mirror over the fireplace, with a broad gilt frame, carved into huge representations of crabs and lobsters, and all crawling sea-crea-tures with shells on them—very ugly, and very strange?"

She would have interrupted me before, but I would not be stopped.

"I must tell you, my dear Duncan," she answered, "that in none of these trances, or whatever you please to call them, did I ever see a mirror. It has struck me before as a curious thing, that a mirror is then an absolute blank to me—I see nothing on which I could put a name. It does not even seem a vacant space to me. A mirror must have nothing in common with the state I am then in, for I feel a kind of repulsion from it; and indeed it would be rather an awful thing to look at, for of course I should see no reflection of myself in it."

(Here I beg once more to remind the reader, that Margaret spoke in Gaelic, and that my translation into ordinary English does not in the least represent the extreme simplicity of the forms of her specu-lations, any more than of the language which conveyed them.)

"But," she continued, "I have a vague recollection of seeing some broad, big, gilded thing with figures on it. It might be something else, though, altogether."

"I will go in hope," I answered, rising at once.

"Not already, Duncan?"

"Why should I stay longer?"

"Stay over to-night."

"What is the use? I cannot."

"For my sake, Duncan!"

"Yes, dear Margaret; for your sake. Yes, surely."

"Thank you," she answered. "I will not keep you longer now. But if I send Janet to you, come at once. And, Duncan, wear this for my sake."

She put into my hand an ancient gold cross, much worn. To my amazement I recognised the counterpart of one Lady Alice had always worn. I pressed it to my heart.

"I am a Catholic; you are a Protestant, Duncan; but never mind: that's the same sign to both of us. You won't part with it. It has been in our family for many long years."

"Not while I live," I answered, and went out, half wild with hope, into the keen mountain air. How deliciously it breathed upon me!

I passed the afternoon in attempting to form some plan of action at Hilton Hall, whither I intended to proceed as soon as Margaret set me at liberty. That liberty came sooner than I expected; and yet I did not go at once. Janet came for me towards sundown. I thought she looked troubled. I rose at once and followed her, but asked no questions. As I entered the cottage, the sun was casting the shadow of the edge of the hollow in which the cottage stood just at my feet; that is, the sun was more than half set to one who stood at the cottage door. I entered.

Margaret sat, propped with pillows. I saw some change had passed upon her. She held out her hand to me. I took it. She smiled feebly, closed her eyes, and went with the sun, down the hill of night. But down the hill of night is up the hill of morning in other lands, and no doubt Margaret soon found that she was more at home there than here.

I sat holding the dead hand, as if therein lay some communion still with the departed. Perhaps she who saw more than others while yet alive, could see when dead that I held her cold hand in my warm grasp. Had I not good cause to love her? She had exhausted the last remnants of her life in that effort to find for me my lost Alice. Whether she had succeeded I had yet to discover. Perhaps she knew now.

I hastened the funeral a little, that I might follow my quest. I had her grave dug amidst her own people and mine; for they lay side by side. The whole neighbourhood for twenty miles round followed Margaret to the grave. Such was her character and reputation, that the belief in her supernatural powers had only heightened the notion of her venerableness.

When I had seen the last sod placed on her grave, I turned and went, with a desolate but hopeful heart. I had a kind of feeling that her death had sealed the truth of her last vision. I mounted old Constancy at the churchyard gate, and set out for Hilton Hall.

21
Hilton

It was a dark, drizzling night when I arrived at the little village of Hilton, within a mile of the Hall. I knew a respectable second-rate inn on the side next the Hall, to which the gardener and other servants had been in the habit of repairing of an evening; and I thought I might there stumble upon some information, especially as the old-fashioned place had a large kitchen in which all sorts of guests met. When I reflected on the utter change which time, weather, and a great scar must have made upon me, I feared no recognition. But what was my surprise when, by one of those coincidences which have so often happened to me, I found in the ostler one of my own troop at Waterloo! His countenance and salute convinced me that he recognised me. I said to him:

"I know you perfectly, Wood; but you must not know me. I will go with you to the stable."

He led the way instantly.

"Wood," I said, when we had reached the shelter of the stable, "I don't want to be known here, for reasons which I will explain to you another time."

"Very well, sir. You may depend on me, sir."

"I know I may, and I shall. Do you know anybody about the Hall?"

"Yes, sir. The gardener comes here sometimes, sir. I believe he's in the house now. Shall I ask him to step this way, sir?"

"No. All I want is to learn who is at the Hall now. Will you get him talking? I shall be by, having something to drink."

"Yes, sir. As soon as I have rubbed down the old horse, sir—bless him!"

"You'll find me there."

I went in, and, with my condition for an excuse, ordered something hot by the kitchen-fire. Several country people were sitting about it. They made room for me, and I took my place at a table on one side. I soon discovered the gardener, although time had done what he could to disguise him. Wood came in presently, and, loitering about, began to talk to him.

"What's the last news at the Hall, William?" he said.

"News!" answered the old man, somewhat querulously. "There's never nothing but news up there, and very new-fangled news, too. What do you think, now, John? They do talk of turning all them greenhouses into hothouses; for, to be sure, there's nothing the new missus cares about but just the finest grapes in the country; and the flowers, purty creatures, may go to the devil for her. There's a lady for ye!"

"But you'll be glad to have her home, and see what she's like, won't you? It's rather dull up there now, isn't it?"

"I don't know what you call dull," replied the old man, as if half offended at the suggestion. "I don't believe a soul missed his lordship when he died; and there's always Mrs. Blakesley and me, as is the best friends in the world, besides the three maids and the stableman, who helps me in the garden, now there's no horses. And then there's Jacob and—"

"But you don't mean," said Wood, interrupting him, "that there's none o' the family at home now?"

"No. Who should there be? Leastways, only the poor lady. And she hardly counts now—bless her sweet face!"

"Do you ever see her?" interposed one of the by-sitters.

"Sometimes."

"Is she quite crazy?"

"Al-to-gether; but that quiet and gentle, you would think she was an angel instead of a mad woman. But not a notion has she in her head, no more than the babe unborn."

It was a dreadful shock to me. Was this to be the end of all? Were it not better she had died? For me, life was worthless now. And there were no wars, with the chance of losing it honestly.

I rose, and went to my own room. As I sat in dull misery by the fire, it struck me that it might not have been Lady Alice after all that the old man spoke about. That moment a tap came to my door, and Wood entered. After a few words, I asked him who was the lady the gardener had said was crazy.

"Lady Alice," he answered, and added: "A love story, that came to a bad end up at the Hall years ago. A tutor was in it, they say. But I don't know the rights of it."

When he left me, I sat in a cold stupor, in which the thoughts—if thoughts they could be called—came and went of themselves. Overcome by the appearances of things—as what man the strongest may not sometimes be?—I felt as if I had lost her utterly, as if there was no Lady Alice anywhere, and as if, to add to the vacant horror of the world without her, a shadow of her, a goblin simulacrum, soul-less, unreal, yet awfully like her, went wandering about the place which had once been glorified by her presence—as to the eyes of seers the phantoms of events which have happened years before are still visible, clinging to the room in which they have indeed taken place. But, in a little while, something warm began to throb and flow in my being; and I thought that if she were dead, I should love her still; that now she was not worse than dead; it was only that her soul was out of sight. Who could tell but it might be wandering in worlds of too noble shapes and too high a speech, to permit of representation in the language of the world in which her bodily presentation remained, and therefore her speech and behaviour seemed to men to be mad? Nay, was it not in some sense better for me that it should be so? To see once the pictured likeness of her of whom I had no such memorial, would I not give years of my poverty-stricken life? And here was such a statue of her, as that of his wife which the widowed king was bending before, when he said:—

"What fine chisel
Could ever yet cut breath?"

This statue I might see, "looking like an angel," as the gardener had said. And, while the bond of visibility remained, must not the soul be, somehow, nearer to the earth, than if the form lay decaying beneath it? Was there not some possibility that the love for whose sake the reason had departed, might be able to recall that reason once more to the windows of sense,—make it look forth at those eyes, and lie listening in the recesses of those ears? In her somnambulic sleeps, the present body was the sign that the soul was within reach: so it might be still.

Mrs. Blakesley was still at the lodge, then: I would call upon her to-morrow. I went to bed, and dreamed all night that Alice was sitting somewhere in a land "full of dark mountains," and that I was wandering about in the darkness, alternately calling and listening; sometimes fancying I heard a faint reply, which might be her voice or an echo of my own; but never finding her. I woke in an outburst of despairing tears, and my despair was not comforted by my waking.

22

The Sleeper

It was a lovely morning in autumn. I walked to the Hall. I entered at the same gate by which I had entered first, so many years before. But it was not Mrs. Blakesley that opened it. I inquired after her, and the woman told me that she lived at the Hall now, and took care of Lady Alice. So far, this was hopeful news.

I went up the same avenue, through the same wide grassy places, saw the same statue from whose base had arisen the lovely form which soon became a part of my existence. Then everything looked rich, because I had come from a poor, grand country. In all my wanderings I had seen nothing so rich; yet now it seemed poverty-stricken. That it was autumn could not account for this; for I had always found that the sadness of autumn vivified the poetic sense; and that the colours of decay had a pathetic glory more beautiful than the glory of the most gorgeous summer with all its flowers. It was winter within me—that was the reason; and I could feel no autumn around me, because I saw no spring beyond me. It had fared with my mind as with the garden in the Sensitive Plant, when the lady was dead. I was amazed and troubled at the stolidity with which I walked up to the door, and, having rung the bell, waited. No sweet memories of the past arose in my mind; not one of the well-known objects around looked at me as claiming a recognition. Yet, when the door was opened, my heart beat so violently at the thought that I might see her, that I could hardly stammer out my inquiry after Mrs. Blakesley.

I was shown to a room. None of the sensations I had had on first crossing the threshold were revived. I remembered them all; I felt none of them. Mrs. Blakesley came. She did not recognise me. I told her who I was. She stared at me for a moment, seemed to see the same face she had known still glimmering through all the changes that had crowded upon it, held out both her hands, and burst into tears.

"Mr. Campbell," she said, "you are changed! But not like her. She's the same to look at; but, oh dear!"

We were both silent for some time. At length she resumed:—

"Come to my room; I have been mistress here for some time now."

I followed her to the room Mrs. Wilson used to occupy. She put wine on the table. I told her my story. My labours, and my wounds, and my illness, slightly touched as I trust they were in the course of the tale, yet moved all her womanly sympathies.

"What can I do for you, Mr. Campbell?" she said.

"Let me see her," I replied.

She hesitated for a moment.

"I dare not, sir. I don't know what it might do to her. It might send her raving; and she is so quiet."

"Has she ever raved?"

"Not often since the first week or two. Now and then occasionally, for an hour or so, she would be wild, wanting to get out. But she gave that over altogether; and she has had her liberty now for a long time. But, Heaven bless her! at the worst she was always a lady."

"And am I to go away without even seeing her?"

"I am very sorry for you, Mr. Campbell."

I felt hurt—foolishly, I confess—and rose. She put her hand on my arm.

"I'll tell you what I'll do, sir. She always falls asleep in the afternoon; you may see her asleep, if you like."

"Thank you; thank you," I answered. "That will be much better. When shall I come?"

"About three o'clock."

I went wandering about the woods, and at three I was again in the housekeeper's room. She came to me presently, looking rather troubled.

"It is very odd," she began, the moment she entered, "but for the first time, I think, for years, she's not for her afternoon sleep."

"Does she sleep at night?" I asked.

"Like a bairn. But she sleeps a great deal; and the doctor says that's what keeps her so quiet. She would go raving again, he says, if the sleep did not soothe her poor brain."

"Could you not let me see her when she is asleep to-night?"

Again she hesitated, but presently replied:—

"I will, sir; but I trust to you never to mention it."

"Of course I will not."

"Come at ten o'clock, then. You will find the outer door on this side open. Go straight to my room."

With renewed thanks I left her and, once again betaking myself to the woods, wandered about till night, notwithstanding signs of an approaching storm. I thus kept within the boundaries of the demesne, and had no occasion to request re-admittance at any of the gates.

As ten struck on the tower-clock, I entered Mrs. Blakesley's room. She was not there. I sat down. In a few minutes she came.

"She is fast asleep," she said. "Come this way."

I followed, trembling. She led me to the same room Lady Alice used to occupy. The door was a little open. She pushed it gently, and I followed her in. The curtains towards the door were drawn. Mrs. Blakesley took me round to the other side.—There lay the lovely head, so phantom-like for years, coming only in my dreams; filling now, with a real presence, the eyes that had longed for it, as if in them dwelt an appetite of sight. It calmed my heart at once, which had been almost choking me with the violence of its palpitation. "That is not the face of insanity," I said to myself. "It is clear as the morning light." As I stood gazing, I made no comparisons between the past and the present, although I was aware of some difference—of some measure of the unknown fronting me; I was filled with the delight of behold-ing the face I loved—full, as it seemed to me, of mind and woman-hood; sleeping—nothing more. I murmured a fervent "Thank God!" and was turning away with a feeling of satisfaction for all the future, and a strange great hope beginning to throb in my heart, when, after a little restless motion of her head on the pillow, her patient lips be-gan to tremble. My soul rushed into my ears.

"Mr. Campbell," she murmured, "I cannot spell; what am I to do to learn?"

The unexpected voice, naming my name, sounded in my ears like a voice from the far-off regions where sighing is over. Then a smile gleamed up from the depths unseen, and broke and melted away all over her face. But her nurse had heard her speak, and now approached in alarm. She laid hold of my arm, and drew me towards the door. I yielded at once, but heard a moan from the bed as I went. I looked back—the curtains hid her from my view. Outside the door, Mrs. Blakesley stood listening for a moment, and then led the way down-stairs.

"You made her restless. You see, sir, she never was like other people, poor dear!"

"Her face is not like one insane," I rejoined.

"I often think she looks more like herself when she's asleep," an-swered she. "And then I have often seen her smile. She never smiles when she's awake. But, gracious me, Mr. Campbell! what shall I do?"

This exclamation was caused by my suddenly falling back in my chair and closing my eyes. I had almost fainted. I had eaten nothing since breakfast; and had been wandering about in a state of excite-ment all day. I greedily swallowed the glass of wine she brought me, and then first became aware that the storm which I had seen gathering while I was in the woods had now broken loose. "What a night in the old hall!" thought I. The wind was dashing itself like a thousand eagles against the house, and the rain was trampling the roofs and the court like troops of galloping steeds. I rose to go.

But Mrs. Blakesley interfered.

"You don't leave this house to-night, Mr. Campbell," she said. "I won't have your death laid at my door."

I laughed.

"Dear Mrs. Blakesley,—" I said, seeing her determined.

"I won't hear a word," she interrupted. "I wouldn't let a horse out in such a tempest. No, no; you shall just sleep in your old quarters, across the passage there."

I did not care for any storm. It hardly even interested me. That beautiful face filled my whole being. But I yielded to Mrs. Blakesley, and not unwillingly.

23
My Old Room

Once more I was left alone in that room of dark oak, looking out on the little ivy-mantled court, of which I was now reminded by the howling of the storm within its high walls. Mrs. Blakesley had extemporised a bed for me on the old sofa; and the fire was already blazing away splendidly. I sat down beside it, and the sombre-hued Past rolled back upon me.

After I had floated, as it were, upon the waves of memory for some time, I suddenly glanced behind me and around the room, and a new and strange experience dawned upon me. Time became to my consciousness what some metaphysicians say it is in itself—only a form of human thought. For the Past had returned and had become the Present. I could not be sure that the Past had passed, that I had not been dreaming through the whole series of years and adventures, upon which I was able to look back. For here was the room, all as before; and here was I, the same man, with the same love glowing in my heart. I went on thinking. The storm went on howling. The logs went on cheerily burning. I rose and walked about the room, looking at everything as I had looked at it on the night of my first arrival. I said to myself, "How strange that I should feel as if all this had happened to me before!" And then I said, "Perhaps it has happened to me before." Again I said, "And when it did happen before, I felt as if it had happened before that; and perhaps it has been happening to me at intervals for ages." I opened the door of the closet, and looked at the door behind it, which led into the hall of the old house. It was bolted. But the bolt slipped back at my touch; twelve years were nothing in the history of its rust; or was it only yesterday I had forced the iron free from the adhesion of the rust-welded surfaces? I stood for a moment hesitating whether to open the door, and have one peep into the wide hall, full of intent echoes, listening breathless for one air of sound, that they might catch it up jubilant and dash it into the ears of—Silence—their ancient enemy—their Death. But I drew back, leaving the door unopened; and, sitting down again by my fire, sank into a kind of unconscious weariness. Perhaps I slept—I do not know; but as I became once more aware of myself, I awoke, as it were, in the midst of an old long-buried night. I was sitting in my own room, waiting for Lady Alice. And, as I sat waiting, and wishing she would come, by slow degrees my wishes intensified themselves, till I found myself, with all my gathered might, willing that she should come. The minutes passed, but the will remained.

How shall I tell what followed? The door of the closet opened—slowly, gently—and in walked Lady Alice, pale as death, her eyes closed, her whole person asleep. With a gliding motion as in a dream, where the volition that produces motion is unfelt, she seemed to me to dream herself across the floor to my couch, on which she laid herself down as gracefully, as simply, as in the old beautiful time. Her appearance did not startle me, for my whole condition was in harmony with the phenomenon. I rose noiselessly, covered her lightly from head to foot, and sat down, as of old to watch. How beautiful she was! I thought she had grown taller; but, perhaps, it was only that she had gained in form without losing anything in grace. Her face was, as it had always been, colourless; but neither it nor her figure showed any signs of suffering. The holy sleep had fed her physical as well as shielded her mental nature. But what would the waking be? Not all the power of the revived past could shut out the anticipation of the dreadful difference to be disclosed, the moment she should open those sleeping eyes. To what a frightfully farther distance was that soul now removed, whose return I had been wont to watch, as from the depths of the unknown world! That was strange; this was terrible. Instead of the dawn of rosy intelligence I had now to look for the fading of the loveliness as she woke, till her face withered into the bewildered and indigent expression of the insane.

She was waking. My love with the unknown face was at hand. The reviving flush came, grew, deepened. She opened her eyes. God be praised! They were lovelier than ever. And the smile that broke over her face was the very sunlight of the soul.

"Come again, you see!" she said gently, as she stretched her beautiful arms towards me.

I could not speak. I could only submit to her embrace, and hold myself with all my might, lest I should burst into helpless weeping. But a sob or two broke their prison, and she felt the emotion she had not seen. Relaxing her hold, she pushed me gently from her, and looked at me with concern that grew as she looked.

"You are dreadfully changed, my Duncan! What is the matter? Has Lord Hilton been rude to you? You look so much older, somehow. What can it be?"

I understood at once how it was. The whole of those dreary twelve years was gone. The thread of her consciousness had been cut, those years dropped out, and the ends reunited. She thought this was one of her old visits to me, when, as now, she had walked in her sleep. I answered,

"I will tell you all another time. I don't want to waste the moments with you, my Alice, in speaking about it. Lord Hilton has behaved very badly to me; but never mind."

She half rose in anger; and her eyes looked insane for the first time.

"How dares he?" she said, and then checked herself with a sigh at her own helplessness.

"But it will all come right, Alice," I went on in terror lest I should disturb her present conception of her circumstances. I felt as if the very face I wore, with the changes of those twelve forgotten years, which had passed over her like the breath of a spring wind, were a mask of which I had to be ashamed before her. Her consciousness was my involuntary standard of fact. Hope of my life as she was, there was thus mingled with my delight in her presence a restless fear that made me wish fervently that she would go. I wanted time to quiet my thoughts and resolve how I should behave to her.

"Alice," I said, "it is nearly morning. You were late to-night. Don't you think you had better go—for fear, you know?"

"Ah!" she said, with a smile, in which there was no doubt of fear, "you are tired of me already! But I will go at once to dream about you."

She rose.

"Go, my darling," I said; "and mind you get some right sleep. Shall I go with you?"

Much to my relief, she answered,

"No, no; please not. I can go alone as usual. When a ghost meets me, I just walk through him, and then he's nowhere; and I laugh."

One kiss, one backward lingering look, and the door closed behind her. I heard the echo of the great hall. I was alone. But what a loneliness—a loneliness crowded with presence! I paced up and down the room, threw myself on the couch she had left, started up, and paced again. It was long before I could think. But the conviction grew upon me that she would be mine yet. Mine yet? Mine she was, beyond all the power of madness or demons; and mine I trusted she would be beyond the dispute of the world. About me, at least, she was not insane. But what should I do? The only chance of her recovery lay in seeing me still; but I could resolve on nothing till I knew whether Mrs. Blakesley had discovered her absence from her room; because, if I drew her, and she were watched and prevented from coming, it would kill her, or worse. I must take to-morrow to think.

Yet at the moment, by a sudden impulse, I opened the window gently, stepped into the little grassy court, where the last of the storm was still moaning, and withdrew the bolts of a door which led into an alley of trees running along one side of the kitchen-garden. I felt like a housebreaker; but I said, "It is her right." I pushed the bolts forward again, so as just to touch the sockets and look as if they went in, and then retreated into my own room, where I paced about till the household was astir.

24
Prison-Breaking

It was with considerable anxiety that I repaired to Mrs. Blakesley's room. There I found the old lady at the breakfast-table, so thoroughly composed, that I was at once reassured as to her ignorance of what had occurred while she slept. But she seemed uneasy till I should take my departure, which I attributed to the fear that I might happen to meet Lady Alice.

Arrived at my inn, I kept my room, my dim-seen plans rendering it desirable that I should attract as little attention in the neighbourhood as might be. I had now to concentrate these plans, and make them definite to myself. It was clear that there was no chance of spending another night at Hilton Hall by invitation: would it be honourable to go there without one, as I, knowing all the outs and ins of the place, could, if I pleased? I went over the whole question of Alice's position in that house, and of the crime committed against her. I saw that, if I could win my wife by restoring to her the exercise of reason, that very success would justify the right I already possessed in her. And could she not demand of me to climb over any walls, or break open whatsoever doors, to free her from her prison—from the darkness of a clouded brain? Let them say what they would of the meanness and wickedness of gaining such access to, and using such power over, the insane—she was mine, and as safe with me as with her mother. There is a love that tears and destroys; and there is a love that enfolds and saves. I hated mesmerism and its vulgar impertinences; but here was a power I possessed, as far as I knew, only over one, and that one allied to me by a reciprocal influence, as well as long-tried affection.—Did not love give me the right to employ this power?

My cognitions concluded in the resolve to use the means in my hands for the rescue of Lady Alice. Midnight found me in the alley of the kitchen-garden. The door of the little court opened easily. Nor had I withdrawn its bolts without knowing that I could manage to open the window of my old room from the outside. I stood in the dark, a stranger and housebreaker, where so often I had sat waiting the visits of my angel. I secured the door of the room, struck a light, lighted a remnant of taper which I found on the table, threw myself on the couch, and said to my Alice— "Come."

And she came. I rose. She laid herself down. I pulled off my coat— it was all I could find—and laid it over her. The night was chilly. She revived with the same sweet smile, but, giving a little shiver, said:

"Why have you no fire, Duncan? I must give orders about it. That's some trick of old Clankshoe."

"Dear Alice, do not breath a word about me to any one. I have quarrelled with Lord Hilton. He has turned me away, and I have no business to be in the house."

"Oh!" she replied, with a kind of faint recollecting hesitation. "That must be why you never come to the haunted chamber now. I go there every night, as soon as the sun is down."

"Yes, that is it, Alice."

"Ah! that must be what makes the day so strange to me too."

She looked very bewildered for a moment, and then resumed:

"Do you know, Duncan, I feel very strange all day—as if I was walking about in a dull dream that would never come to an end? But it is very different at night—is it not, dear?"

She had not yet discovered any distinction between my presence to her dreams and my presence to her waking sight. I hardly knew what reply to make; but she went on:

"They won't let me come to you now, I suppose. I shall forget my Euclid and everything. I feel as if I had forgotten it all already. But you won't be vexed with your poor Alice, will you? She's only a beggar-girl, you know."

I could answer only by a caress.

"I had a strange dream the other night. I thought I was sitting on a stone in the dark. And I heard your voice calling me. And it went all round about me, and came nearer, and went farther off, but I could not move to go to you. I tried to answer you, but I could only make a queer sound, not like my own voice at all."

"I dreamed it too, Alice."

"The same dream?"

"Yes, the very same."

"I am so glad. But I didn't like the dream. Duncan, my head feels so strange sometimes. And I am so sleepy. Duncan, dearest—am I dreaming now? Oh! tell me that I am awake and that I hold you; for to-morrow, when I wake, I shall fancy that I have lost you. They've spoiled my poor brain, somehow. I am all right, I know, but I cannot get at it. The red is withered, somehow."

"You are wide awake, my Alice. I know all about it. I will help you to understand it all, only you must do exactly as I tell you."

"Yes, yes."

"Then go to bed now, and sleep as much as you can; else I will not let you come to me at night."

"That would be too cruel, when it is all I have."

"Then go, dearest, and sleep."

"I will."

She rose and went. I, too, went, making all close behind me. The moon was going down. Her light looked to me strange, and almost malignant. I feared that when she came to the full she would hurt my darling's brain, and I longed to climb the sky, and cut her in pieces. Was I too going mad? I needed rest, that was all.

Next morning, I called again upon Mrs. Blakesley, to inquire after Lady Alice, anxious to know how yesterday had passed.

"Just the same," answered the old lady. "You need not look for any change. Yesterday I did see her smile once, though."

And was that nothing?

In her case there was a reversal of the usual facts of nature—(I say facts, not laws): the dreams of most people are more or less insane; those of Lady Alice were sound; thus, with her, restoring the balance of sane life. That smile was the sign of the dream-life beginning to leaven the waking and false life.

"Have you heard of young Lord Hilton's marriage?" asked Mrs. Blakesley.

"I have only heard some rumours about it," I answered. "Who is the new countess?"

"The daughter of a rich merchant somewhere. They say she isn't the best of tempers. They're coming here in about a month. I am just terrified to think how it may fare with my lamb now. They won't let her go wandering about wherever she pleases, I doubt. And if they shut her up, she will die."

I vowed inwardly that she should be free, if I carried her off, madness and all.

25
New Entrenchments.

But this way of breaking into the house every night did not afford me the facility I wished. For I wanted to see Lady Alice during the day, or at least in the evening before she went to sleep; as otherwise I could not thoroughly judge of her condition. So I got Wood to pack up a small stock of provisions for me in his haversack, which I took with me; and when I entered the house that night, I bolted the door of the court behind me, and made all fast.

I waited till the usual time for her appearance had passed; and, always apprehensive now, as was very natural, I had begun to grow uneasy, when I heard her voice, as I had heard it once before, singing. Fearful of disturbing her, I listened for a moment. Whether the song was her own or not, I cannot be certain. When I questioned her afterwards, she knew nothing about it. It was this,—

> Days of old,
> Ye are not dead, though gone from me;
> Ye are not cold,
> But like the summer-birds gone o'er the sea.
> The sun brings back the swallows fast,
> O'er the sea:
> When thou comest at the last,
> The days of old come back to me.

She ceased singing. Still she did not enter. I went into the closet, and found that the door was bolted. When I opened it, she entered, as usual; and, when she came to herself, seemed still better than before.

"Duncan," she said, "I don't know how it is, but I believe I must have forgotten everything I ever knew. I feel as if I had. I don't think I can even read. Will you teach me my letters?"

She had a book in her hand. I hailed this as another sign that her waking and sleeping thoughts bordered on each other; for she must have taken the book during her somnambulic condition. I did as she desired. She seemed to know nothing till I told her. But the moment I told her anything, she knew it perfectly. Before she left me that night she was reading tolerably, with many pauses of laughter that she should ever have forgotten how. The moment she shared the light of my mind, all was plain; where that had not shone, all was dark. The fact was, she was living still in the shadow of that shock which her nervous constitution had received from our discovery and my ejection.

As she was leaving me, I said,

"Shall you be in the haunted room at sunset tomorrow, Alice?"

"Of course I shall," she answered.

"You will find me there then," I rejoined— "that is, if you think there is no danger of being seen."

"Not the least," she answered. "No one follows me there; not even Mrs. Blakesley, good soul! They are all afraid, as usual."

"And you won't be frightened to see me there?"

"Frightened? No. Why? Oh! you think me queer too, do you?"

She looked vexed, but tried to smile.

"I? I would trust you with my life," I said. "That's not much, though—with my soul, whatever that means, Alice."

"Then don't talk nonsense," she rejoined coaxingly, "about my being frightened to see you."

When she had gone, I followed into the old hall, taking my sack with me; for, after having found the door in the closet bolted, I was determined not to spend one night more in my old quarters, and never to allow Lady Alice to go there again, if I could prevent her. And I had good hopes that, if we met in the day, the same consequences would follow as had followed long ago—namely, that she would sleep at night.

It was just such a night as that on which I had first peeped into the hall. The moon shone through one of the high windows, scarcely more dim than before, and showed all the dreariness of the place. I went up the great old staircase, hoping I trod in the very footsteps of Lady Alice, and reached the old gallery in which I had found her on that night when our strangely-knit intimacy began. My object was to choose one of the deserted rooms in which I might establish myself without chance of discovery. I had not turned many corners, or gone through many passages, before I found one exactly to my mind. I will not trouble my reader with a description of its odd position and shape. All I wanted was concealment, and that it provided plentifully. I lay down on the floor, and was soon fast asleep.

Next morning, having breakfasted from the contents of my bag, I proceeded to make myself thoroughly acquainted with the bearings, etc., of this portion of the house. Before evening, I knew it all thoroughly.

But I found it very difficult to wait for the evening. By the windows of one of the rooms looking westward, I sat watching the down-going of the sun. When he set, my moon would rise. As he touched the horizon, I went the old, well-known way to the haunted chamber. What a night had passed for me since I left Alice in that charmed room! I had a vague feeling, however, notwithstanding the misfortune that had befallen us there, that the old phantoms that haunted it were friendly to Alice and me. But I waited her arrival in fear. Would she come? Would she be as in the night? Or should I find her but half awake to life, and perhaps asleep to me?

One moment longer, and a light hand was laid on the door. It opened gently, and Alice, entering, flitted across the room straight to my arms. How beautiful she was! her old-fashioned dress bringing her into harmony with the room and its old consecrated twilight! For this room looked eastward, and there was only twilight here. She brought me some water, at my request; and then we read, and laughed over our reading. Every moment she not only knew something fresh, but knew that she had known it before. The dust of the years had to be swept away; but it was only dust, and flew at a breath. The light soon failed us in that dusky chamber; and we sat and whispered, till only when we kissed could we see each other's eyes. At length Lady Alice said:

"They are looking for me; I had better go. Shall I come at night?"

"No," I answered. "Sleep, and do not move."

"Very well, I will."

She went, and I returned to my den. There I lay and thought. Had she ever been insane at all? I doubted it. A kind of mental sleep or stupor had come upon her—nothing more. True it might be allied to madness; but is there a strong emotion that man or woman experiences that is not allied to madness? Still her mind was not clear enough to reflect the past. But if she never recalled that entirely, not the less were her love and tenderness—all womanliness—entire in her.

Next evening we met again, and the next, and many evenings. Every time I was more convinced than before that she was thoroughly sane in every practical sense, and that she would recall everything as soon as I reminded her. But this I forbore to do, fearing a reaction.

Meantime, after a marvellous fashion, I was living over again the old lovely time that had gone by twelve years ago; living it over again, partly in virtue of the oblivion that had invaded the companion and source of the blessedness of the time. She had never ceased to live it; but had renewed it in dreams, unknown as such, from which she awoke to forgetfulness and quiet, while I awoke from my troubled fancies to tears and battles.

It was strange, indeed, to live the past over again thus.

26
Escape

It was time, however, to lay some plan, and make some preparations, for our departure. The first thing to be secured was a convenient exit from the house. I searched in all directions, but could discover none better than that by which I had entered. Leaving the house one evening, as soon as Lady Alice had retired, I communicated my situation to Wood, who entered with all his heart into my projects. Most fortunately, through all her so-called madness, Lady Alice had retained and cherished the feeling that there was something sacred about the diamond-ring and the little money which had been intended for our flight before; and she had kept them carefully concealed, where she could find them in a moment. I had sent the ring to a friend in London, to sell it for me; and it produced more than I expected. I had then commissioned Wood to go to the county town and buy a light gig for me; and in this he had been very fortunate. My dear old Constancy had the accomplishment, not at all common to chargers, of going admirably in harness; and I had from the first enjoined upon Wood to get him into as good condition as possible. I now fixed a certain hour at which Wood was to be at a certain spot on one of the roads skirting the park, where I had found a crazy door in the plank-fence—with Constancy in the dogcart, and plenty of wraps for Alice.

"And for Heaven's sake, Wood," I concluded, "look to his shoes."

It may seem strange that I should have been able to go and come thus without detection; but it must be remembered that I had made myself more familiar with the place than any of its inhabitants, and that there were only a very few domestics in the establishment. The gardener and stableman slept in the house, for its protection; but I knew their windows perfectly, and most of their movements. I could watch them all day long, if I liked, from some loophole or other of my quarter; where, indeed, I sometimes found that the only occupation I could think of.

The next evening I said, "Alice, I must leave the house: will you go with me?"

"Of course I will, Duncan. When?"

"The night after to-morrow, as soon as every one is in bed and the house quiet. If you have anything you value very much, take it; but the lighter we go the better."

"I have nothing, Duncan. I will take a little bag—that will do for me."

"But dress as warmly as you can. It will be cold."

"Oh, yes; I won't forget that. Good night."

She took it as quietly as going to church.

I had not seen Mrs. Blakesley since she had told me that the young earl and countess were expected in about a month; else I might have learned one fact which it was very important I should have known, namely, that their arrival had been hastened by eight or ten days. The very morning of our intended departure, I was looking into the court through a little round hole I had cleared for observation in the dust of one of the windows, believing I had observed signs of unusual preparation on the part of the household, when a carriage drove up, followed by two others, and Lord and Lady Hilton descended and entered, with an attendance of some eight or ten.

There was a great bustle in the house all day. Of course I felt uneasy, for if anything should interfere with our flight, the presence of so many would increase whatever difficulty might occur. I was also uneasy about the treatment my Alice might receive from the newcomers. Indeed, it might be put out of her power to meet me at all. It had been arranged between us that she should not come to the haunted chamber at the usual hour, but towards midnight.

I was there waiting for her. The hour arrived; the house seemed quiet; but she did not come. I began to grow very uneasy. I waited half an hour more, and then, unable to endure it longer, crept to her door. I tried to open it, but found it fast. At the same moment I heard a light sob inside. I put my lips to the keyhole, and called "Alice." She answered in a moment:— "They have locked me in."

The key was gone. There was no time to be lost. Who could tell what they might do to-morrow, if already they were taking precautions against her madness? I would try the key of a neighbouring door, and if that would not fit, I would burst the door open, and take the chance. As it was, the key fitted the lock, and the door opened. We locked it again on the outside, restored the key, and in another moment were in the haunted chamber. Alice was dressed, ready for flight. To me, it was very pathetic to see her in the shapes of years gone by. She looked faded and ancient, notwithstanding that this was the dress in which I had seen her so often of old. Her stream had been standing still, while mine had flowed on. She was a portrait of my own young Alice, a picture of her own former self.

One or two lights glancing about below detained us for a little
while. We were standing near the window, feeling now very anxious
to be clear of the house; Alice was holding me and leaning on me with
the essence of trust; when, all at once, she dropped my arm, covered
her face with her hands, and called out: "The horse with the clanking
shoe!" At the same moment, the heavy door which communicated with
this part of the house flew open with a crash, and footsteps came hurrying along the passage. A light gleamed into the room, and by it I
saw that Lady Alice, who was standing close to me still, was gazing,
with flashing eyes, at the door. She whispered hurriedly:

"I remember it all now, Duncan. My brain is all right. It is come
again. But they shall not part us this time. You follow me for once."

As she spoke, I saw something glitter in her hand. She had caught
up an old Malay creese that lay in a corner, and was now making for
the door, at which half a dozen domestics were by this time gathered.
They, too, saw the glitter, and made way. I followed close, ready to
fell the first who offered to lay hands on her. But she walked through
them unmenaced, and, once clear, sped like a bird into the recesses
of the old house. One fellow started to follow. I tripped him up. I was
collared by another. The same instant he lay by his companion, and I
followed Alice. She knew the route well enough, and I overtook her in
the great hall. We heard pursuing feet rattling down the echoing stair.
To enter my room and bolt the door behind us was a moment's work;
and a few moments more took us into the alley of the kitchen-garden.
With speedy, noiseless steps, we made our way to the park, and across
it to the door in the fence, where Wood was waiting for us, old Constancy pawing the ground with impatience for a good run.

He had had enough of it before twelve hours were over.

Was I not well recompensed for my long years of despair? The
cold stars were sparkling overhead; a wind blew keen against us—the
wind of our own flight; Constancy stepped out with a will; and I urged
him on, for he bore my beloved and me into the future life. Close beside
me she sat, wrapped warm from the cold, rejoicing in her deliverance, and now and then looking up with tear-bright eyes into my face.
Once and again I felt her sob, but I knew it was a sob of joy, and not
of grief. The spell was broken at last, and she was mine. I felt that not
all the spectres of the universe could tear her from me, though now
and then a slight shudder would creep through me, when the clank of
Constancy's bit would echo sharply back from the trees we swept past.

We rested no more than was absolutely necessary; and in as short
a space as ever horse could perform the journey, we reached the Scotch
border, and before many more hours had gone over us, Alice was my
wife.

27

Freedom

Honest Wood joined us in the course of a week or two, and has continued in my service ever since. Nor was it long before Mrs. Blakesley was likewise added to our household, for she had been instantly dismissed from the countess's service on the charge of complicity in Lady Alice's abduction.

We lived for some months in a cottage on a hill-side, overlooking one of the loveliest of the Scotch lakes. Here I was once more tutor to my Alice. And a quick scholar she was, as ever. Nor, I trust, was I slow in my part. Her character became yet clearer to me, every day. I understood her better and better.

She could endure marvellously; but without love and its joy she could not live, in any real sense. In uncongenial society, her whole mental faculty had frozen; when love came, her mental world, like a garden in the spring sunshine, blossomed and budded. When she lost me, the Present vanished, or went by her like an ocean that has no milestones; she caring only for the Past, living only in the Past, and that reflection of it in the dim glass of her hope, which prefigured the Future.

We have never again heard the clanking shoe. Indeed, after we had passed a few months in the absorption of each other's society, we began to find that we doubted a great deal of what seemed to have happened to us. It was as if the gates of the unseen world were closing against us, because we had shut ourselves up in the world of the present. But we let it go gladly. We felt that love was the gate to an unseen world infinitely beyond that region of the psychological in which we had hitherto moved; for this love was teaching us to love all men, and live for all men. In fact, we are now, I am glad to say, very much like other people; and wonder, sometimes, how much of the story of our lives might be accounted for on the supposition that unusual coincidences had fallen in with psychological peculiarities. Dr. Ruthwell, who is sometimes our most welcome guest, has occasionally hinted at the sabre-cut as the key to all the mysteries of the story, seeing nothing of it was at least recorded before I came under his charge. But I have only to remind him of one or two circumstances, to elicit from his honesty and immediate confession of bewilderment, followed by silence; although he evidently still clings to the notion that in that sabre-cut lies the solution of much of the marvel. At all events, he considers me sane enough now, else he would hardly honour me with so much of his confidence as he does. Having examined into Lady Alice's affairs, I claimed the fortune which she had inherited. Lord Hilton, my former pupil, at once acknowledged the justice of the claim, and was considerably astonished to find how much more might have been demanded of him, which had been spent over the allowance made from her income for her maintenance. But we had enough without claiming that.

My wife purchased for me the possession of my forefathers, and there we live in peace and hope. To her I owe the delight which I feel every day of my life in looking upon the haunts of my childhood as still mine. They help me to keep young. And so does my Alice's hair; for although much grey now mingles with mine, hers is as dark as ever. For her heart, I know that cannot grow old; and while the heart is young, man may laugh old Time in the face, and dare him to do his worst.

At the Back of the North Wind

(1871)

1
The Hay-Loft

I have been asked to tell you about the back of the north wind. An old Greek writer mentions a people who lived there, and were so comfortable that they could not bear it any longer, and drowned themselves. My story is not the same as his. I do not think Herodotus had got the right account of the place. I am going to tell you how it fared with a boy who went there.

He lived in a low room over a coach-house; and that was not by any means at the back of the north wind, as his mother very well knew. For one side of the room was built only of boards, and the boards were so old that you might run a penknife through into the north wind. And then let them settle between them which was the sharper! I know that when you pulled it out again the wind would be after it like a cat after a mouse, and you would know soon enough you were not at the back of the north wind. Still, this room was not very cold, except when the north wind blew stronger than usual: the room I have to do with now was always cold, except in summer, when the sun took the matter into his own hands. Indeed, I am not sure whether I ought to call it a room at all; for it was just a loft where they kept hay and straw and oats for the horses.

And when little Diamond—but stop: I must tell you that his father, who was a coachman, had named him after a favourite horse, and his mother had had no objection:—when little Diamond, then, lay there in bed, he could hear the horses under him munching away in the dark, or moving sleepily in their dreams. For Diamond's father had built him a bed in the loft with boards all round it, because they had so little room in their own end over the coach-house; and Diamond's father put old Diamond in the stall under the bed, because he was a quiet horse, and did not go to sleep standing, but lay down like a reasonable creature. But, although he was a surprisingly reasonable creature, yet, when young Diamond woke in the middle of the night, and felt the bed shaking in the blasts of the north wind, he could not help wondering whether, if the wind should blow the house down, and he were to fall through into the manger, old Diamond mightn't eat him up before he knew him in his night-gown. And although old Diamond was very quiet all night long, yet when he woke he got up like an earthquake, and then young Diamond knew what o'clock it was, or at least what was to be done next, which was—to go to sleep again as fast as he could.

There was hay at his feet and hay at his head, piled up in great trusses to the very roof. Indeed it was sometimes only through a little lane with several turnings, which looked as if it had been sawn out for him, that he could reach his bed at all. For the stock of hay was, of course, always in a state either of slow ebb or of sudden flow. Sometimes the whole space of the loft, with the little panes in the roof for the stars to look in, would lie open before his open eyes as he lay in bed; sometimes a yellow wall of sweet-smelling fibres closed up his view at the distance of half a yard. Sometimes, when his mother had undressed him in her room, and told him to trot to bed by himself, he would creep into the heart of the hay, and lie there thinking how cold it was outside in the wind, and how warm it was inside there in his bed, and how he could go to it when he pleased, only he wouldn't just yet; he would get a little colder first. And ever as he grew colder, his bed would grow warmer, till at last he would scramble out of the hay, shoot like an arrow into his bed, cover himself up, and snuggle down, thinking what a happy boy he was. He had not the least idea that the wind got in at a chink in the wall, and blew about him all night. For the back of his bed was only of boards an inch thick, and on the other side of them was the north wind.

Now, as I have already said, these boards were soft and crumbly. To be sure, they were tarred on the outside, yet in many places they were more like tinder than timber. Hence it happened that the soft part having worn away from about it, little Diamond found one night, after he lay down, that a knot had come out of one of them, and that the wind was blowing in upon him in a cold and rather imperious fashion. Now he had no fancy for leaving things wrong that might be set right; so he jumped out of bed again, got a little strike of hay, twisted it up, folded it in the middle, and, having thus made it into a cork, stuck it into the hole in the wall. But the wind began to blow loud and angrily, and, as Diamond was falling asleep, out blew his cork and hit him on the nose, just hard enough to wake him up quite, and let him hear the wind whistling shrill in the hole. He searched for his hay-cork, found it, stuck it in harder, and was just dropping off once more, when, pop! with an angry whistle behind it, the cork struck him again, this time on the cheek. Up he rose once more, made a fresh stopple of hay, and corked the hole severely. But he was hardly down again before—pop! it came on his forehead. He gave it up, drew the clothes above his head, and was soon fast asleep.

Although the next day was very stormy, Diamond forgot all about the hole, for he was busy making a cave by the side of his mother's fire with a broken chair, a three-legged stool, and a blanket, and then sitting in it. His mother, however, discovered it, and pasted a bit of brown paper over it, so that, when Diamond had snuggled down the next night, he had no occasion to think of it.

Presently, however, he lifted his head and listened. Who could that be talking to him? The wind was rising again, and getting very loud, and full of rushes and whistles. He was sure some one was talking—and very near him, too, it was. But he was not frightened, for he had not yet learned how to be; so he sat up and hearkened. At last the voice, which, though quite gentle, sounded a little angry, appeared to come from the back of the bed. He crept nearer to it, and laid his ear against the wall. Then he heard nothing but the wind, which sounded very loud indeed. The moment, however, that he moved his head from the wall, he heard the voice again, close to his ear. He felt about with his hand, and came upon the piece of paper his mother had pasted over the hole. Against this he laid his ear, and then he heard the voice quite distinctly. There was, in fact, a little corner of the paper loose, and through that, as from a mouth in the wall, the voice came.

"What do you mean, little boy—closing up my window?"

"What window?" asked Diamond.

"You stuffed hay into it three times last night. I had to blow it out again three times."

"You can't mean this little hole! It isn't a window; it's a hole in my bed."

"I did not say it was a window: I said it was my window."

"But it can't be a window, because windows are holes to see out of."

"Well, that's just what I made this window for."

"But you are outside: you can't want a window."

"You are quite mistaken. Windows are to see out of, you say. Well, I'm in my house, and I want windows to see out of it."

"But you've made a window into my bed."

"Well, your mother has got three windows into my dancing room, and you have three into my garret."

"But I heard father say, when my mother wanted him to make a window through the wall, that it was against the law, for it would look into Mr. Dyves's garden."

The voice laughed.

"The law would have some trouble to catch me!" it said.

"But if it's not right, you know," said Diamond, "that's no matter. You shouldn't do it."

"I am so tall I am above that law," said the voice.

"You must have a tall house, then," said Diamond.

"Yes; a tall house: the clouds are inside it."

"Dear me!" said Diamond, and thought a minute. "I think, then, you can hardly expect me to keep a window in my bed for you. Why don't you make a window into Mr. Dyves's bed?"

"Nobody makes a window into an ash-pit," said the voice, rather sadly. "I like to see nice things out of my windows."

"But he must have a nicer bed than I have, though mine is very nice—so nice that I couldn't wish a better."

"It's not the bed I care about: it's what is in it.—But you just open that window."

"Well, mother says I shouldn't be disobliging; but it's rather hard. You see the north wind will blow right in my face if I do."

"I am the North Wind."

"O-o-oh!" said Diamond, thoughtfully. "Then will you promise not to blow on my face if I open your window?"

"I can't promise that."

"But you'll give me the toothache. Mother's got it already."

"But what's to become of me without a window?"

"I'm sure I don't know. All I say is, it will be worse for me than for you."

"No; it will not. You shall not be the worse for it—I promise you that. You will be much the better for it. Just you believe what I say, and do as I tell you."

"Well, I can pull the clothes over my head," said Diamond, and feeling with his little sharp nails, he got hold of the open edge of the paper and tore it off at once.

In came a long whistling spear of cold, and struck his little naked chest. He scrambled and tumbled in under the bedclothes, and covered himself up: there was no paper now between him and the voice, and he felt a little—not frightened exactly—I told you he had not learned that yet—but rather queer; for what a strange person this North Wind must be that lived in the great house— "called Out-of-Doors, I suppose," thought Diamond—and made windows into people's beds! But the voice began again; and he could hear it quite plainly, even with his head under the bed-clothes. It was a still more gentle voice now, although six times as large and loud as it had been, and he thought it sounded a little like his mother's.

"What is your name, little boy?" it asked.

"Diamond," answered Diamond, under the bed-clothes.

"What a funny name!"

"It's a very nice name," returned its owner.

"I don't know that," said the voice.

"Well, I do," retorted Diamond, a little rudely.

"Do you know to whom you are speaking!"

"No," said Diamond.

And indeed he did not. For to know a person's name is not always to know the person's self.

"Then I must not be angry with you.—You had better look and see, though."

"Diamond is a very pretty name," persisted the boy, vexed that it should not give satisfaction.

"Diamond is a useless thing rather," said the voice.

"That's not true. Diamond is very nice—as big as two—and so quiet all night! And doesn't he make a jolly row in the morning, getting upon his four great legs! It's like thunder."

"You don't seem to know what a diamond is."

"Oh, don't I just! Diamond is a great and good horse; and he sleeps right under me. He is old Diamond, and I am young Diamond; or, if you like it better, for you're very particular, Mr. North Wind, he's big Diamond, and I'm little Diamond; and I don't know which of us my father likes best."

A beautiful laugh, large but very soft and musical, sounded somewhere beside him, but Diamond kept his head under the clothes.

"I'm not Mr. North Wind," said the voice.

"You told me that you were the North Wind," insisted Diamond.

"I did not say Mister North Wind," said the voice.

"Well, then, I do; for mother tells me I ought to be polite."

"Then let me tell you I don't think it at all polite of you to say Mister to me."

"Well, I didn't know better. I'm very sorry."

"But you ought to know better."

"I don't know that."

"I do. You can't say it's polite to lie there talking—with your head under the bed-clothes, and never look up to see what kind of person you are talking to.—I want you to come out with me."

"I want to go to sleep," said Diamond, very nearly crying, for he did not like to be scolded, even when he deserved it.

"You shall sleep all the better to-morrow night."

"Besides," said Diamond, "you are out in Mr. Dyves's garden, and I can't get there. I can only get into our own yard."

"Will you take your head out of the bed-clothes?" said the voice, just a little angrily.

"No!" answered Diamond, half peevish, half frightened.

The instant he said the word, a tremendous blast of wind crashed in a board of the wall, and swept the clothes off Diamond. He started up in terror. Leaning over him was the large, beautiful, pale face of a woman. Her dark eyes looked a little angry, for they had just begun to flash; but a quivering in her sweet upper lip made her look as if she were going to cry. What was the most strange was that away from her head streamed out her black hair in every direction, so that the darkness in the hay-loft looked as if it were made of her, hair but as Diamond gazed at her in speechless amazement, mingled with confidence—for the boy was entranced with her mighty beauty—her hair began to gather itself out of the darkness, and fell down all about her again, till her face looked out of the midst of it like a moon out of a cloud. From her eyes came all the light by which Diamond saw her face and her, hair; and that was all he did see of her yet. The wind was over and gone.

"Will you go with me now, you little Diamond? I am sorry I was forced to be so rough with you," said the lady.

"I will; yes, I will," answered Diamond, holding out both his arms. "But," he added, dropping them, "how shall I get my clothes? They are in mother's room, and the door is locked."

"Oh, never mind your clothes. You will not be cold. I shall take care of that. Nobody is cold with the north wind."

"I thought everybody was," said Diamond.

"That is a great mistake. Most people make it, however. They are cold because they are not with the north wind, but without it."

If Diamond had been a little older, and had supposed himself a good deal wiser, he would have thought the lady was joking. But he was not older, and did not fancy himself wiser, and therefore understood her well enough. Again he stretched out his arms. The lady's face drew back a little.

"Follow me, Diamond," she said.

"Yes," said Diamond, only a little ruefully.

"You're not afraid?" said the North Wind.

"No, ma'am; but mother never would let me go without shoes: she never said anything about clothes, so I dare say she wouldn't mind that."

"I know your mother very well," said the lady. "She is a good woman. I have visited her often. I was with her when you were born. I saw her laugh and cry both at once. I love your mother, Diamond."

"How was it you did not know my name, then, ma'am? Please am I to say ma'am to you, ma'am?"

"One question at a time, dear boy. I knew your name quite well, but I wanted to hear what you would say for it. Don't you remember that day when the man was finding fault with your name—how I blew the window in?"

"Yes, yes," answered Diamond, eagerly. "Our window opens like a door, right over the coach-house door. And the wind—you, ma'am—came in, and blew the Bible out of the man's hands, and the leaves went all flutter, flutter on the floor, and my mother picked it up and gave it back to him open, and there—"

"Was your name in the Bible—the sixth stone in the high priest's breastplate."

"Oh!—a stone, was it?" said Diamond. "I thought it had been a horse—I did."

"Never mind. A horse is better than a stone any day. Well, you see, I know all about you and your mother."

"Yes. I will go with you."

"Now for the next question: you're not to call me ma'am. You must call me just my own name—respectfully, you know—just North Wind."

"Well, please, North Wind, you are so beautiful, I am quite ready to go with you."

"You must not be ready to go with everything beautiful all at once, Diamond."

"But what's beautiful can't be bad. You're not bad, North Wind?"

"No; I'm not bad. But sometimes beautiful things grow bad by doing bad, and it takes some time for their badness to spoil their beauty. So little boys may be mistaken if they go after things because they are beautiful."

"Well, I will go with you because you are beautiful and good, too."

"Ah, but there's another thing, Diamond:—What if I should look ugly without being bad—look ugly myself because I am making ugly things beautiful?—What then?"

"I don't quite understand you, North Wind. You tell me what then."

"Well, I will tell you. If you see me with my face all black, don't be frightened. If you see me flapping wings like a bat's, as big as the whole sky, don't be frightened. If you hear me raging ten times worse than Mrs. Bill, the blacksmith's wife—even if you see me looking in at people's windows like Mrs. Eve Dropper, the gardener's wife—you must believe that I am doing my work. Nay, Diamond, if I change into a serpent or a tiger, you must not let go your hold of me, for my hand will never change in yours if you keep a good hold. If you keep a hold, you will know who I am all the time, even when you look at me and can't see me the least like the North Wind. I may look something very awful. Do you understand?"

"Quite well," said little Diamond.

"Come along, then," said North Wind, and disappeared behind the mountain of hay.

Diamond crept out of bed and followed her.

2
The Lawn

When Diamond got round the corner of the hay, for a moment he hesitated. The stair by which he would naturally have gone down to the door was at the other side of the loft, and looked very black indeed; for it was full of North Wind's hair, as she descended before him. And just beside him was the ladder going straight down into the stable, up which his father always came to fetch the hay for Diamond's dinner. Through the opening in the floor the faint gleam of the-stable lantern was enticing, and Diamond thought he would run down that way.

The stair went close past the loose-box in which Diamond the horse lived. When Diamond the boy was half-way down, he remembered that it was of no use to go this way, for the stable-door was locked. But at the same moment there was horse Diamond's great head poked out of his box on to the ladder, for he knew boy Diamond although he was in his night-gown, and wanted him to pull his ears for him. This Diamond did very gently for a minute or so, and patted and stroked his neck too, and kissed the big horse, and had begun to take the bits of straw and hay out of his mane, when all at once he recollected that the Lady North Wind was waiting for him in the yard.

"Good night, Diamond," he said, and darted up the ladder, across the loft, and down the stair to the door. But when he got out into the yard, there was no lady.

Now it is always a dreadful thing to think there is somebody and find nobody. Children in particular have not made up their minds to it; they generally cry at nobody, especially when they wake up at night. But it was an especial disappointment to Diamond, for his little heart had been beating with joy: the face of the North Wind was so grand! To have a lady like that for a friend—with such long hair, too! Why, it was longer than twenty Diamonds' tails! She was gone. And there he stood, with his bare feet on the stones of the paved yard.

It was a clear night overhead, and the stars were shining. Orion in particular was making the most of his bright belt and golden sword.

But the moon was only a poor thin crescent. There was just one great, jagged, black and gray cloud in the sky, with a steep side to it like a precipice; and the moon was against this side, and looked as if she had tumbled off the top of the cloud-hill, and broken herself in rolling down the precipice. She did not seem comfortable, for she was looking down into the deep pit waiting for her. At least that was what Diamond thought as he stood for a moment staring at her. But he was quite wrong, for the moon was not afraid, and there was no pit she was going down into, for there were no sides to it, and a pit without sides to it is not a pit at all. Diamond, however, had not been out so late before in all his life, and things looked so strange about him!— just as if he had got into Fairyland, of which he knew quite as much as anybody; for his mother had no money to buy books to set him wrong on the subject. I have seen this world—only sometimes, just now and then, you know—look as strange as ever I saw Fairyland. But I confess that I have not yet seen Fairyland at its best. I am always going to see it so some time. But if you had been out in the face and not at the back of the North Wind, on a cold rather frosty night, and in your night-gown, you would have felt it all quite as strange as Diamond did. He cried a little, just a little, he was so disappointed to lose the lady: of course, you, little man, wouldn't have done that! But for my part, I don't mind people crying so much as I mind what they cry about, and how they cry—whether they cry quietly like ladies and gentlemen, or go shrieking like vulgar emperors, or ill-natured cooks; for all emperors are not gentlemen, and all cooks are not ladies—nor all queens and princesses for that matter, either.

But it can't be denied that a little gentle crying does one good. It did Diamond good; for as soon as it was over he was a brave boy again.

"She shan't say it was my fault, anyhow!" said Diamond. "I daresay she is hiding somewhere to see what I will do. I will look for her."

So he went round the end of the stable towards the kitchen-garden. But the moment he was clear of the shelter of the stable, sharp as a knife came the wind against his little chest and his bare legs. Still he would look in the kitchen-garden, and went on. But when he got round the weeping-ash that stood in the corner, the wind blew much stronger, and it grew stronger and stronger till he could hardly fight against it. And it was so cold! All the flashy spikes of the stars seemed to have got somehow into the wind. Then he thought of what the lady had said about people being cold because they were not with the North Wind. How it was that he should have guessed what she meant at that very moment I cannot tell, but I have observed that the most wonderful thing in the world is how people come to understand anything. He turned his back to the wind, and trotted again towards the yard;

whereupon, strange to say, it blew so much more gently against his calves than it had blown against his shins that he began to feel almost warm by contrast.

You must not think it was cowardly of Diamond to turn his back to the wind: he did so only because he thought Lady North Wind had said something like telling him to do so. If she had said to him that he must hold his face to it, Diamond would have held his face to it. But the most foolish thing is to fight for no good, and to please nobody.

Well, it was just as if the wind was pushing Diamond along. If he turned round, it grew very sharp on his legs especially, and so he thought the wind might really be Lady North Wind, though he could not see her, and he had better let her blow him wherever she pleased. So she blew and blew, and he went and went, until he found himself standing at a door in a wall, which door led from the yard into a little belt of shrubbery, flanking Mr. Coleman's house. Mr. Coleman was his father's master, and the owner of Diamond. He opened the door, and went through the shrubbery, and out into the middle of the lawn, still hoping to find North Wind. The soft grass was very pleasant to his bare feet, and felt warm after the stones of the yard; but the lady was nowhere to be seen. Then he began to think that after all he must have done wrong, and she was offended with him for not following close after her, but staying to talk to the horse, which certainly was neither wise nor polite.

There he stood in the middle of the lawn, the wind blowing his night-gown till it flapped like a loose sail. The stars were very shiny over his head; but they did not give light enough to show that the grass was green; and Diamond stood alone in the strange night, which looked half solid all about him. He began to wonder whether he was in a dream or not. It was important to determine this; "for," thought Diamond, "if I am in a dream, I am safe in my bed, and I needn't cry. But if I'm not in a dream, I'm out here, and perhaps I had better cry, or, at least, I'm not sure whether I can help it." He came to the conclusion, however, that, whether he was in a dream or not, there could be no harm in not crying for a little while longer: he could begin whenever he liked.

The back of Mr. Coleman's house was to the lawn, and one of the drawing-room windows looked out upon it. The ladies had not gone to bed; for the light was still shining in that window. But they had no idea that a little boy was standing on the lawn in his night-gown, or they would have run out in a moment. And as long as he saw that light, Diamond could not feel quite lonely. He stood staring, not at the great warrior Orion in the sky, nor yet at the disconsolate, neglected moon going down in the west, but at the drawing-room window with the light shining through its green curtains. He had been in that room once or twice that he could remember at Christmas times; for the Colemans were kind people, though they did not care much about children.

All at once the light went nearly out: he could only see a glimmer of the shape of the window. Then, indeed, he felt that he was left alone. It was so dreadful to be out in the night after everybody was gone to bed! That was more than he could bear. He burst out crying in good earnest, beginning with a wail like that of the wind when it is waking up.

Perhaps you think this was very foolish; for could he not go home to his own bed again when he liked? Yes; but it looked dreadful to him to creep up that stair again and lie down in his bed again, and know that North Wind's window was open beside him, and she gone, and he might never see her again. He would be just as lonely there as here. Nay, it would be much worse if he had to think that the window was nothing but a hole in the wall.

At the very moment when he burst out crying, the old nurse who had grown to be one of the family, for she had not gone away when Miss Coleman did not want any more nursing, came to the back door, which was of glass, to close the shutters. She thought she heard a cry, and, peering out with a hand on each side of her eyes like Diamond's blinkers, she saw something white on the lawn. Too old and too wise to be frightened, she opened the door, and went straight towards the white thing to see what it was. And when Diamond saw her coming he was not frightened either, though Mrs. Crump was a little cross some-times; for there is a good kind of crossness that is only disagreeable, and there is a bad kind of crossness that is very nasty indeed. So she came up with her neck stretched out, and her head at the end of it, and her eyes foremost of all, like a snail's, peering into the night to see what it could be that went on glimmering white before her. When she did see, she made a great exclamation, and threw up her hands. Then without a word, for she thought Diamond was walking in his sleep, she caught hold of him, and led him towards the house. He made no objection, for he was just in the mood to be grateful for notice of any sort, and Mrs. Crump led him straight into the drawing-room.

Now, from the neglect of the new housemaid, the fire in Miss Coleman's bedroom had gone out, and her mother had told her to brush her hair by the drawing-room fire—a disorderly proceeding which a mother's wish could justify. The young lady was very lovely, though not nearly so beautiful as North Wind; and her hair was ex-tremely long, for it came down to her knees—though that was nothing at all to North Wind's hair. Yet when she looked round, with her hair all about her, as Diamond entered, he thought for one moment that it was North Wind, and, pulling his hand from Mrs. Crump's, he stretched out his arms and ran towards Miss Coleman. She was so pleased that she threw down her brush, and almost knelt on the floor to receive him in her arms. He saw the next moment that she was not Lady North Wind, but she looked so like her he could not help running into her arms and bursting into tears afresh. Mrs. Crump said the poor child had walked out in his sleep, and Diamond thought she ought to know, and did not contradict her for anything he knew, it might be so indeed. He let them talk on about him, and said nothing; and when, after their astonishment was over, and Miss Coleman had given him a sponge-cake, it was decreed that Mrs. Crump should take him to his mother, he was quite satisfied.

His mother had to get out of bed to open the door when Mrs. Crump knocked. She was indeed surprised to see her, boy; and having taken him in her arms and carried him to his bed, returned and had a long confabulation with Mrs. Crump, for they were still talking when Diamond fell fast asleep, and could hear them no longer.

3
Old Diamond

Diamond woke very early in the morning, and thought what a curious dream he had had. But the memory grew brighter and brighter in his head, until it did not look altogether like a dream, and he began to doubt whether he had not really been abroad in the wind last night. He came to the conclusion that, if he had really been brought home to his mother by Mrs. Crump, she would say something to him about it, and that would settle the matter. Then he got up and dressed himself, but, finding that his father and mother were not yet stirring, he went down the ladder to the stable. There he found that even old Diamond was not awake yet, for he, as well as young Diamond, always got up the moment he woke, and now he was lying as flat as a horse could lie upon his nice trim bed of straw.

"I'll give old Diamond a surprise," thought the boy; and creeping up very softly, before the horse knew, he was astride of his back. Then it was young Diamond's turn to have more of a surprise than he had expected; for as with an earthquake, with a rumbling and a rocking hither and thither, a sprawling of legs and heaving as of many backs, young Diamond found himself hoisted up in the air, with both hands twisted in the horse's mane. The next instant old Diamond lashed out with both his hind legs, and giving one cry of terror young Diamond found himself lying on his neck, with his arms as far round it as they would go. But then the horse stood as still as a stone, except that he lifted his head gently up to let the boy slip down to his back. For when he heard young Diamond's cry he knew that there was nothing to kick about; for young Diamond was a good boy, and old Diamond was a good horse, and the one was all right on the back of the other.

As soon as Diamond had got himself comfortable on the saddle place, the horse began pulling at the hay, and the boy began thinking. He had never mounted Diamond himself before, and he had never got off him without being lifted down. So he sat, while the horse ate, wondering how he was to reach the ground.

But while he meditated, his mother woke, and her first thought was to see her boy. She had visited him twice during the night, and found him sleeping quietly. Now his bed was empty, and she was frightened.

"Diamond! Diamond! Where are you, Diamond?" she called out.

Diamond turned his head where he sat like a knight on his steed in enchanted stall, and cried aloud,—

"Here, mother!"

"Where, Diamond?" she returned.

"Here, mother, on Diamond's back."

She came running to the ladder, and peeping down, saw him aloft on the great horse.

"Come down, Diamond," she said.

"I can't," answered Diamond.

"How did you get up?" asked his mother.

"Quite easily," answered he; "but when I got up, Diamond would get up too, and so here I am."

His mother thought he had been walking in his sleep again, and hurried down the ladder. She did not much like going up to the horse, for she had not been used to horses; but she would have gone into a lion's den, not to say a horse's stall, to help her boy. So she went and lifted him off Diamond's back, and felt braver all her life after. She carried him in her arms up to her room; but, afraid of frightening him at his own sleep-walking, as she supposed it, said nothing about last night. Before the next day was over, Diamond had almost concluded the whole adventure a dream.

For a week his mother watched him very carefully—going into the loft several times a night—as often, in fact, as she woke. Every time she found him fast asleep.

All that week it was hard weather. The grass showed white in the morning with the hoar-frost which clung like tiny comfits to every blade. And as Diamond's shoes were not good, and his mother had not quite saved up enough money to get him the new pair she so much wanted for him, she would not let him run out. He played all his games over and over indoors, especially that of driving two chairs harnessed to the baby's cradle; and if they did not go very fast, they went as fast as could be expected of the best chairs in the world, although one of them had only three legs, and the other only half a back.

At length his mother brought home his new shoes, and no sooner did she find they fitted him than she told him he might run out in the yard and amuse himself for an hour.

The sun was going down when he flew from the door like a bird from its cage. All the world was new to him. A great fire of sunset burned on the top of the gate that led from the stables to the house; above the fire in the sky lay a large lake of green light, above that a golden cloud, and over that the blue of the wintry heavens. And Diamond thought that, next to his own home, he had never seen any place he would like so much to live in as that sky. For it is not fine things that make home a nice place, but your mother and your father.

As he was looking at the lovely colours, the gates were thrown open, and there was old Diamond and his friend in the carriage, dancing with impatience to get at their stalls and their oats. And in they came. Diamond was not in the least afraid of his father driving over him, but, careful not to spoil the grand show he made with his fine horses and his multitudinous cape, with a red edge to every fold, he slipped out of the way and let him dash right on to the stables. To be quite safe he had to step into the recess of the door that led from the yard to the shrubbery.

As he stood there he remembered how the wind had driven him to this same spot on the night of his dream. And once more he was almost sure that it was no dream. At all events, he would go in and see whether things looked at all now as they did then. He opened the door, and passed through the little belt of shrubbery. Not a flower was to be seen in the beds on the lawn. Even the brave old chrysanthemums and Christmas roses had passed away before the frost. What? Yes! There was one! He ran and knelt down to look at it.

It was a primrose—a dwarfish thing, but perfect in shape—a baby-wonder. As he stooped his face to see it close, a little wind began to blow, and two or three long leaves that stood up behind the flower shook and waved and quivered, but the primrose lay still in the green hollow, looking up at the sky, and not seeming to know that the wind was blowing at all. It was just a one eye that the dull black wintry earth had opened to look at the sky with. All at once Diamond thought it was saying its prayers, and he ought not to be staring at it so. He ran to the stable to see his father make Diamond's bed. Then his father took him in his arms, carried him up the ladder, and set him down at the table where they were going to have their tea.

"Miss is very poorly," said Diamond's father. "Mis'ess has been to the doctor with her to-day, and she looked very glum when she came out again. I was a-watching of them to see what doctor had said."

"And didn't Miss look glum too?" asked his mother.

"Not half as glum as Mis'ess," returned the coachman. "You see—"

But he lowered his voice, and Diamond could not make out more than a word here and there. For Diamond's father was not only one of the finest of coachmen to look at, and one of the best of drivers, but one of the most discreet of servants as well. Therefore he did not talk

about family affairs to any one but his wife, whom he had proved better than himself long ago, and was careful that even Diamond should
hear nothing he could repeat again concerning master and his family.

It was bed-time soon, and Diamond went to bed and fell fast
asleep.

He awoke all at once, in the dark.

"Open the window, Diamond," said a voice.

Now Diamond's mother had once more pasted up North Wind's
window.

"Are you North Wind?" said Diamond: "I don't hear you blowing."

"No; but you hear me talking. Open the window, for I haven't over-
much time."

"Yes," returned Diamond. "But, please, North Wind, where's the
use? You left me all alone last time."

He had got up on his knees, and was busy with his nails once more
at the paper over the hole in the wall. For now that North Wind spoke
again, he remembered all that had taken place before as distinctly as
if it had happened only last night.

"Yes, but that was your fault," returned North Wind. "I had work
to do; and, besides, a gentleman should never keep a lady waiting."

"But I'm not a gentleman," said Diamond, scratching away at the
paper.

"I hope you won't say so ten years after this."

"I'm going to be a coachman, and a coachman is not a gentleman,"
persisted Diamond.

"We call your father a gentleman in our house," said North Wind.

"He doesn't call himself one," said Diamond.

"That's of no consequence: every man ought to be a gentleman,
and your father is one."

Diamond was so pleased to hear this that he scratched at the paper like ten mice, and getting hold of the edge of it, tore it off. The
next instant a young girl glided across the bed, and stood upon the
floor.

"Oh dear!" said Diamond, quite dismayed; "I didn't know—who
are you, please?"

"I'm North Wind."

"Are you really?"

"Yes. Make haste."

"But you're no bigger than me."

"Do you think I care about how big or how little I am? Didn't you
see me this evening? I was less then."

"No. Where was you?"

"Behind the leaves of the primrose. Didn't you see them blowing?"

"Yes."

"Make haste, then, if you want to go with me."

"But you are not big enough to take care of me. I think you are only Miss North Wind."

"I am big enough to show you the way, anyhow. But if you won't come, why, you must stay."

"I must dress myself. I didn't mind with a grown lady, but I couldn't go with a little girl in my night-gown."

"Very well. I'm not in such a hurry as I was the other night. Dress as fast as you can, and I'll go and shake the primrose leaves till you come."

"Don't hurt it," said Diamond.

North Wind broke out in a little laugh like the breaking of silver bubbles, and was gone in a moment. Diamond saw—for it was a star-lit night, and the mass of hay was at a low ebb now—the gleam of something vanishing down the stair, and, springing out of bed, dressed himself as fast as ever he could. Then he crept out into the yard, through the door in the wall, and away to the primrose. Behind it stood North Wind, leaning over it, and looking at the flower as if she had been its mother.

"Come along," she said, jumping up and holding out her hand.

Diamond took her hand. It was cold, but so pleasant and full of life, it was better than warm. She led him across the garden. With one bound she was on the top of the wall. Diamond was left at the foot.

"Stop, stop!" he cried. "Please, I can't jump like that."

"You don't try" said North Wind, who from the top looked down a foot taller than before.

"Give me your hand again, and I will, try" said Diamond.

She reached down, Diamond laid hold of her hand, gave a great spring, and stood beside her.

"This is nice!" he said.

Another bound, and they stood in the road by the river. It was full tide, and the stars were shining clear in its depths, for it lay still, waiting for the turn to run down again to the sea. They walked along its side. But they had not walked far before its surface was covered with ripples, and the stars had vanished from its bosom.

And North Wind was now tall as a full-grown girl. Her hair was flying about her head, and the wind was blowing a breeze down the river. But she turned aside and went up a narrow lane, and as she went her hair fell down around her.

"I have some rather disagreeable work to do to-night," she said, "before I get out to sea, and I must set about it at once. The disagreeable work must be looked after first."

So saying, she laid hold of Diamond and began to run, gliding along faster and faster. Diamond kept up with her as well as he could. She made many turnings and windings, apparently because it was not quite easy to get him over walls and houses. Once they ran through a hall where they found back and front doors open. At the foot of the stair North Wind stood still, and Diamond, hearing a great growl, started in terror, and there, instead of North Wind, was a huge wolf by his side. He let go his hold in dismay, and the wolf bounded up the stair. The windows of the house rattled and shook as if guns were firing, and the sound of a great fall came from above. Diamond stood with white face staring up at the landing.

"Surely," he thought, "North Wind can't be eating one of the children!" Coming to himself all at once, he rushed after her with his little fist clenched. There were ladies in long trains going up and down the stairs, and gentlemen in white neckties attending on them, who stared at him, but none of them were of the people of the house, and they said nothing. Before he reached the head of the stair, however, North Wind met him, took him by the hand, and hurried down and out of the house.

"I hope you haven't eaten a baby, North Wind!" said Diamond, very solemnly.

North Wind laughed merrily, and went tripping on faster. Her grassy robe swept and swirled about her steps, and wherever it passed over withered leaves, they went fleeing and whirling in spirals, and running on their edges like wheels, all about her feet.

"No," she said at last, "I did not eat a baby. You would not have had to ask that foolish question if you had not let go your hold of me. You would have seen how I served a nurse that was calling a child bad names, and telling her she was wicked. She had been drinking. I saw an ugly gin bottle in a cupboard."

"And you frightened her?" said Diamond.

"I believe so!" answered North Wind laughing merrily. "I flew at her throat, and she tumbled over on the floor with such a crash that they ran in. She'll be turned away to-morrow—and quite time, if they knew as much as I do."

"But didn't you frighten the little one?"

"She never saw me. The woman would not have seen me either if she had not been wicked."

"Oh!" said Diamond, dubiously.

"Why should you see things," returned North Wind, "that you wouldn't understand or know what to do with? Good people see good things; bad people, bad things."

"Then are you a bad thing?"

"No. For you see me, Diamond, dear," said the girl, and she looked down at him, and Diamond saw the loving eyes of the great lady beaming from the depths of her falling hair.

"I had to make myself look like a bad thing before she could see me. If I had put on any other shape than a wolf's she would not have seen me, for that is what is growing to be her own shape inside of her."

"I don't know what you mean," said Diamond, "but I suppose it's all right."

They were now climbing the slope of a grassy ascent. It was Primrose Hill, in fact, although Diamond had never heard of it. The moment they reached the top, North Wind stood and turned her face towards London The stars were still shining clear and cold overhead. There was not a cloud to be seen. The air was sharp, but Diamond did not find it cold.

"Now," said the lady, "whatever you do, do not let my hand go. I might have lost you the last time, only I was not in a hurry then: now I am in a hurry."

Yet she stood still for a moment.

4

North Wind

And as she stood looking towards London, Diamond saw that she was trembling.

"Are you cold, North Wind?" he asked.

"No, Diamond," she answered, looking down upon him with a smile; "I am only getting ready to sweep one of my rooms. Those careless, greedy, untidy children make it in such a mess."

As she spoke he could have told by her voice, if he had not seen with his eyes, that she was growing larger and larger. Her head went up and up towards the stars; and as she grew, still trembling through all her body, her hair also grew—longer and longer, and lifted itself from her head, and went out in black waves. The next moment, however, it fell back around her, and she grew less and less till she was only a tall woman. Then she put her hands behind her head, and gathered some of her hair, and began weaving and knotting it together. When she had done, she bent down her beautiful face close to his, and said—

"Diamond, I am afraid you would not keep hold of me, and if I were to drop you, I don't know what might happen; so I have been making a place for you in my hair. Come."

Diamond held out his arms, for with that grand face looking at him, he believed like a baby. She took him in her hands, threw him over her shoulder, and said, "Get in, Diamond."

And Diamond parted her hair with his hands, crept between, and feeling about soon found the woven nest. It was just like a pocket, or like the shawl in which gipsy women carry their children. North Wind put her hands to her back, felt all about the nest, and finding it safe, said—

"Are you comfortable, Diamond?"

"Yes, indeed," answered Diamond.

The next moment he was rising in the air. North Wind grew towering up to the place of the clouds. Her hair went streaming out from her, till it spread like a mist over the stars. She flung herself abroad in space.

Diamond held on by two of the twisted ropes which, parted and interwoven, formed his shelter, for he could not help being a little afraid. As soon as he had come to himself, he peeped through the woven meshes, for he did not dare to look over the top of the nest. The earth was rushing past like a river or a sea below him. Trees and water and green grass hurried away beneath. A great roar of wild animals rose as they rushed over the Zoological Gardens, mixed with a chattering of monkeys and a screaming of birds; but it died away in a moment behind them. And now there was nothing but the roofs of houses, sweeping along like a great torrent of stones and rocks. Chimney-pots fell, and tiles flew from the roofs; but it looked to him as if they were left behind by the roofs and the chimneys as they scudded away. There was a great roaring, for the wind was dashing against London like a sea; but at North Wind's back Diamond, of course, felt nothing of it all. He was in a perfect calm. He could hear the sound of it, that was all.

By and by he raised himself and looked over the edge of his nest. There were the houses rushing up and shooting away below him, like a fierce torrent of rocks instead of water. Then he looked up to the sky, but could see no stars; they were hidden by the blinding masses of the lady's hair which swept between. He began to wonder whether she would hear him if he spoke. He would try.

"Please, North Wind," he said, "what is that noise?"

From high over his head came the voice of North Wind, answering him, gently—

"The noise of my besom. I am the old woman that sweeps the cobwebs from the sky; only I'm busy with the floor now."

"What makes the houses look as if they were running away?"

"I am sweeping so fast over them."

"But, please, North Wind, I knew London was very big, but I didn't know it was so big as this. It seems as if we should never get away from it."

"We are going round and round, else we should have left it long ago."

"Is this the way you sweep, North Wind?"

"Yes; I go round and round with my great besom."

"Please, would you mind going a little slower, for I want to see the streets?"

"You won't see much now."

"Why?"

"Because I have nearly swept all the people home."

"Oh! I forgot," said Diamond, and was quiet after that, for he did not want to be troublesome.

But she dropped a little towards the roofs of the houses, and Diamond could see down into the streets. There were very few people about, though. The lamps flickered and flared again, but nobody seemed to want them.

Suddenly Diamond espied a little girl coming along a street. She was dreadfully blown by the wind, and a broom she was trailing behind her was very troublesome. It seemed as if the wind had a spite at her—it kept worrying her like a wild beast, and tearing at her rags. She was so lonely there!

"Oh! please, North Wind," he cried, "won't you help that little girl?"

"No, Diamond; I mustn't leave my work."

"But why shouldn't you be kind to her?"

"I am kind to her. I am sweeping the wicked smells away."

"But you're kinder to me, dear North Wind. Why shouldn't you be as kind to her as you are to me?"

"There are reasons, Diamond. Everybody can't be done to all the same. Everybody is not ready for the same thing."

"But I don't see why I should be kinder used than she."

"Do you think nothing's to be done but what you can see, Diamond, you silly! It's all right. Of course you can help her if you like. You've got nothing particular to do at this moment; I have."

"Oh! do let me help her, then. But you won't be able to wait, perhaps?"

"No, I can't wait; you must do it yourself. And, mind, the wind will get a hold of you, too."

"Don't you want me to help her, North Wind?"

"Not without having some idea what will happen. If you break down and cry, that won't be much of a help to her, and it will make a goose of little Diamond."

"I want to go," said Diamond. "Only there's just one thing—how am I to get home?"

"If you're anxious about that, perhaps you had better go with me. I am bound to take you home again, if you do."

"There!" cried Diamond, who was still looking after the little girl. "I'm sure the wind will blow her over, and perhaps kill her. Do let me go."

They had been sweeping more slowly along the line of the street. There was a lull in the roaring.

"Well, though I cannot promise to take you home," said North Wind, as she sank nearer and nearer to the tops of the houses, "I can

promise you it will be all right in the end. You will get home somehow. Have you made up your mind what to do?"

"Yes; to help the little girl," said Diamond firmly.

The same moment North Wind dropt into the street and stood,
only a tall lady, but with her hair flying up over the housetops. She
put her hands to her back, took Diamond, and set him down in the
street. The same moment he was caught in the fierce coils of the blast,
and all but blown away. North Wind stepped back a step, and at once
towered in stature to the height of the houses. A chimney-pot clashed
at Diamond's feet. He turned in terror, but it was to look for the little
girl, and when he turned again the lady had vanished, and the wind
was roaring along the street as if it had been the bed of an invisible
torrent. The little girl was scudding before the blast, her hair flying
too, and behind her she dragged her broom. Her little legs were going as fast as ever they could to keep her from falling. Diamond crept
into the shelter of a doorway, thinking to stop her; but she passed
him like a bird, crying gently and pitifully.

"Stop! stop! little girl," shouted Diamond, starting in pursuit.

"I can't," wailed the girl, "the wind won't leave go of me."

Diamond could run faster than she, and he had no broom. In a
few moments he had caught her by the frock, but it tore in his hand,
and away went the little girl. So he had to run again, and this time he
ran so fast that he got before her, and turning round caught her in his
arms, when down they went both together, which made the little girl
laugh in the midst of her crying.

"Where are you going?" asked Diamond, rubbing the elbow that
had stuck farthest out. The arm it belonged to was twined round a
lamp-post as he stood between the little girl and the wind.

"Home," she said, gasping for breath.

"Then I will go with you," said Diamond.

And then they were silent for a while, for the wind blew worse
than ever, and they had both to hold on to the lamp-post.

"Where is your crossing?" asked the girl at length.

"I don't sweep," answered Diamond.

"What do you do, then?" asked she. "You ain't big enough for most
things."

"I don't know what I do do," answered he, feeling rather ashamed.
"Nothing, I suppose. My father's Mr. Coleman's coachman."

"Have you a father?" she said, staring at him as if a boy with a
father was a natural curiosity.

"Yes. Haven't you?" returned Diamond.

"No; nor mother neither. Old Sal's all I've got." And she began to
cry again.

"I wouldn't go to her if she wasn't good to me," said Diamond.

"But you must go somewheres."

"Move on," said the voice of a policeman behind them.

"I told you so," said the girl. "You must go somewheres. They're always at it."

"But old Sal doesn't beat you, does she?"

"I wish she would."

"What do you mean?" asked Diamond, quite bewildered.

"She would if she was my mother. But she wouldn't lie abed a-cuddlin' of her ugly old bones, and laugh to hear me crying at the door."

"You don't mean she won't let you in to-night?"

"It'll be a good chance if she does."

"Why are you out so late, then?" asked Diamond.

"My crossing's a long way off at the West End, and I had been indulgin' in door-steps and mewses."

"We'd better have a try anyhow," said Diamond. "Come along."

As he spoke Diamond thought he caught a glimpse of North Wind turning a corner in front of them; and when they turned the corner too, they found it quiet there, but he saw nothing of the lady.

"Now you lead me," he said, taking her hand, "and I'll take care of you."

The girl withdrew her hand, but only to dry her eyes with her frock, for the other had enough to do with her broom. She put it in his again, and led him, turning after turning, until they stopped at a cellar-door in a very dirty lane. There she knocked.

"I shouldn't like to live here," said Diamond.

"Oh, yes, you would, if you had nowhere else to go to," answered the girl. "I only wish we may get in."

"I don't want to go in," said Diamond.

"Where do you mean to go, then?"

"Home to my home."

"Where's that?"

"I don't exactly know."

"Then you're worse off than I am."

"Oh no, for North Wind—" began Diamond, and stopped, he hardly knew why.

"What?" said the girl, as she held her ear to the door listening.

But Diamond did not reply. Neither did old Sal.

"I told you so," said the girl. "She is wide awake hearkening. But we don't get in."

"What will you do, then?" asked Diamond.

"Move on," she answered.

"Where?"

"Oh, anywheres. Bless you, I'm used to it."

"Hadn't you better come home with me, then?"

"That's a good joke, when you don't know where it is. Come on."

"But where?"

"Oh, nowheres in particular. Come on."

Diamond obeyed. The wind had now fallen considerably. They wandered on and on, turning in this direction and that, without any reason for one way more than another, until they had got out of the thick of the houses into a waste kind of place. By this time they were both very tired. Diamond felt a good deal inclined to cry, and thought he had been very silly to get down from the back of North Wind; not that he would have minded it if he had done the girl any good; but he thought he had been of no use to her. He was mistaken there, for she was far happier for having Diamond with her than if she had been wandering about alone. She did not seem so tired as he was.

"Do let us rest a bit," said Diamond.

"Let's see," she answered. "There's something like a railway there. Perhaps there's an open arch."

They went towards it and found one, and, better still, there was an empty barrel lying under the arch.

"Hallo! here we are!" said the girl. "A barrel's the jolliest bed going—on the tramp, I mean. We'll have forty winks, and then go on again."

She crept in, and Diamond crept in beside her. They put their arms round each other, and when he began to grow warm, Diamond's courage began to come back.

"This is jolly!" he said. "I'm so glad!"

"I don't think so much of it," said the girl. "I'm used to it, I suppose. But I can't think how a kid like you comes to be out all alone this time o' night."

She called him a kid, but she was not really a month older than he was; only she had had to work for her bread, and that so soon makes people older.

"But I shouldn't have been out so late if I hadn't got down to help you," said Diamond. "North Wind is gone home long ago."

"I think you must ha' got out o' one o' them Hidget Asylms," said the girl. "You said something about the north wind afore that I couldn't get the rights of."

So now, for the sake of his character, Diamond had to tell her the whole story.

She did not believe a word of it. She said he wasn't such a flat as to believe all that bosh. But as she spoke there came a great blast of wind through the arch, and set the barrel rolling. So they made haste to get out of it, for they had no notion of being rolled over and over as if they had been packed tight and wouldn't hurt, like a barrel of herrings.

"I thought we should have had a sleep," said Diamond; "but I can't say I'm very sleepy after all. Come, let's go on again."

They wandered on and on, sometimes sitting on a door-step, but always turning into lanes or fields when they had a chance.

They found themselves at last on a rising ground that sloped rather steeply on the other side. It was a waste kind of spot below, bounded by an irregular wall, with a few doors in it. Outside lay broken things in general, from garden rollers to flower-pots and wine-bottles. But the moment they reached the brow of the rising ground, a gust of wind seized them and blew them down hill as fast as they could run. Nor could Diamond stop before he went bang against one of the doors in the wall. To his dismay it burst open. When they came to themselves they peeped in. It was the back door of a garden.

"Ah, ah!" cried Diamond, after staring for a few moments, "I thought so! North Wind takes nobody in! Here I am in master's garden! I tell you what, little girl, you just bore a hole in old Sal's wall, and put your mouth to it, and say, 'Please, North Wind, mayn't I go out with you?' and then you'll see what'll come."

"I daresay I shall. But I'm out in the wind too often already to want more of it."

"I said with the North Wind, not in it."

"It's all one."

"It's not all one."

"It is all one."

"But I know best."

"And I know better. I'll box your ears," said the girl.

Diamond got very angry. But he remembered that even if she did box his ears, he musn't box hers again, for she was a girl, and all that boys must do, if girls are rude, is to go away and leave them. So he went in at the door.

"Good-bye, mister" said the girl.

This brought Diamond to his senses.

"I'm sorry I was cross," he said. "Come in, and my mother will give you some breakfast."

"No, thank you. I must be off to my crossing. It's morning now."

"I'm very sorry for you," said Diamond.

"Well, it is a life to be tired of—what with old Sal, and so many holes in my shoes."

"I wonder you're so good. I should kill myself."

"Oh, no, you wouldn't! When I think of it, I always want to see what's coming next, and so I always wait till next is over. Well! I suppose there's somebody happy somewheres. But it ain't in them carriages. Oh my! how they do look sometimes—fit to bite your head off! Good-bye!"

She ran up the hill and disappeared behind it. Then Diamond shut the door as he best could, and ran through the kitchen-garden to the stable. And wasn't he glad to get into his own blessed bed again!

5
The Summer-House

Diamond said nothing to his mother about his adventures. He had half a notion that North Wind was a friend of his mother, and that, if she did not know all about it, at least she did not mind his going anywhere with the lady of the wind. At the same time he doubted whether he might not appear to be telling stories if he told all, especially as he could hardly believe it himself when he thought about it in the middle of the day, although when the twilight was once half-way on to night he had no doubt about it, at least for the first few days after he had been with her. The girl that swept the crossing had certainly refused to believe him. Besides, he felt sure that North Wind would tell him if he ought to speak.

It was some time before he saw the lady of the wind again. Indeed nothing remarkable took place in Diamond's history until the following week. This was what happened then. Diamond the horse wanted new shoes, and Diamond's father took him out of the stable, and was just getting on his back to ride him to the forge, when he saw his little boy standing by the pump, and looking at him wistfully. Then the coachman took his foot out of the stirrup, left his hold of the mane and bridle, came across to his boy, lifted him up, and setting him on the horse's back, told him to sit up like a man. He then led away both Diamonds together.

The boy atop felt not a little tremulous as the great muscles that lifted the legs of the horse knotted and relaxed against his legs, and he cowered towards the withers, grasping with his hands the bit of mane worn short by the collar; but when his father looked back at him, saying once more, "Sit up, Diamond," he let the mane go and sat up, notwithstanding that the horse, thinking, I suppose, that his master had said to him, "Come up, Diamond," stepped out faster. For both the Diamonds were just grandly obedient. And Diamond soon found that, as he was obedient to his father, so the horse was obedient to him. For he had not ridden far before he found courage to reach forward and catch hold of the bridle, and when his father, whose hand was upon it, felt the boy pull it towards him, he looked up and smiled, and, well pleased, let go his hold, and left Diamond to guide Diamond; and the boy soon found that he could do so perfectly. It was a grand thing to be able to guide a great beast like that. And another discovery he made was that, in order to guide the horse, he had in a measure to obey the horse first. If he did not yield his body to the motions of the horse's body, he could not guide him; he must fall off.

The blacksmith lived at some distance, deeper into London. As they crossed the angle of a square, Diamond, who was now quite comfortable on his living throne, was glancing this way and that in a gentle pride, when he saw a girl sweeping a crossing scuddingly before a lady. The lady was his father's mistress, Mrs. Coleman, and the little girl was she for whose sake he had got off North Wind's back. He drew Diamond's bridle in eager anxiety to see whether her outstretched hand would gather a penny from Mrs. Coleman. But she had given one at the last crossing, and the hand returned only to grasp its broom. Diamond could not bear it. He had a penny in his pocket, a gift of the same lady the day before, and he tumbled off his horse to give it to the girl. He tumbled off, I say, for he did tumble when he reached the ground. But he got up in an instant, and ran, searching his pocket as he ran. She made him a pretty courtesy when he offered his treasure, but with a bewildered stare. She thought first: "Then he was on the back of the North Wind after all!" but, looking up at the sound of the horse's feet on the paved crossing, she changed her idea, saying to herself, "North Wind is his father's horse! That's the secret of it! Why couldn't he say so?" And she had a mind to refuse the penny. But his smile put it all right, and she not only took his penny but put it in her mouth with a "Thank you, mister. Did they wollop you then?"

"Oh no!" answered Diamond. "They never wollops me."

"Lor!" said the little girl, and was speechless.

Meantime his father, looking up, and seeing the horse's back bare, suffered a pang of awful dread, but the next moment catching sight of him, took him up and put him on, saying—

"Don't get off again, Diamond. The horse might have put his foot on you."

"No, father," answered the boy, and rode on in majestic safety.

The summer drew near, warm and splendid. Miss Coleman was a little better in health, and sat a good deal in the garden. One day she saw Diamond peeping through the shrubbery, and called him. He talked to her so frankly that she often sent for him after that, and by degrees it came about that he had leave to run in the garden as he pleased. He never touched any of the flowers or blossoms, for he was not like some boys who cannot enjoy a thing without pulling it to pieces, and so preventing every one from enjoying it after them.

A week even makes such a long time in a child's life, that Diamond had begun once more to feel as if North Wind were a dream of some far-off year.

One hot evening, he had been sitting with the young mistress, as they called her, in a little summer-house at the bottom of the lawn—a wonderful thing for beauty, the boy thought, for a little window in the side of it was made of coloured glass. It grew dusky, and the lady began to feel chill, and went in, leaving the boy in the summer-house. He sat there gazing out at a bed of tulips, which, although they had closed for the night, could not go quite asleep for the wind that kept waving them about. All at once he saw a great bumble-bee fly out of one of the tulips.

"There! that is something done," said a voice—a gentle, merry, childish voice, but so tiny. "At last it was. I thought he would have had to stay there all night, poor fellow! I did."

Diamond could not tell whether the voice was near or far away, it was so small and yet so clear. He had never seen a fairy, but he had heard of such, and he began to look all about for one. And there was the tiniest creature sliding down the stem of the tulip!

"Are you the fairy that herds the bees?" he asked, going out of the summer-house, and down on his knees on the green shore of the tulip-bed.

"I'm not a fairy," answered the little creature.

"How do you know that?"

"It would become you better to ask how you are to know it."

"You've just told me."

"Yes. But what's the use of knowing a thing only because you're told it?"

"Well, how am I to know you are not a fairy? You do look very like one."

"In the first place, fairies are much bigger than you see me."

"Oh!" said Diamond reflectively; "I thought they were very little."

"But they might be tremendously bigger than I am, and yet not very big. Why, I could be six times the size I am, and not be very huge. Besides, a fairy can't grow big and little at will, though the nursery-tales do say so: they don't know better. You stupid Diamond! have you never seen me before?"

And, as she spoke, a moan of wind bent the tulips almost to the ground, and the creature laid her hand on Diamond's shoulder. In a moment he knew that it was North Wind.

"I am very stupid," he said; "but I never saw you so small before, not even when you were nursing the primrose."

"Must you see me every size that can be measured before you know me, Diamond?"

"But how could I think it was you taking care of a great stupid bumble-bee?"

"The more stupid he was the more need he had to be taken care of. What with sucking honey and trying to open the door, he was nearly dated; and when it opened in the morning to let the sun see the tulip's heart, what would the sun have thought to find such a stupid thing lying there—with wings too?"

"But how do you have time to look after bees?"

"I don't look after bees. I had this one to look after. It was hard work, though."

"Hard work! Why, you could blow a chimney down, or—or a boy's cap off," said Diamond.

"Both are easier than to blow a tulip open. But I scarcely know the difference between hard and easy. I am always able for what I have to do. When I see my work, I just rush at it—and it is done. But I mustn't chatter. I have got to sink a ship to-night."

"Sink a ship! What! with men in it?"

"Yes, and women too."

"How dreadful! I wish you wouldn't talk so."

"It is rather dreadful. But it is my work. I must do it."

"I hope you won't ask me to go with you."

"No, I won't ask you. But you must come for all that."

"I won't then."

"Won't you?" And North Wind grew a tall lady, and looked him in the eyes, and Diamond said—

"Please take me. You cannot be cruel."

"No; I could not be cruel if I would. I can do nothing cruel, although I often do what looks like cruel to those who do not know what I really am doing. The people they say I drown, I only carry away to—to—to—well, the back of the North Wind—that is what they used to call it long ago, only I never saw the place."

"How can you carry them there if you never saw it?"

"I know the way."

"But how is it you never saw it?"

"Because it is behind me."

"But you can look round."

"Not far enough to see my own back. No; I always look before me. In fact, I grow quite blind and deaf when I try to see my back. I only mind my work."

"But how does it be your work?"

"Ah, that I can't tell you. I only know it is, because when I do it I feel all right, and when I don't I feel all wrong. East Wind says—only one does not exactly know how much to believe of what she says, for she is very naughty sometimes—she says it is all managed by a baby; but whether she is good or naughty when she says that, I don't know. I just stick to my work. It is all one to me to let a bee out of a tulip, or to sweep the cobwebs from the sky. You would like to go with me to-night?"

"I don't want to see a ship sunk."

"But suppose I had to take you?"

"Why, then, of course I must go."

"There's a good Diamond.—I think I had better be growing a bit. Only you must go to bed first. I can't take you till you're in bed. That's the law about the children. So I had better go and do something else first."

"Very well, North Wind," said Diamond. "What are you going to do first, if you please?"

"I think I may tell you. Jump up on the top of the wall, there."

"I can't."

"Ah! and I can't help you—you haven't been to bed yet, you see. Come out to the road with me, just in front of the coach-house, and I will show you."

North Wind grew very small indeed, so small that she could not have blown the dust off a dusty miller, as the Scotch children call a yellow auricula. Diamond could not even see the blades of grass move as she flitted along by his foot. They left the lawn, went out by the wicket in the-coach-house gates, and then crossed the road to the low wall that separated it from the river.

"You can get up on this wall, Diamond," said North Wind.

"Yes; but my mother has forbidden me."

"Then don't," said North Wind.

"But I can see over," said Diamond.

"Ah! to be sure. I can't."

So saying, North Wind gave a little bound, and stood on the top of the wall. She was just about the height a dragon-fly would be, if it stood on end.

"You darling!" said Diamond, seeing what a lovely little toy-woman she was.

"Don't be impertinent, Master Diamond," said North Wind. "If there's one thing makes me more angry than another, it is the way you humans judge things by their size. I am quite as respectable now as I shall be six hours after this, when I take an East Indiaman by the royals, twist her round, and push her under. You have no right to address me in such a fashion."

But as she spoke, the tiny face wore the smile of a great, grand woman. She was only having her own beautiful fun out of Diamond, and true woman's fun never hurts.

"But look there!" she resumed. "Do you see a boat with one man in it—a green and white boat?"

"Yes; quite well."

"That's a poet."

"I thought you said it was a bo-at."

"Stupid pet! Don't you know what a poet is?"

"Why, a thing to sail on the water in."

"Well, perhaps you're not so far wrong. Some poets do carry people over the sea. But I have no business to talk so much. The man is a poet."

"The boat is a boat," said Diamond.

"Can't you spell?" asked North Wind.

"Not very well."

"So I see. A poet is not a bo-at, as you call it. A poet is a man who is glad of something, and tries to make other people glad of it too."

"Ah! now I know. Like the man in the sweety-shop."

"Not very. But I see it is no use. I wasn't sent to tell you, and so I can't tell you. I must be off. Only first just look at the man."

"He's not much of a rower" said Diamond— "paddling first with one fin and then with the other."

"Now look here!" said North Wind.

And she flashed like a dragon-fly across the water, whose surface rippled and puckered as she passed. The next moment the man in the boat glanced about him, and bent to his oars. The boat flew over the rippling water. Man and boat and river were awake. The same instant almost, North Wind perched again upon the river wall.

"How did you do that?" asked Diamond.

"I blew in his face," answered North Wind. "I don't see how that could do it," said Diamond. "I daresay not. And therefore you will say you don't believe it could."

"No, no, dear North Wind. I know you too well not to believe you."

"Well, I blew in his face, and that woke him up."

"But what was the good of it?"

"Why! don't you see? Look at him—how he is pulling. I blew the mist out of him."

"How was that?"

"That is just what I cannot tell you."

"But you did it."

"Yes. I have to do ten thousand things without being able to tell how."

"I don't like that," said Diamond.

He was staring after the boat. Hearing no answer, he looked down to the wall.

North Wind was gone. Away across the river went a long ripple—what sailors call a cat's paw. The man in the boat was putting up a sail. The moon was coming to herself on the edge of a great cloud, and the sail began to shine white. Diamond rubbed his eyes, and wondered what it was all about. Things seemed going on around him, and all to understand each other, but he could make nothing of it. So he put his hands in his pockets, and went in to have his tea. The night was very hot, for the wind had fallen again.

"You don't seem very well to-night, Diamond," said his mother.

"I am quite well, mother," returned Diamond, who was only puzzled.

"I think you had better go to bed," she added.

"Very well, mother," he answered.

He stopped for one moment to look out of the window. Above the moon the clouds were going different ways. Somehow or other this troubled him, but, notwithstanding, he was soon fast asleep.

He woke in the middle of the night and the darkness. A terrible noise was rumbling overhead, like the rolling beat of great drums echoing through a brazen vault. The roof of the loft in which he lay had no ceiling; only the tiles were between him and the sky. For a while he could not come quite awake, for the noise kept beating him down, so that his heart was troubled and fluttered painfully. A second peal of thunder burst over his head, and almost choked him with fear. Nor did he recover until the great blast that followed, having torn some tiles off the roof, sent a spout of wind down into his bed and over his face, which brought him wide awake, and gave him back his courage. The same moment he heard a mighty yet musical voice calling him.

"Come up, Diamond," it said. "It's all ready. I'm waiting for you."

He looked out of the bed, and saw a gigantic, powerful, but most lovely arm—with a hand whose fingers were nothing the less ladylike that they could have strangled a boa-constrictor, or choked a tigress off its prey—stretched down through a big hole in the roof. Without a moment's hesitation he reached out his tiny one, and laid it in the grand palm before him.

6
Out in the Storm

The hand felt its way up his arm, and, grasping it gently and strongly above the elbow, lifted Diamond from the bed. The moment he was through the hole in the roof, all the winds of heaven seemed to lay hold upon him, and buffet him hither and thither. His hair blew one way, his night-gown another, his legs threatened to float from under him, and his head to grow dizzy with the swiftness of the invisible assailant. Cowering, he clung with the other hand to the huge hand which held his arm, and fear invaded his heart.

"Oh, North Wind!" he murmured, but the words vanished from his lips as he had seen the soap-bubbles that burst too soon vanish from the mouth of his pipe. The wind caught them, and they were nowhere. They couldn't get out at all, but were torn away and strangled. And yet North Wind heard them, and in her answer it seemed to Diamond that just because she was so big and could not help it, and just because her ear and her mouth must seem to him so dreadfully far away, she spoke to him more tenderly and graciously than ever before. Her voice was like the bass of a deep organ, without the groan in it; like the most delicate of violin tones without the wail in it; like the most glorious of trumpet-ejaculations without the defiance in it; like the sound of falling water without the clatter and clash in it: it was like all of them and neither of them—all of them without their faults, each of them without its peculiarity: after all, it was more like his mother's voice than anything else in the world.

"Diamond, dear," she said, "be a man. What is fearful to you is not the least fearful to me."

"But it can't hurt you," murmured Diamond, "for you're it."

"Then if I'm it, and have you in my arms, how can it hurt you?"

"Oh yes! I see," whispered Diamond. "But it looks so dreadful, and it pushes me about so."

"Yes, it does, my dear. That is what it was sent for."

At the same moment, a peal of thunder which shook Diamond's heart against the sides of his bosom hurtled out of the heavens: I cannot say out of the sky, for there was no sky. Diamond had not seen the lightning, for he had been intent on finding the face of North Wind. Every moment the folds of her garment would sweep across his eyes and blind him, but between, he could just persuade himself that he saw great glories of woman's eyes looking down through rifts in the mountainous clouds over his head.

He trembled so at the thunder, that his knees failed him, and he sunk down at North Wind's feet, and clasped her round the column of her ankle. She instantly stooped, lifted him from the roof—up—up into her bosom, and held him there, saying, as if to an inconsolable child—

"Diamond, dear, this will never do."

"Oh yes, it will," answered Diamond. "I am all right now—quite comfortable, I assure you, dear North Wind. If you will only let me stay here, I shall be all right indeed."

"But you will feel the wind here, Diamond."

"I don't mind that a bit, so long as I feel your arms through it," answered Diamond, nestling closer to her grand bosom.

"Brave boy!" returned North Wind, pressing him closer.

"No," said Diamond, "I don't see that. It's not courage at all, so long as I feel you there."

"But hadn't you better get into my hair? Then you would not feel the wind; you will here."

"Ah, but, dear North Wind, you don't know how nice it is to feel your arms about me. It is a thousand times better to have them and the wind together, than to have only your hair and the back of your neck and no wind at all."

"But it is surely more comfortable there?"

"Well, perhaps; but I begin to think there are better things than being comfortable."

"Yes, indeed there are. Well, I will keep you in front of me. You will feel the wind, but not too much. I shall only want one arm to take care of you; the other will be quite enough to sink the ship."

"Oh, dear North Wind! how can you talk so?"

"My dear boy, I never talk; I always mean what I say."

"Then you do mean to sink the ship with the other hand?"

"Yes."

"It's not like you."

"How do you know that?"

"Quite easily. Here you are taking care of a poor little boy with one arm, and there you are sinking a ship with the other. It can't be like you."

"Ah! but which is me? I can't be two mes, you know."

"No. Nobody can be two mes."

"Well, which me is me?"

"Now I must think. There looks to be two."

"Yes. That's the very point.—You can't be knowing the thing you don't know, can you?"

"No."

"Which me do you know?"

"The kindest, goodest, best me in the world," answered Diamond, clinging to North Wind.

"Why am I good to you?"

"I don't know."

"Have you ever done anything for me?"

"No."

"Then I must be good to you because I choose to be good to you."

"Yes."

"Why should I choose?"

"Because—because—because you like."

"Why should I like to be good to you?"

"I don't know, except it be because it's good to be good to me."

"That's just it; I am good to you because I like to be good."

"Then why shouldn't you be good to other people as well as to me?"

"That's just what I don't know. Why shouldn't I?"

"I don't know either. Then why shouldn't you?"

"Because I am."

"There it is again," said Diamond. "I don't see that you are. It looks quite the other thing."

"Well, but listen to me, Diamond. You know the one me, you say, and that is good."

"Yes."

"Do you know the other me as well?"

"No. I can't. I shouldn't like to."

"There it is. You don't know the other me. You are sure of one of them?"

"Yes."

"And you are sure there can't be two mes?"

"Yes."

"Then the me you don't know must be the same as the me you do know,—else there would be two mes?"

"Yes."

"Then the other me you don't know must be as kind as the me you do know?"

"Yes."

"Besides, I tell you that it is so, only it doesn't look like it. That I confess freely. Have you anything more to object?"

"No, no, dear North Wind; I am quite satisfied."

"Then I will tell you something you might object. You might say that the me you know is like the other me, and that I am cruel all through."

"I know that can't be, because you are so kind."

"But that kindness might be only a pretence for the sake of being more cruel afterwards."

Diamond clung to her tighter than ever, crying—

"No, no, dear North Wind; I can't believe that. I don't believe it. I won't believe it. That would kill me. I love you, and you must love me, else how did I come to love you? How could you know how to put on such a beautiful face if you did not love me and the rest? No. You may sink as many ships as you like, and I won't say another word. I can't say I shall like to see it, you know."

"That's quite another thing," said North Wind; and as she spoke she gave one spring from the roof of the hay-loft, and rushed up into the clouds, with Diamond on her left arm close to her heart. And as if the clouds knew she had come, they burst into a fresh jubilation of thunderous light. For a few moments, Diamond seemed to be borne up through the depths of an ocean of dazzling flame; the next, the winds were writhing around him like a storm of serpents. For they were in the midst of the clouds and mists, and they of course took the shapes of the wind, eddying and wreathing and whirling and shooting and dashing about like grey and black water, so that it was as if the wind itself had taken shape, and he saw the grey and black wind tossing and raving most madly all about him. Now it blinded him by smiting him upon the eyes; now it deafened him by bellowing in his ears; for even when the thunder came he knew now that it was the billows of the great ocean of the air dashing against each other in their haste to fill the hollow scooped out by the lightning; now it took his breath quite away by sucking it from his body with the speed of its rush. But he did not mind it. He only gasped first and then laughed, for the arm of North Wind was about him, and he was leaning against her bosom. It is quite impossible for me to describe what he saw. Did you ever watch a great wave shoot into a winding passage amongst rocks? If you ever did, you would see that the water rushed every way at once, some of it even turning back and opposing the rest; greater confusion you might see nowhere except in a crowd of frightened people. Well, the wind was like that, except that it went much faster, and therefore was much wilder, and twisted and shot and curled and dodged and clashed and raved ten times more madly than anything

else in creation except human passions. Diamond saw the threads of
the lady's hair streaking it all. In parts indeed he could not tell which
was hair and which was black storm and vapour. It seemed sometimes
that all the great billows of mist-muddy wind were woven out of the
crossing lines of North Wind's infinite hair, sweeping in endless
intertwistings. And Diamond felt as the wind seized on his hair, which
his mother kept rather long, as if he too was a part of the storm, and
some of its life went out from him. But so sheltered was he by North
Wind's arm and bosom that only at times, in the fiercer onslaught of
some curl-billowed eddy, did he recognise for a moment how wild was
the storm in which he was carried, nestling in its very core and for-
mative centre.

It seemed to Diamond likewise that they were motionless in this
centre, and that all the confusion and fighting went on around them.
Flash after flash illuminated the fierce chaos, revealing in varied yellow
and blue and grey and dusky red the vapourous contention; peal after
peal of thunder tore the infinite waste; but it seemed to Diamond that
North Wind and he were motionless, all but the hair. It was not so.
They were sweeping with the speed of the wind itself towards the sea.

7
The Cathedral

I must not go on describing what cannot be described, for nothing is more wearisome.

Before they reached the sea, Diamond felt North Wind's hair just beginning to fall about him.

"Is the storm over, North Wind?" he called out.

"No, Diamond. I am only waiting a moment to set you down. You would not like to see the ship sunk, and I am going to give you a place to stop in till I come back for you."

"Oh! thank you," said Diamond. "I shall be sorry to leave you, North Wind, but I would rather not see the ship go down. And I'm afraid the poor people will cry, and I should hear them. Oh, dear!"

"There are a good many passengers on board; and to tell the truth, Diamond, I don't care about your hearing the cry you speak of. I am afraid you would not get it out of your little head again for a long time."

"But how can you bear it then, North Wind? For I am sure you are kind. I shall never doubt that again."

"I will tell you how I am able to bear it, Diamond: I am always hearing, through every noise, through all the noise I am making myself even, the sound of a far-off song. I do not exactly know where it is, or what it means; and I don't hear much of it, only the odour of its music, as it were, flitting across the great billows of the ocean outside this air in which I make such a storm; but what I do hear is quite enough to make me able to bear the cry from the drowning ship. So it would you if you could hear it."

"No, it wouldn't," returned Diamond, stoutly. "For they wouldn't hear the music of the far-away song; and if they did, it wouldn't do them any good. You see you and I are not going to be drowned, and so we might enjoy it."

"But you have never heard the psalm, and you don't know what it is like. Somehow, I can't say how, it tells me that all is right; that it is coming to swallow up all cries."

"But that won't do them any good—the people, I mean," persisted Diamond.

"It must. It must," said North Wind, hurriedly. "It wouldn't be the song it seems to be if it did not swallow up all their fear and pain too, and set them singing it themselves with the rest. I am sure it will. And do you know, ever since I knew I had hair, that is, ever since it began to go out and away, that song has been coming nearer and nearer. Only I must say it was some thousand years before I heard it."

"But how can you say it was coming nearer when you did not hear it?" asked doubting little Diamond.

"Since I began to hear it, I know it is growing louder, therefore I judge it was coming nearer and nearer until I did hear it first. I'm not so very old, you know—a few thousand years only—and I was quite a baby when I heard the noise first, but I knew it must come from the voices of people ever so much older and wiser than I was. I can't sing at all, except now and then, and I can never tell what my song is going to be; I only know what it is after I have sung it.—But this will never do. Will you stop here?"

"I can't see anywhere to stop," said Diamond. "Your hair is all down like a darkness, and I can't see through it if I knock my eyes into it ever so much."

"Look, then," said North Wind; and, with one sweep of her great white arm, she swept yards deep of darkness like a great curtain from before the face of the boy.

And lo! it was a blue night, lit up with stars. Where it did not shine with stars it shimmered with the milk of the stars, except where, just opposite to Diamond's face, the grey towers of a cathedral blotted out each its own shape of sky and stars.

"Oh! what's that?" cried Diamond, struck with a kind of terror, for he had never seen a cathedral, and it rose before him with an awful reality in the midst of the wide spaces, conquering emptiness with grandeur.

"A very good place for you to wait in," said North Wind. "But we shall go in, and you shall judge for yourself."

There was an open door in the middle of one of the towers, leading out upon the roof, and through it they passed. Then North Wind set Diamond on his feet, and he found himself at the top of a stone stair, which went twisting away down into the darkness for only a little light came in at the door. It was enough, however, to allow Diamond to see that North Wind stood beside him. He looked up to find her face, and saw that she was no longer a beautiful giantess, but the tall gracious lady he liked best to see. She took his hand, and, giving him the broad part of the spiral stair to walk on, led him down a good way; then, opening another little door, led him out upon a narrow gallery that ran all round the central part of the church, on the ledges of the windows of the clerestory, and through openings in the parts of the wall that divided the windows from each other. It was very narrow, and except when they were passing through the wall, Diamond saw nothing to keep him from falling into the church. It lay below him like a great silent gulf hollowed in stone, and he held his breath for fear as he looked down.

"What are you trembling for, little Diamond?" said the lady, as she walked gently along, with her hand held out behind her leading him, for there was not breadth enough for them to walk side by side.

"I am afraid of falling down there," answered Diamond. "It is so deep down."

"Yes, rather," answered North Wind; "but you were a hundred times higher a few minutes ago."

"Ah, yes, but somebody's arm was about me then," said Diamond, putting his little mouth to the beautiful cold hand that had a hold of his.

"What a dear little warm mouth you've got!" said North Wind. "It is a pity you should talk nonsense with it. Don't you know I have a hold of you?"

"Yes; but I'm walking on my own legs, and they might slip. I can't trust myself so well as your arms."

"But I have a hold of you, I tell you, foolish child."

"Yes, but somehow I can't feel comfortable."

"If you were to fall, and my hold of you were to give way, I should be down after you in a less moment than a lady's watch can tick, and catch you long before you had reached the ground."

"I don't like it though," said Diamond.

"Oh! oh! oh!" he screamed the next moment, bent double with terror, for North Wind had let go her hold of his hand, and had vanished, leaving him standing as if rooted to the gallery.

She left the words, "Come after me," sounding in his ears.

But move he dared not. In a moment more he would from very terror have fallen into the church, but suddenly there came a gentle breath of cool wind upon his face, and it kept blowing upon him in little puffs, and at every puff Diamond felt his faintness going away, and his fear with it. Courage was reviving in his little heart, and still the cool wafts of the soft wind breathed upon him, and the soft wind was so mighty and strong within its gentleness, that in a minute more Diamond was marching along the narrow ledge as fearless for the time as North Wind herself.

He walked on and on, with the windows all in a row on one side of him, and the great empty nave of the church echoing to every one of his brave strides on the other, until at last he came to a little open door, from which a broader stair led him down and down and down, till at last all at once he found himself in the arms of North Wind, who held him close to her, and kissed him on the forehead. Diamond nestled to her, and murmured into her bosom,— "Why did you leave me, dear North Wind?"

"Because I wanted you to walk alone," she answered.

"But it is so much nicer here!" said Diamond.

"I daresay; but I couldn't hold a little coward to my heart. It would make me so cold!"

"But I wasn't brave of myself," said Diamond, whom my older readers will have already discovered to be a true child in this, that he was given to metaphysics. "It was the wind that blew in my face that made me brave. Wasn't it now, North Wind?"

"Yes: I know that. You had to be taught what courage was. And you couldn't know what it was without feeling it: therefore it was given you. But don't you feel as if you would try to be brave yourself next time?"

"Yes, I do. But trying is not much."

"Yes, it is—a very great deal, for it is a beginning. And a beginning is the greatest thing of all. To try to be brave is to be brave. The coward who tries to be brave is before the man who is brave because he is made so, and never had to try."

"How kind you are, North Wind!"

"I am only just. All kindness is but justice. We owe it."

"I don't quite understand that."

"Never mind; you will some day. There is no hurry about understanding it now."

"Who blew the wind on me that made me brave?"

"I did."

"I didn't see you."

"Therefore you can believe me."

"Yes, yes; of course. But how was it that such a little breath could be so strong?"

"That I don't know."

"But you made it strong?"

"No: I only blew it. I knew it would make you strong, just as it did the man in the boat, you remember. But how my breath has that power I cannot tell. It was put into it when I was made. That is all I know. But really I must be going about my work."

"Ah! the poor ship! I wish you would stop here, and let the poor ship go."

"That I dare not do. Will you stop here till I come back?"

"Yes. You won't be long?"

"Not longer than I can help. Trust me, you shall get home before the morning."

In a moment North Wind was gone, and the next Diamond heard a moaning about the church, which grew and grew to a roaring. The storm was up again, and he knew that North Wind's hair was flying.

The church was dark. Only a little light came through the windows, which were almost all of that precious old stained glass which is so much lovelier than the new. But Diamond could not see how beautiful they were, for there was not enough of light in the stars to show the colours of them. He could only just distinguish them from the walls, He looked up, but could not see the gallery along which he had passed. He could only tell where it was far up by the faint glimmer of the windows of the clerestory, whose sills made part of it. The church grew very lonely about him, and he began to feel like a child whose mother has forsaken it. Only he knew that to be left alone is not always to be forsaken.

He began to feel his way about the place, and for a while went wandering up and down. His little footsteps waked little answering echoes in the great house. It wasn't too big to mind him. It was as if the church knew he was there, and meant to make itself his house. So it went on giving back an answer to every step, until at length Diamond thought he should like to say something out loud, and see what the church would answer. But he found he was afraid to speak. He could not utter a word for fear of the loneliness. Perhaps it was as well that he did not, for the sound of a spoken word would have made him feel the place yet more deserted and empty. But he thought he could sing. He was fond of singing, and at home he used to sing, to tunes of his own, all the nursery rhymes he knew. So he began to try 'Hey diddle diddle', but it wouldn't do. Then he tried 'Little Boy Blue', but it was no better. Neither would 'Sing a Song of Sixpence' sing itself at all. Then he tried 'Poor old Cockytoo', but he wouldn't do. They all sounded so silly! and he had never thought them silly before. So he was quiet, and listened to the echoes that came out of the dark corners in answer to his footsteps.

At last he gave a great sigh, and said, "I'm so tired." But he did not hear the gentle echo that answered from far away over his head, for at the same moment he came against the lowest of a few steps that stretched across the church, and fell down and hurt his arm. He cried a little first, and then crawled up the steps on his hands and knees. At the top he came to a little bit of carpet, on which he lay down; and there he lay staring at the dull window that rose nearly a hundred feet above his head.

Now this was the eastern window of the church, and the moon was at that moment just on the edge of the horizon. The next, she was peeping over it. And lo! with the moon, St. John and St. Paul, and the rest of them, began to dawn in the window in their lovely garments. Diamond did not know that the wonder-working moon was behind, and he thought all the light was coming out of the window itself, and that the good old men were appearing to help him, growing out of the night and the darkness, because he had hurt his arm, and was very tired and lonely, and North Wind was so long in coming. So he lay and looked at them backwards over his head, wondering when they would come down or what they would do next. They were very dim, for the moonlight was not strong enough for the colours, and he had enough to do with his eyes trying to make out their shapes. So his eyes grew tired, and more and more tired, and his eyelids grew so heavy that they would keep tumbling down over his eyes. He kept lifting them and lifting them, but every time they were heavier than the last. It was no use: they were too much for him. Sometimes before he had got them half up, down they were again; and at length he gave it up quite, and the moment he gave it up, he was fast asleep.

8
The East Window

That Diamond had fallen fast asleep is very evident from the strange things he now fancied as taking place. For he thought he heard a sound as of whispering up in the great window. He tried to open his eyes, but he could not. And the whispering went on and grew louder and louder, until he could hear every word that was said. He thought it was the Apostles talking about him. But he could not open his eyes.

"And how comes he to be lying there, St. Peter?" said one.

"I think I saw him a while ago up in the gallery, under the Nicodemus window. Perhaps he has fallen down.

"What do you think, St. Matthew?"

"I don't think he could have crept here after falling from such a height. He must have been killed."

"What are we to do with him? We can't leave him lying there. And we could not make him comfortable up here in the window: it's rather crowded already. What do you say, St. Thomas?"

"Let's go down and look at him."

There came a rustling, and a chinking, for some time, and then there was a silence, and Diamond felt somehow that all the Apostles were standing round him and looking down on him. And still he could not open his eyes.

"What is the matter with him, St. Luke?" asked one.

"There's nothing the matter with him," answered St. Luke, who must have joined the company of the Apostles from the next window, one would think. "He's in a sound sleep."

"I have it," cried another. "This is one of North Wind's tricks. She has caught him up and dropped him at our door, like a withered leaf or a foundling baby. I don't understand that woman's conduct, I must say. As if we hadn't enough to do with our money, without going taking care of other people's children! That's not what our forefathers built cathedrals for."

Now Diamond could not bear to hear such things against North Wind, who, he knew, never played anybody a trick. She was far too busy with her own work for that. He struggled hard to open his eyes, but without success.

"She should consider that a church is not a place for pranks, not to mention that we live in it," said another.

"It certainly is disrespectful of her. But she always is disrespectful. What right has she to bang at our windows as she has been doing the whole of this night? I daresay there is glass broken somewhere. I know my blue robe is in a dreadful mess with the rain first and the dust after. It will cost me shillings to clean it."

Then Diamond knew that they could not be Apostles, talking like this. They could only be the sextons and vergers and such-like, who got up at night, and put on the robes of deans and bishops, and called each other grand names, as the foolish servants he had heard his father tell of call themselves lords and ladies, after their masters and mistresses. And he was so angry at their daring to abuse North Wind, that he jumped up, crying— "North Wind knows best what she is about. She has a good right to blow the cobwebs from your windows, for she was sent to do it. She sweeps them away from grander places, I can tell you, for I've been with her at it."

This was what he began to say, but as he spoke his eyes came wide open, and behold, there were neither Apostles nor vergers there—not even a window with the effigies of holy men in it, but a dark heap of hay all about him, and the little panes in the roof of his loft glimmering blue in the light of the morning. Old Diamond was coming awake down below in the stable. In a moment more he was on his feet, and shaking himself so that young Diamond's bed trembled under him.

"He's grand at shaking himself," said Diamond. "I wish I could shake myself like that. But then I can wash myself, and he can't. What fun it would be to see Old Diamond washing his face with his hoofs and iron shoes! Wouldn't it be a picture?"

So saying, he got up and dressed himself. Then he went out into the garden. There must have been a tremendous wind in the night, for although all was quiet now, there lay the little summer-house crushed to the ground, and over it the great elm-tree, which the wind had broken across, being much decayed in the middle. Diamond almost cried to see the wilderness of green leaves, which used to be so far up in the blue air, tossing about in the breeze, and liking it best when the wind blew it most, now lying so near the ground, and without any hope of ever getting up into the deep air again.

"I wonder how old the tree is!" thought Diamond. "It must take a long time to get so near the sky as that poor tree was."

"Yes, indeed," said a voice beside him, for Diamond had spoken the last words aloud.

Diamond started, and looking around saw a clergyman, a brother of Mrs. Coleman, who happened to be visiting her. He was a great scholar, and was in the habit of rising early.

"Who are you, my man?" he added.

"Little Diamond," answered the boy.

"Oh! I have heard of you. How do you come to be up so early?"

"Because the sham Apostles talked such nonsense, they waked me up."

The clergyman stared. Diamond saw that he had better have held his tongue, for he could not explain things.

"You must have been dreaming, my little man," said he. "Dear! dear!" he went on, looking at the tree, "there has been terrible work here. This is the north wind's doing. What a pity! I wish we lived at the back of it, I'm sure."

"Where is that sir?" asked Diamond.

"Away in the Hyperborean regions," answered the clergyman, smiling.

"I never heard of the place," returned Diamond.

"I daresay not," answered the clergyman; "but if this tree had been there now, it would not have been blown down, for there is no wind there."

"But, please, sir, if it had been there," said Diamond, "we should not have had to be sorry for it."

"Certainly not."

"Then we shouldn't have had to be glad for it, either."

"You're quite right, my boy," said the clergyman, looking at him very kindly, as he turned away to the house, with his eyes bent towards the earth. But Diamond thought within himself, "I will ask North Wind next time I see her to take me to that country. I think she did speak about it once before."

9

How Diamond Got to the Back of the North Wind

When Diamond went home to breakfast, he found his father and mother already seated at the table. They were both busy with their bread and butter, and Diamond sat himself down in his usual place. His mother looked up at him, and, after watching him for a moment, said:

"I don't think the boy is looking well, husband."

"Don't you? Well, I don't know. I think he looks pretty bobbish. How do you feel yourself, Diamond, my boy?"

"Quite well, thank you, father; at least, I think I've got a little headache."

"There! I told you," said his father and mother both at once.

"The child's very poorly" added his mother.

"The child's quite well," added his father.

And then they both laughed.

"You see," said his mother, "I've had a letter from my sister at Sandwich."

"Sleepy old hole!" said his father.

"Don't abuse the place; there's good people in it," said his mother.

"Right, old lady," returned his father; "only I don't believe there are more than two pair of carriage-horses in the whole blessed place."

"Well, people can get to heaven without carriages—or coachmen either, husband. Not that I should like to go without my coachman, you know. But about the boy?"

"What boy?"

"That boy, there, staring at you with his goggle-eyes."

"Have I got goggle-eyes, mother?" asked Diamond, a little dismayed.

"Not too goggle," said his mother, who was quite proud of her boy's eyes, only did not want to make him vain.

"Not too goggle; only you need not stare so."

"Well, what about him?" said his father.

"I told you I had got a letter."

"Yes, from your sister; not from Diamond."

"La, husband! you've got out of bed the wrong leg first this morning, I do believe."

"I always get out with both at once," said his father, laughing.

"Well, listen then. His aunt wants the boy to go down and see her."

"And that's why you want to make out that he ain't looking well."

"No more he is. I think he had better go."

"Well, I don't care, if you can find the money," said his father.

"I'll manage that," said his mother; and so it was agreed that Diamond should go to Sandwich.

I will not describe the preparations Diamond made. You would have thought he had been going on a three months' voyage. Nor will I describe the journey, for our business is now at the place. He was met at the station by his aunt, a cheerful middle-aged woman, and conveyed in safety to the sleepy old town, as his father called it. And no wonder that it was sleepy, for it was nearly dead of old age.

Diamond went about staring with his beautiful goggle-eyes, at the quaint old streets, and the shops, and the houses. Everything looked very strange, indeed; for here was a town abandoned by its nurse, the sea, like an old oyster left on the shore till it gaped for weariness. It used to be one of the five chief seaports in England, but it began to hold itself too high, and the consequence was the sea grew less and less intimate with it, gradually drew back, and kept more to itself, till at length it left it high and dry: Sandwich was a seaport no more; the sea went on with its own tide-business a long way off, and forgot it. Of course it went to sleep, and had no more to do with ships. That's what comes to cities and nations, and boys and girls, who say, "I can do without your help. I'm enough for myself."

Diamond soon made great friends with an old woman who kept a toyshop, for his mother had given him twopence for pocket-money before he left, and he had gone into her shop to spend it, and she got talking to him. She looked very funny, because she had not got any teeth, but Diamond liked her, and went often to her shop, although he had nothing to spend there after the twopence was gone.

One afternoon he had been wandering rather wearily about the streets for some time. It was a hot day, and he felt tired. As he passed the toyshop, he stepped in.

"Please may I sit down for a minute on this box?" he said, thinking the old woman was somewhere in the shop. But he got no answer, and sat down without one. Around him were a great many toys of all prices, from a penny up to shillings. All at once he heard a gentle whirring somewhere amongst them. It made him start and look behind

him. There were the sails of a windmill going round and round almost close to his ear. He thought at first it must be one of those toys
which are wound up and go with clockwork; but no, it was a common
penny toy, with the windmill at the end of a whistle, and when the
whistle blows the windmill goes. But the wonder was that there was
no one at the whistle end blowing, and yet the sails were turning round
and round—now faster, now slower, now faster again.

"What can it mean?" said Diamond, aloud.

"It means me," said the tiniest voice he had ever heard.

"Who are you, please?" asked Diamond.

"Well, really, I begin to be ashamed of you," said the voice. "I
wonder how long it will be before you know me; or how often I might
take you in before you got sharp enough to suspect me. You are as
bad as a baby that doesn't know his mother in a new bonnet."

"Not quite so bad as that, dear North Wind," said Diamond, "for I
didn't see you at all, and indeed I don't see you yet, although I
recognise your voice. Do grow a little, please."

"Not a hair's-breadth," said the voice, and it was the smallest voice
that ever spoke. "What are you doing here?"

"I am come to see my aunt. But, please, North Wind, why didn't
you come back for me in the church that night?"

"I did. I carried you safe home. All the time you were dreaming
about the glass Apostles, you were lying in my arms."

"I'm so glad," said Diamond. "I thought that must be it, only I
wanted to hear you say so. Did you sink the ship, then?"

"Yes."

"And drown everybody?"

"Not quite. One boat got away with six or seven men in it."

"How could the boat swim when the ship couldn't?"

"Of course I had some trouble with it. I had to contrive a bit, and
manage the waves a little. When they're once thoroughly waked up, I
have a good deal of trouble with them sometimes. They're apt to get
stupid with tumbling over each other's heads. That's when they're
fairly at it. However, the boat got to a desert island before noon next
day."

"And what good will come of that?"

"I don't know. I obeyed orders. Good bye."

"Oh! stay, North Wind, do stay!" cried Diamond, dismayed to see
the windmill get slower and slower.

"What is it, my dear child?" said North Wind, and the windmill
began turning again so swiftly that Diamond could scarcely see it.
"What a big voice you've got! and what a noise you do make with it?
What is it you want? I have little to do, but that little must be done."

"I want you to take me to the country at the back of the north wind."

"That's not so easy," said North Wind, and was silent for so long that Diamond thought she was gone indeed. But after he had quite given her up, the voice began again.

"I almost wish old Herodotus had held his tongue about it. Much he knew of it!"

"Why do you wish that, North Wind?"

"Because then that clergyman would never have heard of it, and set you wanting to go. But we shall see. We shall see. You must go home now, my dear, for you don't seem very well, and I'll see what can be done for you. Don't wait for me. I've got to break a few of old Goody's toys; she's thinking too much of her new stock. Two or three will do. There! go now."

Diamond rose, quite sorry, and without a word left the shop, and went home.

It soon appeared that his mother had been right about him, for that same afternoon his head began to ache very much, and he had to go to bed.

He awoke in the middle of the night. The lattice window of his room had blown open, and the curtains of his little bed were swinging about in the wind.

"If that should be North Wind now!" thought Diamond.

But the next moment he heard some one closing the window, and his aunt came to his bedside. She put her hand on his face, and said—

"How's your head, dear?"

"Better, auntie, I think."

"Would you like something to drink?"

"Oh, yes! I should, please."

So his aunt gave him some lemonade, for she had been used to nursing sick people, and Diamond felt very much refreshed, and laid his head down again to go very fast asleep, as he thought. And so he did, but only to come awake again, as a fresh burst of wind blew the lattice open a second time. The same moment he found himself in a cloud of North Wind's hair, with her beautiful face, set in it like a moon, bending over him.

"Quick, Diamond!" she said. "I have found such a chance!"

"But I'm not well," said Diamond.

"I know that, but you will be better for a little fresh air. You shall have plenty of that."

"You want me to go, then?"

"Yes, I do. It won't hurt you."

"Very well," said Diamond; and getting out of the bed-clothes, he jumped into North Wind's arms.

"We must make haste before your aunt comes," said she, as she glided out of the open lattice and left it swinging.

The moment Diamond felt her arms fold around him he began to feel better. It was a moonless night, and very dark, with glimpses of stars when the clouds parted.

"I used to dash the waves about here," said North Wind, "where cows and sheep are feeding now; but we shall soon get to them. There they are."

And Diamond, looking down, saw the white glimmer of breaking water far below him.

"You see, Diamond," said North Wind, "it is very difficult for me to get you to the back of the north wind, for that country lies in the very north itself, and of course I can't blow northwards."

"Why not?" asked Diamond.

"You little silly!" said North Wind. "Don't you see that if I were to blow northwards I should be South Wind, and that is as much as to say that one person could be two persons?"

"But how can you ever get home at all, then?"

"You are quite right—that is my home, though I never get farther than the outer door. I sit on the doorstep, and hear the voices inside. I am nobody there, Diamond."

"I'm very sorry."

"Why?"

"That you should be nobody."

"Oh, I don't mind it. Dear little man! you will be very glad some day to be nobody yourself. But you can't understand that now, and you had better not try; for if you do, you will be certain to go fancying some egregious nonsense, and making yourself miserable about it."

"Then I won't," said Diamond.

"There's a good boy. It will all come in good time."

"But you haven't told me how you get to the doorstep, you know."

"It is easy enough for me. I have only to consent to be nobody, and there I am. I draw into myself and there I am on the doorstep. But you can easily see, or you have less sense than I think, that to drag you, you heavy thing, along with me, would take centuries, and I could not give the time to it."

"Oh, I'm so sorry!" said Diamond.

"What for now, pet?"

"That I'm so heavy for you. I would be lighter if I could, but I don't know how."

"You silly darling! Why, I could toss you a hundred miles from me if I liked. It is only when I am going home that I shall find you heavy."

"Then you are going home with me?"

"Of course. Did I not come to fetch you just for that?"

"But all this time you must be going southwards."

"Yes. Of course I am."

"How can you be taking me northwards, then?"

"A very sensible question. But you shall see. I will get rid of a few of these clouds—only they do come up so fast! It's like trying to blow a brook dry. There! What do you see now?"

"I think I see a little boat, away there, down below."

"A little boat, indeed! Well! She's a yacht of two hundred tons; and the captain of it is a friend of mine; for he is a man of good sense, and can sail his craft well. I've helped him many a time when he little thought it. I've heard him grumbling at me, when I was doing the very best I could for him. Why, I've carried him eighty miles a day, again and again, right north."

"He must have dodged for that," said Diamond, who had been watching the vessels, and had seen that they went other ways than the wind blew.

"Of course he must. But don't you see, it was the best I could do? I couldn't be South Wind. And besides it gave him a share in the business. It is not good at all—mind that, Diamond—to do everything for those you love, and not give them a share in the doing. It's not kind. It's making too much of yourself, my child. If I had been South Wind, he would only have smoked his pipe all day, and made himself stupid."

"But how could he be a man of sense and grumble at you when you were doing your best for him?"

"Oh! you must make allowances," said North Wind, "or you will never do justice to anybody.—You do understand, then, that a captain may sail north—"

"In spite of a north wind—yes," supplemented Diamond.

"Now, I do think you must be stupid, my dear" said North Wind. "Suppose the north wind did not blow where would he be then?"

"Why then the south wind would carry him."

"So you think that when the north wind stops the south wind blows. Nonsense. If I didn't blow, the captain couldn't sail his eighty miles a day. No doubt South Wind would carry him faster, but South Wind is sitting on her doorstep then, and if I stopped there would be a dead calm. So you are all wrong to say he can sail north in spite of me; he sails north by my help, and my help alone. You see that, Diamond?"

"Yes, I do, North Wind. I am stupid, but I don't want to be stupid."

"Good boy! I am going to blow you north in that little craft, one of the finest that ever sailed the sea. Here we are, right over it. I shall be blowing against you; you will be sailing against me; and all will be just as we want it. The captain won't get on so fast as he would like, but he will get on, and so shall we. I'm just going to put you on board. Do you see in front of the tiller—that thing the man is working, now to one side, now to the other—a round thing like the top of a drum?"

"Yes," said Diamond.

"Below that is where they keep their spare sails, and some stores of that sort. I am going to blow that cover off. The same moment I will drop you on deck, and you must tumble in. Don't be afraid, it is of no depth, and you will fall on sail-cloth. You will find it nice and warm and dry-only dark; and you will know I am near you by every roll and pitch of the vessel. Coil yourself up and go to sleep. The yacht shall be my cradle and you shall be my baby."

"Thank you, dear North Wind. I am not a bit afraid," said Diamond.

In a moment they were on a level with the bulwarks, and North Wind sent the hatch of the after-store rattling away over the deck to leeward. The next, Diamond found himself in the dark, for he had tumbled through the hole as North Wind had told him, and the cover was replaced over his head. Away he went rolling to leeward, for the wind began all at once to blow hard. He heard the call of the captain, and the loud trampling of the men over his head, as they hauled at the main sheet to get the boom on board that they might take in a reef in the mainsail. Diamond felt about until he had found what seemed the most comfortable place, and there he snuggled down and lay.

Hours after hours, a great many of them, went by; and still Diamond lay there. He never felt in the least tired or impatient, for a strange pleasure filled his heart. The straining of the masts, the creaking of the boom, the singing of the ropes, the banging of the blocks as they put the vessel about, all fell in with the roaring of the wind above, the surge of the waves past her sides, and the thud with which every now and then one would strike her; while through it all Diamond could hear the gurgling, rippling, talking flow of the water against her planks, as she slipped through it, lying now on this side, now on that—like a subdued air running through the grand music his North Wind was making about him to keep him from tiring as they sped on towards the country at the back of her doorstep.

How long this lasted Diamond had no idea. He seemed to fall asleep sometimes, only through the sleep he heard the sounds going on. At length the weather seemed to get worse. The confusion and trampling of feet grew more frequent over his head; the vessel lay over more and more on her side, and went roaring through the waves,

which banged and thumped at her as if in anger. All at once arose a
terrible uproar. The hatch was blown off; a cold fierce wind swept in
upon him; and a long arm came with it which laid hold of him and
lifted him out. The same moment he saw the little vessel far below
him righting herself. She had taken in all her sails and lay now tossing on the waves like a sea-bird with folded wings. A short distance
to the south lay a much larger vessel, with two or three sails set, and
towards it North Wind was carrying Diamond. It was a German ship,
on its way to the North Pole.

"That vessel down there will give us a lift now," said North Wind;
"and after that I must do the best I can."

She managed to hide him amongst the flags of the big ship, which
were all snugly stowed away, and on and on they sped towards the
north. At length one night she whispered in his ear, "Come on deck,
Diamond;" and he got up at once and crept on deck. Everything looked
very strange. Here and there on all sides were huge masses of floating ice, looking like cathedrals, and castles, and crags, while away
beyond was a blue sea.

"Is the sun rising or setting?" asked Diamond.

"Neither or both, which you please. I can hardly tell which myself. If he is setting now, he will be rising the next moment."

"What a strange light it is!" said Diamond. "I have heard that the
sun doesn't go to bed all the summer in these parts. Miss Coleman
told me that. I suppose he feels very sleepy, and that is why the light
he sends out looks so like a dream."

"That will account for it well enough for all practical purposes,"
said North Wind.

Some of the icebergs were drifting northwards; one was passing
very near the ship. North Wind seized Diamond, and with a single
bound lighted on one of them—a huge thing, with sharp pinnacles
and great clefts. The same instant a wind began to blow from the
south. North Wind hurried Diamond down the north side of the iceberg, stepping by its jags and splintering; for this berg had never got
far enough south to be melted and smoothed by the summer sun. She
brought him to a cave near the water, where she entered, and, letting
Diamond go, sat down as if weary on a ledge of ice.

Diamond seated himself on the other side, and for a while was
enraptured with the colour of the air inside the cave. It was a deep,
dazzling, lovely blue, deeper than the deepest blue of the sky. The
blue seemed to be in constant motion, like the blackness when you
press your eyeballs with your fingers, boiling and sparkling. But when
he looked across to North Wind he was frightened; her face was worn
and livid.

"What is the matter with you, dear North Wind?" he said.

"Nothing much. I feel very faint. But you mustn't mind it, for I can bear it quite well. South Wind always blows me faint. If it were not for the cool of the thick ice between me and her, I should faint altogether. Indeed, as it is, I fear I must vanish."

Diamond stared at her in terror, for he saw that her form and face were growing, not small, but transparent, like something dissolving, not in water, but in light. He could see the side of the blue cave through her very heart. And she melted away till all that was left was a pale face, like the moon in the morning, with two great lucid eyes in it.

"I am going, Diamond," she said.

"Does it hurt you?" asked Diamond.

"It's very uncomfortable," she answered; "but I don't mind it, for I shall come all right again before long. I thought I should be able to go with you all the way, but I cannot. You must not be frightened though. Just go straight on, and you will come all right. You'll find me on the doorstep."

As she spoke, her face too faded quite away, only Diamond thought he could still see her eyes shining through the blue. When he went closer, however, he found that what he thought her eyes were only two hollows in the ice. North Wind was quite gone; and Diamond would have cried, if he had not trusted her so thoroughly. So he sat still in the blue air of the cavern listening to the wash and ripple of the water all about the base of the iceberg, as it sped on and on into the open sea northwards. It was an excellent craft to go with the current, for there was twice as much of it below water as above. But a light south wind was blowing too, and so it went fast.

After a little while Diamond went out and sat on the edge of his floating island, and looked down into the ocean beneath him. The white sides of the berg reflected so much light below the water, that he could see far down into the green abyss. Sometimes he fancied he saw the eyes of North Wind looking up at him from below, but the fancy never lasted beyond the moment of its birth. And the time passed he did not know how, for he felt as if he were in a dream. When he got tired of the green water, he went into the blue cave; and when he got tired of the blue cave he went out and gazed all about him on the blue sea, ever sparkling in the sun, which kept wheeling about the sky, never going below the horizon. But he chiefly gazed northwards, to see whether any land were appearing. All this time he never wanted to eat. He broke off little bits of the berg now and then and sucked them, and he thought them very nice.

At length, one time he came out of his cave, he spied far off on the horizon, a shining peak that rose into the sky like the top of some tremendous iceberg; and his vessel was bearing him straight towards it. As it went on the peak rose and rose higher and higher above the horizon; and other peaks rose after it, with sharp edges and jagged ridges connecting them. Diamond thought this must be the place he was going to; and he was right; for the mountains rose and rose, till he saw the line of the coast at their feet and at length the iceberg drove into a little bay, all around which were lofty precipices with snow on their tops, and streaks of ice down their sides. The berg floated slowly up to a projecting rock. Diamond stepped on shore, and without looking behind him began to follow a natural path which led windingly towards the top of the precipice.

When he reached it, he found himself on a broad table of ice, along which he could walk without much difficulty. Before him, at a considerable distance, rose a lofty ridge of ice, which shot up into fantastic pinnacles and towers and battlements. The air was very cold, and seemed somehow dead, for there was not the slightest breath of wind.

In the centre of the ridge before him appeared a gap like the opening of a valley. But as he walked towards it, gazing, and wondering whether that could be the way he had to take, he saw that what had appeared a gap was the form of a woman seated against the ice front of the ridge, leaning forwards with her hands in her lap, and her hair hanging down to the ground.

"It is North Wind on her doorstep," said Diamond joyfully, and hurried on.

He soon came up to the place, and there the form sat, like one of the great figures at the door of an Egyptian temple, motionless, with drooping arms and head. Then Diamond grew frightened, because she did not move nor speak. He was sure it was North Wind, but he thought she must be dead at last. Her face was white as the snow, her eyes were blue as the air in the ice-cave, and her hair hung down straight, like icicles. She had on a greenish robe, like the colour in the hollows of a glacier seen from far off.

He stood up before her, and gazed fearfully into her face for a few minutes before he ventured to speak. At length, with a great effort and a trembling voice, he faltered out—

"North Wind!"

"Well, child?" said the form, without lifting its head.

"Are you ill, dear North Wind?"

"No. I am waiting."

"What for?"

"Till I'm wanted."

"You don't care for me any more," said Diamond, almost crying now.

"Yes I do. Only I can't show it. All my love is down at the bottom of my heart. But I feel it bubbling there."

"What do you want me to do next, dear North Wind?" said Diamond, wishing to show his love by being obedient.

"What do you want to do yourself?"

"I want to go into the country at your back."

"Then you must go through me."

"I don't know what you mean."

"I mean just what I say. You must walk on as if I were an open door, and go right through me."

"But that will hurt you."

"Not in the least. It will hurt you, though."

"I don't mind that, if you tell me to do it."

"Do it," said North Wind.

Diamond walked towards her instantly. When he reached her knees, he put out his hand to lay it on her, but nothing was there save an intense cold. He walked on. Then all grew white about him; and the cold stung him like fire. He walked on still, groping through the whiteness. It thickened about him. At last, it got into his heart, and he lost all sense. I would say that he fainted—only whereas in common faints all grows black about you, he felt swallowed up in whiteness. It was when he reached North Wind's heart that he fainted and fell. But as he fell, he rolled over the threshold, and it was thus that Diamond got to the back of the north wind.

10

At the Back of the North Wind

I have now come to the most difficult part of my story. And why? Because I do not know enough about it. And why should I not know as much about this part as about any other part? For of course I could know nothing about the story except Diamond had told it; and why should not Diamond tell about the country at the back of the north wind, as well as about his adventures in getting there? Because, when he came back, he had forgotten a great deal, and what he did remember was very hard to tell. Things there are so different from things here! The people there do not speak the same language for one thing. Indeed, Diamond insisted that there they do not speak at all. I do not think he was right, but it may well have appeared so to Diamond. The fact is, we have different reports of the place from the most trustworthy people. Therefore we are bound to believe that it appears somewhat different to different people. All, however, agree in a general way about it.

I will tell you something of what two very different people have reported, both of whom knew more about it, I believe, than Herodotus. One of them speaks from his own experience, for he visited the country; the other from the testimony of a young peasant girl who came back from it for a month's visit to her friends. The former was a great Italian of noble family, who died more than five hundred years ago; the latter a Scotch shepherd who died not forty years ago.

The Italian, then, informs us that he had to enter that country through a fire so hot that he would have thrown himself into boiling glass to cool himself. This was not Diamond's experience, but then Durante—that was the name of the Italian, and it means Lasting, for his books will last as long as there are enough men in the world worthy of having them—Durante was an elderly man, and Diamond was a little boy, and so their experience must be a little different. The peasant girl, on the other hand, fell fast asleep in a wood, and woke in the same country.

In describing it, Durante says that the ground everywhere smelt sweetly, and that a gentle, even-tempered wind, which never blew faster or slower, breathed in his face as he went, making all the leaves point one way, not so as to disturb the birds in the tops of the trees, but, on the contrary, sounding a bass to their song. He describes also a little river which was so full that its little waves, as it hurried along, bent the grass, full of red and yellow flowers, through which it flowed. He says that the purest stream in the world beside this one would look as if it were mixed with something that did not belong to it, even although it was flowing ever in the brown shadow of the trees, and neither sun nor moon could shine upon it. He seems to imply that it is always the month of May in that country. It would be out of place to describe here the wonderful sights he saw, for the music of them is in another key from that of this story, and I shall therefore only add from the account of this traveller, that the people there are so free and so just and so healthy, that every one of them has a crown like a king and a mitre like a priest.

The peasant girl—Kilmeny was her name—could not report such grand things as Durante, for, as the shepherd says, telling her story as I tell Diamond's—

> "Kilmeny had been she knew not where,
>   And Kilmeny had seen what she could not declare;
>   Kilmeny had been where the cock never crew,
>   Where the rain never fell, and the wind never blew.
>   But it seemed as the harp of the sky had rung,
>   And the airs of heaven played round her tongue,
>   When she spoke of the lovely forms she had seen,
>   And a land where sin had never been;
>   A land of love and a land of light,
>   Withouten sun, or moon, or night;
>   Where the river swayed a living stream,
>   And the light a pure and cloudless beam:
>   The land of vision it would seem,
>   And still an everlasting dream."

The last two lines are the shepherd's own remark, and a matter of opinion. But it is clear, I think, that Kilmeny must have described the same country as Durante saw, though, not having his experience, she could neither understand nor describe it so well.

Now I must give you such fragments of recollection as Diamond was able to bring back with him.

When he came to himself after he fell, he found himself at the back of the north wind. North Wind herself was nowhere to be seen.

Neither was there a vestige of snow or of ice within sight. The sun too had vanished; but that was no matter, for there was plenty of a certain still rayless light. Where it came from he never found out; but he thought it belonged to the country itself. Sometimes he thought it came out of the flowers, which were very bright, but had no strong colour. He said the river—for all agree that there is a river there—flowed not only through, but over grass: its channel, instead of being rock, stones, pebbles, sand, or anything else, was of pure meadow grass, not over long. He insisted that if it did not sing tunes in people's ears, it sung tunes in their heads, in proof of which I may mention that, in the troubles which followed, Diamond was often heard singing; and when asked what he was singing, would answer, "One of the tunes the river at the back of the north wind sung." And I may as well say at once that Diamond never told these things to any one but—no, I had better not say who it was; but whoever it was told me, and I thought it would be well to write them for my child-readers.

He could not say he was very happy there, for he had neither his father nor mother with him, but he felt so still and quiet and patient and contented, that, as far as the mere feeling went, it was something better than mere happiness. Nothing went wrong at the back of the north wind. Neither was anything quite right, he thought. Only everything was going to be right some day. His account disagreed with that of Durante, and agreed with that of Kilmeny, in this, that he protested there was no wind there at all. I fancy he missed it. At all events we could not do without wind. It all depends on how big our lungs are whether the wind is too strong for us or not.

When the person he told about it asked him whether he saw anybody he knew there, he answered, "Only a little girl belonging to the gardener, who thought he had lost her, but was quite mistaken, for there she was safe enough, and was to come back some day, as I came back, if they would only wait."

"Did you talk to her, Diamond?"

"No. Nobody talks there. They only look at each other, and understand everything."

"Is it cold there?"

"No."

"Is it hot?"

"No."

"What is it then?"

"You never think about such things there."

"What a queer place it must be!"

"It's a very good place."

"Do you want to go back again?"

"No; I don't think I have left it; I feel it here, somewhere."

"Did the people there look pleased?"

"Yes—quite pleased, only a little sad."

"Then they didn't look glad?"

"They looked as if they were waiting to be gladder some day."

This was how Diamond used to answer questions about that country. And now I will take up the story again, and tell you how he got back to this country.

11
How Diamond Got Home Again

When one at the back of the north wind wanted to know how things were going with any one he loved, he had to go to a certain tree, climb the stem, and sit down in the branches. In a few minutes, if he kept very still, he would see something at least of what was going on with the people he loved.

One day when Diamond was sitting in this tree, he began to long very much to get home again, and no wonder, for he saw his mother crying. Durante says that the people there may always follow their wishes, because they never wish but what is good. Diamond's wish was to get home, and he would fain follow his wish.

But how was he to set about it? If he could only see North Wind! But the moment he had got to her back, she was gone altogether from his sight. He had never seen her back. She might be sitting on her doorstep still, looking southwards, and waiting, white and thin and blue-eyed, until she was wanted. Or she might have again become a mighty creature, with power to do that which was demanded of her, and gone far away upon many missions. She must be somewhere, however. He could not go home without her, and therefore he must find her. She could never have intended to leave him always away from his mother. If there had been any danger of that, she would have told him, and given him his choice about going. For North Wind was right honest. How to find North Wind, therefore, occupied all his thoughts.

In his anxiety about his mother, he used to climb the tree every day, and sit in its branches. However many of the dwellers there did so, they never incommoded one another; for the moment one got into the tree, he became invisible to every one else; and it was such a wide-spreading tree that there was room for every one of the people of the country in it, without the least interference with each other. Sometimes, on getting down, two of them would meet at the root, and then they would smile to each other more sweetly than at any other time, as much as to say, "Ah, you've been up there too!"

One day he was sitting on one of the outer branches of the tree, looking southwards after his home. Far away was a blue shining sea, dotted with gleaming and sparkling specks of white. Those were the icebergs. Nearer he saw a great range of snow-capped mountains, and down below him the lovely meadow-grass of the country, with the stream flowing and flowing through it, away towards the sea. As he looked he began to wonder, for the whole country lay beneath him like a map, and that which was near him looked just as small as that which he knew to be miles away. The ridge of ice which encircled it appeared but a few yards off, and no larger than the row of pebbles with which a child will mark out the boundaries of the kingdom he has appropriated on the sea-shore. He thought he could distinguish the vapoury form of North Wind, seated as he had left her, on the other side. Hastily he descended the tree, and to his amazement found that the map or model of the country still lay at his feet. He stood in it. With one stride he had crossed the river; with another he had reached the ridge of ice; with the third he stepped over its peaks, and sank wearily down at North Wind's knees. For there she sat on her doorstep. The peaks of the great ridge of ice were as lofty as ever behind her, and the country at her back had vanished from Diamond's view.

North Wind was as still as Diamond had left her. Her pale face was white as the snow, and her motionless eyes were as blue as the caverns in the ice. But the instant Diamond touched her, her face began to change like that of one waking from sleep. Light began to glimmer from the blue of her eyes.

A moment more, and she laid her hand on Diamond's head, and began playing with his hair. Diamond took hold of her hand, and laid his face to it. She gave a little start.

"How very alive you are, child!" she murmured. "Come nearer to me."

By the help of the stones all around he clambered up beside her, and laid himself against her bosom. She gave a great sigh, slowly lifted her arms, and slowly folded them about him, until she clasped him close. Yet a moment, and she roused herself, and came quite awake; and the cold of her bosom, which had pierced Diamond's bones, vanished.

"Have you been sitting here ever since I went through you, dear North Wind?" asked Diamond, stroking her hand.

"Yes," she answered, looking at him with her old kindness.

"Ain't you very tired?"

"No; I've often had to sit longer. Do you know how long you have been?"

"Oh! years and years," answered Diamond.

"You have just been seven days," returned North Wind.

"I thought I had been a hundred years!" exclaimed Diamond.

"Yes, I daresay," replied North Wind. "You've been away from here seven days; but how long you may have been in there is quite another thing. Behind my back and before my face things are so different! They don't go at all by the same rule."

"I'm very glad," said Diamond, after thinking a while.

"Why?" asked North Wind.

"Because I've been such a long time there, and such a little while away from mother. Why, she won't be expecting me home from Sandwich yet!"

"No. But we mustn't talk any longer. I've got my orders now, and we must be off in a few minutes."

Next moment Diamond found himself sitting alone on the rock. North Wind had vanished. A creature like a great humble-bee or cockchafer flew past his face; but it could be neither, for there were no insects amongst the ice. It passed him again and again, flying in circles around him, and he concluded that it must be North Wind herself, no bigger than Tom Thumb when his mother put him in the nutshell lined with flannel. But she was no longer vapoury and thin. She was solid, although tiny. A moment more, and she perched on his shoulder.

"Come along, Diamond," she said in his ear, in the smallest and highest of treble voices; "it is time we were setting out for Sandwich."

Diamond could just see her, by turning his head towards his shoulder as far as he could, but only with one eye, for his nose came between her and the other.

"Won't you take me in your arms and carry me?" he said in a whisper, for he knew she did not like a loud voice when she was small.

"Ah! you ungrateful boy," returned North Wind, smiling "how dare you make game of me? Yes, I will carry you, but you shall walk a bit for your impertinence first. Come along."

She jumped from his shoulder, but when Diamond looked for her upon the ground, he could see nothing but a little spider with long legs that made its way over the ice towards the south. It ran very fast indeed for a spider, but Diamond ran a long way before it, and then waited for it. It was up with him sooner than he had expected, however, and it had grown a good deal. And the spider grew and grew and went faster and faster, till all at once Diamond discovered that it was not a spider, but a weasel; and away glided the weasel, and away went Diamond after it, and it took all the run there was in him to keep up with the weasel. And the weasel grew, and grew, and grew, till all at once Diamond saw that the weasel was not a weasel but a cat. And away went the cat, and Diamond after it. And when he had run half a mile, he found the cat waiting for him, sitting up and washing her face not to lose time. And away went the cat again, and Diamond after it. But the next time he came up with the cat, the cat was not a cat, but a hunting-leopard. And the hunting-leopard grew to a jaguar, all covered with spots like eyes. And the jaguar grew to a Bengal tiger. And at none of them was Diamond afraid, for he had been at North Wind's back, and he could be afraid of her no longer whatever she did or grew. And the tiger flew over the snow in a straight line for the south, growing less and less to Diamond's eyes till it was only a black speck upon the whiteness; and then it vanished altogether. And now Diamond felt that he would rather not run any farther, and that the ice had got very rough. Besides, he was near the precipices that bounded the sea, so he slackened his pace to a walk, saying aloud to himself:

"When North Wind has punished me enough for making game of her, she will come back to me; I know she will, for I can't go much farther without her."

"You dear boy! It was only in fun. Here I am!" said North Wind's voice behind him.

Diamond turned, and saw her as he liked best to see her, standing beside him, a tall lady.

"Where's the tiger?" he asked, for he knew all the creatures from a picture book that Miss Coleman had given him. "But, of course," he added, "you were the tiger. I was puzzled and forgot. I saw it such a long way off before me, and there you were behind me. It's so odd, you know."

"It must look very odd to you, Diamond: I see that. But it is no more odd to me than to break an old pine in two."

"Well, that's odd enough," remarked Diamond.

"So it is! I forgot. Well, none of these things are odder to me than it is to you to eat bread and butter."

"Well, that's odd too, when I think of it," persisted Diamond. "I should just like a slice of bread and butter! I'm afraid to say how long it is—how long it seems to me, that is—since I had anything to eat."

"Come then," said North Wind, stooping and holding out her arms. "You shall have some bread and butter very soon. I am glad to find you want some."

Diamond held up his arms to meet hers, and was safe upon her bosom. North Wind bounded into the air. Her tresses began to lift and rise and spread and stream and flow and flutter; and with a roar from her hair and an answering roar from one of the great glaciers beside them, whose slow torrent tumbled two or three icebergs at once into the waves at their feet, North Wind and Diamond went flying southwards.

12
Who Met Diamond at Sandwich

As they flew, so fast they went that the sea slid away from under them like a great web of shot silk, blue shot with grey, and green shot with purple. They went so fast that the stars themselves appeared to sail away past them overhead, "like golden boats," on a blue sea turned upside down. And they went so fast that Diamond himself went the other way as fast—I mean he went fast asleep in North Wind's arms.

When he woke, a face was bending over him; but it was not North Wind's; it was his mother's. He put out his arms to her, and she clasped him to her bosom and burst out crying. Diamond kissed her again and again to make her stop. Perhaps kissing is the best thing for crying, but it will not always stop it.

"What is the matter, mother?" he said.

"Oh, Diamond, my darling! you have been so ill!" she sobbed.

"No, mother dear. I've only been at the back of the north wind," returned Diamond.

"I thought you were dead," said his mother.

But that moment the doctor came in.

"Oh! there!" said the doctor with gentle cheerfulness; "we're better to-day, I see."

Then he drew the mother aside, and told her not to talk to Diamond, or to mind what he might say; for he must be kept as quiet as possible. And indeed Diamond was not much inclined to talk, for he felt very strange and weak, which was little wonder, seeing that all the time he had been away he had only sucked a few lumps of ice, and there could not be much nourishment in them.

Now while he is lying there, getting strong again with chicken broth and other nice things, I will tell my readers what had been taking place at his home, for they ought to be told it.

They may have forgotten that Miss Coleman was in a very poor state of health. Now there were three reasons for this. In the first place, her lungs were not strong. In the second place, there was a

gentleman somewhere who had not behaved very well to her. In the
third place, she had not anything particular to do. These three nots
together are enough to make a lady very ill indeed. Of course she could
not help the first cause; but if the other two causes had not existed,
that would have been of little consequence; she would only have to be
a little careful. The second she could not help quite; but if she had
had anything to do, and had done it well, it would have been very
difficult for any man to behave badly to her. And for this third cause
of her illness, if she had had anything to do that was worth doing, she
might have borne his bad behaviour so that even that would not have
made her ill. It is not always easy, I confess, to find something to do
that is worth doing, but the most difficult things are constantly being
done, and she might have found something if she had tried. Her fault
lay in this, that she had not tried. But, to be sure, her father and
mother were to blame that they had never set her going. Only then
again, nobody had told her father and mother that they ought to set
her going in that direction. So as none of them would find it out of
themselves, North Wind had to teach them.

We know that North Wind was very busy that night on which she
left Diamond in the cathedral. She had in a sense been blowing
through and through the Colemans' house the whole of the night. First,
Miss Coleman's maid had left a chink of her mistress's window open,
thinking she had shut it, and North Wind had wound a few of her
hairs round the lady's throat. She was considerably worse the next
morning. Again, the ship which North Wind had sunk that very night
belonged to Mr. Coleman. Nor will my readers understand what a
heavy loss this was to him until I have informed them that he had
been getting poorer and poorer for some time. He was not so successful in his speculations as he had been, for he speculated a great deal
more than was right, and it was time he should be pulled up. It is a
hard thing for a rich man to grow poor; but it is an awful thing for
him to grow dishonest, and some kinds of speculation lead a man deep
into dishonesty before he thinks what he is about. Poverty will not
make a man worthless—he may be worth a great deal more when he is
poor than he was when he was rich; but dishonesty goes very far indeed to make a man of no value—a thing to be thrown out in the dust-
hole of the creation, like a bit of a broken basin, or a dirty rag. So
North Wind had to look after Mr. Coleman, and try to make an honest
man of him. So she sank the ship which was his last venture, and he
was what himself and his wife and the world called ruined.

Nor was this all yet. For on board that vessel Miss Coleman's lover
was a passenger; and when the news came that the vessel had gone
down, and that all on board had perished, we may be sure she did not

think the loss of their fine house and garden and furniture the greatest misfortune in the world.

Of course, the trouble did not end with Mr. Coleman and his family. Nobody can suffer alone. When the cause of suffering is most deeply hidden in the heart, and nobody knows anything about it but the man himself, he must be a great and a good man indeed, such as few of us have known, if the pain inside him does not make him behave so as to cause all about him to be more or less uncomfortable. But when a man brings money-troubles on himself by making haste to be rich, then most of the people he has to do with must suffer in the same way with himself. The elm-tree which North Wind blew down that very night, as if small and great trials were to be gathered in one heap, crushed Miss Coleman's pretty summer-house: just so the fall of Mr. Coleman crushed the little family that lived over his coach-house and stable. Before Diamond was well enough to be taken home, there was no home for him to go to. Mr. Coleman—or his creditors, for I do not know the particulars—had sold house, carriage, horses, furniture, and everything. He and his wife and daughter and Mrs. Crump had gone to live in a small house in Hoxton, where he would be unknown, and whence he could walk to his place of business in the City. For he was not an old man, and hoped yet to retrieve his fortunes. Let us hope that he lived to retrieve his honesty, the tail of which had slipped through his fingers to the very last joint, if not beyond it.

Of course, Diamond's father had nothing to do for a time, but it was not so hard for him to have nothing to do as it was for Miss Coleman. He wrote to his wife that, if her sister would keep her there till he got a place, it would be better for them, and he would be greatly obliged to her. Meantime, the gentleman who had bought the house had allowed his furniture to remain where it was for a little while.

Diamond's aunt was quite willing to keep them as long as she could. And indeed Diamond was not yet well enough to be moved with safety.

When he had recovered so far as to be able to go out, one day his mother got her sister's husband, who had a little pony-cart, to carry them down to the sea-shore, and leave them there for a few hours. He had some business to do further on at Ramsgate, and would pick them up as he returned. A whiff of the sea-air would do them both good, she said, and she thought besides she could best tell Diamond what had happened if she had him quite to herself.

13
The Seaside

Diamond and his mother sat down upon the edge of the rough grass that bordered the sand. The sun was just far enough past its highest not to shine in their eyes when they looked eastward. A sweet little wind blew on their left side, and comforted the mother without letting her know what it was that comforted her. Away before them stretched the sparkling waters of the ocean, every wave of which flashed out its own delight back in the face of the great sun, which looked down from the stillness of its blue house with glorious silent face upon its flashing children. On each hand the shore rounded out-wards, forming a little bay. There were no white cliffs here, as further north and south, and the place was rather dreary, but the sky got at them so much the better. Not a house, not a creature was within sight. Dry sand was about their feet, and under them thin wiry grass, that just managed to grow out of the poverty-stricken shore.

"Oh dear!" said Diamond's mother, with a deep sigh, "it's a sad world!"

"Is it?" said Diamond. "I didn't know."

"How should you know, child? You've been too well taken care of, I trust."

"Oh yes, I have," returned Diamond. "I'm sorry! I thought you were taken care of too. I thought my father took care of you. I will ask him about it. I think he must have forgotten."

"Dear boy!" said his mother, "your father's the best man in the world."

"So I thought!" returned Diamond with triumph. "I was sure of it!—Well, doesn't he take very good care of you?"

"Yes, yes, he does," answered his mother, bursting into tears. "But who's to take care of him? And how is he to take care of us if he's got nothing to eat himself?"

"Oh dear!" said Diamond with a gasp; "hasn't he got anything to eat? Oh! I must go home to him."

"No, no, child. He's not come to that yet. But what's to become of us, I don't know."

"Are you very hungry, mother? There's the basket. I thought you put something to eat in it."

"O you darling stupid! I didn't say I was hungry," returned his mother, smiling through her tears.

"Then I don't understand you at all," said Diamond. "Do tell me what's the matter."

"There are people in the world who have nothing to eat, Diamond."

"Then I suppose they don't stop in it any longer. They—they—what you call—die—don't they?"

"Yes, they do. How would you like that?"

"I don't know. I never tried. But I suppose they go where they get something to eat."

"Like enough they don't want it," said his mother, petulantly.

"That's all right then," said Diamond, thinking I daresay more than he chose to put in words.

"Is it though? Poor boy! how little you know about things! Mr. Coleman's lost all his money, and your father has nothing to do, and we shall have nothing to eat by and by."

"Are you sure, mother?"

"Sure of what?"

"Sure that we shall have nothing to eat."

"No, thank Heaven! I'm not sure of it. I hope not."

"Then I can't understand it, mother. There's a piece of ginger-bread in the basket, I know."

"O you little bird! You have no more sense than a sparrow that picks what it wants, and never thinks of the winter and the frost and, the snow."

"Ah—yes—I see. But the birds get through the winter, don't they?"

"Some of them fall dead on the ground."

"They must die some time. They wouldn't like to be birds always. Would you, mother?"

"What a child it is!" thought his mother, but she said nothing.

"Oh! now I remember," Diamond went on. "Father told me that day I went to Epping Forest with him, that the rose-bushes, and the may-bushes, and the holly-bushes were the bird's barns, for there were the hips, and the haws, and the holly-berries, all ready for the winter."

"Yes; that's all very true. So you see the birds are provided for. But there are no such barns for you and me, Diamond."

"Ain't there?"

"No. We've got to work for our bread."

"Then let's go and work," said Diamond, getting up.

"It's no use. We've not got anything to do."

"Then let's wait."

"Then we shall starve."

"No. There's the basket. Do you know, mother, I think I shall call that basket the barn."

"It's not a very big one. And when it's empty—where are we then?"

"At auntie's cupboard," returned Diamond promptly.

"But we can't eat auntie's things all up and leave her to starve."

"No, no. We'll go back to father before that. He'll have found a cupboard somewhere by that time."

"How do you know that?"

"I don't know it. But I haven't got even a cupboard, and I've always had plenty to eat. I've heard you say I had too much, sometimes."

"But I tell you that's because I've had a cupboard for you, child."

"And when yours was empty, auntie opened hers."

"But that can't go on."

"How do you know? I think there must be a big cupboard somewhere, out of which the little cupboards are filled, you know, mother."

"Well, I wish I could find the door of that cupboard," said his mother. But the same moment she stopped, and was silent for a good while. I cannot tell whether Diamond knew what she was thinking, but I think I know. She had heard something at church the day before, which came back upon her—something like this, that she hadn't to eat for tomorrow as well as for to-day; and that what was not wanted couldn't be missed. So, instead of saying anything more, she stretched out her hand for the basket, and she and Diamond had their dinner.

And Diamond did enjoy it. For the drive and the fresh air had made him quite hungry; and he did not, like his mother, trouble himself about what they should dine off that day week. The fact was he had lived so long without any food at all at the back of the north wind, that he knew quite well that food was not essential to existence; that in fact, under certain circumstances, people could live without it well enough.

His mother did not speak much during their dinner. After it was over she helped him to walk about a little, but he was not able for much and soon got tired. He did not get fretful, though. He was too glad of having the sun and the wind again, to fret because he could not run about. He lay down on the dry sand, and his mother covered him with a shawl. She then sat by his side, and took a bit of work from her pocket. But Diamond felt rather sleepy, and turned on his side and gazed sleepily over the sand. A few yards off he saw something fluttering.

"What is that, mother?" he said.

"Only a bit of paper," she answered.

"It flutters more than a bit of paper would, I think," said Diamond.

"I'll go and see if you like," said his mother. "My eyes are none of the best."

So she rose and went and found that they were both right, for it was a little book, partly buried in the sand. But several of its leaves were clear of the sand, and these the wind kept blowing about in a very flutterful manner. She took it up and brought it to Diamond.

"What is it, mother?" he asked.

"Some nursery rhymes, I think," she answered.

"I'm too sleepy," said Diamond. "Do read some of them to me."

"Yes, I will," she said, and began one.— "But this is such non-sense!" she said again. "I will try to find a better one."

She turned the leaves searching, but three times, with sudden puffs, the wind blew the leaves rustling back to the same verses.

"Do read that one," said Diamond, who seemed to be of the same mind as the wind. "It sounded very nice. I am sure it is a good one."

So his mother thought it might amuse him, though she couldn't find any sense in it. She never thought he might understand it, although she could not.

Now I do not exactly know what the mother read, but this is what Diamond heard, or thought afterwards that he had heard. He was, however, as I have said, very sleepy. And when he thought he understood the verses he may have been only dreaming better ones. This is how they went—

I know a river whose waters run asleep run run ever singing in the shallows dumb in the hollows sleeping so deep and all the swallows that dip their feathers in the hollows or in the shallows are the merriest swallows of all for the nests they bake with the clay they cake with the water they shake from their wings that rake the water out of the shallows or the hollows will hold together in any weather and so the swallows are the merriest fellows and have the merriest children and are built so narrow like the head of an arrow to cut the air and go just where the nicest water is flowing and the nicest dust is blowing for each so narrow like head of an arrow is only a barrow to carry the mud he makes from the nicest water flowing and the nicest dust that is blowing to build his nest for her he loves best with the nicest cakes which the sunshine bakes all for their merry children all so callow with beaks that follow gaping and hollow wider and wider after their father or after their mother the food-provider who brings them a spider or a worm the poor hider down in the earth so there's no dearth for their beaks as yellow as the buttercups growing beside the flowing of the singing river always and ever growing and blowing for fast as the

sheep awake or asleep crop them and crop them they cannot stop them
but up they creep and on they go blowing and so with the daisies the
little white praises they grow and they blow and they spread out their
crown and they praise the sun and when he goes down their praising
is done and they fold up their crown and they sleep every one till over
the plain he's shining amain and they're at it again praising and praising such low songs raising that no one hears them but the sun who
rears them and the sheep that bite them are the quietest sheep awake
or asleep with the merriest bleat and the little lambs are the merriest
lambs they forget to eat for the frolic in their feet and the lambs and
their dams are the whitest sheep with the woolliest wool and the longest wool and the trailingest tails and they shine like snow in the
grasses that grow by the singing river that sings for ever and the sheep
and the lambs are merry for ever because the river sings and they
drink it and the lambs and their dams are quiet and white because of
their diet for what they bite is buttercups yellow and daisies white
and grass as green as the river can make it with wind as mellow to
kiss it and shake it as never was seen but here in the hollows beside
the river where all the swallows are merriest of fellows for the nests
they make with the clay they cake in the sunshine bake till they are
like bone as dry in the wind as a marble stone so firm they bind the
grass in the clay that dries in the wind the sweetest wind that blows
by the river flowing for ever but never you find whence comes the
wind that blows on the hollows and over the shallows where dip the
swallows alive it blows the life as it goes awake or asleep into the
river that sings as it flows and the life it blows into the sheep awake
or asleep with the woolliest wool and the trailingest tails and it never
fails gentle and cool to wave the wool and to toss the grass as the
lambs and the sheep over it pass and tug and bite with their teeth so
white and then with the sweep of their trailing tails smooth it again
and it grows amain and amain it grows and the wind as it blows tosses
the swallows over the hollows and down on the shallows till every
feather doth shake and quiver and all their feathers go all together
blowing the life and the joy so rife into the swallows that skim the
shallows and have the yellowest children for the wind that blows is
the life of the river flowing for ever that washes the grasses still as it
passes and feeds the daisies the little white praises and buttercups
bonny so golden and sunny with butter and honey that whiten the
sheep awake or asleep that nibble and bite and grow whiter than white
and merry and quiet on the sweet diet fed by the river and tossed for
ever by the wind that tosses the swallow that crosses over the shallows dipping his wings to gather the water and bake the cake that the
wind shall make as hard as a bone as dry as a stone it's all in the wind

that blows from behind and all in the river that flows for ever and all in the grasses and the white daisies and the merry sheep awake or asleep and the happy swallows skimming the shallows and it's all in the wind that blows from behind.

Here Diamond became aware that his mother had stopped reading.

"Why don't you go on, mother dear?" he asked.

"It's such nonsense!" said his mother. "I believe it would go on for ever."

"That's just what it did," said Diamond.

"What did?" she asked.

"Why, the river. That's almost the very tune it used to sing."

His mother was frightened, for she thought the fever was coming on again. So she did not contradict him.

"Who made that poem?" asked Diamond.

"I don't know," she answered. "Some silly woman for her children, I suppose—and then thought it good enough to print."

"She must have been at the back of the north wind some time or other, anyhow," said Diamond. "She couldn't have got a hold of it anywhere else. That's just how it went." And he began to chant bits of it here and there; but his mother said nothing for fear of making him, worse; and she was very glad indeed when she saw her brother-in-law jogging along in his little cart. They lifted Diamond in, and got up themselves, and away they went, "home again, home again, home again," as Diamond sang. But he soon grew quiet, and before they reached Sandwich he was fast asleep and dreaming of the country at the back of the north wind.

14
Old Diamond

After this Diamond recovered so fast, that in a few days he was quite able to go home as soon as his father had a place for them to go. Now his father having saved a little money, and finding that no situation offered itself, had been thinking over a new plan. A strange occurrence it was which turned his thoughts in that direction. He had a friend in the Bloomsbury region, who lived by letting out cabs and horses to the cabmen. This man, happening to meet him one day as he was returning from an unsuccessful application, said to him:

"Why don't you set up for yourself now—in the cab line, I mean?"

"I haven't enough for that," answered Diamond's father.

"You must have saved a goodish bit, I should think. Just come home with me now and look at a horse I can let you have cheap. I bought him only a few weeks ago, thinking he'd do for a Hansom, but I was wrong. He's got bone enough for a waggon, but a waggon ain't a Hansom. He ain't got go enough for a Hansom. You see parties as takes Hansoms wants to go like the wind, and he ain't got wind enough, for he ain't so young as he once was. But for a four-wheeler as takes families and their luggages, he's the very horse. He'd carry a small house any day. I bought him cheap, and I'll sell him cheap."

"Oh, I don't want him," said Diamond's father. "A body must have time to think over an affair of so much importance. And there's the cab too. That would come to a deal of money."

"I could fit you there, I daresay," said his friend. "But come and look at the animal, anyhow."

"Since I lost my own old pair, as was Mr. Coleman's," said Diamond's father, turning to accompany the cab-master, "I ain't almost got the heart to look a horse in the face. It's a thousand pities to part man and horse."

"So it is," returned his friend sympathetically.

But what was the ex-coachman's delight, when, on going into the stable where his friend led him, he found the horse he wanted him to buy was no other than his own old Diamond, grown very thin and bony and long-legged, as if they, had been doing what they could to fit him for Hansom work!

"He ain't a Hansom horse," said Diamond's father indignantly.

"Well, you're right. He ain't handsome, but he's a good un" said his owner.

"Who says he ain't handsome? He's one of the handsomest horses a gentleman's coachman ever druv," said Diamond's father; remarking to himself under his breath— "though I says it as shouldn't"—for he did not feel inclined all at once to confess that his own old horse could have sunk so low.

"Well," said his friend, "all I say is—There's a animal for you, as strong as a church; an'll go like a train, leastways a parly," he added, correcting himself.

But the coachman had a lump in his throat and tears in his eyes. For the old horse, hearing his voice, had turned his long neck, and when his old friend went up to him and laid his hand on his side, he whinnied for joy, and laid his big head on his master's breast. This settled the matter. The coachman's arms were round the horse's neck in a moment, and he fairly broke down and cried. The cab-master had never been so fond of a horse himself as to hug him like that, but he saw in a moment how it was. And he must have been a good-hearted fellow, for I never heard of such an idea coming into the head of any other man with a horse to sell: instead of putting something on to the price because he was now pretty sure of selling him, he actually took a pound off what he had meant to ask for him, saying to himself it was a shame to part old friends.

Diamond's father, as soon as he came to himself, turned and asked how much he wanted for the horse.

"I see you're old friends," said the owner.

"It's my own old Diamond. I liked him far the best of the pair, though the other was good. You ain't got him too, have you?"

"No; nothing in the stable to match him there."

"I believe you," said the coachman. "But you'll be wanting a long price for him, I know."

"No, not so much. I bought him cheap, and as I say, he ain't for my work."

The end of it was that Diamond's father bought old Diamond again, along with a four-wheeled cab. And as there were some rooms to be had over the stable, he took them, wrote to his wife to come home, and set up as a cabman.

15
The Mews

It was late in the afternoon when Diamond and his mother and the baby reached London. I was so full of Diamond that I forgot to tell you a baby had arrived in the meantime. His father was waiting for them with his own cab, but they had not told Diamond who the horse was; for his father wanted to enjoy the pleasure of his surprise when he found it out. He got in with his mother without looking at the horse, and his father having put up Diamond's carpet-bag and his mother's little trunk, got upon the box himself and drove off; and Diamond was quite proud of riding home in his father's own carriage. But when he got to the mews, he could not help being a little dismayed at first; and if he had never been to the back of the north wind, I am afraid he would have cried a little. But instead of that, he said to himself it was a fine thing all the old furniture was there. And instead of helping his mother to be miserable at the change, he began to find out all the advantages of the place; for every place has some advantages, and they are always better worth knowing than the disadvantages. Certainly the weather was depressing, for a thick, dull, persistent rain was falling by the time they reached home. But happily the weather is very changeable; and besides, there was a good fire burning in the room, which their neighbour with the drunken husband had attended to for them; and the tea-things were put out, and the kettle was boiling on the fire. And with a good fire, and tea and bread and butter, things cannot be said to be miserable.

Diamond's father and mother were, notwithstanding, rather miserable, and Diamond began to feel a kind of darkness beginning to spread over his own mind. But the same moment he said to himself, "This will never do. I can't give in to this. I've been to the back of the north wind. Things go right there, and so I must try to get things to go right here. I've got to fight the miserable things. They shan't make me miserable if I can help it." I do not mean that he thought these very words. They are perhaps too grown-up for him to have thought, but they represent the kind of thing that was in his heart and his head. And when heart and head go together, nothing can stand before them.

"What nice bread and butter this is!" said Diamond.

"I'm glad you like it, my dear" said his father. "I bought the butter myself at the little shop round the corner."

"It's very nice, thank you, father. Oh, there's baby waking! I'll take him."

"Sit still, Diamond," said his mother. "Go on with your bread and butter. You're not strong enough to lift him yet."

So she took the baby herself, and set him on her knee. Then Diamond began to amuse him, and went on till the little fellow was shrieking with laughter. For the baby's world was his mother's arms; and the drizzling rain, and the dreary mews, and even his father's troubled face could not touch him. What cared baby for the loss of a hundred situations? Yet neither father nor mother thought him hard-hearted because he crowed and laughed in the middle of their troubles. On the contrary, his crowing and laughing were infectious. His little heart was so full of merriment that it could not hold it all, and it ran over into theirs. Father and mother began to laugh too, and Diamond laughed till he had a fit of coughing which frightened his mother, and made them all stop. His father took the baby, and his mother put him to bed.

But it was indeed a change to them all, not only from Sandwich, but from their old place, instead of the great river where the huge barges with their mighty brown and yellow sails went tacking from side to side like little pleasure-skiffs, and where the long thin boats shot past with eight and sometimes twelve rowers, their windows now looked out upon a dirty paved yard. And there was no garden more for Diamond to run into when he pleased, with gay flowers about his feet, and solemn sun-filled trees over his head. Neither was there a wooden wall at the back of his bed with a hole in it for North Wind to come in at when she liked. Indeed, there was such a high wall, and there were so many houses about the mews, that North Wind seldom got into the place at all, except when something must be done, and she had a grand cleaning out like other housewives; while the partition at the head of Diamond's new bed only divided it from the room occupied by a cabman who drank too much beer, and came home chiefly to quarrel with his wife and pinch his children. It was dreadful to Diamond to hear the scolding and the crying. But it could not make him miserable, because he had been at the back of the north wind.

If my reader find it hard to believe that Diamond should be so good, he must remember that he had been to the back of the north wind. If he never knew a boy so good, did he ever know a boy that had been to the back of the north wind? It was not in the least strange of Diamond to behave as he did; on the contrary, it was thoroughly sensible of him.

We shall see how he got on.

16
Diamond Makes a Beginning

The wind blew loud, but Diamond slept a deep sleep, and never heard it. My own impression is that every time when Diamond slept well and remembered nothing about it in the morning, he had been all that night at the back of the north wind. I am almost sure that was how he woke so refreshed, and felt so quiet and hopeful all the day. Indeed he said this much, though not to me—that always when he woke from such a sleep there was a something in his mind, he could not tell what—could not tell whether it was the last far-off sounds of the river dying away in the distance, or some of the words of the endless song his mother had read to him on the sea-shore. Sometimes he thought it must have been the twittering of the swallows—over the shallows, you, know; but it may have been the chirping of the dingy sparrows picking up their breakfast in the yard—how can I tell? I don't know what I know, I only know what I think; and to tell the truth, I am more for the swallows than the sparrows. When he knew he was coming awake, he would sometimes try hard to keep hold of the words of what seemed a new song, one he had not heard before—a song in which the words and the music somehow appeared to be all one; but even when he thought he had got them well fixed in his mind, ever as he came awaker—as he would say—one line faded away out of it, and then another, and then another, till at last there was nothing left but some lovely picture of water or grass or daisies, or something else very common, but with all the commonness polished off it, and the lovely soul of it, which people so seldom see, and, alas! yet seldomer believe in, shining out. But after that he would sing the oddest, loveliest little songs to the baby—of his own making, his mother said; but Diamond said he did not make them; they were made somewhere inside him, and he knew nothing about them till they were coming out.

When he woke that first morning he got up at once, saying to himself, "I've been ill long enough, and have given a great deal of trouble; I must try and be of use now, and help my mother." When he went

into her room he found her lighting the fire, and his father just getting out of bed. They had only the one room, besides the little one,
not much more than a closet, in which Diamond slept. He began at
once to set things to rights, but the baby waking up, he took him, and
nursed him till his mother had got the breakfast ready. She was looking gloomy, and his father was silent; and indeed except Diamond
had done all he possibly could to keep out the misery that was trying
to get in at doors and windows, he too would have grown miserable,
and then they would have been all miserable together. But to try to
make others comfortable is the only way to get right comfortable ourselves, and that comes partly of not being able to think so much about
ourselves when we are helping other people. For our Selves will always
do pretty well if we don't pay them too much attention. Our Selves
are like some little children who will be happy enough so long as they
are left to their own games, but when we begin to interfere with them,
and make them presents of too nice playthings, or too many sweet
things, they begin at once to fret and spoil.

"Why, Diamond, child!" said his mother at last, "you're as good to
your mother as if you were a girl—nursing the baby, and toasting the
bread, and sweeping up the hearth! I declare a body would think you
had been among the fairies."

Could Diamond have had greater praise or greater pleasure? You
see when he forgot his Self his mother took care of his Self, and loved
and praised his Self. Our own praises poison our Selves, and puff and
swell them up, till they lose all shape and beauty, and become like
great toadstools. But the praises of father or mother do our Selves
good, and comfort them and make them beautiful. They never do them
any harm. If they do any harm, it comes of our mixing some of our own
praises with them, and that turns them nasty and slimy and poisonous.

When his father had finished his breakfast, which he did rather
in a hurry, he got up and went down into the yard to get out his horse
and put him to the cab.

"Won't you come and see the cab, Diamond?" he said.

"Yes, please, father—if mother can spare me a minute," answered
Diamond.

"Bless the child! I don't want him," said his mother cheerfully.

But as he was following his father out of the door, she called him
back.

"Diamond, just hold the baby one minute. I have something to
say to your father."

So Diamond sat down again, took the baby in his lap, and began
poking his face into its little body, laughing and singing all the while,
so that the baby crowed like a little bantam. And what he sang was

something like this—such nonsense to those that couldn't understand it! but not to the baby, who got all the good in the world out of it:— baby's a-sleeping wake up baby for all the swallows are the merriest fellows and have the yellowest children who would go sleeping and snore like a gaby disturbing his mother and father and brother and all a-boring their ears with his snoring snoring snoring for himself and no other for himself in particular wake up baby sit up perpendicular hark to the gushing hark to the rushing where the sheep are the woolliest and the lambs the unruliest and their tails the whitest and their eyes the brightest and baby's the bonniest and baby's the funniest and baby's the shiniest and baby's the tiniest and baby's the merriest and baby's the worriest of all the lambs that plague their dams and mother's the whitest of all the dams that feed the lambs that go crop-cropping without stop-stopping and father's the best of all the swallows that build their nest out of the shining shallows and he has the merriest children that's baby and Diamond and Diamond and baby and baby and Diamond and Diamond and baby—

Here Diamond's knees went off in a wild dance which tossed the baby about and shook the laughter out of him in immoderate peals. His mother had been listening at the door to the last few lines of his song, and came in with the tears in her eyes. She took the baby from him, gave him a kiss, and told him to run to his father.

By the time Diamond got into the yard, the horse was between the shafts, and his father was looping the traces on. Diamond went round to look at the horse. The sight of him made him feel very queer. He did not know much about different horses, and all other horses than their own were very much the same to him. But he could not make it out. This was Diamond and it wasn't Diamond. Diamond didn't hang his head like that; yet the head that was hanging was very like the one that Diamond used to hold so high. Diamond's bones didn't show through his skin like that; but the skin they pushed out of shape so was very like Diamond's skin; and the bones might be Diamond's bones, for he had never seen the shape of them. But when he came round in front of the old horse, and he put out his long neck, and began sniffing at him and rubbing his upper lip and his nose on him, then Diamond saw it could be no other than old Diamond, and he did just as his father had done before—put his arms round his neck and cried—but not much.

"Ain't it jolly, father?" he said. "Was there ever anybody so lucky as me? Dear old Diamond!"

And he hugged the horse again, and kissed both his big hairy cheeks. He could only manage one at a time, however—the other cheek was so far off on the other side of his big head.

His father mounted the box with just the same air, as Diamond thought, with which he had used to get upon the coach-box, and Diamond said to himself, "Father's as grand as ever anyhow." He had kept his brown livery-coat, only his wife had taken the silver buttons off and put brass ones instead, because they did not think it polite to Mr. Coleman in his fallen fortunes to let his crest be seen upon the box of a cab. Old Diamond had kept just his collar; and that had the silver crest upon it still, for his master thought nobody would notice that, and so let it remain for a memorial of the better days of which it reminded him—not unpleasantly, seeing it had been by no fault either of his or of the old horse's that they had come down in the world together.

"Oh, father, do let me drive a bit," said Diamond, jumping up on the box beside him.

His father changed places with him at once, putting the reins into his hands. Diamond gathered them up eagerly.

"Don't pull at his mouth," said his father, "just feel, at it gently to let him know you're there and attending to him. That's what I call talking to him through the reins."

"Yes, father, I understand," said Diamond. Then to the horse he said, "Go on Diamond." And old Diamond's ponderous bulk began at once to move to the voice of the little boy.

But before they had reached the entrance of the mews, another voice called after young Diamond, which, in his turn, he had to obey, for it was that of his mother. "Diamond! Diamond!" it cried; and Diamond pulled the reins, and the horse stood still as a stone.

"Husband," said his mother, coming up, "you're never going to trust him with the reins—a baby like that?"

"He must learn some day, and he can't begin too soon. I see already he's a born coachman," said his father proudly. "And I don't see well how he could escape it, for my father and my grandfather, that's his great-grandfather, was all coachmen, I'm told; so it must come natural to him, any one would think. Besides, you see, old Diamond's as proud of him as we are our own selves, wife. Don't you see how he's turning round his ears, with the mouths of them open, for the first word he speaks to tumble in? He's too well bred to turn his head, you know."

"Well, but, husband, I can't do without him to-day. Everything's got to be done, you know. It's my first day here. And there's that baby!"

"Bless you, wife! I never meant to take him away—only to the bottom of Endell Street. He can watch his way back."

"No thank you, father; not to-day," said Diamond. "Mother wants me. Perhaps she'll let me go another day."

"Very well, my man," said his father, and took the reins which Diamond was holding out to him.

Diamond got down, a little disappointed of course, and went with his mother, who was too pleased to speak. She only took hold of his hand as tight as if she had been afraid of his running away instead of glad that he would not leave her.

Now, although they did not know it, the owner of the stables, the same man who had sold the horse to his father, had been standing just inside one of the stable-doors, with his hands in his pockets, and had heard and seen all that passed; and from that day John Stonecrop took a great fancy to the little boy. And this was the beginning of what came of it.

The same evening, just as Diamond was feeling tired of the day's work, and wishing his father would come home, Mr. Stonecrop knocked at the door. His mother went and opened it.

"Good evening, ma'am," said he. "Is the little master in?"

"Yes, to be sure he is—at your service, I'm sure, Mr. Stonecrop," said his mother.

"No, no, ma'am; it's I'm at his service. I'm just a-going out with my own cab, and if he likes to come with me, he shall drive my old horse till he's tired."

"It's getting rather late for him," said his mother thoughtfully. "You see he's been an invalid."

Diamond thought, what a funny thing! How could he have been an invalid when he did not even know what the word meant? But, of course, his mother was right.

"Oh, well," said Mr. Stonecrop, "I can just let him drive through Bloomsbury Square, and then he shall run home again."

"Very good, sir. And I'm much obliged to you," said his mother. And Diamond, dancing with delight, got his cap, put his hand in Mr. Stonecrop's, and went with him to the yard where the cab was waiting. He did not think the horse looked nearly so nice as Diamond, nor Mr. Stonecrop nearly so grand as his father; but he was none, the less pleased. He got up on the box, and his new friend got up beside him.

"What's the horse's name?" whispered Diamond, as he took the reins from the man.

"It's not a nice name," said Mr. Stonecrop. "You needn't call him by it. I didn't give it him. He'll go well enough without it. Give the boy a whip, Jack. I never carries one when I drive old—"

He didn't finish the sentence. Jack handed Diamond a whip, with which, by holding it half down the stick, he managed just to flack the haunches of the horse; and away he went.

"Mind the gate," said Mr. Stonecrop; and Diamond did mind the gate, and guided the nameless horse through it in safety, pulling him this way and that according as was necessary. Diamond learned to drive all the sooner that he had been accustomed to do what he was told, and could obey the smallest hint in a moment. Nothing helps one to get on like that. Some people don't know how to do what they are told; they have not been used to it, and they neither understand quickly nor are able to turn what they do understand into action quickly. With an obedient mind one learns the rights of things fast enough; for it is the law of the universe, and to obey is to understand.

"Look out!" cried Mr. Stonecrop, as they were turning the corner into Bloomsbury Square.

It was getting dusky now. A cab was approaching rather rapidly from the opposite direction, and Diamond pulling aside, and the other driver pulling up, they only just escaped a collision. Then they knew each other.

"Why, Diamond, it's a bad beginning to run into your own father," cried the driver.

"But, father, wouldn't it have been a bad ending to run into your own son?" said Diamond in return; and the two men laughed heartily.

"This is very kind of you, I'm sure, Stonecrop," said his father.

"Not a bit. He's a brave fellow, and'll be fit to drive on his own hook in a week or two. But I think you'd better let him drive you home now, for his mother don't like his having over much of the night air, and I promised not to take him farther than the square."

"Come along then, Diamond," said his father, as he brought his cab up to the other, and moved off the box to the seat beside it. Diamond jumped across, caught at the reins, said "Good-night, and thank you, Mr. Stonecrop," and drove away home, feeling more of a man than he had ever yet had a chance of feeling in all his life. Nor did his father find it necessary to give him a single hint as to his driving. Only I suspect the fact that it was old Diamond, and old Diamond on his way to his stable, may have had something to do with young Diamond's success.

"Well, child," said his mother, when he entered the room, "you've not been long gone."

"No, mother; here I am. Give me the baby."

"The baby's asleep," said his mother.

"Then give him to me, and I'll lay him down."

But as Diamond took him, he woke up and began to laugh. For he was indeed one of the merriest children. And no wonder, for he was as plump as a plum-pudding, and had never had an ache or a pain that lasted more than five minutes at a time. Diamond sat down with him and began to sing to him.

Baby baby babbing
your father's gone a-cabbing
to catch a shilling for its pence
to make the baby babbing dance
for old Diamond's a duck
they say he can swim
but the duck of diamonds
is baby that's him
and of all the swallows
the merriest fellows
that bake their cake
with the water they shake
out of the river
flowing for ever
and make dust into clay
on the shiniest day
to build their nest
father's the best
and mother's the whitest
and her eyes are the brightest
of all the dams
that watch their lambs
cropping the grass
where the waters pass
singing for ever
and of all the lambs
with the shakingest tails
and the jumpingest feet
baby's the funniest
baby's the bonniest
and he never wails
and he's always sweet
and Diamond's his nurse
and Diamond's his nurse
and Diamond's his nurse

When Diamond's rhymes grew scarce, he always began dancing the baby. Some people wondered that such a child could rhyme as he did, but his rhymes were not very good, for he was only trying to remember what he had heard the river sing at the back of the north wind.

17
Diamond Goes On

Diamond became a great favourite with all the men about the mews. Some may think it was not the best place in the world for him to be brought up in; but it must have been, for there he was. At first, he heard a good many rough and bad words; but he did not like them, and so they did him little harm. He did not know in the least what they meant, but there was something in the very sound of them, and in the tone of voice in which they were said, which Diamond felt to be ugly. So they did not even stick to him, not to say get inside him. He never took any notice of them, and his face shone pure and good in the middle of them, like a primrose in a hailstorm. At first, because his face was so quiet and sweet, with a smile always either awake or asleep in his eyes, and because he never heeded their ugly words and rough jokes, they said he wasn't all there, meaning that he was half an idiot, whereas he was a great deal more there than they had the sense to see. And before long the bad words found themselves ashamed to come out of the men's mouths when Diamond was near. The one would nudge the other to remind him that the boy was within hearing, and the words choked themselves before they got any farther. When they talked to him nicely he had always a good answer, sometimes a smart one, ready, and that helped much to make them change their minds about him.

One day Jack gave him a curry-comb and a brush to try his hand upon old Diamond's coat. He used them so deftly, so gently, and yet so thoroughly, as far as he could reach, that the man could not help admiring him.

"You must make haste and, grow" he said. "It won't do to have a horse's belly clean and his back dirty, you know."

"Give me a leg," said Diamond, and in a moment he was on the old horse's back with the comb and brush. He sat on his withers, and reaching forward as he ate his hay, he curried and he brushed, first at one side of his neck, and then at the other. When that was done he asked for a dressing-comb, and combed his mane thoroughly. Then he pushed himself on to his back, and did his shoulders as far down as he could reach. Then he sat on his croup, and did his back and sides; then he turned around like a monkey, and attacked his hind-quarters, and combed his tail. This last was not so easy to manage, for he had to lift it up, and every now and then old Diamond would whisk it out of his hands, and once he sent the comb flying out of the stable door, to the great amusement of the men. But Jack fetched it again, and Diamond began once more, and did not leave off until he had done the whole business fairly well, if not in a first-rate, experienced fashion. All the time the old horse went on eating his hay, and, but with an occasional whisk of his tail when Diamond tickled or scratched him, took no notice of the proceeding. But that was all a pretence, for he knew very well who it was that was perched on his back, and rubbing away at him with the comb and the brush. So he was quite pleased and proud, and perhaps said to himself something like this—

"I'm a stupid old horse, who can't brush his own coat; but there's my young godson on my back, cleaning me like an angel."

I won't vouch for what the old horse was thinking, for it is very difficult to find out what any old horse is thinking.

"Oh dear!" said Diamond when he had done, "I'm so tired!"

And he laid himself down at full length on old Diamond's back.

By this time all the men in the stable were gathered about the two Diamonds, and all much amused. One of them lifted him down, and from that time he was a greater favourite than before. And if ever there was a boy who had a chance of being a prodigy at cab-driving, Diamond was that boy, for the strife came to be who should have him out with him on the box.

His mother, however, was a little shy of the company for him, and besides she could not always spare him. Also his father liked to have him himself when he could; so that he was more desired than enjoyed among the cabmen.

But one way and another he did learn to drive all sorts of horses, and to drive them well, and that through the most crowded streets in London City. Of course there was the man always on the box-seat beside him, but before long there was seldom the least occasion to take the reins from out of his hands. For one thing he never got frightened, and consequently was never in too great a hurry. Yet when the moment came for doing something sharp, he was always ready for it. I must once more remind my readers that he had been to the back of the north wind.

One day, which was neither washing-day, nor cleaning-day nor marketing-day, nor Saturday, nor Monday—upon which consequently

Diamond could be spared from the baby—his father took him on his own cab. After a stray job or two by the way, they drew up in the row upon the stand between Cockspur Street and Pall Mall. They waited a long time, but nobody seemed to want to be carried anywhere. By and by ladies would be going home from the Academy exhibition, and then there would be a chance of a job.

"Though, to be sure," said Diamond's father—with what truth I cannot say, but he believed what he said— "some ladies is very hard, and keeps you to the bare sixpence a mile, when every one knows that ain't enough to keep a family and a cab upon. To be sure it's the law; but mayhap they may get more law than they like some day themselves."

As it was very hot, Diamond's father got down to have a glass of beer himself, and give another to the old waterman. He left Diamond on the box.

A sudden noise got up, and Diamond looked round to see what was the matter.

There was a crossing near the cab-stand, where a girl was sweeping. Some rough young imps had picked a quarrel with her, and were now hauling at her broom to get it away from her. But as they did not pull all together, she was holding it against them, scolding and entreating alternately.

Diamond was off his box in a moment, and running to the help of the girl. He got hold of the broom at her end and pulled along with her. But the boys proceeded to rougher measures, and one of them hit Diamond on the nose, and made it bleed; and as he could not let go the broom to mind his nose, he was soon a dreadful figure. But presently his father came back, and missing Diamond, looked about. He had to look twice, however, before he could be sure that that was his boy in the middle of the tumult. He rushed in, and sent the assailants flying in all directions. The girl thanked Diamond, and began sweeping as if nothing had happened, while his father led him away. With the help of old Tom, the waterman, he was soon washed into decency, and his father set him on the box again, perfectly satisfied with the account he gave of the cause of his being in a fray.

"I couldn't let them behave so to a poor girl—could I, father?" he said.

"Certainly not, Diamond," said his father, quite pleased, for Diamond's father was a gentleman.

A moment after, up came the girl, running, with her broom over her shoulder, and calling, "Cab, there! cab!"

Diamond's father turned instantly, for he was the foremost in the rank, and followed the girl. One or two other passing cabs heard the cry, and made for the place, but the girl had taken care not to call till she was near enough to give her friends the first chance. When they reached the curbstone—who should it be waiting for the cab but Mrs. and Miss Coleman! They did not look at the cabman, however. The girl opened the door for them; they gave her the address, and a penny; she told the cabman, and away they drove.

When they reached the house, Diamond's father got down and rang the bell. As he opened the door of the cab, he touched his hat as he had been wont to do. The ladies both stared for a moment, and then exclaimed together:

"Why, Joseph! can it be you?"

"Yes, ma'am; yes, miss," answered he, again touching his hat, with all the respect he could possibly put into the action. "It's a lucky day which I see you once more upon it."

"Who would have thought it?" said Mrs. Coleman. "It's changed times for both of us, Joseph, and it's not very often we can have a cab even; but you see my daughter is still very poorly, and she can't bear the motion of the omnibuses. Indeed we meant to walk a bit first before we took a cab, but just at the corner, for as hot as the sun was, a cold wind came down the street, and I saw that Miss Coleman must not face it. But to think we should have fallen upon you, of all the cabmen in London! I didn't know you had got a cab."

"Well, you see, ma'am, I had a chance of buying the old horse, and I couldn't resist him. There he is, looking at you, ma'am. Nobody knows the sense in that head of his."

The two ladies went near to pat the horse, and then they noticed Diamond on the box.

"Why, you've got both Diamonds with you," said Miss Coleman. "How do you do, Diamond?"

Diamond lifted his cap, and answered politely.

"He'll be fit to drive himself before long," said his father, proudly. "The old horse is a-teaching of him."

"Well, he must come and see us, now you've found us out. Where do you live?"

Diamond's father gave the ladies a ticket with his name and address printed on it; and then Mrs. Coleman took out her purse, saying:

"And what's your fare, Joseph?"

"No, thank you, ma'am," said Joseph. "It was your own old horse as took you; and me you paid long ago."

He jumped on his box before she could say another word, and with a parting salute drove off, leaving them on the pavement, with the maid holding the door for them.

It was a long time now since Diamond had seen North Wind, or even thought much about her. And as his father drove along, he was thinking not about her, but about the crossing-sweeper, and was wondering what made him feel as if he knew her quite well, when he could not remember anything of her. But a picture arose in his mind of a little girl running before the wind and dragging her broom after her; and from that, by degrees, he recalled the whole adventure of the night when he got down from North Wind's back in a London street. But he could not quite satisfy himself whether the whole affair was not a dream which he had dreamed when he was a very little boy. Only he had been to the back of the north wind since—there could be no doubt of that; for when he woke every morning, he always knew that he had been there again. And as he thought and thought, he recalled another thing that had happened that morning, which, although it seemed a mere accident, might have something to do with what had happened since. His father had intended going on the stand at King's Cross that morning, and had turned into Gray's Inn Lane to drive there, when they found the way blocked up, and upon inquiry were informed that a stack of chimneys had been blown down in the night, and had fallen across the road. They were just clearing the rubbish away. Diamond's father turned, and made for Charing Cross.

That night the father and mother had a great deal to talk about.

"Poor things!" said the mother. "it's worse for them than it is for us. You see they've been used to such grand things, and for them to come down to a little poky house like that—it breaks my heart to think of it."

"I don't know" said Diamond thoughtfully, "whether Mrs. Coleman had bells on her toes."

"What do you mean, child?" said his mother.

"She had rings on her fingers, anyhow," returned Diamond.

"Of course she had, as any lady would. What has that to do with it?"

"When we were down at Sandwich," said Diamond, "you said you would have to part with your mother's ring, now we were poor."

"Bless the child; he forgets nothing," said his mother. "Really, Diamond, a body would need to mind what they say to you."

"Why?" said Diamond. "I only think about it."

"That's just why," said the mother.

"Why is that why?" persisted Diamond, for he had not yet learned that grown-up people are not often so much grown up that they never talk like children—and spoilt ones too.

"Mrs. Coleman is none so poor as all that yet. No, thank Heaven! she's not come to that."

"Is it a great disgrace to be poor?" asked Diamond, because of the tone in which his mother had spoken.

But his mother, whether conscience-stricken I do not know hurried him away to bed, where after various attempts to understand her, resumed and resumed again in spite of invading sleep, he was conquered at last, and gave in, murmuring over and over to himself, "Why is why?" but getting no answer to the question.

18
The Drunken Cabman

A few nights after this, Diamond woke up suddenly, believing he heard North Wind thundering along. But it was something quite different. South Wind was moaning round the chimneys, to be sure, for she was not very happy that night, but it was not her voice that had wakened Diamond. Her voice would only have lulled him the deeper asleep. It was a loud, angry voice, now growling like that of a beast, now raving like that of a madman; and when Diamond came a little wider awake, he knew that it was the voice of the drunken cabman, the wall of whose room was at the head of his bed. It was anything but pleasant to hear, but he could not help hearing it. At length there came a cry from the woman, and then a scream from the baby. Thereupon Diamond thought it time that somebody did something, and as himself was the only somebody at hand, he must go and see whether he could not do something. So he got up and put on part of his clothes, and went down the stair, for the cabman's room did not open upon their stair, and he had to go out into the yard, and in at the next door. This, fortunately, the cabman, being drunk, had left open. By the time he reached their stair, all was still except the voice of the crying baby, which guided him to the right door. He opened it softly, and peeped in. There, leaning back in a chair, with his arms hanging down by his sides, and his legs stretched out before him and supported on his heels, sat the drunken cabman. His wife lay in her clothes upon the bed, sobbing, and the baby was wailing in the cradle. It was very miserable altogether.

Now the way most people do when they see anything very miserable is to turn away from the sight, and try to forget it. But Diamond began as usual to try to destroy the misery. The little boy was just as much one of God's messengers as if he had been an angel with a flaming sword, going out to fight the devil. The devil he had to fight just then was Misery. And the way he fought him was the very best. Like a wise soldier, he attacked him first in his weakest point—that was the baby; for Misery can never get such a hold of a baby as of a grown person. Diamond was knowing in babies, and he knew he could do something to make the baby, happy; for although he had only known one baby as yet, and although not one baby is the same as another, yet they are so very much alike in some things, and he knew that one baby so thoroughly, that he had good reason to believe he could do something for any other. I have known people who would have begun to fight the devil in a very different and a very stupid way. They would have begun by scolding the idiotic cabman; and next they would make his wife angry by saying it must be her fault as well as his, and by leaving ill-bred though well-meant shabby little books for them to read, which they were sure to hate the sight of; while all the time they would not have put out a finger to touch the wailing baby. But Diamond had him out of the cradle in a moment, set him up on his knee, and told him to look at the light. Now all the light there was came only from a lamp in the yard, and it was a very dingy and yellow light, for the glass of the lamp was dirty, and the gas was bad; but the light that came from it was, notwithstanding, as certainly light as if it had come from the sun itself, and the baby knew that, and smiled to it; and although it was indeed a wretched room which that lamp lighted— so dreary, and dirty, and empty, and hopeless!—there in the middle of it sat Diamond on a stool, smiling to the baby, and the baby on his knees smiling to the lamp. The father of him sat staring at nothing, neither asleep nor awake, not quite lost in stupidity either, for through it all he was dimly angry with himself, he did not know why. It was that he had struck his wife. He had forgotten it, but was miserable about it, notwithstanding. And this misery was the voice of the great Love that had made him and his wife and the baby and Diamond, speaking in his heart, and telling him to be good. For that great Love speaks in the most wretched and dirty hearts; only the tone of its voice depends on the echoes of the place in which it sounds. On Mount Sinai, it was thunder; in the cabman's heart it was misery; in the soul of St. John it was perfect blessedness.

By and by he became aware that there was a voice of singing in the room. This, of course, was the voice of Diamond singing to the baby—song after song, every one as foolish as another to the cabman, for he was too tipsy to part one word from another: all the words mixed up in his ear in a gurgle without division or stop; for such was the way he spoke himself, when he was in this horrid condition. But the baby was more than content with Diamond's songs, and Diamond himself was so contented with what the songs were all about, that he did not care a bit about the songs themselves, if only baby liked them. But they did the cabman good as well as the baby and Diamond, for they put him to sleep, and the sleep was busy all the time it lasted, smoothing the wrinkles out of his temper.

At length Diamond grew tired of singing, and began to talk to the baby instead. And as soon as he stopped singing, the cabman began to wake up. His brain was a little clearer now, his temper a little smoother, and his heart not quite so dirty. He began to listen and he went on listening, and heard Diamond saying to the baby something like this, for he thought the cabman was asleep:

"Poor daddy! Baby's daddy takes too much beer and gin, and that makes him somebody else, and not his own self at all. Baby's daddy would never hit baby's mammy if he didn't take too much beer. He's very fond of baby's mammy, and works from morning to night to get her breakfast and dinner and supper, only at night he forgets, and pays the money away for beer. And they put nasty stuff in beer, I've heard my daddy say, that drives all the good out, and lets all the bad in. Daddy says when a man takes a drink, there's a thirsty devil creeps into his inside, because he knows he will always get enough there. And the devil is always crying out for more drink, and that makes the man thirsty, and so he drinks more and more, till he kills himself with it. And then the ugly devil creeps out of him, and crawls about on his belly, looking for some other cabman to get into, that he may drink, drink, drink. That's what my daddy says, baby. And he says, too, the only way to make the devil come out is to give him plenty of cold water and tea and coffee, and nothing at all that comes from the public-house; for the devil can't abide that kind of stuff, and creeps out pretty soon, for fear of being drowned in it. But your daddy will drink the nasty stuff, poor man! I wish he wouldn't, for it makes mammy cross with him, and no wonder! and then when mammy's cross, he's crosser, and there's nobody in the house to take care of them but baby; and you do take care of them, baby—don't you, baby? I know you do. Babies always take care of their fathers and mothers—don't they, baby? That's what they come for—isn't it, baby? And when daddy stops drinking beer and nasty gin with turpentine in it, father says, then mammy will be so happy, and look so pretty! and daddy will be so good to baby! and baby will be as happy as a swallow, which is the merriest fellow! And Diamond will be so happy too! And when Diamond's a man, he'll take baby out with him on the box, and teach him to drive a cab."

He went on with chatter like this till baby was asleep, by which time he was tired, and father and mother were both wide awake—only rather confused—the one from the beer, the other from the blow—and staring, the one from his chair, the other from her bed, at Diamond. But he was quite unaware of their notice, for he sat half-asleep, with his eyes wide open, staring in his turn, though without knowing it, at the cabman, while the cabman could not withdraw his gaze from Diamond's white face and big eyes. For Diamond's face was always rather pale, and now it was paler than usual with sleeplessness, and the light of the street-lamp upon it. At length he found himself nodding, and he knew then it was time to put the baby down, lest he should let him fall. So he rose from the little three-legged stool, and laid the baby in the cradle, and covered him up—it was well it was a warm night, and he did not want much covering—and then he all but staggered out of the door, he was so tipsy himself with sleep.

"Wife," said the cabman, turning towards the bed, "I do somehow believe that wur a angel just gone. Did you see him, wife? He warn't wery big, and he hadn't got none o' them wingses, you know. It wur one o' them baby-angels you sees on the gravestones, you know."

"Nonsense, hubby!" said his wife; "but it's just as good. I might say better, for you can ketch hold of him when you like. That's little Diamond as everybody knows, and a duck o' diamonds he is! No woman could wish for a better child than he be."

"I ha' heerd on him in the stable, but I never see the brat afore. Come, old girl, let bygones be bygones, and gie us a kiss, and we'll go to bed."

The cabman kept his cab in another yard, although he had his room in this. He was often late in coming home, and was not one to take notice of children, especially when he was tipsy, which was oftener than not. Hence, if he had ever seen Diamond, he did not know him. But his wife knew him well enough, as did every one else who lived all day in the yard. She was a good-natured woman. It was she who had got the fire lighted and the tea ready for them when Diamond and his mother came home from Sandwich. And her husband was not an ill-natured man either, and when in the morning he recalled not only Diamond's visit, but how he himself had behaved to his wife, he was very vexed with himself, and gladdened his poor wife's heart by telling her how sorry he was. And for a whole week after, he did not go near the public-house, hard as it was to avoid it, seeing a certain rich brewer had built one, like a trap to catch souls and bodies in, at almost every corner he had to pass on his way home. Indeed, he was never quite so bad after that, though it was some time before he began really to reform.

19
Diamond's Friends

One day when old Diamond was standing with his nose in his bag between Pall Mall and Cockspur Street, and his master was reading the newspaper on the box of his cab, which was the last of a good many in the row, little Diamond got down for a run, for his legs were getting cramped with sitting. And first of all he strolled with his hands in his pockets up to the crossing, where the girl and her broom were to be found in all weathers. Just as he was going to speak to her, a tall gentleman stepped upon the crossing. He was pleased to find it so clean, for the streets were muddy, and he had nice boots on; so he put his hand in his pocket, and gave the girl a penny. But when she gave him a sweet smile in return, and made him a pretty courtesy, he looked at her again, and said:

"Where do you live, my child?"

"Paradise Row," she answered; "next door to the Adam and Eve—down the area."

"Whom do you live with?" he asked.

"My wicked old grannie," she replied.

"You shouldn't call your grannie wicked," said the gentleman.

"But she is," said the girl, looking up confidently in his face. "If you don't believe me, you can come and take a look at her."

The words sounded rude, but the girl's face looked so simple that the gentleman saw she did not mean to be rude, and became still more interested in her.

"Still you shouldn't say so," he insisted.

"Shouldn't I? Everybody calls her wicked old grannie—even them that's as wicked as her. You should hear her swear. There's nothing like it in the Row. Indeed, I assure you, sir, there's ne'er a one of them can shut my grannie up once she begins and gets right a-going. You must put her in a passion first, you know. It's no good till you do that—she's so old now. How she do make them laugh, to be sure!"

Although she called her wicked, the child spoke so as plainly to indicate pride in her grannie's pre-eminence in swearing.

The gentleman looked very grave to hear her, for he was sorry that such a nice little girl should be in such bad keeping. But he did not know what to say next, and stood for a moment with his eyes on the ground. When he lifted them, he saw the face of Diamond looking up in his.

"Please, sir," said Diamond, "her grannie's very cruel to her sometimes, and shuts her out in the streets at night, if she happens to be late."

"Is this your brother?" asked the gentleman of the girl.

"No, sir."

"How does he know your grandmother, then? He does not look like one of her sort."

"Oh no, sir! He's a good boy—quite."

Here she tapped her forehead with her finger in a significant manner.

"What do you mean by that?" asked the gentleman, while Diamond looked on smiling.

"The cabbies call him God's baby," she whispered. "He's not right in the head, you know. A tile loose."

Still Diamond, though he heard every word, and understood it too, kept on smiling. What could it matter what people called him, so long as he did nothing he ought not to do? And, besides, God's baby was surely the best of names!

"Well, my little man, and what can you do?" asked the gentleman, turning towards him—just for the sake of saying something.

"Drive a cab," said Diamond.

"Good; and what else?" he continued; for, accepting what the girl had said, he regarded the still sweetness of Diamond's face as a sign of silliness, and wished to be kind to the poor little fellow.

"Nurse a baby," said Diamond.

"Well—and what else?"

"Clean father's boots, and make him a bit of toast for his tea."

"You're a useful little man," said the gentleman. "What else can you do?"

"Not much that I know of," said Diamond. "I can't curry a horse, except somebody puts me on his back. So I don't count that."

"Can you read?"

"No. But mother can and father can, and they're going to teach me some day soon."

"Well, here's a penny for you."

"Thank you, sir."

"And when you have learned to read, come to me, and I'll give you sixpence and a book with fine pictures in it."

"Please, sir, where am I to come?" asked Diamond, who was too much a man of the world not to know that he must have the gentleman's address before he could go and see him.

"You're no such silly!" thought he, as he put his hand in his pocket, and brought out a card. "There," he said, "your father will be able to read that, and tell you where to go."

"Yes, sir. Thank you, sir," said Diamond, and put the card in his pocket.

The gentleman walked away, but turning round a few paces off, saw Diamond give his penny to the girl, and, walking slower heard him say:

"I've got a father, and mother, and little brother, and you've got nothing but a wicked old grannie. You may have my penny."

The girl put it beside the other in her pocket, the only trustworthy article of dress she wore. Her grandmother always took care that she had a stout pocket.

"Is she as cruel as ever?" asked Diamond.

"Much the same. But I gets more coppers now than I used to, and I can get summats to eat, and take browns enough home besides to keep her from grumbling. It's a good thing she's so blind, though."

"Why?" asked Diamond.

"'Cause if she was as sharp in the eyes as she used to be, she would find out I never eats her broken wittles, and then she'd know as I must get something somewheres."

"Doesn't she watch you, then?"

"O' course she do. Don't she just! But I make believe and drop it in my lap, and then hitch it into my pocket."

"What would she do if she found you out?"

"She never give me no more."

"But you don't want it!"

"Yes, I do want it."

"What do you do with it, then?"

"Give it to cripple Jim."

"Who's cripple Jim?"

"A boy in the Row. His mother broke his leg when he wur a kid, so he's never come to much; but he's a good boy, is Jim, and I love Jim dearly. I always keeps off a penny for Jim—leastways as often as I can.— But there I must sweep again, for them busses makes no end o' dirt."

"Diamond! Diamond!" cried his father, who was afraid he might get no good by talking to the girl; and Diamond obeyed, and got up again upon the box. He told his father about the gentleman, and what he had promised him if he would learn to read, and showed him the gentleman's card.

"Why, it's not many doors from the Mews!" said his father, giving him back the card. "Take care of it, my boy, for it may lead to something. God knows, in these hard times a man wants as many friends as he's ever likely to get."

"Haven't you got friends enough, father?" asked Diamond.

"Well, I have no right to complain; but the more the better, you know."

"Just let me count," said Diamond.

And he took his hands from his pockets, and spreading out the fingers of his left hand, began to count, beginning at the thumb.

"There's mother, first, and then baby, and then me. Next there's old Diamond—and the cab—no, I won't count the cab, for it never looks at you, and when Diamond's out of the shafts, it's nobody. Then there's the man that drinks next door, and his wife, and his baby."

"They're no friends of mine," said his father.

"Well, they're friends of mine," said Diamond.

His father laughed.

"Much good they'll do you!" he said.

"How do you know they won't?" returned Diamond.

"Well, go on," said his father.

"Then there's Jack and Mr. Stonecrop, and, deary me! not to have mentioned Mr. Coleman and Mrs. Coleman, and Miss Coleman, and Mrs. Crump. And then there's the clergyman that spoke to me in the garden that day the tree was blown down."

"What's his name!"

"I don't know his name."

"Where does he live?"

"I don't know."

"How can you count him, then?"

"He did talk to me, and very kindlike too."

His father laughed again.

"Why, child, you're just counting everybody you know. That don't make 'em friends."

"Don't it? I thought it did. Well, but they shall be my friends. I shall make 'em."

"How will you do that?"

"They can't help themselves then, if they would. If I choose to be their friend, you know, they can't prevent me. Then there's that girl at the crossing."

"A fine set of friends you do have, to be sure, Diamond!"

"Surely she's a friend anyhow, father. If it hadn't been for her, you would never have got Mrs. Coleman and Miss Coleman to carry home."

His father was silent, for he saw that Diamond was right, and was ashamed to find himself more ungrateful than he had thought.

"Then there's the new gentleman," Diamond went on.

"If he do as he say," interposed his father.

"And why shouldn't he? I daresay sixpence ain't too much for him to spare. But I don't quite understand, father: is nobody your friend but the one that does something for you?"

"No, I won't say that, my boy. You would have to leave out baby then."

"Oh no, I shouldn't. Baby can laugh in your face, and crow in your ears, and make you feel so happy. Call you that nothing, father?"

The father's heart was fairly touched now. He made no answer to this last appeal, and Diamond ended off with saying:

"And there's the best of mine to come yet—and that's you, daddy—except it be mother, you know. You're my friend, daddy, ain't you? And I'm your friend, ain't I?"

"And God for us all," said his father, and then they were both silent for that was very solemn.

20
Diamond Learns To Read

The question of the tall gentleman as to whether Diamond could read or not set his father thinking it was high time he could; and as soon as old Diamond was suppered and bedded, he began the task that very night. But it was not much of a task to Diamond, for his father took for his lesson-book those very rhymes his mother had picked up on the sea-shore; and as Diamond was not beginning too soon, he learned very fast indeed. Within a month he was able to spell out most of the verses for himself.

But he had never come upon the poem he thought he had heard his mother read from it that day. He had looked through and through the book several times after he knew the letters and a few words, fancying he could tell the look of it, but had always failed to find one more like it than another. So he wisely gave up the search till he could really read. Then he resolved to begin at the beginning, and read them all straight through. This took him nearly a fortnight. When he had almost reached the end, he came upon the following verses, which took his fancy much, although they were certainly not very like those he was in search of.

Little Boy Blue

Little Boy Blue lost his way in a wood.
    Sing apples and cherries, roses and honey;
He said, "I would not go back if I could,
    It's all so jolly and funny."

He sang, "This wood is all my own,
    Apples and cherries, roses and honey;
So here I'll sit, like a king on my throne,
    All so jolly and funny."

A little snake crept out of the tree,
   Apples and cherries, roses and honey;
"Lie down at my feet, little snake," said he,
   All so jolly and funny.

A little bird sang in the tree overhead,
   Apples and cherries, roses and honey;
"Come and sing your song on my finger instead,
   All so jolly and funny."

The snake coiled up; and the bird flew down,
And sang him the song of Birdie Brown.

Little Boy Blue found it tiresome to sit,
And he thought he had better walk on a bit.

So up he got, his way to take,
And he said, "Come along, little bird and snake."

And waves of snake o'er the damp leaves passed,
And the snake went first and Birdie Brown last;

By Boy Blue's head, with flutter and dart,
Flew Birdie Brown with its song in its heart.

He came where the apples grew red and sweet:
"Tree, drop me an apple down at my feet."

He came where the cherries hung plump and red:
"Come to my mouth, sweet kisses," he said.

And the boughs bow down, and the apples they dapple
The grass, too many for him to grapple.

And the cheeriest cherries, with never a miss,
Fall to his mouth, each a full-grown kiss.

He met a little brook singing a song.
He said, "Little brook, you are going wrong.

"You must follow me, follow me, follow, I say
Do as I tell you, and come this way."

And the song-singing, sing-songing forest brook
Leaped from its bed and after him took,

Followed him, followed. And pale and wan,
The dead leaves rustled as the water ran.

And every bird high up on the bough,
And every creature low down below,

He called, and the creatures obeyed the call,
Took their legs and their wings and followed him all;

Squirrels that carried their tails like a sack,
Each on his own little humpy brown back;

Householder snails, and slugs all tails,
And butterflies, flutterbies, ships all sails;

And weasels, and ousels, and mice, and larks,
And owls, and rere-mice, and harkydarks,

All went running, and creeping, and flowing,
After the merry boy fluttering and going;

The dappled fawns fawning, the fallow-deer following,
The swallows and flies, flying and swallowing;

Cockchafers, henchafers, cockioli-birds,
Cockroaches, henroaches, cuckoos in herds.

The spider forgot and followed him spinning,
And lost all his thread from end to beginning.

The gay wasp forgot his rings and his waist,
He never had made such undignified haste.

The dragon-flies melted to mist with their hurrying.
The mole in his moleskins left his barrowing burrowing.

The bees went buzzing, so busy and beesy,
And the midges in columns so upright and easy.

But Little Boy Blue was not content,

Calling for followers still as he went,

Blowing his horn, and beating his drum,
And crying aloud, "Come all of you, come!"

He said to the shadows, "Come after me;"
And the shadows began to flicker and flee,

And they flew through the wood all flattering and fluttering,
Over the dead leaves flickering and muttering.

And he said to the wind, "Come, follow; come, follow,
With whistle and pipe, and rustle and hollo."

And the wind wound round at his desire,
As if he had been the gold cock on the spire.

And the cock itself flew down from the church,
And left the farmers all in the lurch.

They run and they fly, they creep and they come,
Everything, everything, all and some.

The very trees they tugged at their roots,
Only their feet were too fast in their boots,

After him leaning and straining and bending,
As on through their boles he kept walking and wending,

Till out of the wood he burst on a lea,
Shouting and calling, "Come after me!"

And then they rose up with a leafy hiss,
And stood as if nothing had been amiss.

Little Boy Blue sat down on a stone,
And the creatures came round him every one.

And he said to the clouds, "I want you there."
And down they sank through the thin blue air.

And he said to the sunset far in the West,
"Come here; I want you; I know best."

And the sunset came and stood up on the wold,
And burned and glowed in purple and gold.

Then Little Boy Blue began to ponder:
"What's to be done with them all, I wonder."

Then Little Boy Blue, he said, quite low,
"What to do with you all I am sure I don't know."

Then the clouds clodded down till dismal it grew;
The snake sneaked close; round Birdie Brown flew;

The brook sat up like a snake on its tail;
And the wind came up with a what-will-you wail;

And all the creatures sat and stared;
The mole opened his very eyes and glared;

And for rats and bats and the world and his wife,
Little Boy Blue was afraid of his life.

Then Birdie Brown began to sing,
And what he sang was the very thing:

"You have brought us all hither, Little Boy Blue,
Pray what do you want us all to do?"

"Go away! go away!" said Little Boy Blue;
"I'm sure I don't want you—get away—do."

"No, no; no, no; no, yes, and no, no,"
Sang Birdie Brown, "it mustn't be so.

"We cannot for nothing come here, and away.
Give us some work, or else we stay."

"Oh dear! and oh dear!" with sob and with sigh,
Said Little Boy Blue, and began to cry.

But before he got far, he thought of a thing;
And up he stood, and spoke like a king.

"Why do you hustle and jostle and bother?

Off with you all! Take me back to my mother."

The sunset stood at the gates of the west.
"Follow me, follow me" came from Birdie Brown's breast.

"I am going that way as fast as I can,"
Said the brook, as it sank and turned and ran.

Back to the woods fled the shadows like ghosts:
"If we stay, we shall all be missed from our posts."

Said the wind with a voice that had changed its cheer,
"I was just going there, when you brought me here."

"That's where I live," said the sack-backed squirrel,
And he turned his sack with a swing and a swirl.

Said the cock of the spire, "His father's churchwarden."
Said the brook running faster, "I run through his garden."

Said the mole, "Two hundred worms—there I caught 'em
Last year, and I'm going again next autumn."

Said they all, "If that's where you want us to steer for,
What in earth or in water did you bring us here for?"

"Never you mind," said Little Boy Blue;
"That's what I tell you. If that you won't do,

"I'll get up at once, and go home without you.
I think I will; I begin to doubt you."

He rose; and up rose the snake on its tail,
And hissed three times, half a hiss, half a wail.

Little Boy Blue he tried to go past him;
But wherever he turned, sat the snake and faced him.

"If you don't get out of my way," he said,
"I tell you, snake, I will break your head."

The snake he neither would go nor come;
So he hit him hard with the stick of his drum.

The snake fell down as if he were dead,
And Little Boy Blue set his foot on his head.

And all the creatures they marched before him,
And marshalled him home with a high cockolorum.

And Birdie Brown sang Twirrrr twitter twirrrr twee—
    Apples and cherries, roses and honey;
Little Boy Blue has listened to me—
    All so jolly and funny.

21
Sal's Nanny

Diamond managed with many blunders to read this rhyme to his mother.

"Isn't it nice, mother?" he said.

"Yes, it's pretty," she answered.

"I think it means something," returned Diamond.

"I'm sure I don't know what," she said.

"I wonder if it's the same boy—yes, it must be the same—Little Boy Blue, you know. Let me see—how does that rhyme go?

Little Boy Blue, come blow me your horn—

Yes, of course it is—for this one went 'blowing his horn and beating his drum.' He had a drum too.

Little Boy Blue, come blow me your horn;
The sheep's in the meadow, the cow's in the corn,

He had to keep them out, you know. But he wasn't minding his work. It goes—

Where's the little boy that looks after the sheep?
He's under the haystack, fast asleep.

There, you see, mother! And then, let me see—

Who'll go and wake him? No, not I;
For if I do, he'll be sure to cry.

So I suppose nobody did wake him. He was a rather cross little boy, I daresay, when woke up. And when he did wake of himself, and saw the mischief the cow had done to the corn, instead of running home to his mother, he ran away into the wood and lost himself. Don't you think that's very likely, mother?"

"I shouldn't wonder," she answered.

"So you see he was naughty; for even when he lost himself he did not want to go home. Any of the creatures would have shown him the way if he had asked it—all but the snake. He followed the snake, you know, and he took him farther away. I suppose it was a young one of the same serpent that tempted Adam and Eve. Father was telling us about it last Sunday, you remember."

"Bless the child!" said his mother to herself; and then added aloud, finding that Diamond did not go on, "Well, what next?"

"I don't know, mother. I'm sure there's a great deal more, but what it is I can't say. I only know that he killed the snake. I suppose that's what he had a drumstick for. He couldn't do it with his horn."

"But surely you're not such a silly as to take it all for true, Diamond?"

"I think it must be. It looks true. That killing of the snake looks true. It's what I've got to do so often."

His mother looked uneasy. Diamond smiled full in her face, and added—

"When baby cries and won't be happy, and when father and you talk about your troubles, I mean."

This did little to reassure his mother; and lest my reader should have his qualms about it too, I venture to remind him once more that Diamond had been to the back of the north wind.

Finding she made no reply, Diamond went on—

"In a week or so, I shall be able to go to the tall gentleman and tell him I can read. And I'll ask him if he can help me to understand the rhyme."

But before the week was out, he had another reason for going to Mr. Raymond.

For three days, on each of which, at one time or other, Diamond's father was on the same stand near the National Gallery, the girl was not at her crossing, and Diamond got quite anxious about her, fearing she must be ill. On the fourth day, not seeing her yet, he said to his father, who had that moment shut the door of his cab upon a fare—

"Father, I want to go and look after the girl, She can't be well."

"All right," said his father. "Only take care of yourself, Diamond."

So saying he climbed on his box and drove off.

He had great confidence in his boy, you see, and would trust him anywhere. But if he had known the kind of place in which the girl lived, he would perhaps have thought twice before he allowed him to go alone. Diamond, who did know something of it, had not, however, any fear. From talking to the girl he had a good notion of where about it was, and he remembered the address well enough; so by asking his way some twenty times, mostly of policemen, he came at length pretty near the place. The last policeman he questioned looked down upon him from the summit of six feet two inches, and replied with another question, but kindly:

"What do you want there, my small kid? It ain't where you was bred, I guess."

"No sir," answered Diamond. "I live in Bloomsbury."

"That's a long way off," said the policeman.

"Yes, it's a good distance," answered Diamond; "but I find my way about pretty well. Policemen are always kind to me."

"But what on earth do you want here?"

Diamond told him plainly what he was about, and of course the man believed him, for nobody ever disbelieved Diamond. People might think he was mistaken, but they never thought he was telling a story.

"It's an ugly place," said the policeman.

"Is it far off?" asked Diamond.

"No. It's next door almost. But it's not safe."

"Nobody hurts me," said Diamond.

"I must go with you, I suppose."

"Oh, no! please not," said Diamond. "They might think I was going to meddle with them, and I ain't, you know."

"Well, do as you please," said the man, and gave him full directions.

Diamond set off, never suspecting that the policeman, who was a kind-hearted man, with children of his own, was following him close, and watching him round every corner. As he went on, all at once he thought he remembered the place, and whether it really was so, or only that he had laid up the policeman's instructions well in his mind, he went straight for the cellar of old Sal.

"He's a sharp little kid, anyhow, for as simple as he looks," said the man to himself. "Not a wrong turn does he take! But old Sal's a rum un for such a child to pay a morning visit to. She's worse when she's sober than when she's half drunk. I've seen her when she'd have torn him in pieces."

Happily then for Diamond, old Sal had gone out to get some gin. When he came to her door at the bottom of the area-stair and knocked, he received no answer. He laid his ear to the door, and thought he heard a moaning within. So he tried the door, and found it was not locked! It was a dreary place indeed,—and very dark, for the window was below the level of the street, and covered with mud, while over the grating which kept people from falling into the area, stood a chest of drawers, placed there by a dealer in second-hand furniture, which shut out almost all the light. And the smell in the place was dreadful. Diamond stood still for a while, for he could see next to nothing, but he heard the moaning plainly enough now, When he got used to the darkness, he discovered his friend lying with closed eyes and a white suffering face on a heap of little better than rags in a corner of the den. He went up to her and spoke; but she made him no answer. Indeed, she was not in the least aware of his presence, and Diamond saw that he could do nothing for her without help. So taking a lump of barley-sugar from his pocket, which he had bought for her as he came along, and laying it beside her, he left the place, having already made up his mind to go and see the tall gentleman, Mr. Raymond, and ask him to do something for Sal's Nanny, as the girl was called.

By the time he got up the area-steps, three or four women who had seen him go down were standing together at the top waiting for him. They wanted his clothes for their children; but they did not follow him down lest Sal should find them there. The moment he appeared, they laid their hands on him, and all began talking at once, for each wanted to get some advantage over her neighbours. He told them quite quietly, for he was not frightened, that he had come to see what was the matter with Nanny.

"What do you know about Nanny?" said one of them fiercely. "Wait till old Sal comes home, and you'll catch it, for going prying into her house when she's out. If you don't give me your jacket directly, I'll go and fetch her."

"I can't give you my jacket," said Diamond. "It belongs to my father and mother, you know. It's not mine to give. Is it now? You would not think it right to give away what wasn't yours—would you now?"

"Give it away! No, that I wouldn't; I'd keep it," she said, with a rough laugh. "But if the jacket ain't yours, what right have you to keep it? Here, Cherry, make haste. It'll be one go apiece."

They all began to tug at the jacket, while Diamond stooped and kept his arms bent to resist them. Before they had done him or the jacket any harm, however, suddenly they all scampered away; and Diamond, looking in the opposite direction, saw the tall policeman coming towards him.

"You had better have let me come with you, little man," he said, looking down in Diamond's face, which was flushed with his resistance.

"You came just in the right time, thank you," returned Diamond. "They've done me no harm."

"They would have if I hadn't been at hand, though."

"Yes; but you were at hand, you know, so they couldn't."

Perhaps the answer was deeper in purport than either Diamond or the policeman knew. They walked away together, Diamond telling his new friend how ill poor Nanny was, and that he was going to let the tall gentleman know. The policeman put him in the nearest way for Bloomsbury, and stepping out in good earnest, Diamond reached Mr. Raymond's door in less than an hour. When he asked if he was at home, the servant, in return, asked what he wanted.

"I want to tell him something."

"But I can't go and trouble him with such a message as that."

"He told me to come to him—that is, when I could read—and I can."

"How am I to know that?"

Diamond stared with astonishment for one moment, then answered:

"Why, I've just told you. That's how you know it."

But this man was made of coarser grain than the policeman, and, instead of seeing that Diamond could not tell a lie, he put his answer down as impudence, and saying, "Do you think I'm going to take your word for it?" shut the door in his face.

Diamond turned and sat down on the doorstep, thinking with himself that the tall gentleman must either come in or come out, and he was therefore in the best possible position for finding him. He had not waited long before the door opened again; but when he looked round, it was only the servant once more.

"Get, away" he said. "What are you doing on the doorstep?"

"Waiting for Mr. Raymond," answered Diamond, getting up.

"He's not at home."

"Then I'll wait till he comes," returned Diamond, sitting down again with a smile.

What the man would have done next I do not know, but a step sounded from the hall, and when Diamond looked round yet again, there was the tall gentleman.

"Who's this, John?" he asked.

"I don't know, sir. An imperent little boy as will sit on the doorstep."

"Please sir," said Diamond, "he told me you weren't at home, and I sat down to wait for you."

"Eh, what!" said Mr. Raymond. "John! John! This won't do. Is it a habit of yours to turn away my visitors? There'll be some one else to turn away, I'm afraid, if I find any more of this kind of thing. Come in, my little man. I suppose you've come to claim your sixpence?"

"No, sir, not that."

"What! can't you read yet?"

"Yes, I can now, a little. But I'll come for that next time. I came to tell you about Sal's Nanny."

"Who's Sal's Nanny?"

"The girl at the crossing you talked to the same day."

"Oh, yes; I remember. What's the matter? Has she got run over?"

Then Diamond told him all.

Now Mr. Raymond was one of the kindest men in London. He sent at once to have the horse put to the brougham, took Diamond with him, and drove to the Children's Hospital. There he was well known to everybody, for he was not only a large subscriber, but he used to go and tell the children stories of an afternoon. One of the doctors promised to go and find Nanny, and do what could be done—have her brought to the hospital, if possible.

That same night they sent a litter for her, and as she could be of no use to old Sal until she was better, she did not object to having her removed. So she was soon lying in the fever ward—for the first time in her life in a nice clean bed. But she knew nothing of the whole affair. She was too ill to know anything.

22
Mr. Raymond's Riddle

Mr. Raymond took Diamond home with him, stopping at the Mews to tell his mother that he would send him back soon. Diamond ran in with the message himself, and when he reappeared he had in his hand the torn and crumpled book which North Wind had given him.

"Ah! I see," said Mr. Raymond: "you are going to claim your sixpence now."

"I wasn't thinking of that so much as of another thing," said Diamond. "There's a rhyme in this book I can't quite understand. I want you to tell me what it means, if you please."

"I will if I can," answered Mr. Raymond. "You shall read it to me when we get home, and then I shall see."

Still with a good many blunders, Diamond did read it after a fashion. Mr. Raymond took the little book and read it over again.

Now Mr. Raymond was a poet himself, and so, although he had never been at the back of the north wind, he was able to understand the poem pretty well. But before saying anything about it, he read it over aloud, and Diamond thought he understood it much better already.

"I'll tell you what I think it means," he then said. "It means that people may have their way for a while, if they like, but it will get them into such troubles they'll wish they hadn't had it."

"I know, I know!" said Diamond. "Like the poor cabman next door. He drinks too much."

"Just so," returned Mr. Raymond. "But when people want to do right, things about them will try to help them. Only they must kill the snake, you know."

"I was sure the snake had something to do with it," cried Diamond triumphantly.

A good deal more talk followed, and Mr. Raymond gave Diamond his sixpence.

"What will you do with it?" he asked.

"Take it home to my mother," he answered. "She has a teapot—such a black one!—with a broken spout, and she keeps all her money in it. It ain't much; but she saves it up to buy shoes for me. And there's baby coming on famously, and he'll want shoes soon. And every sixpence is something—ain't it, sir?"

"To be sure, my man. I hope you'll always make as good a use of your money."

"I hope so, sir," said Diamond.

"And here's a book for you, full of pictures and stories and poems. I wrote it myself, chiefly for the children of the hospital where I hope Nanny is going. I don't mean I printed it, you know. I made it," added Mr. Raymond, wishing Diamond to understand that he was the author of the book.

"I know what you mean. I make songs myself. They're awfully silly, but they please baby, and that's all they're meant for."

"Couldn't you let me hear one of them now?" said Mr. Raymond.

"No, sir, I couldn't. I forget them as soon as I've done with them. Besides, I couldn't make a line without baby on my knee. We make them together, you know. They're just as much baby's as mine. It's he that pulls them out of me."

"I suspect the child's a genius," said the poet to himself, "and that's what makes people think him silly."

Now if any of my child readers want to know what a genius is—shall I try to tell them, or shall I not? I will give them one very short answer: it means one who understands things without any other body telling him what they mean. God makes a few such now and then to teach the rest of us.

"Do you like riddles?" asked Mr. Raymond, turning over the leaves of his own book.

"I don't know what a riddle is," said Diamond.

"It's something that means something else, and you've got to find out what the something else is."

Mr. Raymond liked the old-fashioned riddle best, and had written a few—one of which he now read.

> I have only one foot, but thousands of toes;
> My one foot stands, but never goes.
> I have many arms, and they're mighty all;
> And hundreds of fingers, large and small.
> From the ends of my fingers my beauty grows.
> I breathe with my hair, and I drink with my toes.
> I grow bigger and bigger about the waist,
> And yet I am always very tight laced.

None e'er saw me eat—I've no mouth to bite;
Yet I eat all day in the full sunlight.
In the summer with song I shave and quiver,
But in winter I fast and groan and shiver.

"Do you know what that means, Diamond?" he asked, when he had finished.

"No, indeed, I don't," answered Diamond.

"Then you can read it for yourself, and think over it, and see if you can find out," said Mr. Raymond, giving him the book. "And now you had better go home to your mother. When you've found the riddle, you can come again."

If Diamond had had to find out the riddle in order to see Mr. Raymond again, I doubt if he would ever have seen him.

"Oh then," I think I hear some little reader say, "he could not have been a genius, for a genius finds out things without being told."

I answer, "Genius finds out truths, not tricks." And if you do not understand that, I am afraid you must be content to wait till you grow older and know more.

23
The Early Bird

When Diamond got home he found his father at home already, sitting by the fire and looking rather miserable, for his head ached and he felt sick. He had been doing night work of late, and it had not agreed with him, so he had given it up, but not in time, for he had taken some kind of fever. The next day he was forced to keep his bed, and his wife nursed him, and Diamond attended to the baby. If he had not been ill, it would have been delightful to have him at home; and the first day Diamond sang more songs than ever to the baby, and his father listened with some pleasure. But the next he could not bear even Diamond's sweet voice, and was very ill indeed; so Diamond took the baby into his own room, and had no end of quiet games with him there. If he did pull all his bedding on the floor, it did not matter, for he kept baby very quiet, and made the bed himself again, and slept in it with baby all the next night, and many nights after.

But long before his father got well, his mother's savings were all but gone. She did not say a word about it in the hearing of her husband, lest she should distress him; and one night, when she could not help crying, she came into Diamond's room that his father might not hear her. She thought Diamond was asleep, but he was not. When he heard her sobbing, he was frightened, and said—

"Is father worse, mother?"

"No, Diamond," she answered, as well as she could; "he's a good bit better."

"Then what are you crying for, mother?"

"Because my money is almost all gone," she replied.

"O mammy, you make me think of a little poem baby and I learned out of North Wind's book to-day. Don't you remember how I bothered you about some of the words?"

"Yes, child," said his mother heedlessly, thinking only of what she should do after to-morrow.

Diamond began and repeated the poem, for he had a wonderful memory.

A little bird sat on the edge of her nest;
    Her yellow-beaks slept as sound as tops;
That day she had done her very best,
    And had filled every one of their little crops.
She had filled her own just over-full,
    And hence she was feeling a little dull.

"Oh, dear!" she sighed, as she sat with her head
    Sunk in her chest, and no neck at all,
While her crop stuck out like a feather bed
    Turned inside out, and rather small;
"What shall I do if things don't reform?
    I don't know where there's a single worm.

"I've had twenty to-day, and the children five each,
    Besides a few flies, and some very fat spiders:
No one will say I don't do as I preach—
    I'm one of the best of bird-providers;
But where's the use? We want a storm—
    I don't know where there's a single worm."

"There's five in my crop," said a wee, wee bird,
    Which woke at the voice of his mother's pain;
"I know where there's five." And with the word
    He tucked in his head, and went off again.
"The folly of childhood," sighed his mother,
    "Has always been my especial bother."

The yellow-beaks they slept on and on—
    They never had heard of the bogy To-morrow;
But the mother sat outside, making her moan—
    She'll soon have to beg, or steal, or borrow.
For she never can tell the night before,
    Where she shall find one red worm more.

The fact, as I say, was, she'd had too many;
    She couldn't sleep, and she called it virtue,
Motherly foresight, affection, any
    Name you may call it that will not hurt you,
So it was late ere she tucked her head in,
    And she slept so late it was almost a sin.

But the little fellow who knew of five
  Nor troubled his head about any more,
Woke very early, felt quite alive,
  And wanted a sixth to add to his store:
He pushed his mother, the greedy elf,
  Then thought he had better try for himself.

When his mother awoke and had rubbed her eyes,
  Feeling less like a bird, and more like a mole,
She saw him—fancy with what surprise—
  Dragging a huge worm out of a hole!
'Twas of this same hero the proverb took form:
  'Tis the early bird that catches the worm.

"There, mother!" said Diamond, as he finished; "ain't it funny?"

"I wish you were like that little bird, Diamond, and could catch worms for yourself," said his mother, as she rose to go and look after her husband.

Diamond lay awake for a few minutes, thinking what he could do to catch worms. It was very little trouble to make up his mind, however, and still less to go to sleep after it.

24
Another Early Bird

He got up in the morning as soon as he heard the men moving in the yard. He tucked in his little brother so that he could not tumble out of bed, and then went out, leaving the door open, so that if he should cry his mother might hear him at once. When he got into the yard he found the stable-door just opened.

"I'm the early bird, I think," he said to himself. "I hope I shall catch the worm."

He would not ask any one to help him, fearing his project might meet with disapproval and opposition. With great difficulty, but with the help of a broken chair he brought down from his bedroom, he managed to put the harness on Diamond. If the old horse had had the least objection to the proceeding, of course he could not have done it; but even when it came to the bridle, he opened his mouth for the bit, just as if he had been taking the apple which Diamond sometimes gave him. He fastened the cheek-strap very carefully, just in the usual hole, for fear of choking his friend, or else letting the bit get amongst his teeth. It was a job to get the saddle on; but with the chair he managed it. If old Diamond had had an education in physics to equal that of the camel, he would have knelt down to let him put it on his back, but that was more than could be expected of him, and then Diamond had to creep quite under him to get hold of the girth. The collar was almost the worst part of the business; but there Diamond could help Diamond. He held his head very low till his little master had got it over and turned it round, and then he lifted his head, and shook it on to his shoulders. The yoke was rather difficult; but when he had laid the traces over the horse's neck, the weight was not too much for him. He got him right at last, and led him out of the stable.

By this time there were several of the men watching him, but they would not interfere, they were so anxious to see how he would get over the various difficulties. They followed him as far as the stable-door, and there stood watching him again as he put the horse between the shafts, got them up one after the other into the loops, fastened the traces, the belly-band, the breeching, and the reins.

Then he got his whip. The moment he mounted the box, the men broke into a hearty cheer of delight at his success. But they would not let him go without a general inspection of the harness; and although they found it right, for not a buckle had to be shifted, they never allowed him to do it for himself again all the time his father was ill.

The cheer brought his mother to the window, and there she saw her little boy setting out alone with the cab in the gray of morning. She tugged at the window, but it was stiff; and before she could open it, Diamond, who was in a great hurry, was out of the mews, and almost out of the street. She called "Diamond! Diamond!" but there was no answer except from Jack.

"Never fear for him, ma'am," said Jack. "It 'ud be only a devil as would hurt him, and there ain't so many o' them as some folk 'ud have you believe. A boy o' Diamond's size as can 'arness a 'oss t'other Diamond's size, and put him to, right as a trivet—if he do upset the keb—'ll fall on his feet, ma'am."

"But he won't upset the cab, will he, Jack?"

"Not he, ma'am. Leastways he won't go for to do it."

"I know as much as that myself. What do you mean?"

"I mean he's a little likely to do it as the oldest man in the stable. How's the gov'nor to-day, ma'am?"

"A good deal better, thank you," she answered, closing the window in some fear lest her husband should have been made anxious by the news of Diamond's expedition. He knew pretty well, however, what his boy was capable of, and although not quite easy was less anxious than his mother. But as the evening drew on, the anxiety of both of them increased, and every sound of wheels made his father raise himself in his bed, and his mother peep out of the window.

Diamond had resolved to go straight to the cab-stand where he was best known, and never to crawl for fear of getting annoyed by idlers. Before he got across Oxford Street, however, he was hailed by a man who wanted to catch a train, and was in too great a hurry to think about the driver. Having carried him to King's Cross in good time, and got a good fare in return, he set off again in great spirits, and reached the stand in safety. He was the first there after all.

As the men arrived they all greeted him kindly, and inquired after his father.

"Ain't you afraid of the old 'oss running away with you?" asked one.

"No, he wouldn't run away with me," answered Diamond. "He knows I'm getting the shillings for father. Or if he did he would only run home."

"Well, you're a plucky one, for all your girl's looks!" said the man; "and I wish ye luck."

"Thank you, sir," said Diamond. "I'll do what I can. I came to the old place, you see, because I knew you would let me have my turn here."

In the course of the day one man did try to cut him out, but he was a stranger; and the shout the rest of them raised let him see it would not do, and made him so far ashamed besides, that he went away crawling.

Once, in a block, a policeman came up to him, and asked him for his number. Diamond showed him his father's badge, saying with a smile:

"Father's ill at home, and so I came out with the cab. There's no fear of me. I can drive. Besides, the old horse could go alone."

"Just as well, I daresay. You're a pair of 'em. But you are a rum 'un for a cabby—ain't you now?" said the policeman. "I don't know as I ought to let you go."

"I ain't done nothing," said Diamond. "It's not my fault I'm no bigger. I'm big enough for my age."

"That's where it is," said the man. "You ain't fit."

"How do you know that?" asked Diamond, with his usual smile, and turning his head like a little bird.

"Why, how are you to get out of this ruck now, when it begins to move?"

"Just you get up on the box," said Diamond, "and I'll show you. There, that van's a-moving now. Jump up."

The policeman did as Diamond told him, and was soon satisfied that the little fellow could drive.

"Well," he said, as he got down again, "I don't know as I should be right to interfere. Good luck to you, my little man!"

"Thank you, sir," said Diamond, and drove away.

In a few minutes a gentleman hailed him.

"Are you the driver of this cab?" he asked.

"Yes, sir" said Diamond, showing his badge, of which, he was proud.

"You're the youngest cabman I ever saw. How am I to know you won't break all my bones?"

"I would rather break all my own," said Diamond. "But if you're afraid, never mind me; I shall soon get another fare."

"I'll risk it," said the gentleman; and, opening the door himself, he jumped in.

He was going a good distance, and soon found that Diamond got him over the ground well. Now when Diamond had only to go straight ahead, and had not to mind so much what he was about, his thoughts always turned to the riddle Mr. Raymond had set him; and this gentleman looked so clever that he fancied he must be able to read it for him. He had given up all hope of finding it out for himself, and he could not plague his father about it when he was ill. He had thought of the answer himself, but fancied it could not be the right one, for to see how it all fitted required some knowledge of physiology. So, when he reached the end of his journey, he got down very quickly, and with his head just looking in at the window, said, as the gentleman gathered his gloves and newspapers:

"Please, sir, can you tell me the meaning of a riddle?"

"You must tell me the riddle first," answered the gentleman, amused.

Diamond repeated the riddle.

"Oh! that's easy enough," he returned. "It's a tree."

"Well, it ain't got no mouth, sure enough; but how then does it eat all day long?"

"It sucks in its food through the tiniest holes in its leaves," he answered. "Its breath is its food. And it can't do it except in the daylight."

"Thank you, sir, thank you," returned Diamond. "I'm sorry I couldn't find it out myself; Mr. Raymond would have been better pleased with me."

"But you needn't tell him any one told you."

Diamond gave him a stare which came from the very back of the north wind, where that kind of thing is unknown.

"That would be cheating," he said at last.

"Ain't you a cabby, then?"

"Cabbies don't cheat."

"Don't they? I am of a different opinion."

"I'm sure my father don't."

"What's your fare, young innocent?"

"Well, I think the distance is a good deal over three miles—that's two shillings. Only father says sixpence a mile is too little, though we can't ask for more."

"You're a deep one. But I think you're wrong. It's over four miles—not much, but it is."

"Then that's half-a-crown," said Diamond.

"Well, here's three shillings. Will that do?"

"Thank you kindly, sir. I'll tell my father how good you were to me—first to tell me my riddle, then to put me right about the distance, and then to give me sixpence over. It'll help father to get well again, it will."

"I hope it may, my man. I shouldn't wonder if you're as good as you look, after all."

As Diamond returned, he drew up at a stand he had never been on before: it was time to give Diamond his bag of chopped beans and oats. The men got about him, and began to chaff him. He took it all good-humouredly, until one of them, who was an ill-conditioned fellow, began to tease old Diamond by poking him roughly in the ribs, and making general game of him. That he could not bear, and the tears came in his eyes. He undid the nose-bag, put it in the boot, and was just going to mount and drive away, when the fellow interfered, and would not let him get up. Diamond endeavoured to persuade him, and was very civil, but he would have his fun out of him, as he said. In a few minutes a group of idle boys had assembled, and Diamond found himself in a very uncomfortable position. Another cab drew up at the stand, and the driver got off and approached the assemblage.

"What's up here?" he asked, and Diamond knew the voice. It was that of the drunken cabman.

"Do you see this young oyster? He pretends to drive a cab," said his enemy.

"Yes, I do see him. And I sees you too. You'd better leave him alone. He ain't no oyster. He's a angel come down on his own business. You be off, or I'll be nearer you than quite agreeable."

The drunken cabman was a tall, stout man, who did not look one to take liberties with.

"Oh! if he's a friend of yours," said the other, drawing back.

Diamond got out the nose-bag again. Old Diamond should have his feed out now.

"Yes, he is a friend o' mine. One o' the best I ever had. It's a pity he ain't a friend o' yourn. You'd be the better for it, but it ain't no fault of hisn."

When Diamond went home at night, he carried with him one pound one shilling and sixpence, besides a few coppers extra, which had followed some of the fares.

His mother had got very anxious indeed—so much so that she was almost afraid, when she did hear the sound of his cab, to go and look, lest she should be yet again disappointed, and should break down before her husband. But there was the old horse, and there was the cab all right, and there was Diamond in the box, his pale face looking triumphant as a full moon in the twilight.

When he drew up at the stable-door, Jack came out, and after a good many friendly questions and congratulations, said:

"You go in to your mother, Diamond. I'll put up the old 'oss. I'll take care on him. He do deserve some small attention, he do."

"Thank you, Jack," said Diamond, and bounded into the house, and into the arms of his mother, who was waiting him at the top of the stair.

The poor, anxious woman led him into his own room, sat down on his bed, took him on her lap as if he had been a baby, and cried.

"How's father?" asked Diamond, almost afraid to ask.

"Better, my child," she answered, "but uneasy about you, my dear."

"Didn't you tell him I was the early bird gone out to catch the worm?"

"That was what put it in your head, was it, you monkey?" said his mother, beginning to get better.

"That or something else," answered Diamond, so very quietly that his mother held his head back and stared in his face.

"Well! of all the children!" she said, and said no more.

"And here's my worm," resumed Diamond.

But to see her face as he poured the shillings and sixpences and pence into her lap! She burst out crying a second time, and ran with the money to her husband.

And how pleased he was! It did him no end of good. But while he was counting the coins, Diamond turned to baby, who was lying awake in his cradle, sucking his precious thumb, and took him up, saying:

"Baby, baby! I haven't seen you for a whole year."

And then he began to sing to him as usual. And what he sang was this, for he was too happy either to make a song of his own or to sing sense. It was one out of Mr. Raymond's book.

The True Story of the Cat and the Fiddle

Hey, diddle, diddle!
    The cat and the fiddle!
He played such a merry tune,
    That the cow went mad
    With the pleasure she had,
And jumped right over the moon.
    But then, don't you see?
    Before that could be,
The moon had come down and listened.
    The little dog hearkened,
    So loud that he barkened,
"There's nothing like it, there isn't."

Hey, diddle, diddle!
    Went the cat and the fiddle,

Hey diddle, diddle, dee, dee!
   The dog laughed at the sport
   Till his cough cut him short,
It was hey diddle, diddle, oh me!
   And back came the cow
   With a merry, merry low,
For she'd humbled the man in the moon.
   The dish got excited,
   The spoon was delighted,
And the dish waltzed away with the spoon.

But the man in the moon,
   Coming back too soon
From the famous town of Norwich,
   Caught up the dish,
   Said, "It's just what I wish
To hold my cold plum-porridge!"
   Gave the cow a rat-tat,
   Flung water on the cat,
And sent him away like a rocket.
   Said, "O Moon there you are!"
   Got into her car,
And went off with the spoon in his pocket

Hey ho! diddle, diddle!
   The wet cat and wet fiddle,
They made such a caterwauling,
   That the cow in a fright
   Stood bolt upright
Bellowing now, and bawling;
   And the dog on his tail,
   Stretched his neck with a wail.
But "Ho! ho!" said the man in the moon—
   "No more in the South
   Shall I burn my mouth,
For I've found a dish and a spoon."

25
Diamond's Dream

"There, baby!" said Diamond; "I'm so happy that I can only sing nonsense. Oh, father, think if you had been a poor man, and hadn't had a cab and old Diamond! What should I have done?"

"I don't know indeed what you could have done," said his father from the bed.

"We should have all starved, my precious Diamond," said his mother, whose pride in her boy was even greater than her joy in the shillings. Both of them together made her heart ache, for pleasure can do that as well as pain.

"Oh no! we shouldn't," said Diamond. "I could have taken Nanny's crossing till she came back; and then the money, instead of going for Old Sal's gin, would have gone for father's beef-tea. I wonder what Nanny will do when she gets well again. Somebody else will be sure to have taken the crossing by that time. I wonder if she will fight for it, and whether I shall have to help her. I won't bother my head about that. Time enough yet! Hey diddle! hey diddle! hey diddle diddle! I wonder whether Mr. Raymond would take me to see Nanny. Hey diddle! hey diddle! hey diddle diddle! The baby and fiddle! O, mother, I'm such a silly! But I can't help it. I wish I could think of something else, but there's nothing will come into my head but hey diddle diddle! the cat and the fiddle! I wonder what the angels do—when they're extra happy, you know—when they've been driving cabs all day and taking home the money to their mothers. Do you think they ever sing nonsense, mother?"

"I daresay they've got their own sort of it," answered his mother, "else they wouldn't be like other people." She was thinking more of her twenty-one shillings and sixpence, and of the nice dinner she would get for her sick husband next day, than of the angels and their nonsense, when she said it. But Diamond found her answer all right.

"Yes, to be sure," he replied. "They wouldn't be like other people if they hadn't their nonsense sometimes. But it must be very pretty nonsense, and not like that silly hey diddle diddle! the cat and the fiddle! I wish I could get it out of my head. I wonder what the angels' nonsense is like. Nonsense is a very good thing, ain't it, mother?—a little of it now and then; more of it for baby, and not so much for grown people like cabmen and their mothers? It's like the pepper and salt that goes in the soup—that's it—isn't it, mother? There's baby fast asleep! Oh, what a nonsense baby it is—to sleep so much! Shall I put him down, mother?"

Diamond chattered away. What rose in his happy little heart ran out of his mouth, and did his father and mother good. When he went to bed, which he did early, being more tired, as you may suppose, than usual, he was still thinking what the nonsense could be like which the angels sang when they were too happy to sing sense. But before coming to any conclusion he fell fast asleep. And no wonder, for it must be acknowledged a difficult question.

That night he had a very curious dream which I think my readers would like to have told them. They would, at least, if they are as fond of nice dreams as I am, and don't have enough of them of their own.

He dreamed that he was running about in the twilight in the old garden. He thought he was waiting for North Wind, but she did not come. So he would run down to the back gate, and see if she were there. He ran and ran. It was a good long garden out of his dream, but in his dream it had grown so long and spread out so wide that the gate he wanted was nowhere. He ran and ran, but instead of coming to the gate found himself in a beautiful country, not like any country he had ever been in before. There were no trees of any size; nothing bigger in fact than hawthorns, which were full of may-blossom. The place in which they grew was wild and dry, mostly covered with grass, but having patches of heath. It extended on every side as far as he could see. But although it was so wild, yet wherever in an ordinary heath you might have expected furze bushes, or holly, or broom, there grew roses—wild and rare—all kinds. On every side, far and near, roses were glowing. There too was the gum-cistus, whose flowers fall every night and come again the next morning, lilacs and syringas and labur-nums, and many shrubs besides, of which he did not know the names; but the roses were everywhere. He wandered on and on, wondering when it would come to an end. It was of no use going back, for there was no house to be seen anywhere. But he was not frightened, for you know Diamond was used to things that were rather out of the way. He threw himself down under a rose-bush, and fell asleep.

He woke, not out of his dream, but into it, thinking he heard a child's voice, calling "Diamond, Diamond!" He jumped up, but all was still about him. The rose-bushes were pouring out their odours in clouds. He could see the scent like mists of the same colour as the rose, issuing like a slow fountain and spreading in the air till it joined the thin rosy vapour which hung over all the wilderness. But again came the voice calling him, and it seemed to come from over his head. He looked up, but saw only the deep blue sky full of stars—more brilliant, however, than he had seen them before; and both sky and stars looked nearer to the earth.

While he gazed up, again he heard the cry. At the same moment he saw one of the biggest stars over his head give a kind of twinkle and jump, as if it went out and came in again. He threw himself on his back, and fixed his eyes upon it. Nor had he gazed long before it went out, leaving something like a scar in the blue. But as he went on gazing he saw a face where the star had been—a merry face, with bright eyes. The eyes appeared not only to see Diamond, but to know that Diamond had caught sight of them, for the face withdrew the same moment. Again came the voice, calling "Diamond, Diamond;" and in jumped the star to its place.

Diamond called as loud as he could, right up into the sky:

"Here's Diamond, down below you. What do you want him to do?"

The next instant many of the stars round about that one went out, and many voices shouted from the sky,—

"Come up; come up. We're so jolly! Diamond! Diamond!"

This was followed by a peal of the merriest, kindliest laughter, and all the stars jumped into their places again.

"How am I to come up?" shouted Diamond.

"Go round the rose-bush. It's got its foot in it," said the first voice.

Diamond got up at once, and walked to the other side of the rose-bush.

There he found what seemed the very opposite of what he wanted—a stair down into the earth. It was of turf and moss. It did not seem to promise well for getting into the sky, but Diamond had learned to look through the look of things. The voice must have meant that he was to go down this stair; and down this stair Diamond went, without waiting to think more about it.

It was such a nice stair, so cool and soft—all the sides as well as the steps grown with moss and grass and ferns! Down and down Diamond went—a long way, until at last he heard the gurgling and splashing of a little stream; nor had he gone much farther before he met it—yes, met it coming up the stairs to meet him, running up just as naturally as if it had been doing the other thing. Neither was Diamond in the least surprised to see it pitching itself from one step to another as it climbed towards him: he never thought it was odd—and no more it was, there. It would have been odd here. It made a merry tune as it came, and its voice was like the laughter he had heard from the sky. This appeared promising; and he went on, down and down the stair, and up and up the stream, till at last he came where it hurried out from under a stone, and the stair stopped altogether. And as the stream bubbled up, the stone shook and swayed with its force; and Diamond thought he would try to lift it. Lightly it rose to his hand, forced up by the stream from below; and, by what would have seemed an unaccountable perversion of things had he been awake, threatened to come tumbling upon his head. But he avoided it, and when it fell, got upon it. He now saw that the opening through which the water came pouring in was over his head, and with the help of the stone he scrambled out by it, and found himself on the side of a grassy hill which rounded away from him in every direction, and down which came the brook which vanished in the hole. But scarcely had he noticed so much as this before a merry shouting and laughter burst upon him, and a number of naked little boys came running, every one eager to get to him first. At the shoulders of each fluttered two little wings, which were of no use for flying, as they were mere buds; only being made for it they could not help fluttering as if they were flying. Just as the foremost of the troop reached him, one or two of them fell, and the rest with shouts of laughter came tumbling over them till they heaped up a mound of struggling merriment. One after another they extricated themselves, and each as he got free threw his arms round Diamond and kissed him. Diamond's heart was ready to melt within him from clear delight. When they had all embraced him,—

"Now let us have some fun," cried one, and with a shout they all scampered hither and thither, and played the wildest gambols on the grassy slopes. They kept constantly coming back to Diamond, however, as the centre of their enjoyment, rejoicing over him as if they had found a lost playmate.

There was a wind on the hillside which blew like the very embodiment of living gladness. It blew into Diamond's heart, and made him so happy that he was forced to sit down and cry.

"Now let's go and dig for stars," said one who seemed to be the captain of the troop.

They all scurried away, but soon returned, one after another, each with a pickaxe on his shoulder and a spade in his hand. As soon as they were gathered, the captain led them in a straight line to another part of the hill. Diamond rose and followed.

"Here is where we begin our lesson for to-night," he said. "Scatter and dig."

There was no more fun. Each went by himself, walking slowly with bent shoulders and his eyes fixed on the ground. Every now and then one would stop, kneel down, and look intently, feeling with his hands and parting the grass. One would get up and walk on again, another spring to his feet, catch eagerly at his pickaxe and strike it into the ground once and again, then throw it aside, snatch up his spade, and commence digging at the loosened earth. Now one would sorrowfully shovel the earth into the hole again, trample it down with his little bare white feet, and walk on. But another would give a joyful shout, and after much tugging and loosening would draw from the hole a lump as big as his head, or no bigger than his fist; when the under side of it would pour such a blaze of golden or bluish light into Diamond's eyes that he was quite dazzled. Gold and blue were the commoner colours: the jubilation was greater over red or green or purple. And every time a star was dug up all the little angels dropped their tools and crowded about it, shouting and dancing and fluttering their wing-buds.

When they had examined it well, they would kneel down one after the other and peep through the hole; but they always stood back to give Diamond the first look. All that Diamond could report, however, was, that through the star-holes he saw a great many things and places and people he knew quite well, only somehow they were different—there was something marvellous about them—he could not tell what. Every time he rose from looking through a star-hole, he felt as if his heart would break for, joy; and he said that if he had not cried, he did not know what would have become of him.

As soon as all had looked, the star was carefully fitted in again, a little mould was strewn over it, and the rest of the heap left as a sign that the star had been discovered.

At length one dug up a small star of a most lovely colour—a colour Diamond had never seen before. The moment the angel saw what it was, instead of showing it about, he handed it to one of his neighbours, and seated himself on the edge of the hole, saying:

"This will do for me. Good-bye. I'm off."

They crowded about him, hugging and kissing him; then stood back with a solemn stillness, their wings lying close to their shoulders. The little fellow looked round on them once with a smile, and then shot himself headlong through the star-hole. Diamond, as privileged, threw himself on the ground to peep after him, but he saw nothing. "It's no use," said the captain. "I never saw anything more of one that went that way."

"His wings can't be much use," said Diamond, concerned and fearful, yet comforted by the calm looks of the rest.

"That's true," said the captain. "He's lost them by this time. They all do that go that way. You haven't got any, you see."

"No," said Diamond. "I never did have any."

"Oh! didn't you?" said the captain.

"Some people say," he added, after a pause, "that they come again.
I don't know. I've never found the colour I care about myself. I suppose I shall some day."

Then they looked again at the star, put it carefully into its hole,
danced around it and over it—but solemnly, and called it by the name
of the finder.

"Will you know it again?" asked Diamond.

"Oh, yes. We never forget a star that's been made a door of."

Then they went on with their searching and digging.

Diamond having neither pickaxe nor spade, had the more time to
think.

"I don't see any little girls," he said at last.

The captain stopped his shovelling, leaned on his spade, rubbed
his forehead thoughtfully with his left hand—the little angels were all
left-handed—repeated the words "little girls," and then, as if a thought
had struck him, resumed his work, saying—

"I think I know what you mean. I've never seen any of them, of
course; but I suppose that's the sort you mean. I'm told—but mind I
don't say it is so, for I don't know—that when we fall asleep, a troop
of angels very like ourselves, only quite different, goes round to all
the stars we have discovered, and discovers them after us. I suppose
with our shovelling and handling we spoil them a bit; and I daresay
the clouds that come up from below make them smoky and dull sometimes. They say—mind, I say they say—these other angels take them
out one by one, and pass each round as we do, and breathe over it,
and rub it with their white hands, which are softer than ours, because
they don't do any pick-and-spade work, and smile at it, and put it in
again: and that is what keeps them from growing dark."

"How jolly!" thought Diamond. "I should like to see them at their
work too.—When do you go to sleep?" he asked the captain.

"When we grow sleepy," answered the captain. "They do say—but
mind I say they say—that it is when those others—what do you call
them? I don't know if that is their name; I am only guessing that may
be the sort you mean—when they are on their rounds and come near
any troop of us we fall asleep. They live on the west side of the hill.
None of us have ever been to the top of it yet."

Even as he spoke, he dropped his spade. He tumbled down beside it,
and lay fast asleep. One after the other each of the troop dropped his
pickaxe or shovel from his listless hands, and lay fast asleep by his work.

"Ah!" thought Diamond to himself, with delight, "now the girl-
angels are coming, and I, not being an angel, shall not fall asleep like
the rest, and I shall see the girl-angels."

But the same moment he felt himself growing sleepy. He struggled hard with the invading power. He put up his fingers to his eyelids and pulled them open. But it was of no use. He thought he saw a glimmer of pale rosy light far up the green hill, and ceased to know.

When he awoke, all the angels were starting up wide awake too. He expected to see them lift their tools, but no, the time for play had come. They looked happier than ever, and each began to sing where he stood. He had not heard them sing before.

"Now," he thought, "I shall know what kind of nonsense the angels sing when they are merry. They don't drive cabs, I see, but they dig for stars, and they work hard enough to be merry after it."

And he did hear some of the angels' nonsense; for if it was all sense to them, it had only just as much sense to Diamond as made good nonsense of it. He tried hard to set it down in his mind, listening as closely as he could, now to one, now to another, and now to all together. But while they were yet singing he began, to his dismay, to find that he was coming awake—faster and faster. And as he came awake, he found that, for all the goodness of his memory, verse after verse of the angels' nonsense vanished from it. He always thought he could keep the last, but as the next began he lost the one before it, and at length awoke, struggling to keep hold of the last verse of all. He felt as if the effort to keep from forgetting that one verse of the vanishing song nearly killed him. And yet by the time he was wide awake he could not be sure of that even. It was something like this:

> White hands of whiteness
>   Wash the stars' faces,
> Till glitter, glitter, glit, goes their brightness
>   Down to poor places.

This, however, was so near sense that he thought it could not be really what they did sing.

26
Diamond Takes a Fare the Wrong Way Right

The next morning Diamond was up almost as early as before. He had nothing to fear from his mother now, and made no secret of what he was about. By the time he reached the stable, several of the men were there. They asked him a good many questions as to his luck the day before, and he told them all they wanted to know. But when he proceeded to harness the old horse, they pushed him aside with rough kindness, called him a baby, and began to do it all for him. So Diamond ran in and had another mouthful of tea and bread and butter; and although he had never been so tired as he was the night before, he started quite fresh this morning. It was a cloudy day, and the wind blew hard from the north—so hard sometimes that, perched on the box with just his toes touching the ground, Diamond wished that he had some kind of strap to fasten himself down with lest he should be blown away. But he did not really mind it.

His head was full of the dream he had dreamed; but it did not make him neglect his work, for his work was not to dig stars but to drive old Diamond and pick up fares. There are not many people who can think about beautiful things and do common work at the same time. But then there are not many people who have been to the back of the north wind.

There was not much business doing. And Diamond felt rather cold, notwithstanding his mother had herself put on his comforter and helped him with his greatcoat. But he was too well aware of his dignity to get inside his cab as some do. A cabman ought to be above minding the weather—at least so Diamond thought. At length he was called to a neighbouring house, where a young woman with a heavy box had to be taken to Wapping for a coast-steamer.

He did not find it at all pleasant, so far east and so near the river; for the roughs were in great force. However, there being no block, not even in Nightingale Lane, he reached the entrance of the wharf, and set down his passenger without annoyance. But as he turned to go back, some idlers, not content with chaffing him, showed a mind to the fare the young woman had given him. They were just pulling him off the box, and Diamond was shouting for the police, when a pale-faced man, in very shabby clothes, but with the look of a gentleman somewhere about him, came up, and making good use of his stick, drove them off.

"Now, my little man," he said, "get on while you can. Don't lose any time. This is not a place for you."

But Diamond was not in the habit of thinking only of himself. He saw that his new friend looked weary, if not ill, and very poor.

"Won't you jump in, sir?" he said. "I will take you wherever you like."

"Thank you, my man; but I have no money; so I can't."

"Oh! I don't want any money. I shall be much happier if you will get in. You have saved me all I had. I owe you a lift, sir."

"Which way are you going?"

"To Charing Cross; but I don't mind where I go."

"Well, I am very tired. If you will take me to Charing Cross, I shall be greatly obliged to you. I have walked from Gravesend, and had hardly a penny left to get through the tunnel."

So saying, he opened the door and got in, and Diamond drove away.

But as he drove, he could not help fancying he had seen the gentleman—for Diamond knew he was a gentleman—before. Do all he could, however, he could not recall where or when. Meantime his fare, if we may call him such, seeing he was to pay nothing, whom the relief of being carried had made less and less inclined to carry himself, had been turning over things in his mind, and, as they passed the Mint, called to Diamond, who stopped the horse, got down and went to the window.

"If you didn't mind taking me to Chiswick, I should be able to pay you when we got there. It's a long way, but you shall have the whole fare from the Docks—and something over."

"Very well, sir" said Diamond. "I shall be most happy."

He was just clambering up again, when the gentleman put his head out of the window and said—

"It's The Wilderness—Mr. Coleman's place; but I'll direct you when we come into the neighbourhood."

It flashed upon Diamond who he was. But he got upon his box to arrange his thoughts before making any reply.

The gentleman was Mr. Evans, to whom Miss Coleman was to have been married, and Diamond had seen him several times with her in the garden. I have said that he had not behaved very well to Miss

Coleman. He had put off their marriage more than once in a cowardly fashion, merely because he was ashamed to marry upon a small income, and live in a humble way. When a man thinks of what people will say in such a case, he may love, but his love is but a poor affair. Mr. Coleman took him into the firm as a junior partner, and it was in a measure through his influence that he entered upon those speculations which ruined him. So his love had not been a blessing. The ship which North Wind had sunk was their last venture, and Mr. Evans had gone out with it in the hope of turning its cargo to the best advantage. He was one of the single boat-load which managed to reach a desert island, and he had gone through a great many hardships and sufferings since then. But he was not past being taught, and his troubles had done him no end of good, for they had made him doubt himself, and begin to think, so that he had come to see that he had been foolish as well as wicked. For, if he had had Miss Coleman with him in the desert island, to build her a hut, and hunt for her food, and make clothes for her, he would have thought himself the most fortunate of men; and when he was at home, he would not marry till he could afford a man-servant. Before he got home again, he had even begun to understand that no man can make haste to be rich without going against the will of God, in which case it is the one frightful thing to be successful. So he had come back a more humble man, and longing to ask Miss Coleman to forgive him. But he had no idea what ruin had fallen upon them, for he had never made himself thoroughly acquainted with the firm's affairs. Few speculative people do know their own affairs. Hence he never doubted he should find matters much as he left them, and expected to see them all at The Wilderness as before. But if he had not fallen in with Diamond, he would not have thought of going there first.

What was Diamond to do? He had heard his father and mother drop some remarks concerning Mr. Evans which made him doubtful of him. He understood that he had not been so considerate as he might have been. So he went rather slowly till he should make up his mind. It was, of course, of no use to drive Mr. Evans to Chiswick. But if he should tell him what had befallen them, and where they lived now, he might put off going to see them, and he was certain that Miss Coleman, at least, must want very much to see Mr. Evans. He was pretty sure also that the best thing in any case was to bring them together, and let them set matters right for themselves.

The moment he came to this conclusion, he changed his course from westward to northward, and went straight for Mr. Coleman's poor little house in Hoxton. Mr. Evans was too tired and too much occupied with his thoughts to take the least notice of the streets they passed through, and had no suspicion, therefore, of the change of direction.

By this time the wind had increased almost to a hurricane, and as they had often to head it, it was no joke for either of the Diamonds. The distance, however, was not great. Before they reached the street where Mr. Coleman lived it blew so tremendously, that when Miss Coleman, who was going out a little way, opened the door, it dashed against the wall with such a bang, that she was afraid to venture, and went in again. In five minutes after, Diamond drew up at the door. As soon as he had entered the street, however, the wind blew right behind them, and when he pulled up, old Diamond had so much ado to stop the cab against it, that the breeching broke. Young Diamond jumped off his box, knocked loudly at the door, then turned to the cab and said—before Mr. Evans had quite begun to think something must be amiss:

"Please, sir, my harness has given away. Would you mind stepping in here for a few minutes? They're friends of mine. I'll take you where you like after I've got it mended. I shan't be many minutes, but you can't stand in this wind."

Half stupid with fatigue and want of food, Mr. Evans yielded to the boy's suggestion, and walked in at the door which the maid held with difficulty against the wind. She took Mr. Evans for a visitor, as indeed he was, and showed him into the room on the ground-floor. Diamond, who had followed into the hall, whispered to her as she closed the door—

"Tell Miss Coleman. It's Miss Coleman he wants to see."

"I don't know" said the maid. "He don't look much like a gentleman."

"He is, though; and I know him, and so does Miss Coleman."

The maid could not but remember Diamond, having seen him when he and his father brought the ladies home. So she believed him, and went to do what he told her.

What passed in the little parlour when Miss Coleman came down does not belong to my story, which is all about Diamond. If he had known that Miss Coleman thought Mr. Evans was dead, perhaps he would have managed differently. There was a cry and a running to and fro in the house, and then all was quiet again.

Almost as soon as Mr. Evans went in, the wind began to cease, and was now still. Diamond found that by making the breeching just a little tighter than was quite comfortable for the old horse he could do very well for the present; and, thinking it better to let him have his bag in this quiet place, he sat on the box till the old horse should have eaten his dinner. In a little while Mr. Evans came out, and asked him to come in. Diamond obeyed, and to his delight Miss Coleman put her arms round him and kissed him, and there was payment for him! Not to mention the five precious shillings she gave him, which he could not refuse because his mother wanted them so much at home for his father. He left them nearly as happy as they were themselves.

The rest of the day he did better, and, although he had not so much to take home as the day before, yet on the whole the result was satisfactory. And what a story he had to tell his father and mother about his adventures, and how he had done, and what was the result! They asked him such a multitude of questions! some of which he could answer, and some of which he could not answer; and his father seemed ever so much better from finding that his boy was already not only useful to his family but useful to other people, and quite taking his place as a man who judged what was wise, and did work worth doing.

For a fortnight Diamond went on driving his cab, and keeping his family. He had begun to be known about some parts of London, and people would prefer taking his cab because they liked what they heard of him. One gentleman who lived near the mews engaged him to carry him to the City every morning at a certain hour; and Diamond was punctual as clockwork—though to effect that required a good deal of care, for his father's watch was not much to be depended on, and had to be watched itself by the clock of St. George's church. Between the two, however, he did make a success of it.

After that fortnight, his father was able to go out again. Then Diamond went to make inquiries about Nanny, and this led to something else.

27
The Children's Hospital

The first day his father resumed his work, Diamond went with him
as usual. In the afternoon, however, his father, having taken a fare to
the neighbourhood, went home, and Diamond drove the cab the rest
of the day. It was hard for old Diamond to do all the work, but they
could not afford to have another horse. They contrived to save him as
much as possible, and fed him well, and he did bravely.

The next morning his father was so much stronger that Diamond
thought he might go and ask Mr. Raymond to take him to see Nanny. He
found him at home. His servant had grown friendly by this time, and
showed him in without any cross-questioning. Mr. Raymond received him
with his usual kindness, consented at once, and walked with him to the
Hospital, which was close at hand. It was a comfortable old-fashioned
house, built in the reign of Queen Anne, and in her day, no doubt, inhabited by rich and fashionable people: now it was a home for poor sick children, who were carefully tended for love's sake. There are regions in London where a hospital in every other street might be full of such children,
whose fathers and mothers are dead, or unable to take care of them.

When Diamond followed Mr. Raymond into the room where those
children who had got over the worst of their illness and were growing
better lay, he saw a number of little iron bedsteads, with their heads
to the walls, and in every one of them a child, whose face was a story
in itself. In some, health had begun to appear in a tinge upon the
cheeks, and a doubtful brightness in the eyes, just as out of the cold
dreary winter the spring comes in blushing buds and bright crocuses.
In others there were more of the signs of winter left. Their faces reminded you of snow and keen cutting winds, more than of sunshine
and soft breezes and butterflies; but even in them the signs of suffering told that the suffering was less, and that if the spring-time had
but arrived, it had yet arrived.

Diamond looked all round, but could see no Nanny. He turned to
Mr. Raymond with a question in his eyes.

"Well?" said Mr. Raymond.

"Nanny's not here," said Diamond.

"Oh, yes, she is."

"I don't see her."

"I do, though. There she is."

He pointed to a bed right in front of where Diamond was standing.

"That's not Nanny," he said.

"It is Nanny. I have seen her many times since you have. Illness makes a great difference."

"Why, that girl must have been to the back of the north wind!" thought Diamond, but he said nothing, only stared; and as he stared, something of the old Nanny began to dawn through the face of the new Nanny. The old Nanny, though a good girl, and a friendly girl, had been rough, blunt in her speech, and dirty in her person. Her face would always have reminded one who had already been to the back of the north wind of something he had seen in the best of company, but it had been coarse notwithstanding, partly from the weather, partly from her living amongst low people, and partly from having to defend herself: now it was so sweet, and gentle, and refined, that she might have had a lady and gentleman for a father and mother. And Diamond could not help thinking of words which he had heard in the church the day before: "Surely it is good to be afflicted;" or something like that. North Wind, somehow or other, must have had to do with her! She had grown from a rough girl into a gentle maiden.

Mr. Raymond, however, was not surprised, for he was used to see such lovely changes—something like the change which passes upon the crawling, many-footed creature, when it turns sick and ill, and revives a butterfly, with two wings instead of many feet. Instead of her having to take care of herself, kind hands ministered to her, making her comfortable and sweet and clean, soothing her aching head, and giving her cooling drink when she was thirsty; and kind eyes, the stars of the kingdom of heaven, had shone upon her; so that, what with the fire of the fever and the dew of tenderness, that which was coarse in her had melted away, and her whole face had grown so refined and sweet that Diamond did not know her. But as he gazed, the best of the old face, all the true and good part of it, that which was Nanny herself, dawned upon him, like the moon coming out of a cloud, until at length, instead of only believing Mr. Raymond that this was she, he saw for himself that it was Nanny indeed—very worn but grown beautiful.

He went up to her. She smiled. He had heard her laugh, but had never seen her smile before.

"Nanny, do you know me?" said Diamond.

She only smiled again, as if the question was amusing.

She was not likely to forget him; for although she did not yet know it was he who had got her there, she had dreamed of him often, and had talked much about him when delirious. Nor was it much wonder, for he was the only boy except Joe who had ever shown her kindness.

Meantime Mr. Raymond was going from bed to bed, talking to the little people. Every one knew him, and every one was eager to have a look, and a smile, and a kind word from him.

Diamond sat down on a stool at the head of Nanny's bed. She laid her hand in his. No one else of her old acquaintance had been near her.

Suddenly a little voice called aloud—

"Won't Mr. Raymond tell us a story?"

"Oh, yes, please do! please do!" cried several little voices which also were stronger than the rest. For Mr. Raymond was in the habit of telling them a story when he went to see them, and they enjoyed it far more than the other nice things which the doctor permitted him to give them.

"Very well," said Mr. Raymond, "I will. What sort of a story shall it be?"

"A true story," said one little girl.

"A fairy tale," said a little boy.

"Well," said Mr. Raymond, "I suppose, as there is a difference, I may choose. I can't think of any true story just at this moment, so I will tell you a sort of a fairy one."

"Oh, jolly!" exclaimed the little boy who had called out for a fairy tale.

"It came into my head this morning as I got out of bed," continued Mr. Raymond; "and if it turns out pretty well, I will write it down, and get somebody to print it for me, and then you shall read it when you like."

"Then nobody ever heard it before?" asked one older child.

"No, nobody."

"Oh!" exclaimed several, thinking it very grand to have the first telling; and I daresay there might be a peculiar freshness about it, because everything would be nearly as new to the story-teller himself as to the listeners.

Some were only sitting up and some were lying down, so there could not be the same busy gathering, bustling, and shifting to and fro with which children generally prepare themselves to hear a story; but their faces, and the turning of their heads, and many feeble exclamations of expected pleasure, showed that all such preparations were making within them.

Mr. Raymond stood in the middle of the room, that he might turn from side to side, and give each a share of seeing him. Diamond kept his place by Nanny's side, with her hand in his. I do not know how much of Mr. Raymond's story the smaller children understood; indeed, I don't quite know how much there was in it to be understood, for in such a story every one has just to take what he can get. But they all listened with apparent satisfaction, and certainly with great attention. Mr. Raymond wrote it down afterwards, and here it is—somewhat altered no doubt, for a good story-teller tries to make his stories better every time he tells them. I cannot myself help thinking that he was somewhat indebted for this one to the old story of The Sleeping Beauty.

28
Little Daylight

No house of any pretension to be called a palace is in the least worthy of the name, except it has a wood near it—very near it—and the nearer the better. Not all round it—I don't mean that, for a palace ought to be open to the sun and wind, and stand high and brave, with weathercocks glittering and flags flying; but on one side of every palace there must be a wood. And there was a very grand wood indeed beside the palace of the king who was going to be Daylight's father; such a grand wood, that nobody yet had ever got to the other end of it. Near the house it was kept very trim and nice, and it was free of brushwood for a long way in; but by degrees it got wild, and it grew wilder, and wilder, and wilder, until some said wild beasts at last did what they liked in it. The king and his courtiers often hunted, however, and this kept the wild beasts far away from the palace.

One glorious summer morning, when the wind and sun were out together, when the vanes were flashing and the flags frolicking against the blue sky, little Daylight made her appearance from somewhere—nobody could tell where—a beautiful baby, with such bright eyes that she might have come from the sun, only by and by she showed such lively ways that she might equally well have come out of the wind. There was great jubilation in the palace, for this was the first baby the queen had had, and there is as much happiness over a new baby in a palace as in a cottage.

But there is one disadvantage of living near a wood: you do not know quite who your neighbours may be. Everybody knew there were in it several fairies, living within a few miles of the palace, who always had had something to do with each new baby that came; for fairies live so much longer than we, that they can have business with a good many generations of human mortals. The curious houses they lived in were well known also,—one, a hollow oak; another, a birch-tree, though nobody could ever find how that fairy made a house of it; another, a hut of growing trees intertwined, and patched up with turf and moss. But there was another fairy who had lately come to the place, and nobody even knew she was a fairy except the other fairies. A wicked old thing she was, always concealing her power, and being as disagreeable as she could, in order to tempt people to give her offence, that she might have the pleasure of taking vengeance upon them. The people about thought she was a witch, and those who knew her by sight were careful to avoid offending her. She lived in a mud house, in a swampy part of the forest.

In all history we find that fairies give their remarkable gifts to prince or princess, or any child of sufficient importance in their eyes, always at the christening. Now this we can understand, because it is an ancient custom amongst human beings as well; and it is not hard to explain why wicked fairies should choose the same time to do unkind things; but it is difficult to understand how they should be able to do them, for you would fancy all wicked creatures would be powerless on such an occasion. But I never knew of any interference on the part of the wicked fairy that did not turn out a good thing in the end. What a good thing, for instance, it was that one princess should sleep for a hundred years! Was she not saved from all the plague of young men who were not worthy of her? And did she not come awake exactly at the right moment when the right prince kissed her? For my part, I cannot help wishing a good many girls would sleep till just the same fate overtook them. It would be happier for them, and more agreeable to their friends.

Of course all the known fairies were invited to the christening. But the king and queen never thought of inviting an old witch.

For the power of the fairies they have by nature; whereas a witch gets her power by wickedness. The other fairies, however, knowing the danger thus run, provided as well as they could against accidents from her quarter. But they could neither render her powerless, nor could they arrange their gifts in reference to hers beforehand, for they could not tell what those might be.

Of course the old hag was there without being asked. Not to be asked was just what she wanted, that she might have a sort of reason for doing what she wished to do. For somehow even the wickedest of creatures likes a pretext for doing the wrong thing.

Five fairies had one after the other given the child such gifts as each counted best, and the fifth had just stepped back to her place in the surrounding splendour of ladies and gentlemen, when, mumbling a laugh between her toothless gums, the wicked fairy hobbled out into the middle of the circle, and at the moment when the archbishop was handing the baby to the lady at the head of the nursery department of state affairs, addressed him thus, giving a bite or two to every word before she could part with it:

"Please your Grace, I'm very deaf: would your Grace mind repeating the princess's name?"

"With pleasure, my good woman," said the archbishop, stooping to shout in her ear: "the infant's name is little Daylight."

"And little daylight it shall be," cried the fairy, in the tone of a dry axle, "and little good shall any of her gifts do her. For I bestow upon her the gift of sleeping all day long, whether she will or not. Ha, ha! He, he! Hi, hi!"

Then out started the sixth fairy, who, of course, the others had arranged should come after the wicked one, in order to undo as much as she might.

"If she sleep all day," she said, mournfully, "she shall, at least, wake all night."

"A nice prospect for her mother and me!" thought the poor king; for they loved her far too much to give her up to nurses, especially at night, as most kings and queens do—and are sorry for it afterwards.

"You spoke before I had done," said the wicked fairy. "That's against the law. It gives me another chance."

"I beg your pardon," said the other fairies, all together.

"She did. I hadn't done laughing," said the crone. "I had only got to Hi, hi! and I had to go through Ho, ho! and Hu, hu! So I decree that if she wakes all night she shall wax and wane with its mistress, the moon. And what that may mean I hope her royal parents will live to see. Ho, ho! Hu, hu!"

But out stepped another fairy, for they had been wise enough to keep two in reserve, because every fairy knew the trick of one.

"Until," said the seventh fairy, "a prince comes who shall kiss her without knowing it."

The wicked fairy made a horrid noise like an angry cat, and hobbled away. She could not pretend that she had not finished her speech this time, for she had laughed Ho, ho! and Hu, hu!

"I don't know what that means," said the poor king to the seventh fairy.

"Don't be afraid. The meaning will come with the thing itself," said she.

The assembly broke up, miserable enough—the queen, at least, prepared for a good many sleepless nights, and the lady at the head of the nursery department anything but comfortable in the prospect before her, for of course the queen could not do it all. As for the king, he made up his mind, with what courage he could summon, to meet the demands of the case, but wondered whether he could with any propriety require the First Lord of the Treasury to take a share in the burden laid upon him.

I will not attempt to describe what they had to go through for some time. But at last the household settled into a regular system—a very irregular one in some respects. For at certain seasons the palace rang all night with bursts of laughter from little Daylight, whose heart the old fairy's curse could not reach; she was Daylight still, only a little in the wrong place, for she always dropped asleep at the first hint of dawn in the east. But her merriment was of short duration. When the moon was at the full, she was in glorious spirits, and as beautiful as it was possible for a child of her age to be. But as the moon waned, she faded, until at last she was wan and withered like the poorest, sickliest child you might come upon in the streets of a great city in the arms of a homeless mother. Then the night was quiet as the day, for the little creature lay in her gorgeous cradle night and day with hardly a motion, and indeed at last without even a moan, like one dead. At first they often thought she was dead, but at last they got used to it, and only consulted the almanac to find the moment when she would begin to revive, which, of course, was with the first appearance of the silver thread of the crescent moon. Then she would move her lips, and they would give her a little nourishment; and she would grow better and better and better, until for a few days she was splendidly well. When well, she was always merriest out in the moonlight; but even when near her worst, she seemed better when, in warm summer nights, they carried her cradle out into the light of the waning moon. Then in her sleep she would smile the faintest, most pitiful smile.

For a long time very few people ever saw her awake. As she grew older she became such a favourite, however, that about the palace there were always some who would contrive to keep awake at night, in order to be near her. But she soon began to take every chance of getting away from her nurses and enjoying her moonlight alone. And thus things went on until she was nearly seventeen years of age. Her father and mother had by that time got so used to the odd state of things that they had ceased to wonder at them. All their arrangements had reference to the state of the Princess Daylight, and it is amazing how things contrive to accommodate themselves. But how any prince was ever to find and deliver her, appeared inconceivable.

As she grew older she had grown more and more beautiful, with the sunniest hair and the loveliest eyes of heavenly blue, brilliant and profound as the sky of a June day. But so much more painful and sad was the change as her bad time came on. The more beautiful she was in the full moon, the more withered and worn did she become as the moon waned. At the time at which my story has now arrived, she looked, when the moon was small or gone, like an old woman exhausted with suffering. This was the more painful that her appearance was unnatural; for her hair and eyes did not change. Her wan face was both drawn and wrinkled, and had an eager hungry look. Her skinny hands moved as if wishing, but unable, to lay hold of something. Her shoulders were bent forward, her chest went in, and she stooped as if she were eighty years old. At last she had to be put to bed, and there await the flow of the tide of life. But she grew to dislike being seen, still more being touched by any hands, during this season. One lovely summer evening, when the moon lay all but gone upon the verge of the horizon, she vanished from her attendants, and it was only after searching for her a long time in great terror, that they found her fast asleep in the forest, at the foot of a silver birch, and carried her home.

A little way from the palace there was a great open glade, covered with the greenest and softest grass. This was her favourite haunt; for here the full moon shone free and glorious, while through a vista in the trees she could generally see more or less of the dying moon as it crossed the opening. Here she had a little rustic house built for her, and here she mostly resided. None of the court might go there without leave, and her own attendants had learned by this time not to be officious in waiting upon her, so that she was very much at liberty. Whether the good fairies had anything to do with it or not I cannot tell, but at last she got into the way of retreating further into the wood every night as the moon waned, so that sometimes they had great trouble in finding her; but as she was always very angry if she discovered they were watching her, they scarcely dared to do so. At length one night they thought they had lost her altogether. It was morning before they found her. Feeble as she was, she had wandered into a thicket a long way from the glade, and there she lay—fast asleep, of course.

Although the fame of her beauty and sweetness had gone abroad, yet as everybody knew she was under a bad spell, no king in the neighbourhood had any desire to have her for a daughter-in-law. There were serious objections to such a relation.

About this time in a neighbouring kingdom, in consequence of the wickedness of the nobles, an insurrection took place upon the death of the old king, the greater part of the nobility was massacred, and the young prince was compelled to flee for his life, disguised like a peasant. For some time, until he got out of the country, he suffered much from hunger and fatigue; but when he got into that ruled by the princess's father, and had no longer any fear of being recognised, he fared better, for the people were kind. He did not abandon his disguise, however. One tolerable reason was that he had no other clothes to put on, and another that he had very little money, and did not know where to get any more. There was no good in telling everybody he met that he was a prince, for he felt that a prince ought to be able to get on like other people, else his rank only made a fool of him. He had read of princes setting out upon adventure; and here he was out in similar case, only without having had a choice in the matter. He would go on, and see what would come of it.

For a day or two he had been walking through the palace-wood, and had had next to nothing to eat, when he came upon the strangest little house, inhabited by a very nice, tidy, motherly old woman. This was one of the good fairies. The moment she saw him she knew quite well who he was and what was going to come of it; but she was not at liberty to interfere with the orderly march of events. She received him with the kindness she would have shown to any other traveller, and gave him bread and milk, which he thought the most delicious food he had ever tasted, wondering that they did not have it for dinner at the palace sometimes. The old woman pressed him to stay all night. When he awoke he was amazed to find how well and strong he felt. She would not take any of the money he offered, but begged him, if he found occasion of continuing in the neighbourhood, to return and occupy the same quarters.

"Thank you much, good mother," answered the prince; "but there is little chance of that. The sooner I get out of this wood the better."

"I don't know that," said the fairy.

"What do you mean?" asked the prince.

"Why, how should I know?" returned she.

"I can't tell," said the prince.

"Very well," said the fairy.

"How strangely you talk!" said the prince.

"Do I?" said the fairy.

"Yes, you do," said the prince.

"Very well," said the fairy.

The prince was not used to be spoken to in this fashion, so he felt a little angry, and turned and walked away. But this did not offend the fairy. She stood at the door of her little house looking after him till the trees hid him quite. Then she said "At last!" and went in.

The prince wandered and wandered, and got nowhere. The sun sank and sank and went out of sight, and he seemed no nearer the end of the wood than ever. He sat down on a fallen tree, ate a bit of bread the old woman had given him, and waited for the moon; for, although he was not much of an astronomer, he knew the moon would rise some time, because she had risen the night before. Up she came, slow and slow, but of a good size, pretty nearly round indeed; whereupon, greatly refreshed with his piece of bread, he got up and went— he knew not whither.

After walking a considerable distance, he thought he was coming to the outside of the forest; but when he reached what he thought the last of it, he found himself only upon the edge of a great open space in it, covered with grass. The moon shone very bright, and he thought he had never seen a more lovely spot. Still it looked dreary because of its loneliness, for he could not see the house at the other side. He sat down, weary again, and gazed into the glade. He had not seen so much room for several days.

All at once he spied something in the middle of the grass. What could it be? It moved; it came nearer. Was it a human creature, gliding across—a girl dressed in white, gleaming in the moonshine? She came nearer and nearer. He crept behind a tree and watched, wondering. It must be some strange being of the wood—a nymph whom the moonlight and the warm dusky air had enticed from her tree. But when she came close to where he stood, he no longer doubted she was human—for he had caught sight of her sunny hair, and her clear blue eyes, and the loveliest face and form that he had ever seen. All at once she began singing like a nightingale, and dancing to her own music, with her eyes ever turned towards the moon. She passed close to where he stood, dancing on by the edge of the trees and away in a great circle towards the other side, until he could see but a spot of white in the yellowish green of the moonlit grass. But when he feared it would vanish quite, the spot grew, and became a figure once more. She approached him again, singing and dancing, and waving her arms over her head, until she had completed the circle. Just opposite his tree she stood, ceased her song, dropped her arms, and broke out into a long clear laugh, musical as a brook. Then, as if tired, she threw herself on the grass, and lay gazing at the moon. The prince was almost afraid to breathe lest he should startle her, and she should vanish from his sight. As to venturing near her, that never came into his head.

She had lain for a long hour or longer, when the prince began again to doubt concerning her. Perhaps she was but a vision of his own fancy. Or was she a spirit of the wood, after all? If so, he too would haunt the wood, glad to have lost kingdom and everything for the hope of being near her. He would build him a hut in the forest, and there he would live for the pure chance of seeing her again. Upon nights like this at least she would come out and bask in the moonlight, and make his soul blessed. But while he thus dreamed she sprang to her feet, turned her face full to the moon, and began singing as she would draw her down from the sky by the power of her entrancing voice. She looked more beautiful than ever. Again she began dancing to her own music, and danced away into the distance. Once more she returned in a similar manner; but although he was watching as eagerly as before, what with fatigue and what with gazing, he fell fast asleep before she came near him. When he awoke it was broad daylight, and the princess was nowhere.

He could not leave the place. What if she should come the next night! He would gladly endure a day's hunger to see her yet again: he would buckle his belt quite tight. He walked round the glade to see if he could discover any prints of her feet. But the grass was so short, and her steps had been so light, that she had not left a single trace behind her. He walked half-way round the wood without seeing anything to account for her presence. Then he spied a lovely little house, with thatched roof and low eaves, surrounded by an exquisite garden, with doves and peacocks walking in it. Of course this must be where the gracious lady who loved the moonlight lived. Forgetting his appearance, he walked towards the door, determined to make inquiries, but as he passed a little pond full of gold and silver fishes, he caught sight of himself and turned to find the door to the kitchen. There he knocked, and asked for a piece of bread. The good-natured cook brought him in, and gave him an excellent breakfast, which the prince found nothing the worse for being served in the kitchen. While he ate, he talked with his entertainer, and learned that this was the favourite retreat of the Princess Daylight. But he learned nothing more, both because he was afraid of seeming inquisitive, and because the cook did not choose to be heard talking about her mistress to a peasant lad who had begged for his breakfast.

As he rose to take his leave, it occurred to him that he might not be so far from the old woman's cottage as he had thought, and he asked the cook whether she knew anything of such a place, describing it as well as he could. She said she knew it well enough, adding with a smile—

"It's there you're going, is it?"

"Yes, if it's not far off."

"It's not more than three miles. But mind what you are about, you know."

"Why do you say that?"

"If you're after any mischief, she'll make you repent it."

"The best thing that could happen under the circumstances," remarked the prince.

"What do you mean by that?" asked the cook.

"Why, it stands to reason," answered the prince "that if you wish to do anything wrong, the best thing for you is to be made to repent of it."

"I see," said the cook. "Well, I think you may venture. She's a good old soul."

"Which way does it lie from here?" asked the prince.

She gave him full instructions; and he left her with many thanks.

Being now refreshed, however, the prince did not go back to the cottage that day: he remained in the forest, amusing himself as best he could, but waiting anxiously for the night, in the hope that the princess would again appear. Nor was he disappointed, for, directly the moon rose, he spied a glimmering shape far across the glade. As it drew nearer, he saw it was she indeed—not dressed in white as before: in a pale blue like the sky, she looked lovelier still. He thought it was that the blue suited her yet better than the white; he did not know that she was really more beautiful because the moon was nearer the full. In fact the next night was full moon, and the princess would then be at the zenith of her loveliness.

The prince feared for some time that she was not coming near his hiding-place that night; but the circles in her dance ever widened as the moon rose, until at last they embraced the whole glade, and she came still closer to the trees where he was hiding than she had come the night before. He was entranced with her loveliness, for it was indeed a marvellous thing. All night long he watched her, but dared not go near her. He would have been ashamed of watching her too, had he not become almost incapable of thinking of anything but how beautiful she was. He watched the whole night long, and saw that as the moon went down she retreated in smaller and smaller circles, until at last he could see her no more.

Weary as he was, he set out for the old woman's cottage, where he arrived just in time for her breakfast, which she shared with him. He then went to bed, and slept for many hours. When he awoke the sun was down, and he departed in great anxiety lest he should lose a glimpse of the lovely vision. But, whether it was by the machinations of the swamp-fairy, or merely that it is one thing to go and another to return by the same road, he lost his way. I shall not attempt to describe his misery when the moon rose, and he saw nothing but trees, trees, trees.

She was high in the heavens before he reached the glade. Then indeed his troubles vanished, for there was the princess coming dancing towards him, in a dress that shone like gold, and with shoes that glimmered through the grass like fireflies. She was of course still more beautiful than before. Like an embodied sunbeam she passed him, and danced away into the distance.

Before she returned in her circle, the clouds had begun to gather about the moon. The wind rose, the trees moaned, and their lighter branches leaned all one way before it. The prince feared that the princess would go in, and he should see her no more that night. But she came dancing on more jubilant than ever, her golden dress and her sunny hair streaming out upon the blast, waving her arms towards the moon, and in the exuberance of her delight ordering the clouds away from off her face. The prince could hardly believe she was not a creature of the elements, after all.

By the time she had completed another circle, the clouds had gathered deep, and there were growlings of distant thunder. Just as she passed the tree where he stood, a flash of lightning blinded him for a moment, and when he saw again, to his horror, the princess lay on the ground. He darted to her, thinking she had been struck; but when she heard him coming, she was on her feet in a moment.

"What do you want?" she asked.

"I beg your pardon. I thought—the lightning" said the prince, hesitating.

"There's nothing the matter," said the princess, waving him off rather haughtily.

The poor prince turned and walked towards the wood.

"Come back," said Daylight: "I like you. You do what you are told. Are you good?"

"Not so good as I should like to be," said the prince.

"Then go and grow better," said the princess.

Again the disappointed prince turned and went.

"Come back," said the princess.

He obeyed, and stood before her waiting.

"Can you tell me what the sun is like?" she asked.

"No," he answered. "But where's the good of asking what you know?"

"But I don't know," she rejoined.

"Why, everybody knows."

"That's the very thing: I'm not everybody. I've never seen the sun."

"Then you can't know what it's like till you do see it."

"I think you must be a prince," said the princess.

"Do I look like one?" said the prince.

"I can't quite say that."

"Then why do you think so?"

"Because you both do what you are told and speak the truth.—Is the sun so very bright?"

"As bright as the lightning."

"But it doesn't go out like that, does it?"

"Oh, no. It shines like the moon, rises and sets like the moon, is much the same shape as the moon, only so bright that you can't look at it for a moment."

"But I would look at it," said the princess.

"But you couldn't," said the prince.

"But I could," said the princess.

"Why don't you, then?"

"Because I can't."

"Why can't you?"

"Because I can't wake. And I never shall wake until—"

Here she hid her face in her hands, turned away, and walked in the slowest, stateliest manner towards the house. The prince ventured to follow her at a little distance, but she turned and made a repellent gesture, which, like a true gentleman-prince, he obeyed at once. He waited a long time, but as she did not come near him again, and as the night had now cleared, he set off at last for the old woman's cottage.

It was long past midnight when he reached it, but, to his surprise, the old woman was paring potatoes at the door. Fairies are fond of doing odd things. Indeed, however they may dissemble, the night is always their day. And so it is with all who have fairy blood in them.

"Why, what are you doing there, this time of the night, mother?" said the prince; for that was the kind way in which any young man in his country would address a woman who was much older than himself.

"Getting your supper ready, my son," she answered.

"Oh, I don't want any supper," said the prince.

"Ah! you've seen Daylight," said she.

"I've seen a princess who never saw it," said the prince.

"Do you like her?" asked the fairy.

"Oh! don't I?" said the prince. "More than you would believe, mother."

"A fairy can believe anything that ever was or ever could be," said the old woman.

"Then are you a fairy?" asked the prince.

"Yes," said she.

"Then what do you do for things not to believe?" asked the prince.

"There's plenty of them—everything that never was nor ever could be."

"Plenty, I grant you," said the prince. "But do you believe there could be a princess who never saw the daylight? Do you believe that now?"

This the prince said, not that he doubted the princess, but that he wanted the fairy to tell him more. She was too old a fairy, however, to be caught so easily.

"Of all people, fairies must not tell secrets. Besides, she's a princess."

"Well, I'll tell you a secret. I'm a prince."

"I know that."

"How do you know it?"

"By the curl of the third eyelash on your left eyelid."

"Which corner do you count from?"

"That's a secret."

"Another secret? Well, at least, if I am a prince, there can be no harm in telling me about a princess."

"It's just the princes I can't tell."

"There ain't any more of them—are there?" said the prince.

"What! you don't think you're the only prince in the world, do you?"

"Oh, dear, no! not at all. But I know there's one too many just at present, except the princess—"

"Yes, yes, that's it," said the fairy.

"What's it?" asked the prince.

But he could get nothing more out of the fairy, and had to go to bed unanswered, which was something of a trial.

Now wicked fairies will not be bound by the law which the good fairies obey, and this always seems to give the bad the advantage over the good, for they use means to gain their ends which the others will not. But it is all of no consequence, for what they do never succeeds; nay, in the end it brings about the very thing they are trying to prevent. So you see that somehow, for all their cleverness, wicked fairies are dreadfully stupid, for, although from the beginning of the world they have really helped instead of thwarting the good fairies, not one of them is a bit wiser for it. She will try the bad thing just as they all did before her; and succeeds no better of course.

The prince had so far stolen a march upon the swamp-fairy that she did not know he was in the neighbourhood until after he had seen the princess those three times. When she knew it, she consoled herself by thinking that the princess must be far too proud and too modest for any young man to venture even to speak to her before he had seen her six times at least. But there was even less danger than the wicked fairy thought; for, however much the princess might desire to be set free, she was dreadfully afraid of the wrong prince. Now, however, the fairy was going to do all she could.

She so contrived it by her deceitful spells, that the next night the prince could not by any endeavour find his way to the glade. It would take me too long to tell her tricks. They would be amusing to us, who know that they could not do any harm, but they were something other than amusing to the poor prince. He wandered about the forest till daylight, and then fell fast asleep. The same thing occurred for seven following days, during which neither could he find the good fairy's cottage. After the third quarter of the moon, however, the bad fairy thought she might be at ease about the affair for a fortnight at least, for there was no chance of the prince wishing to kiss the princess during that period. So the first day of the fourth quarter he did find the cottage, and the next day he found the glade. For nearly another week he haunted it. But the princess never came. I have little doubt she was on the farther edge of it some part of every night, but at this period she always wore black, and, there being little or no light, the prince never saw her. Nor would he have known her if he had seen her. How could he have taken the worn decrepit creature she was now, for the glorious Princess Daylight?

At last, one night when there was no moon at all, he ventured near the house. There he heard voices talking, although it was past midnight; for her women were in considerable uneasiness, because the one whose turn it was to watch her had fallen asleep, and had not seen which way she went, and this was a night when she would probably wander very far, describing a circle which did not touch the open glade at all, but stretched away from the back of the house, deep into that side of the forest—a part of which the prince knew nothing. When he understood from what they said that she had disappeared, and that she must have gone somewhere in the said direction, he plunged at once into the wood to see if he could find her. For hours he roamed with nothing to guide him but the vague notion of a circle which on one side bordered on the house, for so much had he picked up from the talk he had overheard.

It was getting towards the dawn, but as yet there was no streak of light in the sky, when he came to a great birch-tree, and sat down weary at the foot of it. While he sat—very miserable, you may be sure—full of fear for the princess, and wondering how her attendants could take it so quietly, he bethought himself that it would not be a bad plan to light a fire, which, if she were anywhere near, would attract her. This he managed with a tinder-box, which the good fairy had given him. It was just beginning to blaze up, when he heard a moan, which seemed to come from the other side of the tree. He sprung to his feet, but his heart throbbed so that he had to lean for a moment against the tree before he could move. When he got round, there lay a human form in a little dark heap on the earth. There was light enough from his fire to show that it was not the princess. He lifted it in his arms, hardly heavier than a child, and carried it to the flame. The countenance was that of an old woman, but it had a fearfully strange look. A black hood concealed her hair, and her eyes were closed. He laid her down as comfortably as he could, chafed her hands, put a little cordial from a bottle, also the gift of the fairy, into her mouth; took off his coat and wrapped it about her, and in short did the best he could. In a little while she opened her eyes and looked at him—so pitifully! The tears rose and flowed from her grey wrinkled cheeks, but she said never a word. She closed her eyes again, but the tears kept on flowing, and her whole appearance was so utterly pitiful that the prince was near crying too. He begged her to tell him what was the matter, promising to do all he could to help her; but still she did not speak. He thought she was dying, and took her in his arms again to carry her to the princess's house, where he thought the good-natured cook might be able to do something for her. When he lifted her, the tears flowed yet faster, and she gave such a sad moan that it went to his very heart.

"Mother, mother!" he said. "Poor mother!" and kissed her on the withered lips.

She started; and what eyes they were that opened upon him! But he did not see them, for it was still very dark, and he had enough to do to make his way through the trees towards the house.

Just as he approached the door, feeling more tired than he could have imagined possible—she was such a little thin old thing—she began to move, and became so restless that, unable to carry her a moment longer, he thought to lay her on the grass. But she stood upright on her feet. Her hood had dropped, and her hair fell about her. The first gleam of the morning was caught on her face: that face was bright as the never-aging Dawn, and her eyes were lovely as the sky of darkest blue. The prince recoiled in overmastering wonder. It was Daylight herself whom he had brought from the forest! He fell at her feet, nor dared to look up until she laid her hand upon his head. He rose then.

"You kissed me when I was an old woman: there! I kiss you when I am a young princess," murmured Daylight.— "Is that the sun coming?"

29
Ruby

The children were delighted with the story, and made many amusing remarks upon it. Mr. Raymond promised to search his brain for another, and when he had found one to bring it to them. Diamond having taken leave of Nanny, and promised to go and see her again soon, went away with him.

Now Mr. Raymond had been turning over in his mind what he could do both for Diamond and for Nanny. He had therefore made some acquaintance with Diamond's father, and had been greatly pleased with him. But he had come to the resolution, before he did anything so good as he would like to do for them, to put them all to a certain test. So as they walked away together, he began to talk with Diamond as follows:—

"Nanny must leave the hospital soon, Diamond."

"I'm glad of that, sir."

"Why? Don't you think it's a nice place?"

"Yes, very. But it's better to be well and doing something, you know, even if it's not quite so comfortable."

"But they can't keep Nanny so long as they would like. They can't keep her till she's quite strong. There are always so many sick children they want to take in and make better. And the question is, What will she do when they send her out again?"

"That's just what I can't tell, though I've been thinking of it over and over, sir. Her crossing was taken long ago, and I couldn't bear to see Nanny fighting for it, especially with such a poor fellow as has taken it. He's quite lame, sir."

"She doesn't look much like fighting, now, does she, Diamond?"

"No, sir. She looks too like an angel. Angels don't fight—do they, sir?"

"Not to get things for themselves, at least," said Mr. Raymond.

"Besides," added Diamond, "I don't quite see that she would have any better right to the crossing than the boy who has got it. Nobody gave it to her; she only took it. And now he has taken it."

"If she were to sweep a crossing—soon at least—after the illness she has had, she would be laid up again the very first wet day," said Mr. Raymond.

"And there's hardly any money to be got except on the wet days," remarked Diamond reflectively. "Is there nothing else she could do, sir?"

"Not without being taught, I'm afraid."

"Well, couldn't somebody teach her something?"

"Couldn't you teach her, Diamond?"

"I don't know anything myself, sir. I could teach her to dress the baby; but nobody would give her anything for doing things like that: they are so easy. There wouldn't be much good in teaching her to drive a cab, for where would she get the cab to drive? There ain't fathers and old Diamonds everywhere. At least poor Nanny can't find any of them, I doubt."

"Perhaps if she were taught to be nice and clean, and only speak gentle words."

"Mother could teach her that," interrupted Diamond.

"And to dress babies, and feed them, and take care of them," Mr. Raymond proceeded, "she might get a place as a nurse somewhere, you know. People do give money for that."

"Then I'll ask mother," said Diamond.

"But you'll have to give her her food then; and your father, not being strong, has enough to do already without that."

"But here's me," said Diamond: "I help him out with it. When he's tired of driving, up I get. It don't make any difference to old Diamond. I don't mean he likes me as well as my father—of course he can't, you know—nobody could; but he does his duty all the same. It's got to be done, you know, sir; and Diamond's a good horse—isn't he, sir?"

"From your description I should say certainly; but I have not the pleasure of his acquaintance myself."

"Don't you think he will go to heaven, sir?"

"That I don't know anything about," said Mr. Raymond. "I confess I should be glad to think so," he added, smiling thoughtfully.

"I'm sure he'll get to the back of the north wind, anyhow," said Diamond to himself; but he had learned to be very careful of saying such things aloud.

"Isn't it rather too much for him to go in the cab all day and every day?" resumed Mr. Raymond.

"So father says, when he feels his ribs of a morning. But then he says the old horse do eat well, and the moment he's had his supper, down he goes, and never gets up till he's called; and, for the legs of him, father says that makes no end of a differ. Some horses, sir! they won't lie down all night long, but go to sleep on their four pins, like a haystack, father says. I think it's very stupid of them, and so does old Diamond. But then I suppose they don't know better, and so they can't help it. We mustn't be too hard upon them, father says."

"Your father must be a good man, Diamond." Diamond looked up in Mr. Raymond's face, wondering what he could mean.

"I said your father must be a good man, Diamond."

"Of course," said Diamond. "How could he drive a cab if he wasn't?"

"There are some men who drive cabs who are not very good," objected Mr. Raymond.

Diamond remembered the drunken cabman, and saw that his friend was right.

"Ah, but," he returned, "he must be, you know, with such a horse as old Diamond."

"That does make a difference," said Mr. Raymond. "But it is quite enough that he is a good man without our trying to account for it. Now, if you like, I will give you a proof that I think him a good man. I am going away on the Continent for a while—for three months, I believe—and I am going to let my house to a gentleman who does not want the use of my brougham. My horse is nearly as old, I fancy, as your Diamond, but I don't want to part with him, and I don't want him to be idle; for nobody, as you say, ought to be idle; but neither do I want him to be worked very hard. Now, it has come into my head that perhaps your father would take charge of him, and work him under certain conditions."

"My father will do what's right," said Diamond. "I'm sure of that."

"Well, so I think. Will you ask him when he comes home to call and have a little chat with me—to-day, some time?"

"He must have his dinner first," said Diamond. "No, he's got his dinner with him to-day. It must be after he's had his tea."

"Of course, of course. Any time will do. I shall be at home all day."

"Very well, sir. I will tell him. You may be sure he will come. My father thinks you a very kind gentleman, and I know he is right, for I know your very own self, sir."

Mr. Raymond smiled, and as they had now reached his door, they parted, and Diamond went home. As soon as his father entered the house, Diamond gave him Mr. Raymond's message, and recounted the conversation that had preceded it. His father said little, but took thought-sauce to his bread and butter, and as soon as he had finished his meal, rose, saying:

"I will go to your friend directly, Diamond. It would be a grand thing to get a little more money. We do want it." Diamond accompanied his father to Mr. Raymond's door, and there left him.

He was shown at once into Mr. Raymond's study, where he gazed with some wonder at the multitude of books on the walls, and thought what a learned man Mr. Raymond must be.

Presently Mr. Raymond entered, and after saying much the same about his old horse, made the following distinct proposal—one not over-advantageous to Diamond's father, but for which he had reasons—namely, that Joseph should have the use of Mr. Raymond's horse while he was away, on condition that he never worked him more than six hours a day, and fed him well, and that, besides, he should take Nanny home as soon as she was able to leave the hospital, and provide for her as one of his own children, neither better nor worse—so long, that is, as he had the horse.

Diamond's father could not help thinking it a pretty close bargain. He should have both the girl and the horse to feed, and only six hours' work out of the horse.

"It will save your own horse," said Mr. Raymond.

"That is true," answered Joseph; "but all I can get by my own horse is only enough to keep us, and if I save him and feed your horse and the girl—don't you see, sir?"

"Well, you can go home and think about it, and let me know by the end of the week. I am in no hurry before then."

So Joseph went home and recounted the proposal to his wife, adding that he did not think there was much advantage to be got out of it.

"Not much that way, husband," said Diamond's mother; "but there would be an advantage, and what matter who gets it!"

"I don't see it," answered her husband. "Mr. Raymond is a gentleman of property, and I don't discover any much good in helping him to save a little more. He won't easily get one to make such a bargain, and I don't mean he shall get me. It would be a loss rather than a gain—I do think—at least if I took less work out of our own horse."

"One hour would make a difference to old Diamond. But that's not the main point. You must think what an advantage it would be to the poor girl that hasn't a home to go to!"

"She is one of Diamond's friends," thought his father.

"I could be kind to her, you know," the mother went on, "and teach her housework, and how to handle a baby; and, besides, she would help me, and I should be the stronger for it, and able to do an odd bit of charing now and then, when I got the chance."

"I won't hear of that," said her husband. "Have the girl by all means. I'm ashamed I did not think of both sides of the thing at once. I wonder if the horse is a great eater. To be sure, if I gave Diamond two hours' additional rest, it would be all the better for the old bones of him, and there would be four hours extra out of the other horse.

That would give Diamond something to do every day. He could drive old Diamond after dinner, and I could take the other horse out for six hours after tea, or in the morning, as I found best. It might pay for the keep of both of them,—that is, if I had good luck. I should like to oblige Mr. Raymond, though he be rather hard, for he has been very kind to our Diamond, wife. Hasn't he now?"

"He has indeed, Joseph," said his wife, and there the conversation ended.

Diamond's father went the very next day to Mr. Raymond, and accepted his proposal; so that the week after having got another stall in the same stable, he had two horses instead of one. Oddly enough, the name of the new horse was Ruby, for he was a very red chestnut. Diamond's name came from a white lozenge on his forehead. Young Diamond said they were rich now, with such a big diamond and such a big ruby.

30
Nanny's Dream

Nanny was not fit to be moved for some time yet, and Diamond went to see her as often as he could. But being more regularly engaged now, seeing he went out every day for a few hours with old Diamond, and had his baby to mind, and one of the horses to attend to, he could not go so often as he would have liked.

One evening, as he sat by her bedside, she said to him:

"I've had such a beautiful dream, Diamond! I should like to tell it you."

"Oh! do," said Diamond; "I am so fond of dreams!"

"She must have been to the back of the north wind," he said to himself.

"It was a very foolish dream, you know. But somehow it was so pleasant! What a good thing it is that you believe the dream all the time you are in it!"

My readers must not suppose that poor Nanny was able to say what she meant so well as I put it down here. She had never been to school, and had heard very little else than vulgar speech until she came to the hospital. But I have been to school, and although that could never make me able to dream so well as Nanny, it has made me able to tell her dream better than she could herself. And I am the more desirous of doing this for her that I have already done the best I could for Diamond's dream, and it would be a shame to give the boy all the advantage.

"I will tell you all I know about it," said Nanny. "The day before yesterday, a lady came to see us—a very beautiful lady, and very beautifully dressed. I heard the matron say to her that it was very kind of her to come in blue and gold; and she answered that she knew we didn't like dull colours. She had such a lovely shawl on, just like redness dipped in milk, and all worked over with flowers of the same colour. It didn't shine much, it was silk, but it kept in the shine. When she came to my bedside, she sat down, just where you are sitting, Diamond, and laid her hand on the counterpane. I was sitting up, with my table before me ready for my tea. Her hand looked so pretty in its blue glove, that I was tempted to stroke it. I thought she wouldn't be angry, for everybody that comes to the hospital is kind. It's only in the streets they ain't kind. But she drew her hand away, and I almost cried, for I thought I had been rude. Instead of that, however, it was only that she didn't like giving me her glove to stroke, for she drew it off, and then laid her hand where it was before. I wasn't sure, but I ventured to put out my ugly hand."

"Your hand ain't ugly, Nanny," said Diamond; but Nanny went on—

"And I stroked it again, and then she stroked mine,—think of that! And there was a ring on her finger, and I looked down to see what it was like. And she drew it off, and put it upon one of my fingers. It was a red stone, and she told me they called it a ruby."

"Oh, that is funny!" said Diamond. "Our new horse is called Ruby. We've got another horse—a red one—such a beauty!"

But Nanny went on with her story.

"I looked at the ruby all the time the lady was talking to me,—it was so beautiful! And as she talked I kept seeing deeper and deeper into the stone. At last she rose to go away, and I began to pull the ring off my finger; and what do you think she said?— 'Wear it all night, if you like. Only you must take care of it. I can't give it you, for some one gave it to me; but you may keep it till to-morrow.' Wasn't it kind of her? I could hardly take my tea, I was so delighted to hear it; and I do think it was the ring that set me dreaming; for, after I had taken my tea, I leaned back, half lying and half sitting, and looked at the ring on my finger. By degrees I began to dream. The ring grew larger and larger, until at last I found that I was not looking at a red stone, but at a red sunset, which shone in at the end of a long street near where Grannie lives. I was dressed in rags as I used to be, and I had great holes in my shoes, at which the nasty mud came through to my feet. I didn't use to mind it before, but now I thought it horrid. And there was the great red sunset, with streaks of green and gold between, standing looking at me. Why couldn't I live in the sunset instead of in that dirt? Why was it so far away always? Why did it never come into our wretched street? It faded away, as the sunsets always do, and at last went out altogether. Then a cold wind began to blow, and flutter all my rags about—"

"That was North Wind herself," said Diamond.

"Eh?" said Nanny, and went on with her story.

"I turned my back to it, and wandered away. I did not know where I was going, only it was warmer to go that way. I don't think it was a north wind, for I found myself in the west end at last. But it doesn't matter in a dream which wind it was."

"I don't know that," said Diamond. "I believe North Wind can get into our dreams—yes, and blow in them. Sometimes she has blown me out of a dream altogether."

"I don't know what you mean, Diamond," said Nanny.

"Never mind," answered Diamond. "Two people can't always understand each other. They'd both be at the back of the north wind directly, and what would become of the other places without them?"

"You do talk so oddly!" said Nanny. "I sometimes think they must have been right about you."

"What did they say about me?" asked Diamond.

"They called you God's baby."

"How kind of them! But I knew that."

"Did you know what it meant, though? It meant that you were not right in the head."

"I feel all right," said Diamond, putting both hands to his head, as if it had been a globe he could take off and set on again.

"Well, as long as you are pleased I am pleased," said Nanny.

"Thank you, Nanny. Do go on with your story. I think I like dreams even better than fairy tales. But they must be nice ones, like yours, you know."

"Well, I went on, keeping my back to the wind, until I came to a fine street on the top of a hill. How it happened I don't know, but the front door of one of the houses was open, and not only the front door, but the back door as well, so that I could see right through the house— and what do you think I saw? A garden place with green grass, and the moon shining upon it! Think of that! There was no moon in the street, but through the house there was the moon. I looked and there was nobody near: I would not do any harm, and the grass was so much nicer than the mud! But I couldn't think of going on the grass with such dirty shoes: I kicked them off in the gutter, and ran in on my bare feet, up the steps, and through the house, and on to the grass; and the moment I came into the moonlight, I began to feel better."

"That's why North Wind blew you there," said Diamond.

"It came of Mr. Raymond's story about Princess Daylight," returned Nanny. "Well, I lay down upon the grass in the moonlight without thinking how I was to get out again. Somehow the moon suited me exactly. There was not a breath of the north wind you talk about; it was quite gone."

"You didn't want her any more, just then. She never goes where she's not wanted," said Diamond. "But she blew you into the moonlight, anyhow."

"Well, we won't dispute about it," said Nanny: "you've got a tile loose, you know."

"Suppose I have," returned Diamond, "don't you see it may let in the moonlight, or the sunlight for that matter?"

"Perhaps yes, perhaps no," said Nanny.

"And you've got your dreams, too, Nanny."

"Yes, but I know they're dreams."

"So do I. But I know besides they are something more as well."

"Oh! do you?" rejoined Nanny. "I don't."

"All right," said Diamond. "Perhaps you will some day."

"Perhaps I won't," said Nanny.

Diamond held his peace, and Nanny resumed her story.

"I lay a long time, and the moonlight got in at every tear in my clothes, and made me feel so happy—"

"There, I tell you!" said Diamond.

"What do you tell me?" returned Nanny.

"North Wind—"

"It was the moonlight, I tell you," persisted Nanny, and again Diamond held his peace.

"All at once I felt that the moon was not shining so strong. I looked up, and there was a cloud, all crapey and fluffy, trying to drown the beautiful creature. But the moon was so round, just like a whole plate, that the cloud couldn't stick to her. She shook it off, and said there and shone out clearer and brighter than ever. But up came a thicker cloud,—and 'You shan't,' said the moon; and 'I will,' said the cloud,—but it couldn't: out shone the moon, quite laughing at its impudence. I knew her ways, for I've always been used to watch her. She's the only thing worth looking at in our street at night."

"Don't call it your street," said Diamond. "You're not going back to it. You're coming to us, you know."

"That's too good to be true," said Nanny.

"There are very few things good enough to be true," said Diamond; "but I hope this is. Too good to be true it can't be. Isn't true good? and isn't good good? And how, then, can anything be too good to be true? That's like old Sal—to say that."

"Don't abuse Grannie, Diamond. She's a horrid old thing, she and her gin bottle; but she'll repent some day, and then you'll be glad not to have said anything against her."

"Why?" said Diamond.

"Because you'll be sorry for her."

"I am sorry for her now."

"Very well. That's right. She'll be sorry too. And there'll be an end of it."

"All right. You come to us," said Diamond.

"Where was I?" said Nanny.

"Telling me how the moon served the clouds."

"Yes. But it wouldn't do, all of it. Up came the clouds and the clouds, and they came faster and faster, until the moon was covered up. You couldn't expect her to throw off a hundred of them at once—could you?"

"Certainly not," said Diamond.

"So it grew very dark; and a dog began to yelp in the house. I looked and saw that the door to the garden was shut. Presently it was opened—not to let me out, but to let the dog in—yelping and bounding. I thought if he caught sight of me, I was in for a biting first, and the police after. So I jumped up, and ran for a little summer-house in the corner of the garden. The dog came after me, but I shut the door in his face. It was well it had a door—wasn't it?"

"You dreamed of the door because you wanted it," said Diamond.

"No, I didn't; it came of itself. It was there, in the true dream."

"There—I've caught you!" said Diamond. "I knew you believed in the dream as much as I do."

"Oh, well, if you will lay traps for a body!" said Nanny. "Anyhow, I was safe inside the summer-house. And what do you think?—There was the moon beginning to shine again—but only through one of the panes—and that one was just the colour of the ruby. Wasn't it funny?"

"No, not a bit funny," said Diamond.

"If you will be contrary!" said Nanny.

"No, no," said Diamond; "I only meant that was the very pane I should have expected her to shine through."

"Oh, very well!" returned Nanny.

What Diamond meant, I do not pretend to say. He had curious notions about things.

"And now," said Nanny, "I didn't know what to do, for the dog kept barking at the door, and I couldn't get out. But the moon was so beautiful that I couldn't keep from looking at it through the red pane. And as I looked it got larger and larger till it filled the whole pane and outgrew it, so that I could see it through the other panes; and it grew till it filled them too and the whole window, so that the summer-house was nearly as bright as day.

"The dog stopped barking, and I heard a gentle tapping at the door, like the wind blowing a little branch against it."

"Just like her," said Diamond, who thought everything strange and beautiful must be done by North Wind.

"So I turned from the window and opened the door; and what do you think I saw?"

"A beautiful lady," said Diamond.

"No—the moon itself, as big as a little house, and as round as a ball, shining like yellow silver. It stood on the grass—down on the very grass: I could see nothing else for the brightness of it: And as I stared and wondered, a door opened in the side of it, near the ground, and a curious little old man, with a crooked thing over his shoulder, looked out, and said: 'Come along, Nanny; my lady wants you. We're come to fetch you.' I wasn't a bit frightened. I went up to the beautiful bright thing, and the old man held down his hand, and I took hold of it, and gave a jump, and he gave me a lift, and I was inside the moon. And what do you think it was like? It was such a pretty little house, with blue windows and white curtains! At one of the windows sat a beautiful lady, with her head leaning on her hand, looking out. She seemed rather sad, and I was sorry for her, and stood staring at her.

"'You didn't think I had such a beautiful mistress as that!' said the queer little man. 'No, indeed!' I answered: 'who would have thought it?' 'Ah! who indeed? But you see you don't know everything.' The little man closed the door, and began to pull at a rope which hung behind it with a weight at the end. After he had pulled a while, he said— 'There, that will do; we're all right now.' Then he took me by the hand and opened a little trap in the floor, and led me down two or three steps, and I saw like a great hole below me. 'Don't be frightened,' said the tittle man. 'It's not a hole. It's only a window. Put your face down and look through.' I did as he told me, and there was the garden and the summer-house, far away, lying at the bottom of the moonlight. 'There!' said the little man; 'we've brought you off! Do you see the little dog barking at us down there in the garden?' I told him I couldn't see anything so far. 'Can you see anything so small and so far off?' I said. 'Bless you, child!' said the little man; 'I could pick up a needle out of the grass if I had only a long enough arm. There's one lying by the door of the summer-house now.' I looked at his eyes. They were very small, but so bright that I think he saw by the light that went out of them. Then he took me up, and up again by a little stair in a corner of the room, and through another trapdoor, and there was one great round window above us, and I saw the blue sky and the clouds, and such lots of stars, all so big and shining as hard as ever they could!"

"The little girl-angels had been polishing them," said Diamond.

"What nonsense you do talk!" said Nanny.

"But my nonsense is just as good as yours, Nanny. When you have done, I'll tell you my dream. The stars are in it—not the moon, though. She was away somewhere. Perhaps she was gone to fetch you then. I don't think that, though, for my dream was longer ago than yours. She might have been to fetch some one else, though; for we can't fancy it's only us that get such fine things done for them. But do tell me what came next."

Perhaps one of my child-readers may remember whether the moon came down to fetch him or her the same night that Diamond had his dream. I cannot tell, of course. I know she did not come to fetch me, though I did think I could make her follow me when I was a boy—not a very tiny one either.

"The little man took me all round the house, and made me look out of every window. Oh, it was beautiful! There we were, all up in the air, in such a nice, clean little house! 'Your work will be to keep the windows bright,' said the little man. 'You won't find it very difficult, for there ain't much dust up here. Only, the frost settles on them sometimes, and the drops of rain leave marks on them.' 'I can easily clean them inside,' I said; 'but how am I to get the frost and rain off the outside of them?' 'Oh!' he said, 'it's quite easy. There are ladders all about. You've only got to go out at the door, and climb about. There are a great many windows you haven't seen yet, and some of them look into places you don't know anything about. I used to clean them myself, but I'm getting rather old, you see. Ain't I now?' 'I can't tell,' I answered. 'You see I never saw you when you were younger.' 'Never saw the man in the moon?' said he. 'Not very near,' I answered, 'not to tell how young or how old he looked. I have seen the bundle of sticks on his back.' For Jim had pointed that out to me. Jim was very fond of looking at the man in the moon. Poor Jim! I wonder he hasn't been to see me. I'm afraid he's ill too."

"I'll try to find out," said Diamond, "and let you know."

"Thank you," said Nanny. "You and Jim ought to be friends."

"But what did the man in the moon say, when you told him you had seen him with the bundle of sticks on his back?"

"He laughed. But I thought he looked offended too. His little nose turned up sharper, and he drew the corners of his mouth down from the tips of his ears into his neck. But he didn't look cross, you know."

"Didn't he say anything?"

"Oh, yes! He said: 'That's all nonsense. What you saw was my bundle of dusters. I was going to clean the windows. It takes a good many, you know. Really, what they do say of their superiors down there!' 'It's only because they don't know better,' I ventured to say. 'Of course, of course,' said the little man. 'Nobody ever does know better. Well, I forgive them, and that sets it all right, I hope.' 'It's very good of you,' I said. 'No!' said he, 'it's not in the least good of me. I couldn't be comfortable otherwise.' After this he said nothing for a while, and I laid myself on the floor of his garret, and stared up and around at the great blue beautifulness. I had forgotten him almost, when at last he said: 'Ain't you done yet?' 'Done what?' I asked. 'Done saying your prayers,' says he. 'I wasn't saying my prayers,' I answered. 'Oh, yes, you were,' said he, 'though you didn't know it! And now I must show you something else.'

"He took my hand and led me down the stair again, and through a narrow passage, and through another, and another, and another. I don't know how there could be room for so many passages in such a little house. The heart of it must be ever so much farther from the sides than they are from each other. How could it have an inside that was so independent of its outside? There's the point. It was funny— wasn't it, Diamond?"

"No," said Diamond. He was going to say that that was very much the sort of thing at the back of the north wind; but he checked himself and only added, "All right. I don't see it. I don't see why the inside should depend on the outside. It ain't so with the crabs. They creep out of their outsides and make new ones. Mr. Raymond told me so."

"I don't see what that has got to do with it," said Nanny.

"Then go on with your story, please," said Diamond. "What did you come to, after going through all those winding passages into the heart of the moon?"

"I didn't say they were winding passages. I said they were long and narrow. They didn't wind. They went by corners."

"That's worth knowing," remarked Diamond. "For who knows how soon he may have to go there? But the main thing is, what did you come to at last?"

"We came to a small box against the wall of a tiny room. The little man told me to put my ear against it. I did so, and heard a noise something like the purring of a cat, only not so loud, and much sweeter. 'What is it?' I asked. 'Don't you know the sound?' returned the little man. 'No,' I answered. 'Don't you know the sound of bees?' he said. I had never heard bees, and could not know the sound of them. 'Those are my lady's bees,' he went on. I had heard that bees gather honey from the flowers. 'But where are the flowers for them?' I asked. 'My lady's bees gather their honey from the sun and the stars,' said the little man. 'Do let me see them,' I said. 'No. I daren't do that,' he answered. 'I have no business with them. I don't understand them. Besides, they are so bright that if one were to fly into your eye, it would blind you altogether.' 'Then you have seen them?' 'Oh, yes! Once or twice, I think. But I don't quite know: they are so very bright—like buttons of lightning. Now I've showed you all I can to-night, and we'll go back to the room.' I followed him, and he made me sit down under a lamp that hung from the roof, and gave me some bread and honey.

"The lady had never moved. She sat with her forehead leaning on her hand, gazing out of the little window, hung like the rest with white cloudy curtains. From where I was sitting I looked out of it too, but I could see nothing. Her face was very beautiful, and very white, and very still, and her hand was as white as the forehead that leaned on it. I did not see her whole face—only the side of it, for she never moved to turn it full upon me, or even to look at me.

"How long I sat after I had eaten my bread and honey, I don't know. The little man was busy about the room, pulling a string here, and a string there, but chiefly the string at the back of the door. I was thinking with some uneasiness that he would soon be wanting me to go out and clean the windows, and I didn't fancy the job. At last he came up to me with a great armful of dusters. 'It's time you set about the windows,' he said; 'for there's rain coming, and if they're quite clean before, then the rain can't spoil them.' I got up at once. 'You needn't be afraid,' he said. 'You won't tumble off. Only you must be careful. Always hold on with one hand while you rub with the other.' As he spoke, he opened the door. I started back in a terrible fright, for there was nothing but blue air to be seen under me, like a great water without a bottom at all. But what must be must, and to live up here was so much nicer than down in the mud with holes in my shoes, that I never thought of not doing as I was told. The little man showed me how and where to lay hold while I put my foot round the edge of the door on to the first round of a ladder. 'Once you're up,' he said, 'you'll see how you have to go well enough.' I did as he told me, and crept out very carefully. Then the little man handed me the bundle of dusters, saying, 'I always carry them on my reaping hook, but I don't think you could manage it properly. You shall have it if you like.' I wouldn't take it, however, for it looked dangerous.

"I did the best I could with the dusters, and crawled up to the top of the moon. But what a grand sight it was! The stars were all over my head, so bright and so near that I could almost have laid hold of them. The round ball to which I clung went bobbing and floating away through the dark blue above and below and on every side. It was so beautiful that all fear left me, and I set to work diligently. I cleaned window after window. At length I came to a very little one, in at which I peeped. There was the room with the box of bees in it! I laid my ear to the window, and heard the musical hum quite distinctly. A great longing to see them came upon me, and I opened the window and crept in. The little box had a door like a closet. I opened it—the tiniest crack—when out came the light with such a sting that I closed it again in terror—not, however, before three bees had shot out into the room, where they darted about like flashes of lightning. Terribly frightened, I tried to get out of the window again, but I could not: there was no way to the outside of the moon but through the door; and that was in the room where the lady sat. No sooner had I reached the room, than the three bees, which had followed me, flew at once to the lady, and settled upon her hair. Then first I saw her move. She started, put up her hand, and caught them; then rose and, having held them into the flame of the lamp one after the other, turned to me. Her face was not so sad now as stern. It frightened me much. 'Nanny, you have got me into trouble,' she said. 'You have been letting out my bees, which it is all I can do to manage. You have forced me to burn them. It is a great loss, and there will be a storm.' As she spoke, the clouds had gathered all about us. I could see them come crowding up white about the windows. 'I am sorry to find,' said the lady, 'that you are not to be trusted. You must go home again—you won't do for us.' Then came a great clap of thunder, and the moon rocked and swayed. All grew dark about me, and I fell on the floor and lay half-stunned. I could hear everything but could see nothing. 'Shall I throw her out of the door, my lady?' said the little man. 'No,' she answered; 'she's not quite bad enough for that. I don't think there's much harm in her; only she'll never do for us. She would make dreadful mischief up here. She's only fit for the mud. It's a great pity. I am sorry for her. Just take that ring off her finger. I am sadly afraid she has stolen it.' The little man caught hold of my hand, and I felt him tugging at the ring. I tried to speak what was true about it, but, after a terrible effort, only gave a groan. Other things began to come into my head. Somebody else had a hold of me. The little man wasn't there. I opened my eyes at last, and saw the nurse. I had cried out in my sleep, and she had come and waked me. But, Diamond, for all it was only a dream, I cannot help being ashamed of myself yet for opening the lady's box of bees."

"You wouldn't do it again—would you—if she were to take you back?" said Diamond.

"No. I don't think anything would ever make me do it again. But where's the good? I shall never have the chance."

"I don't know that," said Diamond.

"You silly baby! It was only a dream," said Nanny.

"I know that, Nanny, dear. But how can you tell you mayn't dream it again?"

"That's not a bit likely."

"I don't know that," said Diamond.

"You're always saying that," said Nanny. "I don't like it."

"Then I won't say it again—if I don't forget." said Diamond. "But it was such a beautiful dream!—wasn't it, Nanny? What a pity you opened that door and let the bees out! You might have had such a long dream, and such nice talks with the moon-lady. Do try to go again, Nanny. I do so want to hear more."

But now the nurse came and told him it was time to go; and Diamond went, saying to himself, "I can't help thinking that North Wind had something to do with that dream. It would be tiresome to lie there all day and all night too—without dreaming. Perhaps if she hadn't done that, the moon might have carried her to the back of the north wind—who knows?"

31
The North Wind Doth Blow

It was a great delight to Diamond when at length Nanny was well enough to leave the hospital and go home to their house. She was not very strong yet, but Diamond's mother was very considerate of her, and took care that she should have nothing to do she was not quite fit for. If Nanny had been taken straight from the street, it is very probable she would not have been so pleasant in a decent household, or so easy to teach; but after the refining influences of her illness and the kind treatment she had had in the hospital, she moved about the house just like some rather sad pleasure haunting the mind. As she got better, and the colour came back to her cheeks, her step grew lighter and quicker, her smile shone out more readily, and it became certain that she would soon be a treasure of help. It was great fun to see Diamond teaching her how to hold the baby, and wash and dress him, and often they laughed together over her awkwardness. But she had not many such lessons before she was able to perform those duties quite as well as Diamond himself.

Things however did not go well with Joseph from the very arrival of Ruby. It almost seemed as if the red beast had brought ill luck with him. The fares were fewer, and the pay less. Ruby's services did indeed make the week's income at first a little beyond what it used to be, but then there were two more to feed. After the first month he fell lame, and for the whole of the next Joseph dared not attempt to work him. I cannot say that he never grumbled, for his own health was far from what it had been; but I can say that he tried to do his best. During all that month, they lived on very short commons indeed, seldom tasting meat except on Sundays, and poor old Diamond, who worked hardest of all, not even then—so that at the end of it he was as thin as a clothes-horse, while Ruby was as plump and sleek as a bishop's cob.

Nor was it much better after Ruby was able to work again, for it was a season of great depression in business, and that is very soon felt amongst the cabmen. City men look more after their shillings, and their wives and daughters have less to spend. It was besides a wet autumn, and bread rose greatly in price. When I add to this that Diamond's mother was but poorly, for a new baby was coming, you will see that these were not very jolly times for our friends in the mews.

Notwithstanding the depressing influences around him, Joseph was able to keep a little hope alive in his heart; and when he came home at night, would get Diamond to read to him, and would also make Nanny produce her book that he might see how she was getting on. For Diamond had taken her education in hand, and as she was a clever child, she was very soon able to put letters and words together.

Thus the three months passed away, but Mr. Raymond did not return. Joseph had been looking anxiously for him, chiefly with the desire of getting rid of Ruby—not that he was absolutely of no use to him, but that he was a constant weight upon his mind. Indeed, as far as provision went, he was rather worse off with Ruby and Nanny than he had been before, but on the other hand, Nanny was a great help in the house, and it was a comfort to him to think that when the new baby did come, Nanny would be with his wife.

Of God's gifts a baby is of the greatest; therefore it is no wonder that when this one came, she was as heartily welcomed by the little household as if she had brought plenty with her. Of course she made a great difference in the work to be done—far more difference than her size warranted, but Nanny was no end of help, and Diamond was as much of a sunbeam as ever, and began to sing to the new baby the first moment he got her in his arms. But he did not sing the same songs to her that he had sung to his brother, for, he said, she was a new baby and must have new songs; and besides, she was a sister-baby and not a brother-baby, and of course would not like the same kind of songs. Where the difference in his songs lay, however, I do not pretend to be able to point out. One thing I am sure of, that they not only had no small share in the education of the little girl, but helped the whole family a great deal more than they were aware.

How they managed to get through the long dreary expensive winter, I can hardly say. Sometimes things were better, sometimes worse. But at last the spring came, and the winter was over and gone, and that was much. Still, Mr. Raymond did not return, and although the mother would have been able to manage without Nanny now, they could not look for a place for her so long as they had Ruby; and they were not altogether sorry for this. One week at last was worse than they had yet had. They were almost without bread before it was over. But the sadder he saw his father and mother looking, the more Diamond set himself to sing to the two babies.

One thing which had increased their expenses was that they had been forced to hire another little room for Nanny. When the second baby came, Diamond gave up his room that Nanny might be at hand to help his mother, and went to hers, which, although a fine place to what she had been accustomed to, was not very nice in his eyes. He did not mind the change though, for was not his mother the more comfortable for it? And was not Nanny more comfortable too? And indeed was not Diamond himself more comfortable that other people were more comfortable? And if there was more comfort every way, the change was a happy one.

32
Diamond and Ruby

It was Friday night, and Diamond, like the rest of the household, had had very little to eat that day. The mother would always pay the week's rent before she laid out anything even on food. His father had been very gloomy—so gloomy that he had actually been cross to his wife. It is a strange thing how pain of seeing the suffering of those we love will sometimes make us add to their suffering by being cross with them. This comes of not having faith enough in God, and shows how necessary this faith is, for when we lose it, we lose even the kindness which alone can soothe the suffering. Diamond in consequence had gone to bed very quiet and thoughtful—a little troubled indeed.

It had been a very stormy winter, and even now that the spring had come, the north wind often blew. When Diamond went to his bed, which was in a tiny room in the roof, he heard it like the sea moaning; and when he fell asleep he still heard the moaning. All at once he said to himself, "Am I awake, or am I asleep?" But he had no time to answer the question, for there was North Wind calling him. His heart beat very fast, it was such a long time since he had heard that voice. He jumped out of bed, and looked everywhere, but could not see her. "Diamond, come here," she said again and again; but where the here was he could not tell. To be sure the room was all but quite dark, and she might be close beside him.

"Dear North Wind," said Diamond, "I want so much to go to you, but I can't tell where."

"Come here, Diamond," was all her answer.

Diamond opened the door, and went out of the room, and down the stair and into the yard. His little heart was in a flutter, for he had long given up all thought of seeing her again. Neither now was he to see her. When he got out, a great puff of wind came against him, and in obedience to it he turned his back, and went as it blew. It blew him right up to the stable-door, and went on blowing.

"She wants me to go into the stable," said Diamond to himself, "but the door is locked."

He knew where the key was, in a certain hole in the wall—far too high for him to get at. He ran to the place, however: just as he reached it there came a wild blast, and down fell the key clanging on the stones at his feet. He picked it up, and ran back and opened the stable-door, and went in. And what do you think he saw?

A little light came through the dusty window from a gas-lamp, sufficient to show him Diamond and Ruby with their two heads up, looking at each other across the partition of their stalls. The light showed the white mark on Diamond's forehead, but Ruby's eye shone so bright, that he thought more light came out of it than went in. This is what he saw.

But what do you think he heard?

He heard the two horses talking to each other—in a strange language, which yet, somehow or other, he could understand, and turn over in his mind in English. The first words he heard were from Diamond, who apparently had been already quarrelling with Ruby.

"Look how fat you are Ruby!" said old Diamond. "You are so plump and your skin shines so, you ought to be ashamed of yourself."

"There's no harm in being fat," said Ruby in a deprecating tone. "No, nor in being sleek. I may as well shine as not."

"No harm?" retorted Diamond. "Is it no harm to go eating up all poor master's oats, and taking up so much of his time grooming you, when you only work six hours—no, not six hours a day, and, as I hear, get along no faster than a big dray-horse with two tons behind him?— So they tell me."

"Your master's not mine," said Ruby. "I must attend to my own master's interests, and eat all that is given me, and be sleek and fat as I can, and go no faster than I need."

"Now really if the rest of the horses weren't all asleep, poor things—they work till they're tired—I do believe they would get up and kick you out of the stable. You make me ashamed of being a horse. You dare to say my master ain't your master! That's your gratitude for the way he feeds you and spares you! Pray where would your carcass be if it weren't for him?"

"He doesn't do it for my sake. If I were his own horse, he would work me as hard as he does you."

"And I'm proud to be so worked. I wouldn't be as fat as you—not for all you're worth. You're a disgrace to the stable. Look at the horse next you. He's something like a horse—all skin and bone. And his master ain't over kind to him either. He put a stinging lash on his whip last week. But that old horse knows he's got the wife and children to keep—as well as his drunken master—and he works like a horse. I daresay he grudges his master the beer he drinks, but I don't believe he grudges anything else."

"Well, I don't grudge yours what he gets by me," said Ruby.

"Gets!" retorted Diamond. "What he gets isn't worth grudging. It comes to next to nothing—what with your fat and shine.

"Well, at least you ought to be thankful you're the better for it. You get a two hours' rest a day out of it."

"I thank my master for that—not you, you lazy fellow! You go along like a buttock of beef upon castors—you do."

"Ain't you afraid I'll kick, if you go on like that, Diamond?"

"Kick! You couldn't kick if you tried. You might heave your rump up half a foot, but for lashing out—oho! If you did, you'd be down on your belly before you could get your legs under you again. It's my belief, once out, they'd stick out for ever. Talk of kicking! Why don't you put one foot before the other now and then when you're in the cab? The abuse master gets for your sake is quite shameful. No decent horse would bring it on him. Depend upon it, Ruby, no cabman likes to be abused any more than his fare. But his fares, at least when you are between the shafts, are very much to be excused. Indeed they are."

"Well, you see, Diamond, I don't want to go lame again."

"I don't believe you were so very lame after all—there!"

"Oh, but I was."

"Then I believe it was all your own fault. I'm not lame. I never was lame in all my life. You don't take care of your legs. You never lay them down at night. There you are with your huge carcass crushing down your poor legs all night long. You don't even care for your own legs—so long as you can eat, eat, and sleep, sleep. You a horse indeed!"

"But I tell you I was lame."

"I'm not denying there was a puffy look about your off-pastern. But my belief is, it wasn't even grease—it was fat."

"I tell you I put my foot on one of those horrid stones they make the roads with, and it gave my ankle such a twist."

"Ankle indeed! Why should you ape your betters? Horses ain't got any ankles: they're only pasterns. And so long as you don't lift your feet better, but fall asleep between every step, you'll run a good chance of laming all your ankles as you call them, one after another. It's not your lively horse that comes to grief in that way. I tell you I believe it wasn't much, and if it was, it was your own fault. There! I've done. I'm going to sleep. I'll try to think as well of you as I can. If you would but step out a bit and run off a little of your fat!" Here Diamond began to double up his knees; but Ruby spoke again, and, as young Diamond thought, in a rather different tone.

"I say, Diamond, I can't bear to have an honest old horse like you think of me like that. I will tell you the truth: it was my own fault that I fell lame."

"I told you so," returned the other, tumbling against the partition as he rolled over on his side to give his legs every possible privilege in their narrow circumstances.

"I meant to do it, Diamond."

At the words, the old horse arose with a scramble like thunder, shot his angry head and glaring eye over into Ruby's stall, and said—

"Keep out of my way, you unworthy wretch, or I'll bite you. You a horse! Why did you do that?"

"Because I wanted to grow fat."

"You grease-tub! Oh! my teeth and tail! I thought you were a humbug! Why did you want to get fat? There's no truth to be got out of you but by cross-questioning. You ain't fit to be a horse."

"Because once I am fat, my nature is to keep fat for a long time; and I didn't know when master might come home and want to see me."

"You conceited, good-for-nothing brute! You're only fit for the knacker's yard. You wanted to look handsome, did you? Hold your tongue, or I'll break my halter and be at you—with your handsome fat!"

"Never mind, Diamond. You're a good horse. You can't hurt me."

"Can't hurt you! Just let me once try."

"No, you can't."

"Why then?"

"Because I'm an angel."

"What's that?"

"Of course you don't know."

"Indeed I don't."

"I know you don't. An ignorant, rude old human horse, like you, couldn't know it. But there's young Diamond listening to all we're saying; and he knows well enough there are horses in heaven for angels to ride upon, as well as other animals, lions and eagles and bulls, in more important situations. The horses the angels ride, must be angel-horses, else the angels couldn't ride upon them. Well, I'm one of them."

"You ain't."

"Did you ever know a horse tell a lie?"

"Never before. But you've confessed to shamming lame."

"Nothing of the sort. It was necessary I should grow fat, and necessary that good Joseph, your master, should grow lean. I could have pretended to be lame, but that no horse, least of all an angel-horse would do. So I must be lame, and so I sprained my ankle—for the angel-horses have ankles—they don't talk horse-slang up there—and it hurt me very much, I assure you, Diamond, though you mayn't be good enough to be able to believe it."

Old Diamond made no reply. He had lain down again, and a sleepy snort, very like a snore, revealed that, if he was not already asleep, he was past understanding a word that Ruby was saying. When young Diamond found this, he thought he might venture to take up the dropt shuttlecock of the conversation.

"I'm good enough to believe it, Ruby," he said.

But Ruby never turned his head, or took any notice of him. I suppose he did not understand more of English than just what the coachman and stableman were in the habit of addressing him with. Finding, however, that his companion made no reply, he shot his head over the partition and looking down at him said—

"You just wait till to-morrow, and you'll see whether I'm speaking the truth or not.—I declare the old horse is fast asleep!—Diamond!—No I won't."

Ruby turned away, and began pulling at his hayrack in silence.

Diamond gave a shiver, and looking round saw that the door of the stable was open. He began to feel as if he had been dreaming, and after a glance about the stable to see if North Wind was anywhere visible, he thought he had better go back to bed.

33
The Prospect Brightens

The next morning, Diamond's mother said to his father, "I'm not quite comfortable about that child again."

"Which child, Martha?" asked Joseph. "You've got a choice now."

"Well, Diamond I mean. I'm afraid he's getting into his queer ways again. He's been at his old trick of walking in his sleep. I saw him run up the stair in the middle of the night."

"Didn't you go after him, wife?"

"Of course I did—and found him fast asleep in his bed. It's because he's had so little meat for the last six weeks, I'm afraid."

"It may be that. I'm very sorry. But if it don't please God to send us enough, what am I to do, wife?"

"You can't help it, I know, my dear good man," returned Martha. "And after all I don't know. I don't see why he shouldn't get on as well as the rest of us. There I'm nursing baby all this time, and I get along pretty well. I'm sure, to hear the little man singing, you wouldn't think there was much amiss with him."

For at that moment Diamond was singing like a lark in the clouds. He had the new baby in his arms, while his mother was dressing herself.

Joseph was sitting at his breakfast—a little weak tea, dry bread, and very dubious butter—which Nanny had set for him, and which he was enjoying because he was hungry. He had groomed both horses, and had got old Diamond harnessed ready to put to.

"Think of a fat angel, Dulcimer!" said Diamond.

The baby had not been christened yet, but Diamond, in reading his Bible, had come upon the word dulcimer, and thought it so pretty that ever after he called his sister Dulcimer!

"Think of a red, fat angel, Dulcimer!" he repeated; "for Ruby's an angel of a horse, Dulcimer. He sprained his ankle and got fat on purpose."

"What purpose, Diamond?" asked his father.

"Ah! that I can't tell. I suppose to look handsome when his master comes," answered Diamond.— "What do you think, Dulcimer? It must be for some good, for Ruby's an angel."

"I wish I were rid of him, anyhow," said his father; "for he weighs heavy on my mind."

"No wonder, father: he's so fat," said Diamond. "But you needn't be afraid, for everybody says he's in better condition than when you had him."

"Yes, but he may be as thin as a tin horse before his owner comes. It was too bad to leave him on my hands this way."

"Perhaps he couldn't help it," suggested Diamond. "I daresay he has some good reason for it."

"So I should have said," returned his father, "if he had not driven such a hard bargain with me at first."

"But we don't know what may come of it yet, husband," said his wife. "Mr. Raymond may give a little to boot, seeing you've had more of the bargain than you wanted or reckoned upon."

"I'm afraid not: he's a hard man," said Joseph, as he rose and went to get his cab out.

Diamond resumed his singing. For some time he carolled snatches of everything or anything; but at last it settled down into something like what follows. I cannot tell where or how he got it.

Where did you come from, baby dear?
Out of the everywhere into here.

Where did you get your eyes so blue?
Out of the sky as I came through.

What makes the light in them sparkle and spin?
Some of the starry spikes left in.

Where did you get that little tear?
I found it waiting when I got here.

What makes your forehead so smooth and high?
A soft hand stroked it as I went by.

What makes your cheek like a warm white rose?
I saw something better than any one knows.

Whence that three-cornered smile of bliss?
Three angels gave me at once a kiss.

Where did you get this pearly ear?
God spoke, and it came out to hear.

Where did you get those arms and hands?
Love made itself into hooks and bands.

Feet, whence did you come, you darling things?
From the same box as the cherubs' wings.

How did they all just come to be you?
God thought about me, and so I grew.

But how did you come to us, you dear?
God thought about you, and so I am here.

"You never made that song, Diamond," said his mother.

"No, mother. I wish I had. No, I don't. That would be to take it from somebody else. But it's mine for all that."

"What makes it yours?"

"I love it so."

"Does loving a thing make it yours?"

"I think so, mother—at least more than anything else can. If I didn't love baby (which couldn't be, you know) she wouldn't be mine a bit. But I do love baby, and baby is my very own Dulcimer."

"The baby's mine, Diamond."

"That makes her the more mine, mother."

"How do you make that out?"

"Because you're mine, mother."

"Is that because you love me?"

"Yes, just because. Love makes the only myness," said Diamond.

When his father came home to have his dinner, and change Diamond for Ruby, they saw him look very sad, and he told them he had not had a fare worth mentioning the whole morning.

"We shall all have to go to the workhouse, wife," he said.

"It would be better to go to the back of the north wind," said Diamond, dreamily, not intending to say it aloud.

"So it would," answered his father. "But how are we to get there, Diamond?"

"We must wait till we're taken," returned Diamond.

Before his father could speak again, a knock came to the door, and in walked Mr. Raymond with a smile on his face. Joseph got up and received him respectfully, but not very cordially. Martha set a chair for him, but he would not sit down.

"You are not very glad to see me," he said to Joseph. "You don't want to part with the old horse."

"Indeed, sir, you are mistaken there. What with anxiety about him, and bad luck, I've wished I were rid of him a thousand times. It was only to be for three months, and here it's eight or nine."

"I'm sorry to hear such a statement," said Mr. Raymond. "Hasn't he been of service to you?"

"Not much, not with his lameness"

"Ah!" said Mr. Raymond, hastily— "you've been laming him—have you? That accounts for it. I see, I see."

"It wasn't my fault, and he's all right now. I don't know how it happened, but—"

"He did it on purpose," said Diamond. "He put his foot on a stone just to twist his ankle."

"How do you know that, Diamond?" said his father, turning to him. "I never said so, for I could not think how it came."

"I heard it—in the stable," answered Diamond.

"Let's have a look at him," said Mr. Raymond.

"If you'll step into the yard," said Joseph, "I'll bring him out."

They went, and Joseph, having first taken off his harness, walked Ruby into the middle of the yard.

"Why," said Mr. Raymond, "you've not been using him well."

"I don't know what you mean by that, sir. I didn't expect to hear that from you. He's sound in wind and limb—as sound as a barrel."

"And as big, you might add. Why, he's as fat as a pig! You don't call that good usage!"

Joseph was too angry to make any answer.

"You've not worked him enough, I say. That's not making good use of him. That's not doing as you'd be done by."

"I shouldn't be sorry if I was served the same, sir."

"He's too fat, I say."

"There was a whole month I couldn't work him at all, and he did nothing but eat his head off. He's an awful eater. I've taken the best part of six hours a day out of him since, but I'm always afraid of his coming to grief again, and so I couldn't make the most even of that. I declare to you, sir, when he's between the shafts, I sit on the box as miserable as if I'd stolen him. He looks all the time as if he was a bottling up of complaints to make of me the minute he set eyes on you again. There! look at him now, squinting round at me with one eye! I declare to you, on my word, I haven't laid the whip on him more than three times."

"I'm glad to hear it. He never did want the whip."

"I didn't say that, sir. If ever a horse wanted the whip, he do. He's brought me to beggary almost with his snail's pace. I'm very glad you've come to rid me of him."

"I don't know that," said Mr. Raymond. "Suppose I were to ask you to buy him of me—cheap."

"I wouldn't have him in a present, sir. I don't like him. And I wouldn't drive a horse that I didn't like—no, not for gold. It can't come to good where there's no love between 'em."

"Just bring out your own horse, and let me see what sort of a pair they'd make."

Joseph laughed rather bitterly as he went to fetch Diamond.

When the two were placed side by side, Mr. Raymond could hardly keep his countenance, but from a mingling of feelings. Beside the great, red, round barrel, Ruby, all body and no legs, Diamond looked like a clothes-horse with a skin thrown over it. There was hardly a spot of him where you could not descry some sign of a bone underneath. Gaunt and grim and weary he stood, kissing his master, and heeding no one else.

"You haven't been using him well," said Mr. Raymond.

"I must say," returned Joseph, throwing an arm round his horse's neck, "that the remark had better have been spared, sir. The horse is worth three of the other now."

"I don't think so. I think they make a very nice pair. If the one's too fat, the other's too lean—so that's all right. And if you won't buy my Ruby, I must buy your Diamond."

"Thank you, sir," said Joseph, in a tone implying anything but thanks.

"You don't seem to like the proposal," said Mr. Raymond.

"I don't," returned Joseph. "I wouldn't part with my old Diamond for his skin as full of nuggets as it is of bones."

"Who said anything about parting with him?"

"You did now, sir."

"No; I didn't. I only spoke of buying him to make a pair with Ruby. We could pare Ruby and patch Diamond a bit. And for height, they are as near a match as I care about. Of course you would be the coachman—if only you would consent to be reconciled to Ruby."

Joseph stood bewildered, unable to answer.

"I've bought a small place in Kent," continued Mr. Raymond, "and I must have a pair to my carriage, for the roads are hilly thereabouts. I don't want to make a show with a pair of high-steppers. I think these will just do. Suppose, for a week or two, you set yourself to take Ruby down and bring Diamond up. If we could only lay a pipe from Ruby's sides into Diamond's, it would be the work of a moment. But I fear that wouldn't answer."

A strong inclination to laugh intruded upon Joseph's inclination to cry, and made speech still harder than before.

"I beg your pardon, sir," he said at length. "I've been so miserable, and for so long, that I never thought you was only a chaffing of me when you said I hadn't used the horses well. I did grumble at you, sir, many's the time in my trouble; but whenever I said anything, my little Diamond would look at me with a smile, as much as to say: 'I know him better than you, father;' and upon my word, I always thought the boy must be right."

"Will you sell me old Diamond, then?"

"I will, sir, on one condition—that if ever you want to part with him or me, you give me the option of buying him. I could not part with him, sir. As to who calls him his, that's nothing; for, as Diamond says, it's only loving a thing that can make it yours—and I do love old Diamond, sir, dearly."

"Well, there's a cheque for twenty pounds, which I wrote to offer you for him, in case I should find you had done the handsome thing by Ruby. Will that be enough?"

"It's too much, sir. His body ain't worth it—shoes and all. It's only his heart, sir—that's worth millions—but his heart'll be mine all the same—so it's too much, sir."

"I don't think so. It won't be, at least, by the time we've got him fed up again. You take it and welcome. Just go on with your cabbing for another month, only take it out of Ruby and let Diamond rest; and by that time I shall be ready for you to go down into the country."

"Thank you, sir, thank you. Diamond set you down for a friend, sir, the moment he saw you. I do believe that child of mine knows more than other people."

"I think so, too," said Mr. Raymond as he walked away.

He had meant to test Joseph when he made the bargain about Ruby, but had no intention of so greatly prolonging the trial. He had been taken ill in Switzerland, and had been quite unable to return sooner. He went away now highly gratified at finding that he had stood the test, and was a true man.

Joseph rushed in to his wife who had been standing at the window anxiously waiting the result of the long colloquy. When she heard that the horses were to go together in double harness, she burst forth into an immoderate fit of laughter.

Diamond came up with the baby in his arms and made big anxious eyes at her, saying—

"What is the matter with you, mother dear? Do cry a little. It will do you good. When father takes ever so small a drop of spirits, he puts water to it."

"You silly darling!" said his mother; "how could I but laugh at the notion of that great fat Ruby going side by side with our poor old Diamond?"

"But why not, mother? With a month's oats, and nothing to do, Diamond'll be nearer Ruby's size than you will father's. I think it's very good for different sorts to go together. Now Ruby will have a chance of teaching Diamond better manners."

"How dare you say such a thing, Diamond?" said his father, angrily. "To compare the two for manners, there's no comparison possible. Our Diamond's a gentleman."

"I don't mean to say he isn't, father; for I daresay some gentlemen judge their neighbours unjustly. That's all I mean. Diamond shouldn't have thought such bad things of Ruby. He didn't try to make the best of him."

"How do you know that, pray?"

"I heard them talking about it one night."

"Who?"

"Why Diamond and Ruby. Ruby's an angel."

Joseph stared and said no more. For all his new gladness, he was very gloomy as he re-harnessed the angel, for he thought his darling Diamond was going out of his mind.

He could not help thinking rather differently, however, when he found the change that had come over Ruby. Considering his fat, he exerted himself amazingly, and got over the ground with incredible speed. So willing, even anxious, was he to go now, that Joseph had to hold him quite tight.

Then as he laughed at his own fancies, a new fear came upon him lest the horse should break his wind, and Mr. Raymond have good cause to think he had not been using him well. He might even suppose that he had taken advantage of his new instructions, to let out upon the horse some of his pent-up dislike; whereas in truth, it had so utterly vanished that he felt as if Ruby, too, had been his friend all the time.

34

In the Country

Before the end of the month, Ruby had got respectably thin, and Diamond respectably stout. They really began to look fit for double harness.

Joseph and his wife got their affairs in order, and everything ready for migrating at the shortest notice; and they felt so peaceful and happy that they judged all the trouble they had gone through well worth enduring. As for Nanny, she had been so happy ever since she left the hospital, that she expected nothing better, and saw nothing attractive in the notion of the country. At the same time, she had not the least idea of what the word country meant, for she had never seen anything about her but streets and gas-lamps. Besides, she was more attached to Jim than to Diamond: Jim was a reasonable being, Diamond in her eyes at best only an amiable, over-grown baby, whom no amount of expostulation would ever bring to talk sense, not to say think it. Now that she could manage the baby as well as he, she judged herself altogether his superior. Towards his father and mother, she was all they could wish.

Diamond had taken a great deal of pains and trouble to find Jim, and had at last succeeded through the help of the tall policeman, who was glad to renew his acquaintance with the strange child. Jim had moved his quarters, and had not heard of Nanny's illness till some time after she was taken to the hospital, where he was too shy to go and inquire about her. But when at length she went to live with Diamond's family, Jim was willing enough to go and see her. It was after one of his visits, during which they had been talking of her new prospects, that Nanny expressed to Diamond her opinion of the country.

"There ain't nothing in it but the sun and moon, Diamond."

"There's trees and flowers," said Diamond.

"Well, they ain't no count," returned Nanny.

"Ain't they? They're so beautiful, they make you happy to look at them."

"That's because you're such a silly."

Diamond smiled with a far-away look, as if he were gazing through clouds of green leaves and the vision contented him. But he was thinking with himself what more he could do for Nanny; and that same evening he went to find Mr. Raymond, for he had heard that he had returned to town.

"Ah! how do you do, Diamond?" said Mr. Raymond; "I am glad to see you."

And he was indeed, for he had grown very fond of him. His opinion of him was very different from Nanny's.

"What do you want now, my child?" he asked.

"I'm always wanting something, sir," answered Diamond.

"Well, that's quite right, so long as what you want is right. Everybody is always wanting something; only we don't mention it in the right place often enough. What is it now?"

"There's a friend of Nanny's, a lame boy, called Jim."

"I've heard of him," said Mr. Raymond. "Well?"

"Nanny doesn't care much about going to the country, sir."

"Well, what has that to do with Jim?"

"You couldn't find a corner for Jim to work in—could you, sir?"

"I don't know that I couldn't. That is, if you can show good reason for it."

"He's a good boy, sir."

"Well, so much the better for him."

"I know he can shine boots, sir."

"So much the better for us."

"You want your boots shined in the country—don't you, sir?"

"Yes, to be sure."

"It wouldn't be nice to walk over the flowers with dirty boots—would it, sir?"

"No, indeed."

"They wouldn't like it—would they?"

"No, they wouldn't."

"Then Nanny would be better pleased to go, sir."

"If the flowers didn't like dirty boots to walk over them, Nanny wouldn't mind going to the country? Is that it? I don't quite see it."

"No, sir; I didn't mean that. I meant, if you would take Jim with you to clean your boots, and do odd jobs, you know, sir, then Nanny would like it better. She's so fond of Jim!"

"Now you come to the point, Diamond. I see what you mean, exactly. I will turn it over in my mind. Could you bring Jim to see me?"

"I'll try, sir. But they don't mind me much. They think I'm silly," added Diamond, with one of his sweetest smiles.

What Mr. Raymond thought, I dare hardly attempt to put down here. But one part of it was, that the highest wisdom must ever appear folly to those who do not possess it.

"I think he would come though—after dark, you know," Diamond continued. "He does well at shining boots. People's kind to lame boys, you know, sir. But after dark, there ain't so much doing."

Diamond succeeded in bringing Jim to Mr. Raymond, and the consequence was that he resolved to give the boy a chance. He provided new clothes for both him and Nanny; and upon a certain day, Joseph took his wife and three children, and Nanny and Jim, by train to a certain station in the county of Kent, where they found a cart waiting to carry them and their luggage to The Mound, which was the name of Mr. Raymond's new residence. I will not describe the varied feelings of the party as they went, or when they arrived. All I will say is, that Diamond, who is my only care, was full of quiet delight—a gladness too deep to talk about.

Joseph returned to town the same night, and the next morning drove Ruby and Diamond down, with the carriage behind them, and Mr. Raymond and a lady in the carriage. For Mr. Raymond was an old bachelor no longer: he was bringing his wife with him to live at The Mound. The moment Nanny saw her, she recognised her as the lady who had lent her the ruby-ring. That ring had been given her by Mr. Raymond.

The weather was very hot, and the woods very shadowy. There were not a great many wild flowers, for it was getting well towards autumn, and the most of the wild flowers rise early to be before the leaves, because if they did not, they would never get a glimpse of the sun for them. So they have their fun over, and are ready to go to bed again by the time the trees are dressed. But there was plenty of the loveliest grass and daisies about the house, and Diamond's chief pleasure seemed to be to lie amongst them, and breathe the pure air. But all the time, he was dreaming of the country at the back of the north wind, and trying to recall the songs the river used to sing. For this was more like being at the back of the north wind than anything he had known since he left it. Sometimes he would have his little brother, sometimes his little sister, and sometimes both of them in the grass with him, and then he felt just like a cat with her first kittens, he said, only he couldn't purr—all he could do was to sing.

These were very different times from those when he used to drive the cab, but you must not suppose that Diamond was idle. He did not do so much for his mother now, because Nanny occupied his former place; but he helped his father still, both in the stable and the harness-room, and generally went with him on the box that he might learn to drive a pair, and be ready to open the carriage-door. Mr. Raymond advised his father to give him plenty of liberty.

"A boy like that," he said, "ought not to be pushed."

Joseph assented heartily, smiling to himself at the idea of pushing Diamond. After doing everything that fell to his share, the boy had a wealth of time at his disposal. And a happy, sometimes a merry time it was. Only for two months or so, he neither saw nor heard anything of North Wind.

35

I Make Diamond's Acquaintance

Mr. Raymond's house was called The Mound, because it stood upon a little steep knoll, so smooth and symmetrical that it showed itself at once to be artificial. It had, beyond doubt, been built for Queen Elizabeth as a hunting tower—a place, namely, from the top of which you could see the country for miles on all sides, and so be able to follow with your eyes the flying deer and the pursuing hounds and horsemen. The mound had been cast up to give a good basement-advantage over the neighbouring heights and woods. There was a great quarry-hole not far off, brim-full of water, from which, as the current legend stated, the materials forming the heart of the mound—a kind of stone unfit for building—had been dug. The house itself was of brick, and they said the foundations were first laid in the natural level, and then the stones and earth of the mound were heaped about and between them, so that its great height should be well buttressed.

Joseph and his wife lived in a little cottage a short way from the house. It was a real cottage, with a roof of thick thatch, which, in June and July, the wind sprinkled with the red and white petals it shook from the loose topmost sprays of the rose-trees climbing the walls. At first Diamond had a nest under this thatch—a pretty little room with white muslin curtains, but afterwards Mr. and Mrs. Raymond wanted to have him for a page in the house, and his father and mother were quite pleased to have him employed without his leaving them. So he was dressed in a suit of blue, from which his pale face and fair hair came out like the loveliest blossom, and took up his abode in the house.

"Would you be afraid to sleep alone, Diamond?" asked his mistress.

"I don't know what you mean, ma'am," said Diamond. "I never was afraid of anything that I can recollect—not much, at least."

"There's a little room at the top of the house—all alone," she returned; "perhaps you would not mind sleeping there?"

"I can sleep anywhere, and I like best to be high up. Should I be able to see out?"

"I will show you the place," she answered; and taking him by the hand, she led him up and up the oval-winding stair in one of the two towers.

Near the top they entered a tiny little room, with two windows from which you could see over the whole country. Diamond clapped his hands with delight.

"You would like this room, then, Diamond?" said his mistress.

"It's the grandest room in the house," he answered. "I shall be near the stars, and yet not far from the tops of the trees. That's just what I like."

I daresay he thought, also, that it would be a nice place for North Wind to call at in passing; but he said nothing of that sort. Below him spread a lake of green leaves, with glimpses of grass here and there at the bottom of it. As he looked down, he saw a squirrel appear suddenly, and as suddenly vanish amongst the topmost branches.

"Aha! little squirrel," he cried, "my nest is built higher than yours."

"You can be up here with your books as much as you like," said his mistress. "I will have a little bell hung at the door, which I can ring when I want you. Half-way down the stair is the drawing-room."

So Diamond was installed as page, and his new room got ready for him.

It was very soon after this that I came to know Diamond. I was then a tutor in a family whose estate adjoined the little property belonging to The Mound. I had made the acquaintance of Mr. Raymond in London some time before, and was walking up the drive towards the house to call upon him one fine warm evening, when I saw Diamond for the first time. He was sitting at the foot of a great beech-tree, a few yards from the road, with a book on his knees. He did not see me. I walked up behind the tree, and peeping over his shoulder, saw that he was reading a fairy-book.

"What are you reading?" I said, and spoke suddenly, with the hope of seeing a startled little face look round at me. Diamond turned his head as quietly as if he were only obeying his mother's voice, and the calmness of his face rebuked my unkind desire and made me ashamed of it.

"I am reading the story of the Little Lady and the Goblin Prince," said Diamond.

"I am sorry I don't know the story," I returned. "Who is it by?"

"Mr. Raymond made it."

"Is he your uncle?" I asked at a guess.

"No. He's my master."

"What do you do for him?" I asked respectfully.

"Anything he wishes me to do," he answered. "I am busy for him now. He gave me this story to read. He wants my opinion upon it."

"Don't you find it rather hard to make up your mind?"

"Oh dear no! Any story always tells me itself what I'm to think about it. Mr. Raymond doesn't want me to say whether it is a clever story or not, but whether I like it, and why I like it. I never can tell what they call clever from what they call silly, but I always know whether I like a story or not."

"And can you always tell why you like it or not?"

"No. Very often I can't at all. Sometimes I can. I always know, but I can't always tell why. Mr. Raymond writes the stories, and then tries them on me. Mother does the same when she makes jam. She's made such a lot of jam since we came here! And she always makes me taste it to see if it'll do. Mother knows by the face I make whether it will or not."

At this moment I caught sight of two more children approaching. One was a handsome girl, the other a pale-faced, awkward-looking boy, who limped much on one leg. I withdrew a little, to see what would follow, for they seemed in some consternation. After a few hurried words, they went off together, and I pursued my way to the house, where I was as kindly received by Mr. and Mrs. Raymond as I could have desired. From them I learned something of Diamond, and was in consequence the more glad to find him, when I returned, seated in the same place as before.

"What did the boy and girl want with you, Diamond?" I asked.

"They had seen a creature that frightened them."

"And they came to tell you about it?"

"They couldn't get water out of the well for it. So they wanted me to go with them."

"They're both bigger than you."

"Yes, but they were frightened at it."

"And weren't you frightened at it?"

"No."

"Why?"

"Because I'm silly. I'm never frightened at things."

I could not help thinking of the old meaning of the word silly.

"And what was it?" I asked.

"I think it was a kind of an angel—a very little one. It had a long body and great wings, which it drove about it so fast that they grew a thin cloud all round it. It flew backwards and forwards over the well, or hung right in the middle, making a mist of its wings, as if its business was to take care of the water."

"And what did you do to drive it away?"

"I didn't drive it away. I knew, whatever the creature was, the well was to get water out of. So I took the jug, dipped it in, and drew the water."

"And what did the creature do?"

"Flew about."

"And it didn't hurt you?"

"No. Why should it? I wasn't doing anything wrong."

"What did your companions say then?"

"They said— 'Thank you, Diamond. What a dear silly you are!'"

"And weren't you angry with them?"

"No! Why should I? I should like if they would play with me a little; but they always like better to go away together when their work is over. They never heed me. I don't mind it much, though. The other creatures are friendly. They don't run away from me. Only they're all so busy with their own work, they don't mind me much."

"Do you feel lonely, then?"

"Oh, no! When nobody minds me, I get into my nest, and look up. And then the sky does mind me, and thinks about me."

"Where is your nest?"

He rose, saying, "I will show you," and led me to the other side of the tree.

There hung a little rope-ladder from one of the lower boughs. The boy climbed up the ladder and got upon the bough. Then he climbed farther into the leafy branches, and went out of sight.

After a little while, I heard his voice coming down out of the tree.

"I am in my nest now," said the voice.

"I can't see you," I returned.

"I can't see you either, but I can see the first star peeping out of the sky. I should like to get up into the sky. Don't you think I shall, some day?"

"Yes, I do. Tell me what more you see up there."

"I don't see anything more, except a few leaves, and the big sky over me. It goes swinging about. The earth is all behind my back. There comes another star! The wind is like kisses from a big lady. When I get up here I feel as if I were in North Wind's arms."

This was the first I heard of North Wind.

The whole ways and look of the child, so full of quiet wisdom, yet so ready to accept the judgment of others in his own dispraise, took hold of my heart, and I felt myself wonderfully drawn towards him. It seemed to me, somehow, as if little Diamond possessed the secret of life, and was himself what he was so ready to think the lowest living thing—an angel of God with something special to say or do. A gush of reverence came over me, and with a single goodnight, I turned and left him in his nest.

I saw him often after this, and gained so much of his confidence that he told me all I have told you. I cannot pretend to account for it. I leave that for each philosophical reader to do after his own fashion. The easiest way is that of Nanny and Jim, who said often to each other that Diamond had a tile loose. But Mr. Raymond was much of my opinion concerning the boy; while Mrs. Raymond confessed that she often rang her bell just to have once more the pleasure of seeing the lovely stillness of the boy's face, with those blue eyes which seemed rather made for other people to look into than for himself to look out of.

It was plainer to others than to himself that he felt the desertion of Nanny and Jim. They appeared to regard him as a mere toy, except when they found he could minister to the scruple of using him—generally with success. They were, however, well-behaved to a wonderful degree; while I have little doubt that much of their good behaviour was owing to the unconscious influence of the boy they called God's baby.

One very strange thing is that I could never find out where he got some of his many songs. At times they would be but bubbles blown out of a nursery rhyme, as was the following, which I heard him sing one evening to his little Dulcimer. There were about a score of sheep feeding in a paddock near him, their white wool dyed a pale rose in the light of the setting sun. Those in the long shadows from the trees were dead white; those in the sunlight were half glorified with pale rose.

> Little Bo Peep, she lost her sheep,
>   And didn't know where to find them;
> They were over the height and out of sight,
>   Trailing their tails behind them.
>
> Little Bo Peep woke out of her sleep,
>   Jump'd up and set out to find them:
> "The silly things, they've got no wings,
>   And they've left their trails behind them:
>
> "They've taken their tails, but they've left their trails,
>   And so I shall follow and find them;"
> For wherever a tail had dragged a trail,
>   The long grass grew behind them.
>
> And day's eyes and butter-cups, cow's lips and crow's feet
>   Were glittering in the sun.

She threw down her book, and caught up her crook,
    And after her sheep did run.

She ran, and she ran, and ever as she ran,
    The grass grew higher and higher;
Till over the hill the sun began
    To set in a flame of fire.

She ran on still—up the grassy hill,
    And the grass grew higher and higher;
When she reached its crown, the sun was down,
    And had left a trail of fire.

The sheep and their tails were gone, all gone—
    And no more trail behind them!
Yes, yes! they were there—long-tailed and fair,
    But, alas! she could not find them.

Purple and gold, and rosy and blue,
    With their tails all white behind them,
Her sheep they did run in the trail of the sun;
    She saw them, but could not find them.

After the sun, like clouds they did run,
    But she knew they were her sheep:
She sat down to cry, and look up at the sky,
    But she cried herself asleep.

And as she slept the dew fell fast,
    And the wind blew from the sky;
And strange things took place that shun the day's face,
    Because they are sweet and shy.

Nibble, nibble, crop! she heard as she woke:
    A hundred little lambs
Did pluck and eat the grass so sweet
    That grew in the trails of their dams.

Little Bo Peep caught up her crook,
    And wiped the tears that did blind her.
And nibble, nibble crop! without a stop!
    The lambs came eating behind her.

Home, home she came, both tired and lame,
    With three times as many sheep.
In a month or more, they'll be as big as before,
    And then she'll laugh in her sleep.

But what would you say, if one fine day,
    When they've got their bushiest tails,
Their grown up game should be just the same,
    And she have to follow their trails?

Never weep, Bo Peep, though you lose your sheep,
    And do not know where to find them;
'Tis after the sun the mothers have run,
    And there are their lambs behind them.

I confess again to having touched up a little, but it loses far more in Diamond's sweet voice singing it than it gains by a rhyme here and there.

Some of them were out of books Mr. Raymond had given him. These he always knew, but about the others he could seldom tell. Sometimes he would say, "I made that one." but generally he would say, "I don't know; I found it somewhere;" or "I got it at the back of the north wind."

One evening I found him sitting on the grassy slope under the house, with his Dulcimer in his arms and his little brother rolling on the grass beside them. He was chanting in his usual way, more like the sound of a brook than anything else I can think of. When I went up to them he ceased his chant.

"Do go on, Diamond. Don't mind me," I said.

He began again at once. While he sang, Nanny and Jim sat a little way off, one hemming a pocket-handkerchief, and the other reading a story to her, but they never heeded Diamond. This is as near what he sang as I can recollect, or reproduce rather.

What would you see if I took you up
    To my little nest in the air?
You would see the sky like a clear blue cup
    Turned upside downwards there.

What would you do if I took you there
    To my little nest in the tree?
My child with cries would trouble the air,
    To get what she could but see.

What would you get in the top of the tree
    For all your crying and grief?
Not a star would you clutch of all you see—
    You could only gather a leaf.

But when you had lost your greedy grief,
    Content to see from afar,
You would find in your hand a withering leaf,
    In your heart a shining star.

As Diamond went on singing, it grew very dark, and just as he ceased there came a great flash of lightning, that blinded us all for a moment. Dulcimer crowed with pleasure; but when the roar of thunder came after it, the little brother gave a loud cry of terror. Nanny and Jim came running up to us, pale with fear. Diamond's face, too, was paler than usual, but with delight. Some of the glory seemed to have clung to it, and remained shining.

"You're not frightened—are you, Diamond?" I said.

"No. Why should I be?" he answered with his usual question, looking up in my face with calm shining eyes.

"He ain't got sense to be frightened," said Nanny, going up to him and giving him a pitying hug.

"Perhaps there's more sense in not being frightened, Nanny," I returned. "Do you think the lightning can do as it likes?"

"It might kill you," said Jim.

"Oh, no, it mightn't!" said Diamond.

As he spoke there came another great flash, and a tearing crack.

"There's a tree struck!" I said; and when we looked round, after the blinding of the flash had left our eyes, we saw a huge bough of the beech-tree in which was Diamond's nest hanging to the ground like the broken wing of a bird.

"There!" cried Nanny; "I told you so. If you had been up there you see what would have happened, you little silly!"

"No, I don't," said Diamond, and began to sing to Dulcimer. All I could hear of the song, for the other children were going on with their chatter, was—

The clock struck one,
And the mouse came down.
Dickery, dickery, dock!

Then there came a blast of wind, and the rain followed in straight-pouring lines, as if out of a watering-pot. Diamond jumped up with his little Dulcimer in his arms, and Nanny caught up the little boy, and they ran for the cottage. Jim vanished with a double shuffle, and I went into the house.

When I came out again to return home, the clouds were gone, and the evening sky glimmered through the trees, blue, and pale-green towards the west, I turned my steps a little aside to look at the stricken beech. I saw the bough torn from the stem, and that was all the twilight would allow me to see. While I stood gazing, down from the sky came a sound of singing, but the voice was neither of lark nor of nightingale: it was sweeter than either: it was the voice of Diamond, up in his airy nest:—

> The lightning and thunder,
> They go and they come;
> But the stars and the stillness
> Are always at home.

And then the voice ceased.

"Good-night, Diamond," I said.

"Good-night, sir," answered Diamond.

As I walked away pondering, I saw the great black top of the beech swaying about against the sky in an upper wind, and heard the murmur as of many dim half-articulate voices filling the solitude around Diamond's nest.

36
Diamond Questions North Wind

My Readers will not wonder that, after this, I did my very best to gain the friendship of Diamond. Nor did I find this at all difficult, the child was so ready to trust. Upon one subject alone was he reticent—the story of his relations with North Wind. I fancy he could not quite make up his mind what to think of them. At all events it was some little time before he trusted me with this, only then he told me everything. If I could not regard it all in exactly the same light as he did, I was, while guiltless of the least pretence, fully sympathetic, and he was satisfied without demanding of me any theory of difficult points involved. I let him see plainly enough, that whatever might be the explanation of the marvellous experience, I would have given much for a similar one myself.

On an evening soon after the thunderstorm, in a late twilight, with a half-moon high in the heavens, I came upon Diamond in the act of climbing by his little ladder into the beech-tree.

"What are you always going up there for, Diamond?" I heard Nanny ask, rather rudely, I thought.

"Sometimes for one thing, sometimes for another, Nanny," answered Diamond, looking skywards as he climbed.

"You'll break your neck some day," she said.

"I'm going up to look at the moon to-night," he added, without heeding her remark.

"You'll see the moon just as well down here," she returned.

"I don't think so."

"You'll be no nearer to her up there."

"Oh, yes! I shall. I must be nearer her, you know. I wish I could dream as pretty dreams about her as you can, Nanny."

"You silly! you never have done about that dream. I never dreamed but that one, and it was nonsense enough, I'm sure."

"It wasn't nonsense. It was a beautiful dream—and a funny one too, both in one."

"But what's the good of talking about it that way, when you know it was only a dream? Dreams ain't true."

"That one was true, Nanny. You know it was. Didn't you come to grief for doing what you were told not to do? And isn't that true?"

"I can't get any sense into him," exclaimed Nanny, with an expression of mild despair. "Do you really believe, Diamond, that there's a house in the moon, with a beautiful lady and a crooked old man and dusters in it?"

"If there isn't, there's something better," he answered, and vanished in the leaves over our heads.

I went into the house, where I visited often in the evenings. When I came out, there was a little wind blowing, very pleasant after the heat of the day, for although it was late summer now, it was still hot. The tree-tops were swinging about in it. I took my way past the beech, and called up to see if Diamond were still in his nest in its rocking head.

"Are you there, Diamond?" I said.

"Yes, sir," came his clear voice in reply.

"Isn't it growing too dark for you to get down safely?"

"Oh, no, sir—if I take time to it. I know my way so well, and never let go with one hand till I've a good hold with the other."

"Do be careful," I insisted—foolishly, seeing the boy was as careful as he could be already.

"I'm coming," he returned. "I've got all the moon I want to-night."

I heard a rustling and a rustling drawing nearer and nearer. Three or four minutes elapsed, and he appeared at length creeping down his little ladder. I took him in my arms, and set him on the ground.

"Thank you, sir," he said. "That's the north wind blowing, isn't it, sir?"

"I can't tell," I answered. "It feels cool and kind, and I think it may be. But I couldn't be sure except it were stronger, for a gentle wind might turn any way amongst the trunks of the trees."

"I shall know when I get up to my own room," said Diamond. "I think I hear my mistress's bell. Good-night, sir."

He ran to the house, and I went home.

His mistress had rung for him only to send him to bed, for she was very careful over him and I daresay thought he was not looking well. When he reached his own room, he opened both his windows, one of which looked to the north and the other to the east, to find how the wind blew. It blew right in at the northern window. Diamond was very glad, for he thought perhaps North Wind herself would come now: a real north wind had never blown all the time since he left London. But, as she always came of herself, and never when he was looking for her, and indeed almost never when he was thinking of her, he shut the east window, and went to bed. Perhaps some of my readers may wonder that he could go to sleep with such an expectation; and, indeed, if I had not known him, I should have wondered at it myself; but it was one of his peculiarities, and seemed nothing strange in him. He was so full of quietness that he could go to sleep almost any time, if he only composed himself and let the sleep come. This time he went fast asleep as usual.

But he woke in the dim blue night. The moon had vanished. He thought he heard a knocking at his door. "Somebody wants me," he said to himself, and jumping out of bed, ran to open it.

But there was no one there. He closed it again, and, the noise still continuing, found that another door in the room was rattling. It belonged to a closet, he thought, but he had never been able to open it. The wind blowing in at the window must be shaking it. He would go and see if it was so.

The door now opened quite easily, but to his surprise, instead of a closet he found a long narrow room. The moon, which was sinking in the west, shone in at an open window at the further end. The room was low with a coved ceiling, and occupied the whole top of the house, immediately under the roof. It was quite empty. The yellow light of the half-moon streamed over the dark floor. He was so delighted at the discovery of the strange, desolate, moonlit place close to his own snug little room, that he began to dance and skip about the floor. The wind came in through the door he had left open, and blew about him as he danced, and he kept turning towards it that it might blow in his face. He kept picturing to himself the many places, lovely and desolate, the hill-sides and farm-yards and tree-tops and meadows, over which it had blown on its way to The Mound. And as he danced, he grew more and more delighted with the motion and the wind; his feet grew stronger, and his body lighter, until at length it seemed as if he were borne up on the air, and could almost fly. So strong did his feeling become, that at last he began to doubt whether he was not in one of those precious dreams he had so often had, in which he floated about on the air at will. But something made him look up, and to his unspeakable delight, he found his uplifted hands lying in those of North Wind, who was dancing with him, round and round the long bare room, her hair now falling to the floor, now filling the arched ceiling, her eyes shining on him like thinking stars, and the sweetest of grand smiles playing breezily about her beautiful mouth. She was, as so often before, of the height of a rather tall lady. She did not stoop in order to dance with him, but held his hands high in hers. When he saw her, he gave one spring, and his arms were about her neck, and her arms holding him to her bosom. The same moment she swept with him through the open window in at which the moon was shining, made a circuit like a bird about to alight, and settled with him in his nest on the top of the great beech-tree. There she placed him on her lap and began to hush him as if he were her own baby, and Diamond was so entirely happy that he did not care to speak a word. At length, however, he found that he was going to sleep, and that would be to lose so much, that, pleasant as it was, he could not consent.

"Please, dear North Wind," he said, "I am so happy that I'm afraid it's a dream. How am I to know that it's not a dream?"

"What does it matter?" returned North Wind.

"I should, cry" said Diamond.

"But why should you cry? The dream, if it is a dream, is a pleasant one—is it not?"

"That's just why I want it to be true."

"Have you forgotten what you said to Nanny about her dream?"

"It's not for the dream itself—I mean, it's not for the pleasure of it," answered Diamond, "for I have that, whether it be a dream or not; it's for you, North Wind; I can't bear to find it a dream, because then I should lose you. You would be nobody then, and I could not bear that. You ain't a dream, are you, dear North Wind? Do say No, else I shall cry, and come awake, and you'll be gone for ever. I daren't dream about you once again if you ain't anybody."

"I'm either not a dream, or there's something better that's not a dream, Diamond," said North Wind, in a rather sorrowful tone, he thought.

"But it's not something better—it's you I want, North Wind," he persisted, already beginning to cry a little.

She made no answer, but rose with him in her arms and sailed away over the tree-tops till they came to a meadow, where a flock of sheep was feeding.

"Do you remember what the song you were singing a week ago says about Bo-Peep—how she lost her sheep, but got twice as many lambs?" asked North Wind, sitting down on the grass, and placing him in her lap as before.

"Oh yes, I do, well enough," answered Diamond; "but I never just quite liked that rhyme."

"Why not, child?"

"Because it seems to say one's as good as another, or two new ones are better than one that's lost. I've been thinking about it a great deal, and it seems to me that although any one sixpence is as good as any other sixpence, not twenty lambs would do instead of one sheep whose face you knew. Somehow, when once you've looked into anybody's eyes, right deep down into them, I mean, nobody will do for that one any more. Nobody, ever so beautiful or so good, will make up for that one going out of sight. So you see, North Wind, I can't help being frightened to think that perhaps I am only dreaming, and you are nowhere at all. Do tell me that you are my own, real, beautiful North Wind."

Again she rose, and shot herself into the air, as if uneasy because she could not answer him; and Diamond lay quiet in her arms, waiting for what she would say. He tried to see up into her face, for he was dreadfully afraid she was not answering him because she could not say that she was not a dream; but she had let her hair fall all over her face so that he could not see it. This frightened him still more.

"Do speak, North Wind," he said at last.

"I never speak when I have nothing to say," she replied.

"Then I do think you must be a real North Wind, and no dream," said Diamond.

"But I'm looking for something to say all the time."

"But I don't want you to say what's hard to find. If you were to say one word to comfort me that wasn't true, then I should know you must be a dream, for a great beautiful lady like you could never tell a lie."

"But she mightn't know how to say what she had to say, so that a little boy like you would understand it," said North Wind. "Here, let us get down again, and I will try to tell you what I think. You musn't suppose I am able to answer all your questions, though. There are a great many things I don't understand more than you do."

She descended on a grassy hillock, in the midst of a wild furzy common. There was a rabbit-warren underneath, and some of the rabbits came out of their holes, in the moonlight, looking very sober and wise, just like patriarchs standing in their tent-doors, and looking about them before going to bed. When they saw North Wind, instead of turning round and vanishing again with a thump of their heels, they cantered slowly up to her and snuffled all about her with their long upper lips, which moved every way at once. That was their way of kissing her; and, as she talked to Diamond, she would every now and then stroke down their furry backs, or lift and play with their long ears. They would, Diamond thought, have leaped upon her lap, but that he was there already.

"I think," said she, after they had been sitting silent for a while, "that if I were only a dream, you would not have been able to love me so. You love me when you are not with me, don't you?"

"Indeed I do," answered Diamond, stroking her hand. "I see! I see! How could I be able to love you as I do if you weren't there at all, you know? Besides, I couldn't be able to dream anything half so beautiful all out of my own head; or if I did, I couldn't love a fancy of my own like that, could I?"

"I think not. You might have loved me in a dream, dreamily, and forgotten me when you woke, I daresay, but not loved me like a real being as you love me. Even then, I don't think you could dream anything that hadn't something real like it somewhere. But you've seen me in many shapes, Diamond: you remember I was a wolf once—don't you?"

"Oh yes—a good wolf that frightened a naughty drunken nurse."

"Well, suppose I were to turn ugly, would you rather I weren't a dream then?"

"Yes; for I should know that you were beautiful inside all the same. You would love me, and I should love you all the same. I shouldn't like you to look ugly, you know. But I shouldn't believe it a bit."

"Not if you saw it?"

"No, not if I saw it ever so plain."

"There's my Diamond! I will tell you all I know about it then. I don't think I am just what you fancy me to be. I have to shape myself various ways to various people. But the heart of me is true. People call me by dreadful names, and think they know all about me. But they don't. Sometimes they call me Bad Fortune, sometimes Evil Chance, sometimes Ruin; and they have another name for me which they think the most dreadful of all."

"What is that?" asked Diamond, smiling up in her face.

"I won't tell you that name. Do you remember having to go through me to get into the country at my back?"

"Oh yes, I do. How cold you were, North Wind! and so white, all but your lovely eyes! My heart grew like a lump of ice, and then I forgot for a while."

"You were very near knowing what they call me then. Would you be afraid of me if you had to go through me again?"

"No. Why should I? Indeed I should be glad enough, if it was only to get another peep of the country at your back."

"You've never seen it yet."

"Haven't I, North Wind? Oh! I'm so sorry! I thought I had. What did I see then?"

"Only a picture of it. The real country at my real back is ever so much more beautiful than that. You shall see it one day—perhaps before very long."

"Do they sing songs there?"

"Don't you remember the dream you had about the little boys that dug for the stars?"

"Yes, that I do. I thought you must have had something to do with that dream, it was so beautiful."

"Yes; I gave you that dream."

"Oh! thank you. Did you give Nanny her dream too—about the moon and the bees?"

"Yes. I was the lady that sat at the window of the moon."

"Oh, thank you. I was almost sure you had something to do with that too. And did you tell Mr. Raymond the story about the Princess Daylight?"

"I believe I had something to do with it. At all events he thought about it one night when he couldn't sleep. But I want to ask you whether you remember the song the boy-angels sang in that dream of yours."

"No. I couldn't keep it, do what I would, and I did try."

"That was my fault."

"How could that be, North Wind?"

"Because I didn't know it properly myself, and so I couldn't teach it to you. I could only make a rough guess at something like what it would be, and so I wasn't able to make you dream it hard enough to remember it. Nor would I have done so if I could, for it was not correct. I made you dream pictures of it, though. But you will hear the very song itself when you do get to the back of—"

"My own dear North Wind," said Diamond, finishing the sentence for her, and kissing the arm that held him leaning against her.

"And now we've settled all this—for the time, at least," said North Wind.

"But I can't feel quite sure yet," said Diamond.

"You must wait a while for that. Meantime you may be hopeful, and content not to be quite sure. Come now, I will take you home again, for it won't do to tire you too much."

"Oh, no, no. I'm not the least tired," pleaded Diamond.

"It is better, though."

"Very well; if you wish it," yielded Diamond with a sigh.

"You are a dear good, boy" said North Wind. "I will come for you again to-morrow night and take you out for a longer time. We shall make a little journey together, in fact, we shall start earlier, and as the moon will be later, we shall have a little moonlight all the way."

She rose, and swept over the meadow and the trees. In a few moments the Mound appeared below them. She sank a little, and floated in at the window of Diamond's room. There she laid him on his bed, covered him over, and in a moment he was lapt in a dreamless sleep.

37
Once More

The next night Diamond was seated by his open window, with his head on his hand, rather tired, but so eagerly waiting for the promised visit that he was afraid he could not sleep. But he started suddenly, and found that he had been already asleep. He rose, and looking out of the window saw something white against his beech-tree. It was North Wind. She was holding by one hand to a top branch. Her hair and her garments went floating away behind her over the tree, whose top was swaying about while the others were still.

"Are you ready, Diamond?" she asked.

"Yes," answered Diamond, "quite ready."

In a moment she was at the window, and her arms came in and took him. She sailed away so swiftly that he could at first mark nothing but the speed with which the clouds above and the dim earth below went rushing past. But soon he began to see that the sky was very lovely, with mottled clouds all about the moon, on which she threw faint colours like those of mother-of-pearl, or an opal. The night was warm, and in the lady's arms he did not feel the wind which down below was making waves in the ripe corn, and ripples on the rivers and lakes. At length they descended on the side of an open earthy hill, just where, from beneath a stone, a spring came bubbling out.

"I am going to take you along this little brook," said North Wind. "I am not wanted for anything else to-night, so I can give you a treat."

She stooped over the stream and holding Diamond down close to the surface of it, glided along level with its flow as it ran down the hill. And the song of the brook came up into Diamond's ears, and grew and grew and changed with every turn. It seemed to Diamond to be singing the story of its life to him. And so it was. It began with a musical tinkle which changed to a babble and then to a gentle rushing. Sometimes its song would almost cease, and then break out again, tinkle, babble, and rush, all at once. At the bottom of the hill they came to a small river, into which the brook flowed with a muffled but merry sound. Along the surface of the river, darkly clear below them in the moonlight, they floated; now, where it widened out into a little lake, they would hover for a moment over a bed of water-lilies, and watch them swing about, folded in sleep, as the water on which they leaned swayed in the presence of North Wind; and now they would watch the fishes asleep among their roots below. Sometimes she would hold Diamond over a deep hollow curving into the bank, that he might look far into the cool stillness. Sometimes she would leave the river and sweep across a clover-field. The bees were all at home, and the clover was asleep. Then she would return and follow the river. It grew wider and wider as it went. Now the armies of wheat and of oats would hang over its rush from the opposite banks; now the willows would dip low branches in its still waters; and now it would lead them through stately trees and grassy banks into a lovely garden, where the roses and lilies were asleep, the tender flowers quite folded up, and only a few wide-awake and sending out their life in sweet, strong odours. Wider and wider grew the stream, until they came upon boats lying along its banks, which rocked a little in the flutter of North Wind's garments. Then came houses on the banks, each standing in a lovely lawn, with grand trees; and in parts the river was so high that some of the grass and the roots of some of the trees were under water, and Diamond, as they glided through between the stems, could see the grass at the bottom of the water. Then they would leave the river and float about and over the houses, one after another—beautiful rich houses, which, like fine trees, had taken centuries to grow. There was scarcely a light to be seen, and not a movement to be heard: all the people in them lay fast asleep.

"What a lot of dreams they must be dreaming!" said Diamond.

"Yes," returned North Wind. "They can't surely be all lies—can they?"

"I should think it depends a little on who dreams them," suggested Diamond.

"Yes," said North Wind. "The people who think lies, and do lies, are very likely to dream lies. But the people who love what is true will surely now and then dream true things. But then something depends on whether the dreams are home-grown, or whether the seed of them is blown over somebody else's garden-wall. Ah! there's some one awake in this house!"

They were floating past a window in which a light was burning. Diamond heard a moan, and looked up anxiously in North Wind's face.

"It's a lady," said North Wind. "She can't sleep for pain."

"Couldn't you do something for her?" said Diamond.

"No, I can't. But you could."

"What could I do?"

"Sing a little song to her."

"She wouldn't hear me."

"I will take you in, and then she will hear you."

"But that would be rude, wouldn't it? You can go where you please, of course, but I should have no business in her room."

"You may trust me, Diamond. I shall take as good care of the lady as of you. The window is open. Come."

By a shaded lamp, a lady was seated in a white wrapper, trying to read, but moaning every minute. North Wind floated behind her chair, set Diamond down, and told him to sing something. He was a little frightened, but he thought a while, and then sang:—

> The sun is gone down,
> And the moon's in the sky;
> But the sun will come up,
> And the moon be laid by.
>
> The flower is asleep
> But it is not dead;
> When the morning shines,
> It will lift its head.
>
> When winter comes,
> It will die—no, no;
> It will only hide
> From the frost and the snow.
>
> Sure is the summer,
> Sure is the sun;
> The night and the winter
> Are shadows that run.

The lady never lifted her eyes from her book, or her head from her hand.

As soon as Diamond had finished, North Wind lifted him and carried him away.

"Didn't the lady hear me?" asked Diamond when they were once more floating down the river.

"Oh, yes, she heard you," answered North Wind.

"Was she frightened then?"

"Oh, no."

"Why didn't she look to see who it was?"

"She didn't know you were there."

"How could she hear me then?"

"She didn't hear you with her ears."

"What did she hear me with?"

"With her heart."

"Where did she think the words came from?"

"She thought they came out of the book she was reading. She will search all through it to-morrow to find them, and won't be able to understand it at all."

"Oh, what fun!" said Diamond. "What will she do?"

"I can tell you what she won't do: she'll never forget the meaning of them; and she'll never be able to remember the words of them."

"If she sees them in Mr. Raymond's book, it will puzzle her, won't it?"

"Yes, that it will. She will never be able to understand it."

"Until she gets to the back of the north wind," suggested Diamond.

"Until she gets to the back of the north wind," assented the lady.

"Oh!" cried Diamond, "I know now where we are. Oh! do let me go into the old garden, and into mother's room, and Diamond's stall. I wonder if the hole is at the back of my bed still. I should like to stay there all the rest of the night. It won't take you long to get home from here, will it, North Wind?"

"No," she answered; "you shall stay as long as you like."

"Oh, how jolly," cried Diamond, as North Wind sailed over the house with him, and set him down on the lawn at the back.

Diamond ran about the lawn for a little while in the moonlight. He found part of it cut up into flower-beds, and the little summer-house with the coloured glass and the great elm-tree gone. He did not like this, and ran into the stable. There were no horses there at all. He ran upstairs. The rooms were empty. The only thing left that he cared about was the hole in the wall where his little bed had stood; and that was not enough to make him wish to stop. He ran down the stair again, and out upon the lawn. There he threw himself down and began to cry. It was all so dreary and lost!

"I thought I liked the place so much," said Diamond to himself, "but I find I don't care about it. I suppose it's only the people in it that make you like a place, and when they're gone, it's dead, and you don't care a bit about it. North Wind told me I might stop as long as I liked, and I've stopped longer already. North Wind!" he cried aloud, turning his face towards the sky.

The moon was under a cloud, and all was looking dull and dismal. A star shot from the sky, and fell in the grass beside him. The moment it lighted, there stood North Wind.

"Oh!" cried Diamond, joyfully, "were you the shooting star?"

"Yes, my child."

"Did you hear me call you then?"

"Yes."

"So high up as that?"

"Yes; I heard you quite well."

"Do take me home."

"Have you had enough of your old home already?"

"Yes, more than enough. It isn't a home at all now."

"I thought that would be it," said North Wind. "Everything, dreaming and all, has got a soul in it, or else it's worth nothing, and we don't care a bit about it. Some of our thoughts are worth nothing, because they've got no soul in them. The brain puts them into the mind, not the mind into the brain."

"But how can you know about that, North Wind? You haven't got a body."

"If I hadn't you wouldn't know anything about me. No creature can know another without the help of a body. But I don't care to talk about that. It is time for you to go home."

So saying, North Wind lifted Diamond and bore him away.

38
At the Back of the North Wind

I did not see Diamond for a week or so after this, and then he told me what I have now told you. I should have been astonished at his being able even to report such conversations as he said he had had with North Wind, had I not known already that some children are profound in metaphysics. But a fear crosses me, lest, by telling so much about my friend, I should lead people to mistake him for one of those consequential, priggish little monsters, who are always trying to say clever things, and looking to see whether people appreciate them. When a child like that dies, instead of having a silly book written about him, he should be stuffed like one of those awful big-headed fishes you see in museums. But Diamond never troubled his head about what people thought of him. He never set up for knowing better than others. The wisest things he said came out when he wanted one to help him with some difficulty he was in. He was not even offended with Nanny and Jim for calling him a silly. He supposed there was something in it, though he could not quite understand what. I suspect however that the other name they gave him, God's Baby, had some share in reconciling him to it.

Happily for me, I was as much interested in metaphysics as Diamond himself, and therefore, while he recounted his conversations with North Wind, I did not find myself at all in a strange sea, although certainly I could not always feel the bottom, being indeed convinced that the bottom was miles away.

"Could it be all dreaming, do you think, sir?" he asked anxiously.

"I daren't say, Diamond," I answered. "But at least there is one thing you may be sure of, that there is a still better love than that of the wonderful being you call North Wind. Even if she be a dream, the dream of such a beautiful creature could not come to you by chance."

"Yes, I know," returned Diamond; "I know."

Then he was silent, but, I confess, appeared more thoughtful than satisfied.

The next time I saw him, he looked paler than usual.

"Have you seen your friend again?" I asked him.

"Yes," he answered, solemnly.

"Did she take you out with her?"

"No. She did not speak to me. I woke all at once, as I generally do when I am going to see her, and there she was against the door into the big room, sitting just as I saw her sit on her own doorstep, as white as snow, and her eyes as blue as the heart of an iceberg. She looked at me, but never moved or spoke."

"Weren't you afraid?" I asked.

"No. Why should I have been?" he answered. "I only felt a little cold."

"Did she stay long?"

"I don't know. I fell asleep again. I think I have been rather cold ever since though," he added with a smile.

I did not quite like this, but I said nothing.

Four days after, I called again at the Mound. The maid who opened the door looked grave, but I suspected nothing. When I reached the drawing-room, I saw Mrs. Raymond had been crying.

"Haven't you heard?" she said, seeing my questioning looks.

"I've heard nothing," I answered.

"This morning we found our dear little Diamond lying on the floor of the big attic-room, just outside his own door—fast asleep, as we thought. But when we took him up, we did not think he was asleep. We saw that—"

Here the kind-hearted lady broke out crying afresh.

"May I go and see him?" I asked.

"Yes," she sobbed. "You know your way to the top of the tower."

I walked up the winding stair, and entered his room. A lovely figure, as white and almost as clear as alabaster, was lying on the bed. I saw at once how it was. They thought he was dead. I knew that he had gone to the back of the north wind.

The Flight of the Shadow

(1891)

1

Mrs. Day Begins the Story

I am old, else, I think, I should not have the courage to tell the story I am going to tell. All those concerned in it about whose feelings I am careful, are gone where, thank God, there are no secrets! If they know what I am doing, I know they do not mind. If they were alive to read as I record, they might perhaps now and again look a little paler and wish the leaf turned, but to see the things set down would not make them unhappy: they do not love secrecy. Half the misery in the world comes from trying to look, instead of trying to be, what one is not. I would that not God only but all good men and women might see me through and through. They would not be pleased with everything they saw, but then neither am I, and I would have no coals of fire in my soul's pockets! But my very nature would shudder at the thought of letting one person that loved a secret see into it. Such a one never sees things as they are—would not indeed see what was there, but something shaped and coloured after his own likeness. No one who loves and chooses a secret can be of the pure in heart that shall see God.

Yet how shall I tell even who I am? Which of us is other than a secret to all but God! Which of us can tell, with poorest approximation, what he or she is! Not to touch the mystery of life—that one who is not myself has made me able to say *I*, how little can any of us tell about even those ancestors whose names we know, while yet the nature, and still more the character, of hundreds of them, have shared in determining what *I* means every time one of us utters the word! For myself, I remember neither father nor mother, nor one of their fathers or mothers: how little then can I say as to what I am! But I will tell as much as most of my readers, if ever I have any, will care to know.

I come of a long yeoman-line of the name of Whichcote. In Scotland the Whichcotes would have been called *lairds*; in England they were not called *squires*. Repeatedly had younger sons of it risen to rank and honour, and in several generations would his property have entitled the head of the family to rank as a squire, but at the time when I began to be aware of existence, the family possessions had dwindled to one large farm, on which I found myself. Naturally, while some of the family had risen, others had sunk in the social scale; and of the latter was Miss Martha Moon, far more to my life than can appear in my story. I should imagine there are few families in England covering a larger range of social difference than ours. But I begin to think the chief difficulty in writing a book must be to keep out what does not belong to it.

I may mention, however, my conviction, that I owe many special delights to the gradual development of my race in certain special relations to the natural ways of the world. That I was myself brought up in such relations, appears not enough to account for the intensity of my pleasure in things belonging to simplest life—in everything of the open air, in animals of all kinds, in the economy of field and meadow and moor. I can no more understand my delight in the sweet breath of a cow, than I can explain the process by which, that day in the garden—but I must not forestall, and will say rather—than I can account for the tears which, now I am an old woman, fill my eyes just as they used when I was a child, at sight of the year's first primrose. A harebell, much as I have always loved harebells, never moved me that way! Some will say the cause, whatever it be, lies in my nature, not in my ancestry; that, anyhow, it must have come first to some one—and why not to me? I answer, Everything lies in everyone of us, but has to be brought to the surface. It grows a little in one, more in that one's child, more in that child's child, and so on and on—with curious breaks as of a river which every now and then takes to an underground course. One thing I am sure of—that, however any good thing came, I did not make it; I can only be glad and thankful that in me it came to the surface, to tell me how beautiful must he be who thought of it, and made it in me. Then surely one is nearer, if not to God himself, yet to the things God loves, in the country than amid ugly houses—things that could not have been invented by God, though he made the man that made them. It is not the fashionable only that love the town and not the country; the men and women who live in dirt and squalor— their counterparts in this and worse things far more than they think— are afraid of loneliness, and hate God's lovely dark.

2
Miss Martha Moon

Let me look back and see what first things I first remember!

All about my uncle first; but I keep him to the last. Next, all about Rover, the dog—though for roving, I hardly remember him away from my side! Alas, he did not live to come into the story, but I must mention him here, for I shall not write another book, and, in the briefest summary of my childhood, to make no allusion to him would be disloyalty. I almost believe that at one period, had I been set to say who I was, I should have included Rover as an essential part of myself. His tail was my tail; his legs were my legs; his tongue was my tongue!—so much more did I, as we gambolled together, seem conscious of his joy than of my own! Surely, among other and greater mercies, I shall find him again! The next person I see busy about the place, now here now there in the house, and seldom outside it, is Miss Martha Moon. The house is large, built at a time when the family was one of consequence, and there was always much to be done in it. The largest room in it is now called the kitchen, but was doubtless called the hall when first it was built. This was Miss Martha Moon's headquarters.

She was my uncle's second cousin, and as he always called her Martha, so did I, without rebuke: every one else about the place called her Miss Martha.

Of much greater worth and much more genuine refinement than tens of thousands the world calls ladies, she never claimed the distinction. Indeed she strongly objected to it. If you had said or implied she was a lady, she would have shrunk as from a covert reflection on the quality of her work. Had she known certain of such as nowadays call themselves lady-helps, I could have understood her objection. I think, however, it came from a stern adherence to the factness—if I may coin the word—of things. She never called a lie a fib.

When she was angry, she always held her tongue; she feared being unfair. She had indeed a rare power of silence. To this day I do not *know*, but am nevertheless sure that, by an instinct of understanding, she saw into my uncle's trouble, and descried, more or less plainly, the secret of it, while yet she never even alluded to the existence of such a trouble. She had a regard for woman's dignity as profound as silent. She was not of those that prate or rave about their rights, forget their duties, and care only for what they count their victories.

She declared herself dead against marriage. One day, while yet hardly more than a child, I said to her thoughtfully,

"I wonder why you hate gentlemen, Martha!"

"Hate 'em! What on earth makes you say such a wicked thing, Orbie?" she answered. "Hate 'em, the poor dears! I love 'em! What did you ever see to make you think I hated your uncle now?"

"Oh! of course! uncle!" I returned; for my uncle was all the world to me. "Nobody could hate uncle!"

"She'd be a bad woman, anyhow, that did!" rejoined Martha. "But did anybody ever hate the person that couldn't do without her, Orbie?"

My name—suggested by my uncle because my mother died at my birth—was a curious one; I believe he made it himself. *Belorba* it was, and it means *Fair Orphan.*

"I don't know, Martha," I replied.

"Well, you watch and see!" she returned. "Do you think I would stay here and work from morning to night if I hadn't some reason for it?—Oh, I like work!" she went on; "I don't deny that. I should be miserable if I didn't work. But I'm not bound to this sort of work. I have money of my own, and I'm no beggar for house-room. But rather than leave your uncle, poor man! I would do the work of a ploughman for him."

"Then why don't you marry him, Martha?" I said, with innocent impertinence.

"Marry him! I wouldn't marry him for ten thousand pounds, child!"

"Why not, if you love him so much? I'm sure he wouldn't mind!"

"Marry him!" repeated Miss Martha, and stood looking at me as if here at last was a creature she could *not* understand; "marry the poor dear man, and make him miserable! I could love any man better than that! Just you open your eyes, my dear, and see what goes on about you. Do you see so many men made happy by their wives? I don't say it's all the wives' fault, poor things! But the fact's the same: there's the poor husbands all the time trying hard to bear it! What with the babies, and the headaches, and the rest of it, that's what it comes to— the husbands are not happy! No, no! A woman can do better for a man than marry him!"

"But mayn't it be the husband's fault—sometimes, Martha?"

"It may; but what better is it for that? What better is the wife for knowing it, or how much happier the husband for not knowing it? As soon as you come to weighing who's in fault, and counting how much, it's all up with the marriage. There's no more comfort in life for either of them! Women are sent into the world to make men happy. I was sent to your uncle, and I'm trying to do my duty. It's nothing to me what other women think; I'm here to serve your uncle. What comes of me, I don't care, so long as I do my work, and don't keep him waiting that made me for it. You may think it a small thing to make a man happy! I don't. God thought him worth making, and he wouldn't be if he was miserable. I've seen one woman make ten men unhappy! I know my calling, Orbie. Nothing would make me marry one of them, poor things!"

"But if they all said as you do, Martha?"

"No doubt the world would come to an end, but it would go out singing, not crying. I don't see that would matter. There would be enough to make each other happy in heaven, and the Lord could make more as they were wanted."

"Uncle says it takes God a long time to make a man!" I ventured to remark.

Miss Martha was silent for a moment. She did not see how my remark bore on the matter in hand, but she had such respect for anything my uncle said, that when she did not grasp it she held her peace.

"Anyhow there's no fear of it for the present!" she answered. "You heard the screed of banns last Sunday!"

I thought you would have a better idea of Miss Martha Moon from hearing her talk, than from any talk about her. To hear one talk is better than to see one. But I would not have you think she often spoke at such length. She was in truth a woman of few words, never troubled or troubling with any verbal catarrh. Especially silent she was when any one she loved was in distress. I have seen her stand moveless for moments, with a look that was the incarnation of essential motherhood—as if her eyes were swallowing up sorrow; as if her soul was ready to be the sacrifice for sin. Then she would turn away with a droop of the eye-lids that seemed to say she saw what it was, but saw also how little she could do for it. Oh the depth of the love-trouble in those eyes of hers!

Martha never set herself to teach me anything, but I could not know Martha without learning something of the genuine human heart. I gathered from her by unconscious assimilation. Possibly, a spiritual action analogous to exosmose and endosmose, takes place between certain souls.

3

My Uncle

Now I must tell you what my uncle was like.

The first thing that struck you about him would have been, how tall and thin he was. The next thing would have been, how he stooped; and the next, how sad he looked. It scarcely seemed that Martha Moon had been able to do much for him. Yet doubtless she had done, and was doing, more than either he or she knew. He had rather a small head on the top of his long body; and when he stood straight up, which was not very often, it seemed so far away, that some one said he took him for Zacchaeus looking down from the sycamore. *I* never thought of analyzing his appearance, never thought of comparing him with any one else. To me he was the best and most beautiful of men—the first man in all the world. Nor did I change my mind about him ever— I only came to want another to think of him as I did.

His features were in fine proportion, though perhaps too delicate. Perhaps they were a little too small to be properly beautiful. When first I saw a likeness of the poet Shelley, I called out "My uncle!" and immediately began to see differences. He wore a small but long moustache, brushed away from his mouth; and over it his eyes looked large. They were of a clear gray, and very gentle. I know from the testimony of others, that I was right in imagining him a really learned man. That small head of his contained more and better than many a larger head of greater note. He was constantly reading—that is, when not thinking, or giving me the lessons which make me now thank him for half my conscious soul.

Reading or writing or thinking, he made me always welcome to share his room with him; but he seldom took me out walking. He was by no means regular in his habits—regarded neither times nor seasons—went and came like a bird. His hour for going out was unknown to himself, was seldom two days together the same. He would rise up suddenly, even in the middle of a lesson—he always called it "a lesson together"—and without a word walk from the room and the house.

I had soon observed that in gloomy weather he went out often, in the sunshine seldom.

The house had a large garden, of a very old-fashioned sort, such a place for the charm of both glory and gloom as I have never seen elsewhere. I have had other eyes opened within me to deeper beauties than I saw in that garden then; my remembrance of it is none the less of an enchanted ground. But my uncle never walked in it. When he walked, it was always out on the moor he went, and what time he would return no one ever knew. His meals were uninteresting to him— no concern to any one but Martha, who never uttered a word of impatience, and seldom a word of anxiety. At whatever hour of the day he went, it was almost always night when he came home, often late night. In the house he much preferred his own room to any other.

This room, not so large as the kitchen-hall, but quite as long, seems to me, when I look back, my earliest surrounding. It was the centre from which my roving fancies issued as from their source, and the end of their journey to which as to their home they returned. It was a curious place. Were you to see first the inside of the house and then the outside, you would find yourself at a loss to conjecture where within it could be situated such a room. It was not, however, contained in what, to a cursory glance, passed for the habitable house, and a stranger would not easily have found the entrance to it.

Both its nature and situation were in keeping with certain peculiarities of my uncle's mental being. He was given to curious inquiries. He would set out to solve now one now another historical point as odd as uninteresting to any but a mind capable of starting such a question. To determine it, he would search book after book, as if it were a live thing, in whose memory must remain, darkly stored, thousands of facts, requiring only to be recollected: amongst them might nestle the thing he sought, and he would dig for it as in a mine that went branching through the hardened dust of ages. I fancy he read any old book whatever of English history with the haunting sense that next moment he might come upon the trace of certain of his own ancestors of whom he specially desired to enlarge his knowledge. Whether he started any new thing in mathematics I cannot tell, but he would sit absorbed, every day and all day long, for weeks, over his slate, suddenly throw it down, walk out for the rest of the day, and leave his calculus, or whatever it was, for months. He read Shakespeare as with a microscope, propounding and answering the most curious little questions. It seemed to me sometimes, I confess, that he missed a plain point from his eyes being so sharp that they looked through it without seeing it, having focused themselves beyond it.

A specimen of the kind of question he would ask and answer himself, occurs to me as I write, for he put it to me once as we read together.

"Why," he said, "did Margaret, in *Much ado about Nothing*, try to
persuade Hero to wear her other rabato?"

And the answer was,

"Because she feared her mistress would find out that she had been
wearing it—namely, the night before, when she personated her."

And here I may put down a remark I heard him make in reference
to a theory which itself must seem nothing less than idiotic to any
one who knows Shakespeare as my uncle knew him. The remark was
this—that whoever sought to enhance the fame of lord St. Alban's—
he was careful to use the real title—by attributing to him the works of
Shakespeare, must either be a man of weak intellect, of great ignorance, or of low moral perception; for he cast on the memory of a
man already more to be pitied than any, a weight of obloquy such as
it were hard to believe anyone capable of deserving. A being with
Shakespeare's love of human nature, and Bacon's insight into essential truth, guilty of the moral and social atrocities into which his
lordship's eagerness after money for scientific research betrayed him,
would be a monster as grotesque as abominable.

I record the remark the rather that it shows my uncle could look
at things in a large way as well as hunt with a knife-edge. At the same
time, devoutly as I honour him, I cannot but count him intended for
thinkings of larger scope than such as then seemed characteristic of
him. I imagine his early history had affected his faculties, and influ-
enced the mode of their working. How indeed could it have been otherwise!

4
My Uncle's Room, and My Uncle in It

At right angles to the long, black and white house, stood a building behind it, of possibly earlier date, but uncertain intent. It had been used for many things before my uncle's time—once as part of a small brewery. My uncle was positive that, whether built for the purpose or not, it had been used as a chapel, and that the house was originally the out-lying cell of some convent. The signs on which he founded this conclusion, I was never able to appreciate: to me, as containing my uncle's study, the wonder-house of my childhood, it was far more interesting than any history could have made it. It had very thick walls, two low stories, and a high roof. Entering it from the court behind the house, every portion of it would seem to an ordinary beholder quite accounted for; but it might have suggested itself to a more comprehending observer, that a considerable space must lie between the roof and the low ceiling of the first floor, which was taken up with the servants' rooms. Of the ground floor, part was used as a dairy, part as a woodhouse, part for certain vegetables, while part stored the turf dug for fuel from the neighbouring moor.

Between this building and the house was a smaller and lower erection, a mere out-house. It also was strongly built, however, and the roof, in perfect condition, seemed newer than the walls: it had been raised and strengthened when used by my uncle to contain a passage leading from the house to the roof of the building just described, in which he was fashioning for himself the retreat which he rightly called his study, for few must be the rooms more continuously thought and read in during one lifetime than this.

I have now to tell how it was reached from the house. You could hardly have found the way to it, even had you set yourself seriously to the task, without having in you a good share of the constructive faculty. The whole was my uncle's contrivance, but might well have been supposed to belong to the troubled times when a good hiding-place would have added to the value of any home.

There was a large recess in the kitchen, of which the hearth, raised a foot or so above the flagged floor, had filled the whole—a huge chimney in fact, built out from the wall. At some later time an oblong space had been cut out of the hearth to a level with the floor, and in it an iron grate constructed for the more convenient burning of coal. Hence the remnant of the raised hearth looked like wide hobs to the grate. The recess as a chimney-corner was thereby spoiled, for coal makes a very different kind of smoke from the aromatic product of wood or peat.

Right and left within the recess, were two common, unpainted doors, with latches. If you opened either, you found an ordinary shallow cupboard, that on the right filled with shelves and crockery, that on the left with brooms and other household implements.

But if, in the frame of the door to the left, you pressed what looked like the head of a large nail, not its door only but the whole cupboard turned inward on unseen hinges, and revealed an ascending stair, which was the approach to my uncle's room. At the head of the stair you went through the wall of the house to the passage under the roof of the out-house, at the end of which a few more steps led up to the door of the study. By that door you entered the roof of the more ancient building. Lighted almost entirely from above, there was no indication outside of the existence of this floor, except one tiny window, with vaguely pointed arch, almost in the very top of the gable. Here lay my nest; this was the bower of my bliss.

Its walls rose but about three feet from the floor ere the slope of the roof began, so that there was a considerable portion of the room in which my tall uncle could not stand upright. There was width enough notwithstanding, in which four as tall as he might have walked abreast up and down a length of at least five and thirty feet.

Not merely the low walls, but the slopes of the roof were filled with books as high as the narrow level portion of the ceiling. On the slopes the bookshelves had of course to be peculiar. My uncle had contrived, and partly himself made them, with the assistance of a carpenter he had known all his life. They were individually fixed to the rafters, each projecting over that beneath it. To get at the highest, he had to stand on a few steps; to reach the lowest, he had to stoop at a right angle. The place was almost a tunnel of books.

By setting a chair on an ancient chest that stood against the gable, and a footstool on the chair, I could mount high enough to get into the deep embrasure of the little window, whence alone to gain a glimpse of the lower world, while from the floor I could see heaven through six skylights, deep framed in books. As far back as I can remember, it was my care to see that the inside of their glass was always bright, so that sun and moon and stars might look in.

The books were mostly in old and dingy bindings, but there were a few to attract the eyes of a child—especially some annuals, in red skil, or embossed leather, or, most bewitching of all, in paper, protected by a tight case of the same, from which, with the help of a ribbon, you drew out the precious little green volume, with its gilt edges and lovely engravings—one of which in particular I remember—a castle in the distance, a wood, a ghastly man at the head of a rearing horse, and a white, mist-like, fleeting ghost, the cause of the consternation. These books had a large share in the witchery of the chamber.

At the end of the room, near the gable-window, but under one of the skylights, was a table of white deal, without cover, at which my uncle generally sat, sometimes writing, oftener leaning over a book. Occasionally, however, he would occupy a large old-fashioned easy chair, under the slope of the roof, in the same end of the room, sitting silent, neither writing nor reading, his eyes fixed straight before him, but plainly upon nothing. They looked as if sights were going out of them rather than coming in at them. When he sat thus, I would sit gazing at him. Oh how I loved him—loved every line of his gentle, troubled countenance! I do not remember the time when I did not know that his face was troubled. It gave the last finishing tenderness to my love for him. It was from no meddlesome curiosity that I sat watching him, from no longing to learn what he was thinking about, or what pictures were going and coming before the eyes of his mind, but from such a longing to comfort him as amounted to pain. I think it was the desire to be near him—in spirit, I mean, for I could be near him in the body any time except when he was out on one of his lonely walks or rides—that made me attend so closely to my studies. He taught me everything, and I yearned to please him, but without this other half-conscious yearning I do not believe I should ever have made the progress he praised. I took indeed a true delight in learning, but I would not so often have shut the book I was enjoying to the full and taken up another, but for the sight or the thought of my uncle's countenance.

I think he never once sat down in the chair I have mentioned without sooner or later rising hurriedly, and going out on one of his solitary rambles.

When we were having our lessons together, as he phrased it, we sat at the table side by side, and he taught me as if we were two children finding out together what it all meant. Those lessons had, I think, the largest share in the charm of the place; yet when, as not unfrequently, my uncle would, in the middle of one of them, rise abruptly and leave me without a word, to go, I knew, far away from the house, I was neither dismayed nor uneasy: I had got used to the thing before I could wonder what it meant. I would just go back to the book I had been reading, or to any other that attracted me: he never required the preparation of any lessons. It was of no use to climb to the window in the hope of catching sight of him, for thence was nothing to be seen immediately below but the tops of high trees and a corner of the yard into which the cow-houses opened, and my uncle was never there. He neither understood nor cared about farming. His elder brother, my father, had been bred to carry on the yeoman-line of the family, and my uncle was trained to the medical profession. My father dying rather suddenly, my uncle, who was abroad at the time, and had not begun to practise, returned to take his place, but never paid practical attention to the farming any more than to his profession. He gave the land in charge to a bailiff, and at once settled down, Martha told me, into what we now saw him. She seemed to imply that grief at my father's death was the cause of his depression, but I soon came to the conclusion that it lasted too long to be so accounted for. Gradually I grew aware—so gradually that at length I seemed to have known it from the first—that the soul of my uncle was harassed with an undying trouble, that some worm lay among the very roots of his life. What change could ever dispel such a sadness as I often saw in that chair! Now and then he would sit there for hours, an open book in his hand perhaps, at which he cast never a glance, all un-aware of the eyes of the small maiden fixed upon him, with a whole world of sympathy behind them. I suspect, however, as I believe I have said, that Martha Moon, in her silence, had pierced the heart of the mystery, though she *knew* nothing.

One practical lesson given me now and then in varying form by my uncle, I at length, one day, suddenly and involuntarily associated with the darkness that haunted him. In substance it was this: "Never, my little one, hide anything from those that love you. Never let any-thing that makes itself a nest in your heart, grow into a secret, for then at once it will begin to eat a hole in it." He would so often say the kind of thing, that I seemed to know when it was coming. But I had heard it as a thing of course, never realizing its truth, and listen-ing to it only because he whom I loved said it.

I see with my mind's eye the fine small head and large eyes so far above me, as we sit beside each other at the deal table. He looked down on me like a bird of prey. His hair—gray, Martha told me, before he was thirty—was tufted out a little, like ruffled feathers, on each side. But the eyes were not those of an eagle; they were a dove's eyes.

"A secret, little one, is a mole that burrows," said my uncle.

The moment of insight was come. A voice seemed suddenly to say within me, "He has a secret; it is biting his heart!" My affection, my devotion, my sacred concern for him, as suddenly swelled to twice their size. It was as if a God were in pain, and I could not help him. I had no desire to learn his secret; I only yearned heart and soul to comfort him. Before long, I had a secret myself for half a day: ever after, I shared so in the trouble of his secret, that I seemed myself to possess or rather to be possessed by one—such a secret that I did not myself know it.

But in truth I had a secret then; for the moment I knew that he had a secret, his secret—the outward fact of its existence, I mean—was my secret. And besides this secret of his, I had then a secret of my own. For I knew that my uncle had a secret, and he did not know that I knew. Therewith came, of course, the question—Ought I to tell him? At once, by the instinct of love, I saw that to tell him would put him in a great difficulty. He might wish me never to let any one else know of it, and how could he say so when he had been constantly warning me to let nothing grow to a secret in my heart? As to telling Martha Moon, much as I loved her, much as I knew she loved my uncle, and sure as I was that anything concerning him was as sacred to her as to me, I dared not commit such a breach of confidence as even to think in her presence that my uncle had a secret. From that hour I had recurrent fits of a morbid terror at the very idea of a secret—as if a secret were in itself a treacherous, poisonous guest, that ate away the life of its host.

But to return, my half-day-secret came in this wise.

5
My First Secret

I was one morning with my uncle in his room. Lessons were over, and I was reading a marvellous story in one of my favourite annuals: my uncle had so taught me from infancy the right handling of books, that he would have trusted me with the most valuable in his possession. I do not know how old I was, but that is no matter; man or woman is aged according to the development of the conscience. Looking up, I saw him stooping over an open drawer in a cabinet behind the door. I sat on the great chest under the gable-window, and was away from him the whole length of the room. He had never told me not to look at him, had never seemed to object to the presence of my eyes on anything he did, and as a matter of course I sat observing him, partly because I had never seen any portion of that cabinet open. He turned towards the sky-light near him, and held up between him and it a small something, of which I could just see that it was red, and shone in the light. Then he turned hurriedly, threw it in the drawer, and went straight out, leaving the drawer open. I knew I had lost his company for the day.

The moment he was gone, the phantasm of the pretty thing he had been looking at so intently, came back to me. Somehow I seemed to understand that I had no right to know what it was, seeing my uncle had not shown it me! At the same time I had no law to guide me. He had never said I was not to look at this or that in the room. If he had, even if the cabinet had not been mentioned, I do not think I should have offended; but that does not make the fault less. For which is the more guilty—the man who knows there is a law against doing a certain thing and does it, or the man who feels an authority in the depth of his nature forbidding the thing, and yet does it? Surely the latter is greatly the more guilty.

I rose, and went to the cabinet. But when the contents of the drawer began to show themselves as I drew near, "I closed my lids, and kept them close," until I had seated myself on the floor, with my

back to the cabinet, and the drawer projecting over my head like the
shelf of a bracket over its supporting figure. I could touch it with the
top of my head by straightening my back. How long I sat there motionless, I cannot say, but it seems in retrospect at least a week, such a
multitude of thinkings went through my mind. The logical discussion
of a thing that has to be done, a thing awaiting action and not decision—the experiment, that is, whether the duty or the temptation has
the more to say for itself, is one of the straight roads to the pit. Similarly, there are multitudes who lose their lives pondering what they
ought to believe, while something lies at their door waiting to be done,
and rendering it impossible for him who makes it wait, ever to know
what to believe. Only a pure heart can understand, and a pure heart
is one that sends out ready hands. I knew perfectly well what I ought
to do—namely, to shut that drawer with the back of my head, then get
up and do something, and forget the shining stone I had seen betwixt
my uncle's finger and thumb; yet there I sat debating whether I was
not at liberty to do in my uncle's room what he had not told me not to
do.

I will not weary my reader with any further description of the evil
path by which I arrived at the evil act. To myself it is pain even now
to tell that I got on my feet, saw a blaze of shining things, banged to
the drawer, and knew that Eve had eaten the apple. The eyes of my
consciousness were opened to the evil in me, through the evil done
by me. Evil seemed now a part of myself, so that nevermore should I
get rid of it. It may be easy for one regarding it from afar, through the
telescope only of a book, to exclaim, "Such a little thing!" but it was I
who did it, and not another! it was I, and only I, who could know
what I had done, and it was not a little thing! That peep into my uncle's
drawer lies in my soul the type of sin. Never have I done anything
wrong with such a clear assurance that I was doing wrong, as when I
did the thing I had taken most pains to reason out as right.

Like one stunned by an electric shock, I had neither feeling nor
care left for anything. I walked to the end of the long room, as far as
I could go from the scene of my crime, and sat down on the great
chest, with my coffin, the cabinet, facing me in the distance. The first
thing, I think, that I grew conscious of, was dreariness. There was
nothing interesting anywhere. What should I do? There was nothing
to do, nothing to think about, not a book worth reading. Story was
suddenly dried up at its fountain. Life was a plain without water-
brooks. If the sky was not "a foul and pestilent congregation of
vapours," it was nothing better than a canopy of gray and blue. By
degrees my thought settled on what I had done, and in a moment I
realized it as it was—a vile thing, and I had lost my life for it! This is

the nearest I can come to the expression of what I felt. I was simply
in despair. I had done wrong, and the world had closed in upon me;
the sky had come down and was crushing me! The lid of my coffin
was closed! I should come no more out!

But deliverance came speedily—and in how lovely a way! Into my
thought, not into the room, came my uncle! Present to my deepest
consciousness, he stood tall, loving, beautiful, sad. I read no rebuke
in his countenance, only sorrow that I had sinned, and sympathy with
my suffering because of my sin. Then first I knew that I had *wronged*
him in looking into his drawer; then first I saw it was his being that
made the thing I had done an evil thing. If the drawer had been
nobody's, there would have been no wrong in looking into it! And what
made it so very bad was that my uncle was so good to me!

With the discovery came a rush of gladsome relief. Strange to say,
with the clearer perception of the greatness of the wrong I had done,
came the gladness of redemption. It was almost a pure joy to find
that it was against my uncle, my own uncle, that I had sinned! That
joy was the first gleam through a darkness that had seemed settled
on my soul for ever. But a brighter followed; for thus spake the truth
within me: "The thing is in your uncle's hands; he is the lord of the
wrong you have done; it is to him it makes you a debtor:—he loves
you, and will forgive you. Of course he will! He cannot make undone
what is done, but he will comfort you, and find some way of setting
things right. There must be some way! I cannot be doomed to be a
contemptible child to all eternity! It is so easy to go wrong, and so
hard to get right! He must help me!"

I sat the rest of the day alone in that solitary room, away from
Martha and Rover and everybody. I would that even now in my old
age I waited for God as then I waited for my uncle! If only he would
come, that I might pour out the story of my fall, for I had sinned after
the similitude of Adam's transgression!—only I was worse, for neither
serpent nor wife had tempted me!

At tea-time Martha came to find me. I would not go with her. She
would bring me my tea, she said. I would not have any tea. With a
look like that she sometimes cast on my uncle, she left me. Dear
Martha! she had the lovely gift of leaving alone. That evening there
was no tea in the house; Martha did not have any.

With the conceit peculiar to repentance and humiliation, I took a
curious satisfaction in being hard on myself. I could have taken my
meal tolerably well: with the new hope in my uncle as my saviour,
came comfort enough for the natural process of getting hungry, and
desiring food; but with common, indeed vulgar foolishness, my own
righteousness in taking vengeance on my fault was a satisfaction to

me. I did not then see the presumption of the sinner's taking vengeance on her own fault, did not see that I had no right to do that.
For how should a thing defiled punish? With all my great joy in the
discovery that the fault was against my uncle, I forgot that therefore
I was in his jurisdiction, that he only had to deal with it, he alone
could punish, as he alone could forgive it.

It was the end of August, and the night stole swiftly upon the day.
It began to grow very dusk, but I would not stir. I and the cabinet
kept each other dismal company while the gloom deepened into night.
Nor did the night part us, for I and the cabinet filled all the darkness.
Had my uncle remained the whole night away, I believe I should have sat
till he came. But, happily both for my mental suffering and my bodily
endurance, he returned sooner than many a time. I heard the house-
door open. I knew he would come to the study before going to his
bedroom, and my heart gave a bound of awe-filled eagerness. I knew also
that Martha never spoke to him when he returned from one of his late
rambles, and that he would not know I was there: long before she died
Martha knew how grateful he was for her delicate consideration. Martha
Moon was not one of this world's ladies; but there is a country where the
social question is not, "Is she a lady?" but, "How much of a woman is
she?" Martha's name must, I think, stand well up in the book of life.

My uncle, then, approached his room without knowing there was
a live kernel to the dark that filled it. I hearkened to every nearer
step as he came up the stair, along the corridor, and up the short final ascent to the door of the study. I had crept from my place to the
middle of the room, and, without a thought of consequences, stood
waiting the arrival through the dark, of my deliverer from the dark. I
did not know that many a man who would face a battery calmly, will
spring a yard aside if a yelping cur dart at him.

My uncle opened the door, and closed it behind him. His lamp
and matches stood ready on his table: it was my part to see they were
there. With a sigh, which seemed to seek me in the darkness and find
me, he came forward through it. I caught him round the legs, and
clung to him. He gave a great gasp and a smothered cry, staggered,
and nearly fell.

"My God!" he murmured.

"Uncle! uncle!" I cried, in greater terror than he; "it's only Orbie!
It's only your little one!"

"Oh! it's only my little one, is it?" he rejoined, at once recovering
his equanimity, and not for a moment losing the temper so ready,
like nervous cat, to spring from most of us when startled.

He caught me up in his arms, and held me to his heart. I could
feel it beat against my little person.

"Uncle! uncle!" I cried again. "Don't! Don't!"

"Did I hurt you, my little one?" he said, and relaxing his embrace, held me more gently, but did not set me down.

"No, no!" I answered. "But I've got a secret, and you mustn't kiss me till it is gone. I wish there was a swine to send it into!"

"Give it to me, little one. I will treat it better than a swine would."

"But it mustn't be treated, uncle! It might come again!"

"There is no fear of that, my child! As soon as a secret is told, it is dead. It is a secret no longer."

"Will it be dead, uncle?" I returned. "—But it will be there, all the same, when it is dead—an ugly thing. It will only put off its cloak, and show itself!"

"All secrets are not ugly things when their cloaks are off. The cloak may be the ugly thing, and nothing else."

He stood in the dark, holding me in his arms. But the clouds had cleared off a little, and though there was no moon, I could see the dim blue of the sky-lights, and a little shine from the gray of his hair.

"But mine is an ugly thing," I said, "and I hate it. Please let me put it out of my mouth. Perhaps then it will go dead."

"Out with it, little one."

"Put me down, please," I returned.

He walked to the old chest under the gable-window, seated himself on it, and set me down beside him. I slipped from the chest, and knelt on the floor at his feet, a little way in front of him. I did not touch him, and all was again quite dark about us.

I told him my story from beginning to end, along with a great part of my meditations while hesitating to do the deed. I felt very choky, but forced my way through, talking with a throat that did not seem my own, and sending out a voice I seemed never to have heard before. The moment I ceased, a sound like a sob came out of the darkness. Was it possible my big uncle was crying? Then indeed there was no hope for me! He was horrified at my wickedness, and very sorry to have to give me up! I howled like a wild beast.

"Please, uncle, will you kill me!" I cried, through a riot of sobs that came from me like potatoes from a sack.

"Yes, yes, I will kill you, my darling!" he answered, "—this way! this way!" and stretching out his arms he found me in the dark, drew me to him, and covered my face with kisses.

"Now," he resumed, "I've killed you alive again, and the ugly secret is dead, and will never come to life any more. And I think, besides, we have killed the hen that lays the egg-secrets!"

He rose with me in his arms, set me down on the chest, lighted his lamp, and carried it to the cabinet. Then he returned, and taking me by the hand, led me to it, opened wide the drawer of offence, lifted me, and held me so that I could see well into it. The light flashed in a hundred glories of colour from a multitude of cut but unset stones that lay loose in it. I soon learned that most of them were of small money-value, but their beauty was none the less entrancing. There were stones of price among them, however, and these were the first he taught me, because they were the most beautiful. My fault had opened a new source of delight: my stone-lesson was now one of the great pleasures of the week. In after years I saw in it the richness of God not content with setting right what is wrong, but making from it a gain: he will not have his children the worse for the wrong they have done! We shall lose nothing by it: he is our father! For the hurting sand-grain, he gives his oyster a pearl.

"There," said my uncle, "you may look at them as often as you please; only mind you put every one back as soon as you have satisfied your eyes with it. You must not put one in your pocket, or carry it about in your hand."

Then he set me down, saying,

"Now you must go to bed, and dream about the pretty things. I will tell you a lot of stories about them afterward."

We had a way of calling any kind of statement *a story*.

I never cared to ask how it was that, seeing all the same I had done the wrong thing, the whole weight of it was gone from me. So utterly was it gone, that I did not even inquire whether I ought so to let it pass from me. It was nowhere. In the fire of my uncle's love to me and mine to him, the thing vanished. It was annihilated. Should I not be a creature unworthy of life, if, now in my old age, I, who had such an uncle in my childhood, did not with my very life believe in God?

I have wondered whether, if my father had lived to bring me up instead of my uncle, I should have been very different; but the useless speculation has only driven me to believe that the relations on the surface of life are but the symbols of far deeper ties, which may exist without those correspondent external ones. At the same time, now that, being old, I naturally think of the coming change, I feel that, when I see my father, I shall have a different feeling for him just because he is my father, although my uncle did all the fatherly toward me. But we need not trouble ourselves about our hearts, and all their varying hues and shades of feeling. Truth is at the root of all existence, therefore everything must come right if only we are obedient to the truth; and right is the deepest satisfaction of every creature as well as of God. I wait in confidence. If things be not as we think, they will both arouse and satisfy a better *think*, making us glad they are not as we expected.

6
I Lose Myself

I have one incident more to relate ere my narrative begins to flow from a quite clear memory.

I was by no means a small bookworm, neither spent all my time in the enchanted ground of my uncle's study. It is true I loved the house, and often felt like a burrowing animal that would rather not leave its hole; but occasionally even at such times would suddenly wake the passion for the open air: I must get into it or die! I was well known in the farmyard, not to the men only, but to the animals also. In the absence of human playfellows, they did much to keep me from selfishness. But far beyond it I took no unfrequent flight—always alone. Neither Martha nor my uncle ever seemed to think I needed looking after; and I am not aware that I should have gained anything by it. I speak for myself; I have no theories about the bringing up of children. I went where and when I pleased, as little challenged as my uncle himself. Like him, I took now and then a long ramble over the moor, fearing nothing, and knowing nothing to fear. I went sometimes where it seemed as if human foot could never have trod before, so wild and waste was the prospect, so unknown it somehow looked. The house was built on the more sloping side of a high hollow just within the moor, which stretched wide away from the very edge of the farm. If you climbed the slope, following a certain rough country road, at the top of it you saw on the one side the farm, in all the colours and shades of its outspread, well tilled fields; on the other side, the heath. If you went another way, through the garden, through the belt of shrubs and pines that encircled it, and through the wilderness behind that, you were at once upon the heath. If then you went as far as the highest point in sight, wading through the heather, among the rocks and great stones which in childhood I never doubted grew also, you saw before you nothing but a wide, wild level, whose horizon was here and there broken by low hills. But the seeming level was far from flat or smooth, as I found on the day of the adventure I am about to

relate. I wonder I had never lost myself before. I suppose then first
my legs were able to wander beyond the ground with which my eyes
were familiar.

It had rained all the morning and afternoon. When our last lesson
was over, my uncle went out, and I betook myself to the barn, where
I amused myself in the straw. By this time Rover must have gone back
to his maker, for I remember as with me a large, respectable dog of
the old-fashioned mastiff-type, who endured me with a patience that
amounted almost to friendliness, but never followed me about. When
I grew hungry, I went into the house to have my afternoon-meal. It
was called tea, but I knew nothing about tea, while in milk I was a
connoisseur. I could tell perfectly to which of the cows I was indebted
for the milk I happened at any time to be drinking: Miss Martha never
allowed the milks of the different cows to be mingled.

Just as my meal was over, the sun shone with sudden brilliance
into my very eyes. The storm was breaking up, and vanishing in the
west. I threw down my spoon, and ran, hatless as usual, from the
house. The sun was on the edge of the hollow; I made straight for
him. The bracken was so wet that my legs almost seemed walking
through a brook, and my body through a thick rain. In a moment I
was sopping; but to be wet was of no consequence to me. Not for many
years was I able to believe that damp could hurt.

When I reached the top, the sun was yet some distance above the
horizon, and I had gone a good way toward him before he went down.
As he sank he sent up a wind, which blew a sense of coming dark. The
wind of the sunset brings me, ever since, a foreboding of tears: it seems
to say— "Your day is done; the hour of your darkness is at hand." It
grew cold, and a feeling of threat filled the air. All about the grave of
the buried sun, the clouds were angry with dusky yellow and splashes
of gold. They lowered tumulous and menacing. Then, lo! they had lost
courage; their bulk melted off in fierce vapour, gold and gray, and
the sharp outcry of their shape was gone. As I recall the airy scene,
that horizon looks like the void between a cataclysm and the moving
afresh of the spirit of God upon the face of the waters. I went on and
on, I do not know why. Something enticed me, or I was plunged in
some meditation, then absorbing, now forgotten, not necessarily
worthless. I am jealous of moods that can be forgotten, but such may
leave traces in the character. I wandered on. What ups and downs
there were! how uneven was the surface of the moor! The feet learned
what the eyes had not seen.

All at once I woke to the fact that mountains hemmed me in. They
looked mountains, though they were but hills. What had become of
home? where was it? The light lingering in the west might surely have

shown me the direction of it, but I remember no west—nothing but a deep hollow and dark hills. I was lost!

I was not exactly frightened at first. I knew no cause of dread. I had never seen a tramp even; I had no sense of the inimical. I knew nothing of the danger from cold and exposure. But awe of the fading light and coming darkness awoke in me. I began to be frightened, and fear is like other live things: once started, it grows. Then first I thought with dismay, which became terror, of the slimy bogs and the deep pools in them. But just as my heart was dying within me, I looked to the hills—with no hope that from them would come my aid—and there, on the edge of the sky, lifted against it, in a dip between two of the hills, was the form of a lady on horseback. I could see the skirt of her habit flying out against the clouds as she rode. Had she been a few feet lower, so as to come between me and the side of the hill instead of the sky, I should not have seen her; neither should I if she had been a few hundred yards further off. I shrieked at the thought that she did not see me, and I could not make her hear me. She started, turned, seemed to look whence the cry could have come, but kept on her way. Then I shrieked in earnest, and began to run wildly toward her. I think she saw me—that my quicker change of place detached my shape sufficiently to make it discernible. She pulled up, and sat like a statue, waiting me. I kept on calling as I ran, to assure her I was doing my utmost, for I feared she might grow impatient and leave me. But at last it was slowly indeed I staggered up to her, spent. My foot caught, and as I fell, I clasped the leg of her horse: I had no fear of animals more than of human beings. He was startled, and rearing drew his leg from my arms. But he took care not to come down on me. I rose to my feet, and stood panting.

What the lady said, or what I answered, I cannot recall. The next thing I remember is stumbling along by her side, for she made her horse walk that I might keep up with her. She talked a little, but I do not remember what she said. It is all a dream now, a far-off one. It must have been like a dream at the time, I was so exhausted. I remember a voice descending now and then, as if from the clouds—a cold musical voice, with something in it that made me not want to hear it. I remember her saying that we were near her house, and would soon be there. I think she had found out from me where I lived.

All the time I never saw her face: it was too dark. I do not think she once spoke kindly to me. She said I had no business to be out alone; she wondered at my father and mother. I think I was too tired to tell her I had no father or mother. When I did speak, she indicated neither by sound nor movement that she heard or heeded what I said. She sat up above me in the dark, unpleasant, and all but unseen—a riddle which the troubled child stumbling along by her horse's side did not want solved. Had there been anything to call light, I should have run away from her. Vague doubts of witches and ogresses crossed my mind, but I said to myself the stories about them were not true, and kept on as best I could.

Before we reached the house, we had left the heath, and were moving along lanes. The horse seemed to walk with more confidence, and it was harder for me to keep up with him. I was so tired that I could not feel my legs. I stumbled often, and once the horse trod on my foot. I fell; he went on; I had to run limping after him. At last we stopped. I could see nothing. The lady gave a musical cry. A voice and footsteps made answer; and presently came the sound of a gate on its hinges. A long dark piece of road followed. I knew we were among trees, for I heard the wind in them over our heads. Then I saw lights in windows, and presently we stopped at the door of a great house. I remember nothing more of that night.

7

The Mirror

I woke the next morning in a strange bed, and for a long time could not think how I came to be there. A maid appeared, and told me it was time to get up. Greatly to my dislike, she would insist on dressing me. My clothes looked very miserable, I remember, in consequence of what they had gone through the night before. She was kind to me, and asked me a great many questions, but paid no heed to my answers—a treatment to which I had not been used: I think she must have been the lady's maid. When I was ready, she took me to the housekeeper's room, where I had bread and milk for breakfast. Several servants, men and women, came and went, and I thought they all looked at me strangely. I concluded they had no little girls in that house. Assuredly there was small favour for children in it. In some houses the child is as a stranger; in others he rules: neither such house is in the kingdom of heaven. I must have looked a forlorn creature as I sat, or perched rather, on the old horsehair-sofa in that dingy room. Nobody said more than a word or so to me. I wondered what was going to be done with me, but I had long been able to wait for what would come. At length, after, as it seemed, hours of weary waiting, during which my heart grew sick with longing after my uncle, I was, without a word of explanation, led through long passages into a room which appeared enormous. There I was again left a long while—this time alone. It was all white and gold, and had its walls nearly covered with great mirrors from floor to ceiling, which, while it was indeed of great size, was the cause of its looking so immeasurably large. But it was some time before I discovered this, for I was not accustomed to mirrors. Except the small one on my little dressing-table, and one still less on Martha's, I had scarcely seen a mirror, and was not prepared for those sheets of glass in narrow gold frames.

I went about, looking at one thing and another, but handling nothing: my late secret had cured me of that. Weary at last, I dropped upon a low chair, and would probably have soon fallen asleep, had

not the door opened, and some one come in. I could not see the door
without turning, and was too tired and sleepy to move. I sat still, staring, hardly conscious, into the mirror in front of me. All at once I
descried in it my uncle—but only to see him grow white as death, and
turn away, reeling as if he would fall. The sight so bewildered me that,
instead of rushing to embrace him, I sat frozen. He clapped his hands
to his eyes, steadied himself, stood for a moment rigid, then came
straight toward me. But, to my added astonishment, he gave me no
greeting, or showed any sign of joy at having found me. Never before
had he seen me for the first time any day, without giving me a kiss;
never before, it seemed to me, had he spoken to me without a smile: I
had been lost and was found, and he was not glad! The strange reception fell on me like a numbing spell. I had nothing to say, no impulse
to move, no part in the present world. He caught me up in his arms,
hid his face upon me, knocked his shoulder heavily against the door-
post as he went from the room, walked straight through the hall, and
out of the house. I think no one saw us as we went; I am sure neither
of us saw any one. With long strides he walked down the avenue, never
turning his head. Not until we were on the moor, out of sight of the
house, did he stop. Then he set me down; and then first we discovered that he had left his hat behind. For all his carrying of me, and
going so fast—and I must have been rather heavy—his face had no
colour in it.

"Shall I run and get it, uncle?" I said, as I saw him raise his hand
to his head and find no hat there to be taken off. "I should be back in
a minute!"

It was the first word spoken between us. "No, my little one," he
answered, wiping his forehead: his voice sounded far away, like that
of one speaking in a dream; "I can't let you out of my sight. I've been
wandering the moor all night looking for you!"

With that he caught me up again, and pressing his face to mine,
walked with me thus, for a long quarter of a mile, I should think. Oh
how safe I felt!—and how happy!—happy beyond smiling! I loved him
before, but I never knew before what it was to lose him and find him
again.

"Tell me," he said at length.

I told him all, and he did not speak a word until my tale was finished.

"Were you very frightened," he then asked, "when you found you
had lost your way, and darkness was coming?"

"I was frightened, or I would not have gone to the lady. But I wish
I had staid on the moor for you to find me. I knew you would soon be
out looking for me. Until she came I comforted myself with thinking

that perhaps even then you were on the moor, and I might see you any moment."

"What else did you think of?"

"I thought that God was out on the moor, and if you were not there, he would keep me company."

"Ah!" said my uncle, as if thinking to himself; "she but needs him the more when I am with her!"

"Yes, of course!" I answered; "I need him then for you as well as for myself."

"That is very true, my child!—Shall I tell you one thing I thought of while looking for you?"

"Please, uncle."

"I thought how Jesus' father and mother must have felt when they were looking for him."

"And they needn't have been so unhappy if they had thought who he was—need they?"

"Certainly not. And I needn't have been so unhappy if I had thought who you were. But I was terribly frightened, and there I was wrong."

"Who am I, uncle?"

"Another little one of the same father as he."

"Why were you frightened, uncle?"

"I was afraid of your being frightened."

"I hardly had time to be frightened before the lady came."

"Yes; you see I needn't have been so unhappy!"

My uncle always treated me as if I could understand him perfectly. This came, I see now, from the essential childlikeness of his nature, and from no educational theory.

"Sometimes," he went on, "I look all around me to see if Jesus is out anywhere, but I have never seen him yet!"

"We shall see him one day, shan't we?" I said, craning round to look into his eyes, which were my earthly paradise. Nor are they a whit less dear to me, nay, they are dearer, that he has been in God's somewhere, that is, the heavenly paradise, for many a year.

"I think so," he answered, with a sigh that seemed to swell like a sea-wave against me, as I sat on his arm; "—I hope so. I live but for that—and for one thing more."

There are some, I fancy, who would blame him for not being sure, and bring text after text to prove that he ought to have been sure. But oh those text-people! They look to me, not like the clay-sparrows that Jesus made fly, but like bird-skins in a glass-case, stuffed with texts. The doubt of a man like my uncle must be a far better thing than their assurance!

"Would you have been frightened if you had met him on the moor last night, little one?" he asked, after a pause.

"Oh, no, uncle!" I returned. "I should have thought it was you till I came nearer, and then I should have known who it was! He wouldn't like a big girl like me to be frightened at him—would he?"

"Indeed not!'" answered my uncle fervently; but again his words brought with them a great sigh, and he said no more.

When we reached home, he gave me up to Martha, and went out again—nor returned before I was in bed. But he came to my room, and waked me with a kiss, which sent me faster asleep than before.

8

Thanatos and Zoe

I think it must have been soon after this that my uncle bought himself a horse. I know something of horses now—that is, if much riding and much love suffice to give a knowledge of them—and the horse which was a glory and a wonder to me then, is a glory and a wonder to me still. He was large, big-boned, and powerful, with less beauty but more grandeur than a thoroughbred, and full of a fiery gentleness. He was the very horse for Sir Philip Sidney!

One day, after he had had him for several months, and had let no one saddle him but himself, therefore knew him perfectly, and knew that the horse knew his master, I happened to be in the yard as he mounted. The moment he was in the saddle, he bent down to me, and held out his hand.

"Come with me, little one," he said.

Almost ere I knew, I was in the saddle before him. I grasped his hand, instinctively caught with my foot at his, and was astride the pommel. I will not say I sat very comfortably, but the memory of that day's delight will never leave me—not "through all the secular to be." There must be a God to the world that could give any such delight as fell then to the share of one little girl! I think my uncle must soon after have got another saddle, for I have no recollection of any more discomfort; I remember only the delight of the motion of the horse under me.

For, after this, I rode with him often, and he taught me to ride as surely not many have been taught. When he saw me so at home in my seat as to require no support, he made me change my position, and go behind him. There I sat sideways on a cloth, like a lady of old time on a pillion. When I had got used to this, my uncle made me stand on the horse's broad back, holding on by his shoulders; and it was wonderful how soon, and how unconsciously, I accommodated myself to every motion of the strength that bore me, learning to keep my place by pure balance like a rope-dancer. I had soon quite forgotten to hold by my uncle, and without the least support rode as comfortably, and with as much confidence, as any rider in a circus, though with a far less easy pace under me. When my uncle found me capable of this, he was much pleased, though a little nervous at times.

Able now to ride his big horse any way, he brought me one afternoon the loveliest of Shetland ponies, not very small. With the ordinary human distrust in good, I could hardly believe she was meant for me. She was a dappled gray—like the twilight of a morning after rain, my uncle said. He called her Zoe, which means Life. His own horse he called Thanatos, which means Death. Such as understood it, thought it a terrible name to give a horse. For most people are so afraid of Death that they regard his very name with awe.

My uncle had a riding-habit made for me, and after a week found I could give him no more trouble with my horsewomanship. At once I was at home on my new friend's back, with vistas of delight innumerable opening around me, and from that day my uncle seldom rode without me. When he went wandering, it was almost always on foot, and then, as before, he was always alone. The idea of offering to accompany him on such an occasion, had never occurred to me.

But one stormy autumn afternoon—most of my memories seem of the autumn—my uncle looked worse than usual when he went out, and I felt, I think for the first time, a vague uneasiness about him. Perhaps I had been thinking of him more; perhaps I had begun to wonder what the secret could be that made him so often seem unhappy. Anyhow this evening the desire awoke to be with him in his trouble whatever it was. There was no curiosity in the feeling, I think, only the desire to serve him as I had never served him yet. I had been, as long as I could remember, always at his beck or lightest call; now I wanted to come when needed without being called. Was it impossible a girl should do anything for a man in his trouble? He, a great man, had helped a little girl out of the deepest despair; could the little girl do nothing for the great man? That the big people should do everything, did not seem fair! He had told me once that the world was held together by what every one could do that the others could not do: there must be something I could do that he could not do!

The rain was coming down on the roof like the steady tramp of distant squadrons. I was in the study, therefore near the tiles, and that was how the rain always sounded upon them. Tramp, tramp, tramp, came the whole army of things, riding, riding, to befall my uncle and me. Tramp, tramp, came the troops of the future, to take the citadel of the present! I was not afraid of them, neither sought to imagine myself afraid! I had no picture in my mind of any evil that could assail me. A little grove of black poplars under the gable-window,

kept swaying their expostulations, and moaning their entreaties. The
great rushing blasts of the wind through their rooted resistance, made
the music of the band that accompanied the march of the unknown. I
sat and listened, with the vague conviction that something was being
done somewhere. It could not be that only the wind and the trees and
the rain were in all that wailing and marching! The Powers of life and
death must somewhere be at work! Then rose before me the face of
my uncle, as he walked from the room, haloed in a sorrowful stillness. If only I could be with him! If only I knew where to seek him!
Wishing, wishing, I sat and listened to the rain and the wind.

Suddenly I found myself on my feet, making for the door. I would
not have ventured alone upon the moor in such a night, but I should
have Zoe with me, who knew all the ways of it—had doubtless been
used to bogs in her own country, and her mother before her! Like a
small elephant, she would put out her little foot, and tap, and sound,
to see if the surface would bear her—if the questionable spot was what
it looked to her mistress, or what she herself doubted it. When she
had once made up her mind in the negative, no foolish attempt of
mine could overpersuade her—could make her trust our weight on it
a hair's-breadth. In a bog the greenest spots are the most dangerous,
and Zoe knew it: the matted roots might be afloat on a fathomless
depth of water. Backed by my uncle, she soon taught me to be as much
afraid of those green spots as she was herself. I had learned to trust
her thoroughly.

I took my way to the stable, with a hug and a kiss to Martha as I
passed her in the kitchen, I got the cowboy to saddle Zoe, fearing I
might not persuade one of the big men on such a night, and I was not
quite able myself to tighten the girths properly. She had not been out
all day, and when I mounted, she danced at the prospect of a gallop.

I took with me the little lantern I went about the place with when
there was no moon, and with this alight in my hand, we darted off at
a tight-reined gallop into the wet blowing night. What I was going for
I did not know, beyond being with my uncle. So far was I from any
fear, that, but for my shadowy uneasiness about him, I should have
been filled full of the wild joy of battle with the elements. The first
part of the way, I had to cling to the saddle: not otherwise could I
keep my seat against the wind, which blew so fiercely on me sideways, that it threatened to blow me out of it.

I had not gone far before the saddle began to turn round with me;
I was slipping to the ground. I pulled up, dismounted, undid the girths
with difficulty, set the saddle straight, then pulled at every strap with
all my might. It was to no purpose: I could not get another hole out of
one of them. I mounted and set off again; but the moment a stronger

blast came, the saddle began to turn. Then I thought of something to try: dismounting once more, I got up on the off side. The wind now pushed me on to the saddle, freeing it from my leverage, while I had, besides, the use of my legs against the wind, so that we got on bravely, my Zoe and I. But, alas! my lantern was out, and it was impossible to light it again, so that I had now no arrow to shoot at random for my uncle's eye. Before long we reached a tolerable cart-track, which led across the waste to a village, and the wind being now behind us, I resumed the more comfortable seat in the saddle.

We were going at a good speed, and had ridden, as I judged, about three miles, when there came a great flash of lightning—not like any flash I had ever seen before. It was neither the reflection of lightning below the horizon, nor the sudden zigzagged blade, the very idea of force without weight; it was the burst of a ball-headed torrent of fire from a dark cloud, like water sudden from a mountain's heart, which went rushing down a rugged channel, as if the cloud were indeed a mountain, and the fire one of its cataracts. Its endurance was momentary, but its moments might have been counted, for it lasted appreciably longer than an ordinary flash, revealing to my eyes what remains on my mind clear as the picture of some neighbouring tree on the skin of one slain by lightning. The torrent tumbled down the cloud and vanished, but left with me the vision of a man, plainly my uncle, a few hundred yards from me, on a gigantic gray horse, which reared high with fright. But for its size I could have testified before a magistrate, that I had not only seen that horse in the stable as my pony was being saddled, but had stroked and kissed him on the nose. I conceived at once that his apparent size was an illusion caused by the suddenness and keenness of the light, and that my uncle had come home before I had well reached the moor, and had ridden out after me. With a wild cry of delight, I turned at once to leave the road and join him. But the thunder that moment burst with a terrific bellow, and swallowed my cry. The same instant, however, came through it from the other side the voice of my uncle only a few yards away.

"Stay, little one," he shouted; "stay where you are. I will be with you in a moment."

I obeyed, as ever and always without a thought I obeyed the slightest word of my uncle: Zoe and I stood as if never yet parted from chaos and the dark, for Zoe too loved his voice. The wind rose suddenly from a lull to a great roar, emptying a huge cloudful of rain upon us, so that I heard no sound of my uncle's approach; but presently out of the dark an arm was around me, and my head was lying on my uncle's bosom. Then the dark and the rain seemed the natural elements for love and confidence.

"But, uncle," I murmured, full of wonder which had had no time to take shape, "how is it?"

He answered in a whisper that seemed to dread the ear of the wind, lest it should hear him—

"You saw, did you?"

"I saw you upon Death away there in the middle of the lightning. I was going to you. I don't know what to think."

My uncle and I often called the horse by his English name.

"Neither do I," he returned, with a strange half voice, as if he were choking. "It must have been—I don't know what. There is a deep bog away just there. It must be a lake by now!"

"Yes, uncle; I might have remembered! But how was I to think of that when I saw you there—on dear old Death too! He's the last of horses to get into a bog: he knows his own weight too well!"

"But why did you come out on such a night? What possessed you, little one—in such a storm? I begin to be afraid what next you may do."

"I never do anything—now—that I think you would mind me doing," I answered. "But if you will write out a little book of *mays* and *maynots*, I will learn it by heart."

"No, no," he returned; "we are not going back to the tables of the law! You have a better law written in your heart, my child; I will trust to that.—But tell me why you came out on such a night—and as dark as pitch."

"Just because it was such a night, uncle, and you were out in it," I answered. "Ain't I your own little girl? I hope you ain't sorry I came, uncle! I am glad; and I shouldn't like ever to be glad at what made you sorry."

"What are you glad of?"

"That I came—because I've found you. I came to look for you."

"Why did you come to-night more than any other night?"

"Because I wanted so much to see you. I thought I might be of use to you."

"You are always of use to me; but why did you think of it just to-night?"

"I don't know.—I am older than I was last night," I replied.

He seemed to understand me, and asked me no more questions.

All the time, we had been standing still in the storm. He took Zoe's head and turned it toward home. The dear creature set out with slow leisurely step, heedless apparently of storm and stable. She knew who was by her side, and he must set the pace!

As we went my uncle seemed lost in thought—and no wonder! for how could the sight we had seen be accounted for! Or what might it indicate?

Many were the strange tales I had read, and my conviction was
that the vision belonged to the inexplicable. It grew upon me that I
had seen my uncle's double. That he should see his own double would
not in itself have much surprised me—or, indeed, that I should see it;
but I had never read of another person seeing a double at the same
time with the person doubled. During the next few days I sought hard
for some possible explanation of what had occurred, but could find
nothing parallel to it within the scope of my knowledge. I tried *fata
morgana, mirage, parhelion*, and whatever I had learned of recognized illusion, but in vain sought satisfaction, or anything pointing
in the direction of satisfaction. I was compelled to leave the thing
alone. My uncle kept silence about it, but seemed to brood more than
usual. I think he too was convinced that it must have another explanation than present science would afford him. Once I ventured to ask
if he had come to any conclusion; with a sad smile, he answered,

"I am waiting, little one. There is much we have to wait for. Where
would be the good of having your mind made up wrong? It only stands
in the way of getting it made up right!"

By degrees the thing went into the distance, and I ceased even
speculating upon it. But one little fact I may mention ere I leave it—
that, just as I was reaching a state of quiet mental prorogation, I suddenly remembered that, the moment after the flash, my Zoe, startled
as she was, gave out a low whinny; I remembered the quiver of it under me: she too must have seen her master's double!

9
The Garden

I remember nothing more to disturb the even flow of my life till I was nearly seventeen. Many pleasant things had come and gone; many pleasant things kept coming and going. I had studied tolerably well—at least my uncle showed himself pleased with the progress I had made and was making. I know even yet a good deal more than would be required for one of these modern degrees feminine. I had besides read more of the older literature of my country than any one I have met except my uncle. I had also this advantage over most students, that my knowledge was gained without the slightest prick of the spur of emulation—purely in following the same delight in myself that shone radiant in the eyes of my uncle as he read with me. I had this advantage also over many, that, perhaps from impression of the higher mind, I saw and learned a thing not merely as a fact whose glory lay in the mystery of its undeveloped harmonics, but as the harbinger of an unknown advent. For as long as I can remember, my heart was given to expectation, was tuned to long waiting. I constantly felt—felt without thinking—that something was coming. I feel it now. Were I young I dared not say so. How could I, compassed about with so great a cloud of witnesses to the common-place! Do I not see their superior smile, as, with voices sweetly acidulous, they quote in reply—

"Love is well on the way;
He'll be here to-day,
    Or, at latest, the end of the week;
Too soon you will find him,
And the sorrow behind him
    You will not go out to seek!"

Would they not tell me that such expectation was but the shadow of the cloud called love, hanging no bigger than a man's hand on the far horizon, but fraught with storm for mind and soul, which, when it

withdrew, would carry with it the glow and the glory and the hope of
life; being at best but the mirage of an unattainable paradise, therefore direst of deceptions! Little do such suspect that their own
behaviour has withered their faith, and their unbelief dried up their
life. They can now no more believe in what they once felt, than a cloud
can believe in the rainbow it once bore on its bosom. But I am old,
therefore dare to say that I expect more and better and higher and
lovelier things than I have ever had. I am not going home to God to
say— "Father, I have imagined more beautiful things than thou art
able to make true! They were so good that thou thyself art either not
good enough to will them, or not strong enough to make them. Thou
couldst but make thy creature dream of them, because thou canst but
dream of them thyself." Nay, nay! In the faith of him to whom the
Father shows all things he does, I expect lovelier gifts than I ever have
been, ever shall be able to dream of asleep, or imagine awake.

I was now approaching the verge of woman-hood. What lay beyond it I could ill descry, though surely a vague power of undeveloped prophecy dwells in every created thing—even in the bird ere he
chips his shell.

Should I dare, or could I endure to write of what lies now to my
hand, if I did not believe that not our worst but our best moments,
not our low but our lofty moods, not our times logical and scientific,
but our times instinctive and imaginative, are those in which we perceive the truth! In them we behold it with a beholding which is one
with believing. And,

> "Though nothing can bring back the hour
> Of splendour in the grass, of glory in the flower",

could not Wordsworth, and cannot we, call up the vision of that
hour? and has not its memory almost, or even altogether, the potency
of its presence? Is not the very thought of any certain flower enough
to make me believe in that flower—believe it to mean all it ever seemed
to mean? That *these* eyes may never more rest upon it with the old
delight, means little, and matters nothing. I have other eyes, and shall
have yet others. If I thought, as so many have degraded themselves to
think, that the glory of things in the morning of love was a glamour
cast upon the world, no outshine of indwelling radiance, should I care
to breathe one day more the air of this or of any world? Nay, nay, but
there dwells in everything the Father hath made, the fire of the burning bush, as at home in his son dwelt the glory that, set free, broke
out from him on the mount of his transfiguration. The happy-making
vision of things that floods the gaze of the youth, when first he lives

in the marvel of loving, and being loved by, a woman, is the true vision—and the more likely to be the true one, that, when he gives way
to selfishness, he loses faith in the vision, and sinks back into the
commonplace unfaith of the beggarly world—a disappointed, sneer-
ing worshipper of power and money—with this remnant of the light
yet in him, that he grumbles at the gloom its departure has left behind. He confesses by his soreness that the illusion ought to have been
true; he seldom confesses that he loved himself more than the woman,
and so lost her. He lays the blame on God, on the woman, on the soul-
lessness of the universe—anywhere but on the one being in which he
is interested enough to be sure it exists—his own precious, greedy,
vulgar self. Would I dare to write of love, if I did not believe it a true,
that is, an eternal thing!

It was a summer of exceptional splendour in which my eyes were
opened to "the glory of the sum of things." It was not so hot of the
sun as summers I have known, but there were so many gentle and
loving winds about, with never point or knife-edge in them, that it
seemed all the housework of the universe was being done by ladies.
Then the way the odours went and came on those sweet winds! and
the way the twilight fell asleep into the dark! and the way the sun
rushed up in the morning, as if he cried, like a boy, "Here I am! The
Father has sent me! Isn't it jolly!" I saw more sun-rises that year than
any year before or since. And the grass was so thick and soft! There
must be grass in heaven! And the roses, both wild and tame, that grew
together in the wilderness!—I think you would like to hear about the
wilderness.

When I grew to notice, and think, and put things together, I began to wonder how the wilderness came there. I could understand
that the solemn garden, with its great yew-hedges and alleys, and its
oddly cut box-trees, was a survival of the stately old gardens haunted
by ruffs and farthingales; but the wilderness looked so much younger
that I was perplexed with it, especially as I saw nothing like it anywhere else. I asked my uncle about it, and he explained that it was
indeed after an old fashion, but that he had himself made the wilderness, mostly with his own hands, when he was young. This surprised
me, for I had never seen him touch a spade, and hardly ever saw him
in the garden: when I did, I always felt as if something was going to
happen. He said he had in it tried to copy the wilderness laid out by
lord St. Alban's in his essays. I found the volume, and soon came upon
the essay, On Gardens. The passage concerning the wilderness, gave
me, and still gives me so much delight, that I will transplant it like a
rose-bush into this wilderness of mine, hoping it will give like pleasure to my reader.

"For the heath, which was the third part of our plot, I wish it to be framed, as much as may be, to a natural wildness. Trees I would have none in it; but some thickets, made only of sweetbriar, and honnysuckle, and some wild vine amongst; and the ground set with violets, strawberries, and primroses. For these are sweet, and prosper in the shade. And these to be in the heath, here and there not in any order. I like also little heapes, in the nature of mole-hills (such as are in wild heaths) to be set, some with wild thyme; some with pincks; some with germander, that gives a good flower to the eye; some with periwinkle; some with violets; some with strawberries; some with couslips; some with daisies; some with red roses; some with lilium convallium; some with sweet-williams red; some with bearsfoot; and the like low flowers, being withall sweet and sightly. Part of which heapes, to be with standards, of little bushes, prickt upon their top, and part without. The standards to be roses; juniper; holly; beareberries (but here and there, because of the smell of their blossom;) red currans; gooseberries; rosemary; bayes; sweetbriar; and such like. But these standards, to be kept with cutting, that they grow not out of course."

Just such, in all but the gooseberries and currants, was the wilderness of our garden: you came on it by a sudden labyrinthine twist at the end of a narrow alley of yew, and a sudden door in the high wall. My uncle said he liked well to see roses in the kitchen-garden, but not gooseberries in the flower-garden, especially a wild flower-garden. Wherein lies the difference, I never quite made out, but I feel a difference. My main delight in the wilderness was to see the roses among the heather—particularly the wild roses. When I was grown up, the wilderness always affected me like one of Blake's, or one of Beddoes's yet wilder lyrics. To make it, my uncle had taken in a part of the heath, which came close up to the garden, leaving plenty of the heather and ling. The protecting fence enclosed a good bit of the heath just as it was, so that the wilderness melted away into the heath, and into the wide moor—the fence, though contrived so as to be difficult to cross, being so low that one had to look for it.

Everywhere the inner garden was surrounded with brick walls, and hedges of yew within them; but immediately behind the house, the wall to the lane was not very high.

10
Once More a Secret

One day in June I had gone into the garden about one o'clock, whether with or without object I forget. I had just seen my uncle start for Wittenage. Hearing a horse's hoofs in the lane that ran along the outside of the wall, I looked up. The same moment the horse stopped, and the face of his rider appeared over the wall, between two stems of yew, and two great flowers of purple lilac, in shape like two perfect bunches of swarming bees. It was the face of a youth of eighteen, and beautiful with a right manly beauty.

The moment I looked on this face, I fell into a sort of trance—that is, I entered for a moment some condition of existence beyond the ramparts of what commonly we call life. Love at first sight it was that initiated the strange experience. But understand me: real as what immediately followed was to the consciousness, there was no actual fact in it.

I stood gazing. My eyes seemed drawn, and drawing my person toward the vision. Isolate over the garden-wall was the face; the rest of the man and all the horse were hidden behind it. Betwixt the yew stems and the two great lilac flowers—how heart and brain are yet filled with the old scent of them!—my face, my mouth, my lips met his. I grew blind as with all my heart I kissed him. Then came a flash of icy terror, and a shudder which it frights me even now to recall. Instantly I knew that but a moment had passed, and that I had not moved an inch from the spot where first my eyes met his.

But my eyes yet rested on his; I could not draw them away. I could not free myself. Helplessness was growing agony. His voice broke the spell. He lifted his hunting-cap, and begged me to tell him the way to the next village. My self-possession returned, and the joy of its restoration drove from me any lingering embarrassment. I went forward, and without a faltering tone, I believe, gave him detailed directions. He told me afterwards that, himself in a state of bewildered surprise, he thought me the coolest young person he had ever had the fortune to meet. Why should one be pleased to know that she looked quite different from what she felt? There is something wrong there, surely! I acknowledge the something wrong, but do not understand it. He lifted his cap again, and rode away.

I stood still at the foot of the lilac-tree, and, from a vapour, condensed, not to a stone, but to a world, in which a new Flora was about to be developed. If no new spiritual sense was awakened in me, at least I was aware of a new consciousness. I had never been to myself what I was now.

Terror again seized me: the face might once more look over the wall, and find me where it had left me! I turned, and went slowly away from the house, gravitating to the darkest part of the garden.

"What has come to me," I said, "that I seek the darkness? Is this another secret? Am I in the grasp of a new enemy?"

And with that came the whirlwind of perplexity. Must I go the first moment I knew I could find him, and tell my uncle what had happened, and how I felt? or must I have, and hold, and cherish in silent heart, a thing so wondrous, so precious, so absorbing? Had I not deliberately promised—of my own will and at my own instance—never again to have a secret from him? Was this a secret? Was it not a secret?

The storm was up, and went on. The wonder is that, in the fire of the new torment, I did not come to loathe the very thought of the young man—which would have delivered me, if not from the necessity of confession, yet from the main difficulty in confessing.

I said to myself that the old secret was of a wrong done to my uncle; that what had made me miserable then was a bad secret. The perception of this difference gave me comfort for a time, but not for long. The fact remained, that I knew something concerning myself which my best friend did not know. It was, and I could not prevent it from being, a barrier between us!

Yet what was it I was concealing from him? What had I to tell him? How was I to represent a thing of which I knew neither the name nor the nature, a thing I could not describe? Could I confess what I did not understand? The thing might be what, in the tales I had read, was called love, but I did not know that it was. It might be something new, peculiar to myself; something for which there was no word in the language! How was I to tell? I saw plainly that, if I tried to convey my new experience, I should not get beyond the statement that I had a new experience. It did not occur to me that the thing might be so well known, that a mere hint of the feelings concerned, would enable any older person to classify the consciousness. I said to myself I should merely perplex my uncle. And in truth I believe that love, in every

mind in which it arises, will vary in colour and form—will always par-
take of that mind's individual isolation in difference. This, however,
is nothing to the present point.

Comfort myself as I might, that the impossible was required of no
one, and granted that the thing was impossible, it was none the less a
cause of misery, a present disaster: I was aware, and soon my uncle
would be aware, of an impenetrable something separating us. I felt
that we had already begun to grow strange to each other, and the feeling lay like death at my heart.

Our lessons together were still going on; that I was no longer a
child had made only the difference that progress must make; and I
had no thought that they would not thus go on always. They were never
for a moment irksome to me; I might be tired by them, but never of
them. We were regularly at work together by seven, and after half an
hour for breakfast, resumed work; at half-past eleven our lessons were
over. But although the day was then clear of the imperative, much
the greater part of it was in general passed in each other's company.
We might not speak a word, but we would be hours together in the
study. We might not speak a word, but we would be hours together
on horseback.

For this day, then, our lessons were over, and my uncle was from
home. This was an indisputable relief, yet the fact that it was so,
pained me keenly, for I recognized in it the first of the schism. How I
got through the day, I cannot tell. I was in a dream, not all a dream of
delight. Haunted with the face I had seen, and living in the new consciousness it had waked in me, I spent most of it in the garden, now
in the glooms of the yew-walks, and now in the smiling wilderness. It
was odd, however, that, although I was not *expected* to be in my
uncle's room at any time but that of lessons, all the morning I had a
feeling as if I ought to be there, while yet glad that my uncle was not
there.

It was late before he returned, and I went to bed. Perhaps I retired so soon that I might not have to look into his eyes. Usually, I sat
now until he came home. I was long in getting to sleep, and then I
dreamed. I thought I was out in the storm, and the flash came which
revealed the horse and his rider, but they were both different. The
horse in the dream was black as coal, as if carved out of the night
itself; and the man upon him was the beautiful stranger whose horse
I had not seen for the garden-wall. The darkness fell, and the voice of
my uncle called to me. I waited for him in the storm with a troubled
heart, for I knew he had not seen that vision, and I could no more tell
him of it, than could Christabel tell her father what she had seen after
she lay down. I woke, but my waking was no relief.

11
The Mole Burrows

I slept again after my dream, and do not know whether he came into my room as he generally did when he had not said good-night to me. Of course I woke unhappy, and the morning-world had lost something of its natural glow, its lovely freshness: it was not this time a thing new-born of the creating word. I dawdled with my dressing. The face kept coming, and brought me no peace, yet brought me something for which it seemed worth while even to lose my peace. But I did not know then, and do not yet know what the loss of peace actually means. I only know that it must be something far more terrible than anything I have ever known. I remained so far true to my uncle, however, that not even for what the face seemed to promise me, would I have consented to cause him trouble. For what I saw in the face, I would do anything, I thought, except that.

I went to him at the usual hour, determined that nothing should distract me from my work—that he should perceive no difference in me. I was not at the moment awake to the fact that here again were love and deception hand in hand. But another love than mine was there: my uncle loved me immeasurably more than I yet loved that heavenly vision. True love is keen-sighted as the eagle, and my uncle's love was love true, therefore he saw what I sought to hide. It is only the shadow of love, generally a grotesque, ugly thing, like so many other shadows, that is blind either to the troubles or the faults of the shadow it seems to love. The moment our eyes met, I saw that he saw something in mine that was not there when last we parted. But he said nothing, and we sat down to our lessons. Every now and then as they proceeded, however, I felt rather than saw his eyes rest on me for a moment, questioning. I had never known them rest on me so before. Plainly he was aware of some change; and could there be anything different in the relation of two who so long had loved each other, without something being less well and good than before? Nor was it indeed wonderful he should see a difference; for, with all the might of my resolve to do even better than usual, I would now and then find myself unconscious of what either of us had last been saying. The face had come yet again, and driven everything from its presence! I grew angry—not with the youth, but with his face, for appearing so often when I did not invite it. Once I caught myself on the verge of crying out, "Can't you wait? I will come presently!" and my uncle looked up as if I had spoken. Perhaps he had as good as heard the words; he possessed what almost seemed a supernatural faculty of divining the thought of another—not, I was sure, by any effort to perceive it, but by involuntary intuition. He uttered no inquiring word, but a light sigh escaped him, which all but made me burst into tears. I was on one side of a widening gulf, and he on the other!

Our lessons ended, he rose immediately and left the room. Five minutes passed, and then came the clatter of his horse's feet on the stones of the yard. A moment more, and I heard him ride away at a quick trot. I burst into tears where I still sat beside my uncle's empty chair. I was weary like one in a dream searching in vain for a spot whereupon to set down her heart-breaking burden. There was no one but my uncle to whom I could tell any trouble, and the trouble I could not have told him had hitherto been unimaginable! From this my reader may judge what a trouble it was that I could not tell him my trouble. I was a traitor to my only friend! Had I begun to love him less? had I begun to turn away from him? I dared not believe it. That would have been to give eternity to my misery. But it might be that at heart I was a bad, treacherous girl! I had again a secret from him! I was not *with* him!

I went into the garden. The day was sultry and oppressive. Coolness or comfort was nowhere. I sought the shadow of the live yew-walls; there was shelter in the shadow, but it oppressed the lungs while it comforted the eyes. Not a breath of wind breathed; the atmosphere seemed to have lost its life-giving. I went out into the wilderness. There the air was filled and heaped with the odours of the heavenly plants that crowded its humble floor, but they gave me no welcome. Between two bushes that flamed out roses, I lay down, and the heather and the rose-trees closed above me. My mind was in such a confusion of pain and pleasure—not without a hope of deliverance somewhere in its clouded sky—that I could think no more, and fell asleep.

I imagine that, had I never again seen the young man, I should not have suffered. I think that, by slow natural degrees, his phantasmal presence would have ceased to haunt me, and gradually I should have returned to my former condition. I do not mean I should have forgotten him, but neither should I have been troubled when I thought of him. I know I should never have regretted having seen him. In that,

I had nothing to blame myself for, and should have felt—not that a glory had passed away from the earth, but that I had had a vision of bliss. What it was, I should not have had the power to recall, but it would have left with me the faith that I had beheld something too ethereal for my memory to store. I should have consoled myself both with the dream, and with the conviction that I should not dream it again. The peaceful sense of recovered nearness to my uncle would have been far more precious than the dream. The sudden fire of trans-figuration that had for a moment flamed out of the All, and straight-way withdrawn, would have become a memory only; but none the less would that enlargement of the child way of seeing things have re-mained with me. I do not think that would ever have left me: it is the care of the prudent wise that bleaches the grass, and is as the fumes of sulphur to the red rose of life.

Outwearied with inward conflict, I slept a dreamless sleep.

12
A Letter

A cool soft breeze went through the curtains of my couch, and I awoke. The blooms of the peasant-briars and the court-roses were waving together over my head. The sigh of the wind had breathed itself out over the far heath, and ere it died in my fairy forest of lowly plants and bushes, had found and fanned the cheeks that lay down hot and athirst for air. It gave me new life, and I rose refreshed. Something fluttered to the ground. I thought it was a leaf from a white rose above me, but I looked. At my feet lay a piece of paper. I took it up. It had been folded very hastily, and had no address, but who could have a better right to unfold it than I! It might be nothing; it might be a letter. Should I open it? Should I not rather seize the opportunity of setting things right between my heart and my uncle by taking it to him unopened? Only, if it were indeed—I dared hardly even in thought complete the supposition—might it not be a wrong to the youth? Might not the paper contain a confidence? might it not be the messenger of a heart that trusted me before even it knew my name? Would I inaugurate our acquaintance with an act of treachery, or at least distrust? Right or wrong, thus my heart reasoned, and to its reasoning I gave heed. "It will," I said, "be time enough to resolve, when I know concerning what!" This, I now see, was juggling; for the question was whether I should be open with my uncle or not. "It might be," I said to myself, "that, the moment I knew the contents of the paper, I should reproach myself that I had not read it at once!" I sat down on a bush of heather, and unfolded it. This is what I found, written with a pencil:—

"I am the man to whom you talked so kindly over your garden wall yesterday. I fear you may think me presuming and impertinent. Presuming I may be, but impertinent, surely not! If I were, would not my heart tell me so, seeing it is all on your side?

"My name is John Day; I do not yet know yours. I have not dared to inquire after it, lest I should hear of some impassable gulf between us. The fear of such a gulf haunts me. I can think of nothing but the face I saw over the wall through the clusters of lilac: the wall seems to keep rising and rising, as if it would hide you for ever.

"Is it wrong to think thus of you without your leave? If one may not love the loveliest, then is the world but a fly-trap hung in the great heaven, to catch and ruin souls!

"If I am writing nonsense—I cannot tell whether I am or not—it is because my wits wander with my eyes to gaze at you through the leaves of the wild white rose under which you are asleep. Loveliest of faces, may no gentlest wind of thought ripple thy perfect calm, until I have said what I must, and laid it where she will find it!

"I live at Rising, the manor-house over the heath. I am the son of Lady Cairnedge by a former marriage. I am twenty years of age, and have just ended my last term at Oxford. May I come and see you? If you will not see me, why then did you walk into my quiet house, and turn everything upside down? I shall come to-night, in the dusk, and wait in the heather, outside the fence. If you come, thank God! if you do not, I shall believe you could not, and come again and again and again, till hope is dead. But I warn you I am a terrible hoper.

"It would startle, perhaps offend you, to wake and see me; but I cannot bear to leave you asleep. Something might come too near you. I will write until you move, and then make haste to go.

"My heart swells with words too shy to go out. Surely a Will has brought us together! I believe in fate, never in chance!

"When we see each other again, will the wall be down between us, or shall I know it will part us all our mortal lives? Longer than that it cannot. If you say to me, 'I must not see you, but I will think of you,' not one shall ever know I have other than a light heart. Even now I begin the endeavour to be such that, when we meet at last, as meet we must, you shall not say, 'Is this the man, alas, who dared to love me!'

"I love you as one might love a woman-angel who, at the merest breath going to fashion a word unfit, would spread her wings and soar. Do not, I pray you, fear to let me come! There are things that must be done in faith, else they never have being: let this be one of them.— You stir."

As I came to these last words, hurriedly written, I heard behind me, over the height, the quick gallop of a horse, and knew the piece of firm turf he was crossing. The same moment I was there in spirit, and the imagination was almost vision. I saw him speeding away— "to come again!" said my heart, solemn with gladness.

Rising-manor was the house to which the lady took me that dread night when first I knew what it was to be alone in darkness and silence

and space. Was that lady his mother? Had she rescued me for her
son? I was not willing to believe it, though I had never actually seen
her. The way was mostly dark, and during the latter portion of it, I
was much too weary to look up where she sat on her great horse. I
had never to my knowledge heard who lived at Rising. I was not born
inquisitive, and there were miles between us.

I sat still, without impulse to move a finger. I lived essentially.
Now I knew what had come to me. It was no merely idiosyncratic experience, for the youth had the same: it was love! How otherwise could
we thus be drawn together from both sides! Verily it seemed also good
enough to be that wondrous thing ever on the lips of poets and tale-
weaving magicians! Was it not far beyond any notion of it their words
had given me?

But my uncle! There lay bitterness! Was I indeed false to him,
that now the thought of him was a pain? Had I begun a new life apart
from him? To tell him would perhaps check the terrible separation!
But how was I to tell him? For the first time I knew that I had no
mother! Would Mr. Day's mother be my mother too, and help me?
But from no woman save my own mother, hardly even from her, would
I ask mediation with the uncle I had loved and trusted all my life and
with my whole heart. I had never known father or mother, save as he
had been father and mother and everybody to me! What was I to do?
Gladly would I have hurried to some desert place, and there waited
for the light I needed. That I was no longer in any uncertainty as to
the word that described my condition, did not, I found, make it easy
to use the word. "Perhaps," I argued, struggling in the toils of my new
liberty, "my uncle knows nothing of this kind of love, and would be
unable to understand me! Suppose I confessed to him what I felt toward a man I had spoken to but once, and then only to tell him the
way to Dumbleton, would he not think me out of my mind?"

At length I bethought me that, so long as I did not know what to
do, I was not required to do anything; I must wait till I did know what
to do. But with the thought came suffering enough to be the wages of
any sin that, so far as I knew, I had ever committed. For the conviction awoke that already the love that had hitherto been the chief joy
of my being, had begun to pale and fade. Was it possible I was ceasing to
love my uncle? What could any love be worth if mine should fail my
uncle! Love itself must be a mockery, and life but a ceaseless sliding
down to the death of indifference! Even if I never ceased to love him,
it was just as bad to love him less! Had he not been everything to
me?—and this man, what had he ever done for me? Doubtless we are
to love even our enemies; but are we to love them as tenderly as we
love our friends? Or are we to love the friend of yesterday, of whom

we know nothing though we may believe everything, as we love those who have taken all the trouble to make true men and women of us? "What can be the matter with my soul?" I said. "Can that soul be right made, in which one love begins to wither the moment another begins to grow? If I be so made, I cannot help being worthless!"

It was then first, I think, that I received a notion—anything like a true notion, that is, of my need of a God—whence afterward I came to see the one need of the whole race. Of course, not being able to make ourselves, it needed a God to make us; but that making were a small thing indeed, if he left us so unfinished that we could come to nothing right;—if he left us so that we could think or do or be nothing right;—if our souls were created so puny, for instance, that there was not room in them to love as they could not help loving, without ceasing to love where they were bound by every obligation to love right heartily, and more and more deeply! But had I not been growing all the time I had been in the world? There must then be the possibility of growing still! If there was not room in me, there must be room in God for me to become larger! The room in God must be made room in me! God had not done making me, in fact, and I sorely needed him to go on making me; I sorely needed to be made out! What if this new joy and this new terror had come, had been sent, in order to make me grow? At least the doors were open; I could go out and forsake myself! If a living power had caused me—and certainly I did not cause myself—then that living power knew all about me, knew every smallness that distressed me! Where should I find him? He could not be so far that the misery of one of his own children could not reach him! I turned my face into the grass, and prayed as I had never prayed before. I had always gone to church, and made the responses attentively, while I knew that was not praying, and tried to pray better than that; but now I was really asking from God something I sorely wanted. "Father in heaven," I said, "I am so miserable! Please, help me!"

I rose, went into the house, and up to the study, took a sock I was knitting for my uncle, and sat down to wait what would come. I could think no more; I could only wait.

13
Old Love and New

While I waited, as nearly a log, under the weariness of spiritual unrest, as a girl could well be, the door opened. Very seldom did that door open to any one but my uncle or myself: he would let no one but me touch his books, or even dust the room. I jumped from the chest where I sat.

It was only Martha Moon.

"How you startled me, Martha!" I cried.

"No wonder, child!" she answered. "I come with bad news! Your uncle has had a fall. He is laid up at Wittenage with a broken right arm."

I burst into tears.

"Oh, Martha!" I cried; "I must go to him!"

"He has sent for me," she answered quietly.

"Dick is putting the horse to the phaeton."

"He doesn't want me, then!" I said; but it seemed a voice not my own that shrieked the words.

The punishment of my sin was upon me. Never would he have sent for Martha and not me, I thought, had he not seen that I had gone wrong again, and was no more to be trusted.

"My dear," said Martha, "which of us two ought to be the better nurse? You never saw your uncle ill; I've nursed him at death's door!"

"Then you don't think he is angry with me, Martha?" I said, humbled before myself.

"Was he ever angry with you, Orbie? What is there to be angry about? I never saw him even displeased with you!"

I had not realized that my uncle was suffering—only that he was disabled; now the fact flashed upon me, and with it the perception that I had been thinking only of myself: I was fast ceasing to care for him! And then, horrible to tell! a flash of joy went through me, that he would not be home that day, and therefore I *could* not tell him anything!

The moment Martha left me I threw myself on the floor of the desert room. I was in utter misery.

"Gladly would I bear every pang of his pain," I said to myself; "yet I have not asked one question about his accident! He must be in danger, or he would not have sent for Martha instead of me!"

How had the thing happened, I wondered. Had Death fallen with him—perhaps on him? He was such a horseman, I could not think he had been thrown. Besides, Death was a good horse who loved his master—dearly, I was sure, and would never have thrown him or let him fall! A great gush of the old love poured from the fountain in my heart: sympathy with the horse had unsealed it. I sprang from the floor, and ran down to entreat Martha to take me with her: if my uncle did not want me, I could return with Dick! But she was gone. Even the sound of her wheels was gone. I had lain on the floor longer than I knew.

I went back to the study a little relieved. I understood now that I was not glad he was disabled; that I was anything but glad he was suffering; that I had only been glad for an instant that the crisis of my perplexity was postponed. In the meantime I should see John Day, who would help me to understand what I ought to do!

Very strange were my feelings that afternoon in the lonely house. I had always felt it lonely when Martha, never when my uncle was out. Yet when my uncle was in, I was mostly with him, and seldom more than a few minutes at a time with Martha. Our feelings are odd creatures! Now that both were away, there was neither time nor space in my heart for feeling the house desolate; while the world outside was rich as a treasure-house of mighty kings. The moment I was a little more comfortable with myself, my thoughts went in a flock to the face that looked over the garden-wall, to the man that watched me while I slept, the man that wrote that lovely letter. Inside was old Penny with her broom: she took advantage of every absence to sweep or scour or dust; outside was John Day, and the roses of the wilderness! He was waiting the hour to come to me, wondering how I would receive him!

Slowly went the afternoon. I had fallen in love at first sight, it is true; not therefore was I eager to meet my lover. I was only more than willing to see him. It was as sweet, or nearly as sweet, to dream of his coming, as to have him before me—so long as I knew he was indeed coming. I was just a little anxious lest I should not find him altogether so beautiful as I was imagining him. That he was good, I never doubted: could I otherwise have fallen in love with him? And his letter was so straightforward—so manly!

The afternoon was cloudy, and the twilight came the sooner. From the realms of the dark, where all the birds of night build their nests,

lining them with their own sooty down, the sweet odorous filmy dusk
of the summer, haunted with wings of noiseless bats, began at length
to come flickering earthward, in a snow infinitesimal of fluffiest gray
and black: I crept out into the garden. It was dark as wintry night
among the yews, but I could have gone any time through every alley
of them blind-folded. An owl cried and I started, for my soul was sunk
in its own love-dawn. There came a sudden sense of light as I opened
the door into the wilderness, but light how thin and pale, and how
full of expectation! The earth and the vast air, up to the great vault,
seemed to throb and heave with life—or was it that my spirit lay an
open thoroughfare to the life of the All? With the scent of the roses
and the humbler sweet-odoured inhabitants of the wilderness; with
the sound of the brook that ran through it, flowing from the heath
and down the hill; with the silent starbeams, and the insects that make
all the little noises they can; with the thoughts that went out of me,
and returned possessed of the earth;—with all these, and the sense of
thought eternal, the universe was full as it could hold. I stood in the
doorway of the wall, and looked out on the wild: suddenly, by some
strange reaction, it seemed out of creation's doors, out in the illimit-
able, given up to the bare, to the space that had no walls! A shiver ran
through me; I turned back among the yews. It was early; I would wait
yet a while! If he were already there, he too would enjoy the calm of a
lovely little wait.

A small wind came searching about, and found, and caressed me.
I turned to it; it played with my hair, and cooled my face. After a while,
I left the alley, passed out, closed the door behind me, and went straying through the broken ground of the wilderness, among the low
bushes, meandering, as if with some frolicsome brook for a companion—a brook of capricious windings—but still coming nearer to the
fence that parted the wilderness from the heath, my eyes bent down,
partly to avoid the hillocks and bushes, and partly from shyness of
the moment when first I should see him who was in my heart and
somewhere near. Softly the moon rose, round and full. There was still
so much light in the sky that she made no sudden change, and for a
moment I did not feel her presence or look up. In front of me, the
high ground of the moor sank into a hollow, deeply indenting the
horizon-line: the moon was rising just in the gap, and when I did look
up, the lower edge of her disc was just clear of the earth, and the head
of a man looking over the fence was in the middle of the great moon.
It was like the head of a saint in a missal, girt with a halo of solid
gold. I could not see the face, for the halo hid it, as such attributions
are apt to do, but it must be he; and strengthened by the heavenly
vision, I went toward him. Walking less carefully than before, however,

I caught my foot, stumbled, and fell. There came a rush through the bushes; he was by my side, lifted me like a child, and held me in his arms; neither was I more frightened than a child caught up in the arms of any well-known friend: I had been bred in faith and not mistrust! But indeed my head had struck the ground with such force, that, had I been inclined, I could scarcely have resisted—though why should I have resisted, being where I would be! Does not philosophy tell us that growth and development, cause and effect, are all, and that the days and years are of no account? And does not more than philosophy tell us that truth is everything?"

"My darling! Are you hurt?" murmured the voice whose echoes seemed to have haunted me for centuries.

"A little," I answered. "I shall be all right in a minute." I did not add, "Put me down, please;" for I did not want to be put down directly. I could not have stood if he had put me down. I grew faint.

Life came back, and I felt myself growing heavy in his arms.

"I think I can stand now," I said. "Please put me down."

He obeyed immediately.

"I've nearly broken your arms," I said, ashamed of having become a burden to him the moment we met.

"I could run with you to the top of the hill!" he answered.

"I don't think you could," I returned. Perhaps I leaned a little toward him; I do not know. He put his arm round me.

"You are not able to stand," he said. "Shall we sit a moment?"

14
Mother and Uncle

I was glad enough to sink on a clump of white clover. He stretched himself on the heather, a little way from me. Silence followed. He was giving me time to recover myself. As soon, therefore, as I was able, it was my part to speak.

"Where is your horse?" I asked. The first word is generally one hardly worth saying.

"I left him at a little farmhouse, about a mile from here. I was afraid to bring him farther, lest my mother should learn where I had been. She takes pains to know."

"Then will she not find out?"

"I don't know."

"Will she not ask you where you were?"

"Perhaps. There's no knowing."

"You will tell her, of course, if she does?"

"I think not."

"Oughtn't you?"

"No."

"You are sure?"

"Yes."

"You don't mean you will tell her a story?"

"Certainly not."

"What will you do then?"

"I will tell her that I will not tell her."

"Would that be right?"

Through the dusk I could see the light of his smile as he answered, "I think so. I shall not tell her."

"But," I began.

He interrupted me.

My heart was sinking within me. Not only had I wanted him to help me to tell my uncle, but I shuddered at the idea of having with any man a secret from his mother.

"It must look strange to you," he said; "but you do not know my mother!"

"I think I do know your mother," I rejoined. "She saved my poor little life once.—I am not sure it was your mother, but I think it was."

"How was that?" he said, much surprised. "When was it?"

"Many years ago—I cannot tell how many," I answered. "But I remember all about it well enough. I cannot have been more than eight, I imagine."

"Could she have been at the manor then?" he said, putting the question to himself, not me. "How was it? Tell me," he went on, rising to his feet, and looking at me with almost a frightened expression.

I told him the incident, and he heard me in absolute silence. When I had done,—

"It *was* my mother!" he broke out; "I don't know one other woman who would have let a child walk like that! Any other would have taken you up, or put you on the horse and walked beside you!"

"A gentleman would, I know," I replied. "But it would not be so easy for a lady!"

"*She* could have done either well enough. She's as strong as a horse herself, and rides like an Amazon. But I am not in the least surprised: it was just like her! You poor little darling! It nearly makes me cry to think of the tiny feet going tramp, tramp, all that horrible way, and she high up on her big horse! She always rides the biggest horse she can get!—And then never to say a word to you after she brought you home, or see you the next morning!"

"Mr. Day," I returned, "I would not have told you, had I known it would give you occasion to speak so naughtily of your mother. You make me unhappy."

He was silent. I thought he was ashamed of himself, and was sorry for him. But my sympathy was wasted. He broke into a murmuring laugh of merriment.

"When is a mother not a mother?" he said. "—Do you give it up?—When she's a north wind. When she's a Roman emperor. When she's an iceberg. When she's a brass tiger.—There! that'll do. Good-bye, mother, for the present! I mayn't know much, as she's always telling me, but I do know that a noun is not a thing, nor a name a person!"

I would have expostulated.

"For love's sake, dearest," he pleaded, "we will not dispute where only one of us knows! I will tell you all some day—soon, I hope, very soon. I am angry now!—Poor little tramping child!"

I saw I had been behaving presumptuously: I had wanted to argue while yet in absolute ignorance of the thing in hand! Had not my uncle taught me the folly of reasoning from the ideal where I knew nothing of the actual! The ideal must be our guide how to treat the actual, but the actual must be there to treat! One thing more I saw—that there could be no likeness between his mother and my uncle!

"Will you tell me something about yourself, then?" I said.

"That would not be interesting!" he objected.

"Then why are you here?" I returned.

"Can any person without a history be interesting?"

"Yes," he answered: "a person that was going to have a history might be interesting."

"Could a person with a history that was not worth telling, be interesting? But I know yours will interest me in the hearing, therefore it ought to interest you in the telling.

"I see," he rejoined, with his merry laugh, I shall have to be careful! My lady will at once pounce upon the weak points of my logic!"

"I am no logician," I answered; "I only know when I don't know a thing. My uncle has taught me that wisdom lies in that,"

"Yours must be a very unusual kind of uncle!" he returned.

"If God had made many men like my uncle, I think the world wouldn't be the same place."

"I wonder why he didn't!" he said thoughtfully.

"I have wondered much, and cannot tell," I replied.

"What if it wouldn't be good for the world to have many good men in it before it was ready to treat them properly?" he suggested.

The words let me know that at least he could think. Hitherto my uncle had seemed to me the only man that thought. But I had seen very few men.

"Perhaps that is it," I answered. "I will think about it.—Were you brought up at Rising? Have you been there all the time? Were you there that night? I should surely have known had you been in the house!"

He looked at me with a grateful smile.

"I was not brought up there," he answered. "Rising is mine, however—at least it will be when I come of age; it was left me some ten years ago by a great-aunt My father's property will be mine too, of course. My mother's is in Ireland. She ought to be there, not here; but she likes my estates better than her own, and makes the most of being my guardian."

"You would not have her there if she is happier here?"

"All who have land, ought to live on it, or else give it to those who will. What makes it theirs, if their only connection with it is the money it brings them? If I let my horse run wild over the country, how could I claim him, and refuse to pay his damages?"

"I don't quite understand you."

"I only mean there is no bond where both ends are not tied. My mother has no sense of obligation, so far as ever I have been able to see. But do not be afraid: I would as soon take a wife to the house she was in, as I would ask her to creep with me into the den of a hyena."

It was too dreadful! I rose. He sprang to his feet.

"You must excuse me, sir!" I said. "With one who can speak so of his mother, I am where I ought not to be."

"You have a right to know what my mother is," he answered—coldly, I thought; "and I should not be a true man if I spoke of her otherwise than truly."

He would pretend nothing to please me! I saw that I was again in the wrong. Was I so ill read as to imagine that a mother must of necessity be a good woman? Was he to speak of his mother as he did not believe of her, or be unfit for my company? Would untruth be a bond between us?

"I beg your pardon," I said; "I was wrong. But you can hardly wonder I should be shocked to hear a son speak so of his mother—and to one all but a stranger!"

"What!" he returned, with a look of surprise; "do you think of me so? I feel as if I had known you all my life—and before it!"

I felt ashamed, and was silent. If he was such a stranger, why was I there alone with him?

"You must not think I speak so to any one," he went on. "Of those who know my mother, not one has a right to demand of me anything concerning her. But how could I ask you to see me, and hide from you the truth about her? Prudence would tell you to have nothing to do with the son of such a woman: could I be a true man, true to you, and hold my tongue about her? I should be a liar of the worst sort!"

He felt far too strongly, it was plain, to heed a world of commonplaces.

"Forgive me," I said. "May I sit down again?"

He held out his hand. I took it, and reseated myself on the clover-hillock. He laid himself again beside me, and after a little silence began to relate what occurred to him of his external history, while all the time I was watching for hints as to how he had come to be the man he was. It was clear he did not find it easy to talk about himself. But soon I no longer doubted whether I ought to have met him, and loved him a great deal more by the time he had done.

I then told him in return what my life had hitherto been; how I knew nothing of father or mother; how my uncle had been everything to me; how he had taught me all I knew, had helped me to love what was good and hate what was evil, had enabled me to value good books, and turn away from foolish ones. In short, I made him feel that all his mother had not been to him, my uncle had been to me; and that it would take a long time to make me as much indebted to a husband as already I was to my uncle. Then I put the question:

"What would you think of me if I had a secret from an uncle like that?"

"If I had an uncle like that," he answered, "I would sooner cut my throat than keep anything from him!"

"I have not told him," I said, "what happened to-day—or yesterday."

"But you will tell him?"

"The first moment I can. But I hope you understand it is hard to do. My love for my uncle makes it hard. It has the look of turning away from him to love another!"

With that I burst out crying. I could not help it. He let me cry, and did not interfere. I was grateful for that. When at length I raised my head, he spoke.

"It has that look," he said; "but I trust it is only a look. Anyhow, he knows that such things must be; and the more of a good man and a gentleman he is, the less will he be pained that we should love one another!"

"I am sure of that," I replied. "I am only afraid that he may never have been in love himself, and does not know how it feels, and may think I have forsaken him for you."

"Are you with him *always*?"

"No; I am sometimes a good deal alone. I can be alone as much as I like; he always gives me perfect liberty. But I never before wanted to be alone when I could be with him."

"But he *could* live without you?"

"Yes, indeed!" I cried. "He would be a poor creature that could not live without another!"

He said nothing, and I added, "He often goes out alone—sometimes in the darkest nights."

"Then be sure he knows what love is.—But, if you would rather, I will tell him."

"I could not have any one, even you, tell my uncle about me."

"You are right. When will you tell him?"

"I cannot be sure. I would go to him to-morrow, but I am afraid they will not let me until he has got a little over this accident," I answered—and told him what had happened. "It is dreadful to think how he must have suffered," I said, "and how much more I should have thought about it but for you! It tears my heart. Why wasn't it made bigger?"

"Perhaps that is just what is now being done with it!" he answered.

"I hope it may be!" I returned. "—But it is time I went in."

"Shall I not see you again to-morrow evening?" he asked.

"No," I answered. "I must not see you again till I have told my uncle everything."

"You do not mean for weeks and weeks—till he is well enough to come home? How *am* I to live till then!"

"As I shall have to live. But I hope it will be but for a few days at most. Only, then, it will depend on what my uncle thinks of the thing."

"Will he decide for you what you are to do?"

"Yes—I think so. Perhaps if he were—" I was on the point of saying, "like your mother," but I stopped in time—or hardly, for I think he saw what I just saved myself from. It was but the other morning I made the discovery that, all our life together, John has never once pressed me to complete a sentence I broke off.

He looked so sorrowful that I was driven to add something.

"I don't think there is much good," I said, "in resolving what you will or will not do, before the occasion appears, for it may have something in it you never reckoned on. All I can say is, I will try to do what is right. I cannot promise anything without knowing what my uncle thinks."

We rose; he took me in his arms for just an instant; and we parted with the understanding that I was to write to him as soon as I had spoken with my uncle.

15
The Time Between

I now felt quite able to confess to my uncle both what I had thought and what I had done. True, I had much more to confess than when my trouble first awoke; but the growth in the matter of the confession had been such a growth in definiteness as well, as to make its utterance, though more weighty, yet much easier. If I might be in doubt about revealing my thoughts, I could be in none about revealing my actions; and I found it was much less appalling to make known my feelings, when I had the words of John Day to confess as well.

I may here be allowed to remark, how much easier an action is when demanded, than it seems while in the contingent future—how much easier when the thing is before you in its reality, and not as a mere thought-spectre. The thing itself, and the idea of it, are two such different grounds upon which to come either to a decision or to action!

One thing more: when a woman wants to do the right—I do not mean, wants to coax the right to side with her—she will, somehow, be led up to it.

My uncle was very feverish and troubled the first night, and had a good deal of delirium, during which his care and anxiety seemed all about me. Martha had to assure him every other moment that I was well, and in no danger of any sort: he would be silent for a time, and then again show himself tormented with forebodings about me. In the morning, however, he was better; only he looked sadder than usual. She thought he was, for some cause or other, in reality anxious about me. So much I gathered from Martha's letter, by no means scholarly, but graphic enough.

It gave me much pain. My uncle was miserable about me: he had plainly seen, he knew and felt that something had come between us! Alas, it was no fancy of his brain-troubled soul! Whether I was in fault or not, there was that something! It troubled the unity that had hitherto seemed a thing essential and indivisible!

Dared I go to him without a summons? I knew Martha would call me the moment the doctor allowed her: it would not be right to go without that call. What I had to tell might justify far more anxiety than the sight of me would counteract. If I said nothing, the keen eye of his love would assure itself of the something hid in my silence, and he would not see that I was but waiting his improvement to tell him everything. I resolved therefore to remain where I was.

The next two days were perhaps the most uncomfortable ever I spent. A secret one desires to turn out of doors at the first opportunity, is not a pleasant companion. I do not say I was unhappy, still less that once I wished I had not seen John Day, but oh, how I longed to love him openly! how I longed for my uncle's sanction, without which our love could not be perfected! Then John's mother was by no means a gladsome thought—except that he must be a good man indeed, who was good in spite of being unable to love, respect, or trust his mother! The true notion of heaven, is to be with everybody one loves: to him the presence of his mother—such as she was, that is— would destroy any heaven! What a painful but salutary shock it will be to those whose existence is such a glorifying of themselves that they imagine their presence necessary to all about them, when they learn that their disappearance from the world sent a thrill of relief through the hearts of those nearest them! To learn how little they were prized, will one day prove a strong medicine for souls self-absorbed.

"There is nothing covered that shall not be revealed."

16
Fault and No Fault

The next day I kept the house till the evening, and then went walking in the garden in the twilight. Between the dark alleys and the open wilderness I flitted and wandered, alternating gloom and gleam outside me, even as they chased one another within me.

In the wilderness I looked up—and there was John! He stood outside the fence, just as I had seen him the night before, only now there was no aureole about his head: the moon had not yet reached the horizon.

My first feeling was anger: he had broken our agreement! I did not reflect that there was such a thing as breaking a law, or even a promise, and being blameless. He leaped the fence, and clearing every bush like a deer, came straight toward me. It was no use trying to escape him. I turned my back, and stood. He stopped close behind me, a yard or two away.

"Will you not speak to me?" he said. "It is not my fault I am come."

"Whose fault then, pray?" I rejoined, with difficulty keeping my position. "Is it mine?"

"My mother's," he answered.

I turned and looked him in the eyes, through the dusk saw that he was troubled, ran to him, and put my arms about him.

"She has been spying," he said, as soon as he could speak. "She will part us at any risk, if she can. She is having us watched this very moment, most likely. She may be watching us herself. She is a terrible woman when she is for or against anything. Literally, I do not know what she would not do to get her own way. She lives for her own way. The loss of it would be to her as the loss of her soul. She will lose it this time though! She will fail this time—if she never did before!"

"Well," I returned, nowise inclined to take her part, "I hope she will fail! What does she say?"

"She says she would rather go to her grave than see me your husband."

"Why?"

"Your family seems objectionable to her."

"What is there against it?"

"Nothing that I know."

"What is there against my uncle? Is there anything against Martha Moon?" I was indignant at the idea of a whisper against either.

"What have *I* done?" I went on. "We are all of the family I know: what is it?"

"I don't think she has had time to invent anything yet; but she pretends there is something, and says if I don't give you up, if I don't swear never to look at you again, she will tell it."

"What did you answer her?"

"I said no power on earth should make me give you up. Whatever she knew, she could know nothing against *you*, and I was as ready to go to my grave as she was. 'Mother,' I said, 'you may tell my determination by your own! Whether I marry her or not, you and I part company the day I come of age; and if you speak word or do deed against one of her family, my lawyer shall look strictly into your accounts as my guardian.' You see I knew where to touch her!"

"It is dreadful you should have to speak like that to your mother!"

"It is; but you would feel to her just as I do if you knew all—though you wouldn't speak so roughly, I know."

"Can you guess what she has in her mind?"

"Not in the least. She will pretend anything. It is enough that she is determined to part us. How, she cares nothing, so she succeed."

"But she cannot!"

"It rests with you."

"How with me?"

"It will be war to the knife between her and me. If she succeed, it must be with you. I will do anything to foil her except lie."

"What if she should make you see it your duty to give me up?"

"What if there were no difference between right and wrong! We're as good as married!"

"Yes, of course; but I cannot quite promise, you know, until I hear what my uncle will say."

"If your uncle is half so good a man as you have made me think him, he will do what he can on our side. He loves what is fair; and what can be fairer than that those who love each other should marry?"

I knew my uncle would not willingly interfere with my happiness, and for myself, I should never marry another than John Day—that was a thing of course: had he not kissed me? But the best of lovers had been parted, and that which had been might be again, though I could not see how! It *was* good, nevertheless, to hear John talk! It was the right way for a lover to talk! Still, he had no supremacy over what was to be!

"Some would say it cannot be so great a matter to us, when we have known each other such a little while!" I remarked.

"The true time is the long time!" he replied. "Would it be a sign that our love was strong, that it took a great while to come to anything? The strongest things—"

There he stopped, and I saw why: strongest things are not generally of quickest growth! But there was the eucalyptus! And was not St. Paul as good a Christian as any of them? I said nothing, however: there was indeed no rule in the matter!

"You must allow it possible," I said, "that we may not be married!"

"I will not," he answered. "It is true my mother may get me brought in as incapable of managing my own affairs; but—"

"What mother would do such a wicked thing!" I cried.

"*My* mother," he answered.

"Oh!"

"She *would!*"

"I can't believe it."

"I am sure of it."

I held my peace. I could not help a sense of dismay at finding myself so near such a woman. I knew of bad women, but only in books: it would appear they were in other places as well!

"We must be on our guard," he said.

"Against what?"

"I don't know; whatever she may do."

"We can't do anything till she begins!"

"She has begun."

"How?" I asked incredulous.

"Leander is lame," he answered.

"I am so sorry!"

"I am so angry!"

"Is it possible I understand you?"

"Quite. *She* did it."

"How do you know?"

"I can no more prove it than I can doubt it. I cannot inquire into my mother's proceedings. I leave that sort of thing to her. Let her spy on me as she will, I am not going to spy on her."

"Of course not! But if you have no proof, how can you state the thing as a fact?"

"I have what is proof enough for saying it to my own soul."

"But you have spoken of it to me!"

"You are my better soul. If you are not, then I have done wrong in saying it to you."

I hastened to tell him I had only made him say what I hoped he meant—only I wasn't his *better* soul. He wanted me then to promise that I would marry him in spite of any and every thing. I promised that I would never marry any one but him. I could not say more, I said, not knowing what my uncle might think, but so much it was only fair to say. For I had gone so far as to let him know distinctly that I loved him; and what sort would that love be that could regard it as possible, at any distance of time, to marry another! Or what sort of woman could she be that would shrink from such a pledge! The mischief lies in promises made without forecasting thought. I knew what I was about. I saw forward and backward and all around me. A solitary education opens eyes that, in the midst of companions and engagements, are apt to remain shut. Knowledge of the world is no safeguard to man or woman. In the knowledge and love of truth, lies our only safety.

With that promise he had to be, and was content.

17
The Summons

Next morning the post brought me the following letter from my uncle. Whoever of my readers may care to enter into my feelings as I read, must imagine them for herself: I will not attempt to describe them. The letter was not easy to read, as it was written in bed, and with his left hand.

"My little one,—I think I know more than you imagine. I think the secret flew into your heart of itself; you did not take it up and put it there. I think you tried to drive it out, and it would not go: the same Fate that clips the thread of life, had clipped its wings that it could fly no more! Did my little one think I had not a heart big enough to hold her secret? I wish it had not been so: it has made her suffer! I pray my little one to be sure that I am all on her side; that my will is to do and contrive the best for her that lies in my power. Should I be unable to do what she would like, she must yet believe me true to her as to my God, less than whom only I love her:—less, because God is so much bigger, that so much more love will hang upon him. I love you, dear, more than any other creature except one, and that one is not in this world. Be sure that, whatever it may cost me, I will be to you what your own perfected soul will approve. Not to do my best for you, would be to be false, not to God only, but to your father as well, whom I loved and love dearly. Come to me, my child, and tell me all. I know you have done nothing wrong, nothing to be ashamed of. Some things are so difficult to tell, that it needs help to make way for them: I will help you. I am better. Come to me at once, and we will break the creature's shell together, and see what it is like, the shy thing!— Your uncle."

I was so eager to go to him, that it was with difficulty I finished his letter before starting. Death had been sent home, and was in the stable, sorely missing his master. I called Dick, and told him to get ready to ride with me to Wittenage; he must take Thanatos, and be at the door with Zoe in twenty minutes.

We started. As we left the gate, I caught sight of John coming from the other direction, his eyes on the ground, lost in meditation. I stopped. He looked up, saw me, and was at my side in two moments.

"I have heard from my uncle," I said. "He wants me. I am going to him."

"If only I had my horse!" he answered.

"Why shouldn't you take Thanatos?" I rejoined.

"No," he answered, after a moment's hesitation.

"It would be an impertinence. I will walk, and perhaps see you there. It's only sixteen miles, I think.—What a splendid creature he is!"

"He's getting into years now," I replied; "but he has been in the stable several days, and I am doubtful whether Dick will feel quite at home on him."

"Then your uncle would rather I rode him! He knows I am no tailor!" said John.

"How?" I asked.

"I don't mean he knows who I am, but he saw me a fortnight ago, in one of our fields, giving Leander, who is but three, a lesson or two. He stopped and looked on for a good many minutes, and said a kind word about my handling of the horse. He will remember, I am sure."

"How glad I am he knows something of you! If you don't mind being seen with me, then, there is no reason why you should not give me your escort."

Dick was not sorry to dismount, and we rode away together.

I was glad of this for one definite reason, as well as many indefinite: I wanted John to see my letter, and know what cause I had to love my uncle. I forgot for the moment my resolution not to meet him again before telling my uncle everything. Somehow he seemed to be going with me to receive my uncle's approval.

He read the letter, old Death carrying him all the time as gently as he carried myself—I often rode him now—and returned it with the tears in his eyes. For a moment or two he did not speak. Then he said in a very solemn way,

"I see! I oughtn't to have a chance if he be against me! I understand now why I could not get you to promise!—All right! The Lord have mercy upon me!"

"That he will! He is always having mercy upon us!" I answered, loving John and my uncle and God more than ever. I loved John for this especially, at the moment—that his nature remained uninjured toward others by his distrust of her who should have had the first claim on his confidence. I said to myself that, if a man had a bad mother and yet was a good man, there could be no limit to the goodness he must come to. That he was a man after my uncle's own heart,

I had no longer the least doubt. Nor was it a small thing to me that he rode beautifully—never seeming to heed his horse, and yet in constant touch with him.

We reached the town, and the inn where my uncle was lying. On the road we had arranged where he would be waiting me to hear what came next. He went to see the horses put up, and I ran to find Martha. She met me on the stair, and went straight to my uncle to tell him I was come, returned almost immediately, and led me to his room.

I was shocked to see how pale and ill he looked. I feared, and was right in fearing, that anxiety about myself had not a little to do with his condition. His face brightened when he saw me, but his eyes gazed into mine with a searching inquiry. His face brightened yet more when he found his eager look answered by the smile which my perfect satisfaction inspired. I knelt by the bedside, afraid to touch him lest I should hurt his arm.

Slowly he laid his left hand on my head, and I knew he blessed me silently. For a minute or two he lay still.

"Now tell me all about it," he said at length, turning his patient blue eyes on mine. I began at once, and if I did not tell him all, I let it be plain there was more of the sort behind, concerning which he might question me. When I had ended,

"Is that everything?" he asked, with a smile so like all he had ever been to me, that my whole heart seemed to go out to meet it.

"Yes, uncle," I answered; "I think I may say so—except that I have not dwelt upon my feelings. Love, they say, is shy; and I fancy you will pardon me that portion."

"Willingly, my child. More is quite unnecessary."

"Then you know all about it, uncle?" I ventured. "I was afraid you might not understand me. Could any one, do you think, that had not had the same experience?"

He made me no answer. I looked up. He was ghastly white; his head had fallen back against the bed. I started up, hardly smothering a shriek.

"What is it, uncle?" I gasped. "Shall I fetch Martha?"

"No, my child," he answered. "I shall be better in a moment. I am subject to little attacks of the heart, but they do not mean much. Give me some of that medicine on the table."

In a few minutes his colour began to return, and the smile which was forced at first, gradually brightened until it was genuine.

"I will tell you the whole story one day," he said, "—whether in this world, I am doubtful. But *when* is nothing, or *where*, with eternity before us."

"Yes, uncle," I answered vaguely, as I knelt again by the bedside.

"A person," he said, after a while, slowly, and with hesitating effort, "may look and feel a much better person at one time than at another. Upon occasion, he is so happy, or perhaps so well pleased with himself, that the good in him comes all to the surface."

"Would he be the better or the worse man if it did not, uncle?" I asked.

"You must not get me into a metaphysical discussion, little one," he answered. "We have something more important on our hands. I want you to note that, when a person is happy, he may look lovable; whereas, things going as he does not like, another, and very unfinished phase of his character may appear."

"Surely everybody must know that, uncle!"

"Then you can hardly expect me to be confident that your new friend would appear as lovable if he were unhappy!"

"I have seen you, uncle, look as if nothing would ever make you smile again; but I knew you loved me all the time."

"Did you, my darling? Then you were right. I dare not require of any man that he should be as good-tempered in trouble as out of it— though he must come to that at last; but a man must be *just*, whatever mood he is in."

"That is what I always knew you to be, uncle! I never waited for a change in your looks, to tell you anything I wanted to tell you.—I know you, uncle!" I added, with a glow of still triumph.

"Thank you, little one!" he returned, half playfully, yet gravely. "All I want to say comes to this," he resumed after a pause, "that when a man is in love, you see only the best of him, or something better than he really is. Much good may be in a man, for God made him, and the man yet not be good, for he has done nothing, since his making, to make himself. Before you can say you know a man, you must have seen him in a few at least of his opposite moods. Therefore you cannot wonder that I should desire a fuller assurance of this young man, than your testimony, founded on an acquaintance of three or four days, can give me."

"Let me tell you, then, something that happened to-day," I answered. "When first I asked him to come with me this morning, it was a temptation to him of course, not knowing when we might see each other again; but he hadn't his own horse, and said it would be an impertinence to ride yours."

"I hope you did not come alone!"

"Oh, no. I had set out with Dick, but John came after all."

"Then his refusal to ride my horse does not come to much. It is a small thing to have good impulses, if temptation is too much for them."

"But I haven't done telling you, uncle!"

"I am hasty, little one. I beg your pardon."

"I have to tell you what made him give in to riding your horse. I confessed I was a little anxious lest Death, who had not been exercised for some days, should be too much for Dick. John said then he thought he might venture, for you had once spoken very kindly to him of the way he handled his own horse."

"Oh, that's the young fellow, is it!" cried my uncle, in a tone that could not be taken for other than one of pleasure. "That's the fellow, is it?" he repeated. "H'm!"

"I hope you liked the look of him, uncle!" I said.

"The boy is a gentleman anyhow!" he answered.— "You may think whether I was pleased!—I never saw man carry himself better horseward!" he added with a smile.

"Then you won't object to his riding Death home again?"

"Not in the least!" he replied. "The man can ride."

"And may I go with him?—that is, if you do not want me!—I wish I could stay with you!"

"Rather than ride home with him?"

"Yes, indeed, if it were to be of use to you!"

"The only way you can be of use to me, is to ride home with Mr. Day, and not see him again until I have had a little talk with him. Tyranny may be a sense of duty, you know, little one!"

"Tyranny, uncle!" I cried, as I laid my cheek to his hand, which was very cold. "You could not make me think you a tyrant!"

"I should not like you to think me one, darling! Still less would I like to deserve it, whether you thought me one or not! But I could not be a tyrant to you if I would. You may defy me when you please."

"That would be to poison my own soul!" I answered.

"You must understand," he continued, "that I have no authority over you. If you were going to marry Mr. Day to-morrow, I should have no right to interfere. I am but a make-shift father to you, not a legal guardian."

"Don't cast me off, uncle!" I cried. "You *know* I belong to you as much as if you were my very own father! I am sure my father will say so when we see him. He will never come between you and me."

He gave a great sigh, and his face grew so intense that I felt as if I had no right to look on it.

"It is one of the deepest hopes of my existence," he said, "to give you back to him the best of daughters. Be good, my darling, be good, even if you die of sorrow because of it."

The intensity had faded to a deep sadness, and there came a silence.

"Would you like me to go now, uncle?" I asked.

"I wish I could see Mr. Day at once," he returned, "but I am so far from strong, that I fear both weakness and injustice. Tell him I want very much to see him, and will let him know as soon as I am able."

"Thank you, uncle! He will be so glad! Of course he can't feel as I do, but he does feel that to do anything you did not like, would be just horrid."

"And you will not see him again, little one, after he has taken you home, till I have had some talk with him?"

"Of course I will not, uncle."

I bade him good-bye, had a few moments' conference with Martha, and found John at the place appointed.

18
John Sees Something

As we rode, I told him everything. It did not seem in the least strange that I should be so close to one of whom a few days before I had never heard; it seemed as if all my life I had been waiting for him, and now he was come, and everything was only as it should be! We were very quiet in our gladness. Some slight anxiety about my uncle's decision, and the certain foreboding of trouble on the part of his mother, stilled us both, sending the delight of having found each other a little deeper and out of the way of the practical and reasoning.

We did not urge our horses to their speed, but I felt that, for my uncle's sake, I must not prolong the journey, forcing the last farthing of bliss from his generosity, while yet he was uncertain of his duty. The moon was rising just as we reached my home, and I was glad: John would have to walk miles to reach his, for he absolutely refused to take Death on, saying he did not know what might happen to him. As we stopped at the gate I bethought myself that neither of us had eaten since we left in the afternoon. I dismounted, and leaving him with the horses, got what I could find for him, and then roused Dick, who was asleep. John confessed that, now I had made him think of it, he was hungry enough to eat anything less than an ox. We parted merrily, but when next we met, each confessed it had not been without a presentiment of impending danger. For my part, notwithstanding the position I had presumed to take with John when first he spoke of his mother, I was now as distrustful as he, and more afraid of her.

Much the nearest way between the two houses lay across the heath. John walked along, eating the supper I had given him, and now and then casting a glance round the horizon. He had got about half-way, when, looking up, he thought he saw, dim in the ghosty light of the moon, a speck upon the track before him. He said to himself it could hardly be any one on the moor at such a time of the night, and went on with his supper. Looking up again after an interval, he saw that the object was much larger, but hardly less vague, because of a light fog which had in the meantime risen. By and by, however, as they drew nearer to each other, a strange thrill of recognition went through him: on the way before him, which was little better than a footpath, and slowly approaching, came what certainly could be neither the horse that had carried him that day, nor his double, but what was so like him in colour, size, and bone, while so unlike him in muscle and bearing, that he might have been he, worn but for his skin to a skeleton. Straight down upon John he came, spectral through the fog, as if he were asleep, and saw nothing in his way. John stepped aside to let him pass, and then first looked in the face of his rider: with a shock of fear that struck him in the middle of the body, making him gasp and choke, he saw before him—so plainly that, but for the impossibility, he could have sworn to him in any court of justice—the man whom he knew to be at that moment confined to his bed, twenty miles away, with a broken arm. Sole other human being within sight or sound in that still moonlight, on that desolate moor, the horseman never lifted his head, never raised his eyes to look at him. John stood stunned. He hardly doubted he saw an apparition. When at length he roused himself, and looked in the direction in which it went, it had all but vanished in the thickening white mist.

He found the rest of his way home almost mechanically, and went straight to bed, but for a long time could not sleep.

For what might not the apparition portend? Mr. Whichcote lay hurt by a fall from his horse, and he had met his very image on the back of just such a horse, only turned to a skeleton! Was he bearing him away to the tomb?

Then he remembered that the horse's name was Death.

19
John is Taken III

In the middle of the night he woke with a start, ill enough to feel
that he was going to be worse. His head throbbed; the room seemed
turning round with him, and when it settled, he saw strange shapes
in it. A few rays of the sinking moon had got in between the curtains
of one of the windows, and had waked up everything! The furniture
looked odd—unpleasantly odd. Something unnatural, or at least unearthly, must be near him! The room was an old-fashioned one, in
thorough keeping with the age of the house—the very haunt for a
ghost, but he had heard of no ghost in that room! He got up to get
himself some water, and drew the curtains aside. He could have been
in no thraldom to an apprehensive imagination; for what man, with a
brooding terror couched in him, would, in the middle of the night, let
in the moon? To such a passion, she is worse than the deepest darkness, especially when going down, as she was then, with the weary
look she gets by the time her work is about over, and she has long
been forsaken of the poor mortals for whom she has so often to be up
and shining all night. He poured himself some water and drank it,
but thought it did not taste nice. Then he turned to the window, and
looked out.

The house was in a large park. Its few trees served mainly to show
how wide the unbroken spaces of grass. Before the house, motionless
as a statue, stood a great gray horse with hanging neck, his shadow
stretched in mighty grotesque behind him, and on his back the very
effigy of my uncle, motionless too as marble. The horse stood side-
wise to the house, but the face of his rider was turned toward it, as if
scanning its windows in the dying glitter of the moon. John thought
he heard a cry somewhere, and went to his door, but, listening hard,
heard nothing. When he looked again from the window, the apparition seemed fainter, and farther away, though neither horse nor rider
had changed posture. He rubbed his eyes to see more plainly, could
no longer distinguish the appearance, and went back to bed. In the

morning he was in a high fever—unconscious save of restless discomfort and undefined trouble.

He learned afterward from the housekeeper, that his mother herself nursed him, but he would take neither food nor medicine from
her hand. No doctor was sent for. John thought, and I cannot but
think, that the water in his bottle had to do with the sudden illness.
His mother may have merely wished to prevent him from coming to
me; but, for the time at least, the conviction had got possession of
him, that she was attempting his life. He may have argued in semi
conscious moments, that she would not scruple to take again what
she was capable of imagining she had given. Her attentions, however,
may have arisen from alarm at seeing him worse than she had intended
to make him, and desire to counteract what she had done.

For several days he was prostrate with extreme exhaustion. Necessarily, I knew nothing of this; neither was I, notwithstanding my more
than doubt of his mother, in any immediate dread of what she might
do. The cessation of his visits could, of course, cause me no anxiety,
seeing it was thoroughly understood between us that we were not at
liberty to meet.

20
A Strange Visit

On the fifth night after that on which he left me to walk home, I roused, about two o'clock, by a sharp sound as of sudden hail against my window, ceasing as soon as it began. Wondering what it was, for hail it could hardly be, I sprang from the bed, pulled aside the curtain, and looked out. There was light enough in the moon to show me a man looking up at the window, and love enough in my heart to tell me who he was. How he knew the window mine, I have always forgotten to ask him. I would have drawn back, for it vexed me sorely to think him too weak to hold to our agreement, but the face I looked down upon was so ghastly and deathlike, that I perceived at once his coming must have its justification. I did not speak, for I would not have any in the house hear; but, putting on my shoes and a big cloak, I went softly down the stair, opened the door noiselessly, and ran to the other side of the house. There stood John, with his eyes fixed on my window. As I turned the corner I could see, by their weary flashing, that either something terrible had happened, or he was very ill. He stood motionless, unaware of my approach.

"What is it?" I said under my breath, putting a hand on his shoulder.

He did not turn his head or answer me, but grew yet whiter, gasped, and seemed ready to fall. I put my arm round him, and his head sank on the top of mine.

Whatever might be the matter, the first thing was to get him into the house, and make him lie down. I moved a little, holding him fast, and mechanically he followed his support; so that, although with some difficulty, I soon got him round the house, and into the great hall-kitchen, our usual sitting-room; there was fire there that would only want rousing, and, warm as was the night, I felt him very cold. I let him sink on the wide sofa, covered him with my cloak, and ran to rouse old Penny. The aged sleep lightly, and she was up in an instant. I told her that a gentleman I knew had come to the house, either sleep-

438

walking or delirious, and she must come and help me with him. She struck a light, and followed me to the kitchen.

John lay with his eyes closed, in a dead faint. We got him to swallow some brandy, and presently he came to himself a little. Then we put him in my warm bed, and covered him with blankets. In a minute or so he was fast asleep. He had not spoken a word. I left Penny to watch him, and went and dressed myself, thinking hard. The result was, that, having enjoined Penny to let no one near him, *whoever* it might be, I went to the stable, saddled Zoe, and set off for Wittenage.

It was sixteen miles of a ride. The moon went down, and the last of my journey was very dark, for the night was cloudy; but we arrived in safety, just as the dawn was promising to come as soon as it could. No one in the town seemed up, or thinking of getting up. I had learned a lesson from John, however, and I knew Martha's window, which happily looked on the street. I got off Zoe, who was tired enough to stand still, for she was getting old and I had not spared her, and proceeded to search for a stone small enough to throw at the window. The scared face of Martha showed itself almost immediately.

"It's me!" I cried, no louder than she could just hear; "it's me, Martha! Come down and let me in."

Without a word of reply, she left the window, and after some fumbling with the lock, opened the door, and came out to me, looking gray with scare, but none the less with all her wits to her hand.

"How is my uncle, Martha?" I said.

"Much better," she answered.

"Then I must see him at once!"

"He's fast asleep, child! It would be a world's pity to wake him!"

"It would be a worse pity not!" I returned.

"Very well: must-be must!" she answered.

I made Zoe fast to the lamp-post: the night was warm, and hot as she was, she would take no hurt. Then I followed Martha up the stair.

But my uncle was awake. He had heard a little of our motions and whisperings, and lay in expectation of something.

"I thought I should hear from you soon!" he said. "I wrote to Mr. Day on Thursday, but have had no reply. What has happened? Nothing serious, I hope?"

"I hardly know, uncle. John Day is lying at our house, unable to move or speak."

My uncle started up as if to spring from his bed, but fell back again with a groan.

"Don't be alarmed, uncle!" I said. "He is, I hope, safe for the moment, with Penny to watch him; but I am very anxious Dr. Southwell should see him."

"How did it come about, little one?"

"There has been no accident that I know of. But I scarcely know more than you," I replied—and told him all that had taken place within my ken.

He lay silent a moment, thinking.

"I can't say I like his lying there with only Penny to protect him!" he said. "He must have come seeking refuge! I don't like the thing at all! He is in some danger we do not know!"

"I will go back at once, uncle," I replied, and rose from the bedside, where I had seated myself a little tired.

"You must, if we cannot do better. But I think we can. Martha shall go, and you will stay with me. Run at once and wake Dr. Southwell. Ask him to come directly."

I ran all the way—it was not far—and pulled the doctor's nightbell. He answered it himself. I gave him my uncle's message, and he was at the inn a few minutes after me. My uncle told him what had happened, and begged him to go and see the patient, carrying Martha with him in his gig.

The doctor said he would start at once. My uncle begged him to give strictest orders that no one was to see Mr. Day, whoever it might be. Martha heard, and grew like a colonel of dragoons ordered to charge with his regiment.

In less than half an hour they started—at a pace that delighted me.

When Zoe was put up and attended to, and I was alone with my uncle, I got him some breakfast to make up for the loss of his sleep. He told me it was better than sleep to have me near him.

What I went through that night and the following day, I need not recount. Whoever has loved one in danger and out of her reach, will know what it was like. The doctor did not make his appearance until five o'clock, having seen several patients on his way back. The young man, he reported, was certainly in for a fever of some kind—he could not yet pronounce which. He would see him again on the morrow, he said, and by that time it would have declared itself. Some one in the neighbourhood must watch the case; it was impossible for him to give it sufficient attention. My uncle told him he was now quite equal to the task himself, and we would all go together the next day. My delight at the proposal was almost equalled by my satisfaction that the doctor made no objection to it.

For joy I scarcely slept that night: I was going to nurse John! But I was anxious about my uncle. He assured me, however, that in one day more he would in any case have insisted on returning. If it had not been for a little lingering fever, he said, he would have gone much sooner.

"That was because of me, uncle!" I answered with contrition.

"Perhaps," he replied; "but I had a blow on the head, you know!"

"There is one good thing," I said: "you will know John the sooner from seeing him ill! But perhaps you will count that only a mood, uncle, and not to be trusted!"

He smiled. I think he was not *very* anxious about the result of a nearer acquaintance with John Day. I believe he had some faith in my spiritual instinct.

Uncle went with the doctor in his brougham, and I rode Zoe. The back of the house came first in sight, and I saw the window-blinds of my room still down. The doctor had pronounced it the fittest for the invalid, and would not have him moved to the guest-chamber Penny had prepared for him.

In the only room I had ever occupied as my own, I nursed John for a space of three weeks.

From the moment he saw me, he began to improve. My uncle noted this, and I fancy liked John the better for it. Nor did he fail to note the gentleness and gratitude of the invalid.

21
A Foiled Attempt

The morning after my uncle's return, came a messenger from Rising with his lady's compliments, asking if Mr. Whichcote could tell her anything of her son: he had left the house unseen, during a feverish attack, and as she could get no tidings of him, she was in great anxiety. She had accidentally heard that he had made Mr. Whichcote's acquaintance, and therefore took the liberty of extending to him the inquiry she had already made everywhere else among his friends. My uncle wrote in answer, that her son had come to his house in a high fever; that he had been under medical care ever since; and that he hoped in a day or two he might be able to return. If he expressed a desire to see his mother, he would immediately let her know, but in the meantime it was imperative he should be kept quiet.

From this letter, Lady Cairnedge might surmise that her relations with her son were at least suspected. Within two hours came another message—that she would send a close carriage to bring him home the next day. Then indeed were my uncle and I glad that we had come. For though Martha would certainly have defended the citadel to her utmost, she might have been sorely put to it if his mother proceeded to carry him away by force. My uncle, in reply, begged her not to give herself the useless trouble of sending to fetch him: in the state he was in at present, it would be tantamount to murder to remove him, and he would not be a party to it.

When I yielded my place in the sick-room to Martha and went to bed, my heart was not only at ease for the night, but I feared nothing for the next day with my uncle on my side—or rather on John's side.

We were just rising from our early dinner, for we were old-fashioned people, when up drove a grand carriage, with two strong footmen behind, and a servant in plain clothes on the box by the coachman. It pulled up at the door, and the man on the box got down and rang the bell, while his fellows behind got down also, and stood together a little way behind him. My uncle at once went to the hall, but no more than in time, for there was Penny already on her way to open the door. He opened it himself, and stood on the threshold.

"If you please, sir," said the man, not without arrogance, "we're come to take Mr. Day home."

"Tell your mistress," returned my uncle, "that Mr. Day has expressed no desire to return, and is much too unwell to be informed of her ladyship's wish."

"Begging your pardon, sir," said the man, "we have her ladyship's orders to bring him. We'll take every possible care of him. The carriage is an extra-easy one, and I'll sit inside with the young gentleman myself. If he ain't right in his head, he'll never know nothink till he comes to himself in his own bed."

My uncle had let the man talk, but his anger was fast rising.

"I cannot let him go. I would not send a beggar to the hospital in the state he is in."

"But, indeed, sir, you must! We have our orders."

"If you fancy I will dismiss a guest of mine at the order of any human being, were it the queen's own majesty," said my uncle—I heard the words, and with my mind's eyes saw the blue flash of his as he said them— "you will find yourself mistaken."

"I'm sorry," said the man quietly, "but I have my orders! Let me pass, please. It is my business to find the young gentleman, and take him home. No one can have the right to keep him against his mother's will, especially when he's not in a fit state to judge for himself."

"Happily I am in a fit state to judge for him," said my uncle, coldly.

"I dare not go back without him. Let me pass," he returned, raising his voice a little, and approaching the door as if he would force his way.

I ought to have mentioned that, as my uncle went to the door, he took from a rack in the hall a whip with a bamboo stock, which he generally carried when he rode. His answer to the man was a smart, though left-handed blow with the stock across his face: they were too near for the thong. He staggered back, and stood holding his hand to his face. His fellow-servants, who, during the colloquy, had looked on with gentlemanlike imperturbability, made a simultaneous step forward. My uncle sent the thong with a hiss about their ears. They sprang toward him in a fury, but halted immediately and recoiled. He had drawn a small swordlike weapon, which I did not know to be there, from the stock of the whip. He gave one swift glance behind him. I was in the hall at his back.

"Shut the door, Orba," he cried.

I shut him out, and ran to a window in the little drawing-room, which commanded the door. Never had I seen him look as now—his pale face pale no longer, but flushed with anger. Neither, indeed, until that moment had I ever seen the *natural* look of anger, the expression of *pure* anger. There was nothing mean or ugly in it—not an atom of hate. But how his eyes blazed!

"Go back," he cried, in a voice far more stern than loud. "If one of you set foot on the lowest step, and I will run him through."

The men saw he meant it; they saw the closed door, and my uncle with his back to it. They turned and spoke to each other. The coachman sat immovable on his box. They mounted, and he drove away.

I ran and opened the door. My uncle came in with a smile. He went up the stair, and I followed him to the room where the invalid lay. We were both anxious to learn if he had been disturbed.

He was leaning on his elbow, listening. He looked a good deal more like himself.

"I knew you would defend me, sir!" he said, with a respectful confidence which could not but please my uncle.

"You did not want to go home—did you?" he asked with a smile.

"I should have thrown myself out of the carriage!" answered John; "—that is, if they had got me into it. But, please, tell me, sir," he went on, "how it is I find myself in your house? I have been puzzling over it all the morning. I have no recollection of coming."

"You understand, I fancy," rejoined my uncle, "that one of the family has a notion she can take better care of you than anybody else! Is not that enough to account for it?"

"Hardly, sir. Belorba cannot have gone and rescued me from my mother!"

"How do you know that? Belorba is a terrible creature when she is roused. But you have talked enough. Shut your eyes, and don't trouble yourself to recollect. As you get stronger, it will all come back to you. Then you will be able to tell us, instead of asking us to tell you."

He left us together. I quieted John by reading to him, and absolutely declining to talk.

"You are a captive. The castle is enchanted: speak a single word," I said, "and you will find yourself in the dungeon of your own room."

He looked at me an instant, closed his eyes, and in a few minutes was fast asleep. He slept for two hours, and when he woke was quite himself. He was very weak, but the fever was gone, and we had now only to feed him up, and keep him quiet.

22
John Recalls and Remembers

What a weight was off my heart! It seemed as if nothing more could go wrong. But, though John was plainly happy, he was not quite comfortable: he worried himself with trying to remember how he had come to us. The last thing he could definitely recall before finding himself with us, was his mother looking at him through a night that seemed made of blackness so solid that he marvelled she could move in it. She brought him something to drink, but he fancied it blood, and would not touch it. He remembered now that there was a red tumbler in his room. He could recall nothing after, except a cold wind, and a sense of utter weariness but absolute compulsion: he must keep on and on till he found the gate of heaven, to which he seemed only for ever coming nearer. His conclusion was, that he knew what he was about every individual moment, but had no memory; each thing he did was immediately forgotten, while the knowledge of what he had to do next remained with him. It was, he thought, a mental condition analogous with walking, in which every step is a frustrated fall. I set this down here, because, when I told my uncle what John had been saying, myself not sure that I perceived what he meant, he declared the boy a philosopher of the finest grain. But he warned me not to encourage his talking, and especially not to ask him to explain. There was nothing, he said, worse for a weak brain, than to set a strong will to work it.

I tried to obey him, but it grew harder as the days went on. There were not many of them, however; he recovered rapidly. When at length my uncle talked not only to but with him, I regarded it as a virtual withdrawal of his prohibition, and after that spoke to John of whatever came into his or my head.

It was then he told me all he could remember since the moment he left me with his supper in his hand. A great part of his recollection was the vision of my uncle on the moor, and afterward in the park. We did not know what to make of it. I should at once have concluded it caused by prelusive illness, but for my remembrance of what both my uncle and myself had seen, so long before, in the thunderstorm; while John, willing enough to attribute its recurrence to that cause, found it impossible to concede that he was anything but well when crossing the moor. I thought, however, that excitement, fatigue, and lack of food, might have something to do with it, and with his illness too; while, if he was in a state to see anything phantasmal, what shape more likely to appear than that of my uncle!

He would not hear of my mentioning the thing to my uncle. I would for my own part have gone to him with it immediately; but could not with John's prayer in my ears. I resolved, however, to gain his consent if I could.

He had by this time as great a respect for my uncle as I had myself, but could not feel at home with him as I did. Whether the vision was only a vision, or indeed my uncle's double, whatever a double may be, the tale of it could hardly be an agreeable one to him; and naturally John shrank from the risk of causing him the least annoyance.

The question of course came up, what he was to do when able to leave us. He had spoken very plainly to my uncle concerning his relations with his mother—had told him indeed that he could not help suspecting he owed his illness to her.

I was nearly always present when they talked, but remember in especial a part of what passed on one occasion.

"I believe I understand my mother," said John, "—but only after much thinking. I loved her when a child; and if she had not left me for the sake of liberty and influence—that at least is how I account for her doing so—I might at this moment be struggling for personal freedom, instead of having that over."

"There are women," returned my uncle, "some of them of the most admired, who are slaves to a demoniacal love of power. The very pleasure of their consciousness consists in the knowledge that they have power—not power to do things, but power to make other people do things. It is an insanity, but a devilishly immoral and hateful insanity.—I do not say the lady in question is one of such, for I do not know her; I only say I have known such a one."

John replied that certainly the love of power was his mother's special weakness. She was spoiled when a child, he had been told; had her every wish regarded, her every whim respected. This ruinous treatment sprang, he said, from the self-same ambition, in another form, on the part of her mother—the longing, namely, to secure her child's supreme affection—with the natural consequence that they came to hate one another. His father and she had been married but

fifteen months, when he died of a fall, following the hounds. Within
six months she was engaged, but the engagement was broken off, and
she went abroad, leaving him behind her. She married lord Cairnedge
in Venice, and returned to England when John was nearly four, and
seemed to have lost all memory of her. His stepfather was good to
him, but died when he was about eight. His mother was very severe.
Her object plainly was to plant her authority so in his very nature,
that he should never think of disputing her will.

"But," said John, "she killed my love, and so I grew able to cast
off her yoke."

"The world would fare worse, I fancy," remarked my uncle, "if violent women bore patient children. The evil would become irremedi-
able. The children might not be ruined, but they would bring no dis-
cipline to the mother!"

"Her servants," continued John, "obey her implicitly, except when
they are sure she will never know. She treats them so imperiously,
that they admire her, and are proud to have such a mistress. But she
is convinced at last, I believe, that she will never get me to do as she
pleases; and therefore hates me so heartily, that she can hardly keep
her ladylike hands off me. I do not think I have been unreasonable; I
have not found it difficult to obey others that were set over me; but
when I found almost her every requirement part of a system for re-
ducing me to a slavish obedience, I began to lay down lines of my
own. I resolved to do at once whatever she asked me, whether pleasant to me or not, so long as I saw no reason why it should not be
done. Then I was surprised to find how seldom I had to make a stand
against her wishes. At the same time, the mode in which she conveyed
her pleasure, was invariably such as to make a pretty strong effort of
the will necessary for compliance with it. But the effort to overcome
the difficulty caused by her manner, helped to develop in me the
strength to resist where it was not right to yield. By far the most serious difference we had yet had, arose about six months ago, when she
insisted I should make myself agreeable to a certain lady, whom I by
no means disliked. She had planned our marriage, I believe, as one of
her parallels in the siege of the lady's noble father, then a widower of
a year. I told her I would not lay myself out to please any lady, except
I wanted to marry her. 'And why, pray, should you not marry her?'
she returned. I answered that I did not love her, and would not marry
until I saw the woman I could not be happy without, and she accepted
me. She went into a terrible passion, but I found myself quite un-
moved by it: it is a wonderful heartener to know yourself not merely
standing up for a right, but for the right to do the right thing! 'You
wouldn't surely have me marry a woman I didn't care a straw for!' I

said. 'Quench my soul!' she cried—I have often wondered where she learned the oath— 'what would that matter? She wouldn't care a straw for you in a month!'— 'Why should I marry her then?'— 'Because your mother wishes it,' she replied, and turned to march from the room as if that settled the thing. But I could not leave it so. The sooner she understood the better! 'Mother!' I cried, 'I will not marry the lady. I will not pay her the least attention that could be mistaken to mean the possibility of it.' She turned upon me. I have just respect enough left for her, not to say what her face suggested to me. She was pale as a corpse; her very lips were colourless; her eyes—but I will not go on. 'Your father all over!' she snarled—yes, snarled, with an inarticulate cry of fiercest loathing, and turned again and went. If I do not quite think my mother, *at present*, would murder me, I do think she would do anything short of murder to gain her ends with me. But do not be afraid; I am sufficiently afraid to be on my guard.

"My father was a rich man, and left my mother more than enough; there was no occasion for her to marry again, except she loved, and I am sure she did not love lord Cairnedge. I wish, for my sake, not for his, he were alive now. But the moment, I am one and twenty, I shall be my own master, and hope, sir, you will not count me unworthy to be the more Belorba's servant. One thing I am determined upon: my mother shall not cross my threshold but at my wife's invitation; and I shall never ask my wife to invite her. She is too dangerous.

"We had another altercation about Miss Miles, an hour or two before I first saw Orba. They were far from worthy feelings that possessed me up to the moment when I caught sight of her over the wall. It was a leap out of hell into paradise. The glimpse of such a face, without shadow of scheme or plan or selfish end, was salvation to me. I thank God!"

Perhaps I ought not to let those words about myself stand, but he said them.

He had talked too long. He fell back in his chair, and the tears began to gather in his eyes. My uncle rose, put his arm about me, and led me to the study.

"Let him rest a bit, little one," he said as we entered. "It is long since we had a good talk!"

He seated himself in his think-chair—a name which, when a child, I had given it, and I slid to the floor at his feet.

"I cannot help thinking, little one," he began, "that you are going to be a happy woman! I do believe that is a man to be trusted. As for the mother, there is no occasion to think of her, beyond being on your guard against her. You will have no trouble with her after you are married."

"I cannot help fearing she will do us a mischief, uncle," I returned.

"Sir Philip Sidney says— 'Since a man is bound no further to himself than to do wisely, chance is only to trouble them that stand upon chance.' That is, we are responsible only for our actions, not for their results. Trust first in God, then in John Day."

"I was sure you would like him, uncle!" I cried, with a flutter of loving triumph.

"I was nearly as sure myself—such confidence had I in the instinct of my little one. I think that I, of the two of us, may, in this instance, claim the greater faith!"

"You are always before me, uncle!" I said. "I only follow where you lead. But what do you think the woman will do next?"

"I don't think. It is no use. We shall hear of her before long. If all mothers were like her, the world would hardly be saved!"

"It would not be worth saving, uncle."

"Whatever can be saved, must be worth saving, my child."

"Yes, uncle; I shouldn't have said that," I replied.

23
Letter and Answer

We did hear of her before long. The next morning a letter was handed to my uncle as we sat at breakfast. He looked hard at the address, changed countenance, and frowned very dark, but I could not read the frown. Then his face cleared a little; he opened, read, and handed the letter to me.

Lady Cairnedge hoped Mr. Whichcote would excuse one who had so lately come to the neighbourhood, that, until an hour ago, she knew nothing of the position and character of the gentleman in whose house her son had, in a momentary, but, alas! not unusual aberration, sought shelter, and found generous hospitality. She apologized heartily for the unceremonious way in which she had sent for him. In her anxiety to have him home, if possible, before he should realize his awkward position in the house of a stranger, she had been inconsiderate! She left it to the judgment of his kind host whether she should herself come to fetch him, or send her carriage with the medical man who usually attended him. In either case her servants must accompany the carriage, as he would probably object to being removed. He might, however, be perfectly manageable, for he was, when himself, the gentlest creature in the world!

I was in a rage. I looked up, expecting to see my uncle as indignant with the diabolical woman as I was myself. But he seemed sunk in reverie, his body present, his spirit far away. A pang shot through my heart. Could the wicked device have told already?

"May I ask, uncle," I said, and tried hard to keep my voice steady, "how you mean to answer this vile epistle?"

He looked up with a wan smile, such as might have broke from Lazarus when he found himself again in his body.

"I will take it to the young man," he answered.

"Please, let us go at once then, uncle! I cannot sit still."

He rose, and we went together to John's room.

He was much better—sitting up in bed, and eating the breakfast Penny had carried him.

"I have just had a letter from your mother, Day," said my uncle.

"Indeed!" returned John dryly.

"Will you read it, and tell me what answer you would like me to return."

"Hardly like her usual writing—though there's her own strange S!" remarked John as he looked at it.

"Does she always make an S like that?" asked my uncle, with something peculiar in his tone, I thought.

"Always—like a snake just going to strike."

My uncle's face grew ghastly pale. He almost snatched the letter from John's hand, looked at it, gave it back to him, and, to our dismay, left the room.

"What can be the matter, John?" I said, my heart sinking within me.

"Go to him," said John.

I dared not. I had often seen him *like* that before walking out into the night; but there was something in his face now which I had not seen there before. It looked as if some terrible suspicion were suddenly confirmed.

"You see what my mother is after!" said John. "You have now to believe *her*, that I am subject to fits of insanity, or to believe *me*, that there is nothing she will not do to get her way."

"Her object is clear," I replied. "But if she thinks to fool my uncle, she will find herself mistaken!"

"She hopes to fool both you and your uncle," he rejoined. "The only wise thing I could do, she will handle so as to convince any expert of my madness—I mean, my coming to you! My reasons will go for nothing—less than nothing—with any one she chooses to bewitch. She will look at me with an anxious love no doctor could doubt. No one can know *you* do not know that I am not mad—or at least subject to attacks of madness!"

"Oh, John, don't frighten me!" I cried.

"There! you are not sure about it!"

It seemed cruel of him to tease me so; but I saw presently why he did it: he thought his mother's letter had waked a doubt in my uncle; and he wanted me not to be vexed with my uncle, even if he deserted him and went over to his mother's side.

"I love your uncle," he said. "I know he is a true man! I *will* not be angry with him if my mother do mislead him. The time will come when he will know the truth. It must appear at last! I shall have to fight her alone, that's all! The worst is, if he thinks with my mother I shall have to go at once!—If only somebody would sell my horse for me!"

I guessed that his mother kept him short of money, and remembered with gladness that I was not quite penniless at the moment.

"In the meantime, you must keep as quiet as you can, John," I said. "Where is the good of planning upon an *if*? To trust is to get ready, uncle says. Trust is better than foresight."

John required little such persuading. And indeed something very different was in my uncle's mind from what John feared.

Presently I caught a glimpse of him riding out of the yard. I ran to a window from which I could see the edge of the moor, and saw him cross it at an uphill gallop.

He was gone about four hours, and on his return went straight to his own room. Not until nine o'clock did I go to him, and then he came with me to supper.

He looked worn, but was kind and genial as usual. After supper he sent for Dick, and told him to ride to Rising, the first thing in the morning, with a letter he would find on the hall-table.

The letter he read to us before we parted for the night. It was all we could have wished. He wrote that he must not have any one in his house interfered with; so long as a man was his guest, he was his servant. Her ladyship had, however, a perfect right to see her son, and would be welcome; only the decision as to his going or remaining must rest with the young man himself. If he chose to accompany his mother, well and good! though he should be sorry to lose him. If he declined to return with her, he and his house continued at his service.

24
Hand to Hand

We looked for lady Cairnedge all the next day. John was up by
noon, and ready to receive her in the drawing-room; he would not
see her in his bedroom. But the hours passed, and she did not come.

In the evening, however, when the twilight was thickening, and
already all was dark in the alleys of the garden, her carriage drove
quietly up—with a startling scramble of arrest at the door. The same
servants were outside, and a very handsome dame within. As she descended, I saw that she was tall, and, if rather stout, not stouter than
suited her age and style. Her face was pale, but she seemed in perfect
health. When I saw her closer, I found her features the most regular I
had ever seen. Had the soul within it filled the mould of that face, it would
have been beautiful. As it was, it was only handsome—to me repulsive.
The moment I saw it, I knew myself in the presence of a masked battery.

My uncle had insisted that she should be received where we usually sat, and had given Penny orders to show her into the hall-kitchen.

I was alone there, preparing something for John. We were not expecting her, for it seemed now too late to look for her. My uncle was
in the study, and Martha somewhere about the house. My heart sank
as I turned from the window, and sank yet lower when she appeared
in the doorway of the kitchen. But as I advanced, I caught sight of my
uncle, and went boldly to meet the enemy. He had come down his
stair, and had just stepped into a clear blaze of light, which that moment
burst from the wood I had some time ago laid damp upon the fire.
The next instant I saw the lady's countenance ghastly with terror,
looking beyond me. I turned, but saw nothing, save that my uncle
had disappeared. When I faced her again, only a shadow of her fright
remained. I offered her my hand—for she was John's mother, but she
did not take it. She stood scanning me from head to foot.

"I am lady Cairnedge," she said. "Where is my son?"

I turned yet again. My uncle had not come back. I was not prepared to take his part. I was bewildered. A dead silence fell. For the

first time in my life, my uncle seemed to have deserted me, and at the
moment when most I needed him! I turned once more to the lady,
and said, hardly knowing what,

"You wish to see Mr. Day?"

She answered me with a cold stare.

"I will go and tell him you are here," I faltered; and passing her, I
sped along the passage to the drawing-room.

"John!" I cried, bursting in, "she's come! Do you still mean to see
her? Are you able? Uncle—"

There I stopped, for his eyes were stern, and not looking at me,
but at something behind me. One moment I thought his fever had
returned, but following his gaze I looked round:—there stood lady
Cairnedge! John was face to face with his mother, and my uncle was
not there to defend him!

"Are you ready?" she said, nor pretended greeting. She seemed
slightly discomposed, and in haste.

I was by this time well aware of my lover's determination of character, but I was not prepared for the tone in which he addressed the
icy woman calling herself his mother.

"I am ready to listen," he answered.

"John!" she returned, with mingled severity and sharpness, "let
us have no masquerading! You are perfectly fit to come home, and
you must come at once. The carriage is at the door."

"You are quite right, mother," answered John calmly; "I *am* fit to
go home with you. But Rising does not quite agree with me. I dread
such another attack, and do not mean to go."

The drawing-room had a rectangular bay-window, one of whose
three sides commanded the door. The opposite side looked into a little
grove of larches. Lady Cairnedge had already realized the position of
the room. She darted to the window, and saw her carriage but a few
yards away.

She would have thrown up the sash, but found she could not. She
twisted her handkerchief round her gloved hand, and dashed it
through a pane.

"Men!" she cried, in a loud, commanding voice, "come at once."

The moment she went to the window, I sprang to the door, locked
it, put the key in my pocket, and set my back to the door.

I heard the men thundering at the hall-door. Lady Cairnedge
turned as if she would herself go and open to them, but seeing me,
she understood what I had done, and went back to the window.

"Come here! Come to me here—to the window!" she cried.

John had been watching with a calm, determined look. He came
and stood between us.

"John," I said, "leave your mother to me."

"She will kill you!" he answered.

"You might kill her!" I replied.

I darted to the chimney, where a clear fire was burning, caught up the poker, and thrust it between the bars.

"That's for you!" I whispered. "They will not touch you with that in your hand! Never mind me. If your mother move hand or foot to help them, it will be my turn!"

He gave me a smile and a nod, and his eyes lightened. I saw that he trusted me, and I felt fearless as a bull-dog.

In the meantime, she had spoken to her servants, and was now trying to open the window, which had a peculiar catch. I saw that John could defend himself much better at the window than in the room. I went softly behind his mother, put my hands round her neck, and clasping them in front, pulled her backward with all my strength. We fell on the floor together, I under of course, but clutching as if all my soul were in my fingers. Neither should she meddle with John, nor should he lay hand on her! I did not mind much what I did to her myself.

"To the window, John," I cried, "and break their heads!"

He snatched the poker from the fire, and the next moment I heard a crashing of glass, but of course I could not see what was going on. Mine was no grand way of fighting, but what was dignity where John was in danger! For the moment I had the advantage, but, while determined to hold on to the last, I feared she would get the better of me, for she was much bigger and stronger, and crushed and kicked, and dug her elbows into me, struggling like a mad woman.

All at once the tug of her hands on mine ceased. She gave a great shriek, and I felt a shudder go through her. Then she lay still. I relaxed my hold cautiously, for I feared a trick. She did not move. Horror seized me; I thought I had killed her. I writhed from under her to see. As I did so, I caught sight of the pale face of my uncle, looking in at that part of the window next the larch-grove. Immediately I remembered lady Cairnedge's terror in the kitchen, and knew that the cause of it, and of her present cry, must be the same, to wit, the sight of my uncle. I had not hurt her! I was not yet on my feet when my uncle left the window, flew to the other side of it, and fell upon the men with a stick so furiously that he drove them to the carriage. The horses took fright, and went prancing about, rearing and jibbing. At the call of the coachman, two of the men flew to their heads. I saw no more of their assailant.

John, who had not got a fair blow at one of his besiegers, left the window, and came to me where I was trying to restore his mother.

The third man, the butler, came back to the window, put his hand through, undid the catch, and flung the sash wide. John caught up the poker from the floor, and darted to it.

"Set foot within the window, Parker," he cried, "and I will break your head."

The man did not believe he would hurt him, and put foot and head through the window.

Now John had honestly threatened, but to perform he found harder than he had thought: it is one thing to raise a poker, and another to strike a head with it. The window was narrow, and the whole man was not yet in the room, when John raised his weapon; but he could not bring the horrid poker down upon the dumb blind back of the stooping man's head. He threw it from him, and casting his eyes about, spied a huge family-bible on a side-table. He sprang to it, and caught it up—just in time. The man had got one foot firm on the floor, and was slowly drawing in the other, when down came the bible on his head, with all the force John could add to its weight. The butler tumbled senseless on the floor.

"Here, Orbie!" cried John; "help me to bundle him out before he comes to himself—Take what you would have!" he said, as between us we shoved him out on the gravel.

I fetched smelling-salts and brandy, and everything I could think of—fetched Martha too, and between us we got her on the sofa, but lady Cairnedge lay motionless. She breathed indeed, but did not open her eyes. John stood ready to do anything for her, but his countenance revealed little compassion. Whatever the cause of his mother's swoon—he had never seen her in one before—he was certain it had to do with some bad passage in her life. He said so to me that same evening. "But what could the sight of my uncle have to do with it?" I asked. "Probably he knows something, or she thinks he does," he answered.

"Wouldn't it be better to put her to bed, and send for the doctor, John?" I suggested at last.

Perhaps the sound of my voice calling her son by his Christian name, stung her proud ear, for the same moment she sat up, passed her hands over her eyes, and cast a scared gaze about the room.

"Where am I? Is it gone?" she murmured, looking ghastly.

No one answered her.

"Call Parker," she said, feebly, yet imperiously.

Still no one spoke.

She kept glancing sideways at the window, where nothing was to be seen but the gathering night. In a few moments she rose and walked straight from the room, erect, but white as a corpse. I followed, passed her, and opened the hall-door. There stood the carriage, waiting, as if nothing unusual had happened, Parker seated in the rumble, with one of the footmen beside him. The other man stood by the carriage-door. He opened it immediately; her ladyship stepped in, and dropped on the seat; the carriage rolled away.

I went back to John.

"I must leave you, darling!" he said. "I cannot subject you to the risk of such another outrage! I fear sometimes my mother may be what she would have you think me. I ought to have said, I hope she is. It would be the only possible excuse for her behaviour. The natural end of loving one's own way, is to go mad. If you don't get it, you go mad; if you do get it, you go madder—that's all the difference!—I must go!"

I tried to expostulate with him, but it was of no use.

"Where will you go?" I said. "You cannot go home!"

"I would at once," he answered, "if I could take the reins in my own hands. But I will go to London, and see the family-lawyer. He will tell me what I had better do."

"You have no money!" I said.

"How do you know that?" he returned with a smile. "Have you been searching my pockets?"

"John!" I cried.

He broke into a merry laugh.

"Your uncle will lend me a five-pound-note," he said.

"He will lend you as much as you want; but I don't think he's in the house," I answered. "I have two myself, though! I'll run and fetch them."

I bounded away to get the notes. It was like having a common purse already, to lend John ten pounds! But I had no intention of letting him leave the house the same day he was first out of his room after such an illness—that was, if I could help it.

My uncle had given me the use of a drawer in that same cabinet in which were the precious stones; and there, partly, I think, from the pride of sharing the cabinet with my uncle, I had long kept everything I counted precious: I should have kept Zoe there if she had not been alive and too big!

25
A Very Strange Thing

The moment I opened the door of the study, I saw my uncle—in his think-chair, his head against the back of it, his face turned to the ceiling. I ran to his side and dropped on my knees, thinking he was dead. He opened his eyes and looked at me, but with such a wan, woebegone countenance, that I burst into a passion of tears.

"What is it, uncle dear?" I gasped and sobbed.

"Nothing very new, little one," he answered.

"It is something terrible, uncle," I cried, "or you would not look like that! Did those horrid men hurt you? You did give it them well! You came down on them like the angel on the Assyrians!"

"I don't know what you're talking about, little one!" he returned. "What men?"

"The men that came with John's mother to carry him off. If it hadn't been for my beautiful uncle, they would have done it too! How I wondered what had become of you! I was almost in despair. I thought you had left us to ourselves—and you only waiting, like God, for the right moment!"

He sat up, and stared at me, bewildered.

"I had forgotten all about John!" he said.

"As to what you think I did, I know nothing about it. I haven't been out of this room since I saw—that spectre in the kitchen."

"John's mother, you mean, uncle?"

"Ah! she's John's mother, is she? Yes, I thought as much—and it was more than my poor brain could stand! It was too terrible!—My little one, this is death to you and me!"

My heart sank within me. One thought only went through my head—that, come what might, I would no more give up John, than if I were already married to him in the church.

"But why—what is it, uncle?" I said, hardly able to get the words out.

"I will tell you another time," he answered, and rising, went to the door.

"John is going to London," I said, following him.

"Is he?" he returned listlessly.

"He wants to see his lawyer, and try to get things on a footing of some sort between his mother and him."

"That is very proper," he replied, with his hand on the lock.

"But you don't think it would be safe for him to travel to-night—do you, uncle—so soon after his illness?" I asked.

"No, I cannot say I do. It would not be safe. He is welcome to stop till to-morrow."

"Will you not tell him so, uncle? He is bent on going!"

"I would rather not see him! There is no occasion. It will be a great relief to me when he is able—quite able, I mean—to go home to his mother—or where it may suit him best."

It was indeed like death to hear my uncle talk so differently about John. What had he done to be treated in this way—taken up and made a friend of, and then cast off without reason given! My dear uncle was not at all like himself! To say he forgot our trouble and danger, and never came near us in our sore peril, when we owed our deliverance to him! and now to speak like this concerning John! Something was terribly wrong with him! I dared hardly think what it could be.

I stood speechless.

My uncle opened the door, and went down the steps. The sound of his feet along the corridor and down the stair to the kitchen, died away in my ears. My life seemed to go ebbing with it. I was stranded on a desert shore, and he in whom I had trusted was leaving me there!

I came to myself a little, got the two five-pound-notes, and returned to John.

When I reached the door of the room, I found my heart in my throat, and my brains upside down. What was I to say to him? How could I let him go away so late? and how could I let him stay where his departure would be a relief? Even I would have him gone from where he was not wanted! I saw, however, that my uncle must not have John's death at his door—that I must persuade him to stay the night. I went in, and gave him the notes, but begged him, for my love, to go to bed. In the morning, I said, I would drive him to the station.

He yielded with difficulty—but with how little suspicion that all the time I wished him gone! I went to bed only to lie listening for my uncle's return. It was long past midnight ere he came.

In the morning I sent Penny to order the phaeton, and then ran to my uncle's room, in the hope he would want to see John before he left: I was not sure he had realized that he was going.

He was neither in his bed-room nor in the study. I went to the stable. Dick was putting the horse to the phaeton. He told me he had heard his master, two hours before, saddle Thanatos, and ride away. This made me yet more anxious about him. He did not often ride out early—seldom indeed after coming home late! Things seemed to threaten complication!

John looked so much better, and was so eager after the projected interview with his lawyer, that I felt comforted concerning him. I did not tell him what my uncle had said the night before. It would, I felt, be wrong to mention what my uncle might wish forgotten; and as I did not know what he meant, it could serve no end. We parted at the station very much as if we had been married half a century, and I returned home to brood over the strange things that had happened. But before long I found myself in a weltering swamp of futile speculation, and turned my thoughts perforce into other channels, lest I should lose the power of thinking, and be drowned in reverie: my uncle had taught me that reverie is Phaeton in the chariot of Apollo.

The weary hours passed, and my uncle did not come. I had never before been really uneasy at his longest absence; but now I was far more anxious about him than about John. Alas, through me fresh trouble had befallen my uncle as well as John! When the night came, I went to bed, for I was very tired: I must keep myself strong, for something unfriendly was on its way, and I must be able to meet it! I knew well I should not sleep until I heard the sounds of his arrival: those came about one o'clock, and in a moment I was dreaming.

In my dream I was still awake, and still watching for my uncle's return. I heard the sound of Death's hoofs, not on the stones of the yard, but on the gravel before the house, and coming round the house till under my window. There he stopped, and I heard my uncle call to me to come down: he wanted me. In my dream I was a child; I sprang out of bed, ran from the house on my bare feet, jumped into his downstretched arms, and was in a moment seated in front of him. Death gave a great plunge, and went off like the wind, cleared the gate in a flying stride, and rushed up the hill to the heath. The wind was blowing behind us furiously: I could hear it roaring, but did not feel it, for it could not overtake us; we out-stripped and kept ahead of it; if for a moment we slackened speed, it fell upon us raging.

We came at length to the pool near the heart of the heath, and I wondered that, at the speed we were making, we had been such a time in reaching it. It was the dismalest spot, with its crumbling peaty banks, and its water brown as tea. Tradition declared it had no bottom— went down into nowhere.

"Here," said my uncle, bringing his horse to a sudden halt, "we had a terrible battle once, Death and I, with the worm that lives in this hole. You know what worm it is, do you not?"

I had heard of the worm, and any time I happened, in galloping about the heath, to find myself near the pool, the thought would always come back with a fresh shudder—what if the legend were a true one, and the worm was down there biding his time! but anything more about the worm I had never heard.

"No, uncle," I answered; "I don't know what worm it is."

"Ah," he answered, with a sigh, "if you do not take the more care, little one, you will some day learn, not what the worm is called, but what it is! The worm that lives there, is the worm that never dies."

I gave a shriek; I had never heard of the horrible creature before—so it seemed in my dream. To think of its being so near us, and never dying, was too terrible.

"Don't be frightened, little one," he said, pressing me closer to his bosom. "Death and I killed it. Come with me to the other side, and you will see it lying there, stiff and stark."

"But, uncle," I said, "how can it be dead—how can you have killed it, if it never dies?"

"Ah, that is the mystery!" he returned.

"But come and see. It was a terrible fight. I never had such a fight—or dear old Death either. But she's dead now! It was worth living for, to make away with such a monster!"

We rode round the pool, cautiously because of the crumbling banks, to see the worm lie dead. On and on we rode. I began to think we must have ridden many times round the hole.

"I wonder where it can be, uncle!" I said at length.

"We shall come to it very soon," he answered.

"But," I said, "mayn't we have ridden past it without seeing it?"

He laughed a loud and terrible laugh.

"When once you have seen it, little one," he replied, "you too will laugh at the notion of having ridden past it without seeing it. The worm that never dies is hardly a thing to escape notice!"

We rode on and on. All at once my uncle threw up his hands, dropping the reins, and with a fearful cry covered his face.

"It is gone! I have not killed it! No, I have not! It is here! it is here!" he cried, pressing his hand to his heart. "It is here, and it was here all the time I thought it dead! What will become of me! I am lost, lost!"

At the word, old Death gave a scream, and laying himself out, flew with all the might of his swift limbs to get away from the place. But the wind, which was behind us as we came, now stormed in our faces; and presently I saw we should never reach home, for, with all Death's fierce endeavour, we moved but an inch or two in the minute, and that with a killing struggle.

"Little one," said my uncle, "if you don't get down we shall all be lost. I feel the worm rising. It is your weight that keeps poor Death from making any progress."

I turned my head, leaning past my uncle, so as to see behind him. A long neck, surmounted by a head of indescribable horror, was slowly rising straight up out of the middle of the pool. It should not catch them! I slid down by my uncle's leg. The moment I touched the ground and let go, away went Death, and in an instant was out of sight. I was not afraid. My heart was lifted up with the thought that I was going to die for my uncle and old Death. The red worm was on the bank. It was crawling toward me. I went to meet it. It sprang from the ground, threw itself upon me, and twisted itself about me. It was a human embrace, the embrace of some one unknown that loved me!

I awoke and left the dream. But the dream never left me.

26
The Evil Draws Nigher

I rose early, and went to my uncle's room. He was awake, but complained of headache. I took him a cup of tea, and at his request left him.

About noon Martha brought me a letter where I sat alone in the drawing-room. I carried it to my uncle. He took it with a trembling hand, read it, and fell back with his eyes closed. I ran for brandy.

"Don't be frightened, little one," he called after me. "I don't want anything."

"Won't you tell me what is the matter, uncle?" I said, returning. "Is it necessary I should be kept ignorant?"

"Not at all, my little one."

"Don't you think, uncle," I dared to continue, forgetting in my love all difference of years, "that, whatever it be that troubles us, it must be better those who love us should know it? Is there some good in a secret after all?"

"None, my darling," he answered. "The thing that made me talk to you so against secrets when you were a child, was, that I had one myself—one that was, and is, eating the heart out of me. But that woman shall not know and you be ignorant! I will not have a secret with *her!*—Leave me now, please, little one."

I rose at once.

"May I take the letter with me, uncle?" I asked.

He rubbed his forehead with a still trembling hand. The trembling of that beloved hand filled me with such a divine sense of pity, that for the first time I seemed to know God, causing in me that consciousness! The whole human mother was roused in me for my uncle. I would die, I would kill to save him! The worm was welcome to swallow me! My very being was a well of loving pity, pouring itself out over that trembling hand.

He took up the letter, gave it to me, and turned his face away with a groan. I left the room in strange exaltation—the exaltation of merest love.

I went to the study, and there read the hateful letter.

Here it is. Having transcribed it, I shall destroy it.

"Sir,—For one who persists in coming between a woman and her son, who will blame the mother if she cast aside forbearance! I would have spared you as hitherto; I will spare you no longer. You little thought when you crossed me who I was—the one in the world in whose power you lay! I would perish ever-lastingly rather than permit one of my blood to marry one of yours. My words are strong; you are welcome to call them unladylike; but you shall not doubt what I mean. You know perfectly that, if I denounce you as a murderer, I can prove what I say; and as to my silence for so many years, I am able thoroughly to account for it. I shall give you no further warning. You know where my son is: if he is not in my house within two days, I shall have you arrested. *I have made up my mind.*

"Lucretia Cairnedge.

"Rising-Manor, July 15, 18—."

"Whoever be the father, she's the mother of lies!" I exclaimed.—"My uncle—the best and gentlest of men, a murderer!"

I laughed aloud in my indignation and wrath.

But, though the woman was a liar, she must have something to say with a show of truth! How else would she dare intimidation with such a man? How else could her threat have so wrought upon my uncle? What did she know, or imagine she knew? What could be the something on which she founded her lie?—That my uncle was going to tell me, nor did I dread hearing his story. No revelation would lower him in my eyes! Of that I was confident. But I little thought how long it would be before it came, or what a terrible tale it would prove.

I ran down the stair with the vile paper in my hand.

"The wicked woman!" I cried. "If she *be* John's mother, I don't care: she's a devil and a liar!"

"Hush, hush, little one!" said my uncle, with a smile in which the sadness seemed to intensify the sweetness; "you do not *know* anything against her! You do not *know* she is a liar!"

"There are things, uncle, one knows without knowing!"

"What if I said she told no lie?"

"I should say she was a liar although she told no lie. My uncle is not what she threatens to say he is!"

"But men have repented, and grown so different you would not know them: how can you tell it has not been so with me? I may have been a bad man once, and grown better!"

"I know you are trying to prepare me for what you think will be a shock, uncle!" I answered; "but I want no preparing. Out with your worst! I defy you!"

Ah me, confident! But I had not to repent of my confidence!

My uncle gave a great sigh. He looked as if there was nothing for him now but tell all. Evidently he shrank from the task.

He put his hand over his eyes, and said slowly,—

"You belong to a world, little one, of which you know next to nothing. More than Satan have fallen as lightning from heaven!"

He lay silent so long that I was constrained to speak again.

"Well, uncle dear," I said, "are you not going to tell me?"

"I cannot," he answered.

There was absolute silence for, I should think, about twenty minutes. I could not and would not urge him to speak. What right had I to rouse a killing effort! He was not bound to tell *me* anything! But I mourned the impossibility of doing my best for him, poor as that best might be.

"Do not think, my darling," he said at last, and laid his hand on my head as I knelt beside him, "that I have the least difficulty in trusting you; it is only in telling you. I would trust you with my eternal soul. You can see well enough there is something terrible to tell, for would I not otherwise laugh to scorn the threat of that bad woman? No one on the earth has so little right to say what she knows of me. Yet I do share a secret with her which feels as if it would burst my heart. I wish it would. That would open the one way out of all my trouble. Believe me, little one, if any ever needed God, I need him. I need the pardon that goes hand in hand with righteous judgment, the pardon of him who alone can make lawful excuse."

"May God be your judge, uncle, and neither man nor woman!"

"I do not think *you* would altogether condemn me, little one, much as I loathe myself—terribly as I deserve condemnation."

"Condemn you, uncle! I want to know all, just to show you that nothing can make the least difference. If you were as bad as that bad woman says, you should find there was one of your own blood who knew what love meant. But I know you are good, uncle, whatever you may have done."

"Little one, you comfort me," sighed my uncle. "I cannot tell you this thing, for when I had told it, I should want to kill myself more than ever. But neither can I bear that you should not know it. I will *not* have a secret with that woman! I have always intended to tell you everything. I have the whole fearful story set down for your eyes— and those of any you may wish to see it: I cannot speak the words into your ears. The paper I will give you now; but you will not open it until I give you leave."

"Certainly not, uncle."

"If I should die before you have read it, I permit and desire you to read it. I know your loyalty so well, that I believe you would not look

at it even after my death, if I had not given you permission. There are
those who treat the dead as if they had no more rights of any kind.
'Get away to Hades,' they say; 'you are nothing now.' But you will not
behave so to your uncle, little one! When the time comes for you to
read my story, remember that I *now*, in preparation for the knowledge that will give you, ask you to pardon me *then* for all the pain it
will cause you and your husband—John being that husband. I have
tried to do my best for you, Orbie: how much better I might have done
had I had a clear conscience, God only knows. It may be that I was
the tenderer uncle that I could not be a better one."

He hid his face in his hands, and burst into a tempest of weeping.

It was terrible to see the man to whom I had all my life looked
with a reverence that prepared me for knowing the great father, weeping like a bitterly repentant and self-abhorrent child. It seemed sac-
rilege to be present. I felt as if my eyes, only for seeing him thus,
deserved the ravens to pick them out.

I could not contain myself. I rose and threw my arms about him,
got close to him as a child to her mother, and, as soon as the passion
of my love would let me, sobbed out,

"Uncle! darling uncle! I love you more than ever! I did not know
before that I could love so much! I could *kill* that woman with my
own hands! I wish I had killed her when I pulled her down that day!
It is right to kill poisonous creatures: she is worse than any snake!"

He smiled a sad little smile, and shook his head. Then first I
seemed to understand a little. A dull flash went through me.

I stood up, drew back, and gazed at him. My eyes fixed themselves
on his. I stared into them. He had ceased to weep, and lay regarding
me with calm response.

"You don't mean, uncle,—?"

"Yes, little one, I do. That woman was the cause of the action for
which she threatens to denounce me as a murderer. I do not say she
intended to bring it about; but none the less was she the consciously
wicked and wilful cause of it.—And you will marry her son, and be her
daughter!" he added, with a groan as of one in unutterable despair.

I sprang back from him. My very proximity was a pollution to him
while he believed such a thing of me!

"Never, uncle, never!" I cried. "How can you think so ill of one
who loves you as I do! I will denounce *her!* She will be hanged, and
we shall be at peace!"

"And John?" said my uncle.

"John must look after himself!" I answered fiercely. "Because he
chooses to have such a mother, am I to bring her a hair's-breadth
nearer to my uncle! Not for any man that ever was born! John must

discard his mother, or he and I are as we were! A mother! She is a hyena, a shark, a monster! Uncle, she is a *devil!*—I don't care! It is true; and what is true is the right thing to say. I will go to her, and tell her to her face what she is!"

I turned and made for the door. My heart felt as big as the biggest man's.

"If she kill you, little one," said my uncle quietly, "I shall be left with nobody to take care of me!"

I burst into fresh tears. I saw that I was a fool, and could do nothing.

"Poor John!—To have such a mother!" I sobbed. Then in a rage of rebellion I cried, "I don't believe she *is* his mother! Is it possible now, uncle—does it stand to reason, that such a pestilence of a woman should ever have borne such a child as my John? I don't, I can't, I won't believe it!"

"I am afraid there are mysteries in the world quite as hard to explain!" replied my uncle.

"I confess, if I had known who was his mother, I should have been far from ready to yield my consent to your engagement."

"What does it matter?" I said. "Of course I shall not marry him!"

"Not marry him, child!" returned my uncle. "What are you thinking of? Is the poor fellow to suffer for, as well as by the sins of his mother?"

"If you think, uncle, that I will bring you into any kind of relation with that horrible woman, if the worst of it were only that you would have to see her once because she was my husband's mother, you are mistaken. She to threaten you if you did not send back her son, as if John were a horse you had stolen! You have been the angel of God about me all the days of my life, but even to please you, I cannot consent to despise myself. Besides, you know what she threatens!"

"She shall not hurt me. I will take care of myself for your sakes. Your life shall not be clouded by scandal about your uncle."

"How are you to prevent it, uncle dear? Fulfil her threat or not, she would be sure to talk!"

"When she sees it can serve no purpose, she will hardly risk reprisals."

"She will certainly not risk them when she finds we have said good-bye."

"But how would that serve me, little one? What! would you heap on your uncle's conscience, already overburdened, the misery of keeping two lovely lovers apart? I will tell you what I have resolved upon. I will have no more secrets from you, Orba. Oh, how I thank you, dearest, for not casting me off!"

Again I threw myself on my knees by his bed.

"Uncle," I cried, my heart ready to break with the effort to show itself, "if I did not now love you more than ever, I should deserve to be cast out, and trodden under foot!—What do you think of doing?"

"I shall leave the country, not to return while the woman lives."

"I'm ready, uncle," I said, springing to my feet; "—at least I shall be in a few minutes!"

"But hear me out, little one," he rejoined, with a smile of genuine pleasure; "you don't know half my plan yet. How am I to live abroad, if my property go to rack and ruin? Listen, and don't say anything till I have done; I have no time to lose; I must get up at once.—As soon as I am on board at Dover for Paris, you and John must get yourselves married the first possible moment, and settle down here—to make the best of the farm you can, and send me what you can spare. I shall not want much, and John will have his own soon. I know you will be good to Martha!"

"John may take the farm if he will. It would be immeasurably better than living with his mother. For me, I am going with my uncle. Why, uncle, I should be miserable in John's very arms and you out of the country for our sakes! Is there to be nobody in the world but husbands, forsooth! I should love John ever so much more away with you and my duty, than if I had him with me, and you a wanderer. How happy I shall be, thinking of John, and taking care of you!"

He let me run on. When I stopped at length—

"In any case," he said with a smile, "we cannot do much till I am dressed!"

27
An Encounter

I left my uncle's room, and went to my own, to make what preparation I could for going abroad with him. I got out my biggest box,
and put in all my best things, and all the trifles I thought I could not
do without. Then, as there was room, I put in things I could do without, which yet would be useful. Still there was room; the content would
shake about on the continent! So I began to put in things I should
like to have, but which were neither necessary nor useful. Before I
had got these in, the box was more than full, and some of them had to
be taken out again. In choosing which were to go and which to be left,
I lost time; but I did not know anything about the trains, and expected
to be ready before my uncle, who would call me when he thought fit.

My thoughts also hindered my hands. Very likely I should never
marry John; I would not heed that; he would be mine all the same!
but to promise that I would not marry him, because it suited such a
mother's plans to marry him to some one else—that I would not do to
save my life! I would have done it to save my uncle's, but our exile
would render it unnecessary!

At last I was ready, and went to find my uncle, reproaching myself that I had been so long away from him. Besides, I ought to have
been helping him to pack, for neither he nor his arm was quite strong
yet. With a heartful of apology, I sought his room. He was not there.
Neither was he in the study. I went all over the house, and then to the
stable; but he was nowhere, neither had anyone seen him. And Death
was gone too!

The truth burst upon me: I was to see him no more while that
terrible woman lived! No one was to know whither he had gone! He
had given himself for my happiness! Vain intention! I should never
be happy! To be in Paradise without him, would not be to be in
Heaven!

John was in London; I could do nothing! I threw myself on my
uncle's bed, and lay lost in despair! Even if John were with me, and

we found him, what could we do? I knew it now as impossible for him
to separate us that he might be unmolested, as it was for us to accept
the sacrifice of his life that we might be happy. I knew that John's
way would be to leave everything and go with me and my uncle, only
we could not live upon nothing—least of all in a strange land! Martha,
to be sure, could manage well enough with the bailiff, but John could
not burden my uncle, and could not lay his hands on his own! In the
mean time my uncle was gone we knew not whither! I was like one
lost on the dark mountains.—If only John would come to take part in
my despair!

With a sudden agony, I reproached myself that I had made no attempt to overtake my uncle. It was true I did not know, for nobody
could tell me, in what direction he had gone; but Zoe's instinct might
have sufficed where mine was useless! Zoe might have followed and
found Thanatos! It was hopeless now!

But I could no longer be still. I got Zoe, and fled to the moor. All
the rest of the day I rode hither and thither, nor saw a single soul on
its wide expanse. The very life seemed to have gone out of it. When
most we take comfort in loneliness, it is because there is some one
behind it.

The sun was set and the twilight deepening toward night when I
turned to ride home. I had eaten nothing since breakfast, and though
not hungry, was thoroughly tired. Through the great dark hush, where
was no sound of water, though here and there, like lurking live thing,
it lay about me, I rode slowly back. My fasting and the dusk made
everything in turn take a shape that was not its own. I seemed to be
haunted by things unknown. I have sometimes thought whether the
spirits that love solitary places, may not delight in appropriating, for
embodiment momentary and partial, such a present shape as may
happen to fit one of their passing moods; whether it is always the
mere gnarled, crone-like hawthorn, or misshapen rock, that, between
the wanderer and the pale sky, suddenly appalls him with the sense
of *another*. The hawthorn, the rock, the dead pine, is indeed there,
but is it alone there?

Some such thought was, I remember, in my mind, when, about
halfway from home, I grew aware of something a little way in front
that rose between me and a dark part of the sky. It seemed a figure on
a huge horse. My first thought, very naturally, was of my uncle; the
next, of the great gray horse and his rider that John and I had both
seen on the moor. I confess to a little awe at the thought of the latter;
but I am somehow made so as to be capable of awe without terror,
and of the latter I felt nothing. The composite figure drew nearer: it
was a woman on horseback. Immediately I recalled the adventure of

my childhood; and then remembered that John had said his mother always rode the biggest horse she could find: could that shape, towering in the half-dark before me, be indeed my deadly enemy—she who, my uncle had warned me, would kill me if she had the chance? A fear far other than ghostly invaded me, and for a moment I hesitated whether to ride on, or turn and make for some covert, until she should have passed from between me and my home. I hope it was something better than pride that made me hold on my way. If the wicked, I thought, flee when no man pursueth, it ill becomes the righteous to flee before the wicked. By this time it was all but dark night, and I had a vague hope of passing unquestioned: there had been a good deal of rain, and we were in a very marshy part of the heath, so that I did not care to leave the track. But, just ere we met, the lady turned her great animal right across the way, and there made him stand.

"Ah," thought I, "what could Zoe do in a race with that terrible horse!"

He seemed made of the darkness, and rose like the figurehead of a frigate above a yacht.

"Show me the way to Rising," said his rider.

The hard bell-voice was unmistakable.

"When you come where the track forks," I began.

She interrupted me.

"How can I distinguish in the dark?" she returned angrily. "Go on before, and show me the way."

Now I had good reason for thinking she knew the way perfectly well; and still better reason for declining to go on in front of her.

"You must excuse me," I said, "for it is time I were at home; but if you will turn and ride on in front of me, I will show you a better, though rather longer way to Rising."

"Go on, or I will ride you down" she cried, turning her horse's head toward me, and making her whip hiss through the air.

The sound of it so startled Zoe, that she sprang aside, and was off the road a few yards before I could pull her up. Then I saw the woman urging her horse to follow. I knew the danger she was in, and, though tempted to be silent, called to her with a loud warning.

"Mind what you are doing, lady Cairnedge!" I cried. "The ground here will not carry the weight of a horse like yours."

But as I spoke he gave in, and sprang across the ditch at the wayside. There, however, he stood.

"You think to escape me," she answered, in a low, yet clear voice, with a cat-like growl in it. "You make a mistake!"

"Your ladyship will make a worse mistake if you follow me here," I replied.

Her only rejoinder was a cut with her whip to her horse, which had stood motionless since taking his unwilling jump. I spoke to Zoe; she bounded off like a fawn. I pulled her up, and looked back.

Lady Cairnedge continued urging her horse. I heard and saw her whipping him furiously. She had lost her temper.

I warned her once more, but she persisted.

"Then you must take the consequences!" I said; and Zoe and I made for the road, but at a point nearer home.

Had she not been in a passion, she would have seen that her better way was to return to the road, and intercept us; but her anger blinded her both to that and to the danger of the spot she was in.

We had not gone far when we heard behind us the soft plunging and sucking of the big hoofs through the boggy ground. I looked over my shoulder. There was the huge bulk, like Wordsworth's peak, towering betwixt us and the stars!

"Go, Zoe!" I shrieked.

She bounded away. The next moment, a cry came from the horse behind us, and I heard the woman say "Good God!" I stopped, and peered through the dark. I saw something, but it was no higher above the ground than myself. Terror seized me. I turned and rode back.

"My stupid animal has bogged himself!" said lady Cairnedge quietly.

Deep in the dark watery peat, as thick as porridge, her horse gave a fruitless plunge or two, and sank lower.

"For God's sake," I cried, "get off! Your weight is sinking the poor animal! You will smother him!"

"It will serve him right," she said venomously, and gave the helpless creature a cut across the ears.

"You will go down with him, if you do not make haste," I insisted.

Another moment and she stood erect on the back of the slowly sinking horse.

"Come and give me your hand," she cried.

"You want to smother me with him! I think I will not," I answered. "You can get on the solid well enough. I will ride home and bring help for your horse, poor fellow! Stay by him, talk to him, and keep him as quiet as you can. If he go on struggling, nothing will save him."

She replied with a contemptuous laugh.

I got to the road as quickly as possible, and galloped home as fast as Zoe could touch and lift. Ere I reached the stable-yard, I shouted so as to bring out all the men. When I told them a lady had her horse fast in the bog, they bustled and coiled ropes, put collars and chains on four draught-horses, lighted several lanterns, and set out with me. I knew the spot perfectly. No moment was lost either in getting ready, or in reaching the place.

Neither the lady nor her horse was to be seen.

A great horror wrapt me round. I felt a murderess. She might have failed to spring to the bank of the hole for lack of the hand she had asked me to reach out! Or her habit might have been entangled, so that she fell short, and went to the bottom—to be found, one day, hardly changed, by the side of her peat-embalmed steed!—no ill fitting fate for her, but a ghastly thing to have a hand in!

She might, however, be on her way to Rising on foot! I told two of the men to mount a pair of the horses, and go with me on the chance of rendering her assistance.

We took the way to Rising, and had gone about two miles, when we saw her, through the starlight, walking steadily along the track. I rode up to her, and offered her one of the cart-horses: I would not have trusted my Zoe with her any more than with an American lion that lives upon horses. She declined the proffer with quiet scorn. I offered her one or both men to see her home, but the way in which she refused their service, made them glad they had not to go with her. We had no choice, therefore turned and left her to get home as she might.

Not until we were on the way back, did it occur to me that I had not asked Martha whether she knew anything about my uncle's departure. She was never one to volunteer news, and, besides, would naturally think me in his confidence!

I found she knew nothing of our expedition, as no one had gone into the house—had only heard the horses and voices, and wondered. I was able to tell her what had happened; but the moment I began to question her as to any knowledge of my uncle's intentions, my strength gave way, and I burst into tears.

"Don't be silly, Belorba!" cried Martha, almost severely. "You an engaged young lady, and tied so to your uncle's apron-strings that you cry the minute he's out of your sight! You didn't cry when Mr. Day left you!"

"No," I answered; "he was going only for a day or two!"

"And for how many is your uncle gone?"

"That is what I want to know. He means to be away a long time, I fear."

"Then it's nothing but your fancy sets you crying!—But I'll just see!" she returned. "I shall know by the money he left for the house-keeping! Only I won't budge till I see you eat."

Faint for want of food, I had no appetite. But I began at once to eat, and she left me to fetch the money he had given her as he went.

She came back with a pocket-book, opened it, and looked into it. Then she looked at me. Her expression was of unmistakable dismay. I took the pocket-book from her hand: it was full of notes!

I learned afterward, that it was his habit to have money in the house, in readiness for some possible sudden need of it.

28
Another Vision

That same night, within an hour, to my unspeakable relief, John came home—at least he came to me, who he always said was his home. It was rather late, but we went out to the wilderness, where I had a good cry on his shoulder; after which I felt better, and hope began to show signs of life in me. I never asked him how he had got on in London, but told him all that had happened since he went. It was worse than painful to tell him about his mother's letter, and what my uncle told me in consequence of it, also my personal adventure with her so lately; but I felt I must hide nothing. If a man's mother is a devil, it is well he should know it.

He sat like a sleeping hurricane while I spoke, saying never a word. When I had ended,—

"Is that all?" he asked.

"It is all, John: is it not enough?" I answered.

"It is enough," he cried, with an oath that frightened me, and started to his feet. The hurricane was awake.

I threw my arms round him.

"Where are you going?" I said.

"To *her*" he answered.

"What for?"

"To *kill* her," he said—then threw himself on the ground, and lay motionless at my feet.

I kept silence. I thought with myself he was fighting the nature his mother had given him.

He lay still for about two minutes, then quietly rose.

"Good night, dearest!" he said; "—no; good-bye! It is not fit the son of such a mother should marry any honest woman."

"I beg your pardon, John!" I returned; "I hope *I* may have a word in the matter! If I choose to marry you, what right have you to draw back? Let us leave alone the thing that has to be, and remember that my uncle must not be denounced as a murderer! Something must be done. That he is beyond personal danger for the present is something; but is he to be the talk of the country?"

"No harm shall come to him," said John. "If I don't throttle the tigress, I'll muzzle her. I know how to deal with her. She has learned at least, that what her stupid son says, he does! I shall make her understand that, on her slightest movement to disgrace your uncle, I will marry you right off, come what may; and if she goes on, I shall get myself summoned for the defence, that, if I can say nothing for *him*, I may say something against *her*. Besides, I will tell her that, when my time comes, if I find anything amiss with her accounts, I will give her no quarter.— But, Orbie," he continued, "as I will not threaten what I may not be able to perform, you must promise not to prevent me from carrying it out."

"I promise," I said, "that, if it be necessary for your truth, I will marry you at once. I only hope she may not already have taken steps!"

"Her two days are not yet expired. I shall present myself in good time.—But I wonder you are not afraid to trust yourself alone with the son of such a mother!"

"To be what I know you, John," I answered, "and the son of that woman, shows a good angel was not far off at your birth. But why talk of angels? Whoever was your mother, God is your father!"

He made no reply beyond a loving pressure of my hand. Then he asked me whether I could lend him something to ride home upon. I told him there was an old horse the bailiff rode sometimes; I was very sorry he could not have Zoe: she had been out all day and was too tired! He said Zoe was much too precious for a hulking fellow like him to ride, but he would be glad of the old horse.

I went to the stable with him, and saw him mount. What a determined look there was on his face! He seemed quite a middle-aged man.

I have now to tell how he fared on the moor as he rode.

It had turned gusty and rather cold, and was still a dark night. The moon would be up by and by however, and giving light enough, he thought, before he came to the spot where his way parted company with that to Dumbleton. The moon, however, did not see fit to rise so soon as John expected her: he was not at that time quite *up* in moons, any more than in the paths across that moor.

Now as he had not an idea where his rider wanted to be carried, and as John did for a while—he confessed it—fall into a reverie or something worse, old Sturdy had to choose for himself where to go, and took a path he had often had to take some years before; nor did John discover that he was out of the way, until he felt him going steep clown, and thought of Sleipner bearing Hermod to the realm of Hela. But he let him keep on, wishing to know, as he said, what the old fellow was up to. Presently, he came to a dead halt.

John had not the least notion where they were, but I knew the spot the moment he began to describe it. By the removal of the peat on the side of a slope, the skeleton of the hill had been a little exposed, and had for a good many years been blasted for building-stones. Nothing was going on in the quarry at present. Above, it was rather a dangerous place; there was a legend of man and horse having fallen into it, and both being killed. John had never seen or heard of it.

When his horse stopped, he became aware of an indefinite sensation which inclined him to await the expected moon before attempting either to advance or return. He thought afterward it might have been some feeling of the stone about him, but at the time he took the place for an abrupt natural dip of the surface of the moor, in the bottom of which might be a pool. Sturdy stood as still as if he had been part of the quarry, stood as if never of himself would he move again.

The light slowly grew, or rather, the darkness slowly thinned. All at once John became aware that, some yards away from him, there was something whitish. A moment, and it began to move like a flitting mist through the darkness. The same instant Sturdy began to pull his feet from the ground, and move after the mist, which rose and rose until it came for a second or two between John and the sky: it was a big white horse, with my uncle on his back: Death and he, John concluded, were out on one of their dark wanderings! His impulse, of course, was to follow them. But, as they went up the steep way, Sturdy came down on his old knees, and John got off his back to let him recover himself the easier. When they reached the level, where the moon, showing a blunt horn above the horizon, made it possible to see a little, the white horse and his rider had disappeared—in some shadow, or behind some knoll, I fancy; and John, having not the least notion in what part of the moor he was, or in which direction he ought to go, threw the reins on the horse's neck. Sturdy brought him back almost to his stable, before he knew where he was. Then he turned into the road, for he had had enough of the moor, and took the long way home.

29
Mother and Son

In the morning he breakfasted alone. A son with a different sort of mother, might then have sought her in her bedroom; but John had never within his memory seen his mother in her bedroom, and after what lie had heard the night before, could hardly be inclined to go there to her now. Within half an hour, however, a message was brought him, requesting his presence in her ladyship's dressing-room.

He went with his teeth set.

"Whose horse is that in the stable, John?" she said, the moment their eyes met.

"Mr. Whichcote's, madam," answered John: *mother* he could not say.

"You intend to keep up your late relations with those persons?"

"I do."

"You mean to marry the hussy?"

"I mean to marry the lady to whom you give that epithet. There are those who think it not quite safe for you to call other people names!"

She rose and came at him as if she would strike him. John stood motionless. Except a woman had a knife in her hand, he said, he would not even avoid a blow from her. "A woman can't hurt you much; she can only break your heart!" he said. "My mother would not know a heart when she had broken it!" he added.

He stood and looked at her.

She turned away, and sat down again. I think she felt the term of her power at hand.

"The man told you then, that, if you did not return immediately, I would get him into trouble?"

"He has told me nothing. I have not seen him for some days. I have been to London."

"You should have contrived your story better: you contradict yourself."

"I am not aware that I do."

478

"You have the man's horse!"

"His horse is in my stable; he is not himself at home."

"Fled from justice! It shall not avail him!"

"It may avail you though, madam! It is sometimes prudent to let well alone. May I not suggest that a hostile attempt on your part, might lead to awkward revelations?"

"Ah, where could the seed of slander find fitter soil than the heart of a son with whom the prayer of his mother is powerless!"

To all appearance she had thoroughly regained her composure, and looked at him with a quite artistic reproach.

"The prayer of a mother that never prayed in her life!" returned John; "—of a woman that never had an anxiety but for herself!—I don't believe you are my mother. If I was born of you, there must have been some juggling with my soul in antenatal regions! I disown you!" cried John with indignation that grew as he gave it issue.

Her face turned ashy white; but whether it was from conscience or fear, or only with rage, who could tell!

She was silent for a moment. Then again recovering herself,—

"And what, pray, would you make of me?" she said coolly. "Your slave?"

"I would have you an honest woman! I would die for that!—Oh, mother! mother!" he cried bitterly.

"That being apparently impossible, what else does my dutiful son demand of his mother?"

"That she should leave me unmolested in my choice of a wife. It does not seem to me an unreasonable demand!"

"Nor does it seem to me an unreasonable reply, that any mother would object to her son's marrying a girl whose father she could throw into a felon's-prison with a word!"

"That the girl does not happen to be the daughter of the gentleman you mean, signifies nothing: I am very willing she should pass for such. But take care. He is ready to meet whatever you have to say. He is not gone for his own sake, but to be out of the way of our happiness—to prevent you from blasting us with a public scandal. If you proceed in your purpose, we shall marry at once, and make your scheme futile."

"How are you to live, pray?"

"Madam, that is my business," answered John.

"Are you aware of the penalty on your marrying without my consent?" pursued his mother.

"I am not. I do not believe there is any such penalty."

"You dare me?"

"I do."

"Marry, then, and take the consequences."

"If there were any, you would not thus warn me of them."

"John Day, you are no gentleman!"

"I shall not ask your definition of a gentleman, madam."

"Your father was a clown!"

"If my father were present, he would show himself a gentleman by making you no answer. If you say a word more against him, I will leave the room."

"I tell you your father was a clown and a fool—like yourself!"

John turned and went to the stable, had old Sturdy saddled, and came to me.

On his way over the heath, he spent an hour trying to find the place where he had been the night before, but without success. I presume that Sturdy, with his nose in that direction, preferred his stall, and did not choose to find the quarry. As often as John left him to himself, he went homeward. When John turned his head in another direction, he would set out in that direction, but gradually work round for the farm.

John told me all I have just set down, and then we talked.

"I have already begun to learn farming," I said.

"You are the right sort, Orbie!" returned John. "I shall be glad to teach you anything I know."

"If you will show me how a farmer keeps his books," I answered, "that I may understand the bailiff's, I shall be greatly obliged to you. As to the dairy, and poultry-yard, and that kind of thing, Martha can teach me as well as any."

"I'll do my best," said John.

"Come along then, and have a talk with Simmons! I feel as if I could bear anything after what you saw last night. My uncle is not far off! He is somewhere about with the rest of the angels!"

30
Once More, And Yet Again

From that hour I set myself to look after my uncle's affairs. It was the only way to endure his absence. Working for him, thinking what he would like, trying to carry it out, referring every perplexity to him and imagining his answer, he grew so much dearer to me, that his absence was filled with hope. My heart being in it, I had soon learned enough of the management to perceive where, in more than one quarter, improvement, generally in the way of saving, was possible: I do not mean by any lowering of wages; my uncle would have conned me small thanks for such improvement as that! Neither was it long before I began to delight in the feeling that I was in partnership with the powers of life; that I had to do with the operation and government and preservation of things created; that I was doing a work to which I was set by the Highest; that I was at least a floor sweeper in the house of God, a servant for the good of his world. Existence had grown fuller and richer; I had come, like a toad out of a rock, into a larger, therefore truer universe, in which I had work to do that was wanted. Had I not been thus expanded and strengthened, how should I have patiently waited while hearing nothing of my uncle!

It was not many days before John began to press me to let my uncle have his way: where was the good any longer, he said, in our not being married? But I could not endure the thought of being married without my uncle: it would not seem real marriage without his giving me to my husband. And when John was convinced that I could not be prevailed upon, I found him think the more of me because of my resolve, and my persistency in it. For John was always reasonable, and that is more than can be said of most men. Some, indeed, who are reasonable enough with men, are often unreasonable with women. If in course of time the management of affairs be taken from men and given to women—which may God for our sakes forbid—it will be because men have made it necessary by their arrogance. But when they have been kept down long enough to learn that they are not the lords of creation one bit more than the weakest woman, I hope they will be allowed to take the lead again, lest women should become what men were, and go strutting in their importance. Only the true man knows the true woman; only the true woman knows the true man: the difficulty between men and women comes all from the prevailing selfishness, that is, untruth, of both. Who, while such is their character, would be judge or divider between them, save one of their own kind? When such ceases to be their character, they will call for no umpire.

John lived in his own house with his mother, but they did not meet. His mother managed his affairs, to whose advantage I need hardly say; and John helped me to manage my uncle's, to the advantage of all concerned. Every morning he came to see me, and every night rode back to his worse than dreary home. At my earnest request, he had a strong bolt put on his bedroom-door, the use of which he promised me never to neglect. At my suggestion too, he let it be known that he had always a brace of loaded pistols within his reach, and showed himself well practiced in shooting with them. I feared much for John.

After I no longer only believed, but knew the bailiff trustworthy, and had got some few points in his management bettered, I ceased giving so much attention to details, and allowed myself more time to read and walk and ride with John. I laid myself out to make up to him, as much as ever I could, for the miserable lack of any home-life. At Rising he had not the least sense of comfort or even security. He could never tell what his mother might not be plotting against him. He had a very strong close box made for Leander, and always locked him up in it at night, never allowing one of the men there to touch him. The horse had all the attention any master could desire, when, having locked his box behind him, he brought him over to us in the morning.

One lovely, cold day, in the month of March, with ice on some of the pools, and the wind blowing from the north, I mounted Zoe to meet John midway on the moor, and had gone about two-thirds of the distance, when I saw him, as I thought, a long way to my right, and concluded he had not expected me so soon, and had gone exploring. I turned aside therefore to join him; but had gone only a few yards when, from some shift in a shadow, or some change in his position with regard to the light, I saw that the horse was not John's; it was a gray, or rather, a white horse. Could the rider be my uncle? Even at that distance I almost thought I recognized him. It must indeed have been he John saw at the quarry! He was not gone abroad! He had been all this long time lingering about the place, lest ill should befall us! "Just like him!" said my heart, as I gave Zoe the rein, and she sprang off at her best speed. But after riding some distance, I lost sight of the horseman, whoever he was, and then saw that, if I did not turn at once, I should not keep my appointment with John. Of course had I *believed* it was my uncle, I should have followed and followed; and the incident would not have been worth mentioning, for gray horses are not so uncommon that there might not be one upon the heath at any moment, but for something more I saw the same night.

It was bright moonlight. I had taken down a curtain of my window to mend, and the moon shone in so that I could not sleep. My thoughts were all with my uncle—wondering what he was about; whether he was very dull; whether he wanted me much; whether he was going about Paris, or haunting the moor that stretched far into the distance from where I lay. Perhaps at that moment he was out there in the moonlight, would be there alone, in the cold, wide night, while I slept! The thought made me feel lonely myself: one is indeed apt to feel lonely when sleepless; and as the moon was having a night of it, or rather making a day of it, all alone with herself, why should we not keep each other a little company? I rose, drew the other curtain of my window aside, and looked out.

I have said that the house lay on the slope of a hollow: from whichever window of it you glanced, you saw the line of your private horizon either close to you, or but a little way off. If you wanted an outlook, you must climb; and then you were on the moor.

From my window I could see the more distant edge of the hollow: looking thitherward, I saw against the sky the shape of a man on horseback. Not for a moment could I doubt it was my uncle. The figure was plainly his. My heart seemed to stand still with awe, or was it with intensity of gladness? Perhaps every night he was thus near me while I slept—a heavenly sentinel patrolling the house—the visible one of a whole camp unseen, of horses of fire and chariots of fire. So entrancing was the notion, that I stood there a little child, a mere incarnate love, the tears running down my checks for very bliss.

But presently my mood changed: what had befallen him? When first I saw him, horse and man were standing still, and I noted nothing strange, blinded perhaps by the tears of my gladness. But presently they moved on, keeping so to the horizon-line that it was plain my uncle's object was to have the house full in view; and as thus they skirted the edge of heaven, oh, how changed he seemed! His tall figure hung bent over the pommel, his neck drooped heavily. And the horse was so thin that I seemed to see, almost to feel his bones. Poor Thanatos! he looked tired to death, and I fancied his bent knees quivering, each short slow step he took. Ah, how unlike the happy old horse that had been! I thought of Death returning home weary from the

slaughter of many kings, and cast the thought away. I thought of Death
returning home on the eve of the great dawn, worn with his age-long
work, pleased that at last it was over, and no more need of him: I kept
that thought. Along the sky-line they held their slow way, toilsome
through weakness, the rider with weary swing in the saddle, the horse
with long gray neck hanging low to his hoofs, as if picking his path
with purblind eyes. When his rider should collapse and fall from his
back, not a step further would he take, but stand there till he fell to
pieces!

Fancy gave way to reality. I woke up, called myself hard names,
and hurried on a few of my clothes. My blessed uncle out in the night
and weary to dissolution, and I at a window, contemplating him like
a picture! I was an evil, heartless brute!

By the time I had my shoes on, and went again to the window, he
had passed out of its range. I ran to one on the stair that looked at
right angles to mine: he had not yet come within its field. I stood and
waited. Presently he appeared, crawling along, a gray mounted ghost,
in the light that so strangely befits lovers wandering in the May of
hope, and the wasted spectre no less, whose imagination of the past
reveals him to the eyes of men. For an instant I almost wished him
dead and at rest; the next I was out of the house—then up on the moor,
looking eagerly this way and that, poised on the swift feet of love,
ready to spring to his bosom. How I longed to lead him to his own
warm bed, and watch by him as he slept, while the great father kept
watch over every heart in his universe. I gazed and gazed, but nowhere could I see the death-jaded horseman.

I bounded down the hill, through the wilderness and the dark alleys, and hurried to the stable. Trembling with haste I led Zoe out,
sprang on her bare back, and darted off to scout the moor. Not a man
or a horse or a live thing was to be seen in any direction! Once more I
all but concluded I had looked on an apparition. Was my uncle dead?
Had he come back thus to let me know? And was he now gone home
indeed? Cold and disappointed, I returned to bed, full of the conviction that I had seen my uncle, but whether in the body or out of the
body, I could not tell.

When John came, the notion of my having been out alone on the
moor in the middle of the night, did not please him. He would have
me promise not again, for any vision or apparition whatever, to leave
the house without his company. But he could not persuade me. He
asked what I would have done, if, having overtaken the horseman, I
had found neither my uncle nor Death. I told him I would have given
Zoe the use of her heels, when *that* horse would soon have seen the
last of her. At the same time, he was inclined to believe with me, that

I had seen my uncle. His intended proximity would account, he said, for his making no arrangement to hear from me; and if he continued to haunt the moor in such fashion, we could not fail to encounter him before long. In the meantime he thought it well to show no sign of suspecting his neighbourhood.

That I had seen my uncle, John was for a moment convinced when, the very next day, having gone to Wittenage, he saw Thanatos carrying Dr. Southwell, my uncle's friend. On the other hand, Thanatos looked very much alive, and in lovely condition! The doctor would not confess to knowing anything about my uncle, and expressed wonder that he had not yet returned, but said he did not mind how long he had the loan of such a horse.

Things went on as before for a while.

John began again to press me to marry him. I think it was mainly, I am sure it was in part, that I might never again ride the midnight moor— "like a witch out on her own mischievous hook," as he had once said. He knew that, if I caught sight of anything like my uncle anywhere, John or no John, I would go after it.

There was another good reason, however, besides the absence of my uncle, for our not marrying: John was not yet of legal age, and who could tell what might not lurk in his mother's threat! Who could tell what such a woman might not have prevailed on her husband to set down in his will! I was ready enough to marry a poor man, but I was not ready to let my lover become a poor man by marrying me a few months sooner. Were we not happy enough, seeing each other everyday, and mostly all day long? No doubt people talked, but why not let them talk? The mind of the many is not the mind of God! As to society, John called it an oyster of a divinity. He argued, however, that probably my uncle was keeping close until he saw us married. I answered that, if we were married, his mother would only be the more eager to have her revenge on us all, and my uncle the more careful of himself for our sakes. Anyhow, I said, I would not consent to be happier than we were, until we found him. The greater happiness I would receive only from his hand.

31
My Uncle Comes Home

Time went on, and it was now the depth of a cold, miserable winter. I remember the day to which I have now come so well! It was a black day. There was such a thickness of snow in the air, that what light got through had a lost look. It was almost more like a London fog than an honest darkness of the atmosphere, bred in its own bounds. But while the light lasted, the snow did not fall. I went about the house doing what I could find to do, and wondering John did not come.

His horse had again fallen lame—this time through an accident which made it necessary for him to stay with the poor animal long after his usual time of starting to come to me. When he did start, it was on foot, with the short winter afternoon closing in. But he knew the moor by this time nearly as well as I did.

It was quite dark when he drew near the house, which he generally entered through the wilderness and the garden. The snow had begun at last, and was coming down in deliberate earnest. It would lie feet deep over the moor before the morning! He was thinking what a dreary tramp home it would be by the road—for the wind was threatening to wake, and in a snow-wind the moor was a place to be avoided—when he struck his foot against something soft, in the path his own feet had worn to the wilderness, and fell over it. A groan followed, and John rose with the miserable feeling of having hurt some creature. Dropping on his knees to discover what it was, he found a man almost covered with snow, and nearly insensible. He swept the snow off him, contrived to get him on his back, and brought him round to the door, for the fence would have been awkward to cross with him. Just as I began to be really uneasy at his prolonged absence, there he was, with a man on his back apparently lifeless!

I did not stop to stare or question, but made haste to help him. His burden was slipping sideways, so we lowered it on a chair, and then carried it between us into the kitchen, I holding the legs. The moment a ray of light fell upon the face, I saw it was my uncle.

I just saved myself from a scream. My heart stopped, then bumped as if it would break through. I turned sick and cold. We laid him on the sofa, but I still held on to the legs; I was half unconscious. Martha set me on a chair, and in a moment or two I came to myself, and was able to help her. She said never a word, but was quite collected, looking every now and then in the face of her cousin with a doglike devotion, but never stopping an instant to gaze. We got him some brandy first, then some hot milk, and then some soup. He took a little of everything we offered him. We did not ask him a single question, but, the moment he revived, carried him up the stair, and laid him in bed. Once he cast his eyes about, and gave a sigh as of relief to find himself in his own room, then went off into a light doze, which, broken with starts and half-wakings, lasted until next day about noon. Either John or Martha or I was by his bedside all the time, so that he should not wake without seeing one of us near him.

But the sad thing was, that, when he did wake, he did not seem to come to himself. He never spoke, but just lay and looked out of his eyes, if indeed it was more than his eyes that looked, if indeed *he* looked out of them at all!

"He has overdone his strength!" we said to each other. "He has not been taking care of himself!—And then to have lain perhaps hours in the snow! It's a wonder he's alive!"

"He's nothing but skin and bone!" said Martha. "It will take weeks to get him up again!—And just look at his clothes! How ever did he come nigh such! They're fit only for a beggar! They must have knocked him down and stripped him!—Look at his poor boots!" she said pitifully, taking up one of them, and stroking it with her hand. "He'll never recover it!"

"He will," I said. "Here are three of us to give him of our life! He'll soon be himself again, now that we have him!"

But my heart was like to break at the sad sight. I cannot put in words what I felt.

"He would get well much quicker," said John, "if only we could tell him we were married!"

"It will do just as well to invite him to the wedding," I answered.

"I do hope he will give you away," said Martha.

"He will never give me away," I returned; "but he will give me to John. And I will not have the wedding until he is able to do that."

"You are right," said John. "And we mustn't ask him anything, or even refer to anything, till he wants to hear."

Days went and came, and still he did not seem to know quite where he was; if he did know, he seemed so content with knowing it, that he did not want to know anything more in heaven or earth. We grew very anxious about him. He did not heed a word that Dr. Southwell said. His mind seemed as exhausted as his body. The doctor justified John's resolve, saying he must not be troubled with questions, or the least attempt to rouse his memory.

John was now almost constantly with us. One day I asked him whether his mother took any notice of his being now so seldom home at night. He answered she did not; and, but for being up to her ways, he would imagine she knew nothing at all about his doings.

"What does she do herself all day long?" I asked.

"Goes over her books, I imagine," he answered. "She knows the hour is at hand when she must render account of her stewardship, and I suppose she is getting ready to meet it;—how, I would rather not conjecture. She gives me no trouble now, and I have no wish to trouble her."

"Have you no hope of ever being on filial terms with her again?" I said.

"There can be few things more unlikely," he replied.

I was a little troubled, notwithstanding my knowledge of her and my feeling toward her, that he should regard a complete alienation from his mother with such indifference. I could not, however, balance the account between them! If she had a strong claim in the sole fact that she was his mother, how much had she not injured him simply by not being lovable! Love unpaid is the worst possible debt; and to make it impossible to pay it, is the worst of wrongs.

But, oh, what a heart-oppression it was, that my uncle had returned so different! We were glad to have him, but how gladly would we not have let him go again to restore him to himself, even were it never more to rest our eyes upon him in this world! Dearly as I loved John, it seemed as if nothing could make me happy while my uncle remained as he was. It was a kind of cold despair to know him such impassable miles from me. I could not get near him! I went about all day with a sense—not merely of loss, but of a loss that gnawed at me with a sickening pain. He never spoke. He never said *little one* to me now! he never looked in my eyes as if he loved me! He was very gentle, never complained, never even frowned, but lay there with a dead question in his eyes. We feared his mind was utterly gone.

By degrees his health returned, but apparently neither his memory, nor his interest in life. Yet he had a far-away look in his eyes, as if he remembered something, and started and turned at every opening of the door, as if he expected something. He took to wandering about the yard and the stable and the cow-house; would gaze for an hour at some animal in its stall; would watch the men threshing the corn, or twisting straw-ropes. When Dr. Southwell sent back his

horse, it was in great hope that the sight of Death would wake him
up; that he would recognize his old companion, jump on his back,
and be well again; but my uncle only looked at him with a faint admiration, went round him and examined him as if he were a horse he
thought of buying, then turned away and left him. Death was troubled
at his treatment of him. He on his part showed him all the old attention, using every equine blandishment he knew; but having met with
no response, he too turned slowly away, and walked to his stable, Dr.
Southwell would gladly have bought him, but neither John nor I would
hear of parting with him: he was almost a portion of his master! My
uncle might come to himself any moment: how could we look him in
the face if Death was gone from us! Besides, we loved the horse for
his own sake as well as my uncle's, and John would be but too glad to
ride him!

My uncle would wander over the house, up and down, but seemed
to prefer the little drawing-room: I made it my special business to
keep a good fire there. He never went to the study; never opened the
door in the chimney-corner. He very seldom spoke, and seldomer to
me than to any other. It *was* a dreary time! Our very souls had longed
for him back, and thus he came to us!

Sorely I wept over the change that had passed upon the good man.
He must have received some terrible shock! It was just as if his mother,
John said, had got hold of him, and put a knife in his heart! It was
well, however, that he was not wandering about the heath, exposed
to the elements! and there was yet time for many a good thing to come!
Where one *must* wait, one *can* wait.

John had to learn this, for, say what he would, the idea of marrying while my uncle remained in such plight, was to me unendurable.

32
Twice Two is One

The spring came, but brought little change in the condition of my uncle. In the month of May, Dr. Southwell advised our taking him abroad. When we proposed it to him, he passed his hand wearily over his forehead, as if he felt something wrong there, and gave us no reply. We made our preparations, and when the day arrived, he did not object to go.

We were an odd party: John and I, bachelor and spinster; my uncle, a silent, moody man, who did whatever we asked him; and the still, open-eyed Martha Moon, who, I sometimes think, understood more about it all than any of us. I could talk a little French, John a good deal of German. When we got to Paris, we found my uncle considerably at home there. When he cared to speak, he spoke like a native, and was never at a loss for word or phrase.

It was he, indeed, who took us to a quiet little hotel he knew; and when we were comfortably settled in it, he began to take the lead in all our plans. By degrees he assumed the care and guidance of the whole party; and so well did he carry out what he had silently, perhaps almost unconsciously undertaken, that we conceived the greatest hopes of the result to himself. A mind might lie quiescent so long as it was ministered to, and hedged from cares and duties, but wake up when something was required of it! No one would have thought anything amiss with my uncle, that heard him giving his orders for the day, or acting cicerone to the little company—there for his sake, though he did not know it. How often John and I looked at each other, and how glad were our hearts! My uncle was fast coming to himself! It was like watching the dead grow alive.

One day he proposed taking a carriage and a good pair of horses, and driving to Versailles to see the palace. We agreed, and all went well. I had not, in my wildest dreams, imagined a place so grand and beautiful. We wandered about it for hours, and were just tired enough to begin thinking with pleasure of the start homeward, when we found ourselves in a very long, straight corridor. I was walking alone, a little ahead of the rest; my uncle was coming along next, but a good way behind me; a few paces behind my uncle, came John with Martha, to whom he was more scrupulously attentive than to myself.

In front of me was a door, dividing the corridor in two, apparently filled with plain plate-glass, to break the draught without obscuring the effect of the great length of the corridor, which stretched away as far on the other side as we had come on this. I paused and stood aside, leaning against the wall to wait for my uncle, and gazing listlessly out of a window opposite me. But as my uncle came nearer to open the door for us, I happened to cast my eyes again upon it, and saw, as it seemed, my uncle coming in the opposite direction; whence I concluded of course, that I had made a mistake, and that what I had taken for a clear plate of glass, was a mirror, reflecting the corridor behind me. I looked back at my uncle with a little anxiety. My reader may remember that, when he came to fetch me from Rising, the day after I was lost on the moor, encountering a mirror at unawares, he started and nearly fell: from this occurrence, and from the absence of mirrors about the house, I had imagined in his life some painful story connected with a mirror.

Once again I saw him start, and then stand like stone. Almost immediately a marvellous light overspread his countenance, and with a cry he bounded forward. I looked again at the mirror, and there I saw the self-same light-irradiated countenance coming straight, as was natural, to meet that of which it was the reflection. Then all at once the solid foundations of fact seemed to melt into vaporous dream, for as I saw the two figures come together, the one in the mirror, the other in the world, and was starting forward to prevent my uncle from shattering the mirror and wounding himself, the figures fell into each other's arms, and I heard two voices weeping and sobbing, as the substance and the shadow embraced.

Two men had for a moment been deceived like myself: neither glass nor mirror was there—only the frame from which a swing-door had been removed. They walked each into the arms of the other, whom they had at first each taken for himself.

They paused in their weeping, held each other at arm's-length, and gazed as in mute appeal for yet better assurance; then, smiling like two suns from opposing rain-clouds, fell again each on the other's neck, and wept anew. Neither had killed the other! Neither had lost the other! The world had been a graveyard; it was a paradise!

We stood aside in reverence. Martha Moon's eyes glowed, but she manifested no surprise. John and I stared in utter bewilderment. The two embraced each other, kissed and hugged and patted each other, wept and murmured and laughed, then all at once, with one great sigh between them, grew aware of witnesses. They were too happy to blush, yet indeed they could not have blushed, so red were they with the fire of heaven's own delight. Utterly unembarrassed they turned toward us—and then came a fresh astonishment, an old and new joy together out of the treasure of the divine house-holder: the uncle of the mirror, radiant with a joy such as I had never before beheld upon human countenance, came straight to me, cried; "Ah, little one!" took me in his arms, and embraced me with all the old tenderness. Then I knew that my own old uncle was the same as ever I had known him, the same as when I used to go to sleep in his arms.

The jubilation that followed, it is impossible for me to describe; and my husband, who approves of all I have yet written, begs me not to attempt an adumbration of it.

"It would be a pity," he says, "to end a won race with a tumble down at the post!"

33

Half One is One

I am going to give you the whole story, but not this moment; I want to talk a little first. I need not say that I had twin uncles. They were but one man to the world; to themselves only were they a veritable two. The word *twin* means one of two that once were one. To *twin* means to *divide*, they tell me. The opposite action is, of *twain* to make one. To me as well as the world, I believe, but for the close individual contact of all my life with my uncle Edward, the two would have been but as one man. I hardly know that I felt any richer at first for having two uncles; it was long before I should have felt much poorer for the loss of uncle Edmund. Uncle Edward was to me the substance of which uncle Edmund was the shadow. But at length I learned to love him dearly through perceiving how dearly my own uncle loved him. I loved the one because he was what he was, the other because he was not that one. Creative Love commonly differentiates that it may unite; in the case of my uncles it seemed only to have divided that it might unite. I am hardly intelligible to myself; in my mind at least I have got into a bog of confused metaphysics, out of which it is time I scrambled. What I would say is this—that what made the world not care there should be two of them, made the earth a heaven to those two. By their not being one, they were able to love, and so were one. Like twin planets they revolved around each other, and in a common orbit around God their sun. It was a beautiful thing to see how uncle Edmund revived and expanded in the light of his brother's presence, until he grew plainly himself. He had suffered more than my own uncle, and had not had an orphan child to love and be loved by.

What a drive home that was! Paris, anywhere seemed home now! I had John and my uncles; John had me and my uncle; my uncles had each other; and I suspect, if we could have looked into Martha, we should have seen that she, through her lovely unselfishness, possessed us all more than any one of us another. Oh the outbursts of gladness on the way!—the talks!—the silences! The past fell off like an ugly veil from the true face of things; the present was sunshine; the future a rosy cloud.

When we reached our hotel, it was dinner-time, and John ordered champagne. He and I were hungry as two happy children; the brothers ate little, and scarcely drank. They were too full of each other to have room for any animal need. A strange solemnity crowned and dominated their gladness. Each was to the other a Lazarus given back from the grave. But to understand the depth of their rapture, you must know their story. That of Martha and Mary and Lazarus could not have equalled it but for the presence of the Master, for neither sisters nor brother had done each other any wrong. They looked to me like men walking in a luminous mist—a mist of unspeakable suffering radiant with a joy as unspeakable—the very stuff to fashion into glorious dreams.

When we drew round the fire, for the evenings were chilly, they laid their whole history open to us. What a tale it was! and what a telling of it! My own uncle, Edward, was the principal narrator, but was occasionally helped out by my newer uncle, Edmund. I had the story already, my reader will remember, in my uncle's writing, at home: when we returned I read it—not with the same absorption as if it had come first, but with as much interest, and certainly with the more thorough comprehension that I had listened to it before. That same written story I shall presently give, supplemented by what, necessarily, my uncle Edmund had to supply, and with some elucidation from the spoken narrative of my uncle Edward.

As the story proceeded, overcome with the horror of the revelation I foresaw, I forgot myself, and cried out—

"And that woman is John's mother!"

"Whose mother?" asked uncle Edmund, with scornful curiosity.

"John Day's," I answered.

"It cannot be!" he cried, blazing up. "Are you sure of it?"

"I have always been given so to understand," replied John for me; "but I am by no means sure of it. I have doubted it a thousand times."

"No wonder! Then we may go on! But, indeed, to believe you her son, would be to doubt you! I *don't* believe it."

"You could not help doubting me!" responded John. "—I might be true, though, even if I were her son!" he added.

"Ed," said Edmund to Edward, "let us lay our heads together!"

"Ready Ed!" said Edward to Edmund.

Thereupon they began comparing memories and recollections,—to find, however, that they had by no means data enough. One thing was clear to me—that nothing would be too bad for them to believe of her.

"She would pick out the eye of a corpse if she thought a sovereign lay behind it!" said uncle Edmund.

"To have the turning over of his rents,—" said uncle Edward, and checked himself.

"Yes—it would be just one of her devil-tricks!" agreed uncle Edmund.

"I beg your pardon, John," said uncle Edward, as if it were he that had used the phrase, and uncle Edmund nodded to John, as if he had himself made the apology.

John said nothing. His eyes looked wild with hope. He felt like one who, having been taught that he is a child of the devil, begins to know that God is his father—the one discovery worth making by son of man.

Then, at my request, they went on with their story, which I had interrupted.

When it was at length all poured out, and the last drops shaken from the memory of each, there fell a long silence, which my own uncle broke.

"When shall we start, Ed?" he said.

"To-morrow, Ed."

"This business of John's must come first, Ed!"

"It shall, Ed!"

"You know where you were born, John?"

"On my father's estate of Rubworth in Gloucestershire, I *believe*," answered John.

"You must be prepared for the worst, you know!"

"I am prepared. As Orba told me once, God is my father, whoever my mother may be!"

"That's right. Hold by that!" said my uncles, as with one breath.

"Do you know the year you were born?" asked uncle Edmund.

"My *mother* says I was born in 1820."

"You have not seen the entry?"

"No. One does not naturally doubt such statements."

"Assuredly not—until—" He paused.

How uncle Edmund had regained his wits! And how young the brothers looked!

"You mean," said John, "until he has known my mother!"

Now for the story of my twin uncles, mainly as written by my uncle Edward!

34
The Story of My Twin Uncles

"My brother and I were marvellously like. Very few of our friends, none of them with certainty, could name either of us apart—or even together. Only two persons knew absolutely which either of us was, and those two were ourselves. Our mother certainly did not—at least without seeing one or other of our backs. Even we ourselves have each made the blunder occasionally of calling the other by the wrong name. Our indistinguishableness was the source of ever-recurring mistake, of constant amusement, of frequent bewilderment, and sometimes of annoyance in the family. I once heard my father say to a friend, that God had never made two things alike, except his twins. We two enjoyed the fun of it so much, that we did our best to increase the confusions resulting from our resemblance. We did not lie, but we dodged and pretended, questioned and looked mysterious, till I verily believe the person concerned, having in himself so vague an idea of our individuality, not unfrequently forgot which he had blamed, or which he had wanted, and became hopelessly muddled.

"A man might well have started the question what good could lie in the existence of a duality in which the appearance was, if not exactly, yet so nearly identical, that no one but my brother or myself could have pointed out definite differences; but it could have been started only by an outsider: my brother and I had no doubt concerning the advantage of a duality in which each was the other's double; the fact was to us a never ceasing source of delight. Each seemed to the other created such, expressly that he might love him as a special, individual property of his own. It was as if the image of Narcissus had risen bodily out of the watery mirror, to be what it had before but seemed. It was as if we had been made two, that each might love himself, and yet not be selfish.

"We were almost always together, but sometimes we got into individual scrapes, when—which will appear to some incredible—the one accused always accepted punishment without denial or subterfuge or attempt to perplex: it was all one which was the culprit, and which should be the sufferer. Nor did this indistinction work badly: that the other was just as likely to suffer as the doer of the wrong, wrought rather as a deterrent. The mode of behaviour may have had its origin in the instinctive perception of the impossibility of proving innocence; but had we, loving as we did, been capable of truthfully accusing each other, I think we should have been capable of lying also. The delight of existence lay, embodied and objective to each, in the existence of the other.

"At school we learned the same things, and only long after did any differences in taste begin to develop themselves.

"Our brother, elder by five years, who would succeed to the property, had the education my father thought would best fit him for the management of land. We twins were trained to be lawyer and doctor—I the doctor.

"We went to college together, and shared the same rooms.

"Having finished our separate courses, our father sent us to a German university: he would not have us insular!

"There we did not work hard, nor was hard work required of us. We went out a good deal in the evenings, for the students that lived at home in the town were hospitable. We seemed to be rather popular, owing probably to our singular likeness, which we found was regarded as a serious disadvantage. The reason of this opinion we never could find, flattering ourselves indeed that what it typified gave us each double the base and double the strength.

"We had all our friends in common. Every friend to one of us was a friend to both. If one met man or woman he was pleased with, he never rested until the other knew that man or woman also. Our delight in our friends must have been greater than that of other men, because of the constant sharing.

"Our all but identity of form, our inseparability, our unanimity, and our mutual devotion, were often, although we did not know it, a subject of talk in the social gatherings of the place. It was more than once or twice openly mooted—what, in the chances of life, would be likeliest to strain the bond that united us. Not a few agreed that a terrible catastrophe might almost be expected from what they considered such an unnatural relation.

"I think you must already be able to foresee from what the first difference between us would arise: discord itself was rooted in the very unison—for unison it was, not harmony—of our tastes and instincts; and will now begin to understand why it was so difficult, indeed impossible for me, not to have a secret from my little one.

"Among the persons we met in the home-circles of our fellow-students, appeared by and by an English lady—a young widow, they said, though little in her dress or carriage suggested widowhood. We met her again and again. Each thought her the most beautiful woman he had ever seen, but neither was much interested in her at first. Nor do I believe either would, of himself, ever have been. Our likings and dislikings always hitherto had gone together, and, left to themselves, would have done so always, I believe; whence it seems probable that, left to ourselves, we should also have found, when required, a common strength of abnegation. But in the present case, our feelings were not left to themselves; the lady gave the initiative, and the dividing regard was born in the one, and had time to establish itself, ere the provoking influence was brought to bear on the other.

"Within the last few years I have had a visit from an old companion of the period. I daresay you will remember the German gentleman who amused you with the funny way in which he pronounced certain words—one of the truest-hearted and truest-tongued men I have ever known: he gave me much unexpected insight into the evil affair. He had learned certain things from a sister, the knowledge of which, old as the story they concerned by that time was, chiefly moved his coming to England to find me.

"One evening, he told me, when a number of the ladies we were in the habit of meeting happened to be together without any gentleman present, the talk turned, half in a philosophical, half in a gossipy spirit, upon the consequences that might follow, should two men, bound in such strange fashion as my brother and I, fall in love with the same woman—a thing not merely possible, but to be expected. The talk, my friend said, was full of a certain speculative sort of metaphysics which, in the present state of human development, is far from healthy, both because of our incompleteness, and because we are too near to what we seem to know, to judge it aright. One lady was present—a lady by us more admired and trusted than any of the rest—who alone declared a conviction that love of no woman would ever separate us, provided the one fell in love first, and the other knew the fact before he saw the lady. For, she said, no jealousy would in that case be roused; and the relation of the brother to his brother and sister would be so close as to satisfy his heart. In a few days probably he too would fall in love, and his lady in like manner be received by his brother, when they would form a square impregnable to attack. The theory was a good one, and worthy of realization. But, alas, the Prince of the Power of the Air was already present in force, in the heart of the English widow! Young in years, but old in pride and self-confidence, she smiled at the notion of our advocate. She said that the idea of any such friendship between men was nonsense; that she knew more about men than some present could be expected to know: their love was but a matter of custom and use; the moment self took part in the play, it would burst; it was but a bubble-company! As for love proper—she meant the love between man and woman—its law was the opposite to that of friendship; its birth and continuance depended on the parties *not* getting accustomed to each other; the less they knew each other, the more they would love each other.

"Upon this followed much confused talk, during which the English lady declared nothing easier than to prove friendship, or the love of brothers, the kind of thing she had said.

"Most of the company believed the young widow but talking to show off; while not a few felt that they desired no nearer acquaintance with one whose words, whatever might be her thoughts, degraded humanity. The circle was very speedily broken into two segments, one that liked the English lady, and one that almost hated her.

"From that moment, the English widow set before her the devil-victory of alienating two hearts that loved each other—and she gained it for a time—until Death proved stronger than the Devil. People said we could not be parted: *she* would part us! She began with my brother. To tell how I know that she began with him, I should have to tell how she began with me, and that I cannot do; for, little one, I dare not let the tale of the treacheries of a bad woman toward an unsuspecting youth, enter your ears. Suffice it to say, such a woman has well studied those regions of a man's nature into which, being less divine, the devil in her can easier find entrance. There, she knows him better than he knows himself; and makes use of her knowledge, not to elevate, but to degrade him. She fills him with herself, and her animal influences. She gets into his self-consciousness beside himself, by means of his self-love. Through the ever open funnel of his self-greed, she pours in flattery. By depreciation of others, she hints admiration of himself. By the slightest motion of a finger, of an eyelid, of her person, she will pay him a homage of which first he cannot, then he will not, then he dares not doubt the truth. Not such a woman only, but almost any silly woman, may speedily make the most ordinary, and hitherto modest youth, imagine himself the peak of creation, the triumph of the Deity. No man alive is beyond the danger of imagining himself exceptional among men: if such as think well of themselves were right in so doing, truly the world were ill worth God's making! He is the wisest who has learned to 'be naught awhile!' The silly soul becomes so full of his tempter, and of himself in and through her, that he loses interest in all else, cares for nobody but her, prizes nothing but her regard, broods upon nothing but her favours, looks forward to nothing but again her presence and further favours. God is nowhere; fellow-man in the way like a buzzing fly—else no more to be regarded than a speck of dust neither upon his person nor his garment. And this terrible disintegration of life rises out of the most wonderful, mysterious, beautiful, and profound relation in humanity! Its roots go down into the very deeps of God, and out of its foliage creeps the old serpent, and the worm that never dies! Out of it steams the horror of corruption, wrapt in whose living death a man cries out that God himself can do nothing for him. It is but the natural result of his making the loveliest of God's gifts into his God, and worshipping and serving the creature more than the creator. Oh my child, it is a terrible thing to be! Except he knows God the saviour, man stands face to face with a torturing enigma, hopeless of solution!

"The woman sought and found the enemy, my false self, in the house of my life. To that she gave herself, as if she gave herself to me. Oh, how she made me love her!—if that be love which is a deification of self, the foul worship of one's own paltry being!—and that when most it seems swallowed up and lost! No, it is not love! Does love make ashamed? The memories of it may be full of pain, but can the soul ever turn from love with sick contempt? That which at length is loathed, can never have been loved!

"Of my brother she would speak as of a poor creature not for a moment to be compared with myself. How I could have believed her true when she spoke thus, knowing that in the mirror I could not have told myself from my brother, knowing also that our minds, tastes, and faculties bore as strong a resemblance as our bodies, I cannot tell, but she fooled me to a fool through the indwelling folly of my self-love. At other times, wishing to tighten the bonds of my thraldom that she might the better work her evil end, proving herself a powerful devil, she would rouse my jealousy by some sign of strong admiration of Edmund. She must have acted the same way with my brother. I saw him enslaved just as I—knew we were faring alike—knew the very thoughts as well as feelings in his heart, and instead of being consumed with sorrow, chuckled at the *knowledge* that *I* was the favoured one! I suspect now that she showed him more favour than myself, and taught him to put on the look of the hopeless one. I fancied I caught at times a covert flash in his eye: he knew what he knew! If so, poor Edmund, thou hadst the worst of it every way!

"Shall I ever get her kisses off my lips, her poison out of my brain! From my heart, her image was burned in a moment, as utterly as if by years of hell!

"The estrangement between us was sudden; there were degrees only in the widening of it. First came embarrassment at meeting. Then all commerce of wish, thought, and speculation, ended. There was no more merrymaking jugglery with identity; each was himself only, and

for himself alone. Gone was all brother-gladness. We avoided each
other more and more. When we must meet, we made haste to part.
Heaven was gone from home. Each yet felt the same way toward the
other, but it was the way of repelling, not drawing. When we passed
in the street, it was with a look that said, or at least meant— 'You are
my brother! I don't want you!' We ceased even to nod to each other.
Still in our separation we could not separate. Each took a room in
another part of the town, but under the same pseudonym. Our common lodging was first deserted, then formally given up by each. Always
what one did, that did the other, though no longer intending to act in
consort with him. He could not help it though he tried, for the other
tried also, and did the same thing. One of us might for months have
played the part of both without detection—especially if it had been
understood that we had parted company; but I think it was never suspected, although now we were rarely for a moment together, and still
more rarely spoke. A few weeks sufficed to bring us to the verge of
madness.

"To this day I doubt if the woman, our common disease, knew the
one of us from the other. That in any part of her being there was the
least approach to a genuine womanly interest in either of us, I do not
believe. I am very sure she never cared for me. Preference I cannot
think possible; she could not, it seems to me, have felt anything for
one of us without feeling the same for both; I do not see how, with all
she knew of us, we could have made two impressions upon her moral
sensorium.

"It was at length the height of summer, and every one sought
change of scene and air. It was time for us to go home; but I wrote to
my father, and got longer leave."

"I wrote too," interposed my uncle Edmund at this point of the
story, when my own uncle was telling it that evening in Paris.

"The day after the date of his answer to my letter, my father died.
But Edmund and I were already on our way, by different routes, to
the mountain-village whither the lady had preceded us; and having,
in our infatuation, left no address, my brother never saw the letter
announcing our loss, and I not for months.

"A few weeks more, and our elder brother, who had always been
delicate, followed our father. This also remained for a time unknown to
me. My mother had died many years before, and we had now scarce a
relation in the world. Martha Moon is the nearest relative you and I have.
Besides her and you, there were left therefore of the family but myself
and your uncle Edmund—both absorbed in the same worthless woman.

"At the village there were two hostelries. I thought my brother
would go to the better; he thought I would go to the better; so we met

at the worse! I remember a sort of grin on his face when we saw each other, and have no doubt the same grin was on mine. We always did the same thing, just as of old. The next morning we set out, I need hardly say each by himself, to find the lady.

"She had rented a small chalet on the banks of a swift mountain-stream, and thither, for a week or so, we went every day, often encountering. The efforts we made to avoid each other being similar and simultaneous, they oftener resulted in our meeting. When one did nothing, the other generally did nothing also, and when one schemed, the other also schemed, and similarly. Thus what had been the greatest pleasure of our peculiar relation, our mental and moral resemblance, namely, became a large factor in our mutual hate. For with self-loathing shame, and a misery that makes me curse the day I was born, I confess that for a time I hated the brother of my heart; and I have but too good ground for believing that he also hated me!"

"I did! I did!" cried uncle Edmund, when my own uncle, in his verbal narrative, mentioned his belief that his brother hated him; whereupon uncle Edward turned to me, saying—

"Is it not terrible, my little one, that out of a passion called by the same name with that which binds you and John Day, the hellish smoke of such a hate should arise! God must understand it! that is a comfort: in vain I seek to sound it. Even then I knew that I dwelt in an evil house. Amid the highest of such hopes as the woman roused in me, I scented the vapours of the pit. I was haunted by the dim shape of the coming hour when I should hate the woman that enthralled me, more than ever I had loved her. The greater sinner I am, that I yet yielded her dominion over me. I was the willing slave of a woman who sought nothing but the consciousness of power; who, to the indulgence of that vilest of passions, would sacrifice the lives, the loves, the very souls of men! She lived to separate, where Jesus died to make one! How weak and unworthy was I to be caught in her snares! how wicked and vile not to tear myself loose! The woman whose touch would defile the Pharisee, is pure beside such a woman!"

I return to his manuscript.

"The lady must have had plenty of money, and she loved company and show; I cannot but think, therefore, that she had her design in choosing such a solitary place: its loveliness would subserve her intent of enthralling thoroughly heart and soul and brain of the fools she had in her toils. I doubt, however, if the fools were alive to any beauty but hers, if they were not dead to the wavings of God's garment about them. Was I ever truly aware of the presence of those peaks that dwelt alone with their whiteness in the desert of the sky—awfully alone—of the world, but not with the world? I think we saw nothing

save with our bodily eyes, and very little with them; for we were
blinded by a passion fitter to wander the halls of Eblis, than the pal-
aces of God.

"The chalet stood in a little valley, high in the mountains, whose
surface was gently undulating, with here and there the rocks breaking through its rich-flowering meadows. Down the middle of it ran
the deep swift stream, swift with the weight of its fullness, as well as
the steep slope of its descent. It was not more than seven or eight feet
across, but a great body of water went rushing along its deep course.
About a quarter of a mile from the chalet, it reached the first of a
series of falls of moderate height and slope, after which it divided
into a number of channels, mostly shallow, in a wide pebbly torrent-
bed. These, a little lower down, reunited into a narrower and yet
swifter stream—a small fierce river, which presently, at one reckless
bound, shot into the air, to tumble to a valley a thousand feet below,
shattered into spray as it fell.

"The chalet stood alone. The village was at no great distance, but
not a house was visible from any of its windows. It had no garden.
The meadow, one blaze of colour, softened by the green of the mingling grass, came up to its wooden walls, and stretched from them
down to the rocky bank of the river, in many parts to the very water's-
edge. The chalet stood like a yellow rock in a green sea. The meadow
was the drawing-room where the lady generally received us.

"One lovely evening, I strolled out of the hostelry, and went walking up the road that led to the village of Auerbach, so named from the
stream and the meadow I have described. The moon was up, and promised the loveliest night. I was in no haste, for the lady had, in our
common hearing, said, she was going to pass that night with a friend,
in a town some ten miles away. I dawdled along therefore, thinking
only to greet the place, walk with the stream, and lie in the meadow,
sacred with the shadow of her demonian presence. Quit of the restless hope of seeing her, I found myself taking some little pleasure in
the things about me, and spent two hours on the way, amid the sound
of rushing water, now swelling, now sinking, all the time.

"It had not crossed me to wonder where my brother might be. I
banished the thought of him as often as it intruded. Not able to help
meeting, we had almost given up avoiding each other; but when we
met, our desire was to part. I do not know that, apart, we had ever yet
felt actual hate, either to the other.

"The road led through the village. It was asleep. I remember a
gleam in just one of the houses. The moonlight seemed to have
drowned all the lamps of the world. I came to the stream, rushing
cold from its far-off glacier-mother, crossed it, and went down the

bank opposite the chalet: I had taken a fancy to see it from that side. Glittering and glancing under the moon, the wild little river rushed joyous to its fearful fall. A short distance away, it was even now fall-ing—falling from off the face of the world! This moment it was falling from my very feet into the void—falling, falling, unupheld, down, down, through the moonlight, to the ghastly rock-foot below!

"The chalet seemed deserted. With the same woefully desolate look, it constantly comes back in my dreams. I went farther down the valley. The full-rushing stream went with me like a dog. It made no murmur, only a low gurgle as it shot along. It seemed to draw me with it to its last leap. As I looked at its swiftness, I thought how hard it would be to get out of. The swiftness of it comes to me yet in my dreams.

"I came to a familiar rock, which, part of the bank whereon I walked, rose some six or seven feet above the meadow, just opposite a little hollow where the lady oftenest sat. Two were on the grass to-gether, one a lady seated, the other a man, with his head in the lady's lap. I gave a leap as if a bullet had gone through my heart, then instinc-tively drew back behind the rock. There I came to myself, and began to take courage. She had gone away for the night: it could not be she! I peeped. The man had raised his head, and was leaning on his elbow. It was Edmund, I was certain! She stooped and kissed him. I scrambled to the top of the rock, and sprang across the stream, which ran below me like a flooded millrace. Would to God I had missed the bank, and been swept to the great fall! I was careless, and when I lighted, I fell. Her clear mocking laugh rang through the air, and ech-oed from the scoop of some still mountain. When I rose, they were on their feet.

"'Quite a chamois-spring!' remarked the lady with derision.

"She saw the last moment was come. Neither of us two spoke.

"'I told you,' she said, 'neither of you was to trouble me to-night: you have paid no regard to my wish for quiet! It is time the foolery should end! I am weary of it. A woman cannot marry a double man—or half a man either—without at least being able to tell which is which of the two halves!'

"She ended with a toneless laugh, in which my brother joined. She turned upon him with a pitiless mockery which, I see now, must have left in his mind the conviction that she had been but making game of him; while I never doubted myself the dupe. Not once had she re-ceived me as I now saw her: though the night was warm, her deshabille was yet a somewhat prodigal unmasking of her beauty to the moon! The conviction in each of us was, that she and the other were laugh-ing at him.

"We locked in a deadly struggle, with what object I cannot tell. I do not believe either of us had an object. It was a mere blind conflict of pointless enmity, in which each cared but to overpower the other. Which first laid hold, which, if either, began to drag, I have not a suspicion. The next thing I know is, we were in the water, each in the grasp of the other, now rolling, now sweeping, now tumbling along, in deadly embrace.

"The shock of the ice-cold water, and the sense of our danger, brought me to myself. I let my brother go, but he clutched me still. Down we shot together toward the sheer descent. Already we seemed falling. The terror of it over-mastered me. It was not the crash I feared, but the stayless rush through the whistling emptiness. In the agony of my despair, I pushed him from me with all my strength, striking at him a fierce, wild, aimless blow—the only blow struck in the wrestle. His hold relaxed. I remember nothing more."

At this point of the verbal narrative, my uncle Edmund again spoke.

"You never struck me, Ed," he cried; "or if you did, I was already senseless. I remember nothing of the water."

"When I came to myself," the manuscript goes on, "I was lying in a pebbly shoal. The moon was aloft in heaven. I was cold to the heart, cold to the marrow of my bones. I could move neither hand nor foot, and thought I was dead. By slow degrees a little power came back, and I managed at length, after much agonizing effort, to get up on my feet—only to fall again. After several such failures, I found myself capable of dragging myself along like a serpent, and so got out of the water, and on the next endeavour was able to stand. I had forgotten everything; but when my eyes fell on the darting torrent, I remembered all—not as a fact, but as a terrible dream from which I thanked heaven I had come awake.

"But as I tottered along, I came slowly to myself, and a fearful doubt awoke. If it was a dream, where had I dreamt it? How had I come to wake where I found myself? How had the dream turned real about me? Where was I last in my remembrance? Where was my brother? Where was the lady in the moonlight? No, it was not a dream! If my brother had not got out of the water, I was his murderer! I had struck him!—Oh, the horror of it! If only I could stop dreaming it—three times almost every night!"

Again uncle Edmund interposed—not altogether logically:

"I tell you, I don't believe you struck me, Ed! And you must remember, neither of us would have got out if you hadn't!"

"You might have let me go!" said the other.

"On the way down the Degenfall, perhaps!" rejoined uncle Edmund. "—I believe it was that blow brought me to my senses, and made me get out!"

"Thank you, Ed!" said uncle Edward.

Once more I write from the manuscript.

"I said to myself he *must* have got out! It could not be that I had drowned my own brother! Such a ghastly thing could not have been permitted! It was too terrible to be possible!

"How, then, had we been living the last few months? What brothers had we been? Had we been loving one another? Had I been a neighbour to my nearest? Had I been a brother to my twin? Was not murder the natural outcome of it all? He that loveth not his brother is a murderer! If so, where the good of saving me from being in deed what I was in nature? I had cast off my brother for a treacherous woman! My very thought sickened within me.

"My soul seemed to grow luminous, and understand everything. I saw my whole behaviour as it was. The scales fell from my inward eyes, and there came a sudden, total, and absolute revulsion in my conscious self—like what takes place, I presume, at the day of judgment, when the God in every man sits in judgment upon the man. Had the gate of heaven stood wide open, neither angel with flaming sword, nor Peter with the keys to dispute my entrance, I would have turned away from it, and sought the deepest hell. I loathed the woman and myself; in my heart the sealed fountain of old affection had broken out, and flooded it.

"All the time this thinking went on, I was crawling slowly up the endless river toward the chalet, driven by a hope inconsistent with what I knew of my brother. What I felt, he, if he were alive, must be feeling also: how then could I say to myself that I should find him with her? It was the last dying hope that I had not killed him that thus fooled me. 'She will be warming him in her bosom!' I said. But at the very touch, the idea turned and presented its opposite pole. 'Good God!' I cried in my heart, 'how shall I compass his deliverance? Better he lay at the bottom of the fall, than lived to be devoured by that serpent of hell! I will go straight to the den of the monster, and demand my brother!'"

But to see the eyes of uncle Edmund at this point of the story!

"At last I approached the chalet. All was still. A handkerchief lay on the grass, white in the moonlight. I went up to it, hoping to find it my brother's. It was the lady's. I flung it from me like a filthy rag.

"What was the passion worth which in a moment could die so utterly!

"I turned to the house. I would tear him from her: he was mine, not hers!

"My wits were nigh gone. I thought the moonlight was dissolving the chalet, that the two within might escape me. I held it fast with my eyes. The moon drew back: she only possessed and filled it! No; the moon was too pure: she but shone reflected from the windows; she would not go in! *I* would go in! I was Justice! The woman was a thief! She had broken into the house of life, and was stealing!

"I stood for a moment looking up at her window. There was neither motion nor sound. Was she gone away, and my brother with her? Could she be in bed and asleep, after seeing us swept down the river to the Degenfall! Could he be with her and at rest, believing me dashed to pieces? I must be resolved! The door was not bolted; I stole up the stair to her chamber. The door of it was wide open. I entered, and stood. The moon filled the tiny room with a clear, sharp-edged, pale-yellow light. She lay asleep, lovely to look at as an angel of God. Her hair, part of it thrown across the top-rail of the little iron bed, streamed out on each side over the pillow, and in the midst of it lay her face, a radiant isle in a dark sea. I stood and gazed. Fascinated by her beauty? God forbid! I was fascinated by the awful incongruity between that face, pure as the moonlight, and the charnel-house that lay unseen behind it. She was to me, henceforth, not a woman, but a live Death. I had no sense of sacredness, such as always in the chamber even of a little girl. How should I? It was no chamber; it was a den. She was no woman, but a female monster. I stood and gazed.

"My presence was more potent than I knew. She opened her eyes—opened them straight into mine. All the colour sank away out of her face, and it stiffened to that of a corpse. With the staring eyes of one strangled, she lay as motionless as I stood. I moved not an inch, spoke not a word, drew not a step nearer, retreated not a hair's-breadth. Motion was taken from me. Was it hate that fixed my eyes on hers, and turned my limbs into marble? It certainly was not love, but neither was it hate.

"Agony had been burrowing in me like a mole; the half of what I felt I have not told you: I came to find my brother, and found only, in a sweet sleep, the woman who had just killed him. The bewilderment, of it all, with my long insensibility and wet garments, had taken from me either the power of motion or of volition, I do not know which: speechless in the moonlight, I must have looked to the wretched woman both ghostly and ghastly.

"Two or three long moments she gazed with those horror-struck eyes; then a frightful shriek broke from her drawn, death-like lips. She who could sleep after turning love into hate, life into death, would have fled into hell to escape the eyes of the dead! Insensibility is not courage. Wake in the scornfullest mortal the conviction that one of the disembodied stands before him, and he will shiver like an aspen-leaf. Scream followed scream. Volition or strength, whichever it was that had left me, returned. I backed from the room, went noiseless from the house, and fled, as if she had been the ghost, and I the mortal. Would I had been the spectre for which she took me!"

Here uncle Edward again spoke.

"Small wonder she screamed, the wretch!" he cried: "that was her second dose of the horrible that night! You found the door unbolted because I had been there before you. I too entered her room, and saw her asleep as you describe. I went close to her bedside, and cried out, 'Where is my brother?' She woke, and fainted, and I left her."

"Then," said I, "when she came to herself, thinking she had had a bad dream, she rearranged her hair, and went to sleep again!"

"Just so, I daresay, little one!" answered uncle Edward.

"I had not yet begun to think what I should do, when I found myself at our little inn," the manuscript continues. "No idea of danger to myself awoke in my mind, nor was there any cause to heed such an idea, had it come. Nobody there knew the one from the other of us. Not many would know there were two of us. Any one who saw me twice, might well think he had seen us both. If my brother's body were found in the valley stream, it was not likely to be recognized, or to be indeed recognizable. The only one who could tell what happened at the top of the fall, would hardly volunteer information. But, while I knew myself my brother's murderer, I thought no more of these sheltering facts than I did of danger. I made it no secret that my brother had gone over the fall. I went to the foot of the cataract, thence to search and inquire all down the stream, but no one had heard of any dead body being found. They told me that the poor gentleman must, before morning, have been far on his way to the Danube.

"Giving up the quest in despair, I resigned myself to a torture which has hitherto come no nearer expending itself than the consuming fire of God.

"I dared not carry home the terrible news, which must either involve me in lying, or elicit such confession as would multiply tenfold my father's anguish, and was in utter perplexity what to do, when it occurred to me that I ought to inquire after letters at the lodging where last we had lived together. Then first I learned that both my father and my elder brother, your father, little one, were dead.

"The sense of guilt had not destroyed in me the sense of duty. I did not care what became of the property, but I did care for my brother's child, and the interests of her succession.

"Your father had all his life been delicate, and had suffered not a little. When your mother died, about a year after their marriage, leaving us you, it soon grew plain to see that, while he loved you dearly, and was yet more friendly to all about him than before, his heart had given up the world. When I knew he was gone, I shed more tears over him than I had yet shed over my twin: the worm that never dies made my brain too hot to weep much for Edmund. Then first I saw that my elder brother had been a brother indeed; and that we twins had never been real to each other. I saw what nothing but self-loathing would ever have brought me to see, that my love to Edmund had not been profound: while a man is himself shallow, how should his love be deep! I saw that we had each loved our elder brother in a truer and better fashion than we had loved each other. One of the chief active bonds between us had been fun; another, habit; and another, constitutional resemblance—not one of them strong. Underneath were bonds far stronger, but they had never come into conscious play; no strain had reached them. They were there, I say; for wherever is the poorest flower of love, it is there in virtue of the perfect root of love; and love's root must one day blossom into love's perfect rose. My chief consolation under the burden of my guilt is, that I love my brother since I killed him, far more than I loved him when we were all to each other. Had we never quarrelled, and were he alive, I should not be loving him thus!

"That we shall meet again, and live in the devotion of a far deeper love, I feel in the very heart of my soul. That it is my miserable need that has wrought in me this confidence, is no argument against the confidence. As misery alone sees miracles, so is there many a truth into which misery alone can enter. My little one, do not pity your uncle much; I have learned to lift up my heart to God. I look to him who is the saviour of men to deliver me from blood-guiltiness—to lead me into my brother's pardon, and enable me somehow to make up to him for the wrong I did him.

"Some would think I ought to give myself up to justice. But I felt and feel that I owe my brother reparation, not my country the opportunity of retribution. It cannot be demanded of me to pretermit, because of my crime, the duty more strongly required of me because of the crime. Must I not use my best endeavour to turn aside its evil consequences from others? Was I, were it even for the cleansing of my vile soul, to leave the child of my brother alone with a property exposing her to the machinations of prowling selfishness! Would it atone for the wrong of depriving her of one uncle, to take the other from her, and so leave her defenceless with a burden she could not carry? Must I take so-called justice on myself at her expense—to the oppression, darkening, and endangering of her life? Were I accused, I would tell the truth; but I would not volunteer a phantasmal atonement. What comfort would it be to my brother that I was hanged? Let the punishment God pleased come upon me, I said; as far as lay in me, I would live for my brother's child! I have lived for her.

"But I am, and have been, and shall, I trust, throughout my earthly time, and what time thereafter may be needful, always be in Purgatory. I should tremble at the thought of coming out of it a moment ere it had done its part.

"One day, after my return home, as I unpacked a portmanteau, my fingers slipped into the pocket of a waistcoat, and came upon something which, when I brought it to the light, proved a large ruby. A pang went to my heart. I looked at the waistcoat, and found it the one I had worn that terrible night: the ruby was the stone of the ring Edmund always wore. It must have been loose, and had got there in our struggle. Every now and then I am drawn to look at it. At first I saw in it only the blood; now I see the light also. The moon of hope rises higher as the sun of life approaches the horizon.

"I was never questioned about the death of my twin brother. One, of two so like, must seem enough. Our resemblance, I believe, was a bore, which the teasing use we made of it aggravated; therefore the fact that there was no longer a pair of us, could not be regarded as cause for regret, and things quickly settled down to the state in which you so long knew them. If there be one with a suspicion of the terrible truth, it is cousin Martha.

"You will not be surprised that you should never have heard of your uncle Edmund.

"I dare not ask you, my child, not to love me less; for perhaps you ought to do so. If you do, I have my consolation in the fact that my little one cannot make me love *her* less."

Thus ended the manuscript, signed with my uncle's name and address in full, and directed to me at the bottom of the last page.

35
Uncle Edmund's Appendix

When my uncle Edward had told his story, corresponding, though more conversational in form, with that I have now transcribed, my uncle Edmund took up his part of the tale from the moment when he came to himself after their fearful rush down the river. It was to this effect:

He lay on the very verge of the hideous void. How it was that he got thus far and no farther, he never could think. He was out of the central channel, and the water that ran all about him and poured immediately over the edge of the precipice, could not have sufficed to roll him there. Finding himself on his back, and trying to turn on his side in order to rise, his elbow found no support, and lifting his head a little, he looked down into a moon-pervaded abyss, where thin silvery vapours were stealing about. One turn, and he would have been on his way, plumb-down, to the valley below—say, rather, on his way off the face of the world into the vast that bosoms the stars and the systems and the cloudy worlds. His very soul quivered with terror. The pang of it was so keen that it saved him from the swoon in which he might yet have dropped from the edge of the world. Not daring to rise, and unable to roll himself up the slight slope, he shifted himself sideways along the ground, inch by inch, for a few yards, then rose, and ran staggering away, as from a monster that might wake and pursue and overtake him. He doubted if he would ever have recovered the sudden shock of his awful position, of his one glance into the ghastly depth, but for the worse horror of the all-but-conviction that his brother had gone down to Hades through that terrible descent. If only he too had gone, he cried in his misery, they would now be together, with no wicked woman between their hearts! For his love too was changed into loathing. He too was at once, and entirely, and for ever freed from her fascination. The very thought of her was hateful to him.

With straight course, but wavering walk, he made his way through the moonlight to demand his brother. He too picked up the handkerchief, and dropped it with disgust.

What followed in the lady's chamber, I have already given in his own words.

When he fled from the chalet, it was with self-slaughter in his heart. But he endured in the comfort of the thought that the door of death was always open, that he might enter when he would. He sought the foot of the fall the same night; then, as one possessed of demons to the tombs, fled to the solitary places of the dark mountains.

He went through many a sore stress. Ignorant of the death of his father and his elder brother, the dread misery of encountering them with his brother's blood on his soul, barred his way home. He could not bear the thought of reading in their eyes his own horror of himself. His money was soon spent, and for months he had to endure severe hardships—of simple, wholesome human sort. He thought afterward that, if he had had no trouble of that kind, his brain would have yielded. He would have surrendered himself but for the uselessness of it, and the misery and public stare it would bring upon his family.

Knowing German well, and contriving at length to reach Berlin, he found employment there of various kinds, and for a good many years managed to live as well as he had any heart for, and spare a little for some worse off than himself. Having no regard to his health, however, he had at length a terrible attack of brain-fever, and but partially recovering his faculties after it, was placed in an asylum. There he dreamed every night of his home, came awake with the joy of the dream, and could sleep no more for longing—not to go home— that he dared not think of—but to look upon the place, if only once again. The longing grew till it became intolerable. By his talk in his sleep, the good people about him learning his condition, gave and gathered money to send him home. On his way, he came to himself quite, but when he reached England, he found he dared not go near the place of his birth. He remained therefore in London, where he made the barest livelihood by copying legal documents. In this way he spent a few miserable years, and then suddenly set out to walk to the house of his fathers. He had but five shillings in his possession when the impulse came upon him.

He reached the moor, and had fallen exhausted, when a solitary gypsy, rare phenomenon, I presume, with a divine spot awake in his heart, found him, gave him some gin, and took him to a hut he had in the wildest part of the heath. He lay helpless for a week, and then began to recover. When he was sufficiently restored, he helped his host to weave the baskets which, as soon as he had enough to make a load, he took about the country in a cart. He soon became so clever at the work as quite to earn his food and shelter, making more baskets while the gypsy was away selling the others. At home, the old horse managed to live, or rather not to die, on the moor, and, all things considered, had not a very hard life of it. On his back, uncle Edmund, ill able to walk so far—for he was anything but strong now, would sometimes go wandering in the twilight, or when the moon shone, to some spot whence he could see his old home. Occasionally he would even go round and round the house while we slept, like a ghost dreaming of ancient days.

"But," I said, interrupting his narrative, "the horseman I saw that night in the storm could not have been you, uncle; for the horse was a grand creature, rearing like the horse with Peter the Great on his back, in the corner of the map of Russia!"

"Were *you* out that terrible night?" he returned. "The lightning was enough to frighten even an older horse than the gypsy's.—I wonder how my friend is getting on! He must think me very ungrateful! But I daresay he imagines me lying fathom-deep in the bog.—You will do something for him, won't you, Ed?"

"You shall do for him yourself what you please, Ed," answered my own uncle, "and I will help you."

"But, uncle Edmund," I said, "if it was you we saw, the place you were in was a very boggy one always, and nearly a lake then!"

"I thought I should never get out!" he replied. "But for the poor horse and his owner, I should not have minded."

"How *did* you get out of it, uncle?" I persisted. "Lady Cairnedge smothered a splendid black horse not far from there. Through the darkness I heard him going down. It makes me shudder every time I think of it."

"I cannot tell you, child. I suppose my gray was such a skeleton that the bog couldn't hold him. I left it all to him, and he got himself and me too out of it somehow. It was too dark, as you know, to see anything between the flashes. I remember we were pretty deep sometimes."

He went back to London after that, and had come and gone once or twice, he said. When he came he always lodged with his gypsy friend. He had learned that his father was dead, but took the Mr. Whichcote he heard mentioned, for his elder brother, David, my father.

I asked him how it was he appeared to such purpose, and in the very nick of time, that afternoon when lady Cairnedge had come with her servants to carry John away; for of course I knew now that our champion must have been uncle Edmund. He answered he had that very morning made up his mind to present himself at the house, and had walked there for the purpose, resolved to tell his brother all. He got in by the end of the garden, as John was in the way of doing, and had reached the little grove of firs by the house, when he saw a carriage at

the door, and drew back. Hearing then the noises of attack and defence, he came to the window and looked in, heard lady Cairnedge's
shriek, saw her on the floor, and the men attempting to force an entrance at the other side of the window. Hardly knowing what he did,
he rushed at them and beat them off. Then suddenly turning faint,
for his heart was troublesome, he retired into the grove, and lay there
helpless for a time. He recovered only to hear the carriage drive away,
leaving quiet behind it.

To see that woman in the house of his fathers, was a terrible shock
to him. Could it be that David had married her? He stole from his
covert, and crawled across the moor to the gypsy's hut. There he was
consoled by learning that the mistress of the house was a young girl,
whom he rightly concluded to be the daughter of his brother David.

In making a second visit with the same intent, he had another
attack of the heart, and now knew that he would have died in the snow
had not John found him.

36
The End of the First Volume

We returned to England the next day. All the journey through, my uncles were continually reverting to the matter of John's parentage: the more they saw of him, the less could they believe lady Cairnedge his mother. Through questions put to him, and inquiries afterward made, they discovered that, when he went to London, he had gone to lady Cairnedge's lawyer, not his father's, of whom he had never heard—which accounted for his having on that occasion learned nothing of consequence to him. When we reached London, my uncle Edmund, who, having been bred a lawyer, knew how to act, went at once to examine the will left by John's father. That done, he set out for the place where John was born. The rest of us went home.

The second day after our arrival there, uncle Edmund came. He had found perfect proof, not only that lady Cairnedge was John's stepmother, but that she had no authority over him or his property whatever.

A long discussion took place in my uncles' study—I have to shift the apostrophe of possession—as to whether John ought to compel restitution of what she might have wrongfully spent or otherwise appropriated. She had been left an income by each of her husbands, upon either of which incomes she might have lived at ease; but they had a strong suspicion, soon entirely justified, that while spending John's money, she had been saving up far more than her own. But in the discussion, John held to it that, as she had once been the wife of his father, he would spare her so far—provided she had nowise impoverished either of the estates. He would insist only upon her immediate departure.

"Yes, little one," said my uncle, one summer evening, as he and I talked together, seated alone in the wilderness, "what we call misfortune is always the only good fortune. Few will say *yes* in response, but Truth is independent of supporters, being justified by her children.

"Until *misfortune* found us," he went on, "my brother and I had indeed loved one another, but with a love so poor that a wicked woman was able to send it to sleep. To what she might have brought us, had she had full scope, God only knows: *now* all the women in hell could not separate us!"

"And all the women in paradise would but bring you closer!" I ventured to add.

The day after our marriage, which took place within a month of our return from Paris, John went to Rising, on a visit to lady Cairnedge of anything but ceremony, and took his uncles and myself with him.

"Will you tell her ladyship," he said to the footman, "that Mr. Day desires to see her."

The man would have shut the door in our faces, with the words, "I will see if my lady is at home;" but John was prepared for him. He put his foot between the door and the jamb, and his two hands against the door, driving it to the wall with the man behind it. There he held him till we were all in, then closed the door, and said to him, in a tone I had never heard him use till that moment,

"Let lady Cairnedge know at once that Mr. Day desires to see her."

The man went. We walked into the white drawing-room, the same where I sat alone among the mirrors the morning after I was lost on the moor. How well I remembered it! There we waited. The gentlemen stood, but, John insisting, I sat—my eyes fixed on the door by which we had entered. In a few minutes, however, a slight sound in another part of the room, caused me to turn them thitherward. There stood lady Cairnedge, in a riding-habit, with a whip in her hand, staring, pale as death, at my uncles. Then, with a scornful laugh, she turned and went through a door immediately behind her, which closed instantly, and became part of the wainscot, hardly distinguishable. John darted to it. It was bolted on the outside. He sought another door, and ran hither and thither through the house to find the woman. My uncles ran after him, afraid something might befall him. I remained where I was, far from comfortable. Two or three minutes passed, and then I heard the thunder of hoofs. I ran to the window. There she was, tearing across the park at full gallop, on just such a huge black horse as she had smothered in the bog! I was the only one of us that saw her, and not one of us ever set eyes upon her again.

When we went over the house, it soon became plain to us that she had been in readiness for a sudden retreat, having prepared for it after a fashion of her own: not a single small article of value was to be discovered in it. John's great-aunt, who left him the property, died in the house, possessed of a large number of jewels, many of them of great price both in themselves and because of their antiquity: not one of them was ever found.

A report reached us long after, that lady Cairnedge was found dead in her bed in a hotel in the Tyrol.

My uncles lived for many years on the old farm. Uncle Edmund bought a gray horse, as like uncle Edward's as he could find one, only younger. I often wondered what Death must think—to know he had his master on his back, and yet see him mounted by his side. Every day one or the other, most days both, would ride across the moor to see us. For many years Martha walked in at the door at least once every week.

My uncles took no pains, for they had no desire, to be distinguished the one from the other. Each was always ready to meet any obligation of the other. If one made an appointment, few could tell which it was, and nobody which would keep it. No one could tell, except, perhaps, one who had been present, which of them had signed any document: their two hands were absolutely indistinguishable, I do not believe either of them, after a time, always himself knew whether the name was his or his brother's. He could only be always certain it must have been written by one of them. But each indifferently was ready to honour the signature, *Ed. Whichcote.*

They died within a month of each other. Their bodies lie side by side. On their one tombstone is the inscription:

HERE LIE THE DISUSED GARMENTS OF
EDWARD AND EDMUND WHICHCOTE,

BORN FEB. 29, 1804;
DIED JUNE 30, AND
JULY 28, 1864.

THEY ARE NOT HERE; THEY ARE RISEN.

JOHN AND I ARE WAITING.
BELORBA DAY.

ALSO AVAILABLE:

*Shadows from a Veiled Creation:
Classic Tales of Supernatural Fiction
in the Christian Tradition*

ISBN 1-930585-26-8

44 stories, with authors including
Daniel DeFoe, G. K. Chesterton, Sabine
Baring-Gould, M. R. James, Charles
Williams, E. G. Swain, Robert H.
Benson, Mary Wilkins, Henry S.
Whitehead, and Arthur Quiller-Couch.

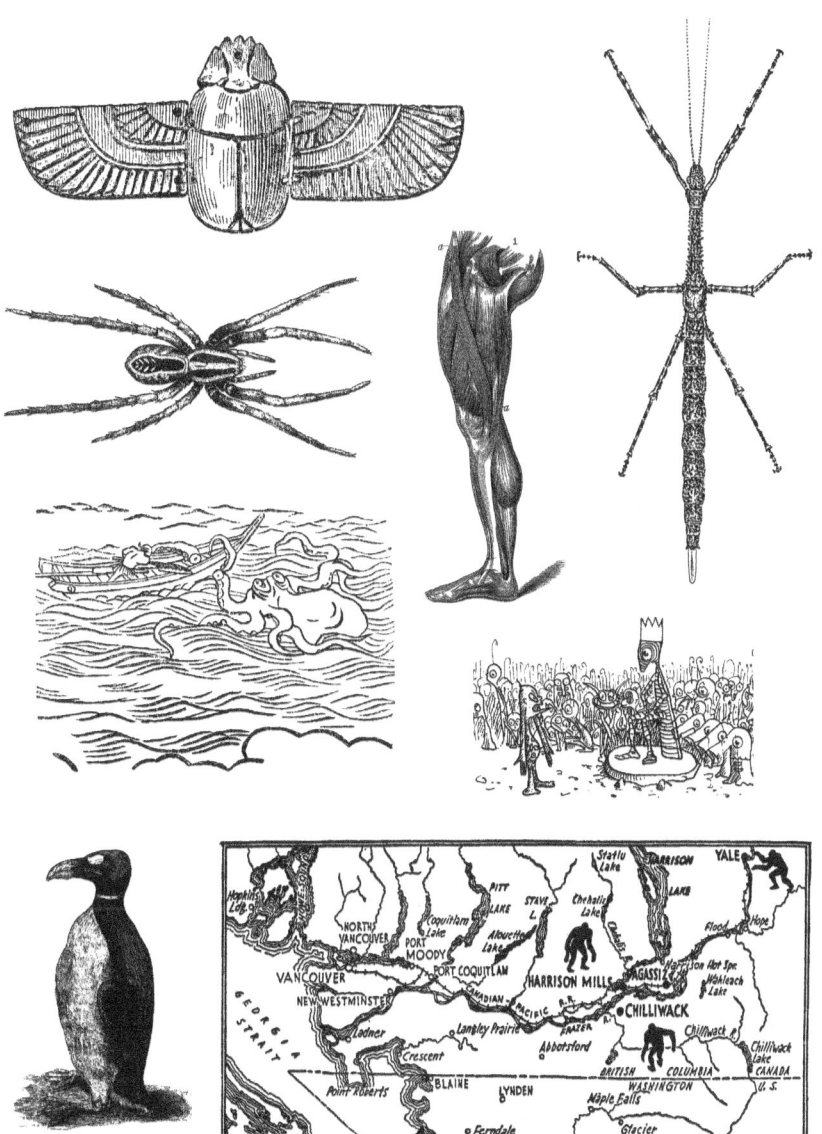